THE SHATTERED CITY

THE SHATTERED CITY

BOOK FOUR IN THE LAST MAGICIAN SERIES

BY LISA MAXWELL

MARGARET K. McELDERRY BOOKS

NEW YORK   LONDON   TORONTO   SYDNEY   NEW DELHI

MARGARET K. McELDERRY BOOKS

An imprint of Simon & Schuster Children's Publishing Division

1230 Avenue of the Americas, New York, New York 10020

Text © 2022 by Lisa Maxwell

Jacket photo-illustration © 2022 by Craig Howell

Series design by Russell Gordon

Jacket design by Greg Stadnyk © 2022 by Simon & Schuster, Inc.

MARGARET K. McELDERRY BOOKS is a trademark of Simon & Schuster, Inc.

For information about special discounts for bulk purchases, please contact Simon & Schuster Special Sales at 1-866-506-1949 or business@simonandschuster.com.

The Simon & Schuster Speakers Bureau can bring authors to your live event. For more information or to book an event, contact the Simon & Schuster Speakers Bureau at 1-866-248-3049 or visit our website at www.simonspeakers.com.

Interior design by Brad Mead and Mike Rosamilia.

The text for this book was set in Bembo Std.

Manufactured in the United States of America

First Edition

2 4 6 8 10 9 7 5 3 1

Library of Congress Cataloging-in-Publication Data

Names: Maxwell, Lisa, 1979– author.

Title: The shattered city / Lisa Maxwell.

Description: First edition. | New York : Margaret K. McElderry Books, [2022] | Series: The last magician ; book 4 | Summary: Hunted by an ancient evil, Esta and Harte have raced through time and across a continent to track down the artifacts needed to bind the mystical Book's devastating power, and now, with only one artifact left, they must find a way to end the threat they have created or the very heart of magic will die.

Identifiers: LCCN 2022012214 (print) | LCCN 2022012215 (ebook)

ISBN 9781534432512 (hardcover) | ISBN 9781534432543 (ebook)

Subjects: CYAC: Magic—Fiction. | Time travel—Fiction. | BISAC: YOUNG ADULT FICTION / Fantasy / Historical | YOUNG ADULT FICTION / Social Themes / Prejudice & Racism | LCGFT: Fantasy fiction. | Time-travel fiction.

Classification: LCC PZ7.M44656 Sh 2022 (print) | LCC PZ7.M44656 (ebook) | DDC [Fic]—dc23

LC record available at https://lccn.loc.gov/2022012214

LC ebook record available at https://lccn.loc.gov/2022012215

This one is for the readers—
Those who have found their home
And those who are still searching.

The Brink

Dead Line

Trinity Church

St. Paul's Chapel

Cela's Place

Bella Strega

The Tombs

Fifth

Wall St.

City Hall

Canal

Paul Kelly's

Elizabeth

The Docks

Five Points

Bowery

Professor Lachlan's Building

Brooklyn→

Broome

Houston

Bridge

Dom's Warehouse

BROOKLYN

THE CITY

The city stirred as the sun dipped below the horizon and night began to rise. With a shuddering sigh, it felt the cool, timeless waters lapping at its shores, heard the endless wailing of children hungry within closed-off rooms. It tasted the fears of the women and men who wandered through the narrow channels of its streets, staking everything they had—everything they were—for a dream they often could not even name.

Far beneath the present, beneath the constant disappointment and the regret, the land remembered what natives and newcomers alike had long since forgotten. It remembered that once it had been a true place, before the land had been carved and flattened and pressed into order.

The city could not forget, because in the darkness, the past was always there. The future too. Alongside what was, the city could see the glimmer of what had been and what could *still* become, especially at night, when the past and future and all the possibilities in between seemed one and the same.

The city had watched itself change many times before and knew it would change again. But on that night, the deepest night in the darkest part of the year, it sensed something that felt like a beginning.

Or perhaps it felt like an end.

That night a dangerous new magic began to stir. Beneath the indifferent stars, cold fires smudged their heavy incense into the sky, and chaos flared. The streets that carved order into bedrock began to burn, and the city felt itself beginning to come undone.

But there were those who would stand and fight for an impossible future.

The city had barely noticed them when they'd first arrived on its banks days or weeks or years before: one with fire in her eyes and a knife in her hand, one who could fold the light but could not uncrease his own heart. They had been no different from any of the other desperate souls who came day after day, year after year, all hoping to carve a life from the unfeeling streets. That night they stood apart, and the city wondered. . . .

And there were others: those held no power at all—at least none that could be remembered. They had been born in the city's own cradle, but now the city took their measure.

Great beasts of smoke and fog rose from the cold fires as a demon raged, and the city watched her children fight. It watched them fall one by one. The assassin, the spy, and those who would help them. Broken and bleeding on a rooftop filled with angry men. A knife to the heart. A bullet to the brain.

And then there were the two. The Magician and the Thief. And the city stirred with interest once more. But in the end, they were too late, and their blood mingled with the rest.

The demon laughed, and the men who dreamed of greatness fled like the rats that tickled the city's ribs day and night. All except one, who stayed tucked into the shadows, eyes glinting at the sight of the broken bodies before him.

The city watched as the Serpent smiled. Like the city, he knew already that time was a circle, unending and infinite until shattered against desire. His hands tightened around a gorgon's head, and his lip curled.

Time went still. The night held its breath. But then, the world spun on. The city shook off its disappointment. And it began to dream.

PART

I

ONLY A DREAM

1920—Brooklyn

Esta stared down at the small book in front of her. If not for the power radiating from it, the Ars Arcana would have been unimpressive. Unremarkable, even. It was smaller than one might expect of such a fabled object, bound in worn leather that had long since cracked and peeled from age. But the design carved into its cover was astounding. Clear and crisp, the geometric shapes were layered and woven into one another to form a complex sigil. The lines were so entangled that it was impossible to tell where one ended and the next began.

So much was riding on what the Book of Mysteries contained—the information *and* the magic within its pages—that Esta hadn't been able to fall asleep. She knew she should probably wait for Harte, but impatience made her a little reckless. She hadn't been able to stop herself from taking the Book from the satchel and running her finger along the intricate design carved into the leather of the cover. At the soft brush of her touch, the Book shuddered. The Aether around her trembled in response. Even the very quintessence of existence seemed to understand that the piece of pure, untouched magic within those pages could remake the world. Or destroy it.

For what was Aether but time, the very substance that carved order from chaos? And what was magic but the promise of power within chaos? Time and magic. Order and chaos. Once, the two had existed in a fragile equilibrium. Like the ouroboros, the ancient image of a serpent fated to forever devour its own tail, time kept magic in check, and the wild chaos of magic spurred time onward. But a mistake—an act of hubris, however well meaning—had changed everything. Now, deep within the Ars Arcana, a piece of the beating heart of magic waited. Severed and separated from time by an act of ritual, it was impossibly potent and dangerous. In the wrong hands, its power could cause unthinkable destruction.

Esta glanced over her shoulder to where Harte was still sleeping on the low sofa. On a makeshift pallet nearby, North's boy, Everett, snored softly as well. Even in sleep, he looked so much like his father. But North wasn't with them any longer. He had sacrificed himself for Everett—for the hope of a better future for all Mageus—in Chicago. And Esta would not allow that sacrifice to go wasted. She would do everything she could to claim them a different fate.

The enigmatic owner of the Nitemarket, Dominic Fusilli, had dropped them off at one of his warehouses in Brooklyn and told them to get some rest. As far as Esta knew, she was alone with the Book in the stillness of the night.

She could wake Harte—she probably *should* wake him—but it had been nearly two days since he'd had any real sleep, and he was still weak from being sick in California. He needed the rest. And also, she wasn't ready to tell him yet—not about what Seshat had revealed back in Chicago nor about what Esta had done to save his life. She'd promised to finish the ritual Seshat had started eons before, a ritual to place that severed piece of magic back into the whole of creation. It was a promise she had no idea how to keep.

The Book trembled again, beckoned. The answers were within those pages.

They have to be.

Her finger had barely made contact with the ancient cover when, suddenly, the Ars Arcana threw itself open, and the most terrible wailing split the silence of the night as the pages began flipping in a seemingly endless wave. Which shouldn't have been possible. The Book wasn't *that* big. There shouldn't have been *that* many pages. Then, just as suddenly as the Book had opened, its pages burst with a blinding flash of light so bright, Esta had to flinch away, shielding her eyes from its brilliance. When the light dimmed and her eyes readjusted, she was no longer in the warehouse in Brooklyn but back on the stage of the Chicago Coliseum. The Book was gone.

In her hand was the hilt of the dagger that held the Pharaoh's Heart, and beneath her, Jack writhed, his eyes open in rage and fear. She lifted the dagger, knowing what she must do—what she *had* done. What she would do a thousand times over. She knew what would happen next, the sickening crunch of bone. The terrible sinking of the ancient dagger's blade as it sucked itself deep into Jack's chest.

You would be so willing to kill for the power in these pages?

A voice echoed inside her head—it was her own voice and not her own at the same time. Startled, she stopped with the dagger over her head. All around, the crowd in the massive arena had gone silent.

Of course she would kill for the Book. She already had.

And now? Will you take the beating heart of magic as your own . . .? Or will you give it over to the one who thinks herself a goddess?

The voice was no longer her own but Thoth's—the same voice that had spoken to her before, in Denver. In Chicago as well.

Will you sacrifice yourself for Seshat's mistakes? Do you trust in her promises so absolutely?

Esta shook her head, trying to shake off the voice. It couldn't be Thoth. She'd destroyed him and the danger he posed along with him, but the memory of him was so strong, and his words were already worming into her mind, poking at her misgivings and fears.

She will not save you, the voice whispered. *Given the chance, Seshat will destroy you and the world itself. For what? For simple vengeance.*

It was no less than Seshat had threatened for months now. But they'd made a bargain. Harte's life for Esta's promise . . .

You will die to keep that promise, the voice threatened. *But there is another way. Give your affinity over willingly, like so many have before you. You need not die. With your affinity, I could control Seshat's power. Your magic could remove Seshat from the Magician without destroying the boy who holds your heart. You could live beyond the reach of time, and your magician with you.*

She wanted to deny the temptation in those words, but she couldn't. *How?*

With the beating heart of magic.

The voice spoke again, a crooning caress along the inside of her mind. *Think of all you could do if only you would have the courage to take what I offer. Think of the chaos you brought into the world. Think of those you could save: Your friend who tumbled from the sky . . . All those who have died because of you . . . Your parents . . . Your magician, who is destined to be consumed by the demon within him.*

Seshat will not save them. She will not save you.

It *was* a temptation. It would have been a lie not to admit that to herself. To save Mari and North. To save Dolph and Leena, the mother she'd never met. To know that Harte would be safe.

Think of what you could do with the power in these pages, the voice tempted. It was her voice now, and Thoth's as well. Both together. Terrible and enticing all the same. *The demon bitch was too weak to truly take it as her own. But you, girl . . . you are more than Seshat could ever be. With the power in these pages, you could become* infinite. *Think of it,* the voice whispered. *Think of what you could accomplish if magic—pure magic, true magic—answered only to you.*

No. Esta recoiled from the idea. She'd seen what the quest for power had done to Seshat. To Jack. To Thoth. She didn't want the power in the Book; she only wanted to replace it into the whole of creation, where it belonged. She only wanted to complete the ritual that Seshat had started so long ago, as she'd promised she would.

I don't want that power, she told the Book. Told herself as well. *I only want to finish what Seshat started. I only want to set things right.*

Ancient laughter bubbled up from within the pages, from within herself.

Ah, the voice said, its amusement surrounding her. *You would reunite the piece of magic that Seshat stole. You would place the beating heart of magic back into balance with the marching of time. But will you be willing to do what is required?*

I'll do whatever it takes, she said.

But what of the cost?

No matter the cost. She'd already blackened her soul with Jack's death, hadn't she? She would pay again and again if she had to. To save the world. To save *Harte.*

The hilt of the dagger felt unnaturally cold in Esta's hand, and the energy of the Pharaoh's Heart pulsed through the Aether around her. She ignored the icy burn and plunged the blade down. The sickening grinding of bone vibrated through her arms as Jack's watery blue eyes widened in pain and surprise. As though he could not believe she could have bested him. As though he could not believe it was possible for him to lose.

And then Thoth was there, rising up, cold and terrible in his fury, and she did not hesitate to reach for her own terrible power, the affinity that was as much a part of her as her own skin. Without hesitation, she pulled at the Aether, the substance that held together all things. Time. Magic and its opposite. And she did not stop until the darkness that lived in the spaces between all things flooded into Thoth and tore him from this world.

That darkness poured from Jack and, as before, his screams and Thoth's mixed. It became a living thing—as alive and prescient as Thoth himself—as it gathered into a malevolent cloud swirling above. When Jack slumped back to the ground, emptied, the dark cloud broke, shattering itself into a million tiny shards. They fell like needles of cold energy onto the crowd—onto Esta—slicing through her too tender skin. It felt like the Brink crashing over her.

And then, all at once, it was over.

Esta was still gripping the hilt of the dagger, still pressing it into Jack's chest, but suddenly she felt the warmth of Jack's hands covering hers. She startled, because this *hadn't* happened before. It wasn't part of the memory. She looked down, but it *wasn't* Jack's hand that had gripped hers. Now it was Harte who lay beneath her. Harte whose lips were frothing with blood and whose hands were wrapped around hers, trying to pull the dagger from his chest. At the sight of his stormy eyes wide and empty, filled with an inky darkness, Esta scrambled away—

And fell off the edge of the world.

Her eyes flew open the second she landed, and it took more than a few seconds before the dream began to burn away and she realized where she was. Not in Chicago. Not in the presence of Thoth. No longer trapped in the nightmare that had felt like truth itself.

Moonlight filtered through the high, clouded windows of Dom's warehouse. *Brooklyn.* They were in Brooklyn now, she told herself, still trying to calm her breathing. Jack was dead and Thoth was gone, and it had been a dream. *Only* a dream.

But it felt too real. Even now, she felt the voice inside her, brushing at the fears deep within her.

Her mouth tasted foul, and her skin felt like ice. She'd fallen off the ratty couch she and Harte had curled themselves up on once they'd arrived. Harte was still asleep there. He shifted, moving into the space she'd just vacated, and though his face was calm and peaceful, Esta couldn't shake the image from her dream: his lips frothing with blood, his beautiful eyes clouded over by an inky black emptiness that obscured their usual stormy gray. There was a part of her that wanted to climb back up next to him, to tuck herself into his warmth and pretend for just a little while longer that everything was okay. But the dream was still too thick, too close.

Instead, Esta pulled herself up from the cold, filthy floor and eased the satchel from beneath Harte's head. She looked down at him, peaceful as he was, and forced the remaining vision of the dream away. Until it was only Harte as he truly was, his dark hair mussed from sleep, his cheekbones still too sharp from nearly dying of plague.

Unable to stop herself, she leaned down until her face was close to his. Even in his sleep, Harte seemed to sense her there and lifted his chin until their lips met. It was the barest brush of a kiss, nothing more than the whisper of their mouths meeting, but Esta felt the last bit of coldness from the dream drain away, and some of the tension she was carrying eased.

Harte was safe. *She* was safe. So what if she'd made a promise to Seshat that she didn't know how to keep? She'd figure it out. She would find a way to finish the ritual Seshat had started centuries before and bring time and magic back into balance. They had the Book now, and with it, all the secrets and spells that Thoth had collected through the years. And they had four of the five artifacts. The fifth waited a few decades before, just beyond the bridge, where Harte had left it with a friend. Seshat, magic, time—Esta would figure out a way to save Harte and in turn save them all.

And if she heard the voice of her dream echoing again in her waking, mocking her certainty? She shrugged it off. Pushed that voice back down deep and ignored it. Just as she tried to ignore the memory of the dream, of Harte bloodied and dead by her own hand.

There was light spilling from beneath a doorway at the other end of the hall. Everett was up, it seemed. She could use the company, especially now. She suspected that he could as well. After all, he'd lost his father just hours ago. He shouldn't be alone.

Clutching the satchel to her chest, she started down the hallway, leaving Harte peaceful and sleeping for a little while longer. The sooner Esta figured out what would need to be done, the better for everyone. But her hand had barely reached for the handle of the door when a sharp pain erupted along the underside of her arm, and she could not stop herself from screaming.

CLAVIS

1920—Brooklyn

T he sound of Esta's screaming ripped Harte from sleep. There was no transition from unconsciousness to waking. The effect was instant. One second he was dead to the world, and the next he was on his feet, already moving before his brain could register where he was.

He was running down an endless hallway, sure that he was already too late—sure that Esta was already gone—when he saw her there in the light spilling from an open doorway, with Everett kneeling next to her.

No. No no no—

Shoving Everett aside, he took Esta in his arms, and it was only when she hissed in pain that he breathed. *Not dead. Not gone.* But she was hurt. Her face was etched with pain, and she was cradling her left arm, which was a bloody mess.

Everett was still there, crouched over them both. "What did she do to her arm?"

"*She* didn't do anything," Harte told him, hearing the fury in his own voice. "I'll kill him for this."

"You'll have to get in line." Esta sucked air through her gritted teeth as she tried to pull away from him to stand up.

He didn't let her go. Couldn't. Not when his sleep-muddled brain still hadn't quite accepted that she wasn't dead, wasn't gone.

"Who?" Everett asked, frowning as he watched Harte help Esta to her feet.

"Nibsy Lorcan." They said it together, because they both knew what the wounds on Esta's arm meant. They both knew who was to blame.

"The *Professor*?" Everett asked, frowning. "What does he have to do with anything?"

"He's the one who did this," Esta told Everett.

The other boy frowned. "How? He's trapped behind the Brink."

On her feet now, Esta winced as she looked over the bloodied mess of her arm. "That never stopped him from touching me before."

Her face was too pale, and Harte wanted to punch something. But he knew that wouldn't help anything—not yet at least. First he had to take care of Esta. "Could you go get some cool water? A clean towel or some gauze?"

"Alcohol if you can find any," Esta added, wincing. "I don't need this getting infected."

While Everett disappeared into the cavernous depths of the warehouse, Harte guided Esta into the warmly lit room. "What the hell did he do to you?"

"I think it's a burn," she told him through gritted teeth. "It feels like my skin's still on fire."

She was probably right. The skin on her forearm was raw and angry, puckered and bleeding. There were already welts forming, but the damage wasn't haphazard. Even with the ragged, swollen flesh, anyone could see the marks were purposeful. It looked like she'd been branded by some invisible iron. The smell of it—burned flesh, *her* flesh—was strong enough to make Harte's stomach turn.

"It's another message," she told him. "But I don't know what it—"

She gasped again, and Harte looked down to see her skin opening again. It looked like an invisible scalpel was slicing through her in thin, neat lines, just below the burn. A second later Harte realized what was happening. They were letters. The bastard was carving letters into her.

C-L-A

There was no way for him to stop what was happening. All Harte could do was cradle her arm, impotent with rage, as blood welled and dripped from Esta's wrist and the lurid letters continued to appear.

V-I-S

"Key," she whispered, her voice unsteady as she spoke in short, staccato breaths. "It means key. In Latin. It's just like before."

"It's nothing like before," Harte snapped, anger lashing through his tone so sharply that Esta flinched. He forced himself to calm his voice. He was still furious but not at her. He was angry that Nibsy had touched her again and that he couldn't do anything to stop it. "Last time, you woke up and discovered a scar that was already healed over. That's not what this is."

"No," she admitted. "But I think the difference is that *this* just happened."

"Clearly," Harte said, frowning.

Esta shook her head. "Last time, the scar appeared because he did something to the girl in the past. It was 1904 when that scar appeared, but he could have cut her—me—anytime after we left the city in 1902. Only the effects of it would have appeared. But I think these new marks are still bleeding because this literally *just* happened. It *is* happening. Here and now, in 1920."

Harte's mouth pressed together. It made sense, but the violence of it? "He's turned into a fucking butcher."

"He always has been," Esta said softly.

She was right. Nibsy had left a trail of broken lives in his wake.

"But why this? Why now?" Harte asked.

"Because he knows we're here. What happened back in Chicago has to be all over the news by now. This," she said, holding up her still-bloodied arm, "is his way of letting us know he hasn't given up. That he won't give up."

Everett had returned with a pitcher of water and some rags that looked nearly clean. "I found—" He stopped short, his face draining of color when he saw the newest injury—and the blood. "Oh god . . ."

"I'm fine," Esta said automatically.

"You're bleeding all over the place," Harte told her. "You're definitely not fine. Bring those over here," he ordered Everett, who was still too shocked to do anything more than obey.

"It's all I could find," Everett said, making the words sound more like an apology than an explanation.

"It's great," Esta said gently as she winced again.

Harte was still too angry—too terrified—to do anything more than make a half-formed grunt of thanks. His hands could manipulate cards right beneath a person's nose or pick a lock in the darkness of an underwater tank, but he could not seem to keep them steady as he dabbed the water over Esta's mangled skin.

"It's okay, Harte," she said, touching his wrist softly to stop him. To steady the shaking that even she must have been able to see. "I can clean my own arm."

"I have it," he said.

"Harte—"

"Just let me look at it, would you?" He could hear the tightness in his own voice. He stopped, closed his eyes, and tried to calm himself. "Let me do this for you," he said, opening his eyes again and meeting her gaze. He knew why she wanted to do this herself—why she felt like she had to do everything on her own—but he couldn't let it go. "Let me help you, Esta." He paused, and when he spoke again, he made his voice softer. "I need to make sure you're okay." He swallowed hard, hating how helpless he felt. "Please."

Any other time, Esta probably would have argued. Even now he could see that she wanted to. But she seemed to understand. Resigned, she offered up her hand.

Everett stood close by, watching as Harte worked as gently as he could to clean and bandage her wounds. His expression was creased with grief and worry, and Esta knew that it was more than her injuries that had put the hollowness in his eyes.

The burns were puckered and nearly indecipherable, but though the cuts were still seeping blood, the word was clear. *Clavis.*

"What does it mean?" Everett asked, frowning. "Is it a name or—"

"It's Latin for key," Esta said softly. "But I don't know what that's supposed to signify."

"Maybe he wants your cuff," Harte said as he covered the burns with some ointment from the kit before moving on to the cuts.

"Ishtar's Key?" Everett asked. "That makes sense."

"It's possible," Esta admitted. "But I can't help feeling like there's more to it. He had the cuff for ages and never did anything with it."

"We'll figure it out," Harte told her, trying to sound more confident than he felt. Hating that there was nothing he could do to protect her—except take care of Nibsy Lorcan once and for all.

"Well, well, well," a voice said from the doorway.

The three of them jumped at the sound of it, turning as one to find Dominic Fusilli, the owner of the Nitemarket and their erstwhile rescuer, standing in the darkened doorway. He had the satchel that had once been secured under Harte's head. Esta must have taken it when she'd woken up, but they'd all forgotten about it in the rush to help her. Dom had already opened it, already removed the small, worn book from within. It was too late to stop him.

The interest that lit Dom's face had Harte's instincts prickling in warning. "What do we have here?"

SACRIFICE AND POWER

1920—Brooklyn

Esta considered her options as she watched Dom flip through the pages of the Ars Arcana. They'd all been so distracted by the mess on her arm that none of them had heard Dom's footsteps approaching, and he'd found the satchel she'd dropped before they could pick it up. Now he had the Book and the artifacts, and Esta wasn't sure how to get them back without upsetting the one ally they seemed to have. It was too late to slip through the seconds and take it from him. He'd already seen the Book, and they were in his warehouse, under his protection. For now they were safe. And the Book wasn't going anywhere—she wouldn't let it.

Maybe she was wrong to be so uneasy. After all, Dom *had* saved them from an impossible situation in Chicago. Whatever magic he'd used on the van to transport them to Brooklyn in the blink of an eye had certainly allowed them to get far, far away from where the authorities would be searching. But Maggie didn't like Dominic Fusilli, so Esta figured that was a good enough reason not to trust him.

One look at Harte told Esta that he felt as uneasy as she did.

If Dom noticed their mood, he didn't show it. He was taking his time, studying the page he was on before turning to the next. "I still can't believe I'm looking at this," he said. "The Book of Mysteries. Here. In my hands. And the lost artifacts—or some of them. When I think of what these would sell for . . ." He let out a low whistle. "I'd be set for life."

"They're not for sale," Harte said flatly.

"Everything's for sale," Dom told them with a shrug. He glanced up at Esta. "Everyone has their price."

"Not us," Harte said, stepping toward Dom. "Not for these."

Esta placed her hand on Harte's arm. Starting a fight with Dom wasn't going to help anything. Better to convince him, to make him think that giving back the Book and the artifacts would help him in some way. "What Harte means to say," Esta told Dom, "is that we can't sell them *yet*. We have to use them first . . . to bring down the Brink."

Dom's brows lifted. "*This* is why you were in Chicago?"

She nodded. "The sooner we figure out how to use those artifacts to control the power in the Book, the sooner we can take care of the Brink. The sooner *you* could expand the Nitemarket like you wanted."

Dom's eyes shifted from the page he was reading back to Esta. "The answers are in here?"

"I don't know where else they'd be," she told him, and it wasn't even a lie. "The Order used that Book to create the Brink. It must describe how they did it and explain how we can end it."

"Maybe, but you'd have to figure out what any of this means first." Dom gestured to the markings on the page.

"I might be able to help with that," Everett said. "I've been studying the Order and their type of magic since I was just a kid."

"You're *still* just a kid," Dom said.

"Everett's the one who knew how to disable the tower in Chicago *and* how to reverse its power," Esta reminded Dom. But at the mention of Chicago, Everett's mouth went tight. She gentled her tone when she continued. "If he says he can figure it out, I believe him. If you're sure? You don't have to do this."

"I do," Everett told her. "I can't have it mean nothing. I need to help. I need to do whatever I can."

She knew he was talking about North, about the way he'd died so tragically the night before. "Okay," she said. "Thank you."

Dom still seemed reluctant to part with the objects in his possession.

"The sooner we know what's in those pages, the sooner you get your New York market. It's just 'good business,'" Esta told him, echoing the very words he'd used the night before.

Dom considered Everett, and Esta felt danger stir in the silence that fell as he thought about his options.

So many people had betrayed them for less, and now Dom held the Book and the artifacts in his literal hands. Esta waited, ready for whatever decision he made. She wouldn't allow him to take the Book, but attacking too early would mean turning their one possible ally into an enemy.

Finally, he made up his mind and slid the Book across the table. "It doesn't leave this room." Then he shot a warning look at Esta and Harte. "I'm gonna make some coffee. You two want some?"

Hours later, the burnt and bitter coffee had long since gone cold, but Everett hadn't made much progress. Harte was clearly getting impatient, but he didn't move far from her side. He'd taken to pacing within arm's reach. Dom seemed less concerned about how long things were taking. He still had the satchel and was examining the stones in each of the artifacts with the same sort of small magnifying glass that jewelers used.

"Amazing," he murmured, setting the Dragon's Eye back onto the table next to the other two. "There isn't anything about these stones that makes them physically different, but the power coming from them is something else." Dom set the crown back on the table and picked up the necklace, turning it over in the light and watching the stone flash and glimmer. "I haven't come across anything like them before. And I've seen plenty."

"That's probably because of how they were made," Everett said. It was the first he'd spoken since he'd started examining the Book.

"You found something?" Esta asked, leaning over the table to look at the page Everett had open. Harte moved closer.

"I think so," Everett told them. "Look at this."

There on the page was a series of sketches that clearly showed the five stones surrounded by detailed notes written in faded ink. On the facing page was a detailed drawing of the hand of the philosopher.

"*Is. Newton*," Esta read, running her finger along the inscription there. "Isaac Newton. This is how he did it, isn't it? This is how he made the stones."

"I think so," Everett confirmed.

Esta had already known that Isaac Newton was the one responsible for infusing artifacts he'd collected from ancient dynasties with the affinities of five powerful Mageus in an attempt to control and use the Book's magic. But the attempt had nearly driven him mad. In Chicago, she'd learned that Newton had been under Thoth's control all along. Somehow, Newton had managed to fight off Thoth before the ritual could be completed. He'd given the stones and the Book to the Order for safekeeping, back when the Order still had magic themselves. Years later, the Order had brought the artifacts across an ocean and tried to replicate Newton's work. They'd used them to create the Brink in an attempt to protect their magic and to keep the Book—and Seshat—under control. But the ritual had never been right—like Seshat's ritual, the Order's had never been finished, and the Order's protective barrier had turned into a trap. And then it had become a weapon.

"It doesn't look that different from the ritual that people still use to make magical objects," Dom said.

"What do you mean?" Esta asked.

"It takes a ritual like this to break part of someone's affinity away from them and infuse it into an object. This here . . ." Dom tapped on an elaborate design that looked strikingly like the one carved into the front cover of the Book. "Writing, like this design here, makes the ritual material."

"Sigils are the earliest forms of ritual magic," Everett told them. "The most common, too."

"I wouldn't be in business without them," Dom said. "But I've never seen one quite this complicated. You can't even really look at it straight, can you?"

"It's definitely ancient," Everett agreed. "Powerful, too. But this is different from the rituals used to make objects nowadays." He glanced at Dom. "My understanding is that most magical objects only contain a part of someone's affinity."

"Sure," Dom said. "That's usually how it works."

"Why would anyone willingly give up even a *part* of their affinity?" Harte asked.

Dom shrugged. "It's not always willing," he told them. "But desperate people do desperate things."

"It sounds like what Dolph did to Leena," Esta said, glancing at Harte.

He was frowning thoughtfully as he stared down at the Book. "Or like what Seshat did to herself by placing parts of her magic into the original stones." He glanced up and met Esta's eyes.

They were onto something here. She could feel it, and the expression Harte wore told Esta that he felt the same.

"This ritual is different, though," Everett said, pointing to a block of text on the page. "It's not meant to take part of an affinity. It's designed to take *everything*. All of a person's magic. And their life along with it."

Dom frowned. *"Everything?"*

Everett nodded. "The people who Newton used to power those stones didn't survive. They weren't supposed to."

This wasn't news. Esta learned that months ago, when the Professor had revealed himself and what he intended to do. But she couldn't help thinking of the Nitemarket and all the objects she'd seen for sale there. She thought, too, of what Dolph had done to Leena. "Why not just take part of their magic?"

"Because a life sacrificed is stronger," Everett told them, and when they all turned to him, he shrugged. "A life is singular. And taking a life can create a rare form of power."

But Esta wasn't sure that made sense. She looked down at the bandage on her arm. If a life was singular, how could there be two of her—the person she was and the other version of herself who was growing up under the thumb of Nibsy?

Because you are nothing. An abomination.

She shivered a little at the memory of Thoth's words back in Denver. She wasn't *nothing*. She couldn't be. She was herself. She wasn't some mistake in the time line.

Harte was staring at her—she could feel the intensity of his gaze—but she didn't look at him. She couldn't let Dom know how important this was, or she worried that he'd never give up the Book.

"Does it say what he planned on doing with the stones?" she asked.

Everett frowned and turned back to the Book. "It looks like his plan was to connect them using the Aether."

"That's what Seshat did," Harte murmured. "When she created the Book. She connected the stones she made with her affinity through the Aether."

"But Seshat was trying to save the old magic," Esta reminded him. "What was Newton trying to do?"

"He was trying to create the philosopher's stone," Everett said. When they all looked at him, he only shrugged. "Isn't that the goal of all the old alchemists? Create the substance that can transmute matter and let you live forever?"

Dom swore softly under his breath. "Did he succeed?"

"No," Esta told them.

Everett looked up at her, frowning.

"Newton never went through with the ritual," she reminded them. "He gave the stones and the Book to the Order for safekeeping instead. They're the ones who finally tried the ritual. But it didn't work the way they expected. It's what created the Brink."

"But the Brink didn't work," Dom said. "The Order doesn't have the philosopher's stone. If they did, we'd all know about it."

"Because the ritual went wrong," Harte told him.

"And also because the philosopher's stone isn't a *thing*," Everett said. "Not according to this . . ." He paused, studying the page.

"Well, go on," Dom directed, leaning forward to look over the page where Everett was reading. "What is it?"

"I don't know, exactly," Everett told them. "Alchemical recipes are more like poems than recipes. They're symbolic. Alchemists used them to obscure as much as to record their work. But it doesn't seem like Newton thinks the philosopher's stone is a thing so much as a state of being. A place. It's what he was trying to create by connecting the stones through the Aether."

"Aether is time," Esta said softly. Newton was creating a boundary made of time—or made from manipulating time. Just like Seshat was trying to do.

"That doesn't explain anything," Dom said, clearly growing impatient.

"Give me a second," Everett said, focusing more intently on the pages. "He united the artifacts to control the power in the Book and then . . ." As Everett turned the page, Esta saw that the next one was torn. The bottom half was gone.

"Then *what?*" Dom demanded.

"I don't know. It's missing." Everett frowned down at the missing page. "Whatever ritual he used, it's gone."

"Your arm, Esta." Harte's voice was soft, but there was a thread of fury in it that she didn't immediately understand.

"My arm?" He was already reaching for her, already pulling back her sleeve and unwinding the gauze. When the burned flesh was exposed, Esta understood. The strange markings there matched the ones on the page. But on the page, one line of markings included a row of Greek letters beneath it.

"It's not gone. It's a cipher," Dom told her, flipping back a few pages to where the images of Newton's gems were. The odd symbols were on that page as well.

"A cipher?" She was still too shocked to see the symbols on her arm replicated on the pages of the Book.

"Newton was hiding the ritual with code," Dom explained. "But half the key is missing."

"Maybe Newton didn't want anyone else to be able to replicate his process," Everett said.

But Esta was already shaking her head. That wasn't it at all.

"Clavis," Esta said, thinking of the newest word cut into her wrist. "Nibsy doesn't want my cuff—I mean, I don't doubt he does. But that's not why he carved 'Clavis' into the girl's arm. He knows we have the Book. He's telling us he has the other half of this page."

"It could be a trick," Harte argued. "Maybe he doesn't have anything."

"No," Esta said. "He tried the ritual before. He has the missing piece. He has the key to this cipher and the answer to how we can complete the ritual. He must have kept a piece of the Book separate when he sent me back with Logan. He must have known he'd need some kind of insurance in case I got away or took the Book from him. How else would he have been able to do this?" She pointed to the burns on her arm, the perfect match to the symbols on the page.

"He's forcing you back," Everett realized.

"Well, you're not going," Harte told her. "It's a trap."

"I know it's a trap," Esta said with a sinking feeling. "But he knows it's one that will work. The answers to controlling Seshat—to controlling the Book's power—are on the other half of this page. We have to get it back from him."

"That's *exactly* what he wants," Harte said. "We don't stand a chance if he's expecting us."

Harte was right, but that didn't change anything.

"We don't have a choice," she told him.

"Maybe not, but we have *time*," he reminded her.

"*No*, we don't," she said, lifting her raw arm to remind him. "I'm not going to sit around while Nibsy keeps carving me up."

His eyes narrowed, and he opened his mouth to argue with her, but before he could get a word out, a pounding sounded from somewhere in the bowels of the building.

Dom came alert instantly, and his eyes shifted to the Book and the artifacts still lying on the table. "Shit. They're early." Dom reached for the satchel and started loading the artifacts back into the canvas bag. "You all have to get out of here."

"Who's early?" Esta asked, already reaching for her affinity.

At first Dom didn't answer. He was too busy securing the Book back into the satchel.

Clearly done with being patient, Harte grabbed Dom, spun him around, took him by the collar, and shook. "*Who* is early?"

Dom licked his lips. His eyes darted from Esta to Everett, as though either would help him. Harte tightened his grip and gave Dom another shake. "Razor Riley and his lot," Dom said finally.

Harte went still, but he didn't release Dom. "From the Five Pointers, Razor Riley?"

"Where else would he be from?" Dom said, jerking away from Harte's grasp. He clutched the satchel close to his chest and turned to go, but Everett stood in his way, blocking the door.

"Why would Razor Riley be out there?" Harte demanded.

"Because he's working for Lorcan," Dom said, not bothering to look back at Harte. He spoke to Everett then, lowering his voice and softening his tone. "Let me go, kid. Lorcan doesn't know about you. Far as I'm concerned, he doesn't need to know. You can walk away now without getting mixed up in this."

"I'm already mixed up," Everett said, squaring his shoulders.

"Look, we don't have time for this." Dom turned back to Harte. "Razor's here to take the two of you to Lorcan, and I don't have any plans to get caught up in that mess. We can stand here arguing about things, or you can let me go, and maybe you get away. Maybe the kid here can even get out clean without the Professor ever knowing he was involved."

"You sold us out," Esta accused, unable to stop the stupid note of disappointment from her voice.

"I saved you from the mess you were in back in Chicago," Dom said, clearly affronted that anyone would be upset. "There's no way you were getting out of there without my help."

"But you were working for Nibsy the whole time," Harte growled.

"I don't work for anyone. I'm an independent businessman," Dom said. "The Professor made me an offer that sounded like a good deal at the time. If it makes you feel any better, I thought I would be helping you. I never intended to—"

"How much?" Harte demanded. "How much were our lives worth?"

"It doesn't matter," Dom said. "I'm not going to be able to collect, not if Razor doesn't get you." He gave them a devilish grin and clutched the satchel holding the Book and the artifacts tighter to his chest. "It's a fair trade, don't you think? You get to walk out of here alive and whole, and I get the payday I was promised."

Harte lunged for Dom, but Esta was already in motion. She didn't wait to warn Harte or make any heroic declarations. She simply took hold of her magic and pulled.

NEVER ENOUGH

1920—Brooklyn

Harte saw red as he lunged for Dom, but Esta had already caught him before he could even take a swing. The world went silent around them as she pulled him back, and it was only her sharp intake of breath, a sign that she was still in pain, that stopped him from breaking away from her and doing everything he could to pummel the conniving bastard who'd betrayed them.

He should have known that getting out of Chicago had been too easy. They should have left Dom's warehouse last night. *He* should have insisted that they go rather than collapsing into sleep on that filthy couch. Instead, he'd let himself believe that fate or chance or whatever higher power there might be had given him a handful of minutes to just breathe and hold Esta in safety. As though fate had been anything but a fickle bitch since he was born.

Esta glanced meaningfully at Harte, and he knew what she was asking: whether Seshat was still quiet. He gave her a small nod. Thanks to the Quellant, there wasn't so much as a rumble from the goddess trapped beneath his skin.

"Come on," she said, pulling him toward the door, where Everett was standing frozen in time. "We have to go. We don't have time for him."

"It wouldn't take long," he growled, thinking about the satisfaction he would feel when his fist landed square on Dominic Fusilli's nose. "And we're not going anywhere without the Book."

"I already have it," Esta told him, patting the satchel she'd slung across her chest. "The Book and the artifacts, too."

Harte took another look at the rat who'd betrayed them, longing to leave Dom with a broken nose to remember him by, but eventually he relented, and they moved together so she could pull Everett into her net of time as well.

Everett gasped, startled for a minute, but he recovered quickly. "If there was a way to bottle what you can do—"

Esta shot Everett a look that shut him up. "We go together. Whatever you do, don't either of you let go of me."

"Not a chance," Harte told her, squeezing her hand slightly. *Not ever again.*

"Let's go," Esta directed, nodding toward the open doorway.

Harte didn't argue this time. Together they moved toward the rear of the building, where they'd parked the truck in a gated yard late the night before. Esta and Everett started toward the vehicle, but Harte pulled them both back.

"What is it?" Esta asked.

The truck was still in the same place. The back loading area seemed to be empty as well.

"This feels too easy," Harte said. They'd slipped away from Dom without any trouble, and now they were just going to walk away? "If Nibsy is behind this, we need to be ready for anything. He knows you. He'll be prepared for what you can do."

"How?" she asked.

"I don't know," he admitted. "But if he knew somehow that we would eventually need that half-torn page in the Book, he certainly could predict that you would try to use your affinity to get away."

"Maybe . . . But his goons can't catch what they can't see," she said.

He admired her confidence, but then he'd always admired that part of her. Still, he couldn't shake his unease. "But what about what happened in Chicago? In the Nitemarket and at the convention, the Order used something that interfered with our affinities."

"He has a point," Everett said.

"If the Order has something to null the Quellant, like they did in Chicago, the Professor might, too," Harte told her.

Esta frowned. "We don't have much of a choice, though. We can't sit here and wait for whatever Nibsy might have planned. Our best chance is to move and hope we're faster than he is."

Harte hated that she was right, even if every instinct he had was screaming at him that this was a trap. "Fine. But we need to think this through. We need a plan."

She considered the truck before turning to Everett. "Can you drive that thing?"

It took a bit of doing, but they got themselves into the truck, with Esta between the two of them. She had her hand wrapped around the bare skin of Everett's wrist, so he could still maneuver the vehicle, and Harte had his fingers tangled with Esta's, so they could all stay within the net of her magic. When Everett turned the key, the sound of the enormous engine cranking to life was the only noise in the otherwise silent day.

Everett put the truck into gear and turned it around, but they'd barely pulled out of the gated area when Harte told Everett to stop. The back part of the building was accessible by a narrow alley that turned sharply left before emptying out onto one of the main streets of Brooklyn. But when they'd turned the corner, Harte saw that his earlier instincts had been right. They definitely had a problem.

Esta swore softly beside him.

"What *is* that?" Everett asked.

Ahead of the truck, the alley was filled with some kind of a thick, fog-like substance. It was dense enough that Harte couldn't make out anything beyond it. There was no way to see what waited for them within the soupy murk—or on the other side of it. Worse, it seemed to be *moving*. With every passing second, it filled more of the alley, approaching them and swelling in size despite the rest of the world being caught and held in Esta's power.

"Whatever that is, it shouldn't be moving," Esta told them, sounding every bit as uneasy as Harte felt.

"I knew this was a mistake," Harte said.

"We could go back?" Everett suggested. "Or, if they're expecting us to take the truck, we could go on foot. Or find another way out of this place."

Esta shook her head. "Nibsy would have accounted for the other exits too. At least the truck gives us a little protection, and it moves a lot faster than we could on foot."

"You're thinking we charge through," Harte said, knowing already it was the only real option.

"I think we have to go for it," she said. "Maybe if we expect the worst . . ." She didn't finish.

At first, none of them spoke. The world hung in the stillness of her magic, and there was no sound except for the nearly deafening rumble of the truck's engine. They all knew what the worst meant: they had the Book and four of the artifacts. If they didn't get through that fog, Nibsy would have almost everything he needed.

"If that fog is anything like what happened in Chicago, we need to worry about Seshat." He looked down at their joined hands. Whatever agreement or truce Esta might have made, he didn't trust the goddess not to take advantage of any opportunity she could. "If that fog destroys the Quellant, I won't be able to stop her."

Harte started to release her hand, but Esta caught his fingers more tightly and didn't let him go.

"He'll be expecting us to use my affinity," Esta said, considering the problem. "So maybe I shouldn't use it. Maybe I should let go of time, and we floor it and see what happens. You can have more Quellant ready, just in case, and once we're on the other side, I'll pull time slow again."

"If you can," Harte said.

"If I can't, at least we'll be in the truck. We'll have the benefit of speed. Maybe we'll be able to lose them."

"It sounds like our best option," Everett said.

"It sounds like our *only* option," Harte muttered, hating everything about the plan.

Ahead of them, the fog was closer still. It seemed to have grown denser, darker since they'd stopped.

"Get the extra Quellant ready," Esta told him. "Just in case." As he pulled the packet of tablets out of the leather satchel, she glanced at Everett. "Ready?"

Everett tightened his grip on the shifter and gave Esta a tight-mouthed nod.

"I'll release time as soon as we're moving." She gave Harte's hand a small squeeze, but before she could pull away, he caught her.

"Wait." He leaned in and pressed his lips against hers, allowing himself one more moment of hope, of *her*, in case everything went wrong, as it probably would. In case the Quellant didn't work again. In case Nibsy got the best of them this time.

Harte wanted to stay there, his mouth against hers, their breath intermingling, and pretend that their life could be easy. But he knew it wasn't possible—wouldn't *ever* be possible as long as Nibsy was chasing them and Seshat lived beneath his skin. The fog was still growing, still creeping malevolently toward them, so he pulled away, but he was glad to see that Esta's expression had turned as soft and dazed as he felt.

Her tongue darted out, licking her lips, and he felt a pull low in his gut. And he knew it didn't matter if they had a thousand years—it wouldn't ever be enough.

When she spoke again, her voice was rough with emotion. "Okay, Everett. Floor it."

GONE

1920—Brooklyn

Even with their lives hanging in the balance, Esta could only focus on the feeling of Harte's kiss still on her lips. Her arm might have been aching from the cuts and burns beneath the bandage before, but she barely felt those wounds now. She hardly felt the pain or the fear or even the weight of what was before them—because suddenly, everything felt *right*.

They'd been running for so long—too long—and even now they were running straight into danger, but when he'd stopped to kiss her, the weight of the world had lifted. Everything narrowed to nothing more than the two of them together. And if that was all she could ever have, she would take the memory, tuck it away, and keep it with her.

But there was no more time. There was only action, because the strange fog was now at the nose of the truck, and in a matter of seconds, they would be covered by it.

Everett threw the truck into gear, and the second it lurched forward, Esta released time and Harte. As the truck punched into the dense soup of the fog, she could feel a cold energy surrounding her. She couldn't see a foot in front of the truck, but she knew the second Seshat had awoken because she felt Harte flinch away like he was suddenly afraid to touch her. It took only a matter of seconds—barely time to take a breath or blink—and they were coming out through the other side. The fog grew thinner, and then daylight broke through.

Esta reached almost immediately for Everett, for her affinity, ready to pull time slow once she was sure they were free of whatever that trap had been, but as the murky light of the overcast day found them, her affinity slipped from her, and gunfire erupted.

"Go!" she screamed, but Everett was already shifting the truck into a higher gear and pushing the heavy vehicle's engine as hard as he could.

Harte's instincts had been right. As they breached the fog, they ran straight into an ambush. The alleyway was blocked by a line of men—Five Pointers, from the looks of it. The sharp, rapid retort of their guns echoed off the brick walls, as the glass of the windshield shattered.

"Get down!" she yelled to Harte as she ducked below the level of the dashboard and tried to shield herself from the shards of glass. She grabbed for Everett's wrist and tried again to pull the seconds slow, but Esta could feel the cold tendrils of the fog's energy still clinging to her. It felt like she'd walked through a particularly thick spiderweb. The sticky coolness of the corrupted magic clung to her skin, making it impossible to get a good grasp on her affinity. She would find the seconds and the world would almost go still, but then they'd slip away from her.

The truck swerved, and the sound of the shots followed them. Then suddenly the truck lurched to the left as they were hit from the side. Horns sounded as Everett steered the truck back into their lane, barely avoiding other traffic.

"You need to do your thing," Everett said, his voice tight and pained. "I don't know if I can shake them."

"I'm trying," she said. She almost had it, though. The cold wisps of the fog's unnatural energy were almost gone. "Just keep them off our tail a little longer."

Next to her on the floor, Harte was drawn and pale. His hands shook as he struggled to bring the tablets of Quellant to his mouth. She wanted to help him, but she knew that Seshat made touching him too dangerous.

"Esta—" Everett's voice was strained. "Please. You have to—"

The truck lurched again, and suddenly her affinity was whole again. Without hesitating, she grabbed the seconds and pulled them slow, but the world had barely gone quiet when Everett's hand fell from the shifter. She looked up to find Everett slumped over the steering wheel. His foot was still on the gas pedal, but he wasn't conscious. She grabbed the wheel and swerved around the stopped car they'd been about to slam into.

The world was silent now except for the roar of the truck. Everett's foot was still wedged on the gas pedal, and the truck was still careening through the Brooklyn streets, but Everett wasn't steering it.

"Everett . . ." She tried to pull him back off the wheel, tried to shake him to get some response, but he slumped back into the seat, his head lolling to one side as he let out a weak groan. That's when she saw the blood.

He'd been hit. She couldn't tell where the blood was coming from, but there was so much of it. His eyes were partially opened, unfocused, but he was still breathing—and still bleeding.

"Everett. You have to hold on, okay?" She let go of his wrist to freeze him in time and keep him from bleeding any more as she swerved the wheel and barely missed a milk truck. His foot was still wedged on the gas pedal, and it was all she could do to guide the truck around the traffic. She knew that if she pushed his leg aside and moved his foot off the gas without depressing the clutch at the same time, the truck would stall. Maybe she should do that. She could switch places with him and drive. But her affinity still felt off, and she didn't know how much longer she could hold the seconds at bay. They were still too close to the Five Pointers—or whoever it was that Nibsy had sent after them—to risk wasting any time. The farther away they could get, the better.

Esta looked down to find Harte frozen and pained-looking on the floor of the passenger side. The Quellant was still in his hands, but he didn't look like he'd been otherwise harmed. He couldn't do anything to help as long as Seshat was freed from the Quellant's effects, and she couldn't let go of time for that to happen as long as they were so close to the warehouse. She was on her own. She had to hold on to every-thing a little bit longer until she could lose Nibsy's guys and get them somewhere safe. So she left Everett's foot where it was, left the truck in gear, and tried to steer them through the silent, stopped Brooklyn traffic without killing anyone. But she had no idea where she was going.

When she turned down one of the side streets, Esta realized she'd made a mistake. The street dead-ended into a strip of land, and beyond that lay the river. At that speed, they would end up in the water. Without much choice, she pushed Everett's foot aside and felt the truck shudder as the engine stalled out. She barely managed to reach the brake before the truck hit the curb of the street and its front tires reached the edge of the grass.

As the engine hissed and shuddered, Esta simply sat there, trying to catch her breath. Unsure of what to do. She had no idea if they'd been followed. Pulling back Everett's jacket without touching any of his skin, she looked for the wound and saw that he'd been hit twice—once in the side and once in the upper thigh. Stuck in her net of time, his wounds weren't bleeding, but the instant she released her hold on the seconds, they would.

In the distance, the city waited beneath a heavy sky. The bridge rose from the water, a pathway toward her eventual fate, summoning her onward, but for now, the world was silent.

She had to release time. She knew that. She needed Harte to help Everett, and Harte needed the Quellant to be any use at all. But she didn't know just how far Nibsy's plans had gone. She had no idea what might happen when she released the seconds. For sure, Everett would start bleeding again. Seshat would likely rise up and fight. And there could be more of the Five Pointers, more of Nibsy's men waiting, ready for when they appeared.

But hesitation wasn't going to help her. She couldn't sit there, stuck in the abeyance of time forever. The minutes had to continue on, and so did she.

Esta let herself take one more breath in the silence, one more breath before everything might explode again, and then she let go of the seconds and watched the world spin back into motion.

Immediately, Harte gasped.

"Get that Quellant in your mouth," she told him as she reached for Everett, trying to put pressure on his wounds. "Everett . . . can you hear me? Can you talk?"

She sensed Harte's struggle, sensed him shuddering from the Quellant, and knew Seshat had receded, because suddenly he was there with her.

"What the hell happened?" Harte asked.

"You were right," she said, tapping lightly at Everett's cheek, willing him to focus on her. Waiting for the attack that didn't come. "It was an ambush. He's hit. We need to get him help."

Everett groaned. "No . . . have to go on."

She ignored him. "Come on, Harte. Help me move him over so I can drive. We need to get him to a hospital or—"

"No." Everett's eyes were open now. "Go."

"We are not leaving you here," Esta said, determined to ignore the grayish pallor of his skin, the way his eyes weren't quite focused on her. She ignored, too, the way her own hands were trembling. The way her heart felt unsteady and her throat felt tight. This couldn't be happening, not after North. Not after all they'd learned and all that had happened. "We're going to get you help."

"Too late," he said, flinching. "Have to go back . . . Make this right."

Esta's eyes were burning. She wanted to deny his request, but she couldn't find the words because she knew he was right. They probably wouldn't be able to find a hospital in time, and even if they did, in 1920 he likely wouldn't make it. But in the future . . . "I can take you forward. We can go where there's help."

She took Everett's hand as she held out her other hand to Harte. But he didn't immediately take hold.

"Esta," Harte said, his voice annoyingly gentle.

She bristled. "Take my hand, Harte."

But Everett was pulling away from her. "Make a good future for us . . . for my parents," he whispered, his voice barely a breath. "Go."

His chest didn't rise again.

"No," she said, shaking him slightly. His blood was still on her hands, and his eyes remained unfocused, glassy.

"He's gone, Esta." Harte was pulling her away, or at least he was trying to. But she didn't want to admit what had just happened, couldn't make herself move. "We have to go before the people who were after us catch up. We have to put as much space between us and Nibsy Lorcan as we can right now. We have to leave him."

"There's no getting away from Nibsy," she said dully, realizing the truth. Everett was gone, another person lost because of her actions.

But there was a way to fix this—there was a way to put everything to right.

She reached forward and closed Everett's eyes. "Being on this side of the Brink isn't going to keep us safe, and you know he's not going to stop coming after us. We have to go back into the city."

"Esta," Harte said. "Let's think this through."

"I have," she said. "It was always the plan to go back. We have to find the ring, and now we also need to get the missing piece of the Book from Nibsy. Without it, we can't end all of this."

"That doesn't mean we have to walk right into another one of his traps," Harte argued. "There has to be another way."

"There isn't. I'm not going to run from this, Harte." She took his hand in hers, belatedly realizing that hers was still marked with Everett's blood. "We're going to make him pay."

THE BRIDGE

1920—Brooklyn

The bridge to Brooklyn had always loomed larger than life in Harte Darrigan's mind. It was an enormous thing, a marvel of modern engineering that was about as old as he was. When he was a boy, he'd dreamed of walking across it, a free man escaping the prison of the city. Later, its wide span and the waters below had offered an answer to the problem of the power that he'd unwittingly accepted by touching the Book. It had always represented freedom to Harte, but now he was on the other side, preparing to cross back into the city he'd worked so hard to escape.

In the distance another bridge loomed, a marvel of steel. But it seemed appropriate somehow that they were there, on the same bridge that had led them out of the city months before. Now that span of steel and stone represented nothing more and nothing less than his fate.

Harte looked over at Esta when she paused at the foot of the long expanse that would lead them up and over the water. She was wearing a shapeless pair of workman's overalls, the only thing she could find in Dom's warehouse to replace her bloodstained dress from Chicago. Her hair was short now, but the humidity hanging in the air had it curling around her face in a way that almost suited her better than the long locks she'd had when they'd first met. Her mouth was set in its familiar determined line. He'd kissed that mouth—though not nearly enough—knew what her lips felt like when they molded against his, what she tasted like when their breath intermingled. Suddenly he felt more helpless than he ever had before, more helpless even than when he was lying in that filthy hole back in San Francisco, barely able to breathe. Barely able to do anything more than hope for death.

The angles of her face had become more than familiar to him—they'd become essential. *She'd* become essential. Maybe she'd always been that for him, though. His life had changed completely from the first moment he'd seen her on the dance floor of the Haymarket.

"What if it doesn't work?" he pressed. "What if we go after Nibsy and it isn't enough? What if he still wins?"

"He won't," Esta said, her jaw going tight. "I'll die before I let that happen."

"That's exactly what I'm afraid of," he told her softly. Because he knew that when Esta set her mind to something, there was no stopping her. And Harte didn't know how he'd keep her safe.

The sky above was growing heavier and more threatening as they started across the span of the bridge. Behind them, Brooklyn lay quiet and still. Ahead, Manhattan promised nothing but danger. His entire life, all he'd wanted was to escape from that very city. He'd plotted and planned, lied and betrayed, all to be on *this* side of the Brink. And he'd made it. Now he found himself in the unbelievable position of preparing to return to the prison he'd been born into.

There was no question that he would return. Esta was right; they had no choice but to cross back into the city, to go after Nibsy Lorcan, and to find the missing part of the Book. And there was nowhere he wanted to be but at her side.

"We need a plan," Harte said. "Once Nibsy realizes we've escaped, he'll be expecting us to come for him and the key. We've already seen what he's capable of. If we want any chance of walking out of this alive, we're going to have to think *around* him. But with all he's capable of, I don't know how to get past his talent."

"There might be a way," Esta said, glancing over at him. "But you're not going to like it."

Harte had a feeling he was going to *hate* it. But he squeezed her hand gently and waited for her to speak.

"We don't have to cross the Brink now," she told him. "We could choose any time to arrive."

"You think we should go back?" he asked, considering the possibilities. "It's where we have to go eventually. We can use the Book to hold the stones and—"

"He'll be expecting that too," she said. "He knows I have to take the cuff back. He's probably been ready for us to return all along—and we have to expect that he *will be* ready, whenever we finally do return." Her expression was thoughtful. "I think we should go forward."

"Forward?" It wasn't really a question of what she meant—Harte *knew* what she meant. But there was a part of him that needed her to say it.

"If we go back to 1902, we play right into his plans. We still don't have any answers about how to control Seshat's power or to use the piece of magic in the Ars Arcana to make things right. We haven't even figured out how to use the Book to take the stones back. But if we go forward in time?" She shrugged. "Professor Lachlan might still be waiting. He probably will be. But half a century is a long time to stay on high alert."

"But it's not impossible," Harte reminded her. "Not when it's Nibsy."

"No, not impossible," she admitted. "But before, there were *decades* when Professor Lachlan was waiting for me to reappear. During that time, he wasn't powerful. He wasn't the leader of the Devil's Own or any gang. He was a college professor, quietly biding his time and trying to keep his unnatural longevity from being noticed. He was alone for a long time before he put together the team I grew up with. At some point, he'd have to start lying low. If he's still using healers, he wouldn't want to draw attention to himself."

"You don't know that for sure," Harte said. "He isn't the same Professor that you grew up with. If he has that fog, he's liable to have more tricks."

"Probably," she admitted. "But we can expect that. We can be ready."

"We can't be ready for everything, Esta. We have no idea what kind of a future we'd be walking into," Harte argued.

"That's true, but right now? Nibsy is a grown man solidly in his prime. That attack back there tells us that he's strong and surrounded by allies. Maybe if we go far enough ahead, he won't be. When he's old, maybe he'll be weaker. Maybe he'll be alone. Maybe we'll have a better shot at getting the piece of the Book back from him."

"Or maybe he would have had even longer to plan," Harte said darkly. "Who knows what we've changed, Esta. He could have surrounded himself with more protection. It might be even harder to get to him. And with his affinity, we have to assume he'll know that we're coming the second we arrive in the city—*whenever* that is."

"Maybe," she said. "But we can plan for that. We know what power he has now. If we go forward, though?" She shrugged. "That's a future that *none* of us can predict. We have a real chance to take advantage of his surprise. We can't be ready for everything, but then, neither can he."

Harte hated the idea every bit as much as he'd expected to, but he couldn't deny that Esta had a point. If they crossed the bridge now, Nibsy would *definitely* be waiting for them on the other side of the bridge. He'd be waiting for them no matter when they came for the missing page, but slipping ahead—dealing with an old man instead of one in his prime—might at least give them the *possibility* of victory.

"Fine. We'll do it your way," Harte said, wishing there were some other option that didn't require multiple trips through time. She'd slipped him through time before, and it was always awful. Worse, once they were . . . *whenever* they were going, he'd be working blind. It wouldn't be the New York he knew. "When will you take us forward? Before we cross or . . . ?"

"Before makes sense," Esta said. "It's likely that Nibsy will have bigger numbers on the other side waiting for us now. And if we slip forward now, we'll still be outside the Brink. In case anything goes wrong. But I think we should get closer—maybe on the bridge. Maybe right before the Brink?"

He gave her a small, resigned nod. "Then I guess we better get going."

They walked on together, hand in hand, and as they approached the midpoint of the enormous span, Harte began to feel the telltale ice of the Brink's energy cutting through the heat of the summer day.

Esta looked up at him, her golden eyes calm and steady. "I'm going to have to release time to slip us forward. Are you ready?"

"Not even a little," he told her. But there wasn't really a choice. There was no way to run from this, no way around what they had to do. All roads had always led here, to this place—this city. The ring waited for them somewhere across the river in the years that had already gone by, and now they knew the key to stopping Seshat—to fixing the Brink—waited there as well, with Nibsy.

In the distance, the world had once more launched back into motion. He could hear the steady clattering rumble of traffic, the far-off wailing of a train's whistle, and over the sound of the wind, the water.

Esta squeezed his hand, and a second later Harte felt the beginning of the same nauseating push-pull he'd felt before. It was like being torn apart, like he was shattering into a million pieces, and then, suddenly, gunfire erupted from the foot of the bridge behind them.

He'd barely had time to look back and see the pair of men shooting at him when in the next second, they were falling. Endlessly tumbling until, all at once, it was over. Day had turned to night, and the summer's heat had transformed itself into the bitter bite of winter.

Harte's vision swirling, he fell to his knees and found himself sinking into the snow. Esta was there, cursing as she knelt beside him and rubbed his back.

"Are you okay?" she asked.

He nodded as he tried to pull himself together. His stomach was still rolling as he got to his feet.

"They threw me off," she told him, shivering when the wind gusted off the frozen river. "I should have expected an attack, but I didn't." She shivered again.

　　　　　　　　　　　　　　LISA MAXWELL

He tried to give her his jacket. She started to shrug him off, but he wrapped it around her anyway.

"We need to get going," she told him.

She was right. Even now, Nibsy might know they had arrived.

Harte noticed, then, just how much the world had changed. The city skyline in 1920 had been a marvel to him, but this? *This* city was nearly impossible to take in. Its buildings towered over the river, and they were lit so dazzlingly bright against the night sky that for a second he couldn't breathe. He'd seen glimpses of this city the time he'd used his affinity on Esta those many months ago, but to her, it had seemed ordinary. He hadn't really understood.

The bridge below vibrated with a steady stream of motorcars. The road was filled with enormous trucks and boxy automobiles that were all square angles and rumbling engines. The buildings on the other side of the river glowed like torches, and in the sky above, there were no stars. There was a scent in the air, heavy like coal smoke but different somehow.

"This is where you're from?" he asked.

"Not exactly," she said, frowning as she looked at the skyline. "But it's close." Esta took in the skyline for another long minute before she let out a long, weary-sounding breath and turned to him, her expression creased with worry and something too close to pain for Harte's liking. "I know what this means for you, Harte. I know what you did to get out of New York, and now you're willingly going to walk back into the prison of the Brink. Maybe you don't have to. You could wait here and—"

"I'm coming with you, Esta." And if part of him almost didn't mind? If he looked up at those soaring buildings, the sheer audacity of late-century Manhattan, and felt a small spark of . . . wonder? For *this* prison of a city? Because it was still a prison. Time hadn't changed that.

He'd have time to consider that later.

"Harte—"

Before she could argue with him any more, he leaned in and kissed her. Again. Because he could and because he wanted to. And because he wasn't stupid enough to take any time they might have together for granted, not *ever* again. He felt her surprise, her annoyance at the way he'd silenced her argument. As he pulled away from her, she was frowning.

Her shoulders sagged a little. "I just wish this could be different. I wish you didn't have to give up everything you wanted just to help me."

He wanted to tell her that he wasn't *only* helping her, that he wasn't giving up everything. He wanted to tell her that before she'd walked into his life, he hadn't had a clue about what he'd *truly* wanted. But he didn't say any of those things. Instead, he cocked his mouth into the wry grin he'd perfected years ago and gave her a wink. "But it's so much more fun when you owe me."

She rolled her eyes at him, but the breathy laugh that came with it was real. It broke the tension between them. "Keep telling yourself that, Darrigan."

He took her hand again, brushed his thumb across her soft skin, and watched with satisfaction as she shivered from something other than the bitter cold. Then all at once, the world went still as Esta pulled time to a stop. There were no more words. Nothing that needed to be said. In silence, together, they walked onward toward the city, with only the sound of their own footsteps to accompany them.

At first it was impossible to tell where the cold of the winter night ended and the power of the Brink began. They were so similar, the bite in the air and the dangerous energy that seemed to be reaching for them. It was still a ways off, but with each step they took, the night deepened. The winter wrapped more firmly around them. And the Brink warned them of what was to come.

When they reached the midpoint of the bridge, Harte felt a sudden change. There was a shifting, a pulse of energy, as the icy magic of the Brink flew toward them, wrapped around them, tried to pull them under.

Everything after that happened too fast, and later, he would never really be able to remember what came first and what followed. One minute they were walking toward the city, forcing themselves forward, step by step, and the next they were running as though their lives depended on it. They hadn't decided to run or even discussed it, but they seemed to know at the same time that they had to go *now*, and quickly, or they'd never make it through.

They were nearly to the other side of the bridge, but not close enough, when a new bolt of cold stabbed through Harte like a jagged, icy blade. And then everything began to fall apart.

THE DELPHI'S TEAR

1902—Bella Strega

James Lorcan twisted the ring on his finger, reveling in the power that seemed to radiate from the crystalline stone. He smiled to himself as the Aether vibrated with possibility. The Delphi's Tear was every bit as powerful as he'd hoped.

Suddenly, though, the Aether shifted, and James came to attention. Something was happening. Something was changing. He'd hoped that with the Delphi's Tear, the Aether would more than suggest. But even with the ring upon his finger, the Aether revealed no more than it had before. It thrummed again, directing him onward with its usual vague urgency.

He made his way down the back staircase to the Strega's barroom, all the while following the wild fluctuations of the Aether. It was early evening, too early for the usual crowd, but when he entered the saloon, he found it louder than usual. The energy felt unsettled and more than a little dangerous, and James saw the cause almost immediately.

Near the zinc bar, a drunken Mooch was speaking loudly enough to be heard over the din. He was gesticulating as he spoke, railing to anyone who would listen, as Werner tried—and failed—to quiet him. Quite a crowd had amassed around the pair, and as Mooch continued to speak, the feeling in the air grew more and more electric. Certain that this was the cause of the disturbance, James paused, biding his time before he made his presence known.

He'd been listening to the whispers filtering through the ranks of the

Devil's Own ever since he'd returned from the Flatiron Building with the Delphi's Tear on his hand—and without Mooch and Werner—two nights before. After Logan had described how the two had left with Viola, how they'd run to save themselves instead of finishing the mission he'd sent them on, James had assumed that he would not see them in the Bowery again—at least not alive. Yet there they were, disrupting his evening and threatening everything he was on the verge of building.

Gripping the cane tighter, he felt the magic within it flare stronger than ever as he took a step into the low-ceilinged room. Even those around the periphery were quiet, trying to listen to Mooch, so at first one noticed James enter. But as he walked through the crowd, an awareness rippled, and slowly people began to move out of his way, giving him room to pass freely.

He was nearly to the bar before he could hear clearly what Mooch was saying.

"It was an impossible job," the redheaded firebrand slurred, waving his glass of Nitewein around so wildly that the contents sloshed over his hand. "A suicide mission."

According to Mooch, they'd been sent into the Order's lair like lambs to the slaughter.

"Dolph Saunders wouldn't never have asked us to do it," Mooch railed, even as Werner tried to shush him. "Dolph would've had our backs."

"Nibsy *does* have our backs," Werner said, trying to take the glass away from his friend.

Mooch jerked his hand back, spilling the remained contents. "Nibsy Lorcan ain't more than a boy. People are following him like he's some-body, but he ain't nothing compared to the man Dolph—"

It was the final statement that had James stepping forward. The thump of his cane shouldn't have been audible over the noise of the saloon, but somehow it was enough for people to turn. The crowd went silent, because everyone understood that a line had been crossed. Everyone seemed to be holding their collective breath, waiting for what would happen next.

When Mooch realized that James had appeared, there was no flash of fear or misgiving. Instead, Mooch lifted his chin, his expression bleary-eyed and smugly indifferent. Next to him, Werner's expression had shifted into an alert wariness. Werner, at least, understood.

Stopping a few feet from Mooch, James leaned on the cane and again reveled in the feel of its power beneath his palm and the way it sang to the nervous energy careening through the room. As the room buzzed, he simply stared at the two boys without speaking.

Because he could. Because the Strega was his to command.

Mooch was a few inches taller than James and older as well. He was mean as a snake and could turn his fire on anyone—and did, often without provocation. But it didn't take a reading of the Aether to know that he wouldn't threaten James. Not here in the heart of the Strega. And not with his fire, at least. Because Mooch wasn't a leader. He was a coward.

"So," James said softly, knowing that nevertheless his voice carried through the room. "I see you have returned to us at last."

"Didn't expect that, did you?" Mooch demanded, too drunk to be nervous and too cocky to be smart.

"What is that supposed to mean?" James asked, his voice deadly calm.

"Don't listen to him none," Werner said, trying to push Mooch behind him. "Look, we would've come back sooner. We meant to. But the Order . . . they're everywhere. They're picking up anyone they suspect of having the old magic." Werner shifted nervously.

"I'm aware." James leaned into the cane, kept his expression free of any emotion. Beneath his hand, the power within the silver top—Leena's power and Dolph's—sizzled against his skin. "The rest of us are *all* aware of the danger we're currently in, no thanks to the two of you. And yet here you stand, blaming others for your own failures."

"Just take back what you said," Werner hissed into Mooch's ear. "Apologize."

But Mooch only lifted his chin higher.

Werner's eyes darted to James. "He's been drinking too much tonight,

Nibs. Nerves, you know. He's just talking shit, but he don't mean nothing by it."

"James," he corrected. "I've asked you to call me James."

"Right. *James*. Sorry." Werner ran a hand through his dark blond hair. "Like I said, Mooch here, he don't mean nothin.' Do ya, Mooch?" He elbowed his drunken friend. *"Tell him."*

Even inebriated as he was, Mooch's confidence suddenly faltered. There was a flicker of misgiving in his expression as he seemed to realize the gravity of the situation.

The smugness drained from his expression. "Yeah, I didn't mean nothing," he muttered half-heartedly. But he looked down, unable or unwilling to meet James' eyes.

"I see." James stepped closer. "But I wonder . . . why would you say something you didn't mean?" he asked, pretending confusion. "You said quite a lot just now."

"I was just talking, is all," Mooch told him. A soft belch highlighted his drunkenness and punctuated his confession.

James cocked his head slightly. "Were you?"

"Sure . . ." Mooch looked more nervous now. "I was just talking."

"You do that often, don't you?" James asked. He kept his voice soft and even.

The entire barroom had gone silent to listen. It felt like the Aether itself was holding its breath and waiting for what would come, and then James felt the shift, the telltale nudge that told him it was time.

"What?" Mooch seemed confused now.

"You often say things you don't mean," James clarified, allowing a bit more menace to color his tone. "You lie."

"I don't—"

"For instance," James continued, not allowing Mooch to explain. "When you told the others just now that you did everything possible to retrieve the ring, you were lying, weren't you?" He took another step forward.

"No. I wasn't lying about that," Mooch said. "Werner was there. He can tell you. There wasn't any way to get the ring out of that place."

Werner was backing away now. Another coward. But there would be time enough to deal with him later.

"You've lied to me before, Mooch. Do you think I don't know? When you told me that the police had released you from the Tombs, it was a lie," James said. "Wasn't it?"

"I don't know what you're talking about," Mooch said, but his voice cracked as he spoke, and his face was drained of color. "They released me, just like I said they did."

"No, Mooch. You had help. And you repaid your saviors by helping them break into my rooms," James said softly. "You allowed them to steal from me."

"No, Nibs—I mean, James," Mooch said, correcting himself as he stumbled over his words and his lies. "I *wouldn't*."

"But you did. Would you like to tell everyone here who it was that you let into the Strega that day back in May, or would you rather I told them?" James asked.

The silence around them now was deafening, but the Aether, it was dancing. Urging him on.

"You see," James said—and he was speaking to the room now, not only to Mooch. "It would be so much easier to believe that you'd done every-thing you could to bring me the ring if you hadn't let Viola Vaccarelli come into our home, our sanctuary. You helped her—a traitor to the Devil's Own—steal from me. From *us*."

"No, I—"

"Save your lies, Mooch." He leaned forward a bit, ignoring the boy's protest. "No one here believes them, just as no one believes you did everything you could at the Flatiron Building."

"But we *did*," Mooch said. "It was impossible to get the artifact like you wanted." Mooch looked to Werner, who wasn't by his side any lon-ger. The other boy had already pressed himself back into the crowd.

"Another lie," James said. He held up his hand, the one bearing the ring, and allowed himself a to feel the satisfaction of seeing the color drain from Mooch's face. "Logan didn't walk away from his duty to the Devil's Own. But *you* did. Maybe you never wanted us to have this artifact." He lowered his voice. "Maybe you were working with Viola—and against *us*—all along."

"No way, Nib—James. That ain't it at all," Mooch said, backing away. But he was blocked by the bar behind him. "That ain't how it happened at all. Tell 'em, Werner. Explain what it was like up there."

Werner's eyes met James', and they widened slightly. But Werner didn't speak to help his friend. He just shook his head slightly and then looked away.

James took in every detail of the crowded saloon. There was not a soul there who hadn't been listening. He stepped toward Mooch. "It seems to me that while the rest of us risked ourselves for what Dolph Saunders built, you were off making nice with those who have betrayed Dolph and the Devil's Own."

"No, Nibs—*James. No.*" He sounded more sober now. "That ain't how it—"

"I think," James said, cutting him off before he could finish his protest, "that those of us who are loyal to Dolph's memory—may his soul rest in peace—should not stand for another lie from the mouth of a traitor."

He turned to the room and sensed that they were with him, every one of them. And why shouldn't they be? Hadn't he led them after Dolph had fallen? Hadn't he protected them from the Five Pointers and the threat of Tammany's police?

Jerking up his sleeve far enough to expose the intertwined snakes on his own arm, James looked around the room and met the eyes of those watching. "We all took this mark when we pledged ourselves to the Devil's Own, but this was never Dolph's mark alone. These intertwined serpents, life and death, were a promise to something larger than

Dolph Saunders. They were a promise to what he believed in. They were a promise of *loyalty*. Not to a man, but to an idea."

James turned back to Mooch now. He allowed his affinity to swell through the power in the cane just a little, testing it. Mooch reacted exactly as James had hoped, immediately grabbing his neck where the edge of a snake barely peeked out over the collar of his shirt. He grimaced and rubbed at the tattoo as though he were trying to rub off the ink inscribed into his skin.

"What the hell, Nibs?" Mooch whimpered.

Around them, the saloon rustled with uneasiness. James understood why. He could sense them all there, sense the marks that connected them to the cane he was holding, and he knew they could sense him as well. The Delphi's Tear might not have revealed the future to him, but the power in the artifact, along with his own connection to the Aether, made the cane he leaned against more powerful—and more dangerous—than it had ever been in Dolph Saunders' hand.

"Does it speak to you, Mooch?" James asked, swallowing the amusement that threatened to show in his expression.

"Please," Mooch said, his eyes filled with the kind of panic that could only be described as satisfying.

"Does your mark know of your betrayal?" James asked, taking another step closer.

"I didn't mean nothing by it," Mooch whined. "Maybe Viola and her rich toff did come and get me out of the Tombs. I know it was wrong to let them in, but she told me she just wanted to get something from her old room. You gotta believe me, Nibs—*James*. You gotta know I wouldn't do nothing to hurt the gang."

"But you did," James said. "Maybe you didn't mean anything by your actions, but they were a betrayal nonetheless. You think to compare me to Dolph Saunders? We all know one thing Dolph never tolerated"—he leaned closer until his face was a breath away from Mooch's—"*disloyalty*."

Before Mooch could so much as flinch away, James lifted the cane, and in a swift, impossible-to-stop motion, he placed the Medusa's head against the tattoo on Mooch's neck. She might have been kissing the dark ink on his skin, but at the touch of her cold silver lips, Mooch's scream tore through the saloon.

As the mark turned bloody, James began to draw on the power of the stone as well. He'd been experimenting with the cane for weeks now, had determined that his connection to the Aether gave him more flexibility to use the marks than Dolph ever had. Dolph had needed to touch someone—skin to skin—to borrow their affinity, but James could feel the marks through the Aether that surrounded a person. Until now, it hadn't been strong enough to do more than send a tingling bit of ice as a subtle warning to a single person. It had been enough to throw Viola off, but not enough to do any real damage.

With the power in the ring now on his finger, though? Things had changed.

Focusing through the Delphi's Tear, connecting it to the power in the Medusa's head, suddenly James could sense *every* person within his sight who wore the mark of the Devil's Own. He felt their link to the magic trapped in the cane head, felt the oaths they had given, and he used that connection to send a warning to everyone in that room. A promise. A threat.

The men and women in the barroom, the dangerous cutthroats, brawlers, and thieves who had once pledged themselves to Dolph Saunders, began to shuffle uncertainly. He could feel their panic rising, sensed that they all understood a new order had begun. And then he watched as, one by one, they began to kneel.

A DIFFERENT CITY

1902—The Bowery

Viola Vaccarelli eyed the darkened entrance to the stables from the mouth of the alleyway where she stood waiting in the shadows with Jianyu. Though she itched to charge in and just begin already, they couldn't risk being reckless. Ever since the events at the Flatiron Building a few weeks before, the city had been simmering. It seemed that every faction in the city had used the night of the Manhattan Solstice to tighten their control or increase their power.

Tammany had taken the Five Pointers' open warfare on the Order and the deadly attack on the plaza near Madison Square as a sign of the Order's weakness. In response, they'd increased the police presence throughout the city, and especially in the Bowery, to show who was truly in charge. The city might not be burning, as it had after Khafre Hall, but Tammany's police patrolled the poorest streets in the city with impunity, looking for any reason to bust open heads.

Having lost Tammany's previous support and help, the Order hadn't simply sat back to lick their wounds, as maybe they should have. Instead, they'd created patrols of their own and filled them with the roughest native-born men they could find. Viola knew their kind. She'd grown up with men like this all her life. Stronzi, tutti. The patrols were more than willing to turn their anger and hatred for the newest waves of immigrants into violence. When they weren't making trouble with the police, they prowled through the poorest tenements, searching for the Order's lost artifacts. It didn't matter if some of the people they injured in their searches weren't actually Mageus.

But the power struggle between Tammany and the Order wasn't the only danger in the city. With Paolo's absence, every gang was out for more territory . . . and for the blood of its rivals. The hole that Dolph Saunders' death had left in the power structure of the Bowery back in March had become the center of a building hurricane. Rival gangs didn't hesitate to take up weapons over the smallest slight. They were making ready for war.

To Viola's irritation, Nibsy had managed to maintain his hold on the Strega and the Devil's Own through his alignment with the Five Pointers. But as more of Dolph's rivals circled, there was no telling who would finally claim the Bella Strega and the territory that came with it.

Something was coming, of that Viola was certain. She'd seen the streets churn with riots enough times before that she knew they would soon erupt again. It was only a matter of when and a question of what might set them off. But this deep into the night, the city was almost quiet. Its ever-present noise was now little more than a gentle hum in the background, and it was almost possible to imagine a different city. *Almost.* But not quite, not when she knew that there was still violence stirring beneath. That violence had brought them to this part of town in the depth of the night.

The stables themselves were on the eastern edge of the Bowery, a little ways from the docks and nestled between buildings that held factories and sweatshops—far enough away from the nearest tenement that no residents milled around the streets. Viola didn't mistake the emptiness for safety, though.

"You're sure they've brought him here?" she whispered, glancing at Jianyu.

He gave her a single, nearly imperceptible nod. "Earlier this evening, but long after the horses were all in for the night."

Another Mageus had been taken up by the Order's patrols. Another soul that would have otherwise been lost.

For the last few weeks, word of abductions had been finding their way to Jianyu. A father taken from his pushcart. A brother who never returned home from his shift at the factory. One of the worried family members would appear on the street corner near the basement apartment where the two of them were currently staying, out of place in the neighborhood and desperate enough to turn to the very people they considered traitors. Jianyu never hesitated to offer his help, and Viola never bothered to argue against it. To her thinking, there was enough pain and suffering in the city without her adding more.

She watched for another long minute, waiting for some evidence of what was happening inside the stables, listening for any sound that might tell them when to make their move. Impatience grated against her already raw nerves. But too early, and they'd all be in danger. Too late, and . . .

They couldn't be too late.

Jianyu was already removing the bronze mirrors from his pockets, small disklike objects that helped him to focus his affinity and pull even the smallest strands of light out of the darkness. And it *was* dark. In this part of town, the shadows fell heavier than normal across the streets. Near the stables, the lamps hadn't been lit for the evening. Another sign that Jianyu's information wasn't incorrect. The Order always preferred to do their dirty work under the cover of night.

"If you are ready?" Jianyu asked, his expression tense with the effort of holding on to the light.

Viola nodded and stepped closer to him, looping one of her arms around his lean waist so he could wrap her in his cloak of magic. Then, hidden from any who might be looking, the two of them moved quickly toward the stables. Using Libitina, Viola made short work of the lock, and once the door was open, they let themselves silently into the building.

The air inside was even warmer than the balmy summer night, thick and moist with the breath of horses and the scent of hay. At first the only sound inside the stable was the soft shuffling of hooves and the occasional snort from a nearby stall. But then she heard it, muffled in the distance—the low moaning of someone in pain.

LISA MAXWELL

She exchanged a silent, knowing glance with Jianyu, and he nodded. Together they moved through the stables, past sleeping horses, until they came to another door. Not the stables then, but the next building over.

Surprisingly, this doorway wasn't secured. A bit of luck, but Viola did not relax. She kept her wits about her as she followed Jianyu into the narrow passage that ran between the two buildings. Another moan echoed in the darkness, but it was closer now. Jianyu sent her a silent look and nodded, before picking up their pace.

Finally, they came to the place where the passageway opened into a larger chamber. It was a factory of sorts. Large machines lurked in the shadowy gloom. In the center of the factory floor, four men stood above a boy who had been tied to a chair. Bruised and bloodied, Josef Salzer was barely recognizable from the beating, but the men—cowards that they were—clearly weren't finished with him. Three looked to be common day laborers, and were nothing more than hired muscle. But the other was dressed in an expensive-looking suit.

Because the Order doesn't trust their hired help. There was always one of their lower-level leccapiedi present, supervising without actually dirtying his hands. The Order's men always asked the questions, and the hired muscle delivered the answers.

"Again," the man in the suit said, his voice filled with bored indifference.

One of the larger men stepped forward and slammed his fist into the boy's face, and Josef's head ricocheted backward with such force that Viola nearly gasped. The Order's man didn't so much as flinch.

Viola sent her affinity out, sensing the heartbeats of every person in the room. Ready.

"Not yet," Jianyu whispered close to her ear. "It has to look as though they've killed him."

She swallowed down her hatred and her impatience. Jianyu was right. The Order could not know that Josef had survived. He looked a mess, but so far, the boy's heart was still beating. He'd lost a lot of blood, but they weren't yet close to killing him. He had a long way to go before death would offer any relief.

Josef let out a keening moan as his head rolled forward. Blood poured from his nose, staining the front of his torn shirt.

"It's very simple, boy. You give us a name, and we let you walk out of here tonight," the man in the suit said. He stood a few feet away, far enough not to be splattered. "Any name will do."

"I told you . . . I don't know anything," Josef said slowly, haltingly through broken teeth and a blood-filled mouth.

"You worked for a man named Dolph Saunders," the suited man said. "A gang boss who was responsible for attacking the Khafre Hall. Word is, you acted as a runner for him, delivering messages. You must know *something.*"

"Dolph's dead," Josef gasped, his chest heaving with the effort. "He's been dead for months."

"So you say," the suited man said. He shrugged, as though it didn't really matter. "Give us another name, then. You must know someone who was involved with the attacks. You must know who was loyal to him, who might have helped him. You give us their names, and we let you go. It's as easy as that."

It was never so easy, and from their previous experience with these late-night rescues, Viola knew that there was no chance of the boy ever walking away from this without Jianyu's and her help. But still they waited. She kept her affinity close, ready to stop the boy's words if it became necessary.

Josef's chest heaved with the effort to draw breath. He could have ended his misery by now. He could have given a name—any name, whether real or fake, involved or innocent. Instead, he lifted his head and glared at the man in the suit through swollen eyes. Then, every line of his broken and battered body defiant, he spit a wad of blood and phlegm at the man. But it fell short of him, landing at his feet.

Incensed, the Order's man lifted his fist.

"Now," Jianyu whispered.

Viola didn't have to be told twice. Without hesitation, she let her affinity flare and found the beating of Josef's heart, the blood thundering erratically through his veins. She slowed the rush nearly to a stop.

The boy's head flopped forward. His body went limp in the chair.

"What the—" The man in the suit froze, his fist still raised. When he realized the boy wasn't moving, his arm fell and he let out a curse. Then he turned on the stocky men with bloodied fists. "I told you that I needed him alive."

One of the larger, rough men thumbed at his nose. "You told us to make him bleed, and that's what we did."

"It ain't our fault if he can't hold his blood," another of the bruisers laughed.

The laugh set the suited man on a tear. Suddenly, they were all arguing, shouting about payment and orders, but Viola didn't care to listen. Her concentration was on the feel of her magic and the roaring in her ears as she focused on Josef's blood, on the beating of his heart. Slowly, she allowed it to beat once more. Twice. Enough to keep him alive. Enough to make the men believe he was dead.

"Shit," the suited man said. "We were close to breaking him. I could feel it."

He was wrong, of course. They hadn't been close, not when Josef Salzer had chosen to use what little strength he had to curse the men who could kill him. Now they wouldn't have the chance.

"Dump him out back," the suited man ordered. He tossed a pile of bills on the floor at the other men's feet, and then, with another disgusted string of curses, he turned and left.

The men lunged for the money. When they'd sorted out their shares, they passed around a flask and laughed about how easily they'd broken the boy. But eventually they got to work dealing with the body. There were saloons to visit and women to find waiting for them in the night.

Only when the men finally cut Josef from the chair and carried him, still unconcious, out the back of the factory did she and Jianyu move, following silently as one. Hidden in the threads of Jianyu's affinity.

The men dumped Josef in the alleyway behind the factory. They didn't even bother to hide the body or cover their tracks. Why should they? No one would care about another piece of the Bowery's trash, dead in the gutter. And for those who did care? Josef's body only served as a warning for what could come for them as well.

Viola's jaw ached from clenching it all evening. She thought for sure her molars would crack from the pressure one of these nights, from the strength it took to keep her temper in check. The willpower it took not to let her affinity unfurl and kill them all.

When the coast was clear, she and Jianyu moved quickly. By the time they reached the boy, he was already sitting up, groggy and disoriented from the beating and from her magic. He wouldn't be able to walk on his own, she realized. One of his legs had been broken. She could help with that, once they were safe, once he was back in the arms of his mother, Golde.

But when Josef saw who was standing over him, it wasn't relief that crossed his face. It never was. His eyes widened, and he tried to back away. Thanks to the poisonous lies Nibsy had spread throughout the Bowery, Josef Salzer believed *they* were the traitors.

With a sigh, Viola sent out her affinity again, pulled on his heartbeat softly, just enough that he passed out once more.

"It's always the same," she muttered, helping Jianyu to support the boy's weight between the two of them. "Always the hate."

"The understanding comes later," Jianyu reminded her. "Golde will explain. She will make him understand."

"She'd better," Viola muttered. The summer's sultry heat had her sweating through her dress from the effort of dragging the boy through the streets. They had not expected a second building, so they had farther to go than they had planned.

"She will," Jianyu assured her.

"And then what?" Viola asked. She stopped short, suddenly exhausted beyond reason. It had already been weeks of this. Weeks and weeks of midnight rescues to save the lives of those who believed them to be villains. Weeks of never knowing when the Order and their men would come for them as well. All in the midst of a city on the verge of exploding.

And who would rescue her if that happened? Who would rescue Jianyu? After all they'd done, after all the lives they'd tried to save, who among the Devil's Own would risk their lives to save the two of them?

No one. She and Jianyu were on their own. Even with souls under their protection, even with life upon life owed to them, they were alone.

With Josef slung between them and the danger of the Conclave marching closer, Viola finally voiced the fear that she knew they both held silently in their hearts: "What if they never return?"

Jianyu didn't bother to ask who she was referring to. They did not often speak of Esta and Harte, but the Thief and the Magician were always there, a silent absence between them. "Then it becomes even more important to carry on," Jianyu said. "We do what we have always intended. We protect those we can protect. And we stop Nibsy and the Order from building any more power."

"*How?*" Viola asked, glancing at him. "Each week brings a new riot in the streets, a new victim to rescue. The Order will not stop searching for their treasures. They will not stop until every Mageus in this city has been damaged by their violence. And we don't even have an artifact to show for all the danger we're in."

"We have the silver discs," Jianyu said, urging her on. They still had quite a distance to cover before they reached the wagon waiting for them.

"Useless trinkets," she grumbled.

"You know that is not true," Jianyu told her. "You would not have taken them if they had not called to you with their power. Perhaps it is time to stop waiting for Darrigan and Esta to rescue us from our future. Perhaps it is time to begin searching for answers of our own."

But the Order had just left the discs sitting there, out in the open.

Unguarded. Unwatched. They could not possibly be so important. "What if there are no answers?"

In the distance, a dog barked, and then they heard the sound of shouting. The clattering of wagon wheels was growing closer. But between them, Josef Salzer was a deadweight, holding them down.

"Cela," Viola said. She was waiting for them around the corner, without any protection.

"We have to go," Jianyu told her. "We must get to her," he said, pulling Josef and Viola onward. "And we must go now."

ANOTHER MANHATTAN

1983—The Bridge

Esta felt her affinity waver as the icy warning of the Brink crashed over them, swelling until it had engulfed them both like a wave cresting over a seawall. The seconds suddenly felt sharp and dangerous, but she gripped them tighter, determined not to let them fly away from her as she dragged Harte onward.

She ran on instinct, their hands still clasped tightly and her breath coming hard, as she pushed through a thick wall of cold energy that seemed endless. The other enormous limestone tower of the Brooklyn Bridge was still fifty yards or more away, but it might as well have been fifty miles. Every step brought a fresh burst of pain as the seconds in the grasp of her affinity sharpened, twisting savagely to be free. Time felt like a live wire.

Suddenly, Esta felt Harte jerk out of the grip of her magic. She turned back to find him frozen with the rest of the world, his face contorted in a kind of desperate agony. This time she allowed the seconds to slip away from her, and as the world slammed back into motion and Harte was free, a wailing moan of sheer pain tore from his chest. She reached for him, but he pulled away.

"No!" His features contorted with another moan. "Don't touch me!"

"Seshat?" she asked.

A grimace was her only answer.

Separate now, they ran. Dimly, Esta was aware of sirens screaming in the distance as they burst through the last few yards of dangerous energy. When they finally broke free of the Brink's power, Harte tumbled to his knees, shivering in the shadows of the bridge's towers. His chest heaved from the exertion of the run, and Esta understood he was shivering from something more than the cold. His hands were pressed over his ears, holding his head, as though trying desperately to keep himself together.

"The Quellant?" she asked, needing to touch him but knowing she couldn't.

"Gone," he said through gritted teeth. "She's . . ." He groaned again, flinching from some unseen torture. "So angry. Can't—" He doubled over again.

Desperate to help him, Esta pulled out the leather pouch Maggie had gifted her so many weeks before, the one filled with various magical concoctions. With half-frozen fingers, she fumbled open the clasp, but when she looked inside, she suddenly couldn't breathe.

It's gone. It's all gone.

Everything inside the pouch had turned to powdery ash. The wind gusted, as if on cue, and she tried to clasp the pouch closed again to protect what was left. But she knew already that it was pointless. The incendiaries and Flash and Bangs—and most important of all, the Quellant—were gone. The Brink had taken everything. Incinerated all of it with its terrible power.

On her arm, her cuff felt icy hot, and she grasped the satchel that was slung diagonally against her chest. To her relief, the Book and the artifacts were still there. But without the Quellant . . .

Esta realized then that the sirens she'd been hearing for the last couple of minutes weren't in the distance any longer. They were coming closer. Behind them on the bridge, she could still feel the warning of the Brink, a devastating cold over the chill of the winter air. Before her, the streets seemed more dangerous than they had been before. The air felt suddenly alive, as though the city itself knew they'd entered. As though it was angry with their trespass.

"We need to go," she told Harte, her instincts prickling. The sirens were even louder now. They couldn't be found there, trapped on the bridge with the Brink behind them and no way to retreat. "Can you walk?"

Harte nodded, but from the agony in his eyes and the way he held himself stiff and hunched against the pain, she wasn't sure she believed him. But she couldn't help him, either. She couldn't even touch him without the Quellant to hold back Seshat.

Luckily, he was able to pull himself to his feet, and on unsteady legs he moved, lurching and stumbling next to her as they hurried along the remaining span of the bridge. They slipped and slid through the filthy slush covering the long, sloping walkway that led to the park where City Hall waited, white and sepulchral, in the snowy night. Even wearing the jacket Harte had given her, she wasn't dressed for the cold, and with the thin leather of her soles already soaked through, she could no longer feel her toes. But the cold that chilled her to the core was more than the weather. The echoing reminder of the Brink's energy still vibrated through her, a warning of what would happen to her affinity—to her very self—if ever she tried to leave the city again.

But somehow none of that mattered—not the slushy snow nor the ache in her frozen toes. Not even the unsettled fear that clung to her bones as sirens drew closer. All that mattered was Harte. Stumbling along beside her, he gasped and shook with each step, but he hadn't given up.

She had to get them somewhere safe. Off the bridge. Out of sight.

Esta led the way around the park that skirted City Hall, trying to make sense of the way this version of the city was different from the one she had known as a child. So much was the same—the height of the buildings and the lights and the speed and the noise of it—but this New York, modern though it seemed, wasn't hers. This city was somehow louder and dirtier. The scent of diesel smoke was heavy in the air, and trash and debris lined the streets, piled up alongside the homeless who'd made their beds beneath makeshift tents in the snowy park.

Harte tried to keep pace beside her, but he was struggling. By the time they reached the sidewalk in front of City Hall, he was breathing hard through clenched teeth. Without warning, he stopped and curled over, grabbing his head again. His whole expression twisted in pain.

"Harte?" Esta stepped toward him, but he flinched away, and when he finally uncurled himself, finally looked up at her, she saw a too-familiar darkness bleeding into the gray of his irises.

She'd made an agreement with Seshat. She'd killed Jack and destroyed Thoth along with him in exchange for Harte's life, but it was clear the goddess had decided not to uphold her side of their bargain.

"Just hold on a little longer," Esta told him, wishing she could do more as she tried to decide where to go. She wanted more than anything to put her arms around him, to keep him from flying apart, but she knew that without the Quellant, she couldn't take the risk.

The flashing red of police lights lit the buildings around them now as the squeal of tires tore through the night. A half dozen bright blue cars with glinting chrome fenders skidded to a stop near the mouth of the bridge, blocking the entrance to the walkway where they had just been.

"We have to keep moving," she told Harte. The police showing up like they had couldn't be a coincidence, even if she didn't understand how they could have known about their arrival. The Brink hadn't ever been monitored as far as she knew. But who was to say how much their movements through the past had changed this present? Who was to say what dangers waited in this version of the time line?

Harte was still huddled over, doubled into himself.

"We have to go. *Now.*" In a few minutes those cops would be out of those cars and would start to fan out. They were clearly looking for something—for someone—and they would see the path the two of them had made through the snow. If they didn't get away before then, there would be no way to explain what she and Harte were doing in the nearly empty park in the middle of the night, coatless and dressed in clothing decades out of style.

The two of them scuttled along behind a row of newspaper boxes covered in graffiti, careful to avoid being seen. Half the windows had been busted out of the few boxes that were still standing. They had to keep moving, but with the police surrounding the area now, their only real choice was to go underground.

The Brooklyn Bridge subway station didn't look that different from the way it had looked in her own time. It still welcomed them with the same mechanical staleness the air underground always carried, that dust-laced scent of machines layered with the strong ammonia reek of urine. But at least the platform was protected from the icy wind and free from snow. At least they were out of sight.

Luckily, the station was mostly empty. A group of three guys in heavy coats huddled together on the far end of the platform. Even from a distance they looked completely strung out.

When Harte groaned again, grabbing at his head, they glanced up from whatever they were dealing, but a second later they turned back to their huddle. Uninterested.

She couldn't hear the sirens anymore, but that didn't put her at ease. She had no idea what was happening aboveground. Still, no one had followed them. At least not yet. Eventually someone would track them down. They had to get on a train, and fast.

Esta looked up. The station clock had been busted open, its hands removed, and its face obscured by graffiti, so she wasn't even sure what time it was. Late, by the emptiness of the streets and the platform, but this wasn't her New York. There were no digital readouts to tell her the schedule. There was nothing they could do but wait and hope that the next train would arrive before the police found them.

Harte crouched down, hunching against the peeling paint of the iron column in the center of the narrow cement platform. He was rocking a little, still moaning to himself, but at least the guys at the other end of the station didn't seem to notice or care. Just another junkie, as far as they knew.

"Is there anything I can do?" She crouched down next to him, wanting more than anything to brush the hair back from his pale, damp forehead. "Anything that would help?"

He shook his head, his teeth still gritted. "Stay back." His lips pressed together, like he was steeling himself against the next wave of whatever pain Seshat was inflicting. "Please. It makes it worse . . . when you're close. She's so angry. Wants you. So *badly*." He grimaced again. "She keeps screaming about Thoth. How she wants to destroy him."

It didn't make sense. "Thoth's gone. I took care of him when I killed Jack."

"Tell that to Seshat," Harte groaned. He looked even more wan in the yellowish glow from the fluorescent lights overhead.

The squeal of an arriving train echoed through the tunnels before Esta could reply.

Harte flinched, clamping his hands more tightly over his ears at the sound of screeching brakes as the train slid into the station. The litter along the edges of the platform fluttered in the gust of air the train brought with it.

The cars were boxier than the ones Esta had grown up riding, and the entire train was covered completely in graffiti, including the windows, so she couldn't see inside. She had no idea how many people might be riding or what might be waiting, but when the doors lurched open, no one exited. A disembodied voice echoed through the dimly lit station, instructing everyone to disembark. It was the last stop on the line.

Esta clenched her jaw in frustration at the worthless train. They couldn't just sit here waiting. Soon, the cops outside would start searching farther from the bridge. Soon enough, they'd search the station. But considering how late it was? She didn't know how long it would be before another train came along—

And then she realized which train it was.

"Come on," she told Harte, pulling him up by his sleeve-covered arm.

Clearly in too much pain to argue and too weak to pull away, he allowed her to drag him onto the train, but the second they were aboard, he seemed to realize how close she was and pulled away again. She understood why, but the rejection still stung as she took a seat in the row closest to the back door of the car. Harte took the bench opposite, making sure to keep his distance.

He flinched again, like another volley of pain had just shot through him. "I can't . . . ," he whispered. "Too much . . ." He rocked as he spoke to himself—or to Seshat. She couldn't hear him enough to be sure.

Esta willed the doors to close before anyone else arrived or tried to board, but she didn't let go of the breath she was holding until the train started to lurch forward slowly, not gathering much speed as it left the station. Harte didn't seem to notice. The rocking had stopped, and now he seemed suddenly too still, hunched as he was against the filthy wall of the train, his eyes closed and his mouth in a pained line.

"Just a little longer," she told him.

He grimaced in response, turning away from her.

The inside of the subway car was as covered in graffiti as the outside, and there was trash collecting beneath the seats. Subway cars in general weren't exactly the cleanest places in the city even in her own time, but this was something else. She'd seen pictures of the city before it was cleaned up back in the 1990s, but she hadn't spent much time in the eighties. The oddness of a city so similar to her own—and yet so different—was unsettling. As the train began to move, a bent syringe rolled to a stop against Esta's foot. She kicked it away.

The train swayed as it started to curve around the next bend, and Esta realized they needed to move. If they missed their chance, she was out of ideas. It was this or nothing.

She stood, bracing herself against the movement in the same way she had her whole life. It steadied her a little, the familiarity of the train's movement beneath her, lurching and swaying. Harte was huddled against the filthy window, his hands over his ears, as if he were trying to hold his head together.

"Let's go, Harte," she said as the train lurched again. She stood and made her way to the door at the end of the car and flung it open, but when she turned back, Esta realized Harte hadn't followed her. He was still curled in the corner of the seat, still grimacing and half-delirious from the pain.

JUST A LITTLE LONGER

1983—Lower Manhattan

Harte heard Esta calling him as if from a distance. It was hard to hear anything over the storm raging inside him. The instant they'd crossed the Brink and the Quellant burned away, Seshat had begun railing against him, swelling and clawing and pushing at the boundary between them. It felt as though his skin might split open if he didn't concentrate on keeping himself together.

He thought he had understood. He thought he'd felt the true extent of Seshat's affinity before. But this was different. Now he understood exactly why Thoth had wanted her magic. She was a force. *More than a force.* She was power and its antithesis. Even ancient and disembodied and half-broken by Thoth's betrayal, Seshat's magic was a living, breathing thing. Her power was astounding, *impossible.* Holding her back felt like he was trying to hold on to lightning.

Worse, Seshat wanted Esta more than ever.

Harte was only half-aware of where they were, and he had no idea where they were going. But he didn't think he could last much longer against Seshat's onslaught, not when he felt utterly decimated by her wrath.

You cannot stop me. I will take all that she is, all that she contains, and tear it from the world.

"No," he said, struggling to hold himself back—to hold Seshat back.

"Harte?" Esta was standing in an open doorway. Her short hair was a wild riot around her face in the gusting wind.

He could hear and see her, but he couldn't respond. All of his focus was on Seshat, pushing her back. On holding her down. *Just a little longer.*

Yes. Go to her, Seshat commanded, her power swelling within until he was on his feet. He couldn't stop his back from arching as she pressed and clawed at him. He could not stop himself from moving steadily toward the open door, toward Esta.

She had no idea the danger she was in.

Esta let the door slide closed and approached him, grabbing him by his sleeve. Seshat roared in triumph as Harte tried to pull away, but Esta was determined.

"We have to go. It's time," she told him, dragging him toward the door of the train again. "I just need you to hold on for a little longer."

Just a little longer. But Harte wasn't sure that he could. The pain of Seshat's power churned within him. The agony of what she was doing inside his skin. She was raging about Thoth. Screaming with a voice that could shatter his sanity.

Oh god, it's too much. He couldn't hold on. Needed it to end. Because this power, the immenseness of all that Seshat was and all that she could do wasn't something he could live through much longer.

He had to protect Esta. He had to keep her safe from the terror beneath his skin.

They were on the platform at the back of the train car now, but the wind whipping at his hair was nothing compared to Seshat's fury, and the darkness of the tunnel was nothing compared to the living, terrifying darkness roiling inside him. The walls of the tunnel slid past at a dizzying speed, and he understood what he had to do. He saw how easily he could end everything. The train was certainly going fast enough, and Esta wouldn't be able to stop him—she knew that she couldn't touch him while Seshat writhed beneath his skin.

Esta was still talking, but Harte could not understand what she was saying. He was too focused on keeping Seshat back. Too focused on the agony of feeling the goddess raging within him. She could not be allowed to touch Esta. He would keep Esta safe. If he could do nothing else, he'd keep Seshat from destroying her. And from destroying the world.

Esta was holding on to the metal railing, unhooking the metal chains that kept people safely on the platform at the end of the car. Then she turned back to him, and he saw the fear in her expression and knew what she must see in his own.

"Harte," she said, her voice coming to him from a distance. It felt as though he were locked tight in a watery box, with the noise of the audience far off. "It's going to be okay. You can do this."

She understands. The relief was almost enough to break Seshat's hold on him.

He'd been *fighting* for so long because he couldn't bear to leave Esta, but now the time had come. He saw it in her eyes, that she knew what had to happen, what needed to be done. He moved toward the edge of the platform as Seshat raged more violently. He wouldn't have thought that was possible, but he should have known better. Every time he thought he understood what she was capable of, the ancient power surprised him with still more.

His hands curled on the railing, wishing there were some other answer. But there wasn't. Even Esta understood that now.

The air around him felt warmer than it should have somehow, thicker too, like the dust and mold and smoke from the ages of trains passing through had lingered on.

Esta was talking again, and Harte watched her mouth move without hearing her. He wanted to kiss her just once more, but that was impossible—far too much a risk when Seshat was so close to the surface now. But while Harte couldn't make out what she was saying, he understood. This was the end.

He held up a hand, wishing he could touch her. With the goddess railing inside him, it took every ounce of his strength to force out the words he needed her to hear. "You . . . are not negotiable. Never have been." He grimaced against the power thrashing inside him. "Not for me."

Her eyes went wide, and the sudden terror there surprised him, but only distantly. Even as he backed away from her, she was trying to tell him something, her mouth moving excitedly and her eyes bright with fear.

"It's okay," he said, taking another step toward the edge of the small platform on the rear of the car. "I'll be okay."

"No!" He didn't need to hear her voice to know what she was saying, but he was already turning, already preparing himself, even as Seshat roared and wailed.

He closed his eyes, wishing he were braver, wishing he could go to his death without so many regrets. He took one last deep breath, hating that it reeked of the filth in the tunnel, and then he released his hold on the train rail and fell.

NOT EVER AGAIN

1983—Under the City

As the train screamed around the bend in the tunnel, Esta held on to the cold metal railing at the back of the car and promised herself that if they made it through the next few minutes, she would kill Harte Darrigan herself.

It was clear Harte wasn't listening to her. He was standing next to her on the edge of the train car's back platform, but his eyes were an inky black. His features were twisted in pain and fear, and his expression looked haunted . . . and determined. She understood exactly what he was preparing to do, and she wasn't about to let him. He'd promised that he would give up the idea of destroying himself to save her. He'd promised that they were in this together. And now she was going to make sure he kept that promise.

Just as the idiot released his hold on the railing, Esta slammed into him, pulling them both off the car and hoping it was enough momentum to get them across the gap. Because she had a hold on Harte, she couldn't stop herself from landing hard on the unforgiving concrete of the abandoned station's platform. Pain lanced through her arm where the skin was still tender and mangled beneath the bandage, but she ignored it and used all her strength to twist, rolling them both back from the edge as the train picked up speed to round the curve and exit the station. They weren't even touching skin to skin, but Esta could practically feel Seshat's power lancing through their brief connection. She moved quickly enough that it wasn't much more than a brush of darkness in her vision and sizzling heat across her skin.

Once she'd put some distance between them, Esta let herself lie there on the cold cement as she tried to catch her breath. Her arm was throbbing from holding on to Harte and from landing so hard, and her pulse felt erratic from the adrenaline still jangling through her. But at least they were safe. Silence surrounded them in the emptiness of the station. No red police lights flashed. No sirens screamed. No one seemed to have seen or followed them.

Above, nearly pristine green and gold tiles lined the vaulted ceilings of the old City Hall station, framing the dark glass of large, snow-covered skylights. The station was dark except for the eerie yellowish glow of emergency lamps that revealed the pedestrian exit.

Harte groaned nearby, and Esta turned her head to see him curled up on the ground a few feet away from her. She pushed herself upright, ignoring the aching in her arm as she listened to the last sounds of the train they'd just been on moving off into the distance on its northward route along the 6 line.

He moaned again, and Esta scooted closer to look at him. She wanted to touch him, to help him in some way, but she knew exactly how dangerous that would be. She let out an unsteady breath as she inched closer. *You are nonnegotiable.* The second Harte had given her those words, she'd understood what he was about to do. If the train hadn't reached the platform when it did, he would have jumped. He would have already been gone.

"You're a complete idiot, you know that?" she said softly, hating the way her voice hitched around the words. She didn't really mean it. She understood why he would have thrown himself from the subway car. Wouldn't she have done the same to keep the world safe? To keep *him* safe?

But she wasn't even sure that Harte could hear her. His eyes opened, wide and unseeing, but he didn't look in her direction. His gray irises had turned completely black, and the inky darkness was spreading to the whites as well. He grimaced, his face contorting, and she understood that he was still fighting Seshat.

Esta was going to make sure he won.

"Go." His mouth was drawn, pained, but his words made it clear he knew she was there. That *he* was still there. "She wants to *destroy* you."

"I don't have any plans to die today, Harte." She wanted to move closer and reassure him, but the air around him was charged and unsettled. "And you'd better not, either."

The City Hall subway station had been closed for nearly forty years. They'd shut it down in the forties, when the subway cars had grown too long and too large to fit into the curved station without creating an unsafe gap between the train and the curve of the platform. It had been empty and abandoned since then, and it wasn't exactly legal to visit it, so there was no one around. No vagrants sleeping in the corners, no junkies dealing on the stairwell, and no graffiti marring the shining ceramic tiles on the walls. Trapped in time, the station platform was silent and lonely. And almost clean. In short, it was exactly what they needed.

"This is where the very first subway train ever departed," she told him, speaking out loud because she had to prove to herself that her voice wouldn't shake.

Professor Lachlan had shown her this secret place when she was a girl. It had been a crisp fall day, and they'd ridden the 6 until the end of the line. They'd remained on the train as it made the loop in the station to turn around and head north, and she'd peered through the scratched windows to see this place, dimly lit but still shining like new. He'd wanted her to know everything about the city. Every nook and every secret.

An unpleasant thought occurred to her: Could he have known she would need this place one day?

She wasn't sure how to feel about that—the idea that even with the tangled knot of time, so much of her training could have been intended to lead her there, right where Professor Lachlan wanted her. Was it possible that despite everything, despite all they'd changed and all she'd thought they'd been able to do to avoid his grasp, he had known all along that this was where she would end up? How was she ever supposed to beat him if, in both the past and the future, he could still move her around like a pawn on a board? Despite the passing of time—despite the *changing* of history?

Harte had curled tightly into a ball, trying to protect himself against Seshat's fury and anger.

Esta looked around, considering her options—*their* options. She wasn't sure how long Harte could last like this, and without the Quellant . . . They needed the missing part of the Book. She needed to stop Seshat from destroying Harte.

"I have to get the key," she said, more to herself than to Harte. But this time he seemed to hear her.

"Esta, no." When he opened his eyes, he looked almost lucid . . . almost like himself. "You know Nibsy's waiting for you. He wants you to come for it, and I can't—" A groan tore from his throat that made her ache.

Without hesitating, she pulled time still, and the world went silent. "You're right, Harte," she said softly, her throat tight with emotion. "You can't."

The station had already been quiet, but now the far-off sounds of trains traveling along the tracks and the creaking of the pipes drained away into complete silence.

Esta took one last look at Harte and hoped that Seshat's powers couldn't harm him while he was held in the grip of her affinity's net. Or at least she hoped he wouldn't be aware and wouldn't remember the minutes that passed until she returned. She wished she could touch him just once before she left him, but she didn't dare. She couldn't risk it.

She'd been a fool for trusting Seshat to keep her word.

Esta had *killed* a man to keep her promise. She'd destroyed Thoth, eliminated the threat he posed, and *this* was how the bitch of a goddess repaid her? By driving Harte to nearly end everything by throwing himself from the train?

No. Esta wasn't going to sit there and hope that Seshat came to her senses. She wouldn't allow Seshat to destroy Harte or to hurt anyone or anything else. *Not ever again.* She'd get the key to Newton's cipher from Professor Lachlan, and then she would take care of Seshat herself. Even if it was the last thing she did.

Esta took the Book from the satchel and considered her options. She might be able to steal time, but she couldn't put off the inevitable. She was going back to Orchard Street.

Considering her options, Esta placed the Book on the floor and gave it a small push, sliding it closer to Harte. She lifted the satchel from her shoulder and slid it toward him as well. It could be a mistake to leave the Book and the artifacts, but it would be a worse mistake to let them fall into Nibsy's hands. The last thing she wanted to do was deliver the Ars Arcana directly to him. Then she took one more look at Harte—his too-sharp cheekbones, his rumpled dark hair. But when she reached his eyes, she saw the hold Seshat had on him.

She hated the blackness there, the dark power already overwhelming him. And she would do anything to destroy it. As she turned away and headed toward the tunnel that led up to the emergency exit, she vowed she'd see his eyes flash storm-gray at her once more.

UNEXPECTED ANSWERS

1902—The Bowery

Jianyu and Viola had barely made it around the corner before the police wagon tore down the street they had just been on. Hanging from its sides were uniformed men, off to round up whatever the disturbance in the distance happened to be.

Jianyu exchanged a look with Viola, and in silent agreement, they began to move faster.

It was not only Josef Salzer's unconscious body that weighed on Jianyu as they worked to get the boy to safety. Viola's words worried him as well.

What if there are no answers?

It had been months since that day on the bridge when Harte and Esta had left him to defend the ring and hold everything together. Months of chaos. Months of failure. He had lost the Delphi's Tear and any chance to reclaim a place in the Devil's Own along with it. And with each day that passed, he could not help but wonder what would become of them if Harte and Esta never returned. But Jianyu forced himself to push aside his worries for the future. They would still be there once Josef was safely in his family's keeping.

Finally they arrived at the side street where Cela waited with the wagon they had borrowed from Mr. Fortune and his newspaper the *New York Age.*

Cela was in the driver's perch behind a single mangy-looking nag. She was dressed in the rough-spun clothes of a common working man, trousers and a jacket that she had tailored to hide her true form. A man's broad-brimmed hat was pulled down low over her brow, shielding her face, but Jianyu did not miss the tightness of her fingers around the worn leather of the reins.

When they neared, he let out a low, soft whistle, the signal that they had arrived.

Cela straightened, the hat tipping back enough for him to see the soft curve of her cheek and the sharp line of her hairless jaw. Only a fool would not notice she was a woman beneath the clothes, but the city was filled with fools.

Her eyes were sharp as they searched the night, but it was only when they were standing at the foot of the wagon that Jianyu finally released his affinity enough to allow her to find him in the darkness.

"You made it in time?" she whispered, climbing down from her perch.

"Barely," Viola told her.

Cela had accompanied them on each of these trips over the last weeks, but even with all she had seen, she gasped when Josef Salzer's head tipped back and she saw his broken and bloodied face. She rushed over to help them.

"Barely is better than not at all," Jianyu told them.

Together they lifted Josef into the back of the covered wagon, and then Viola climbed in with the boy. She would need to stay close to keep his heart beating and his moans quiet until they arrived at the safe house far, far uptown.

When Jianyu lifted the gate of the wagon and secured it, Viola turned back, frowning at him. "You aren't coming with us?"

"I have to tell his mother," Jianyu told her. "Golde will be waiting for news, and she should not have to see the sun rise without it."

"We can wait," Cela said as she climbed back into the driver's perch.

He considered her offer, but when a shout went up in the distance, he shook his head. It was not worth it to risk more than one life. "Not tonight."

Cela did not look pleased, but she also did not argue. "Get back to us safe."

The note of concern in her voice settled deep within him, a reminder that he was not alone—that *they* were not alone—as he pulled his affinity close, opened what little moonlight found its way through the clouds above, and wrapped his magic around himself once more.

With so many police officers patrolling the streets, it took longer than usual for Jianyu to reach Golde Salzer's home. Josef's family lived in a pair of small, lightless rooms on the fourth floor of a tenement not far from the Bella Strega. The building was deep within territory under the control of the Devil's Own and, consequently, territory currently held by Nibsy Lorcan, so Jianyu kept his affinity close as he walked through the part of the city he'd once called home. No good would come of Nibsy knowing that he had been there.

The building where Golde and her children lived was mostly dark. Its inhabitants had no doubt already turned in for the night to prepare for the long day of work that would greet them when the sun rose. But he knew Golde would be up, waiting for word of her son. When Jianyu reached her door, he tapped the softest of rhythms and waited. When the door inched open, Golde's drawn, shadowed face appeared. Only then did he allow the light to recede a little, exposing himself. With a small jerk of his head, he motioned that she should follow, and then, wordlessly, made his way to the stairs and then up toward the roof. He did not look back to see if she was behind him.

Luckily, the roof was empty. All around, the Lower East Side fanned out in a jumbled mess of streets. The city felt quieter here. In the distance, he could almost make out the towers of the bridge in the hazy summer night. This close to the stars, the rot of the gutter and the stench of the streets below were barely detectable. Here, he could almost imagine the city was a different place, a better one.

Perhaps one day it would be.

A few minutes later, Golde stepped out onto the roof. She had a shawl pulled up over her hair, another wrapped around her. In her eyes, she carried the same distrust and the same wariness he regularly saw in the eyes of those who had been turned by Nibsy's honeyed lies. Even when she had come to him for help, she had not quite trusted him.

Golde glanced back at the stairwell once more, as though making sure she had not been followed.

Jianyu understood her nervousness. Golde had told him already that her husband did not approve of her seeking help to find their oldest son. The older man had been injured in a factory accident months before, back when Dolph was still running the Bowery, but the man's leg still had not healed enough to find work. He depended on his children and his wife to keep a roof over their heads and food on their table. They all depended on Josef, who had once worked for Dolph. Which meant that they now depended upon the generosity of Nibsy Lorcan. None of them could risk Nibsy finding out about Jianyu's involvement.

"You found him, my Josef?" she asked, her voice barely a whisper.

Jianyu nodded.

"Truly?" she asked, stepping toward him. The mistrust and hesitation all but vanished. "Where is he? I want to see him. Take me to my boy."

"Golde—" He stopped when her eyes flashed. "*Mrs.* Salzer. You know I cannot."

Her expression hardened. "I want to see my child. I want to see him with my own eyes."

Josef was no more a child than Jianyu himself was. The boy had been hardened by the streets like so many others. Still, he understood a mother's care, even if it had been a lifetime since he had felt it himself.

"Soon," Jianyu promised softly, hoping to calm her. "When we know for sure that it is safe."

"When it's safe," she said, cursing in German that Jianyu could not understand. "When has life for our kind ever been safe here in this blighted city?"

Jianyu could not disagree, but he did not mistake Golde's words as including himself in the sentiment. She meant Mageus, to be sure. But that did not necessarily mean that she considered the two of them as anything alike.

Golde looked up at him, her small face lined beyond its years. But that was what came of rooms full of children and only empty cupboards to feed them. "What do you want? Money? I told you already that I couldn't offer you much."

"Keep your coin," Jianyu said, trying to hide his frustration. "I told you before, there is no need. But your son is not the only one we protect. When we know for sure that the Order no longer searches for him, I can bring you to him."

She frowned. "There must be something I could give you. Something you want. Why else would you risk so much?"

It was a question Jianyu asked himself often. "I know what it is to need rescuing," he told her. "I had a friend once who risked everything for me. I am only repaying his kindness."

"You mean Dolph Saunders," Golde said.

Jianyu nodded.

"They say you betrayed him," Golde told him. "They say you betrayed the Devil's Own, you and that Italian girl. And yet here you are, saving my son, the same as Dolph himself would have."

Jianyu did not speak. He understood that Golde was not really talking to him, but to her own conscience.

"They knew him by name," Jianyu said. "The men who took your boy. It was no accident. They knew he worked for Dolph. Do you have any idea who might have betrayed him?"

Golde's brows drew together thoughtfully, but then she shook her head. "It could have been anyone. After I stopped Josef from taking the mark, a lot of the boys turned away from him."

"What mark?" Jianyu asked, suddenly alert. "Dolph's?"

"It's not his any longer," Golde said dourly. "That *boy* offered it to

Josef, the one who thinks he has the eggs to step into the shoes Dolph Saunders left behind."

"Nibsy Lorcan offered your son protection in exchange for taking the mark?" Jianyu considered the implications of this.

She nodded. "Josef had been running messages for him, the same as he had for Saunders, until about a week ago. The boy wanted him to take the mark. Josef would have, but I stopped him because Dolph Saunders promised me that it wasn't required for the job. If it was good enough for Saunders, it should have been good enough for the one who followed him," she said sourly. "So I said no. I told him that his god was more important than loyalty to any one man, and he's a good boy, my Josef. He listened. He honored me. And he lost the job because of it.

"When those men took him, I went to Lorcan. I told him how they'd taken my Josef—a boy who had always been loyal to the Strega and to the Devil's Own. I told him that Dolph had promised protection. . . ." She shook her head. "Lorcan told me that he wasn't Dolph Saunders, and Josef wasn't one of his. It's the only reason I sent word to you. I would have never sunk so low otherwise."

Jianyu was not surprised. He and Viola were never the first choice of those who the Order had taken. They were always the choice of the desperate. But the news that Nibsy had offered Josef a mark . . . None that they had rescued wore the mark of the Devil's Own.

"I'm sorry for it now," Golde said, surprising him. "I'm sorry for thinking of you so poorly. I shouldn't have listened to the whispers and gossip."

Her words unsettled something in him. How many times had Jianyu rescued someone from the Order's men only to have his actions thrown in his face? "There is no need to apologize," he said, feeling unspeakably awkward. "I will send word as Josef heals, and when it is safe, I will bring you to him."

Golde reached out and touched his arm. "Thank you," she told him, and then, pulling her shawl around her, she turned to go back into the building.

At first Jianyu did not follow. He stayed on the roof, under the sweep of stars with the city breathing around him, struck by what had just happened. Golde's words—her gratitude—were unsettling enough, but the news that Nibsy Lorcan might be building his ranks was more so. Especially if he was culling those who refused to take the mark.

It should not have been so surprising. In these unsettled times, it made sense that Nibsy would want to increase his numbers. With the leadership of the Five Pointers currently sitting in a cell on Blackwell's Island, with Tammany and the Order at odds, and with the gangs of the Bowery at one another's throats, Nibsy would want an army of supporters around him. *Of course* he would demand loyalty as well. The only question was what his next move would be once he'd amassed that army.

It was a question that was answered sooner than Jianyu expected. As he exited the front door of Golde's building, there was the boy himself—Nibsy Lorcan—waiting for him in the pallid shaft of a streetlamp's glow.

Before Jianyu had time to reach for his bronze mirrors or his magic, Werner stepped from the shadows, and he felt the breath being pressed from his chest.

THE LIBRARY'S SECRETS

1983—City Hall Station

W hen she reached the top of the stairs leading out of the subway, Esta made quick work of the locked emergency exit door and then carefully secured it again so it wouldn't look disturbed. She didn't have any plans to let go of time, but just in case . . . There was no use taking any chances.

Finally aboveground and in the icy night air, she turned her back on the steady red glow of the police lights that surrounded the bridge and started walking through the park that skirted the white stone buildings of City Hall. She tucked her hands into her pockets and hunched against the cold, glad that the wind was now as still as the rest of the world, and then she started trudging through the drifting snow in the park toward the redbrick building that had defined her childhood.

Esta hadn't gone very far when something made her pause. She looked back over her shoulder and saw the lights of two unfamiliar towers standing like twin sentinels in the winter night behind her. She'd never seen them before. In all her trips through time, there had never been a reason to. Professor Lachlan had kept her focused and on a tight leash. But the looming presence of the Twin Towers was yet another reminder that while this city might look similar to her own, it wasn't. She was a stranger here, and with all the changes she and Harte might have created to the time line, she could be standing on quicksand.

Turning north, she cut through the park, but before she reached Centre Street, she noticed a statue gracing the intersection that hadn't been there before. The body of a man gleamed almost golden in the dim light, but covered in snow, she couldn't tell who it depicted. There was something about it that sent a chill through her, though, even more than the night air. It was enough to make her pause and see what else had changed, but other than the statue, the area around City Hall seemed the same—past and future, almost identical.

She couldn't help but remember the day not so long ago when she'd first found herself in the past. Viola had still hated her and had brought her downtown to test her mettle on the Dead Line. It had been only a few months ago, but it felt longer. It felt like an eternity.

Esta shook off the past and kept walking, weaving her way through once-familiar streets. Caught in her magic, the cloudy windows of a graffiti-covered bus revealed the single passenger it carried on its late-night run. She wished she could grab the bus or hail a cab, but the city remained caught in her affinity, and it needed to stay that way—for Harte. To protect him for as long as she could.

Though her thin-soled shoes were soaked, the cold hardly touched her now. With each step, determination heated her blood. She would find the fragment of the Book and then—

And then what? As far as she knew, she couldn't do anything without all five of the artifacts—but the ring was in 1902, and Harte was stuck *here*. She couldn't leave him, not without releasing time and leaving him to Seshat's mercy. . . .

Or maybe she could, she thought as she trudged onward through the slush-covered sidewalks. Maybe she *could* slip back and get the ring from this Cela Johnson. If she timed it right, she could return before Harte could give in to Seshat's power or do anything stupid. It would be difficult but not impossible.

With time pulled slow, the streets of lower Manhattan felt like a graveyard. Light glowed from windows, but held in the net of her power, no one and nothing moved. She was alone in a crowded city, a solitary traveler on an impossible quest.

When she reached the Bowery, she couldn't stop herself from cutting down toward where the Bella Strega had been. She could almost see the city as it had once been, still inscribed there beneath the layers of graffiti and grit. But the Strega was lost to the past, and if she didn't succeed in retrieving the key to the cipher from Nibsy, her friends would be as well.

The Bowery was lined with the kind of heavy, boxy cars ladened with chrome that were popular in the 1980s. She passed one with its window busted out, another that was missing a front tire. It was no wonder people had called this part of the city Skid Row. Along the streets, the metal gates sealed off shop entrances for the night, but many of the buildings were boarded up and abandoned. She imagined that even if she released time, this part of the city would feel like a ghost town compared to the other versions of the Bowery she had known.

She reached the place where she thought the Strega should have been, but all she found there was a burned-out building. Something clenched inside her at the sight of it. Her eyes stung as she thought of the last time she'd been inside, but she steeled herself against those memories and turned her grief to resolve. Pulling her determination around her like a cloak, she turned her back on the parts of the past that could not be changed. She had to focus, to keep moving, because there was so much that could be different—so much that she might still change. As long as she didn't fail.

Cutting through the narrow stretch of Roosevelt Park, she finally arrived at Orchard Street. A few blocks more and she found herself standing in front of the building that had once been her home. The storefront on the first floor was still boarded up with plywood covered with layers of graffiti. Someone was curled up in a nearby stairwell with his battered, gloved hands curled around a bag-covered bottle. The building almost looked abandoned, like many of its neighbors, but above, on the topmost floor, a light shone like a beacon.

Esta went to the rear of the building, where a service entrance opened on the staircase that went up the back. She picked the lock in a matter of seconds and then let herself in. She paused, waiting for . . .

She wasn't sure what she was waiting for. An alarm? Some indication that the Professor—that *Nibsy*—knew she'd arrived? But nothing happened. The city remained silent. Time stood still. The air around her stirred only with her movement.

It smelled the same. It was such a strange thing to realize, but the second Esta was out of the cold air, memories of the past overwhelmed her. The back staircase had always had a kind of strange odor that she couldn't place, but now she recognized it as the smell of the tenements, the scent of the past rising up through to the present. Layers of mold and dust that no amount of paint could cover. Even in her childhood, the ghost of this smell had been there, ready to greet her anytime she came home.

But this was no homecoming, she reminded herself as she started up the narrow back staircase. She was there for only one reason—to retrieve the key to the cipher so she could stop Seshat from destroying the world. So she could save Harte.

Professor Lachlan owned the entire building—or he had when she'd been growing up twenty or more years from now. In her own time line, he'd owned the building since the middle of the century or earlier, so she assumed that in *this* version of the time line, things wouldn't be that different, especially considering the power he seemed to have wielded in 1920. The slip of paper she was looking for—the missing fragment of a single page—was somewhere within these walls. It had to be. She could search from the bottom up, but she knew she'd be wasting her time. The key to the cipher would be where Professor Lachlan kept all his treasures, secure in the safe on the top floor of the building.

Esta was almost warm by the time she reached the top of the staircase. It wasn't surprising to find the access door there locked, but she'd been picking locks since she could remember. As the lock gave the satisfying *click* to signal it had surrendered, she couldn't help but feel it was almost too easy. She slowly pushed the door open, making sure to keep her wits about her and time firmly in her grasp. So far, her affinity felt strong and sure.

On the other side of the heavy fire door, the entire floor had been converted into an enormous library. By the time she'd left to go back to 1902, Esta had helped Professor Lachlan turn it into the finest, most extensive collection of documents about New York City that no one had ever heard of. Now the library wasn't quite so full of the city's secrets. But Esta needed only one secret. It had to be there.

The library was lit by a single desk lamp that sat on an enormous oak table at the center of the room. It had been only a few weeks ago—years from now in the future—that Professor Lachlan had used that same table to show her all five of the Order's artifacts. That had been the moment she finally understood what he had been working toward and the first time she'd seen them all together.

The wide table was covered with the usual stacks of newspapers and books. It wouldn't change much, Esta realized. It was like he didn't care about hiding the treasures he'd collected. But then . . . *maybe he doesn't.* Maybe Professor Lachlan didn't care what she saw because he had always been waiting for her to return for the one thing he knew she would need. Or maybe he was just a sloppy old man who never learned how to take care of his own house.

Either way, the sheer amount of stuff to look through felt overwhelming. If the fragment she was looking for wasn't in the safe, she'd have to search the whole library. And if it wasn't there, she'd have to search the rest of the building as well.

It will be in the safe. There was nowhere else Professor Lachlan would keep it. Other than maybe on his own person. Would he have risked carrying around a tiny scrap of fragile paper for decade after decade when he could keep it securely locked away? She doubted it.

On the far side of the library, a painting hung on the wall where the safe should be. It hadn't been there during her childhood, but Esta recognized it. Depicted in finely swirling brushstrokes, Isaac Newton sat beneath a tree with the fabled Book in his hand and two moons above him in the sky. She made her way past the precarious stacks of books and papers until she was standing in front of the painting. The last time she'd seen the painting, it had been hanging in Dolph Saunders' apartment. She'd helped steal it from the Met for Dolph—for her *real* father—but it wasn't the painting she was interested in. It was what lay behind it.

Esta removed the painting carefully and set it aside, but her spirits sank when she saw what waited for her. She'd hoped it was still too early for Professor Lachlan to have installed the biometric safe he'd had when she was growing up. She'd hoped it would be a simpler mechanism, and one she could easily crack, but the flat panel on the front of the safe glared back at her instead. There was no tumbler, no lock for a key. No clear way into the safe.

Then something caught her eye—hanging on the wall nearby were two shadowbox frames, one holding a pair of bronze mirrors inscribed with Chinese characters and another with a glinting silver dagger that had once been Viola's.

Esta's heart lurched. It didn't matter that her two friends would have likely been long dead anyway. Professor Lachlan had no right to these items. He didn't deserve them. Worse, she knew that he hadn't come by them accidentally. Jianyu and Viola's belongings would never have found their way into Professor Lachlan's possession if he hadn't somehow been involved with their deaths.

She took a paperweight from the table and used it to break the glass in one of the frames. Then, careful not to get her finger anywhere close to the blade, Esta lifted Viola's knife from the velvet backing. Its handle was strangely cool to the touch and too heavy for something so delicate, but it was exactly what she needed. She thought Viola would more than approve.

Returning to the safe, Esta jammed the tip of the thin blade into the hairline seam of the safe, and then carefully, she began to cut. The knife sliced through the iron safe as easily as it had once sunk itself into a zinc bar. Methodically, she worked the blade around the door of the safe, tracing the opening until . . . *there*.

The instant the door fell away, something popped, and a second later smoke began to seep from within the safe. *Opium*. Or something like it, from the scent. She didn't have Harte's ability to hold her breath for endless minutes, but she had a little time. Looking at the thick stack of papers and notebooks within the safe, her stomach sank. She'd have to hurry.

OLD FRIENDS

1902—Bella Strega

James dismissed Werner and Logan once they had deposited Jianyu on the low couch in his apartment. It was well past dawn now, and the light from the early morning was enough to see by without using an oil lamp. Thanks to Werner, Jianyu was still unconscious, but in a matter of seconds—his breath finally returned to him—he woke. James watched, unconcerned and unmoved, as Jianyu gasped, lurching upright so violently he nearly fell off the couch. It gave him more than a small satisfaction to see the confusion in Jianyu's eyes and then the fear when he realized where he was.

"Sit down," James commanded at the first glimmer of warmth from Jianyu's magic. "And don't bother with that disappearing trick of yours. There's nowhere you can go in this city that Logan won't be able to find you again, unless, of course, you're willing to part with those mirrors of yours."

Jianyu's hands went immediately to the deep pockets hidden in his tunic to check that his bronze mirrors were still there. Relief swept across the sharp features of his face, making him appear every bit as weak as he truly was. It was exactly as James had expected: Jianyu would never go anywhere without them. Depending on the trinkets made him vulnerable, just as depending on Dolph Saunders to protect him had made him a fool.

"If you try to leave, Werner's outside to ensure that you stay," James told him. "So sit. We have things to discuss."

"I have nothing to discuss with you." The words were spoken through clenched teeth.

"Ah, but I think you do," James told him.

Delightful, really, the anger thrumming through Jianyu. He showed it so rarely, but James had always known it was there, hidden behind the careful facade. Few realized what Jianyu was capable of. They thought him quiet and still, but James had understood the truth almost immediately. He'd used it when it suited him before, and he'd use it again. After all, anger was such a helpful emotion—so easy to use against the one who carried it.

Standing, James made his way to the small kitchen area at the rear of the apartment, unconcerned with whether Jianyu would stay or attack. He already knew that Dolph's old spy would do neither. The Aether had felt off since the day he took care of Mooch. Now it shivered and bunched, anticipating a new path, but James understood that Jianyu was no danger. *Not yet.* He poured two cups of whiskey and brought them back to the sitting area, where Jianyu waited, still strung tight as a bow.

He offered one of the cups. "Take it," he commanded, when Jianyu at first refused. Then, after he'd pushed one glass into Jianyu's reluctant hands, he dragged a chair over, turning it so he could straddle the spindly back. He took his time drinking from his own cup.

"Not thirsty?" he asked when it was clear Jianyu had no intention of drinking. He shrugged. "Suit yourself." He drained his own glass and set it aside, enjoying the way it burned a little, warming his chest and urging him onward.

"What do you want?" Jianyu asked, setting the cup of untouched liquor aside.

"I thought I'd already made that clear. I'd like to talk," James said with a guileless smile. "Can't a couple of old friends have a simple conversation?"

"I am no longer your friend," Jianyu told him coldly. "I think perhaps I never was. And I am not interested in this conversation. I have nothing to say to you."

"Well, I imagine that's a lie," James said, keeping his voice affable, light. "I'm sure there are any number of things you wish to say to me."

Jianyu only glared at him.

"We don't have to be enemies, you know," James said, taking a sip and trying to call up the old version of himself, the boy that no one suspected. "We could work with each other. Fight the Order. Take control of the streets of this city. *Together.* As Dolph would have wanted."

"You killed Dolph," Jianyu said simply.

"You know that I had to," James told him.

"I know no such thing."

"He would have destroyed the Brink," James explained, though in truth, he didn't *need* to explain anything. He could have simply commanded. But for now the Aether whispered patience, and so he spoke gently, attempting logic and persuasion . . . and saved his final cards for later.

Jianyu's brows drew together, and James could see when the truth registered.

"You've talked to Esta," James said. "You know Dolph was wrong. The Brink can't come down, not without destroying magic. Dolph never would have accepted that answer. He was *obsessed* with destroying the Brink, because he thought that was the only way to destroy the Order. He was so convinced the Book was the solution that he never even considered the danger. How could he know more about the old magic than any of us and never realize that it's all connected? How could he not understand that to destroy even one part of it would have doomed us all?"

"That is not why you killed him," Jianyu said.

James let his mouth curl, just a little. "Don't paint him as some kind of saint, my friend. You know he wasn't. None of us is."

Jianyu didn't speak. He simply regarded James with his usual stony, unreadable stare. But all around them the Aether trembled and bunched, and he knew that Jianyu was calculating his chances of escape.

"I have no intention of keeping you here indefinitely," James told him truthfully. Why should he keep Jianyu a prisoner when he was so much more useful out in the city, stirring trouble and the Aether along with it. "Once we've finished our little discussion, you'll be free to go."

Jianyu snorted his disbelief.

"I'll find you again if I have more to discuss," James assured him. Then he finished his drink and set the cup aside. "Or Logan will."

"So talk," Jianyu said. "What is it that you want from me?"

James did smile then. Jianyu might have had more of a backbone than most suspected, but he wasn't a formidable opponent. He was barely even amusing.

"I want what you stole from the Order."

Jianyu's gaze fell, briefly, to the ring glittering on James' right hand. "You already wear the Delphi's Tear, there on your finger."

"Oh, come now," James said, growing impatient. He stood then, leaning on his cane as he drew himself up to loom over Jianyu, who remained seated. "There's no sense in denying it. Werner told me that Viola found something—silver discs. Logan confirmed that she took them." When Jianyu's expression betrayed his surprise, James only smiled. "I may be willing to offer a trade."

"You have nothing I want," Jianyu said.

"Lie," James countered. "I have *exactly* what you want. I have the Strega and the Devil's Own." He watched Jianyu's expression close up, like a house before a storm, and he knew he'd hit his mark. "You want your home. Your family. I can make that happen, Jianyu. I can convince them all it was a simple misunderstanding. I can make sure they welcome you back like the prodigal son."

Jianyu's mouth tightened, but he didn't respond. He also couldn't quite hide the longing in his eyes. And nothing could disguise the way the Aether danced.

"I could also offer you protection," James added.

"As you protected Josef Salzer?" Jianyu asked.

"He wasn't my concern."

"The boy was one of Dolph's," Jianyu charged. "If you believe yourself worthy of taking Dolph Saunders' place, he should have been yours to protect."

"I protect those who are *loyal*," he told Jianyu. "I offered the boy the mark, but Josef refused it. He made his own choices, and he suffered the consequences of them."

"Did he?" Jianyu asked, tilting his head. "Or was he offered up? It strikes me as damning that none of those we have saved from the Order wore the mark."

James didn't so much as blink, despite Jianyu's astuteness. "Josef Salzer was never my concern. None of them were. My only concern is the road that lies ahead. Destroying the Order. Reclaiming the power that once belonged only to those with the old magic." *Taking my place as their leader.*

"Your concern has only ever been for yourself," Jianyu charged, as though it were a failing—a sin of some sort—to survive.

James had had enough. Whatever the Aether signaled, his patience was at an end. "I want the sigils. I'm willing to offer you protection in exchange for them," he told Jianyu. "I'm willing to offer you an alliance."

Jianyu stood. "We are finished here." He started for the door, had his hand on the knob and was already pulling it open before James spoke again.

"The Order's already searching for what you stole," James said. "It's the reason for the patrols."

Jianyu stopped, one foot nearly out the door. He hesitated, his hand still on the doorknob, but eventually he turned back, just as James knew he would.

"I've kept them from you," James said. "I've offered up others to give you time to see reason, but I'm running out of patience. Soon they'll find someone who's willing to talk, and then the Order will come for you and your little crew." He paused, letting this information settle. "What will you do then? How will you protect your Sundren friends? You're alone. Without support or backup . . .

"Oh, I know you have each other," he said, waving away the silent argument he saw shimmering in Jianyu's expression. "But a lone Chinaman and an Italian girl against the Order? It's laughable. Outsiders, all of you.

Mageus on top of that. Face it, Jianyu. Alone, you don't stand a chance against what the richest men in the city are capable of. But under my protection? Under the protection of the Devil's Own?" He shrugged.

Jianyu did not speak at first. It was not hesitation—James understood this—but care. He'd never been rash before, and he would not start now. "What, *exactly*, are you offering?"

"Come back," James said softly. "Repledge yourself to the organization that your dearly departed Dolph Saunders built. Pledge yourself to *me*. Give Newton's Sigils into my keeping, and in turn, I will protect you and yours. Your Sundren will be safe."

"And what of Viola?"

James shrugged. "That depends upon Viola."

"You would take her back willingly after the injury she gave you?" Jianyu asked, eyeing the cane.

"She made a mistake," he said with another affable-looking shrug. "We could come to an arrangement."

The edge of Jianyu's mouth twitched, but he did not smile. "Those discs must be very valuable for you to make such a generous offer."

"They are," James said. He was sure of it.

A long, fraught moment passed between them as the Aether vibrated and danced. But with the strange vibrations that had plagued him for weeks, James could not read the message within it. He could not tell what answer Jianyu might give until he spoke.

"After what you have done, you cannot actually imagine we would simply hand over anything so powerful?" Jianyu said. "You cannot truly believe we would trust you?"

"But I would," James said easily. "In fact, I've imagined much, much more than that." James let the affability slide from his expression. In its place, James revealed the reality of who—of *what*—he had become. His hand caressed the coils on the Medusa's head, felt the cold energy there answering to him, and sent it out into the air. "You see, my old friend. You no longer have a choice."

THE PROFESSOR

1983—Orchard Street

Esta didn't waste time. Still holding her breath, she took the contents from the opened safe and started shuffling through, searching for some sign of the key. Already, her lungs were starting to ache. Soon they would begin to burn. She didn't have much time.

The safe was filled mostly with papers. A stack of ledgers seemed to list the contents of bank accounts—or some kind of accounts. A quick look told her that Nibsy's business holdings went quite a ways into the past. There was also an accordion folder filled with loose-leaf papers— notes, it looked like. As she flipped through the sheets of paper, she realized it was research. Spells. Rituals. There were answers here, she thought, her skin prickling with awareness.

The next item was a small, unremarkable notebook. She almost set it aside, but when she riffled through the pages, she noticed that something was wrong with the writing. The words written on the paper weren't steady or stable. After a certain date, the letters vibrated and changed, rotating through any number of combinations. It looked like the news clipping she'd taken back to the past originally had looked when she changed the past.

It was some kind of diary, she realized from the few stable entries. *Nibsy's diary.* The dates on the pages—nearly a century of them— remained steady, even as the entries blurred and shifted. Occasionally a name she recognized would shimmer to the surface, along with a few words. A phrase here. A sentence there. But before she could finish reading what the words said, they would blur again. Erasing and changing over themselves.

Professor Lachlan had kept a record of everything he'd done. But why were the entries so unstable? Hadn't the past already happened?

She flipped back to one of the few stable entries and allowed her eyes to scan over the contents. *I left him in the cemetery, bleeding into Leena's grave. The great Dolph Saunders. Finally facedown in the dirt. Exactly where he belonged.*

Esta felt grief twist in her chest. She'd never doubted Harte when he'd told her how Dolph had died, how Nibsy had betrayed them all and took more than Dolph's life—took everything he'd worked so long and so hard to build. But to see it there, stark and clear in the too-familiar writing she recognized from her childhood lessons?

She blinked back tears and turned the page.

The last stable entry detailed something about a gala at Morgan's mansion in May of 1902. Every page after was unsettled. Every entry remained indeterminate.

She realized immediately what the notebook meant. History could still be rewritten.

Esta flipped forward through the notebook, taking in page after page of entries that continued to shift and morph, until she found another that wasn't completely impossible to read: December 21, 1902. *The Conclave.*

As she watched, portions of the handwriting grew less erratic, the words solidifying into a clear description of what happened at the Conclave. The entry looked old, with the ink faded from the years, but there were places where words held steady. There on the page were names that she recognized: Viola. Jianyu.

They're dead. There, clear and solid and steady in the middle of the notebook's otherwise chaotic pages, was the description of how they died. They'd turned on each other. *Nibsy* had somehow turned them on each other. The words only grew steadier and more legible as she read, as though her being there, her knowing about their deaths, was somehow stabilizing that version of the past and making it absolute.

Her head spun, and she flipped the pages backward and then ahead, urgently searching for some other outcome. They could go back. They would go back and stop this—

A new line wrote itself into the notebook, an impossible future that couldn't be. The shock of seeing her name there on the page alongside Harte's made her nearly drop the diary. She gasped, trying to catch it, and accidentally inhaled some of the strange fog that had filled the library. Suddenly, she felt off-kilter, but she couldn't tell if it was from the terrible future the notebook had just revealed or from the opium-laced fog. With shaking hands, she picked up the notebook again by the edge of its cover. As it flopped open, a page came loose.

No. Not a page—a *piece* of a page.

The fog was already working on her affinity as she reached for it. Her magic was growing more slippery, but she knew before her fingers grasped the small piece of parchment that *this* was what she had come for.

Time was slipping away from her, but she had to know. Flipping the diary open again, she read the steady lines in the bold, neat hand, and her head spun with a combination of the opium in the air and her complete horror at the knowledge of what was coming—of what she couldn't stop. Viola's death. Jianyu's. And now, added to theirs, her own. And Nibsy Lorcan the victor.

No. She wouldn't let it happen. She knew now, didn't she? Knowing meant she could prepare. Knowing meant she could avoid that particular future. That *had* to change things, didn't it? But the names on the page remained maddeningly steady and clear.

Her head was still spinning, and her lungs were burning with the effort not to take another breath, but the power floating through the air in the strange fog had already done its work. Her affinity wavered, and then she lost hold of the seconds completely.

Esta tried to pull time slow again, but it was pointless. She tucked the notebook into her dress, knowing already that she was out of time. Professor Lachlan had been expecting her to come for the key, and he probably already knew she was there. She had to get outside. She had to get away before he caught her.

She sprinted for the back stairwell and took the steps two at a time, holding the handrails as she went. At the bottom, she reached for the dead bolt she'd resecured, but now the lock wouldn't turn.

Probably another security feature—a trap to keep her in.

It didn't matter, because Esta knew the building like the back of her hand. She knew every corner and niche to hide in, every twist of every hallway. She'd slipped out enough times as a child. Professor Lachlan couldn't keep her there. And besides, she still had Viola's knife.

But she'd barely started to slip it into the space between the door and the jamb when she felt more than heard the presence behind her on the stairs. When she turned, Professor Lachlan was standing on the landing above her, watching. He stepped into the light, allowing the hazy, yellow glow to illuminate him, casting his features in shadows.

On instinct, Esta reached for her affinity, but it was still deadened. Glancing at the hallway and then to the door that led out to the back of the building, she tried to decide which was her better chance for an escape. Neither was ideal.

Again, she pulled at the seconds, but again and again, they slipped through her fingers. She needed to stall.

The man on the steps looked younger than the one who had raised her, but he was dressed in the usual tweed he'd worn through her entire childhood. Even looming above her as he was, the Professor was a small man. He was more than a hundred years old, but he barely looked sixty. Still, Esta wasn't fooled into believing that he was frail, not with his hand resting softly on a familiar cane.

The Professor began to move easily down the steps toward her, and she noticed that he didn't limp anymore. The cane was more an affectation now than a requirement.

"You're looking good, Nibsy," she said, doing her best to conceal her apprehension. "You know, considering that you should be dead."

He ignored her taunting. "I knew you'd come," he told her. "It's a shame you have no hope at all of leaving. Not with your affinity intact."

Esta didn't respond. It wouldn't do any good to engage with him. She couldn't panic or do anything rash. She had to *think*.

She still had the knife. Maybe she'd never be as good an aim as Viola had once been, but her lack of skills wouldn't stop the magic in the blade from cutting. This man had killed so many: Dolph, Leena, Dakari.

No—he hadn't yet killed Dakari. But he would if she allowed him to live. He would hurt so many others.

And yet Esta *had* to allow him to live. There had to be someone waiting here to raise the girl she had once been. Someone had to forge her into the woman she needed to become. Or time would take its due, and it would take Harte with it.

Outside the building, the city beyond had come back to life. Sirens screamed in the distance, and the winter wind howled against the back door, but Esta's complete focus was on the man in front of her. She lifted Viola's knife.

"Will you kill me the same as you killed Jack Grew?" Professor Lachlan asked. He lifted his hands as if in surrender, but there was amusement in his old eyes.

She kept the knife raised, a silent threat. Nothing good could come from a long-winded discussion. Not with this snake of a man. She thought she might almost be able to feel her affinity coming back. A little longer and she'd be able to slip free of him.

His expression was as unreadable as it had ever been. "You made quite the impression on the entire country, you know. The pictures were everywhere—your face twisted in rage with your knife plunging into that poor man's chest. The blood splattered on your dress." His mouth twitched then as he looked her over—her ill-fitting overalls and inappropriate shoes. "How long has it been for you since that day? Have you lived with what you've done for weeks or years . . . or is the memory still fresh? Tell me, do you remember what it felt like as the blade pressed through bone? Do you still think about the life fading from his eyes?"

Esta refused to take the bait. She couldn't let herself think about Jack's death, not when it had barely been hours and not when the horror of what she had done was still too fresh. She couldn't let herself remember the way it had felt for the knife to slip past the bone and breath in Jack's chest. It would be with her, haunt her, always. And it didn't matter that Jack had deserved it. It didn't matter that Thoth would have destroyed everything with Seshat's power. Killing Jack had changed her, just as Harte had warned weeks before in the New Jersey train station.

Professor Lachlan's mouth curved, as though he understood that her thoughts had taken her back there. He took another step down toward her. "Did you enjoy it? It's a heady feeling to take a life."

"You should know," she said, keeping her voice calm. Easy. *Don't let him know.*

"It's true I've taken my share," the old man admitted. "It's something to watch the final breath, to see the light dim from the eyes. It's my one regret that I didn't stay to watch Dolph die. There was too much danger in waiting in the cemetery to stay, to enjoy my final victory." He tilted his head slightly, as though considering her. "You turned Jack Grew into a martyr, you know. By killing him there, in front of the crowded convention, you made him into a saint, not only for the Brotherhoods, but for the *country.* You have no idea what's followed—the gilded statues they've raised in his honor, the horrors they've committed in his name—or you would have come far sooner than now."

Esta remained silent. She wouldn't ask. She would *not* give him that satisfaction, even as dread crept down her spine.

"But you've arrived, as I knew you would. As I *planned* for you to," he said, adjusting his grip on the cane. She could see the silver of the Medusa's face peeking out between his fingers, and on his hand, flashing in the dimly lit stairwell, was the Delphi's Tear.

The last artifact—it was *here*. With that ring, they would have all five artifacts and the Book. They could stop Seshat. They had everything they needed—if only she could get it from him.

Esta schooled her expression. She couldn't let him know how much she wanted the ring. She couldn't broadcast what she was about to do . . . *especially* if he likely already knew. The effects of the opium fog were starting to ebb, but even if she could pull time around her, she'd have to touch the Professor to get the ring. It would draw him into the net of her affinity.

"I'm not here because you planned for me," she told him. *Stall. Keep him talking.* He loved to talk.

Her mind raced for a plan that would work. She spun through ideas, immediately discarding them as she took a step forward. If anyone died today, she would make sure it was him. Even if she had to kill him herself, that ring was what she needed to save Harte. She wasn't leaving without it.

"You know you can't kill me," Professor Lachlan said.

Esta, undeterred, gave him a smile that was all teeth. "I can try."

"You could," he admitted. "But you won't succeed. You should know by now that already I've planned for every possibility. Even this one."

A door to Esta's left opened then, spilling light into the dark vestibule, and when she turned to see what danger was approaching, her breath seized in her chest, and the world seemed to freeze.

Horror jolted through her as she came face-to-face with a ghost from her past.

MISSING

1902—Little Africa

Cela Johnson still felt the exhaustion of the night before, but she thought she was covering it well enough. Crossing her arms over her chest, she faced her brother, Abel, as confidently as she ever had. But even as they talked, she kept one ear alert for any indication that Viola or Jianyu might be returning to the small basement rooms they all shared.

Jianyu had not returned the night before. It wasn't unusual for him to deliver news of their midnight rescues to the waiting families, but he always returned before dawn. As the minutes ticked by and night turned to morning, Cela and Viola had both finally admitted something must have gone wrong.

Viola had gone out to find him. It wasn't any safer for her to be out alone, but at least she could defend herself in ways Cela couldn't. She'd left just after dawn, but it was nearly noon now, and she still hadn't returned. So Cela had more on her mind than Abel's too-familiar argument about why she needed to get out of the city. In the past few weeks, the conversation had become one she was beyond tired of having, especially since it was clear that neither she nor her older brother was going to change their mind.

"You're taking too many risks, Rabbit," Abel said. "One of these times, I'm going to come home and you're not going to be waiting for me."

"I know you're worried, and you're right to be," Cela told him, trying to keep the annoyance out of her voice. He meant well, and she understood his fear. She would have felt the same, would have been worried for his safety just as much if their situations were reversed. And he would have been every bit as determined as she was to stay. "But you know I can't leave now. I promised to help our friends, and I'm going to keep that promise."

Abel's mouth tightened, and the shift in his features made her brother look suddenly even more tired than usual. The dark circles beneath his eyes were deeper today, and the lines bracketing his mouth were grimmer. "You can still help them when things clear up a little. But until then, it's not safe here."

"It's never safe here, Abe."

He rubbed the growth of beard on his chin. "You know what I'm saying, Cela. Things are dangerous now. Police on every corner. Patrols hunting through buildings like they own them. What if you get caught up in that while I'm gone?"

"I'll be okay," she said gently. "I know how to watch out for myself. I've been doing it for long enough."

"What if you don't think of it as leaving? Maybe you could just take a trip," he pressed. "You could go stay with our uncle down on the coast. Get out of the heat of the city for a while."

"Abel Johnson, they don't want me there. You *know* that. And even if they did, I wouldn't want to bring my troubles to their doorstep. If I'm in so much danger, I'm going to stay right here and keep that danger from touching anyone else," she told him. "You need to stop worrying about me and get yourself ready to go. Doesn't your train leave in an hour?"

"I feel like I just got back," he grumbled. "Maybe I could get one of the other fellas to take this route. I'd feel better if you weren't alone."

"*Abel* . . ." She met his exasperated expression with one of her own. "I'm not alone here. I got people to watch over me," she said, trying not to think of what had happened to Jianyu or why Viola hadn't returned yet.

Her brother ran his hand over the dark, short-cropped curls that covered his head. "Too bad they're also the ones who got you into this mess."

She nodded. "And I trust them to get me out of it."

Abel cocked a brow in her direction, a question and a challenge. She wasn't stupid—she understood his worry and his point.

"They're not going to let anything happen to me," she assured him. Hadn't Viola killed Kelly's men just by looking at them? Cela knew exactly how much that single action had cost Viola. The Italian girl seemed perfectly content to kill with a knife but had some kind of strange moral code against using her magic to do the same. The fact that Viola had chosen to save Cela and Abel over her own soul by using her power? That was more than enough for Cela. Even if she was still prickly as a pincushion.

"Please, Cela—"

"I'm done talking about this, Abe." She let out a tired breath. "You trusted me to take care of myself when you went off hiding from those union busters, so you'll just have to trust me now. I'm not running off to the country like some scared mouse. This city is my home, and I'm not leaving it. I'm certainly not leaving my *friends*." She softened her expression and her voice as she stepped toward her brother and took his familiar face gently in her hands. He looked *so* much like their father. Acted like him too, sometimes, come to think of it. "I've lost everything else—our family's home, my job at the theater, the life I had before. I can't leave my city, too. I won't be chased off or sent away for my own good."

"Rabbit—"

"You have to go, so you'll go," she told him, stepping back. "You'll be gone two, maybe three weeks, and I'll be here waiting when you come back. I'll be *fine*, just like I always am. But if you lose this job—"

"I *know*, dammit. I know." He closed his eyes, and she knew he was begging patience and strength. But they both understood what would happen if he lost his position. It wasn't as though jobs that paid as well as working on the Pullman cars were just lying around like overripe fruit. It was thankless and exhausting work, but on good runs with the right kind of passengers, the gratuities he earned more than made up for the money he had to put into buying the bootblack and other supplies he needed just to *do* the job. With the money he earned, they could rebuild their home and their lives.

"I'll be fine. I promise," she said, giving him a brisk, tight hug before letting him go.

"Make sure you keep that promise," Abe said, his shoulders falling a little—a signal she'd won the argument. At least for the time being.

She stepped forward and wrapped her arms around her brother. "I know how to take care of myself, Abe."

He pulled back. "I know you do, Rabbit. But I can't stop myself from worrying. You're my sister, aren't you?"

She gave him another squeeze. "Always."

A whistle came from the street outside, and the two of them froze, listening as it sounded again. In the days that had passed since the Order's solstice ritual, they'd stayed out of sight as much as they could, lying low in the small basement room. They couldn't be sure who might know about their involvement with the theft of the Order's treasures, so they weren't taking any chances.

"That'll be Joshua," Abel said, pulling back. "Hopefully, he'll have some news about a better place."

"You asked him to find one?" she asked, surprised.

"I had a feeling you weren't going to bend any," he said, chucking her gently under the chin. There was still a sadness in his eyes that he couldn't quite hide.

"And you still bothered me with your arguing?" she asked, feigning irritation but feeling nothing but love and pride.

He shrugged. "I had to try, but if you're set on staying like I figured you'd be, I wanted to get you settled somewhere better than this place before I go."

Cela's throat went tight as she gave a small nod, grateful for her brother in every way a person could be grateful. "You better go on and talk to Joshua, then. Make sure he got us one of those big places up on Madison Avenue."

Abel shook his head, and it was clear he was more amused than truly exasperated when he left.

A few seconds after her brother went out to talk to their friend, Viola slipped into the room soundlessly. And alone.

Cela's skin prickled with dread. "You didn't find him?"

"Golde said he left not long after we saw him," Viola told her. "There's no sign of him after then."

"He wouldn't stay away like this on purpose," Cela said.

"I know," Viola agreed. "Something's happened."

"The Order?"

Viola frowned. "Maybe, but we have other enemies. Some closer to home."

"Nibsy," Cela said, thinking of who else might want to harm them. "Or the Five Pointers?"

"It could be any of them," Viola admitted. She stepped forward and laid her hand on Cela's arm. "We'll find him."

The door opened, and Abel entered in a rush. "Get your things," he said, not even noticing the somber mood of the room. "Take only what you can carry." When Cela didn't move fast enough for his liking, he started throwing some of her sewing supplies into a bag himself.

"Abel, what are you doing?" Cela asked, confused by the sudden change in her brother. "What's going on?"

Abel paused long enough to meet her eyes. "There's a group of men checking apartments one building over. And they're headed this way."

LISA MAXWELL

TRUST AND LIES

1983—City Hall Station

The last thing Harte remembered, he'd been tumbling from the moving train and landing hard—so hard that Seshat had been shaken into silence. But she hadn't remained silent for long. He'd barely had time to breathe before she'd started up again, her banshee's voice tearing at him from the inside as her rage bubbled and churned within, threatening to rip the very essence of him to shreds.

Then Esta had appeared above him. She'd been telling him something. Or trying to.

He couldn't hear her over Seshat's terrible noise, but he'd understood her intention. Even with all that had gone wrong, she wouldn't give up. Esta would walk straight into the trap Nibsy Lorcan had set for her, and there was nothing he could do to stop her.

And then, all at once, she was gone. *Gone.* Like she'd never been there at all.

In the distance, Harte heard the rumble of one of the underground trains and understood what must have happened. Esta had used her affinity. She'd left him to go after Nibsy by herself.

Looking around, he tried to get his bearings. The station was a dark, cavernous space. In his own time, they'd already started building the subway system. He'd walked by the opened streets many times, marveling at the audacity of the plan, but he hadn't imagined what it would actually be like to be completely underground. To feel so . . . entombed.

But then, he never could have imagined that the city would become the marvel that it was now. The piles of trash everywhere weren't that different, but the *height* of the skyline. Even through the haze of Seshat's fury, he'd been struck by the wonder of it all. The dizzying brightness of the buildings lit from within and the speed of cars streaming by.

He needed to figure out what to do next, but it was all he could do to keep himself from flying apart. He had to *think*. Esta had gone to deal with Nibsy on her own, but she never would have let go of her hold on time. Not unless something had gone terribly wrong. The fact that he was even aware that she'd left—and the fact that she hadn't returned—meant that she was in trouble.

Harte thought of the fog back in Brooklyn, the strange energy that had blasted through the Nitemarket and the convention in Chicago, and the Quellant that Maggie had invented. Even something as simple as the opium the Veiled Prophet Society had used in St. Louis to protect the necklace. There were so many ways to deaden an affinity and strip someone of their magic, and Nibsy Lorcan likely knew all of them.

Bracing himself against the onslaught from within, Harte tried to get to his feet. He had to find a way out of the station. He had to find Esta.

At the thought of her, Seshat's power slammed against the thin barrier that held her back, and Harte stumbled from the force of it, falling over again. His skin felt both feverishly hot and sickly cold at the same time, and his limbs were trembling. The ancient goddess had been quiet until they'd crossed back into the city. The second they'd breached the Brink, she'd become erratic. Desperate. *Terrified.* And her fear made her power feel even more dangerous.

Seshat screamed and raged as she railed against the bars of her cage, and Harte understood her intentions too clearly. She would destroy Esta and the world itself to keep Thoth from touching her power.

"He's gone. Thoth is dead." His unsteady voice was barely audible in the huge, vaulted chamber, even to himself. "He can't touch you."

Fool, she wailed. *Thoth is not gone. As long as he is anywhere, he is* everywhere. *And if he succeeds in controlling my power, nothing will stop him from claiming the beating heart of magic as his own. He will be unstoppable. Infinite. There will be no time, no place safe from his destruction.*

Harte pulled himself to his knees. Nothing Seshat was telling him was new, but none of it mattered. Not until he found Esta.

Toward the back of the station, there was a tunnel that glowed with a faint light. Possibly the exit? As he inched along, Seshat fought him. She didn't want him to leave the station, and the closer he came to the tunnel, the more erratic her fear became. But he was almost there. He'd nearly made it to the first of the steps that led upward into the darkened staircase.

And then, suddenly, Esta appeared. He'd been alone with Seshat's wailing, and then a heartbeat later she was *there.* She was *safe.*

Seshat froze, her wailing suddenly going silent as she retracted deep within him, and the reprieve was almost enough to make him weep with relief. He was too exhausted from her onslaught to wonder why. All he could do was collapse against the cold, hard wall, trying to catch his breath. He had to gather what strength he could, because he knew Seshat wouldn't stay quiet for long.

When he looked up, Esta's face was drawn and serious. Her eyes were hard, determined, and he knew instinctively that something had happened to her. It was there in her expression. Something had put a distance in her eyes like he'd never seen before.

"Are you okay?" he asked, still leaning against the tiled wall. "Did Nibsy harm you? Because if he touched you—"

"I'm fine." Her voice was strong and sure, but there was a stiffness in her tone that he didn't recognize.

"Esta?" he asked gently. "You can tell me."

"I don't want to talk about it," she told him. "Not right now. *Please.* Don't make me relive it."

The stern set of her usually soft mouth and the hardness in her eyes told the story clearly enough. *Fine then.* He wouldn't ask more of her than she could give, wouldn't drag the details from her. *Not now, at least.* But he desperately wanted to touch her. She'd done too much, taken on too much in the last few days, and there was nothing he could do to help her, to comfort her. Not with the threat of Seshat within him.

"The Book," she said, her gaze finding the scarred leather tome where it lay on the platform. He hadn't even noticed it there. She must have left it with him, and he'd been so distracted by Seshat's rage—so desperate to reach Esta before Nibsy could hurt her—that he hadn't protected it. He'd walked *away* from it.

"I'm sorry," he said. "I didn't—"

Esta wasn't listening. She hurried over to the Ars Arcana and stopped. Standing over it, she paused, clenching her fists at her sides, before she finally picked it up from the ground.

Seshat was still quiet, but Harte realized that it wasn't an easy quiet. The emptiness within him was somehow almost more terrible than her raging. Then, from somewhere deep within him, Harte felt Seshat's fear. It was as though she understood what was coming, what would happen next.

On unsteady legs, Harte made his way to where Esta was standing, paging through the Book. She was looking for something, and then she found it—the page that was half-torn and missing. With the Ars Arcana propped open in one hand, she pulled a small scrap of parchment from her pocket and held it up to the page. The pieces matched exactly, and the second the torn halves touched, Harte felt a jolt of power wash over him as the fragment fused itself back onto the page in a burst of molten light.

"You did it," Harte said, still barely believing it. "You got the key from Nibsy."

Her mouth went tight, but she nodded in a way that made him wonder what it had cost her. Because something had changed. Something had changed *her.*

"Now we'll be able to get the demon's power out of you, and once we have control over it, we'll finally be able to use the piece of pure magic in the Book." She was still looking at the newly complete page rather than him when she spoke. "We'll be able to change *everything*."

Harte felt a wave of panic rush through him. It was all happening too fast. "We still need the Delphi's Tear. We don't have the ring yet."

Esta peered up through her dark lashes, then pulled something from her other pocket. "This ring?"

She was holding the Delphi's Tear. Weeks ago—decades ago now—Harte had given it to Cela Johnson as payment for taking care of his mother. The ring should have been in 1902, waiting for them to retrieve it. Nibsy shouldn't have had possession of it. "How—"

"I'm a thief," Esta said without any irony or humor.

Harte didn't want to think about what it meant that Nibsy Lorcan had come to possess the ring. What had happened to Cela? Had Jianyu not reached her in time to protect her? Or had they both been unable to protect themselves?

"You have the others?" she asked.

He noticed the satchel lying on the ground and scooped it up, ignoring the way Seshat shivered within him. "They're right here, where you left them."

Esta nodded and took a thick piece of charcoal from the same pocket that had been holding the ring. "Go ahead and take them out." She crouched down and started drawing a circle on the ground.

"Wait." He stepped toward her. "Esta, we can't just rush into this. We don't know what this ritual will do to you."

She didn't give any indication that she'd heard him. Ignoring his worry, she continued her tracing, making steady progress on the circle that was quickly forming around her. It was maybe six or seven feet in diameter. Not enormous, but more than large enough for a person to stand in the center and hold out their arms.

"*Esta*," he said again, more forcefully. He stepped toward the line, but Seshat lurched within him, and he stopped short before crossing it. "Would you stop for a second? We have to talk about this."

"There's nothing to talk about." She looked up at him, pausing only long enough to speak. "We don't have time to argue. The police are searching for us. They know we crossed the Brink." Her expression was as brittle as her voice, and there was something of a warning in her words. As though she'd been pushed as far as anyone could be pushed before breaking. "If they find us, they'll take the Book and the artifacts, and everything will have been for *nothing*. I have to finish this *now*."

Harte took an instinctive step back at the forcefulness of her tone. Something terrible must have happened at Nibsy's place for her to be so closed off and distant. She'd faced something, done something, and now she *needed* this. Danger or not.

Seshat started to wail as Esta rolled up her sleeve, slipped the cuff from her arm, and set it along the dark circle she'd drawn on the ground. A little farther along the line, she placed the ring.

When Harte didn't immediately move, impatience flashed in Esta's expression. "I need the others."

"What if the ritual kills you?" he asked softly.

"It won't," she said, lifting her chin. Confident as she ever was.

"How can you know that?" Harte asked.

"I made the old man tell me everything when I took the key from him," she said.

"You can't believe anything Nibsy tells you." Harte shook his head. "You *know* that."

"I believe *this*." She pointed to the page of the Book. "It's all here. See . . . when you put the page together, these symbols aren't some secret code. They're just an older version of Greek. Professor Lachlan taught me to read this years ago." Her mouth formed strange syllables the likes of which Harte had never heard before. "*To catch the serpent with the hand of the philosopher: With power willingly given, mercury ignites. Elements unite. The serpent catches its tail, severs time, consumes. Transforms power to power's like* . . . It's all right here."

None of that was clear enough for him. "Esta—" But before he could say anything else, Seshat wailed and thrashed, causing him to nearly collapse with the effort of holding her back.

"Look at you," Esta said. "We need to get that demon out of *you* and back into the *Book*."

"Not if it means losing you." He grimaced against Seshat again. "Nibsy nearly killed you before, trying to do this same ritual."

"I wasn't willing then, but I am now." Her jaw was set, and her eyes flashed. "My affinity, *willingly* given, will ignite the Aether and unify the artifacts. With them, we can control the demon goddess and use her power. Only the goddess can touch the piece of pure magic in the Ars Arcana, which means we need to get her out of *you* and back into the *Book* where she belongs. Where she can be controlled. I can do this. I know I can."

Lies, Seshat screamed. *You cannot allow her to do this. The only way to unite the stones is through sacrifice. Total and complete sacrifice of her affinity. She will die, willing or no, and whoever possesses the Book will possess my power as well.*

So that's it, he thought. If Seshat was fighting so hard against this, it meant that the ritual would work. *You expect me to believe you care about her at all?*

I'm not your enemy, Seshat said. *I never was. . . .*

But Harte was already shoving her down, back into the recesses of his soul.

"I need the artifacts," Esta said. She'd already placed the Book on the ground in the center of the circle.

His hands were shaking as he took out the crown, the necklace, and the dagger. In the dim lighting of the station, the pieces looked dull, almost ordinary, but he could feel their power thickening the air. He hadn't seen the five of them all in one place since he'd stolen them from the Order's Mysterium. Then he'd had the same foreboding. Now Seshat railed from somewhere deep, deep inside him, but he ignored her protests. If she didn't want this ritual to happen, there had to be a reason.

He stepped into the circle, but he didn't hand over the other three artifacts, not yet. "I can't lose you to this. We need to be sure. This isn't worth dying for."

A soft breath escaped from her lips. A sign that was as much exhaustion as frustration. "I know, Harte. I love you, too."

The shock of hearing those words from her bolted through him. How many times had he wondered, had he wanted to say those words only for them to stick in his throat? And now, after all they'd been through, she was giving them to him here? Just when she was about to take an incalculable risk? "You . . ." He couldn't seem to choke it out.

"Love you." The words still sounded stiff, like the creaking of a gate that needed oiling or the cracking of a lock that rusted shut.

He shook his head, feeling an unexpected dread. This wasn't how it was supposed to happen. "You don't have to say that."

"But I do." She gave him a small, brittle smile. "Now, if you could hand me the satchel? I'll need the other stones."

He was still too shocked, too overwhelmed to move. "Esta, I— Don't. *Please.*" Why wouldn't she look at him? "Don't you dare say your good-byes."

She blinked as though surprised by his assumption. "No. Not a good-bye. I just thought—" Her jaw went tight, and her expression became unreadable once again. "This *will* work," she said, cutting him off before he could say anything more. "It will be fine. Everything is going to turn out the way it's supposed to." She looked at him, her golden eyes pleading. "You *do* trust me, don't you?"

The sharpness in her voice threw him off, but he pulled himself together when she glared at him, and he had the sense again that something was wrong. That there was something she wasn't telling him. "Of course . . ." It was Seshat he didn't trust. Nibsy. *Himself.*

"This is going to work," she repeated, but he wasn't sure that she was talking to him anymore. She held out her hands and looked at him, clearly waiting for the artifacts. "I need you to believe in me." There was a spark of impatience in her eyes, an urgency that reminded him that something must have happened while she was away. There was a flinty determination in her expression he hadn't seen for months. "I thought you loved me?"

He did. After all they'd been through, how could she not know that he loved her? Which meant that, whatever misgivings he might have, he couldn't take the choice from her. It meant that he *had* to trust her. Afraid to get too close, he placed the satchel on the ground at her feet. Her eyes lit as she picked it up.

"Thank you," she whispered, relief softening her expression.

The unease he was feeling dissipated a little. She would be okay. *They* would be okay.

She got to work almost immediately. Completely focused on her task now, Esta placed the artifacts at separate points, evenly spaced along the circle on the floor. Before she placed the dagger that held the Pharaoh's Heart in its place, she used the ancient knife to slice open the tip of her finger.

It took everything Harte had not to stop her when he saw the bright red blood welling. *I trust her*, he reminded himself. More than he'd ever trusted anyone. So he held his tongue and prayed that they weren't wrong.

Back in the center of the circle, Esta knelt before the open Book again. Then slowly, carefully, she used her bleeding fingertip to trace over the design on the page as again she spoke words he couldn't understand, syllables that rattled strangely in his ears. As she worked, Harte could feel the power beginning to swirl around them. Beneath his feet, the space within the circle Esta had sketched onto the floor started to glow, faintly at first and then brighter.

On instinct, Harte took a step back from the Book. He had to get out of the circle, away from the enormous power flowing from the Ars Arcana, but at the edge of the circle, he ran into an invisible wall. Cold, deadly energy sizzled in warning, holding him in place. Stuck within the circle, he watched as light continued to pour from the page of the Book, lifting the short hair around Esta's face and illuminating her.

Another empty train slid into the station, its wheels screaming as it slowed and rounded the bend. But Harte barely noticed it. By now there was a wild energy growing in the cavernous space, a dangerous magic building. Within his skin, Seshat was screaming and wailing, more desperate and terrified than she'd ever been.

As the energy increased, there was a roaring in his ears that grew and grew until it blocked any other noise—the train, the far-off tracks, his own shouting. Even Seshat's screams eventually were drowned out by the ancient and indescribable cacophony that was filling his mind. Something was coming to life—a magic like chaos blooming. He could feel it tearing through the air, and the enormity of it took his breath away.

There was too much magic, too much *power*. But the energy, the chaotic wildness of it, had pinned him in place. He couldn't even begin to stop Esta from finishing the ritual.

He had to stop her. He knew suddenly that she had been wrong. This power? There was no surviving this. There was only sacrifice.

Harte knew what would happen next because he'd seen Seshat start this ritual before in the visions that had assaulted him back in St. Louis. Esta and Seshat, the reality and the memory—he could see them both, superimposed and simultaneous. What had been. What was. What would be.

"Esta," he screamed, but his voice was lost in the noise. She didn't look up. She couldn't hear him. Or if she could, she was too far into the ritual, too far gone into the totality of the magic swirling around her.

One by one the artifacts around him began to lift themselves into the air, floating in the invisible net of Aether that held all of creation together. One by one they began to glow with a strange, ethereal light, and Harte felt another power join the first—a familiar brush of magic that could only be Esta's. She was using her affinity to unite the stones, just as Seshat had eons ago. Just as the Book had instructed her.

There was nothing he could do. He couldn't stop her from sending her affinity outward, into the stones, or from connecting all she was to the artifacts and, with them, to the magic trapped in the Book. They joined together in a swirling eddy of power and light, like a Brink made visible.

Sweat was beading at Esta's temples, and her expression was strained. The power that could only be the piece of original magic trapped in the Book—the portion of the beating heart of magic that Seshat had trapped ages ago—was flowing through Esta now, consuming her. Linking her very self to the stones and to the Book. When she finally raised her eyes to meet his, their usual golden warmth was gone. In its place were bright hollows, empty sockets lit from within.

All at once a terrible bolt of energy coursed through the room, and then through Harte himself.

From somewhere deep, deep within the recesses of his very being, Seshat let out a soul-shattering scream that was anger and pain and terror made real. Harte felt the goddess's anguish as though it were his own. The power tore through him, and suddenly Harte could feel everything: the net of time and Aether that held the whole world together, the individual affinities and lives that had been stolen to power the artifacts, and the thin thread of Esta's own affinity connecting it all. Seshat clawed at him in a last, desperate attempt to stop her inevitable end. And then Harte felt the sureness of what would come, the absolute horror of knowing that he could be destroyed by the very magic that made him whole.

There were tears of blood streaming down Esta's face now, and Harte knew—knew absolutely and without doubt—that she had been wrong. The fear in her eyes—the pure surprised terror there—cracked his heart in two. She'd believed that this would work, and she'd been wrong. This ritual was killing her, *would* kill her. But Harte still couldn't move. He was rooted in place by the terrible beating heart of magic that surrounded him.

Then he, too, was being pulled apart.

When Seshat lost her grip within him, Harte felt himself shattering as the goddess' power drained from him. The pulsing power around him swirled, glowing ever brighter and hotter as Seshat's power joined it, growing like a storm about to crash over them both.

And then it did break. The light trembled and the power shattered, and Harte felt the sucking of some unseen wind drawing him toward the Book. With a flash of light, the Book pulled it all inward, slammed itself shut, and suddenly went dark.

The screaming stopped. Silence filled the station as Esta collapsed to the floor, her body limp over the now-closed Book.

Harte, finally able to move, ran to her. Sliding on his knees, he scooped her up and cupped her face. Begged her to stay with him. Begged any power listening to save her.

Esta's eyes fluttered open, but he wasn't sure if she could see him. She wasn't there, not really.

"He lied," she whispered, the surprise of this fact flashing through her expression. And then she was gone.

OUTSIDERS

1902—Little Africa

Cela took one look at her brother's expression, saw the fear etched in his features, and knew he wasn't exaggerating the danger.

"Police?" Viola asked, already reaching for her knife.

Joshua shook his head. "Whoever they are, they're nobody official. They're trying not to be noticed, but they're not from the neighborhood."

Cela understood immediately what he meant. *White men.*

They'd picked the basement rooms in Little Africa on purpose. Just south of the Village and not far from Washington Square, the neighborhood had historically been the place where African-descended people lived, going way back to when the Dutch thought they were doing enslaved people a favor by giving them a little land to farm. Recently, the neighborhood had grown more mixed and was known for the black-and-tan dives on Thompson Street that kept the social reformers in a tizzy. But the buildings on those blocks were still predominantly populated by Negroes. Abel and Joshua had enough friends and contacts in the nearby buildings that it had felt like the safest place to stay. Since neither the Order nor the police bothered to recruit Negroes, their patrols couldn't get close without drawing attention to themselves as outsiders.

"The Order," Viola said.

Joshua nodded. "Most likely. They're making their way through the building next door," Joshua told them. "But word is they're looking for two specific Mageus." He looked at Viola. "A Chinese man and an Italian girl."

"That seems awful specific," Abel said, cutting his eyes in Cela's direction. She knew what he was thinking: *So much for your protection.*

"You have to go," Cela told Viola. She didn't know how the Order knew to look for them, but she wasn't going to sit around letting her friend get caught. She was already tossing their few belongings into a sack.

"We *all* have to go," Abel said, firmer than ever now.

"If those men are searching for Jianyu, we can't just up and leave without him," Cela explained as she shoved the last few items into the satchel. "What if he runs straight into that patrol? Even if he manages to get around them, he won't know where we've gone if we just disappear."

"Where *is* Jianyu?" Abel asked, his hands on his hips.

Cela glanced at Viola. "We don't exactly know," Cela said finally, unwilling to lie to her brother. "He didn't come back last night like we expected him to."

"What happened last night?" Abel frowned, and when Cela exchanged another silent look with Viola, it was enough to have him scrubbing his hands over his face. "No . . . Tell me you weren't out in the middle of the night *again*, pressing your luck. Not after you promised you'd be more careful."

"I only waited in the wagon," Cela said, knowing it wasn't really an answer.

"You only waited . . ." Abel looked to be at the end of his patience.

"Nothing happened," she said. "I got back fine."

"Jianyu didn't," Abel pointed out. "And now there are men out there searching for the two of them. It's only a matter of time before someone starts looking for you, too." He shook his head, and Cela could see the temper building. "We're not waiting."

"Abel—"

"Jianyu is grown," Abe told her. "He's going to have to take care of himself. My job is to keep *you* safe."

"I'll wait for you out front," Joshua said, clearly uncomfortable with the tension mounting in the small room. "You'll hear the signal if anything else happens."

"Thanks," Abel said, relief roughening the tone of the word. "I owe you."

"You sure do," Joshua told him without an ounce of humor. "Hattie would have me by the short hairs if she knew I was wrapped up in another one of your messes."

Once his friend was gone, Abel turned back to Cela and Viola.

"We're leaving in the next two minutes."

"Abel—"

"*Two minutes.* I'll give you two minutes to gather whatever you can carry, but if Jianyu doesn't show up by then, we're not waiting a second longer."

"Abe—"

"He's right," Jianyu said, appearing out of thin air like some kind of ghost. "You have to go."

No matter how many times she'd seen him do it, Cela was still thrown off by the unexpectedness of Jianyu's affinity. She'd known about magic since before she could remember, but seeing it? Feeling it right there in your presence? That was something else altogether. Something like *wonder.* But this time? Seeing him appear out of thin air, she felt nothing but relief.

Except he didn't look right. His expression was tight, and his color was off. He looked wan and unsteady on his feet.

"Where have you been?" Viola demanded, her voice sharp with the kind of frustration that grows from fear.

"There is no time for explanations," Jianyu said. "We have to leave, now."

"Finally," Abe said, throwing up his hands. "Someone's talking sense."

Cela glared at her brother, but Jianyu was still issuing orders.

"You especially have to go, Cela."

His words felt like a slap. A betrayal. "No," she said, ready to fight him every bit as much as she'd fought her brother on this point. "The patrol isn't looking for me," she told him.

"What patrol?" His brows creased.

"The one in the next building," Abel explained. "They're looking for Mageus that sound an awful lot like you and Viola here."

Jianyu let out a soft string of words she couldn't understand. "He works faster than I expected." He looked up at her. "You need to leave the city."

She started to argue, but Jianyu stepped forward and took her hands. "There is no time for argument," he said, gripping her fingers even more tightly. "You must leave. You must get outside of the Brink, where Nibsy Lorcan cannot touch you. And you must take the silver discs with you."

MERCURY IGNITES

1983—City Hall Station

The air was still warm, thick with the magic that had just exploded through the station. The artifacts were still glowing with their eerie luminescence, and Harte still felt the presence of a boundary around him, trapping him within the circle that Esta had drawn on the ground. Beneath Harte, Esta wasn't moving. He couldn't tell if she was breathing.

"Come on," he pleaded, jostling her softly. "Please, Esta. I can't—" His voice broke, and he swallowed hard against the horror rising in his throat. "*Please.* You have to wake up. You *have* to."

Because I can't do this without you.

But Esta didn't respond. She remained quiet and still, her body limp in his arms.

He lied. Those had been her final words to him, and she'd said them as though she couldn't believe they were true. Who had lied? Nibsy?

Of course Nibsy Lorcan would have lied. Why would she have thought otherwise?

Careful not to touch the Book beneath her, Harte maneuvered Esta to cradle her head on his lap, then brushed her hair back from her too-pale face. Still, she didn't stir. Her skin had gone a sickly gray, and her lips looked pale and bloodless. Her eyes were open, but their amber irises gazed unseeing at the dark skylights above.

He couldn't lose her. *Not like this.* He'd never even told her—

Esta blinked then and took a small, shuddering breath, and relief nearly knocked Harte over. He could tell she wasn't aware of him. He wasn't sure whether she could see or focus on anything at all. But if he leaned down, he could now feel the faintest whisper of breath coming from her mouth.

She was alive, and it was enough. It was *everything*. Esta was alive, and Seshat was trapped back in the Book, and Harte would do anything to make sure Esta kept breathing.

Suddenly there were footsteps coming from the corridor at the back of the station, and suddenly a group of men flooded out of the tunnel, surrounding the circle on the floor and the two of them inside it. They weren't police—at least Harte didn't think they were. Dressed in boxy coats with white sashes, the men wore a familiar silver medallion on their lapel. They looked like a version of the Jefferson Guard, but there was something off about them. It wasn't only the strange cut of their coats. It was their eyes—every single one of them had nothing but endless darkness where their eyes should have been. Pupils and whites together had been obscured, and in their place was a familiar, fathomless black.

"Thoth," Harte whispered, understanding suddenly without understanding anything at all. Seshat had said he was everywhere, but Harte hadn't believed her.

The men's mouths curved up in eerie synchronicity. "Yes," they all said, their voices chanting in unison, but it wasn't human voices that came from their mouths.

Harte had heard that voice before, in visions and in dreams. He still didn't understand how this could be, but he knew that Seshat had been right. Her anger and rage and especially her *terror* made horrible sense now. Esta might have killed Jack back in Chicago, but she hadn't managed to destroy Thoth. He'd escaped somehow, and now he was here, within these men. Years in the future. Controlling them as he'd once controlled Jack.

What did Esta do?

"She freed me," the men said, addressing Harte's unspoken thought in that singular, inhuman voice. "She *unleashed* me. Made me *more* than even I dreamed of being." The men laughed in eerie unison, a dark, mirthless scraping sound.

"No," he said, not willing to believe she had sacrificed so much for *this*.

"She's a mere child," the voices said, echoing through the cavernous chamber. "She never had the power to defeat me. But she released me, allowed me to become *infinite*. And now it seems she has helped me further. She has made it possible for me to take what is and was always destined to be mine." Together, all the men moving as one, they stepped toward the Book.

"No." The word was nothing more than a husk of breath, but the relief Harte felt at the sound of Esta speaking threatened to overwhelm him. She looked up at him then, and though her golden eyes were now rimmed in blood, he knew she wasn't gone—not completely. She could see him.

Suddenly, Harte felt another blast of magic. Power poured from the Ars Arcana, and because it was still connected to the circle and to Esta herself, it began to lift her from his arms as it coursed through her. As he held on to her, energy poured from her eyes and mouth, flooding the station with a magic more intense than anything Harte had ever felt before. He was trying to keep hold of her, but he could feel the heat of the magic vibrating through her. The sheer immensity of it.

Esta's skin grew feverish, and the artifacts began to glow again, now with an *impossible* brightness. The Aether connecting them was a wall of light, a swirling mass of energy and magic that threatened to destroy everything it could touch. The stones lit as though burning from within. The power in the air swirled, filling the entire space with the terrible chaos of pure magic.

It lasted for ages.

It lasted for mere moments.

Time lost meaning as the men who had surrounded the circle screamed and grabbed their heads. One by one, the darkness was pushed from their eyes, replaced with a blinding flash of light, and as their eyes went dark, the men fell to the ground. When the last one fell, the power drained from the air, and Esta collapsed back to the floor.

She was breathing. Barely. But she was unconscious again. Her eyes had closed, and she looked even paler and more lifeless than before. Around them, the men lay dead on the station platform. The circle remained aglow, and the artifacts and the Book were still hovering in the air, floating just above the ground.

Harte was so focused on Esta that at first he didn't hear the shuffling footsteps approaching or the odd tapping sound that punctuated them. He didn't realize that a new danger was approaching until it had already arrived. An old man with a cane stepped from the darkened tunnel into the dim station. Harte might have dismissed the old man, but he immediately recognized the cane—the polished silver of the gorgon's head was visible even from across the platform.

"Nibsy." Harte said the name like a curse.

But the old man only smiled. His eyes were focused on the Ars Arcana, abandoned on the station floor.

THE DEVIL'S MARKS

1902—Little Africa

Jianyu's words had Viola reaching on instinct for the pocket in her skirts, the one Cela had stitched for her to conceal the silver discs. Their now-familiar weight seemed almost a balance to Libitina's heft.

"Che pazzo?" she asked, incredulous. "You cannot send her off, unprotected, with the only leverage we have. Assolutamente no. I took the sigils from the Order's rooms, and so *I* will be the one to keep them here, close by, where I can protect them."

Cela stepped away from Jianyu. "I don't want to take them anywhere, and I'm not leaving my city." Her mouth had gone tight and her eyes thunderous. "I'm not running like some scared rabbit."

"Bene," Viola said, nodding. "Cela, at least, talks sense."

"It is the only way," Jianyu said, looking more desperate than Viola had ever seen him. There was something in his expression that she had not noticed before when he looked at Cela. Something that reminded Viola too much of how she felt when she looked at Ruby Reynolds. A wonder, but a fear as well.

Abel had stepped forward. "We're *all* leaving. That patrol in the next building is going to be here any minute now."

"You must go, but we cannot go with you," Jianyu told him. "Not so long as Nibsy can track us. We cannot risk it."

"What are you talking about?" Viola asked, stepping forward.

"Logan did not die that night," he told her. "He delivered the ring to Nibsy."

She could not stop the curse that slipped from her lips, but the filthy words offered no comfort or relief. When they had seen the body falling from the tower, they had worried that Nibsy might have obtained the Delphi's Tear. They'd suspected *someone* had, considering the desperation of the Order over the past few weeks. But they hadn't known, not for sure. Now they did.

It didn't change their current situation. "Let them come. Nibsy Lorcan can be taken care of easily enough." She had already slipped her blade out, imagining the pleasure it would be to skewer him with it again. "We'll see how long he keeps the ring."

Jianyu turned on her with more emotion in his expression than she'd ever seen there before. "He has the marks, Viola. He can use them."

Viola froze, silenced by this news. *No. It can't be.*

"What marks?" Cela asked. "What are you talking about?"

But Viola understood too well the implications of Jianyu's words. Once, the tattoos had been a simple statement of loyalty, but they were not an oath without consequences. Everyone who took the marks pledged not only themselves, but their affinity, and anyone who broke that oath could be unmade by them.

Everyone. Including Jianyu and herself.

Viola pressed her lips together. "But the cane, it belonged to Dolph."

"Maybe once, but Nibsy has the cane." Jianyu's jaw went tight. "And he does not require the Medusa's kiss to use it."

"No . . ." But then a memory came back to her of a moment in a stairwell weeks before, when Nibsy had threatened her. "I didn't think . . . Madonna," Viola whispered, crossing herself. "I thought I'd been imagining it."

"You knew?" Jianyu asked.

She was shaking her head, unable to admit it even to herself.

"How long have you known this might be a danger to us?"

"I didn't know," she told him. "Not for sure."

"When?" Jianyu demand.

She flinched at the rare fury in his words. "The night of the solstice."

"You kept this information from me?" Jianyu asked. "I thought we were together in this. I thought—"

"I didn't believe it!" Viola snapped, fear warring with the anger she felt at herself for not listening to her instincts. Then her shoulders sagged. "When it happened, I told myself it was nothing. I didn't want to believe it could be possible, but . . ." She shook her head again, as though the motion could shake away the truth. "When we were coming down from the roof that night, before Paolo was taken, Nibsy made another of his stupid threats, and I thought I felt something. But it shouldn't have been possible."

"Perhaps not, but it is," Jianyu told her, reaching behind himself, so he could rub at his own back, where the tattoo of an ouroboros that matched hers lay beneath his tunic.

"No," Viola said, her mouth tight. "I cannot believe this. I *won't*. It must be a trick. If he could truly use the marks as you say, you would not have escaped."

"He *allowed* me to leave," Jianyu told her. "Cat and mouse. He is only toying with us, but when his patience runs out, he will come after the discs. And as long as we wear the marks, he can unmake us."

Viola tightened her grip on the dagger. "He can't use the marks if he's dead."

"Even if you could get close enough to kill him, it is no answer," Jianyu said. "Not when the Devil's Own all still believe in his forked tongue. We cannot fight them all," Jianyu told her. "And I know you, Viola. You do not want to kill those we once counted as friends."

Viola cursed softly, a string of Italian that would have made any of her brother's men blush. But Jianyu had already turned back to Cela, pleading.

"That is why you have to go," Jianyu said, turning to look at Cela. It was there again, that expression of longing in his eyes when he looked at her. The one that made Viola feel bereft.

"He's right," Viola told Cela and Abel. "As long as this danger exists, we cannot protect you." They could not even protect themselves.

"It's what I've been telling her for weeks now," Abel said.

"We don't even know what the discs do yet," Cela argued. "You could be sending me away for no good reason at all."

"If Nibsy Lorcan wants them, it is essential that he never gets them. You are the only one who can do this. You are the only one of us who can cross the Brink and take the discs where Nibsy Lorcan cannot reach them." Jianyu paused. "Where he cannot reach *you*."

A shrill whistle sounded from outside the small, high window in the wall.

"That's Joshua's signal," Abel told them. "It's time to go."

Jianyu felt the mood of the room shift as everyone went silent. From somewhere just outside the building came the sound of shouting.

"We're leaving," Abel told Cela. "And we're leaving right *now*."

But before they could get out the door, Joshua was there, launching himself into the room and shutting it firmly behind him. "They're here!" he said, panting with the exertion of his sprint. "Five men. They saw me before I could get in here."

Through the thin wooden door, the sound of pounding and shouting came from the other end of the hallway.

"I can take care of this," Viola said, stepping toward the door, but Jianyu caught her gently by the arm.

"You cannot touch them," he said. "If they are looking for you, they likely know your affinity. If you harm them here, the Order will know. You will put everyone in this building in the Order's sights."

"He's right," Abel said, his jaw going tight. "If the Order knows Mageus were being hidden here, it would make the entire community look complicit."

Joshua swore. "This is exactly what we were worried about."

"We won't allow that to happen," Viola promised them, looking at Jianyu.

He understood immediately and offered her his hand as the pounding and shouting drew closer. "Take hold. Quickly, and they will not find any of us."

THE SERPENT'S JAWS

1983—City Hall Station

Harte watched as an older version of Nibsy Lorcan stepped into the dimly lit space of the station. He was acutely aware of how bad the current situation was. The artifacts and the Book were exposed and vulnerable, and Esta was still unconscious. He couldn't protect the artifacts or the Book without letting go of Esta, and he couldn't bring himself to do that.

"You know, Darrigan, I haven't been called that name in decades," Nibsy said with a disgusted squint. He wasn't as old as Harte would have expected him to be; the healers he used must have been absurdly talented. However much his appearance had changed, his eyes were the same, as small and as beady as a rat's behind the thick glass of his spectacles' lenses. "I didn't much like it way back when. I find I still don't."

Harte didn't care much what Nibsy Lorcan did or didn't like, but he needed time to think, to get Esta, the Book, and the artifacts out of there. He maneuvered so that his body was between her and Nibsy, protecting her and shielding the Book from Nibsy's view until he figured out a plan.

Nibsy took a small step forward, and when Harte wrapped himself more protectively around Esta, the old man only shook his head. "I'm the least of your worries right now. There'll be more of them coming any minute now." He nodded toward the bodies on the floor. "The amount of power the two of you set off will have every Guard in the city on their way. And there you are, trapped. Easy pickings."

Harte didn't respond. He wouldn't give Nibsy the satisfaction or the ammunition.

"I might not be able to cross that line, but the Guard won't have any issue with it, Sundren as they are. And she's too weak to fight more of them off. They'll drag you both away, and when you break that ritual spell and cross the boundary, it will kill you both as surely as anything."

"There shouldn't *be* any Guards," Harte said, trying to stall.

"Why? Because Esta killed Jack Grew?" the old man asked, amused. "Murdered him in the middle of a crowded arena in front of all the press. There were pictures in every paper. Newsreels played in every cinema for weeks after. Did you really think that would end the Guard and the Brotherhoods? Jack's death showed every Sundren in this country *exactly* how dangerous our kind are. It galvanized the Brotherhoods' cause and handed them popularity and power they never dreamed of wielding." His eyes narrowed. "She made him into a *martyr*, and the idiots in this land turned him into a saint."

Harte thought of the familiar darkness in the dead men's eyes and knew Nibsy was telling the truth, but he wondered whether Nibsy understood that more than Jack Grew's hatred had survived that night in Chicago. Thoth had as well.

"She doesn't have much time, you know, especially after what she's done to these fellows." The old man nudged one of the fallen bodies with his toe. "Even now, her connection to the artifacts and the Book is draining her. They want what they're owed. *Magic* wants what is owed."

The serpent catches its tail, severs time, consumes.

Harte had a million questions, but he didn't voice any of them. He remained silent and considered his options. From the way Nibsy was waiting at the edge of the sigil, Harte had a sense that, unlike the Guard, he couldn't cross the boundary Esta had created. Which meant that he'd been telling the truth. It also meant they had time. But he knew he didn't have *much* time.

"She has to finish what she started. It's the only way." Nibsy used the cane to point at the swirling energy around the sigil. "This is only the beginning of the ritual. Just like the Brink, if you try to leave, the power that she's awoken will take your affinity—both of your affinities. Unless she gives the spell what it desires, what she promised the whole of magic by beginning it, she'll die from what it's taking. That's the only way to end the ritual."

"What she promised?"

"Her power," Nibsy said, his eyes flashing with anticipation. "Her *magic*. It was the mistake the Order made in creating the Brink—believing they could use the power in the Book without offering something in return. They wanted power without the price. Without true sacrifice."

"You lied to her," Harte said, his jaw tight. "You said it wouldn't kill her."

"Of *course* I lied," the old man told him, impatience coloring his words. "About any number of things. The girl shouldn't have been fool-ish enough to believe me. But she's not dead, as far as I can see. The ritual hasn't killed her. Not yet. Now she has to finish what she started. It's the only way out for you. More, it's the only way to stop the Brotherhoods from having the key to infinite power." He took another step forward. "Think of the damage the Order did with the Book and the artifacts *before*. The atrocity of the Brink happened because they didn't understand how to control the demon bitch within those pages. But now that the girl has united the artifacts and reimprisoned Seshat? Think of what the Brotherhoods could do. They could touch the very heart of magic. Her sacrifice would be for nothing if the Brotherhoods gain control of the Book now."

Harte didn't believe for a second that Nibsy cared. He wanted the Book and the power it contained. But Nibsy was right about one thing— if the Brotherhoods got the Book, everything that had happened to them would have been for nothing. But if Esta died there—in that time before she could return the cuff to her younger self—none of it would matter.

"If she dies, we both lose," Harte reminded him.

"Not if she completes the ritual," Nibsy said, amusement glinting in his eyes.

Harte examined the open page that Esta had read before. *The serpent catches its tail, severs time.*

Harte considered those words. Could there be a chance . . . ?

"How can she finish anything?" Harte asked, the words tearing from his throat. "She isn't even conscious."

"You can help her," Nibsy said simply. "Use your affinity. Command her. She has to sacrifice her power. She has to finish what she began."

Harte took Esta's hand. He understood what Nibsy wanted him to do, but accepting it meant admitting defeat. His thumb traced along the rough, scarred skin on her wrist. "You want me to betray her," he said. "You want me to *kill* her."

The old man huffed an impatient breath. "Let's not pretend you're so noble, Darrigan. We've known each other too long to have lies between us. I know what you are."

"You don't know anything about me," he said.

"You expect me to believe that you've changed so much?" Nibsy scoffed. "*You*, the boy who sacrificed your own *mother* to escape this prison of a city. You've betrayed everyone who trusted you. No, Darrigan. People like us never change. We are who and what we are. So why delay the inevitable? Why this ridiculous charade? The girl has served her purpose. For both of us. She has to give her power to the stones. It's your only way out of the cage she's created for you. Unless you want to die at the hands of the Guard. Because once the Brotherhoods get the Book, you're dead either way."

Esta's breath shuddered, and Harte felt the energy in the room waver. He understood that she wouldn't last much longer.

"If she dies before the ritual is completed, you'll never leave that circle alive," the old man said. "When the Guard comes and they drag you across that line, the ritual will take your power and your life as surely as the Brink."

Desperately, Harte tried to remember the vision Seshat had shown him of that original ritual. What had she done? What had she been trying to do? He remembered how Thoth had shattered the stones, how that had doomed Seshat, causing her to flee into the Book. But what would Seshat have done to complete the ritual if Thoth hadn't arrived? Harte couldn't be sure. Seshat had never shared that piece of the puzzle with him. He didn't know what she'd intended to do.

"Help her do what must be done," Nibsy coaxed, looking suddenly more like the fifteen-year-old boy Harte remembered. "Save yourself, Darrigan. The Guard will be here soon. It's the girl's power or both your lives. And you and I both know that you are no martyr."

Beneath him, Esta's breathing was growing shallow. The energy in the room felt increasingly unstable. Harte looked down at her, at the face he knew every soft curve and sharp angle of. His heart twisted at the mess of silvery scars on her arm, awareness prickling at the nape of his neck.

Carefully, he cupped her cheek, considering his options, but she didn't respond. Her skin felt too cool to the touch.

Closing his eyes, Harte opened his affinity and broke the promise he'd made to Esta weeks before. It felt like a betrayal to cross the boundary between them, but he needed to be sure. But instead of Esta, he found nothing but darkness and pain. She was so consumed by the Book and its power, he couldn't sense anything of what she had been. He couldn't sense *her*.

"I'm so sorry," he whispered. "If there were any other way . . ." He kissed her then, brushing his lips against her forehead, and as his lips touched her skin, he sent out a single command.

Her eyes flew open as the power in the room went electric, but Harte didn't let go.

Nibsy was screaming. The cane he'd been holding clattered to the ground, and the old man fell to his knees beside it, writhing in pain.

"No!" Nibsy's face contorted in rage. But there was confusion in his expression as well. "How—"

Harte sent another command through their connection and watched as Seshat's power—the *Book's* power—ripped the affinity from Nibsy Lorcan. Or, most of it. Not enough to kill him, but enough to break him. The old man fell over, unconscious and without the magic that had guided him for so long.

By then the energy in the room felt erratic, and the air was suddenly charged, hot and dangerous. The energy coursing through her felt like fire against his skin, and Harte felt as though he would be burned alive if he kept holding on. He looked down at their joined hands, and he knew what had to be done. There wasn't a choice. Not any longer.

He sent another command through their connection, and the air around him came alive with magic. The artifacts glowed hot and bright before they flickered and then suddenly went dark. Slowly, the circle faded, until it was no more than a dark line on the station floor.

The platform was painfully silent, like the sound of the world had drained away. Esta's body had collapsed back onto the ground, but she wasn't moving. Carefully, Harte edged closer to her. He hesitated—knowing already but not wanting to accept the truth—before he finally reached out and touched her. She didn't respond, didn't move.

She wasn't breathing.

He tried to tell himself that he'd done what he had to do. That it was the only choice he'd had—for both of them. Otherwise, they would have both been trapped here for the Guard to find. Along with the Book. And the artifacts. They would have been sitting ducks, an offering of untold power for whoever found them.

There had been no other way, but he'd hoped . . .

Harte's throat was tight as he looked at the still and lifeless body. The reality of what just happened crashed through him, and panic clawed at his skin. But there was already a numbness settling over him, as absolute as the silence in the cavernous station. He should have felt bowled over. He should have felt destroyed. Instead, he felt . . . nothing. An endless emptiness had hollowed him out.

She was gone. There was no going back, no reversing the choices he'd made. He could only hope he'd chosen right.

A few yards away, the old man wasn't moving either, but he wasn't dead. Harte had made sure of it. He'd left Nibsy Lorcan just enough magic to survive, because he wanted the bastard to live long enough to know life without his affinity. The Guard could deal with him.

Nearby, the Book lay open and inert on the ground. It looked so unimpressive, a tattered old journal, just as it had appeared the first time he'd seen it deep in the bowels of Khafre Hall. But now he knew what waited inside those pages. And he knew what he had to do.

Slowly, Harte pulled himself to his feet. He felt severed from himself, as though he were walking through a terrible dream. The world around him hung unreal, unsteady. His head felt as though it were filled with cotton, but his hearing was slowly returning. Distantly, he heard the squealing of a train. If Nibsy was right, Thoth was still loose in the world. The Book and the artifacts needed his protection now more than ever.

He had to go. *For Esta.*

Harte felt like he was watching himself from a distance as he scooped up the artifacts and then, using the sleeve of his shirt so his skin didn't make contact, took the Book from where it rested on the floor. He put them all into the satchel and slung the canvas bag across his body.

A train was screaming into the station now. It was time.

He took one more look at the bodies, Nibsy and Esta, both lying still on the station platform. Seeing her like that, he felt something crack inside him. But he couldn't stay. If there was any chance for a future, any chance that the girl on the platform hadn't given her life for nothing, he had to go—to stop the Brotherhoods, to stop Thoth—and he had to go *now.*

The train slid into the station, and as it slowed through the curve, he leapt onto the platform of the back car. As it sped away into the darkness of the tunnel, Harte didn't look away from the carnage he was leaving behind. He kept his eyes on the body of the girl he loved until he couldn't see her any longer and hoped he hadn't made a terrible mistake.

LIKE LIGHTNING

1902—Little Africa

Cela understood immediately what Jianyu intended. Relief rocketed through her as she grabbed hold of his outstretched hand. Viola followed a half second later, but Abel and Joshua didn't move.

"Come," Jianyu said. "I can get you past them."

But Abel only shook his head. "You get my sister out of here. Make sure she's safe. Joshua and I will stay back and distract them. We'll meet you at the new place."

"No, Abe." Cela started to release Jianyu, but his fingers tightened around hers.

"They aren't looking for us," Abel told her, and the determination in her brother's expression made her pause. "Don't worry, Rabbit. We'll be right behind you."

But it wasn't enough. The Order's patrols wouldn't care if Abel and Joshua belonged there. She couldn't just leave him behind, not when it was her fault that they were still there. If she hadn't argued so much about waiting for Jianyu, they'd already be gone, and Abel wouldn't be in danger.

"Abe—" She started to plead with him, but a violent pounding shook the door and silenced her.

"Open up!" a man shouted from the other side.

The patrol didn't wait. A second later, the door flew open, the latch splintering at the force of the booted foot that had kicked it down.

Cela felt the world tilt suddenly, and her vision shifted, like she was looking through wobbly old glass. Before the men entering the room could careen into them, Jianyu pulled Cela and Viola back along the wall. Just barely out of reach.

Joshua and her brother were standing shoulder to shoulder, looking every bit as formidable as the light-haired white men who had just destroyed the entrance.

"Can we help you gentlemen?" Joshua said. He kept his voice contrite, almost humble. It was a dance he'd done too many times before. But Cela didn't miss the way he lifted his chin.

Don't start anything, Abe.

Cela felt Jianyu nudging her to the side, but she couldn't just leave them there.

Just hold your temper and get out alive, she pleaded silently.

"We're looking for a couple of maggots who were rumored to be seen in this neighborhood," one of the other men said.

"Maggots?" Abel shot Joshua a doubtful kind of look. "Haven't seen any maggots around here." He paused, giving the men a steady glare. "Haven't seen any Mageus, either."

One of the men stepped forward. His expression was twisted into a sneer of distaste. "Same thing, ain't it, boy?"

A muscle clenched in Abel's jaw, but to Cela's relief, he didn't take the bait. Joshua was silent next to him, but he crossed his arms over his chest in defiance. How many times had they done this, faced men who refused to recognize their manhood? Too many. She knew it wore on him—it wore on her, as well—but it hadn't broken him. It wouldn't. Abel Johnson was too damn strong.

Cela felt Jianyu nudge her again, this time tugging gently at her arm, but she didn't move. She couldn't leave her brother there with those men. Not until she knew he was safe.

"Search the place," the first man commanded. He was still glaring at Abe with open disgust, and he kept his gaze steady as the other two started tearing the meager furnishings apart.

Abel's gaze shifted slightly to glance past the man confronting him, ignoring the pair who were already tearing apart the room. His eyes seemed to find the place she was standing, invisible though she was, as though pulled by magnets. Or maybe like magic.

Go, he told her without saying a word. *Go.* It was a command that she couldn't refuse. Because it would only make it worse to stay—for him, and for them all.

This time she allowed Jianyu to pull her along. Together, they inched into the hallway, where they saw another two doors had been busted open by the other pair of mercenaries. She heard crying and felt Jianyu tug at Viola—a reminder that she could not use her magic here, not without harming the very innocents they were trying to protect.

In a matter of seconds they were out the back of the building in the rank-smelling alley where outhouses stood leaning unevenly in a row. Like every tenement, refuse from the residents was piled along the curb. But the area wasn't empty. There was a single white boy standing there like the whole place belonged to him. Cela had heard enough about Nibsy Lorcan that it took only one glance at the boy's gold-rimmed glasses and silver-topped cane for her to know who the kid was.

Jianyu skidded to a halt. Cela heard his sharp intake of breath, and the world went back into focus as he released her hand and reached for his chest. The boy blocking the way out of the alley only smiled softly as both Jianyu and Viola crumpled to the ground, like marionettes being cut from their strings.

"It's good to see you again, Cela," the boy said, his voice soft and almost conversational.

"Again?" Her skin was crawling with warning. Her friends were on their hands and knees now, struggling against whatever magic this boy was spinning, but she didn't dare look away from him. It was like coming face-to-face with a snake. Any sudden movement, and she didn't doubt he'd bite.

"We've never been formally introduced," the boy said. "But I've been watching." He gave her a small, dangerous smile that sent a skittering of unease down her spine. "You seem like a smart enough girl, but you have dangerous taste in friends."

She sensed Jianyu collapse, and Viola followed quickly after. She wanted to stop whatever was happening to them, but she had the sense that showing how much she cared would be a mistake. Besides, she wasn't about to kneel in front of this kid, not even to tend to her friends. Instead, she kept her eyes focused on the bespectacled boy and pretended that Jianyu and Viola weren't gasping for life at her feet.

"Nibsy Lorcan," she said, squaring her shoulders. "I've heard plenty about you, too."

His eyes flashed at that. "I'm sure you have."

"Wasn't anything good," she told him, proud of herself for keeping her voice from betraying her fear.

"There's usually more than one side to any story," the boy said.

"Looks pretty one-sided to me," she pressed, nodding toward her friends, who were too still now for her liking.

"I'll let them go in a minute," he told her. "But I wanted a chance to meet you first. A chance to talk. You see, we both want the same thing, Cela."

"I doubt that very much," she told him.

"You want your friends to be safe," he said. "I don't want to harm them."

She choked out a nervous burst of laughter. "I'm not sure this is the best way to show it."

"I didn't think their interference would be . . . *productive*." He shrugged. "They don't understand."

Cela clenched her teeth to keep herself from saying all the things she wanted to. But she knew anything she said could be used against them. Talking to this boy was nothing but a trap.

The soft curve of Nibsy's mouth went flat. "Soon, Cela, the Order is going to fall, and power is going to shift in this city. You could be on the winning side. Think of what it would mean for your family—your brother. Think of what it could do for your people."

She kept her expression steady, knowing already that this boy was no more going to help her "people" than any other fool who wanted power. It was probably the first time he'd ever even ventured into this neighborhood.

She was tired of his games, his doublespeak. "Are you planning on telling me what you want?"

"I want to win," Nibsy told her. "I want to make those who've held us down and pushed us back pay. I think you might want that too. The police killed your father, didn't they? Just because of the color of his skin? Think of a world where they don't have the power to hurt you or yours. A city safe for people like us."

There was no "like us," not as far as Cela was concerned. "And you think *you* can make that happen?" she wondered. *Like some kind of white savior come to rescue the poor darker brother.*

"I know I can," he said. "But not alone. I'll need them to help—Jianyu and Viola both. I need my spy and my assassin. With them, I can't fail."

"You would trust them?" she asked.

"No, but in exchange for Newton's Sigils, I might be persuaded." The lenses of his glasses flashed in the sunlight.

The creeping feeling up her spine told Cela that, whatever happened, this boy should never, ever get ahold of those discs.

"We don't have them," Cela bluffed. "Viola dropped them on her way out of the building."

Fury flashed across the boy's face. It was there and gone in an instant, like lightning across the summer sky, but Cela wasn't so foolish as to pretend she hadn't seen it.

"Let's not waste our time with lies, Cela Johnson. I know you have them. I know they're here, close by. I could kill both of your friends and you as well to take them, if I wanted. But I meant what I told you. I'd rather do this with Jianyu's and Viola's help. So give them this message for me: Your friends should come back to the Strega and the Devil's Own. They should pledge themselves to me and to my cause. If they do, I'll welcome them with open arms. I can and will protect them from the dangers of this city." He nodded toward the building. "I'll offer my protection to you and your brother as well. Because it would be quite the tragedy if something happened to you. Or to your dear, *dear* brother. It would be a shame, for instance, if those men in there decide that you or Abel had something to do with the theft at the Flatiron Building."

"You sent them," she realized.

His mouth curved up. "Think of this as a warning. Tell your friends that there's no sense in trying to fight the inevitable. They can give over the sigils willingly, or next time I'll be sure to send someone more suited to finish the job."

"Go to hell," Cela spat.

She'd barely gotten the words out when she suddenly felt a sharpness in her chest as her breath rushed from her. She couldn't breathe. She couldn't do anything but feel the burning of her lungs. It was worse than simply holding her breath. It was like having the air and the life pressed out of her.

Her vision was already going dark around the edges, and her legs felt suddenly weak. She couldn't stop her legs from collapsing beneath her until she found herself kneeling on the ground in front of him. If she fell now, he could take the discs. She couldn't let that happen, but she also couldn't fight him.

"That," the boy said, as her chest burned, "was a mistake."

She was gasping for breath, but she still couldn't draw any air into her lungs. The world was spinning now, as she tried to stay up on her hands and knees, and then she collapsed completely. Above her, the sky was a bright, impossible blue. She blinked up, not understanding how things could have gotten so far out of her control so quickly.

The boy came and stood above her, a dark shadow blocking the beauty of the summer day. "First Darrigan and now these two. You really should pick your friends with more care, Cela Johnson. For your brother's sake, and your own."

A NEW IMPOSSIBLE

1983—The Bowery

As the subway train rounded the corner, the abandoned station platform slipped away, and along with it, Harte's final glimpse of the carnage it held. The new Guard, crumpled on the station platform. Nibsy, old and frail and unconscious.

And Esta's body. *Dead.*

The train continued onward, screaming and clattering as it swayed and shook down the track, but Harte felt like he was sleepwalking. The train's movement and noise were just another part of the nightmare. He didn't know how he managed it, but somehow he released the latch of the door and let himself into the empty train car.

Inside, lights were a glaring, unnatural bluish-white, and as the door slid closed behind him, the noise of the tracks was dampened, leaving him alone, not in silence, but in a muffled quiet that was no relief. Before, Seshat's earsplitting screams had overwhelmed him, and her wailing had drowned out nearly everything—the sounds of the city, Esta's words, his own thoughts. But now his mind was painfully quiet. After weeks of being possessed, occupied by a being that was not himself, Harte felt strangely empty. Or he would have, if he could have felt anything but the frantic clawing of grief.

He'd left her there. How could he have *left* her there?

His chest felt gripped in a vise, and his throat was closing up. He couldn't breathe, not deeply enough to keep his head from swirling. He felt as though he might never breathe again.

He couldn't stop remembering how Esta's eyes had gone white, lit from within by some unbelievable power. He couldn't stop seeing her cheeks stained with bloody tears. Her body, still and lifeless, on the platform. Her wide mouth gone slack and her whiskey-colored eyes dull and empty. He would never stop seeing her like that. As long as he drew breath, that image would be with him, stark and clear and *impossible*. He would *never* be able to forget.

He didn't want to forget. He would carry the memory with him, use it to fuel him and drive him onward.

The train squealed around another curve, nearly throwing Harte over. He couldn't go back, but he wasn't sure what to do next. He had no idea where the train was headed, but Harte knew where he had to go. *For Esta.*

A little while later, the train slowed into a station, and Harte prepared for . . . He had no idea what he was preparing for. An attack? More of the Guard? His hands reflexively tightened around the strap of the satchel that held the Book and the artifacts. Whatever happened next, he couldn't lose them. He *definitely* couldn't allow the Brotherhoods to get control of them. He couldn't let all that had happened have been for nothing.

When the train doors slid open, the noise of an alarm tore through the quiet of the empty car. A disembodied voice blared with a garbled warning to keep a watch for suspicious travelers.

They were searching for unregistered Mageus—for *him*.

He slouched in his seat, peering through a break in the graffiti that covered the window. On the platform, a pair of Guards had surrounded an old man. Another set of Guards stood nearby, blocking the station exit, their silver medallions glinting at their lapels. A group of three guys about his age stepped on board, seemingly unconcerned by the alarm or the Guards. They played at punching one another as their half-drunken laughter filled the silence of the car. When they looked in his direction, Harte turned toward the window, pulling up his collar to obscure his face.

It felt like an eternity before the doors slid shut again, but finally the train lurched onward. Harte kept his head turned away from the other passengers, but he couldn't relax. He had no idea what the next station would bring. Probably more of the Guard.

He couldn't just stay there, stuck on the train like a fish in a barrel. Easy pickings.

As the train sped down the track, Harte glanced back toward the rear of the car, where the new arrivals were standing, their bodies swaying as they held the overhead poles. Their voices were a low rumble, barely audible over the noise of the train, but a single look told him they weren't there for him. They weren't even looking in his direction.

When the train rattled to its next stop, the alarm once again split through the quiet of the car, but there weren't any Guards waiting on the platform. He considered leaving, but he had no idea where he was—or what might be waiting for him on the streets above. The signs were unreadable beneath the mess of graffiti, and he felt frozen with indecision. Once he got off the train, he knew what he needed to do next. But *next* seemed impossible when the memory of Esta's broken body was all he could think about.

The doors slid shut, and he was once again trapped. The train was moving again, but he still couldn't breathe. What if he'd made the wrong choice?

He didn't *want* to breathe. He didn't *deserve* to breathe. Not when he'd killed her. It hadn't been the ritual or Seshat or Nibsy. It had been *him*, the choice *he'd* made to use his affinity, to do what Nibsy had suggested. He'd forced her to give her affinity to the ritual and give magic what it demanded. He'd done it knowing that it would kill her, knowing that she wouldn't survive losing her magic.

Who could?

Maybe Nibsy had been right. Maybe people never changed. Harte had been a conman and a liar his entire life. He did what he did to save himself, knowing the cost.

Harte's skin turned hot at the thought. His head was throbbing as the blood in his veins churned and pounded in his ears. He felt himself break out in a cold sweat. *What if she didn't have to die?* His vision swam, started going dark around the edges as his stomach twisted, heaved.

When the doors opened, Harte lurched out of his seat, nearly falling as he scrambled to get off the train. He had to get out of the tomb-like car, had to get out of the oppressiveness of being underground.

Harte was barely on to the station platform when he heard a shout, and he knew he'd been seen. The guys who had boarded the train had suddenly turned their interest on him and were yelling after him. They'd already started to move toward the exit of the car, but they were too slow. The doors of the car closed on them before they could follow, and the train had started moving, taking the danger they posed along with it.

Even with the noise of the train receding into the distant tunnel, Harte didn't feel any relief. Leaning against one of the filthy, graffiti-covered pillars, he tried to keep himself upright under the burden of his guilt and regret. He had to keep moving, had to make whatever sins he'd committed worth it in the end. *For Esta.* He forced himself to take a breath and was rewarded with the fetid reek of urine and something unmistakably rotten. It turned his stomach. It reminded him of home.

There was a person huddled in the corner, wrapped so deeply in ragged blankets that Harte couldn't tell if they were alive. But he didn't have time to check on some stranger. He had to keep moving. If the other riders had suspected him, they would alert the authorities when they reached the next stop. The Guard would know where he'd disembarked. They'd come for him. But he couldn't be taken. Not yet. He had to keep going, had to make the sacrifice worth it. He forced himself to take one step and then the next. *For Esta.*

Everything he did from that moment forward would be for Esta.

HOLLOW

1902—Little Africa

Breath and air burst back into Viola's lungs as she came to consciousness in a rush of nausea and dread. Only one person she knew of could attack like that—*Werner*. The coniglio. After what she had done to get him to safety? *This* was his repayment? She never should have let him go running off after the mess at the Flatiron Building. She should have made sure he wasn't a liability.

Her cheek was pressed against the filth of the street, but she didn't move. Not right away. Jianyu was lying next to her, and Cela just beyond. Both were starting to stir, but Viola hesitated, sending out her affinity instead. She found their two heartbeats, but not a third. Nibsy was gone.

Her head still swirling, Viola pulled herself up, cursing herself silently for letting down her guard. Cursing Nibsy as well for managing to get the upper hand.

Jianyu was already on his feet, checking Cela for injuries.

"They're gone," Viola told him as she pulled herself up and brushed herself off, trying not to think about the grime that had pressed against her cheek. She turned on Jianyu, furious. "How could you be so stupid? How could you lead him to us? You should have been more careful. You should have—"

"I *was* careful," Jianyu said, frustration flashing in his expression. His voice was sharper than Viola had ever heard it. "I would never put either of you in danger."

"You didn't," Cela said. "He'd already sent the patrols. You didn't lead them here."

"What?" Viola turned to her.

"We had a nice conversation before he knocked me out. It's not just the sigils he wants. It's the two of you as well," Cela told them, her voice filled with unease. "He promised that he could protect me and my brother if you joined him again." She had wrapped her arms around herself as though she'd caught a chill, but there was an edge to her voice that Viola approved of.

"He can go to the devil," Viola snarled. "Nibsy Lorcan is a snake. You can't believe a single word that drops from his mouth." But even her bravado couldn't dispel her unease. She looked to Jianyu. "How could he find us?"

"He did not have to follow me, not when he can *track* us," Jianyu said. "Or, rather, he can track the sigils."

Viola didn't understand his meaning at first . . . and then, all at once, she did. "*Logan*," she said, spitting his name like a curse. She remembered what the boy had told her when they were trapped at the top of that building. "He can find objects infused with magic. Objects like the sigils." *And like my blade.* "But Nibsy, he didn't take the discs?"

Cela shook her head. "He could have. I don't know why he didn't."

"Knowing Nibsy, he has his reasons, and none of them portend well for us." Jianyu turned to Cela. "Can you understand now why I said you must take the sigils out of the city, beyond the Brink? Eventually, he will decide the time has come for him to take them from us. So long as the discs remain here, Nibsy will be able to find them. With Werner's help and control of the marks, he will be able to take them. There is nowhere in the city we can hide them, so you must take them out of his reach."

Viola saw then the reason for the wildness in his eyes, the cause for his desperation to get Cela to safety. He felt something for her. It was no less than she would do to protect the person she loved.

Suddenly, she could not stop herself from thinking of Ruby, who was far across the seas and living a life that Viola could hardly imagine. She could never be a part of that life, but at least Ruby was safe from Nibsy Lorcan and the Order.

"It's not enough," Viola said, her voice heavy with the truth of the matter. She was already reaching through the hidden slit in her skirt for Libitina. "The sigils are not the only objects that put us at risk. What of my knife? Your mirrors? If, as you say, Nibsy has the marks, we cannot allow him to find us so easily again. Libitina, she is a liability now. So are your mirrors." She turned and offered the blade to Cela. "You must take this as well. She will protect you, whenever you need protection."

"I don't want it," Cela said, stepping back, but she ran into Jianyu and couldn't retreat any farther. "He wants the two of you, and he's not going to stop just because I leave the city. I can't just run and leave you two behind to deal with the danger he poses."

"Then don't run," Viola said, offering her blade again, determined. "Help to protect us. Nibsy Lorcan already has the ring and control over the Devil's Own. He cannot be allowed to have any other power."

"The sigils must be kept from him," Jianyu agreed.

Viola took a step forward and gently placed Libitina in Cela's palm. "We trust you, Cela. Not to run, but to fight with us. By keeping them safe, you keep *us* safe. And many more as well."

Finally, Cela's fingers wrapped around the handle of the blade. "Fine," she said, her jaw tight. "I'll go. I'll take them outside the Brink and keep them away from Nibsy. But I'm not staying away forever. This is my city, *my* home. I won't be forced away. I'm going to come back," she vowed. "I'm going to return this to you."

How many times had Viola let her dagger sail through the air, willing it to hit some target or another? But this, *this* was terrifying. To simply hand it over? To watch it disappear into Cela's bag. It did not matter that Viola trusted Cela and Abel, nor that she knew this was the only real choice. Cela needed all the protection they could provide, but giving up Libitina meant she would have only herself, only her affinity, for protection.

"Certo," Viola said, trying not to show how much she wanted to grab her blade and take it back. "Even the Brink could not stop me if you tried to keep her from me." She pulled out the sigils and handed them over as well and watched as Jianyu gave her the bronze mirrors he kept always at his side.

Cela had barely managed to secure them in her bag when the door of the building burst open. Two of the patrolmen came bursting out. "There they are!" one shouted.

"Go," Viola said, turning to face the men.

"But Abel," Cela protested.

"Get her to the bridge," Viola told Jianyu, knowing that they'd been seen. Knowing, too, what that meant not only for Cela and Abel but for everyone in that building. "Va via! I will take care of this and make sure Abel is safe. Go!"

In a blink, Jianyu had taken Cela's hand and wrapped her in light, protecting them from the patrol's view. The men from the patrol were already running toward her and the place where Jianyu and Cela had just vanished from sight.

For so long, Viola had tried to avoid using her magic to kill. She had believed it was the worst sort of sin to use her gift to take life rather than save it, but the past few weeks had shown her how foolish she had been. Even with Libitina, she had been using her affinity all along, channeling her connection to blood through the intention of the blade. Dolph had given her the knife because he'd understood that she needed to have that measure of distance. Now she had come to accept that, affinity or blade, each death on her soul had been a choice she had made.

Once, she had cared for the state of her soul. She had wished for a different future. She had dreamed, perhaps, of being worthy of a different sort of life. But Ruby had wiped away that hope and replaced it with the understanding that the other life she'd imagined would never be.

She let her affinity fly free, and the first man fell. She relished the look of fear in his partner's eyes before she finished him as well.

When the area went silent, when the only sound was the constant hum of the ever-present city beyond, she waited for the regret that always came, the heaviness of remorse that so often weighed down her soul after she took a life. But this time, it did not arrive. In its place was a sort of empty ache, a hollowness that felt neither like salvation nor sin. It felt like the beginning of something she could not name.

Looking over her shoulder, Viola searched for some sign that Jianyu and Cela were still there. But nothing stirred. No one appeared.

Viola knew that she was completely alone in the strange silence of that back alley. She allowed herself a moment of grief to mourn the girl she had once wanted to be—the girl she never would become. Then she pulled herself together. There were still men in the building who hunted them, men who might be doing harm to Abel and Joshua. If it came to the choice between her and them, her soul was already too heavily marked for hesitation or regret.

OMFUG

1983—The Bowery

Harte's skin was still damp with sweat and his legs were unsteady as he carried his worry and regret up the trash-strewn steps of the subway exit into the cold, slush-covered night. When he reached the street above, he stopped short, overwhelmed by the changed city around him. Everything seemed brighter here. But then, beneath the changed facade, he was struck by how familiar it all felt. The low-slung buildings. The people milling about in groups on wide sidewalks. The way the city pulsed in the night. But above him, the sky was starless.

The sign on the corner read BLEECKER STREET. He *knew* that name.

Tucking his arms around himself against the bitter cold, Harte adjusted the strap of the satchel to secure it and started to walk. His shoes slipped on the ice-covered walk as he passed a group of people huddled against the cold, wreaths of smoke and breath circling them. In the distance, he heard the screaming of sirens. It was only a matter of time before someone started looking for him, and he didn't want to give himself away by looking back—or by looking guilty. As he traversed the short blocks of Bleecker, the sirens grew closer, so he picked up his pace.

He turned a corner, and then suddenly he knew where he was. Before him was the broad boulevard that was the Bowery.

The elevated trains were gone. Once, the tracks had shadowed the wide sidewalks, showering coal and ash on the people below. Now, when he looked up, all he could see was the heaviness of the sky. The street, once cobblestone and brick, was now a smooth stretch of dark ribbon marred only by the filthy, drifting snow and the occasional water-filled pothole. The lights lining the street were blindingly bright, turning the night into a false day. It reminded him of how the area around the Haymarket had once been in his own time. That part of the city had been called the Satan's Circus, and rightly so, but this version of the Bowery could likely wear that name just as well.

As he walked along, he saw men sleeping curled beneath old newspapers in freezing doorways. Many buildings in the area were caged or boarded, but the sidewalks weren't empty. Groups of people, young and old, milled about, ignoring the approaching sirens.

Everything had changed, but the city Harte had once known was still there. The names of shops and saloons were different now, but the buildings remained. The bones of the Bowery were the same, and he could almost see the ghost of his own time beneath the strange, new surface.

Still, the changes were disorienting, and he wasn't fooled into confidence by this glimpse of the past. The sirens were even louder now, and he understood it was only a matter of time before the Guard would arrive at the station he'd just exited and begin tracking him on foot. With the tracks he was leaving in the snow, he would be easy enough to find.

He couldn't keep running, and he couldn't chance leading them to the place he was headed. Instead, he needed to find somewhere to hide away until the danger passed and he could continue on.

Across the Bowery, there was a crowd of people gathered beneath a dirty white canopy emblazoned with a series of letters that didn't make sense as any kind of word. He couldn't tell what the place was, exactly—a saloon, maybe? The people seemed to be waiting for something at the entrance. Or perhaps they were just waiting. A perpetual cloud of smoke hung around them, and their laughter and voices carried through the cold night air.

The sirens were nearly there. In the distance came the barking of dogs and shouting, and Harte knew his time was up. The crowd under the awning would give him some cover at least, and if he could get inside . . .

He tried not to hurry across the street, because he didn't want to draw attention to himself. It took everything he had to keep his steps slow and measured, and the wide stretch of even road felt like an endless chasm between him and possible safety. Finally, he reached the building. Keeping his head down and his shoulders hunched, he inched behind a cluster of people waiting in line just as three vehicles emblazoned with the word "police" careened into the nearby intersection. One bore another symbol—Harte didn't need to see the details to recognize it as the Philosopher's Hand.

The same symbol had been proudly displayed on a banner back in Chicago at the Coliseum, where Jack nearly had become the vice presidential nominee. The Hand's appearance here had a chill running down Harte's neck that had nothing to do with the weather.

The sirens had finally drawn the crowd's attention, and the people in line around Harte started craning their necks, peering around one another to see what the commotion was about. Meanwhile, shards of red and blue light chased along the nearby storefronts, glinting off gated windows as uniformed men exited the vehicles. Two of the men were dressed in the boxy coats of the Guard, and their familiar silver medallions glinted in the brightness of the streetlights.

The pair of Guards said something to the others before heading toward the crowd. Harte slipped behind the person nearest to him and then began making his way to the door, using the distracted queue as cover. No one bothered to look at him. They were all too busy watching the action in the street to care that he was bypassing them in the line.

At the entrance, a bouncer sat on a stool, his head also turned toward the commotion in the streets. He was dressed in a dark leather duster and had his hands crossed over a barrel-shaped chest. Harte was nearly past when the guy put out his arm suddenly, blocking his way as he scowled.

"The cover's three." He held out his hand, waiting.

"Three?" Harte didn't know what the man was referring to.

"Dollars," the bouncer said, irritation growing in his expression.

Three dollars? It was an exorbitant sum. More than a day's wage for most working people. Harte couldn't imagine giving over that much money just to enter some sort of saloon. Not that the price mattered. Three dollars or three cents, he didn't have a penny to his name.

But he couldn't simply stand there waiting to be found.

With the Guards and their medallions so close, using his affinity would be dangerous, but he didn't have much choice. Not when the police and the Guards were already searching the groups of people in line on the sidewalk behind him.

Dipping his hand into his coat pocket, Harte pretended to retrieve the money, but instead of handing over the required entrance fee, he touched the guy's hand, sending a small charge of magic toward him. It was the second time in months that he'd used his affinity, and this time he couldn't ignore the thrill of satisfaction that went through him.

He had carried Seshat within his skin for so long. During that time, he hadn't used his affinity more than once or twice because he hadn't wanted to risk hurting anyone with the goddess's angry power. Now Harte realized just how much he'd been closed off from an essential part of himself. He'd always been ambivalent about his magic—at least since using it had been the cause of his mother's pain—but feeling the connection to the old magic again settled something in him. Perhaps his affinity was neither good nor bad. Perhaps it was simply a part of him, as intrinsic as his gray eyes or sharp chin. As essential as Esta was. He could no more deny his magic than he could deny his connection to her.

The bouncer blinked and dropped his hand, looking momentarily confused before waving Harte through. Without hesitating, Harte opened the scarred wood and glass door and plunged headfirst into the darkness and the noise of the saloon.

It was the volume that registered first. Before the filthy floors or graffiti-covered walls, before the smell of stale cigarettes and old liquor, a wall of sound overwhelmed him. The intensity of it, the *absoluteness* of the noise hit him with the force of something like magic. For a second he considered retreating and taking his chances with the police, but he quickly regained his footing and rejected that idea. He'd already used his affinity; the Guards' medallions would certainly have alerted them to his magic by now.

Lifting his hands to his ears, he pressed on through the crowd, who seemed unbothered by the sound, and headed deeper into the heart of the noise. The chaos inside the saloon—as unpleasant as it might be—was his best chance at evading the Guards. At least with the crowded tangle of bodies making it nearly impossible to press through, the police would have trouble finding him.

But the *racket*. He couldn't imagine *anyone* calling it music, but there seemed to be a stage. Performers. A sort of rhythm.

He pushed his way deeper into the crowd, careful to protect both the satchel he was wearing and himself as he was jostled and pummeled by the writhing, thrashing bodies around him. He tried to circle the edge of the room, heading toward the bar on the far side, but as he moved, he found himself caught in the crowd and pulled into the mass of bodies careening around him. There, in the center of the chaos, the noise was even louder. The rumbling of the rhythm thumped through his chest, rubbed up against the emptiness there, and pounded away at the aching grief. He felt utterly lost. All he could do was keep himself upright. Completely adrift in a turbulent, churning sea of bodies.

Harte thought of Esta suddenly. He wondered if she knew of this place or if she'd experienced anything like it before in her own time. Strangely, he imagined she would like it.

No. She would *love* it—the noise and anger and energy that filled the room, terrible and hypnotizing just the same. She would love the possibilities, the careless pockets ripe for picking and the anonymity of the throbbing crowd.

But thinking of Esta immediately brought up the stark memory of her body, crumpled and still on the station platform, and a wave of guilt and regret nearly brought him to his knees. *My fault. All my fault.*

The scream of the singer filled the room, tearing through the hollowness in his chest, echoing the grief there. Echoing, too, the rage. Overcome, he stopped trying to push through the crowd. Instead he gave himself over to it, allowed himself to be carried along by it.

The singer was screaming again, and it no longer mattered that he could not understand the words. He felt the truth in them. The ragged emotion in the voice spoke to him, and suddenly something within him broke and he found himself shouting back. He was screaming with the rest of them because, for some reason, he felt that he *had* to. There was no choice. He could let out the pain or be torn apart by regret.

Minutes or seconds or hours later, something shuddered through the crowd. A cold energy flooded the space, jolting him from the trance-like stupor he'd been in. His clothes were plastered to his skin by sweat beneath his light jacket, and his throat felt raw from screaming, but it took only a second to find the source of the disturbance. There, amid the still-writhing violence of the bodies on the dance floor, were members of the Guard.

Harte had known they would track him. He'd expected it. But he'd gotten so caught up in the crowd and whatever strange magic the music had spun to hold him in its grasp, he'd forgotten himself. He should have been gone already, but now he was trapped.

LIKE TO LIKE

1902—The Bowery

The Bella Strega was usually mostly empty in the afternoons, and that day was no different. When James returned from his errand over in Little Africa, there was only a handful of people curled around cups of Nitewein in the mostly silent bar. The new girl behind the bar, Anna, turned to the opening door and, when she saw who it was, gave him a welcoming smile.

"The usual?" she called.

He nodded before making his way to his regular table, moving slowly to keep his limp from being too obvious as he crossed the barroom. His leg was aching from his trek across the city and from standing on it for so long, but it wouldn't do to let the others know what a weakness it had become. Werner trailed behind like some kind of half-lost pup, but James could sense the hesitation in him. He'd been pliable enough since he'd returned empty-handed from the Flatiron Building with his tail between his legs, but he'd also been uneasy after James had dispensed with Mooch.

Even if Mooch's death hadn't stopped the Aether from rumbling, James did not doubt his decision. Mooch had been a problem for far too long. It was simply a lucky coincidence that the boy had made himself a convenient target for the necessary demonstration of James' power. Thanks to Mooch, no one would dare doubt his control over the Devil's Own now. And no one would dare move against him.

At least, no one who wore the mark.

Dropping into his usual chair, he tested the Aether as he waited for his drink. There was still something there, an indeterminacy that the day's activities had done nothing to calm. The vibration he felt, churning somewhere deep in the Aether, might have been a warning. Or it might have been the promise of more power. He couldn't quite tell. Not yet. And the diary was no help. It remained stubbornly unreadable since the gala. Useless as ever.

He needed something to change. He needed a victory of sorts to buoy him on.

The girl—Anna—approached the table with his usual glass of ale and gave him a flirtatious smile as she placed it on the table before him. When she retreated to the bar, she tossed a blushing glance over her shoulder in his direction. It was as direct an invitation as anything he'd ever seen.

As he drank, he watched Anna move behind the bar, more and more sure that his instincts had been correct. He'd hired her for a reason, and it wasn't just that she was easy to look at with her strawberry hair and milk-white skin. It also wasn't the fact that she'd accepted the position because she was clearly interested in him. After all, she wasn't the first who had tried to catch his eye with a coy smile since he'd taken over the Strega and the Devil's Own. She certainly wouldn't be the last. And he wasn't so desperate to fall for a seductive glance or an airy giggle.

Her willingness might have drawn his attention, but it hadn't been the most beguiling thing about her. The affinity that lived beneath her skin was far more interesting to James. From the first time he'd set eyes on her, he'd sensed the girl's connection to the old magic was a powerful one— and more, it was an affinity that could be of some use to him. He'd had enough of hobbling through the city on his injured leg. It was time to act.

He watched a bit longer, amused at how easily she entranced the men who leaned against the bar, hoping to catch her eye. They didn't see through her act: how she smiled sweetly at those who paid her attention and slipped her extra coins. She could blush on command when she wanted to, dipping her chin and preening when it suited her.

Yes, she was the one. It was time to test his theories about the Delphi's

Tear. What was the worst that might happen? Barmaids were easy enough to find. And James couldn't simply sit around waiting for Logan to return with news. Perhaps it would have been more efficient to simply take the sigils earlier, but the Aether had made it clear that it wasn't the best way forward. He needed Viola and Jianyu for what was coming. Of that, he was certain, even if he still could not completely see why.

He nodded to Werner, who jumped and came scurrying over. Again James noted that the boy was too nervous these days. If he got any jumpier, he might become a liability. Even if his affinity had its uses.

"Have Anna bring a growler of the new ale up to my rooms."

"Your rooms?" Werner looked surprised. "You want her to go to your rooms?"

James glared up at him. "Did I stutter?"

"No." Werner shook his head. "No, Nib—James. Sorry, it's just that I—"

"You *what?*" James asked, glancing up over the rim of his spectacles. He could almost imagine what Werner was thinking, comparing James to the poor, sainted Dolph Saunders, who never took a woman to his room, not even after Leena died.

But James wasn't Dolph, thank god. He was a hell of a lot smarter. And soon he'd be stronger, as well.

"Well?" he pressed. "Did you have something to say?"

Werner frowned as though he wanted to say more, but coward that he was, he kept his mouth shut. "No. I'll have her come right up."

"Give me five minutes," he said. "Then send her."

He didn't wait to see Werner's reaction. It took longer than he liked to climb the steps to the set of rooms above. He honestly didn't understand how Dolph could have stood it for so long, limping along through the city with such a weakness visible to anyone who might count themselves as an enemy. But then, Dolph Saunders hadn't had the benefit of the Delphi's Tear.

The ring was heavy on his finger, and its potent energy was a constant reminder of its potential. James had only to concentrate on his connection to the old magic and he could sense the answering power within the glasslike stone. But he couldn't *quite* join with that power, at least not as he'd hoped to.

Perhaps he should have known. The notebook from his future self had already told him that the stones worked best when they were aligned with affinities closest to the elements the stones were infused with. He could tap into some of the ring's power, but not all of it. Not truly. It hadn't given him any clearer view of the future, not like he'd hoped, but it would give him a more *certain* future . . . as long as Anna was as willing as he expected her to be.

By the time he reached his rooms, he was exhausted from the climb, hopefully for the last time. He had barely sunk into the worn cushions of the low couch when a knock came at the door.

"Come!" he called. "It's open."

Anna entered without any shyness at all. She was young, maybe a year older than himself, but the years without her family for protection had left their mark. Or perhaps that was simply the hunger she'd been born with to have more, to *be* more. It was a hunger he identified with and understood. It was one he could use.

"Where would you like this?" she asked, lifting the growler of ale she'd perched on her hip.

"In a glass," he told her, nodding toward the far corner of the room, where a cast-iron stove anchored the kitchen area. "Pour one for yourself as well and join me."

He didn't miss the flash of satisfaction in her eyes. *Blue. Like my sister Janie's.*

But he brushed away that thought and the sentimentality that came along with it. Janie was gone, along with his mother and father and everyone else. All he had now was himself and the future he could create.

"Oh, I shouldn't," Anna said, giving him a small smile that told him she knew already that she would.

"You definitely should," he encouraged. "Anna, isn't it?" Of course he knew it was.

She nodded, her bow-shaped mouth curving with the pleasure of being known, of being seen. It was almost too easy. She was almost too predictable. It would have been boring if he weren't so tired and in so much pain.

"Well . . . maybe just a wee nip," she said softly, pretending a sudden shyness he didn't buy for one instant. But the sound of her words brushed against memories. She was new enough, fresh enough, that she still sounded like the land of his childhood. His mother had said that—*a wee nip*. It was a reminder of all he'd lost. Of what he must become.

After she poured the ale, she took the seat he offered close to him on the couch without protest. The Aether trembled in response, and he knew that his plan would work.

They talked for a while, or rather she did. She chattered on about how grateful she was to have a place at the Strega, about her family and how they'd been taken by a bout of influenza the previous winter. As they drank one cup of ale after another, she prattled on, becoming bolder with each drink. When he placed his hand upon her knee, she didn't stop him. She only moved closer, practically onto his lap, but the pressure of her body made him wince.

"What is it?" She backed away, wide-eyed. "Oh, lord. It's your hip, isn't it? That injury—" Her hands came up over her mouth. "Oh, I *am* sorry. I shouldn't have—"

"It's fine," he told her. "It's not your fault that it hasn't healed properly. You know what happened, I'm sure . . . when Viola attacked me back in March on the bridge."

"I did hear a bit of something about that," she said. "But I can't imagine it. After all you've done, for her to attack you like that? And to leave you hurting so?" A combination of pity and hope flickered in her expression. "You know, James, after all you've done for me . . . maybe I can help?"

He feigned confusion. "What do you mean? Help how?"

Her mouth quirked. "I've done a fair bit of healing in my days," she said. "Perhaps I could have a go of it? Try to make things a little better for you?"

"You'd do that?" He blinked, waited for her to take the bait.

"Of course!" She moved closer, until her leg was pressed against his, and then rested her hand on his thigh. "You've given me a home, *safety* in a dangerous city. It's the very least I could do."

"I would be indebted to you," he said, and it even sounded as though he meant it.

"No! Never." She shook her head, but he knew it was a lie. It was what she wanted, to harness herself to his growing power. She wasn't even good at hiding it.

Too bad she'd never get what she desired most.

He waited a beat and then another before covering her hand with his and giving her a look that was pure sadness. "It wouldn't work anyway. The injury was made with Viola's knife—a bespelled blade. Natural magic alone wouldn't be enough. . . ." He glanced at her out of the corner of her eye. "But perhaps . . ."

"Yes?" Her voice was breathy as she inched closer yet.

"It's possible that you could focus your affinity through an object of ritual magic," he told her. "It would have to be powerful. . . ."

She took her other hand and ran a single finger over the surface of the ring he was wearing. "What about this?" Her eyes glinted, and he knew in an instant he'd been right.

It was a shame, really. She was so clearly drawn to power, so willing to do whatever it took. They might have been good together. At the very least, she might have been amusing for a while.

"The Delphi's Tear?" He lifted his brows.

She brushed her finger over it again, and this time she shuddered from the power radiating from it. "Maybe it would help?"

"It could be dangerous," he warned. "Channeling that much power. I'm not sure if you should . . ."

"I'd be willing to try. After all you've done for me." Her teeth scraped at her full lower lip, innocence and temptation all at once, but he didn't fall for it. And he certainly didn't have time to be interested. At least not until he was whole again.

He hesitated, only for a heartbeat. Only enough to make her think he was actually concerned for her safety. Then he took the ring, twisted it so it faced down, and grasped her hand so her palm was pressed to the ring between them. "Only if you're sure," he said.

She scooted closer until her whole body was pressed against him and squeezed his hand. Then she closed her eyes.

Almost immediately, energy crackled in the air, and James could feel Anna's affinity brush against the power in the ring. She was stronger than he'd realized. Her affinity swelled, and he felt an echoing call in his hip. He could feel himself knitting back together as the stone in the ring surged with heat. The gold suddenly felt like a brand against his skin.

Anna's eyes flew open. There was pain in her expression. And fear. She started to pull away, but James locked his hand around hers.

"Keep going," he commanded as he tightened his fingers, keeping her trapped with her skin pressed to the ring.

She was shaking her head, and there were tears streaming down her cheeks, but he only reached for the cane. A reminder of the promise she'd made a week ago when she'd allowed the intertwined serpents to be inked onto the skin just above her heart. Even now he could see the very edge of a tail curving up from the neckline of her dress.

"Finish it," he commanded, sensing the power in the silver gorgon's head surge against him.

He could feel everything—the knitting of bone and sinew and muscle healing, the pulsing power of the Delphi's Tear, and the fear coursing through the girl as she obeyed his command. Until the ache burned away to nothing. Until, spent, she slumped unconscious across his lap.

James could hardly breathe. The air was filled with the wild energy of their magic, with the power of the stone. It was only a knock at the door that sent him moving again. He pushed the girl to the side and stood, without pain. And without the aid of the cane.

But the Aether was still thrumming its indecipherable message. Healing his leg had been *an* answer, but it wasn't the one he was looking for.

Werner was waiting on the other side of the door. His eyes shifted to the room behind James, where the girl was lying on the couch. "Sorry," he said, blinking. "I didn't mean to interrupt. . . ."

"You didn't," he said honestly. "What is it?"

"Torrio just arrived," Werner told him. "Something about Eastman's guys roughing up some of the Five Pointers. He's waiting downstairs."

Perhaps that was the cause for the Aether's message.

James looked back over his shoulder and nodded toward the girl. He couldn't tell if she was breathing. He felt a pang of something like regret. She might have been amusing. But the ring was still warm on his finger, and his leg felt sure and steady beneath him, so he couldn't quite bring himself to care. "Take care of that, would you? I'll deal with Torrio myself."

FAMILIAR MAGIC

1983—The Bowery

With the music still pounding through the air and the bodies in the saloon still pulsing along with its rhythm, Harte quickly realized that the Guards weren't making much progress. They were trying to press through the crowded dance floor to search, but no one seemed to care about their authority. If anything, they reacted against their presence, and suddenly Harte felt magic hot and thick in the air. Familiar magic. *Old magic.* It felt like walking into the Strega, and he knew immediately that there were others like him there. The Guards' silver medallions were glowing, but the men who wore them didn't seem to know where to begin looking.

Without hesitating now, Harte touched the person in front of him, sending a small jolt of his affinity into them—just enough to move them aside. Again and again, he repeated the action, moving away from the police and toward—

He didn't know what he was moving toward. He only knew he had to get as far from the Guard as possible.

Before he could touch the next person, a hand grabbed his arm. Flinching away, he turned, ready to fight, but it wasn't a Guard. It was a girl. She barely came up to his chin, but the set of her shoulders and the spark in her eyes made her seem larger somehow. Her hair was a riot of spikes and fringy layers around her face, straw-blond streaked with an unnatural black, and a row of safety pins glinted up the side of her ear.

She jerked her head in the opposite direction from the way he'd been heading and started to lead him. But he pulled away.

Turning back, she glared at him. "They're here for *you*," she shouted, pointing to be clear what she meant over the volume of the music.

"How do you—"

"Just *look* at you," she shouted, glaring at him. "It's clear you don't belong. I don't know what your deal is, but you're going to put everyone in danger standing there like an idiot. Come on. There's a back way out."

Harte hesitated, but then he felt another wash of warm energy— cinnamon and vanilla cut through the reek of smoke.

"You can trust me," the girl said. "We're the same. I'm not letting those bastards win."

This time when she turned, he followed her through the bodies, away from the police searching, and toward a narrow hallway filled with groups of people—couples wrapped around each other and men with their heads together, turned away from the rest.

"Through there." She pointed down the gauntlet of bodies. A group of three men nearby turned to look at the two of them, their eyes like knives. But the girl narrowed her eyes at them, and they turned away.

From where he was standing, Harte couldn't see a door on the other end of the corridor. There were no signs of where the hallway led, but when he turned back to ask, the girl was gone. Behind him, the saloon was still pulsing with the same angry rhythm, and the Guards were still searching for him. Remembering the warmth and the cinnamon of the girl's magic, Harte plunged through the crowded hallway until he reached the end, where he found a door.

It could be a trap. He had no idea who the girl had been, and he'd had enough experience with Mageus who were more than willing to turn against their own kind for the right price to know that he couldn't trust her just because of their shared connection to the old magic. But there was no going back. He couldn't let the Book or the artifacts fall into the wrong hands, especially if Nibsy had told him the truth. If the stones were now unified, the Brotherhoods could use them to control Seshat, and through her, to control the power in the Book. There wasn't really a choice. He'd deal with whatever was on the other side of the door once he was through it.

For Esta.

The alley behind the bar wasn't empty, but to Harte's relief, there weren't any police, either. A few feet from the back door, a group of men laughed as they smoked. They barely noticed him as he walked past. Somewhere close by, sirens wailed their warning, urging him to keep moving.

The icy night air hit his cheeks like a slap, sharp and unexpected after the humid warmth of the saloon, but it was enough to remind him to be on guard. Without delaying any longer, he started walking, but he kept the hot anger of the noise and the crowd wrapped around him like a shield against the night.

Walking through the lower part of Manhattan was like walking through a dreamscape. Although the city he had once known was still there, enormous buildings now rose in the distance. The streets were devoid of horses and carriages, and the automobiles that occasionally passed weren't the slick fishlike sculptures he'd taken in with a kind of awed wonder in San Francisco. These vehicles were enormous, hulking beasts made of angles and shining silver. The city looked as though time had taken its claws to it, leaving it scraped and torn. Shattered. And more dangerous than it had once been.

Harte turned onto First Street and kept walking until he found Houston right where he expected it to be. He crossed the broad street, then cut southeast through the part of the city that had once been his home. East of Bowery, the landscape changed, and he discovered the neighborhood was now divided by a park that hadn't been there before. Where tenements had once tumbled atop one another, a wide stretch of snow-covered darkness now waited, broken only by the halos of an occasional lamp along the walkways. Even this late at night, there were people in the park. Some gathered in small clusters, while others slept on benches and alongside fences. They were likely harmless, but he decided on a longer route, taking Delancey Street instead of walking through the unknown park.

Finally, he turned south onto Orchard, and a few blocks later, he found the place he was looking for, the building where Esta had grown up. The bottom floors had once been a shop of some kind, but they were boarded up now. The tenements on either side looked empty. Their windows were covered with plywood and graffiti.

Actually, the whole building would have seemed abandoned to anyone not paying attention, Harte thought. But to someone looking carefully, the trappings of life were there, even with the windows dark and covered over. If there were answers to be found, they would be inside.

After considering his options, he went around the back. He wasn't expecting Nibsy to return anytime soon—if ever—but Harte wasn't sure who else might be inside. Esta had talked of a man named Dakari, of other team members and healers that Nibsy had used over the years. He'd have to be prepared for anything.

In a matter of seconds, he'd picked the lock and had the back entrance open. He waited, but nothing happened—no alarms sounded, and no one came running—so he stepped carefully across the threshold. Not even a second later, a cold blast of energy crashed over him, and a strange, dense fog began filling the space from the floor up. As it rose, he felt his affinity go dead. Cursing, Harte ran for the stairs, trying to get above the dangerous cloud.

Like most tenements, the building had a narrow, steep staircase running up through the back. The grime of the past had been washed away, and the worn wooden steps that should have been there were now sleek metal risers. The original gas lamps had been replaced with electric, but the lights were dark. He decided against turning them on. If the blast of cold was anything to go by, the entire building was likely set up like a trap.

When he reached the second-floor landing, Harte found that the space where a hallway should have been was now sealed over by a large steel plate. There wasn't a lock to pick or a doorknob to turn, but there was a cold energy radiating from it that indicated some kind of ritual magic at work. He would need to search that floor.

He continued upward to the next floor, searching. The third level had been converted to a series of living spaces. A large room at the front of the house contained couches and a larger version of the television set he'd enjoyed back in San Francisco. There was a comfortable bedchamber with thick velvet draperies and silk paper on the walls. Leather armchairs flanked the fireplace, and over the mantel hung a portrait of Nibsy, older than Harte had known him but younger than the man he'd met in the subway station.

There were two other bedchambers on that floor. One that had clearly been empty and unused for years and another that felt more recently used, but without any of the personality or luxury of Nibsy's own rooms. He made short work of searching the rooms, but there was nothing—and no one—there.

The fourth level had been left untouched and was clearly just storage. Nothing on that floor had changed in nearly a hundred years. The grime from oil lamps still crowned the ceiling and the walls were scraped and scarred from the families who had passed through them over the years. The individual apartments were filled with dusty boxes, but with the windows boarded up, it was too dark to see much more.

At the top of the building, Harte found another locked door. The dead bolt was surprisingly complex, but Harte managed to crack it after a few tries. When the door swung open, he found himself in an open space filled with shelf after shelf of books.

Nibsy's library.

He'd seen this room before, back when he still hadn't trusted Esta and had used his affinity to breach her defenses. Later, she'd told him more about the collection in that room, a collection she'd helped to gather for the man she'd called Professor Lachlan. She'd told him, too, about what the Professor had tried to do to her in that very room after Harte had sent her back to her own time, thinking she would be safer there.

All of Nibsy's secrets were in that library. The answers he needed were hidden there, and in the end, he'd find them all. But before he began searching, a large table in the center of the room covered with piles of newspapers and books caught his attention. Alongside the piles was a familiar glint of steel.

Harte took Viola's knife from the table and turned the stiletto blade over in his hand as he thought about the steel door on the second floor. He started to head back toward the stairs when he noticed the doors of an elevator on the far side of the room. There hadn't been elevator doors on the other floors he'd searched. Intrigued, he went to press the button to call the elevator, and a second later he heard the groaning growl of cables as the elevator approached. When the doors opened, he entered the cage carefully, ready for another trap. When nothing happened, he examined a row of numbered buttons. He pressed one, testing it, but realized it had been stabilized somehow. He pressed another, and it was the same. The only button that actually depressed was the one for the second floor. He depressed the "2," and the elevator shuddered as it began to descend.

When the doors opened, Harte found himself in a windowless vestibule lit by a flickering yellowish bulb. On one side was a row of four closed doors. Across from the doors, a long, broad desk faced a windowless wall. Black-and-white television screens had been stacked on the desk, four across and three high. He stepped closer to examine the pictures flickering on them and realized he was looking at the empty rooms of the building. There was the back entryway, still filled with the fog that had attacked the second he'd entered. The library. The interior of the empty elevator. The living quarters on the third floor.

Someone could have been watching him the entire time.

There was one other screen that depicted a room he had not yet found—a dark cell with a single cot illuminated by a thin beam of light.

Someone was huddled there. He couldn't tell from the flickering footage who the person was or whether they were breathing.

His hands felt damp and unsteady as he took hold of Viola's blade again and moved toward the first of the locked doors. Again, he felt the telltale brush of ritual magic. Cold emanated from the steel doorways. None had knobs or handles or locks, but Harte didn't need them. He didn't care who knew he'd been there.

Jamming the knife into the first one, he wrenched it open and found himself looking into an empty room. It wasn't the room on the screen, though. He tried the next and found a room of boxes. The next was a room that looked a little like the hospital in San Francisco. It held a narrow hospital bed with a bare, stained mattress and a metal stand draped with the same odd tubing that had been attached to his arm. It also wasn't the room on the screen.

There was one door left.

Glancing back at the screens, he saw the lump on the bed hadn't moved. He'd been making enough noise that it should've woken whoever that was. Unless they were already too far gone to move.

His hands shook as he placed the tip of the blade between the door and the jamb and wrenched the final door open.

The room was larger than it looked on the screen. Deeper. Darker, too. There was only a single source of light—a spotlight that illuminated the cot on the other side of the space. The figure lying there didn't move or stir at all.

Harte's breath felt tight in his chest as he took a step into the room. And then another. He waited, trying to listen for any sign of breathing or life.

The attack came from behind. Before he realized what was happening, something had been thrown over his head, blinding him, and arms like vises clamped around his neck. They squeezed. Tighter. Tighter still. He grabbed for his attacker, clawed at the strong arms that held him, but weak and unsteady after weeks of illness in California and days of not sleeping, Harte was barely able to stay on his feet, much less throw off his attacker. Before he could fight them off, his vision started to blur. He dropped the knife in a last attempt to pull away his attacker's arms.

Growling in rage, he tried to free himself. But he knew it was too late. He'd been caught by surprise. He'd failed Esta once again. It was the last thing Harte thought before everything went black.

PART

II

STEALING SECRETS

1902—East Thirty-Sixth Street and Madison Avenue

I t had been nearly three months since Jianyu had sent Cela to safety outside the city, and he was no closer to discovering what Newton's Sigils could do or why Nibsy wanted them. Each day that passed felt like a wasted opportunity, and with each week, the situation in the city grew more tenuous. Over the summer, the Order had only grown more desperate to find their lost objects, and as their desperation grew, so too did their violence.

Perhaps it was good that Cela was outside the city, Jianyu thought. But it had been weeks since he and Viola had received word from her. Abel usually brought news, but with the demands of his job as a porter during the busy summer travel season, his trips into the city had become less frequent. Jianyu knew that Abel had people checking on her, watching over her, but she wouldn't be able to send word if she needed help.

And, even if she could, there would be no way for him to help if word ever came.

He tried to put thoughts of Cela out of his mind and focus on the task before him. Across the street, J. P. Morgan's Madison Avenue mansion loomed. Sweat slid down his back despite the hint of a chill in the late-September afternoon. After weeks of searching, he had narrowed his focus to Morgan himself. That day in the Flatiron Building, it had been Morgan who had immediately recognized the importance of the missing discs. Morgan had been the one to discover they were missing, and he had also been the one to name them—Newton's Sigils—and to explain that without them, the Order could lose control of the Brink.

If Jianyu had stayed a little longer, perhaps he would have already had the information he needed. But that night Jianyu had been too concerned about Cela and Abel, about whether Viola had reached them in time, to tarry for long. The details had not seemed important, not when his friends' lives were in danger.

Now that information had become essential.

It had been years since Jianyu had thought of himself as a thief. There might have been a danger in gathering the city's secrets, but he had always considered the work done for Dolph Saunders as something more than simple theft. After all, secrets could not be *stolen*, not truly. Not when they were given away by those careless enough to speak them aloud. What might be told in the ear of one man could travel for a hundred miles, and whose fault was it if he happened to catch a whisper on the wind?

Thievery, *true* thievery, was different, and Jianyu had enough experience with it in his youth to know the difference. The cracking of a lock, the lifting of an object precious to its owner—precious as well to someone who would pay. The heaviness of guilt and the breathless thrill of danger that came alongside the action. He knew these well. He had learned them young, and they had cost him everything.

The act of breaking into a local merchant's house back in Gwóng-dūng had been the event that had forced him to leave his homeland and come to this wretched country. Or rather, it had been the fact that he had been *caught* that had set his life on its current path. If not for that one fateful night, he likely would still be raiding homes along the Zyū Gōng.

In truth, he would likely have been long dead. Young thieves did not last long in his province.

Jianyu had been in Morgan's house before, at least three separate times, and he had come to understand the rhythm of the servants as they went about their tasks for the day. He was familiar with the wide hallways and towering ceilings, could navigate easily through the maze of rooms to Morgan's personal library. He was ready.

With the sun high overhead, wrapping his affinity around himself was as easy and natural as breathing, but he paused to make certain the light was secure, to be sure that no one could detect even a glimmer of his form. When a carriage pulled up in front of the house, he knew it was time. He crossed the street and mounted the front steps just as the enormous door opened and Morgan's wife stepped out. As she descended to the waiting carriage, he slid into the interior of the home.

The halls were empty, and so nothing stopped him from reaching Morgan's library quickly and without incident. Pausing long enough to be sure no one was near, he opened the door and slipped inside.

Immediately, he felt swallowed by the enormous, masculine space. This was no cozy room for contemplation. It was a room designed to impress, and he easily could imagine Morgan holding court behind the large mahogany desk, directing his empire from the comfort and luxury of the plush leather chair. Floor-to-ceiling shelves lined the walls, and the gilding on the spines of finely made books winked in the soft filtered light. The air smelled of wealth, of tobacco and wood polish, of amber and leather. Beneath his feet, the boldly colored Persian carpet was plush enough to swallow the sound of his steps, so he did not worry about being detected as he moved across the space, invisible as a ghost to any prying eyes.

The mansion was enormous, but Jianyu had decided to focus first on the library, Morgan's personal sanctuary. It seemed the likeliest place for the tycoon to keep his most important pieces—and his most important secrets. During his previous visits, he had made his way through two walls of shelves with no luck. He had opened book after book, but he had not yet found the answer to the question of the strange silver discs Viola had taken from the Order's new headquarters.

They needed those answers. Until they understood how to use Newton's Sigils, Cela had to remain outside the city.

Jianyu turned to the next section of shelving and, tilting his head from side to side to loosen the tightness in his neck and shoulders, he got to work. His fingers grazed the edges of the spines one by one, scanning the letters there. He searched for words that spoke of magic and science or told the tale of ancient lands and terrible power. The first shelf was Shakespeare. Dickens and Thackeray. Goethe and Dostoevsky. Literature and philosophy that Jianyu remembered from Dolph's collection. But not what he was looking for. In the next section over, however, a name shimmered from the spines that sent Jianyu's heart racing: Newton.

With light fingers, he tried to tip the first book toward him but found that it did not move. Not a book, he realized. An entire shelf that appeared to be volumes of Newton's work was actually a single, solid stretch of faux volumes, and with a bit of effort, he was able to fold the entire piece down. Behind it, he found a mechanism that could only be a strange type of combination lock. Its tumblers were cylindrical and inscribed with odd icons rather than the arabic numerals typical in the West.

Jianyu stepped back, considering the problem. There was no clear hinge on the hidden panel behind the false books. Whatever the lock kept safe was larger than the single shelf. Carefully he traced his fingertips along the edges of the section of shelving that he had been searching and realized that there was something more to the molding there than in other places in the library. Perhaps the lock protected a larger chamber, and the entire section of shelf would swing out? But then, this was not an exterior wall. It was more likely a compartment of some sort.

Carefully, he rotated the tumblers, but the images on their surface were nonsense. Hieroglyphs or some sort of cipher, he could not be sure. He could detect the faint rubbing of metal against stone when he moved them, but this was not the sort of thievery he had any experience with. He wished again that Esta or Darrigan had returned. He had no talent with locks.

He was still considering the problem, sure that the answers they needed must wait within, when he became aware of a noise. It came softly at first, barely audible through the thick walls of the mansion, but soon the rumble of male voices was on the other side of the door.

LISA MAXWELL

The door swung open suddenly, and J. P. Morgan entered the room, along with three other men. The same men who had been with him in the Mysterium that night—the High Princept and others from the Order's Inner Circle. Morgan stood in the doorway, ushering the men in, and before Jianyu could slip out, he pulled the door closed behind him, twisted the key in the lock, and pocketed it.

INTRUDERS

1983—Orchard Street

Esta still felt unsteady from whatever Professor Lachlan and the girl had drugged her with, but she was free. She couldn't believe her plan had worked. She hadn't really expected it to. Not when she was sure Professor Lachlan had been watching her every move. Not when the girl who was her exact image had somehow been an even better fighter than she had *ever* been. But she'd managed to outwit them in the end. The body beneath the bedsheet wasn't moving—at least for now—and the door to the cell was wide open.

Glancing up at the camera in the corner, Esta flipped off the red light that had been glowing at her like an all-seeing eye. She didn't care if it—if *they*—were still watching. The door was *open*. She was free.

On the floor at her feet, the person beneath the sheet started to move. It wouldn't take long before he was conscious again. She started to step over his body when she saw the knife that had fallen from his hand. Viola's knife. Frowning, she scooped it up. Professor Lachlan didn't deserve to keep it.

The figure on the floor was already pushing himself up, and she knew it was time to go. He'd be disoriented for a minute or two, but not long enough to waste time. She had just started to pull time slow when the man beneath the sheet moaned.

She stopped in her tracks. She knew the sound of that voice.

"Harte?" Esta turned and pulled the sheet from the body. There, trapped in her hold on time, was Harte.

She hadn't even considered that he'd come for her—how could he have known? If she had pressed a little differently, a little harder, she could have killed him. "Oh, god. *Harte.*"

In an instant Esta was on her knees next to him. She started to reach for him, to bring him into the net of her affinity, but then pulled back when she remembered they'd lost the Quellant and that Seshat was still a danger.

How is he here?

She released time, and with another wincing groan, he wobbled a little, rubbing at his eyes. He'd have a hell of a headache from what she'd done, but he was there. However he'd managed it, he'd come for her. He'd *found* her.

It was only a second, maybe two, before he blinked at her, but that time felt unbearably slow and sticky until his confusion cleared and he really looked at her. She saw as he recognized her—the flash of relief and some other deeper emotion in the depths of his stormy eyes.

"Esta?" He bolted upright then, his hands coming to frame her face. They were trembling a little, and his eyes were searching her face like he barely recognized her. "Tell me it's really you."

She pulled back on instinct from the frenzy in his voice and the wildness in his eyes, but he'd already grabbed her wrist. Without any thought of gentleness, he tore the bandage off. She gasped as the red, angry wounds burned in the open air. He seemed frozen as he stared down at the raw skin on her arm, and then his face split into a smile. He started *laughing*. He sounded like some kind of lunatic.

And then suddenly he wasn't laughing any longer. He was kissing her. His hands framed her face before she could stop him, but she realized that there was no sizzle of Seshat's power, no darkness threatening. He was kissing her, and she kissed him back. All that had happened fell away, and there was only Harte—his lips against hers, claiming her, as his strong fingers threaded through her hair. Pinned her to him.

Breathless, she pulled back. "How—"

"I *knew* it," he said, leaning his forehead against hers. His breathing was still heavy. His hands were still trembling, but then, so was she. "I knew it couldn't be—I didn't want it to be you."

"The girl," she said, understanding what must have happened. She'd hardly been able to believe it when she'd turned in the stairwell and found the other version of herself—the one that should have been an eighty-year-old woman. But the girl hadn't been old. She'd been like looking into a mirror. "He used her to get to you, didn't he?"

Harte nodded, closing his eyes.

She tried to pull back. "Is it safe? Seshat—"

"She's gone," he told her, not allowing her to retreat from him. "Locked back into the Book."

"The girl did the ritual?" The girl—the one who had looked so much like her, the one who had once *been* her in another time line, another reality.

Harte pulled back from her, and his stormy eyes were filled with pain so stark, so *clear*, it took her breath away.

"It killed her," Esta realized. "The ritual killed her."

He nodded. "I couldn't save her. And then I left her there." Closing his eyes, he pressed his forehead against hers. "I didn't mean—" His voice broke, and she felt him shudder.

The ritual killed her. That other girl. That other version of who Esta might have become. Dead. Gone.

She didn't understand how she could still be there, alive and whole, when the injuries on her arm proved that she and the girl shared a connection. Unless it was because the past remained malleable. It was still possible to save the girl—to save herself—by going back and giving her the stone. By putting history on a different path.

Esta had been so confident, so willing to take on the responsibility of removing Seshat from Harte's skin. She'd been ready to make the sacrifice—more than willing—but she knew now that it had only been because, secretly, she'd hoped there was a way to survive it. Now that it

was over, now that she was still here and the truth of the ritual's consequences were irrefutable, Esta realized she'd been wrong. She hadn't been
anywhere near ready to make the sacrifice that had been required. And
she was damn grateful to be there, alive and with Harte.

Esta took Harte's face gently in her hands, her heart aching for him.
She'd never forget finding him in that hellish hole in San Francisco, a
hair's breadth from death, so she understood what he must be feeling. She
knew what it was like to almost lose him. Even if he'd hoped it wasn't
actually her who had returned to him in the subway station, he couldn't
have known for sure. Not really. She and the girl were identical. Nibsy
had made certain of it.

He'd been so damn proud of what he'd done. Because he'd had the
ring, a change from her original time line, Nibsy had been able to augment
the power of the healers he used. He'd been able to slow the girl's aging
because he had known that Esta would come for him eventually. He'd
ensured it by keeping that scrap from the Book, and he'd been ready.

And so had the girl, that other version of herself. It had been like
fighting a better, tougher, and more prepared version of herself—and Esta
had lost in the end.

Could Nibsy know so much? Predict *so much*?

"It wasn't me," Esta said, trying to push away her fear along with
Harte's. Softly, she brushed Harte's hair from where it had fallen over his
forehead. "I'm here. We're both here. We're both *alive*. You did what you
had to do, and now we have a chance, Harte. Now that Seshat's no longer
a threat to you, we have a *real* chance."

"I know. I keep telling myself that, but I just watched you die, Esta."
His expression was bleak, empty. He let out another shuddering breath,
as though expelling all the grief he was carrying. "I watched you die, and
I *left* you there."

"You didn't leave me, Harte." She leaned forward and kissed him
softly. "That wasn't me. I'm still here. You *came* for me."

"Knowing that doesn't seem to matter. I'm not going to be able to forget . . ." He looked at her, his expression fathomless and filled with grief. "The ritual didn't kill her, Esta. *I* did."

"No, Harte—"

"She'd trapped us in a circle of power—a ritual like the one Seshat did," he explained. "And then Nibsy came. The only way out of that circle was for her to finish the ritual by giving her affinity to the stones. But she couldn't do it on her own, not after what it had done to her already . . ."

"You used your magic," she said, understanding what had happened.

"We were trapped there, in that ritual circle, and the Guard was coming. If they'd found us . . . If they'd pulled us across that boundary . . ." He shook his head.

"The Guard?" Esta frowned. "The Jefferson Guard?" That couldn't be right. She'd killed Jack. She'd taken care of Thoth.

Harte nodded. "The power of the ritual must have drawn them into the station," he explained. "He told me it was the only way, but what if it wasn't? She looked so much like you."

From the vestibule outside the cell, a buzzing alarm blared, startling them both.

"Something's happening," Esta said, filing away all that Harte had just told her. She pulled herself to her feet and offered Harte a hand.

Scanning the monitors of the control room, they found the issue— men had entered through the back door. More through the front. Harte had been right. "Those aren't police," she said, noticing the familiar cut of the uniform and the glint of metal at their lapels. "The Guard is here."

The squad of Guardsmen was already climbing the back staircase. In the flickering black-and-white of the screens, the staircase light seemed filtered, like they were walking through a fog. There was a trio outside the door to the second floor—close to where they were currently standing—trying to figure out how to open it, while their comrades continued upward.

"I left Nibsy on the platform too," Harte told her. "It was only a matter of time before they traced him to this place."

Esta watched as a Guard took a small pen-like device from his coat and shot a beam of light toward the space between the door and the jamb. A few seconds later she heard an echoing noise coming from the room beyond that made it clear they were trying to cut through the door.

"You're sure the ritual took care of Seshat?" she asked Harte.

He nodded. "She's back in the Book. I felt her there, through you— through the girl. When I used my affinity to command her, I knew what she'd done to Seshat."

Esta wasn't sure what that meant, exactly, but there would be plenty of time for explanations later, once they were safe. First they had to get out of that building and away from the danger they were currently in.

She took his hand and pulled her affinity around her, silencing the buzzing alarm and the faint hissing from whatever the Guards were doing to the door. The screens stopped flickering, leaving the intruders all frozen in their tracks, caught in her net of time. Still, she didn't move. Not immediately. She waited for the telltale brush of Seshat's energy, the sizzling power that threatened to pull her under. And only after a stretch of seconds, only when she didn't feel Seshat's power, did she breathe again.

"She's really gone," Esta whispered, still only barely believing it.

Harte's mouth went tight. "Not gone but contained."

"I'll take it." Contained was fine. Contained she could work with. Especially since she hadn't been the one to die in the ritual. They still had a chance. As long as they got through the next few minutes.

"My cuff," she said. "Tell me you have it?"

Harte lifted his sleeve and slid it from his forearm.

"You have the rest?" She frowned as she took it and slid the silver cuff over her arm, felt the rightness of the stone's energy against her skin.

He patted the satchel. "They're all here. The Book, too."

But he'd kept her cuff, the artifact that meant the most to her, closer. He'd worn it on his own arm, against his own skin.

She leaned in and kissed him, quickly. Fiercely. Because she understood. And since they weren't dead yet, because she could.

INCONSEQUENTIAL

1902—East Thirty-Sixth Street and Madison Avenue

J ianyu pressed himself into the corner of the room to avoid detection as Morgan took his place behind the enormous desk, opened a box of inlaid wood, and offered cigars to the others as they took their seats.

"Has there been any news at all?" Morgan clipped the end from his cigar and lit the tip. He took a couple of deep puffs, then offered the heavy brass lighter to the older man across from him, a man Jianyu recognized as the High Princept.

"There have been some . . . developments," the old man said, examining the end of his cigar before lighting it.

"What developments?" Morgan asked, the cigar still clenched between his teeth. "Why is this the first I'm hearing of it?"

The other two men exchanged glances, but the High Princept ignored Morgan's outburst as he finished lighting his cigar. He took his time savoring the first few drags on the tobacco before finally licking his thin, papery lips and focusing on Morgan. "We felt it was unnecessary to involve your family any further."

"My family . . ." Morgan's eyes widened slightly.

The Princept took another puff and then settled back into the cushioning of the leather chair, as though this were his room, his meeting.

"You aren't actually considering freezing me out because of my stupid upstart moron of a nephew?" Morgan asked, clearly incredulous. "He's not even a Morgan. He's my wife's problem."

"He became your problem as well when we allowed him membership at your suggestion," one of the other men said. "He's been nothing but a menace ever since."

"I've taken care of that. Jack won't be a menace to anyone out in Cleveland," Morgan said, his temper clearly rising.

"Maybe you did your duty by sending him away, but Barclay's right," the Princept told him. "Because of Jack, we lost Khafre Hall. Because of the fiasco at the Fuller Building, the alliance we were building with Tammany is all but destroyed. We had the Delphi's Tear, and now it's gone. Newton's Sigils are gone as well."

"There's no evidence that was Jack's doing," Morgan said. "Barclay's grandson was named as well."

"Theodore was already on a ship bound for the Continent," the other man—Barclay—said. "And unlike you, I've made sure that he won't cause any problems in the future. How much more do we need to lose?"

Jianyu studied the man closer, startled to recognize the lines of Theo's profile in the older man's face. But where Theo was all affable kindness, the elder Barclay was stone and flint. He had no doubt that anyone who pressed the man was sure to catch his spark.

The nostrils of Morgan's large, bulbous nose flared. He was growing more frustrated by the second, but so far he was smart enough not to lose control of himself, or of the situation.

"This is preposterous," Morgan said, stabbing his cigar into a crystal bowl. "You wouldn't have even realized Newton's Sigils were missing if I hadn't noticed. You clearly didn't understand their importance, or they would have been locked into the Mysterium as they should have been."

"Locking them away would have done little good, considering that the Delphi's Tear managed to escape from that chamber." The Princept leveled a cold glare at Morgan. "Your dear nephew wasn't so lucky. Strange that he was even there."

"I'm not going to sit here and defend Jack," Morgan said. "He's a constant embarrassment to me and to the entire family. But if he had the ring, we would have found it."

"Perhaps," the Princept said.

Morgan stood. "What *exactly* are you implying?"

"We're not implying anything," the last man, who had so far been silent, said. "But it does seem strange that you are so focused on finding the sigils and not on the Delphi's Tear, as the rest of us have been."

"I've been focused on Newton's Sigils because none of you fools seem to realize how important they are to the Order's control over the city."

"So you've told us," the Princept drawled.

By now Morgan's face had turned an alarming shade of red. He stalked over to the bookshelf that Jianyu had just vacated and slammed open the secret compartment. Then, from a chain within his chest, he withdrew a small cylindrical piece of gold. Placing it in the center of the series of icons, he twisted, and the tumblers moved with a soft clicking sound, arranging themselves. With a *click*, they landed on their final combination, and the *snick* of a latch echoed through the waiting room. The other men all leaned forward, clearly curious to see what was about to happen.

From within the safe, Morgan drew out a thick leather envelope. He returned to his place behind his desk and opened the package, riffling through the contents until he drew out a piece of parchment and slipped it across the desk, facing the men.

The room was submersed in silence as the three men pored over the fragile scrap. Jianyu inched forward, trying to get a look at the document without being detected. The parchment was covered with a narrow, pinched script, but there were also diagrams—and the sigils were clear in the faded ink of the sketches.

"What is this?" the Princept demanded. "Where did you get it?"

"I came across it in a bundle of papers I purchased a few years ago," Morgan said.

"And you didn't think it was important to share this with the Inner Circle?" Barclay asked.

"Not particularly," Morgan told them. "As far as I knew at the time, the sigils were being used in the Mysterium to control the Ars Arcana's power. I never expected that anyone would be able to break into that chamber, much less take the Book of Mysteries. Moreover, I never dreamed that the Inner Circle was unaware of what they were capable of. You were using them. I assumed you understood."

"Of course we understood," the Princept huffed. "They old Mysterium used the sigils to protect the Book's power. But with the Ars Arcana missing . . ." There was an uneasiness in his tone now.

"Clearly you understand very little," Morgan told them. "These manuscripts show what our Founders knew and what the rest of you have forgotten. The sigils weren't only to protect the Book's power; they were protection *from* the Book's power." He poked a manicured finger at the diagram. "The Founders used them in the early days to keep the Book's magic under control. They can create a barrier of sorts to neutralize magic. Not unlike the Brink, but more its inverse."

"They form a key," Barclay murmured as he studied the document. "In the wrong hands . . . Maggots could use these to get through the Brink."

"Yes. In the wrong hands, Newton's Sigils could make the Brink inconsequential," Morgan said. "*That* is why I've been so interested in finding them. *That* is why I've personally funded the search for the sigils. Should the wrong person get ahold of them, they would control access in and out of the city. With it, they could undercut our power—with or without the artifacts."

Jianyu leaned closer, but he still could not make out what was written on the document.

"Newton devised the sigils when he discovered how powerful the Book was," Morgan explained, lifting the parchment from the desktop as he spoke and making it clear that it belonged to him. "He was terrified of what the Book could do, and so he gave the Founders of the Order a tool to contain its power."

"If this is true, we would have *known*," the Princept blustered.

"You *should* have known," Morgan sneered. "This history is no secret to the oldest families in the Order. Those of us whose forefathers established this city and this Order and whose families have been here since the beginning remember that there was a time when the Brink was not a weapon but a mistake. The Founders did not realize the danger in the power it contained until it was far too late. It was only through our fathers' and grandfathers' dedication to the occult sciences that the Order was able to use these sigils and transform the Brink into their greatest strength.

"But in recent years, the Inner Circle has become complacent with whom they offer membership to, and newer members, like yourself, never bothered to learn our true history. You thought membership in our hallowed organization would finally wash away the taint of new money that clings to you like manure." Morgan huffed. "You may have managed to claim leadership, but you never really understood the history of our esteemed Order. You never bothered to learn of the struggles that forged us, and so you cannot understand our true greatness. If you had, you never would have allowed Newton's Sigils to go unguarded."

The High Princept had visibly stiffened under the onslaught of Morgan's words. The old man's face had gone a mottled red, and it was clear his temper was about to snap, but before he could open his mouth to speak, a knock sounded at the door. The men froze, their protests and anger silenced, as Morgan set the parchment on the desk again and moved to answer the door.

"What is it?" Morgan barely opened the door, but the maid's voice carried clearly enough.

"Sir." One of the staff was at the door. "You and your friends need to get outside immediately. There's a fire started in the coal cellar and—"

"A fire?" the Princept asked. He was on his feet already, and Barclay quickly followed.

Jianyu looked at the sheet of parchment sitting on the desk, the leather folder filled with other secrets as well, and he waited. Too soon and he might be caught. Too late and the chance would slip away.

"Yes, sir," the maid said, still not entering the room. "In the coal cellar."

"We should go, Morgan." Barclay stepped forward.

"My people will take care of the fire," Morgan growled. "This house is built like a fort. We're not in any real danger."

"I'm not waiting to find out," Barclay said, already pushing past Morgan.

Morgan tried to block his way. "You can't leave yet. You haven't told me what you've heard. You said there was news."

"The news can wait, John. I'm not going to leave my wife a widow because you're too thick-skulled to take the appropriate precautions," Barclay said, pushing past. The other man and the Princept started to follow.

Jianyu saw his opportunity, and without further hesitation, he scooped up the parchment, and the leather envelope as well, tucking them beneath his tunic and obscuring them with the light, just before Morgan turned back to the room and saw the now-empty desk.

Morgan lurched for the desk, giving Jianyu just enough room to slip past him and out the door, dodging around the retreating men of the Inner Circle and harried servants as he went. Behind him, he could hear Morgan cursing.

He slipped out of the mansion with a group of servants, hidden from their sight by the power of his affinity. There was smoke in the air, but there was something else as well—the telltale warmth of magic sizzled through the heat of the summer night. It brushed against Jianyu's neck, lifting the short hair there in warning. He did not have to wait long to figure out where it was coming from. Across the street, Nibsy Lorcan waited, concealed by the crowd of people who had gathered to watch dark smoke pour from Morgan's coal cellar.

Alarms clanged in the distance, growing ever closer, as Jianyu turned away. But he had not taken more than two steps when he felt ice creeping along the ink on his back. His steps froze as the pain intensified and his panic grew.

When he turned, Nibsy was watching him—or, rather, he was watching the spot where Jianyu was standing since Jianyu had not yet released the light. Tentatively, he took a step toward Nibsy, and the ice in his chest eased just a little.

So this is his game. He took another step, and then another, slowly moving toward the crowd of people where Nibsy waited. With each step he took, the icy warning in his skin eased a little. When he was nearly an arm's reach away, Nibsy spoke.

"We need to talk." Nibsy kept his eyes on the column of dark smoke coming from the mansion. He did not bother to look over at the spot where Jianyu stood. Why should he? Jianyu knew he could sense him through the marks. "Come," he said, turning away, back into the crowd.

He hesitated, but as soon as Nibsy began walking away, Jianyu felt the mark etched into his skin surge with a cold energy that turned his blood to ice and his knees weak with fear. Wordlessly he followed. Because he did not have a choice.

NO ONE IS SAFE

1983—Orchard Street

W hen Esta finally drew back from Harte, the warmth of his mouth remained imprinted upon her lips. With the seconds hanging in the net of time and the world silent around them, she paused to catch her breath, to marvel that he was there at all. While she'd been plotting her escape, he'd come for her. Somehow, Harte had known the other Esta wasn't her. Even after he'd watched her die, he'd come to Professor Lachlan's building—to find her. To save her.

Esta Filosik had never been the type to want or need saving, but now, looking into Harte's stormy gray eyes, she wasn't about to complain.

"As nice as that was . . . ," Harte started.

"Nice?" she asked, pretending to be insulted. "You think that was *nice?*"

His eyes softened. "There aren't words for what that was," he said, lifting her hand to his lips and placing a kiss on the center of her palm.

She felt her cheeks go warm. She felt *everything* go warm.

"But we should get going." He lowered their joined hands. "If my experience getting in here is anything to go by, we should expect anything trying to get out."

Together, they moved to the bank of now-frozen monitors, looking for the best path of escape. It was clear that the Guardsmen had already fanned out through the building. Knowing where the Guards were would help in avoiding them, but Esta wasn't ready to leave. Not yet.

"We need to go back up to the library," she told Harte.

"Esta, no." He shook his head. "We have to get out of the building. Now. While we still can."

"Harte, every secret Nibsy ever wanted to hide is up there," she said.

His brows drew together. "We'll come back."

"What if the Guard takes everything before we can? We don't have to go back blind," she said, remembering how fat the file in the safe was. And there was Nibsy's diary as well. "It's more than just knowing what happened in the past, Harte. Nibsy knew how to complete the ritual to neutralize Seshat, didn't he? He wouldn't have bothered if he didn't also know how to use the Book's power. He's been studying and planning for nearly a century, and the information upstairs is our best chance for understanding how to fix everything without making any more mistakes," she told him. "The answers we need are up there. But we're not the only ones who could use that information." She tapped at the image on the screen, the men mounting the staircase. "We have to get his notebooks and files, and we have to get them now. Before they do."

He wanted to argue. Esta could see it there in the sharp lines of his face, the set determination of his expression.

"You know I'm right about this," she told him.

"We have the Book and the artifacts, and thanks to what the girl did, Seshat's trapped within its pages," he argued. "She's not a danger anymore."

"She's not the only danger," Esta told him.

He frowned. "What are you talking about?"

She hadn't had time to tell him—not with all that had happened. Or maybe she'd been avoiding it. "It isn't over, Harte."

"Seshat isn't a threat anymore, Esta."

"But the Book is," she told him. "As long as there's a piece of pure magic in that Book, someone could use it. As long as it remains apart from the whole of magic and vulnerable to time, everything is at risk. Whoever controls it could control time itself. It isn't enough to put Seshat back into the Book. We have to fix the ritual Seshat began."

"We don't—"

"We *do*," she argued. "Until it's done, no one is safe. The world isn't safe. We need to return the piece of magic to the whole. *I* need to, Harte."

"It isn't your job," he said, looking panicked. "You can't save the world. You shouldn't have to."

"Seshat thought I could. And if I can—*because* I can—I *do* have to," she countered. "And what about the Brink? What about the city? We could fix the Brink and free the Mageus trapped here. I could free *you*. Those answers are up there. I *know* they are."

Harte was silent at first, but finally he gave in. "Fine," he said, not sounding like he meant it. "But quickly. And if *anything* else happens, we leave. No arguments."

"But—"

"I've lost you once today, Esta," he told her, his voice breaking around the words. "Don't ask me to do it again."

Her heart clenched. "You're not going to lose me, Harte—"

"I can't," he said. His eyes were determined. "I *won't*. Promise me. If I say we leave, we leave. No questions. No arguments."

She bristled at the command in his tone, but there were too many shadows flickering in the depths of his eyes for her to be truly angry.

"At the first sign of trouble, we're gone," she told him. "I swear."

He didn't look convinced, but his shoulders relaxed a little. "So what's the plan?"

She considered their options. "The elevator," she told him, realizing it wasn't included in any of the images on the monitor screens. "I'll have to let go of time to use it—"

"No—"

"We'll be at risk until it opens," she said, ignoring his protest. "But they haven't entered the library yet. As long as we can get to the top floor before they get through the door, they'll never see us."

He studied the glowing screens. "This is a terrible idea."

"There's no other door, Harte." She pointed to the end of the room, where the doorway had been sealed off by something more than a simple steel plate. "There's only one way in and out of this floor—through the elevator. We might as well go to the library."

His jaw was set, and he still looked unconvinced, but he allowed her to pull him toward the elevator doors.

"Ready?" she asked, hoping that they weren't making a mistake.

He didn't look ready at all. "There has to be a better way."

"There isn't. Not as far as I can see." She gave his hand a sure squeeze.

Not bothering to wait for Harte's next argument, Esta took one more breath before she let go of her affinity and allowed the seconds to spool out. Immediately, the buzzing alarm was back, and so was the sizzling noise from the doorway. Without wasting any time, she pushed the call button. They waited, their hands still clasped tightly together—ready for anything—as they listened to the groaning climb of the lift. The noise of it echoed through the building, louder than it had ever been in her childhood, and she knew the Guardsmen could likely hear it too.

The elevator came to a lumbering stop, and as the doors began to open, she pulled Harte back at the last second. Just before one of the Guard rushed out.

Without hesitating, she pulled at her affinity, cursing as she slammed the seconds to a stop. But the Guard had already seen them. "Shit. Shit. *Shit.*"

The door was open, and the man was caught mid-lunge. Behind him were two others. Harte pulled her back, putting himself between them.

Almost too frustrated to be annoyed with Harte's protectiveness, Esta stepped to his side and considered the situation. She'd hoped to get out of the building without being seen, but it was too late to worry about that now.

"I'm going to have to touch them. To get them out of there," she explained. "They'll see us. Unless you can make it so they don't remember?"

He shook his head, his frustration palpable. "The entrance was booby-trapped. More of that fog. I still can't reach my affinity."

"Okay then." There was nothing they could do about the Guard seeing them. They just had to keep moving. Determined, she nodded, but she knew she was trying to convince herself as much as him. "We can do this." When it looked like he was about to argue—again—she cut him off. "It's the only way out, Harte." Then she stopped the rest of his arguments by grabbing the arm of the Guard closest to them and yanking the man into the room.

The Guard barely had time to register what was happening—and to see them both—before he stumbled forward and froze once again, caught back in the net of time she'd spun around them.

"I'm going to need your help on the next two," she told him.

This time, thankfully, he didn't bother to argue with her. Together, they managed to get the other two men out of the elevator. With each dazed, shocked look, she knew they were backing themselves into a corner. The Brotherhoods—or whoever was now in control of the Guard—would know they'd been there. They'd never stop hunting them.

But that was a worry for later. First they needed to get out of the building, preferably with all of Nibsy's secrets.

Once the elevator was empty, the two of them stepped inside, and Esta released her hold on the seconds. She pushed violently at the button for the top floor, even as the rattled men were pulling themselves to their feet and starting toward the closing door. The door slid shut just before the men reached it, but Esta couldn't feel any relief. They had no idea what might be waiting for them in the library.

Holding tight to Harte's hand, they watched the dial move as the elevator inched upward. They passed the third floor and then the fourth, and she knew with each second that the Guard back in the control room could have already alerted the others. Even now, they could be waiting in the library for them to arrive.

But when they reached the top floor and the door slid open, the library was empty. Without waiting, Esta reached for her magic and pulled time still. The buzzing alarm ceased, and the world fell silent again.

"The door," Harte said, pulling her toward the staircase door that was standing open. But even once the door was secured, even with time pulled close around her, she didn't feel any relief. Not in that room. The lack of Guards wasn't enough. She wouldn't feel any relief until they were out of the building, until she could walk away and never have to look back.

"The papers will be in the safe," she told him, shaking off her apprehension as she pulled him toward the painting on the other side of the room.

When they removed the picture of Newton, she saw that the safe had been repaired from where she'd mangled it earlier with Viola's dagger. Not surprising. She wouldn't have expected anything less of Professor Lachlan. This library was his citadel, and the safe had always been its inner sanctum.

Once more, she pressed Viola's dagger into the seam around the edge of the safe, and the magic-infused blade again sank into the metal. She was nearly through when she heard something from the other side of the library's door.

"That's impossible," she whispered, turning to look over her shoulder. There shouldn't have been *any* noise as long as she held the seconds in her grip.

But a sizzling hiss, like the sound of the Guards trying to cut through the door on the floor below, was coming from the far side of the room.

"Thoth," Harte whispered, and when she turned to him, his expression didn't contain the confusion she felt. It held only fear.

"He's gone," she told him. "I destroyed him in Chicago, when I killed Jack."

"You didn't," Harte said, his expression bleak. He didn't bother to explain. Instead, he took the knife from her and, wrenching it, pried the safe open. He grabbed everything inside. "We have to go."

"Wait, Harte—" The hissing had turned into a pounding now. "What are you talking about?"

"Later." He tugged her toward the elevator.

"We don't even know if we got everything," she said, looking back toward the mess of papers and books scattered around the room. "We have to make sure—"

"You promised, Esta," he said, turning on her. He nodded toward the pounding on the other side of the door. "That is the definition of trouble."

He was right. The stack of ledgers and folders in his arms would have to be enough.

They weren't quite into the elevator when the door fell forward, completely severed from its lock and hinges. Even before she could let go of time, before they could close the elevator and try to escape, two Guards lurched into the room. Their eyes were completely black, and Esta knew for certain that Harte hadn't been wrong.

Thoth wasn't gone.

As the Guard advanced, they spoke in unison. "The Book," they said, Thoth's voice echoing from their lips. "Give me the Book, girl. Or you will both die."

But she'd had enough death for one day—hell, for an entire lifetime. And Esta had no intention of giving *anyone* the Book. Instead, she focused on the seconds, searching for what she needed, and when she found an empty space, she pulled them both through.

The world lurched, and time pressed at her, threatening to tear Harte from her grasp, but Esta held tight, until suddenly, night turned to day and the blaring alarm faded to silence. They were alone in the closed elevator now, with no Guard and no threat of Thoth. Ishtar's Key was warm against her skin, and Harte's hand was still squeezing hers tightly. But he was leaning against the slick metal wall of the lift.

"You okay?" she asked as he let out a small groan. "You aren't going to be sick?"

He shook his head. "I don't think so." But he didn't sound sure. He looked pale and unsteady on his feet.

They needed some air and time to catch their breath and consider what their next step should be. Slipping through time had always been miserable for Logan. Clearly, it was bad for Harte as well. Especially considering what he'd been through in the previous weeks.

She pushed the button for the library, and when the doors slid open, she pulled him into the room. She didn't notice the figure sitting behind the broad desk until it was already too late.

Suddenly, icy fog blasted through them from all sides. Before Esta could grab for her magic, before she could even finish the thought that *the elevator was a trap*, her affinity slid away from her. Dead and cold and empty.

THE CHURCHYARD

1902—The Bowery

As he walked away from the Morgan mansion, James smiled to himself at the fear that he'd seen in Jianyu's eyes. After the girl whose affinity healed him, he had not been able to practice much with the ring and with what he could do to the connections between the marks. He couldn't show such a display around the Devil's Own. Not yet, at least. He wasn't ready to draw their suspicion, or worse, invoke unnecessary fear, because he knew that his control over Dolph's people was still tenuous and in its earliest stages. The wrong move could tip the balance against him. Until he knew for sure what power the Delphi's Tear could truly afford him, until he'd *mastered* that power, he didn't want anyone to suspect what he might be capable of. Jianyu's compliance was an excellent sign, perhaps even a promise of the possibilities to come.

Since the last time they'd talked, Jianyu and Viola had been busy. They'd saved more of his castoffs from the Order's patrols, and they'd been searching for answers. For a while, he'd let them have their small victories, but now he was finished waiting.

With a simple tilt of his head, James signaled that Jianyu should come with him, and then he turned south, toward the Bowery, certain Jianyu would follow.

Neither of them spoke as they walked, not even when Jianyu finally released the light and appeared next to him. In stony, uneasy silence, they traversed the city in tandem as the sun sank lower on the horizon.

It was nearly dusk by the time they reached the church, and neither had uttered a single word. Jianyu remained silent as James opened the graveyard gate and let himself into the churchyard and walked among the weathered monuments until he came to a stop over the small, flat stone that held Leena Rahal's name. He felt Jianyu's frustration—his fear and his impatience—but though the Aether vibrated with that same unreadable tension, there was no other indication of any immediate danger. So James simply waited.

It took him longer to break than James expected, but eventually Jianyu showed himself to be the weaker of the two.

"I assume there is something you want? Some reason you led me on this chase?" Jianyu asked, his voice low and surprisingly unconcerned.

James didn't bother to turn or guard himself, because he knew Jianyu wouldn't strike. *Couldn't strike.* The Devil's Own belonged to him now, and Jianyu and Viola both understood *exactly* how quickly the Devil's Own would turn on them should he come to any harm. In the eyes of those who had once followed and trusted Dolph Saunders, it was Jianyu and Viola who were the traitors. And the remaining members of the gang would be more than happy to make either of them pay.

And if anyone else at the Strega suspected who the real architect of Dolph's demise was? It barely signified. He'd already made it abundantly clear what would happen to anyone who crossed him. Jianyu understood the danger as well.

James tossed a careless glance over his shoulder. "I wanted to pay my respects to an old friend."

"You were no friend to Leena." He took one menacing step toward James.

At the same time, James gripped the gorgon's head and sent a warning pulse through its connection to Jianyu's marks. The cane itself was no more than an affectation now, but he carried it with him anyway. It still had its uses, after all.

Jianyu stopped, his back arching against the place where Dolph's mark lay beneath his clothing, and James held the pulse of energy a second longer before releasing it and Jianyu both.

"I hope you've given serious thought to my offer," James said. "You're running out of time. Soon you'll need my protection."

"I seem to have done well enough on my own these past weeks," Jianyu told him.

"Have you?" James mused. "You can't still really believe you've been able to avoid my notice, not when I found you so easily today."

Jianyu's jaw clenched, but he didn't refute the claim.

"You didn't truly think you were so good at hiding, did you?" James asked, amused despite himself. *How could he have not known?* "This city isn't so big, really. I could have come for you at any time. I could have sent any number of factions after you had I wanted you out of my way. You and Viola have been safe because *I* willed it. It was a gift. And now you'll repay me for my generosity."

Jianyu's eyes were as sharp as any blade Viola had ever wielded. "I would rather die."

Tightening his hold on the Medusa's head, James focused on the Aether, on his connection to it, *through* it. He watched as Jianyu grimaced and went rigid again, fighting against the pain that he'd sent thrumming through the mark. "That can be arranged."

James took a step forward, indifferent to Jianyu's pain. Interested only in what he carried. "I want what you took from Morgan's house."

"What makes you think I took anything?" Jianyu gasped.

"I know you did," James told him. "Thanks to the distraction I helped to provide."

"You—" Jianyu's brows furrowed. "The fire."

"Of course," James said. "You didn't realize I'd been following you, but I had the sense that today could be important for you. For *us*."

"Never for *us*," Jianyu promised, but his words were empty when he could barely remain on his feet.

James tightened his grip on the cane, and Jianyu crumpled to the ground.

A few seconds later, he started to struggle up. The fury in his eyes made it clear he wanted a fight, so James depressed a small lever to release the hidden blade in the tip of the cane. Jianyu froze at the sound, clearly remembering the poisoned blade hidden there, and he remained still as James used it to slice open his tunic, revealing the leather envelope tucked within.

"I'll be taking this," he said, scooping up the package while Jianyu writhed in pain.

The Aether trembled, but the strange hum did not stop.

"They'll come for you," he assured Jianyu. "The Order is already searching for you, but without my protection, the rest will come as well. And when they do, you'll return to me. You'll beg for my protection."

Jianyu's expression was tinged with such fury, such glorious hatred . . . it was almost amusing.

"Oh, I know you'd never come to me to save yourself," James assured him. "You're far too noble and self-sacrificing for that. But you'd beg for those you care for. Those you've promised to protect."

He loosened his grip on the cane and released the connection he'd been holding through it. With a shuddering gasp, Jianyu pulled himself up onto his hands and knees. Then, slowly, he got to his feet.

"You don't want me as your enemy, Jianyu," James said softly, but the threat in his words was clear. "It would be *much* better for everyone involved if you counted me as a friend."

"I will never count you as a friend," Jianyu vowed.

James could practically *taste* his anger, his barely leashed temper. *Delicious.* Jianyu losing hold of his careful control would be more than entertaining. It would be perfect.

"You wound me," he said with a mocking smile. "Never is such a long time, you know. Just like being dead." Then he let his expression go cold. "I'll have the sigils one way or the other. Better to hand them over while you still can."

"You will never get them," Jianyu promised. "They are in a place where you cannot reach them. And they will remain there, far outside your grasp."

"Are they?" Nibsy asked, allowing his lip to curl as he clutched the Medusa's silver-coiled head. The ring's energy urged him on, but he held back. It wasn't time. Not yet. "Tell me, Jianyu . . . is Cela Johnson enjoying her time as a chambermaid in Atlantic City?"

Jianyu's face drained of color. His hands clenched into fists at his sides, but he seemed frozen. Unable to decide whether to attack or flee.

James didn't bother to hide his amusement now as he took another step further. "Did you really think I couldn't reach her simply because she was beyond the Brink? Did you forget that Kelly's men are mine now?" He gave Jianyu a pat on the cheek too sharp to be playful, and when Jianyu flinched, James couldn't help but laugh. "I'll be sure to have Razor Riley give Cela your regards."

"We are finished here," Jianyu said, nostrils flaring. He turned on his heels and slipped into the night.

"No," James said, more to himself than to Jianyu. "We're only just beginning."

TICK-TOCK

1983—Orchard Street

Esta lunged for the elevator buttons, even as she felt her magic hollowing out. But the lift was as dead as her affinity. No matter how violently she pressed, the elevator didn't respond.

"You're not going to be leaving that way." The old man's voice was soft and calm, and Esta knew he was speaking the truth. Somehow, he had known to be there in the library waiting for them.

Harte's hand tightened around hers, and when she looked over at him, they didn't have to speak to understand each other. The cold blast had affected both of them, and with the elevator dead, there was no choice. They'd have to go through the library and down the steps to escape, which meant they'd have to play the old man's game. At least until their affinities returned. She gave Harte a sure nod. They'd face this head-on.

Together, they stepped out of the elevator. Professor Lachlan was there at the other end of the large room, sitting beneath the portrait of Newton and the Book, behind the large table he'd always used as a desk. He had a pistol—the same gun he'd used to kill Dakari—sitting within reach on the tabletop.

"I wondered when you'd show up again," the old man said. "After you disappeared on the Guard a few days ago, I knew I only had to wait. But I suspected you wouldn't risk going too far ahead, because I taught you better than that. It looks like I was right. As usual."

Esta bristled at the presumptive ownership in his tone. "*You* didn't teach me anything." That had been a different version of Professor

Lachlan, one who had been every bit as duplicitous. But the old man sitting before them had lived a different life in a far different world.

I don't know this man, she thought. *Not really.* Though she did know what he was capable of. She'd seen that other version of herself, frozen unnaturally in time, and she understood exactly what he was willing to do in order to win.

But the man sitting at the far end of the library looked different. She hadn't taken them that far forward, but the slumped, wizened creature behind the large, scarred table looked nothing like the man who'd managed to get the best of her. Something had happened to him in the hours since he'd surprised her with the other version of herself and left her locked in the prison cell of a room. One thing was clear—physically at least, he was no longer a threat. She doubted he could even stand. But then, who needed to stand when they had a weapon that could do the job from a distance?

"How the hell did you get out of there?" Harte asked. "I left you for dead."

"Yes," the Professor said, his expression the portrait of mock sadness. "Isn't it terrible that an unregistered Mageus attacked one of the preeminent experts on the occult arts? Even without my affinity, I knew exactly where you would go. How else do you think the Guard found you so quickly?"

"I should've killed you when I had the chance," Harte growled.

"There's a part of me that wishes you had," Nibsy said. "Until you showed up just now, I would have welcomed death."

"Don't worry," Harte told him. "I can rectify that mistake." He started forward, but Esta held him steady. Even in the old man's current state, he could reach the gun before Harte could reach the desk.

Professor Lachlan coughed out something that might have been a laugh. "You always were a smart girl, in whichever life you led." He leaned forward a little. "Not ever as smart as you believed you were. But you did well enough for my purposes."

"I'm not doing anything for your purposes," she told him.

His pale, dry lips twitched at that. "As I said, you're not *nearly* as smart as you think you are. I'm not finished with you yet, girl."

"That's where you're wrong," Esta said. It was a bluff. With the gun in the Professor's reach and her magic cold and dead from whatever had just happened in the elevator, they didn't have the upper hand. But she pulled confidence around herself anyway, the last bit of magic she had left. "We're leaving, and you're not going to do a thing to stop us."

Esta gave Harte another small, sure nod and then turned away from the Professor. Hand in hand, they walked toward the staircase, and neither of them looked back.

"You would leave the answers you need and simply walk away?" the old man asked when they were halfway to the door. There was amusement in his tone, even though his voice sounded like the crackling of leaves.

She froze, hating herself for pausing.

"You have no idea how to use the power in the Book, do you?" the old man asked. "The beating heart of magic . . . Do you have any idea what it's even *capable* of?"

"Esta," Harte murmured, tugging gently on her hand. "He's not going to help us. You can't trust anything he says."

"I got you out of that ritual circle, didn't I?" Nibsy said. "I could have just as easily left you to die."

"Only because you needed the ritual to end so you could get the Book. There was nothing noble about you helping me. You killed that girl," Harte said, anger lashing in his words.

"No," the old man murmured. "*You* did that. I simply handed you the weapon. You're the one who chose to pull the trigger. You chose your life and your freedom over hers." He nodded to Esta.

"I knew it wasn't really Esta," Harte said.

"Did you?" Nibsy murmured, amusement glinting behind the thick lenses of his spectacles. "But you're wrong. It *was* Esta. Just not the version you're used to. That girl was simply another possibility of what could be."

"Then why let her die?" Esta asked. "You groomed her, kept her ageless over *decades*, and for what? She would have been far more willing to help you than I'll ever be."

"She served her purpose," the old man said. "She was an anomaly. An impossibility, and yet she still fulfilled her fate. With her sacrifice, the stones have been unified. Now they can be used to control the goddess and unlock the power in the Book."

"Not by you," Esta said. "You don't have the Book or the artifacts."

"But I will, when you take them back." The old man did smile then. "You see, *this* version of the time line was never my destiny." He turned to focus his cloudy eyes on Esta. "Just as dying in that ritual circle was not supposed to be yours. The girl doesn't matter—not her life, not her death—not so long as you return as you must."

"Or her life will become mine," Esta realized. "Her time line will become the only possibility."

"And the effects on history you created—the chaos and evil you unleashed—will become permanent." Professor Lachlan nodded. He adjusted himself in his seat to reach for a stack of papers, grimacing at the movement. "Your duplicity turned into a gift," he said. "Had you taken the Book directly back to my younger self, I would not have realized the possibilities the Book holds for time itself. Because of you, because you tried to betray me, I had another lifetime to learn. I had another lifetime to prepare."

"It won't matter," Esta promised.

"Oh, but it will," he told her. "Didn't I teach you that time was like a book and history merely the words on the pages? Tear out one page. Write over another. I believed the essence beneath would remain the same." He shrugged. "When you slipped away from Logan, when you saved the Magician from his fate and broke through the Brink, you created another story, a time line written overtop the first. But you didn't change the *essence* of the thing. You never changed time itself. But *I* will.

"The original time line is still there. Like a palimpsest. The life I was meant to have is waiting beneath the surface of *this* lifetime, beneath time and memory. So is yours. It's why you have to return, why you have to send Ishtar's Key forward with the other girl. Your very existence depends upon it. But you know this already. You have the Book and the goddess within it. You have the stones. And when you return to your past, as you must, you'll deliver me my victory."

"We won't deliver you anything," Esta promised.

The old man's expression didn't so much as flicker. "Tell yourself whatever stories you must, but the truth is this—you *will* return to the past. You've already decided, or you wouldn't still be here. Time would have already taken you. You will go back because you know that returning is the only way to save your friends, and now it's also the only way to erase the chaos *you* unleashed on the world. You will return, and when you do, I'll be waiting. You'll bring me everything I need to change time and magic and the world itself."

"We're done here," Esta said, trying to ignore the creeping dread that had started to sink its hooked fingers into her. He wasn't wrong about her returning to the past, but they would never let Nibsy win.

"We're not even close to done." The old man lifted the pistol, pulled back the hammer.

Without hesitating, she turned and placed herself between the old man and Harte.

"Esta, no," Harte said, trying to push her aside.

But she wouldn't budge. Harte was expendable, but she knew the Professor needed her. "He's not going to shoot at me," she said. "He needs me alive."

"She's right," the old man said. He hadn't yet aimed the gun.

"Put the gun down," she demanded, keeping herself in front of Harte. "I'm done with your games, old man."

"No," the Professor said. "You'll play a little longer. I'll even give you a fighting chance—it'll make things that much more interesting. You have a world to save, don't you?" He looked up from the dark body of the pistol. "I have the answers you need to save it. Think of what you could do if you knew how to unlock the secrets of the Book. You could fix the Brink. Free the city. Complete the ritual that the goddess started."

Harte cursed. "He's not going to give you anything real. He's never going to help us."

Esta knew that. But she felt rooted to the spot, like she was under some kind of spell. Because what if this old man *wasn't* lying? True, Nibsy would never help them. He would never willingly hand them the key to his defeat. But if he needed her to take this knowledge back? Games upon games. Those papers might be nothing, or they might hold the answers she needed. Without her affinity, though, she couldn't reach them.

"Come on, Esta," Harte urged, tugging at her gently.

"Tick-tock, girl." The old man lifted the gun. "Your time is running out."

She didn't think or hesitate. Esta simply moved on instinct, shoving Harte down and covering him with her body as the crack of the gunshot rang out.

There was only one. A single shot. And then silence.

Harte was already pushing her aside, checking her for injuries, but the silence in the room was more deafening than the shot itself.

"I'm fine," she told him, taking his face in her hands. Meeting his eyes until he knew it was true.

His gaze shifted behind her, and the color drained from his face. But she didn't need to turn to know what she'd see. Professor Lachlan slumped over a blood-splattered desk, the gun still resting in his lifeless hand.

ONE OF OUR OWN

1902—Atlantic City

Cela Johnson hated scrubbing floors. She hated the acrid smell of the cheap soap powder and the way the water and grime made her fingers prune and crack. She hated spending the day on her hands and knees when she was born to rise. She hated it almost as much as she hated hiding.

Once, her talent with a needle and thread had kept her from the housekeeping that most Negro women were forced into just to survive. Instead, she'd worked her way into the costume shop of a white theater, where the hours were good and the pay was even better. With her skills, she should have been able to find a position with any modiste in New Jersey, but that would be the first place anyone would come looking for her. People knew who she was, which meant she couldn't use her skills now to make her living, not without the possibility of someone taking notice. Her only real choice had been a position as a maid in one of the enormous new Atlantic City hotels that drew crowds away from the heat and stink of the sweltering Manhattan streets. She hated the work, but it paid for her room in a clean and safe boardinghouse, and at least with all the people who came through, she could keep her ears open for any news from the city.

And if the middle-class tourists acted as though she wasn't even good enough to breathe the same air as them? At least they tipped well. Sometimes. After nearly three months of work, she'd been able to save enough that, with what Abel earned as a porter, they would be able to start rebuilding their parents' home come fall.

If I'm back in the city by then.

Pushing aside that thought, Cela lifted herself from the damp and soapy floor. She would be back in the city by then, one way or another. It was her home, wasn't it? And she trusted Jianyu and Viola to figure out what the Order's discs could do, didn't she?

But it had been longer than she'd expected already. *Eighty-seven days.* It couldn't possibly be much longer. At some point, she was going to be done waiting.

She wiped her raw hands on her apron before taking up the bucket of filthy water and starting toward the back hallway, the tucked-away corridor where the hotel staff kept the whole place running. Her shift was nearly over, and she wanted nothing more than to take off the constricting uniform, unpin her hair, and have a nice long soak in a cool bath. Abel's train would be coming in later, and when he arrived, maybe they could grab dinner. It would be nice not to be so alone.

Turning the corner, she twisted just in time to avoid two young boys nearly careening into her and the bucket of dirty water. The water inside sloshed over, splattering on the clean floor, and with a sigh, she bent down to wipe it up before anyone could slip.

"Watch where you're going, girl," the father snapped as he passed. His wife simply lifted her nose, which looked like an overripe tomato from the sun, and gave a disdainful sniff.

Cela didn't say a word, but she ducked her head and kept her eyes focused on the floor until they were gone. She couldn't hide her loathing, and it wouldn't do anyone any good to let them see it. She wished—and not for the first time—that Viola were there. Over the past few weeks, she'd found herself missing the prickly Italian, and for more reason than her ability to stop a heartbeat from ten paces.

She didn't let herself think too much about Jianyu—not about his quiet strength or the way he managed to lead without trying at all. She certainly didn't think about what it meant that he'd come running down the street to find them after the mess of the Flatiron Building. It was easier to believe that she'd imagined the way he'd looked at her, as though she were something rare and precious, especially because he hadn't made any move in the months since then. His notes were terse and impersonal, without any indication that deeper feeling ran through his words. So maybe she'd only seen what she'd wanted to. It was easier not to think about it at all.

She was too busy imagining what Viola could do to the bratty little boys and their awful parents to notice the men who didn't belong when she first stepped into the chambermaids' workroom. But the sound of the flat, guttural New York accents broke through her daydreaming, and she pulled up short just before she could be seen.

"You sure you haven't seen her around?" the man was asking. He and his partner were talking to a trio of maids, their backs turned to the door that Cela had just entered. "She might be going by a different name."

"A Negro girl who can sew?" Flora said, giving the men a doubtful look. "That description could match a dozen of the girls who work here."

"This one's on the darker side," the other man said, turning to examine the other women, as though sizing them up by the color of their skin.

Cela pulled back, ducking into one of the alcoves where the mops and brushes were usually stored, but not before she recognized one of the men. She'd seen him before—at the Morgans' gala and in the saloon she almost hadn't escaped from the night of the Manhattan Solstice. Razor Riley. A Five Pointer. And he was there in Atlantic City. Looking for *her*.

She didn't know whether to be relieved that she didn't have Newton's Sigils on her or worried about how safe they were hidden in the floorboard of the boardinghouse's fruit cellar.

He isn't magic, she reminded herself. He might be close, but he couldn't track her or the discs, not like Logan Sullivan could. And anyway, she had been waiting for something like this to happen for weeks now. She'd known all along it was only a matter of time before someone came looking for her.

From across the room, Hazel caught her eye and lifted a single, arched brow. Cela realized then it had been a mistake to keep to herself so much over the last couple of months. She shouldn't have been so standoffish.

herself back. There was a sort of safety here in their community. A sort of acceptance and welcome, too. She'd forgotten that somehow. "I'd love to come out for a while. Thank you."

"No thanks needed," Hazel said. Her mouth curled into a wry grin. "But you might could get Chef to make up a little something from what's left of the lunch service for the rest of us to share. You know he's sweet on you."

Cela felt her cheeks heat. She hadn't been unaware of the way one of the sous chefs watched her when she was near the kitchen. He was handsome, to be sure. Tall with a sharp jaw and skin the color of deep mahogany, he spoke with an accent that hinted of islands and reminded her of her mother's people. Considering her situation, she hadn't let herself imagine there could be anything between them. But now that these women had reminded her she still had a life to live while she waited for the future to unfold, she couldn't help but wonder . . .

"I think I can manage that," she said, unable to tuck back her smile.

Abel's train wouldn't be in until close to nine, she told herself as she changed out of the soiled uniform and back into her regular clothes. Abel was in contact with Joshua, who was keeping track of Jianyu's and Viola's whereabouts in the city, so it's not like she could do anything much until he arrived. She had plenty of time to venture to the beach for a quick swim and maybe even to flirt with the handsome chef. And if she happened to make some allies while she was there? So much the better.

The kitchens were in the basement at the rear of the hotel, far from where the guests could hear the noise or feel the heat of the ovens. The scent of yeasty bread and the brininess of seafood met her as she turned into the service hall. Her stomach growled in response, and she realized it had been hours since her small lunch of sturdy bread and stale cheese. She hoped Chef was in a generous mood.

She never had a chance to find out. As she started to turn the corner into the passageway of the kitchen, strong arms grabbed her from behind, and a wide hand covered her mouth.

TOGETHER OR NOT AT ALL

1983—Orchard Street

Harte could feel Esta starting to shake. Her eyes were fixed on the far side of the room, where the old man who had once been Nibsy Lorcan had turned the gun on himself.

"Dammit," she whispered. "Why did he—"

"Come on," he said, lifting Esta to her feet. The old man was dead. It didn't matter why he did it, because it didn't change anything. "We have to get moving, in case someone heard that gunshot and comes to investigate."

"It's New York in the 1980s, Harte. Nobody is going to investigate a gunshot." But she slipped her hand into his. "You're okay?" she asked, checking him over again.

"There was only one shot," he reminded her.

"Right." She looked back over her shoulder, hesitating.

He squeezed her hand softly, rubbing his thumb across her cool skin. "He's not worth your pity, Esta."

"I know," she said, but the look in her eyes told a different story. Then he watched as she visibly pulled herself together. "We should take the papers. We should take anything that might help us."

"Nothing he was willing to give us is going to help," Harte told her. "You know Nibsy. It's just more lies."

"You're probably right, but that doesn't mean we should leave it here for someone else to find." She released his hand, and Harte felt suddenly adrift. "You heard him. He thought we would take this back and hand it over to his younger self. Maybe he was willing to risk helping us if he thought it was the way to help himself."

"Or maybe it's another trap."

"Probably," she admitted. "But can you really walk away from the possibility of answers? He knew how to do the ritual that got Seshat out of you, Harte. What if he really did figure out how to use the power in the Book? What if those papers could help us finish this?"

He wanted to reach for her because he felt like she might slip away for good if he wasn't touching her. But he curled his fingers and tucked them at his side instead.

"Fine. But let's make it quick." Thanks to whatever that bit of magic was in the elevator, they were without their affinities. He'd feel better when they were out of the building.

Esta approached the desk slowly, but once there, she hesitated for only a second before taking the stack of papers trapped beneath the old man's lifeless arm. When she made it back to Harte's side, he could see that the edges of some of them were stained red with Nibsy's blood. He took them from her and tucked them into the satchel with everything else.

Together they descended the back stairs. All around them, the building was muffled in an almost oppressive silence, but once they stepped out the back and into the bright chill of the winter day, the noise of the city hit them like a wall.

"This way," Esta said, taking him by the hand again and heading toward the busier thoroughfare of Delancey Street, but they hadn't gone more than a block before Harte felt the clear sense that someone was watching.

Tossing a glance over his shoulder, he cursed softly when he saw two men walking a few hundred feet behind them. They weren't obviously police or Guardsmen, but something about them made Harte think of the authorities. Maybe it was the inky black filling their eyes. "I think we have company."

Esta paused long enough to pretend to look at the wares in a large shop window. But her eyes were focused on the reflection in the glass. "Cops," she said softly, pulling him onward.

"Worse than cops," Harte told her. "Did you see their eyes?" Her jaw tensed, and he knew she had.

"There's a subway station up ahead," she told him. "We have to get away from this neighborhood."

The thought of going back into the subway tunnels made him nearly stumble. "If we go underground, we'll be trapped."

"Not if we keep moving," she said. But he didn't miss the soft "I hope" that she muttered under her breath. "We need a distraction."

The nearest subway entrance was at the end of the next block. Harte didn't have to look back to know the men were still following them, but when they came to the entrance, Esta cut straight through the crowd of people standing nearby, huddled around a barrel of something that was burning. When they were in the middle of the crowd, Harte stopped abruptly and shoved himself backward into one of the men warming his hands over the fire, knocking the guy into someone else. The effect was instantaneous, but he was ready for it. By the time the man caught himself, Harte was already pulling Esta through the crowd, leaving the men to turn on one another.

She gave him a bright, sharp smile and tugged him onward down the slush-covered steps.

Like the other stations, this one reeked of urine and trash, but in a stroke of brilliant luck, a train was already there, waiting. Together, they hopped the turnstiles and slid in just as the doors closed. Harte looked back through the graffiti-covered windows in time to see that the two black-eyed men had arrived at the station, but the train was already pulling away before the men could reach it.

The car was packed. The air was humid and warmer than the cold winter streets above, filled with the combined scents of too many bodies, cologne, stale smoke, and something mechanical. But the crowd wasn't enough to keep them safe.

Harte braced himself against one of the metal poles as the train picked up speed and leaned in to whisper into Esta's ear. "They saw us." The Guard or police—whoever the men were—knew what train they were on and which direction they were traveling.

Their faces were close, and even with the thick, fetid air around them, the light floral scent of the soap she'd been using back in Chicago tickled his nose.

"It doesn't matter," she said. "We're not staying here. Follow me."

Harte held tightly to Esta's hand as she dragged him through the press of bodies toward the rear of the car. When they arrived, she slid the door open, letting in a burst of air and noise. Harte turned to make sure no one was following. But if he'd worried at all that someone was watching and might try to stop them, he quickly realized no one cared. The other passengers kept their eyes forward or down, resolutely ignoring whatever was happening at the back of the train. This New York, for all its changes, wasn't so different from his own time, it seemed.

Quickly they moved across the swinging platform and then through the next car. It was packed, but slightly less so, and they made better time passing through the crowd and out the back end of the car. The train rounded a bend, its wheels squealing, as they arrived at the final car on the line. The crowd was lighter there, and Esta led them through the car and out the rear doors until they were standing on the platform at the back. There was nowhere else to go.

"We need to get off before it enters the station," she told him. "It'll slow when it approaches the next stop, but you have to watch out for the third rail when you jump."

She couldn't be serious. "The what?" He could barely hear her over the noise of the tunnel.

"Third. Rail," she shouted, pointing to the right side of the track. "There. It's electrified. You touch it, and you die."

He looked up at her but saw in less than a heartbeat that she was serious. This time, there was no hidden station, no platform to land on. She wanted him to jump from the train? Only a few hours before, he'd been planning on doing the same thing without any hope of surviving, and now she expected them to not only survive but to land without hitting an electrified part of the track? "Esta, no. This is insane. We can't—"

"How's your affinity? Because mine is dead right now," she said, her expression bunching with frustration. "The men following us back there—*whoever* they were—are going to know there are only two directions heading out of the last station. They'll have people waiting at both stops for us. This is our only chance, Harte." She was already climbing over the back railing of the car. "We can do this."

He wasn't so sure, but there was no choice except to follow her. Once they were both hanging from the back of the car, he looked over to find her staring out into the darkness of the tunnel behind them. Her short hair was whipping around her face, and her jaw was set.

She's afraid. For all her bluster and bravado, he knew by the way she was holding herself—stiff and apart from him—that she wasn't sure this would work.

"There has to be another way," he shouted, willing her to turn to him. To hear him.

She only shook her head. "It's slowing," she said. Finally, she looked at him, and her golden eyes were glinting with determination. "When I say go, you jump first."

"No," he said, moving his hand over so it covered hers. "We go together or not at all."

Her mouth pressed into a tight line, but she nodded. "Together, then. Ready?"

"Not even a little—"

"Now!" she shouted, and together they released the car and tumbled down onto the track.

TRUTH AND LIES

1983—Beneath the City

The instant Esta released the subway car and began to fall, she realized that maybe she'd made a mistake. The tracks were farther down than she'd expected, and she had plenty of time to regret her choices before she hit the unyielding ground below. She landed hard enough to knock the breath from her lungs and make her teeth rattle. Ignoring the pain, she wrenched herself into a ball and rolled away from the deadly third rail.

As the train traveled off to the station, the sound of its squealing brakes receded along with it, but it took a few seconds until she could breathe again.

Nearby, Harte groaned, and she forced herself to sit up, despite the sharp ache coming from the side she'd landed on. "Are you okay?" she asked, pulling herself to her feet and looking back in the direction the train had come from.

The tunnel wasn't completely pitch-black. Every hundred feet or so a fluorescent emergency light projected an unhealthy glow on the tunnel walls. The pattern of dark and light created a trail leading off into the distance.

"We have to get moving before another train comes," she told him, reaching for her magic and still finding it dead. "I think I saw a service tunnel that branched off a little ways back."

Together they stumbled down the track, listening for the telltale rumble of an approaching train. Finally, they found the tunnel. The jaundice-yellow lights lining its walls barely cut through the gloom.

"You don't think they'll search the tunnels once they realize we're not on the train?" Harte asked as they paused in the narrow opening.

"Let's hope we're out of here before they find us," she told him. "Come on."

They made their way into the gloom of the smaller service tunnel until the fluorescent glow of the main tunnel was no longer visible. A train passed by in the distance, making the ground shiver.

"Hopefully we can avoid the Guard, at least until our affinities return."

"What if they don't return completely?" Harte asked, voicing the question that had been worrying Esta since the blast of ice had drained her power. "What if Nibsy's done something to corrupt our magic?"

"They will." *They have to.* Without her affinity, they couldn't return to the past. "Nibsy needs us in 1902," she reminded him. "We're no good to him here—especially now. He wouldn't have done anything to jeopardize our ability to go back."

Harte grunted. She didn't need to see his face to know he wasn't feeling nearly as confident as she had just sounded.

She wished that *she* were as confident as she'd just sounded.

But Esta had to believe that she was right. The old man had only turned the gun on himself to make a point: *This* life didn't matter. This version of history was nothing to him.

"I can practically hear you thinking over there," Harte said. He spoke softly, but the darkness amplified his voice.

She stopped, suddenly overwhelmed by everything, and after a second she felt him step closer, felt him reach for her. His fingers brushed along her neck, finding her face in the darkness. He cupped her cheek gently with one hand, and she stepped into him as he pulled her closer with his free arm.

"Are *you* okay?" he asked, giving her words back to him.

"I will be." It wasn't a lie, but she was glad for the darkness. It was easier to pretend to be strong when he couldn't see the doubt on her face.

"We don't need our affinities," she told him, but it felt like she was really trying to convince herself.

He huffed his disagreement.

"I'm not saying they wouldn't be helpful," she said. "But we're more than our magic, Harte. We always have been. For now we just need to keep moving."

He didn't respond, neither to argue nor to agree.

"For example, we don't need magic to get out of these tunnels," she said, trying to remember one of the many lessons of her youth. She'd studied everything about the city, including the tunnels and rivers that lay beneath the modern streets. Professor Lachlan had prepared her for everything—maybe even for this.

"We don't?"

She stepped back from him. "No, we don't," she said, finally getting her bearings. "This way."

They walked for what felt like an eternity, stopping so Esta could consider their options any time they came to another place where the tunnels branched off. But her knowledge of the tunnels was more theoretical than practical. She couldn't be sure she was taking the right turns.

For a while they didn't speak. It had been only a few hours since they'd crossed the bridge back into the city, but enough had happened to fill entire days. The darkness of the tunnels and the comforting silence between them gave Esta time to think, to realize exactly how much they'd just been through. But one thought—one question—kept rising to the surface.

"How did you know?" she asked. Esta didn't specify what she meant, but Harte seemed to understand immediately.

"You mean, how did I know that it wasn't you?" He let out a long breath. "There were a lot of reasons. The fact that her arm was scarred and healed over was the thing that confirmed it. But that wasn't what made me suspect at first."

"What was?"

He didn't immediately answer. Instead, the crunch of gravel beneath their feet filled the space of words. When he finally spoke, his voice was softer and, despite still having her hand in his, he sounded farther away. "She told me that she loved me."

"And you didn't believe her," Esta said, her stomach twisting with some emotion that she didn't want to name.

"No," Harte said. "I didn't."

"Because . . . you don't believe that I do?"

Harte stopped suddenly. For a long, terrible moment, he didn't speak. But then he took her other hand in his. It was so dark in that part of the tunnel that even with her eyes acclimated to the lack of light, Esta could barely make out the features of his face. But she felt him breathing, steady and slow. Felt the warmth of his hands around hers, sure and steady. "No," he said. "That isn't it at all."

"Then what?" she asked, suddenly uneasy. "You didn't want her— me—to say it, or . . . ?" She tried to pull away, but he didn't let her go.

He let out an amused breath, and she felt the warmth flutter across her face. "That's not it either." There was a smile in the words that had impatience lashing at her.

"Then *what?*"

"She only said those words to prove herself to me," he told her. "But I *know* you, Esta. You've never used what we have between us to prove anything. You've *never* thrown love at me as a weapon."

She frowned, thinking of how they'd first met. Thinking too of the nights in the theater, when she had tried to seduce him for Dolph's cause. "I don't know that we're remembering things the same way."

"I'm not saying you didn't try to tempt me, especially back when we were still at odds," he said wryly, the humor in his words coming clearly through the darkness. "But I knew all along that it was nothing more than simple misdirection."

"Not *so* simple," she argued. But there was no heat in her words, because he was right. Esta might have tried to lure him in, but she never would have toyed with something as serious as love. Especially not once she really knew him. She might be a thief, but she had grown up feeling unwanted. So had he. She never would have used their connection as a weapon against him.

"You've never lied to me about anything that really mattered, especially not when it came to what this is between us." He lifted her hand to his lips, and she felt the warmth of his mouth brushing her knuckles. "Even then, even though Nibsy raised you to be ruthless and effective, you had far too much integrity for those kinds of games. And now?" He kissed her knuckles again. "You know you don't need to prove anything to me, especially not about how you feel. We've been through too much together. You are not negotiable. *We* are not negotiable. That's all there is to it."

His words warmed her. But suddenly his belief in her—in *them*—felt like an overwhelming weight. When had anyone given her that sort of trust so blindly?

Never.

And he was wrong. She had lied, and recently, too. It had been such a stupid, seemingly insignificant lie, but now, with his words wrapping around her, it felt like a wound between them. After everything that had just happened? She couldn't leave it there to fester.

"There's something I have to tell you." She bit her lip, feeling embarrassed and stupid and awful all at once. Harte didn't respond, so she had no choice but to go on. "Back in Chicago . . ." She paused, not knowing how to start.

"Esta?" he asked when she hesitated long enough that the silence had made it too difficult to start again.

"Back in Chicago, I told you something that wasn't completely true." She let out a breath, not knowing why it felt so hard to just say it. "I told you there hadn't been any"—she used his word for it—"*consequences*. To what happened on the train."

Harte didn't respond immediately, and the silence between them had weight now. There was distance within that silence too. "I don't understa—"

"I won't know for a week at least," she blurted.

Again, the silence. The distance. She couldn't quite draw breath, and it had nothing to do with the ache in her ribs. The tightness in her chest went deeper than that.

"You lied," he said—it wasn't a question. "About *that?*"

She wished she could see his face. Why had she thought that darkness would make this confession easier? "Only about knowing," she told him. "I still don't think anything happened. The timing was wrong, and the chances are so slim, and—" She was doing this all wrong. "I didn't think you'd let me do what I needed to do if you were worried about . . . *that.*"

"You thought I would want to protect the child, if there was one." He was standing right next to her, but he sounded so far away.

She nodded, then realized he couldn't see her. "I was worried, but I was wrong. I never should have told you anything until I knew for sure. I don't want that lie between us. I want what you said just now to be true. I don't want *any* more lies between us, especially not about things that matter. And what we have, Harte?" She gave his hands a squeeze. "*This?* It matters."

He pulled away from her, leaving her hands cold. She suddenly wasn't sure what to do with them.

"I'm sorry," she said, wishing it were enough.

He didn't speak. In the distance, the tunnels vibrated, and suddenly she wished she had just swallowed the secret. Or maybe the city could just swallow her up.

"As soon as I told you, I regretted lying. I was going to tell you the truth, but then everything went south and—" She stopped. "I just needed you to see me as an equal, and not like some soft, pointless creature you needed to protect. It's not an excuse. It's not meant as one. But you deserve an explanation. I knew how dangerous it was going into the convention, and I needed you to know I could do whatever it took. I didn't want you to stop me."

"You really think I could have?" he asked. "I know you can do anything."

"After what happened on the train . . ." She felt her cheeks warm with the thought of his hands on her skin, the way they fit together. "When we were together, it was more than just physical. It wasn't something I could laugh off or walk away from, and you bringing up the possibility that it was a mistake?"

"Not a mistake," he said, brushing his fingers against hers again. "Not ever a mistake."

"No," she agreed. "Not a mistake. But you were acting like I was a problem to be solved, and I hated it."

"It was more than just physical for me too, Esta."

His words lifted a little of the weight she'd been carrying. "Things are different where I'm from, Harte. I don't need you to take care of me like that, and I didn't want anything to change between us because of it. From the way you were talking back in Chicago, I was afraid things already had."

Silence sprang up between them again, and Esta had to stop herself from filling it with her own words. She'd said enough. The ball was in his court now.

"I hate that you lied to me," he told her softly. "Especially about that."

"I know," she said. "I'm sorry, Harte. I—"

"But I understand why you did," he said. "I was an idiot."

She couldn't stop the bark of surprised laughter from escaping, but he was still talking.

"I see that now," he told her. "I was so overwhelmed by what had happened between us, and I didn't know what to do with any of it. I know things are different where you came from. I've seen glimpses of that world in the past few weeks. But it's not the world I grew up in, and after everything that happened, I just couldn't let myself become my father."

"You're *not*," she said fiercely, wishing she could see him. "You never would be."

"I know," he said with a small, humorless laugh. "I realized that back in San Francisco, but it didn't stop me from reacting on instinct. I made a mess of things."

"It wasn't just you," she admitted.

He kissed her then without warning and with an urgency that felt almost desperate, and she responded in kind. When their lips met, the last of the weight lifted, and suddenly she was flying. Harte's breath mixed with hers, the only air she needed. His hands were in her hair, angling her closer to deepen the kiss, and as she opened for him—with him—the heat of their mouths, the taste of him, overwhelmed her.

This kiss was a claiming, a homecoming. A match of wills and a promise of more. His hands framed her face, glided down the heated skin of her neck to her shoulders. One hand went to her waist, anchoring her to him, while the other traced the angle of her collarbone so softly that she thought she might die from wanting. They were trapped in an uncertain future, stuck in the muck and darkness of the underground, and it didn't matter. All she needed was this—Harte's mouth tangling with hers, his arms around her, and his hands on her skin. The friction of his fingertips brushing against her skin was perfect.

It was un*bearable*.

His teeth nipped at her lip, and she suddenly couldn't be close enough to him. She needed more. She didn't want anything between them any longer—no lies or regrets or even wanting. Covering his hand with her own, she showed him, helped him along by guiding him lower, until his hand was tracing down over her chest, to the curve of her breast beneath the rough overalls she was wearing, and she felt him deepen the kiss on a groan. But there was too much damn fabric between them. His hands were on her, but it wasn't enough. He was already working at the buttons at her neck and finally he slipped beneath the fabric. The rough pads of his fingers felt like flames tracing across her skin, and she could not stop herself from gasping.

Harte went still. "God, Esta." His voice broke as he pulled his hand away, leaving her feeling suddenly bereft. But his chest was heaving the same as hers. "We shouldn't be doing this."

"Yes," she said, stepping toward him. "Yes, we should."

But the moment had broken already. "I watched you *die*."

"Not me," she said softly, her heart aching a little at the pain in his voice. "You knew it wasn't me." That fact alone felt miraculous, more precious than any treasure she could steal.

"I knew it wasn't you," he agreed. "Deep down, I knew. If I truly thought that girl was you, I would have died in that ritual circle with you. But, Esta, she looked *so* much like you." He reached for her then, framed her face with his hands so gently it brought tears to her eyes. "All I wanted in Chicago was for you to survive. I would have done anything—*said anything*—to make you want to go on, even if I wasn't with you. I never meant to bring up what happened on the train as a way to make you feel smaller. I know I can't protect you—that you don't *need* me to. And it destroys me. But the thought of you still in this world, surviving? That's all I need. That's all I want."

She kissed him then, rising just slightly on her toes to press her mouth against his once more. She meant for the kiss to be brief, but he leaned into it. Deepened it in a way that made her heart race again. It didn't matter that the tunnel smelled of dampness and rot or that she could hear something scurrying in the distance. There was only Harte. Only a perfect new understanding between them.

Breathless again but settled now in a way she hadn't been before, she pulled away. "You're right. We shouldn't do this," she told him, fastening the buttons again with a small smile. "At least not here." She slipped her hands into his. "If I didn't make a wrong turn, the exit should be just around the next bend."

He pulled her closer and pressed another small kiss on the sensitive skin of her neck, just below her ear, and then together they continued on, her head spinning a little from the kiss.

They turned a corner and saw the access door ahead, bathed in the yellowish glow of an emergency light. "Ready to get out of here?" She pulled out Viola's dagger. "You want to do the honors?" she asked, offering it to Harte.

He gave her a small smile, but he'd barely reached for it when that smile slid from his face. He didn't take the blade. "Where are you hurt?"

"What?" she asked, confused at his meaning. But his words seemed to shake something free in her. All at once, she felt the throbbing ache in her side again from where she'd landed after jumping off the train. "I'm fine," she said, refusing to acknowledge the pain.

"You're not fine, Esta," he said, holding up his hand so she could see the dark smear of blood that stained his fingers and palm. "You're bleeding."

TO SKIN A FOX

1902—Uptown

Viola paced around the parlor of the small apartment above the *New York Age*'s offices and print shop, where she and Jianyu had been staying since they'd sent Cela away. She tried not to think of the minutes that had already passed. Jianyu should have been back by long before now.

She hated waiting in the cramped set of rooms while Jianyu went out to search for answers to the question of Newton's Sigils. She would rather have gone with him. With Nibsy in control of the marks, it wouldn't do for them both to be caught. This way, at least, should one of them be found by Nibsy or the Order—or any of the factions that might be hunting for them—the other could go on. Because someone needed to warn the Johnsons and wait for Harte and Esta. Someone would remain to continue fighting.

The door swung open suddenly, and Viola startled to her feet, a knife already in her hand, before she realized it wasn't an attack. The soft warmth of the old magic brushed against her skin as Jianyu appeared in the open doorway.

"Where have you been?" she demanded.

"We need to find Joshua," he said at the same time. "We need to send word to Cela as well. To anyone who could keep her safe."

His words brushed away whatever comforting warmth his magic had just created and replaced it with an icy feeling of dread. Viola lowered the knife that had already been aimed at Jianyu's heart at the same time she registered the panic and fear in his eyes. "What are you talking about?"

"Nibsy knows where Cela is," Jianyu said, his voice tight with a fury that Viola had rarely heard there. He closed the door solidly behind him and latched it for good measure. He was breathing heavily, as though he'd run across the city, and he leaned now against the back of a chair, trying to catch his breath.

"No," she told him, unwilling to believe what he was telling her. "That's not possible."

Jianyu's expression grew grim. "We have to send word to Joshua. She must be warned."

Viola shook her head. "Joshua, he left yesterday, remember? He'll be gone for three weeks."

"Then we must find another messenger," Jianyu said. She'd never seen him so frantic.

"Jianyu, slow down," she told him gently. "How could Nibsy have found Cela?"

"Your brother's men," Jianyu told her, looking more than a little disgusted. "He used the Five Pointers. He's sending them after her."

She knew that Nibsy and the Five Pointers had an alliance, but Johnny the Fox hadn't worked to claim command over Paul Kelly's gang only to hand his power to a boy. Especially not when the Fox hated Mageus every bit as much as her brother. "Why would Torrio follow Nibsy Lorcan's orders?"

"I do not know," Jianyu said, looking more shaken than Viola had ever seen him.

Because he cares for Cela.

"Are you sure Nibsy knows? Are you sure he isn't bluffing?" she asked

Jianyu raked his hand through already disheveled hair and shook his head. "He would not lie about such a thing."

"Of *course* he would," Viola told him. "Nibsy would lie about anything if he thought it would help him get his way."

"He knows she is in Atlantic City, Viola."

Dread curled in her stomach. If Nibsy knew that, he already knew too much.

"What if this is nothing more than a trap?" Viola asked, trying desperately for some other explanation. "Atlantic City, it's a big place, no? Maybe he don't know so much as he says. Maybe he wants us to run like scared rabbits and warn her, so his men, they can follow."

"We cannot take that chance," he told her, worry coloring his sharp features.

She understood what he was feeling. *Madonna*, did she understand. Hadn't she felt the same way when she saw Ruby being attacked by that terrible stone beast at Morgan's gala? She'd felt so helpless, so *desperate*, that she'd acted on impulse and skewered Jianyu with her blade by accident. She wouldn't let him rush in and make the same kind of foolish mistake now.

"Abel will be back soon," she reminded him. "We expect him tomorrow with news."

"Tomorrow may be too late." Jianyu ran a hand through his short hair, making himself look even more disheveled and harried. "I found the information about using the sigils. I had it in my hands. And then Nibsy . . ."

She understood immediately. Nibsy had the marks. "What could you have done? What can any of us do against the marks?"

Jianyu's mouth went tight. "I should have died to defend it."

"If Nibsy Lorcan wanted you dead, he would have made it so," Viola said, trying not to let her own fear show through her words. "He's up to something." Nibsy never would have let Jianyu go if he truly had everything he needed. "We must be careful not to rush and fall into his traps. We must think. *Plan*."

"Cela's safety cannot wait for that," Jianyu said, shoving aside the chair he'd been leaning on. "Not when the sigils can be used to open a doorway—a passage—out of the Brink."

"No. Non é possibile." She shook her head, refusing to believe something so preposterous. "Dolph, he would have known this. He would have wanted them, along with the Book of Mysteries."

Jianyu leaned against the door, his head tipped back. "Dolph was focused only on the Book," he reminded her. "You saw his journal, just as I did. There was no mention of Newton's Sigils. If he had known about them, the information would have been there."

A pounding came at the door, causing Jianyu and Viola both to jump. She reached for Libitina—an instinct she couldn't quite quit—before she realized the voice calling on the other side was familiar. A friend.

"Viola? Jianyu? You all in there?" Abel called, as the pounding came again.

Jianyu let out a breath at the sound of Abel's voice, and Viola heard her own relief echoed in it. Abel was back earlier than they'd expected him. He could get to Cela. Her brother was not trapped, as they were. He could protect her.

"Thank god," Viola said, dizzy with relief as Jianyu opened the door.

But when Abel stepped into the room, the look on his face turned Viola's relief to dread.

"She's gone." His voice broke as he stumbled into the room. "Her landlady said Cela didn't come home last night, and her room looked like it had been ransacked."

She met Jianyu's eyes again, and they exchanged a silent look of under-standing before she turned back to Abel. "We'll get your sister back," she vowed.

"We cannot go after Nibsy," Jianyu told her. "Not with the marks—"

"I'm not going after that snake," Viola said. "Not yet. First, I'm going to go skin myself a fox."

LISA MAXWELL

MORE THAN MAGIC

1983—Times Square

Harte looked down at Esta's blood coating his hand and cursed himself for not realizing that she was hurt. Just seconds ago, that same hand had been touching her in places that, once, he'd only dared dream of. He'd forgotten that they were trapped underground in the filthy darkness of a foul-smelling tunnel filled with who knew what kind of vermin. Once his mouth had touched hers, once his hands had found the soft curve of her waist, none of that had mattered. Nothing had mattered but Esta.

Now he felt like the worst kind of ass. Because she was clearly hurt, and badly, from the amount of blood.

"I'll be okay, Harte." She tugged at her clothes to see where the blood was coming from, but when she twisted, she couldn't stop herself from sucking in a sharp breath.

"Come on," he told her, taking her by the hand and moving toward the doorway that promised to be an exit. He didn't even care what—or *who*—might be waiting as he forced Viola's dagger into the jamb and wrenched the lock in two.

On the other side of the door, they found a small, windowless room with another door. He made quick work of that lock as well, and then they were out. Free. Or, maybe not free, exactly. It was another of the subterranean stations, and there were people *everywhere*. Luckily, no one seemed to care that they'd just emerged from some kind of service door. One or two people might have tossed disinterested looks their way, but for the most part, no one paid them any attention at all.

Harte blinked at the sudden brightness, trying to make sense of the chaotic crowd around him, as Esta took charge.

"This way," she told him, apparently not thrown off by the noise and crush of the people around him. "It's rush hour. That should give us some cover." She tugged him onward through the crowd.

There was a battered mosaic on the wall that told Harte where they were: *Times Sq-42nd St*. Forty-Second Street, he understood, even if the crowds in the subway station didn't make sense this far uptown. That area had been mostly train tracks leading to the Grand Central Depot in the city he had known. And he didn't have any idea what a Times Square was.

But he didn't have long to ponder it before they emerged from the closeness of the subway station into the impossible brightness of enormous buildings covered in lights. Gone was the Forty-Second Street he had known. Gone were the brick streets and carriages of his own time. In their place, a strange new city had erupted. Buildings soared stories above him, and traffic poured by in a constant stream of boxy vehicles, many of which were painted a garish yellow.

He hadn't realized his feet had stopped and that he was standing in the middle of the crowded sidewalk until he felt Esta tugging on his hand.

"I know it's a lot, but keep moving," she told him gently.

She was right. If no one had paid any attention when the two of them had emerged from a maintenance tunnel in the station, people were noticing now. An older man in a heavy overcoat and a sharply brimmed hat glared at him and muttered something about *tourists* as he shoved by.

They joined the river of people moving along the sidewalks beneath the lit canopies of what seemed like a million marquees. There had always been theaters in New York, but not like this. Even Satan's Circus hadn't had lights like this . . . or *shows* like this, Harte thought, feeling his cheeks heat as he read the flashing lights advertising peep shows and barely clad girls, twenty-four-hour theaters and "burlesk." A large silver bus rumbled past, its graffiti-marred windows mostly concealing the tired-looking people within as it spewed a cloud of dark exhaust to mingle with the cigarette smoke already hanging in the air.

Harte coughed, his eyes watering from the bus's noxious fumes as he tried to keep pace with Esta. They crossed one street, then another, and then she stopped suddenly.

"No," she told him, looking completely rattled. "This isn't right."

They were standing in a wedge-shaped plaza in the middle of traffic. Vehicles streamed around them, and now that they paused, Harte could see that the small lit signs on top of the yellow automobiles said "taxi." Standing there in the middle of traffic felt a little like standing in the middle of a stampede, but Esta was unmoved by the bustle and speed around them. She was too busy looking up at a statue that glinted warmly in the setting sun.

Jack.

It wasn't the best likeness of him, but even with the too-broad shoulders, the too-strong jaw, and even without needing to read the placard below, Harte recognized the attempt to represent Jack Grew.

"This should be George M. Cohen," Esta said, horror clear in her voice.

"One of the Vaudeville troupe?" Harte asked, confused. The Cohen family had been a staple on the circuit, but none of them had been famous or important enough to warrant a statue. Especially not one this large or prominent.

Esta didn't answer. She was still staring up at Jack's image cast in something that looked suspiciously like gold. Then, slowly, she turned her head from side to side, taking in the city around her. Her hand tightened on Harte's as she let out a curse that would have made a sailor blush.

He turned and found what she was looking at. There was a wedge-shaped building across the street from them emblazoned with the directive to "Drink Coca-Cola." It was twice the size of any billboard he'd ever seen, far larger even than the one Wallack's had put up for his show.

But Harte understood that the advertisement wasn't what made Esta curse. Twenty or so feet above the street, words made from light chased around the building. They moved like magic, though he suspected it was a simple matter of electricity.

They weren't the only ones who were watching the words scroll past. Around them, others had paused to watch, reading what seemed to be the news of the day. And the news of the day was them.

Escaped unregistereds. Last seen in Bowery Station. Considered extremely dangerous.

"They're looking for us," he said.

Her jaw was set as she nodded. "I knew they would be, but . . . this isn't right," she told him. But he had the sense that she wasn't talking about the risqué signage all around him. "That statue of Jack—" She glanced over at him. "It's not supposed to be like this. He's not supposed to be anyone."

The sign above the words changed suddenly, like magic.

No, not magic, Harte realized. It was a sign made from slats of wood that had rotated to evolve into a new image. Now, instead of Coca-Cola, it displayed an image that looked unmistakably like the banner that had flown from the Coliseum back in Chicago: the Philosopher's Hand. The image shifted again, but this time not from any mechanical manipulation. Like the banner in Chicago, the image *was* enchanted somehow.

Esta cursed again as their faces looked down on the bustling streets from above. The whole street seemed to pause, holding its breath. Excited murmuring whipped through the crowd around them. Suddenly Harte was acutely aware of the dark-suited police officers standing on a corner nearby.

"We have to go," Esta said. She pulled him through the crowd and across the street, dodging the traffic that was slowly inching around the square, but Harte felt more than one set of eyes upon them as they left.

He glanced down at her, saw her skin pale in the bright daylight and noticed the tear in the heavy overalls she was wearing and the dark stain spreading around it. "We can't just keep running. You're still bleeding, Esta."

"I know." She swallowed hard, and he could instantly see the pain she'd been hiding from him. "We need supplies. And we need to find a place to lie low until we figure things out." When she looked up at him, her golden eyes were tight. "But I don't know where to go. I can't quite feel my affinity yet. I don't know what to do other than to keep moving."

Harte reached for his magic, but he couldn't *quite* sense anything more than the faraway feeling that his affinity was still there. Just out of reach. "Me neither. But it's like you said, we're more than our magic."

Her lips pressed tightly together, and he could practically hear her thinking. Finally, she came to some conclusion. "You're right. We'll just have to do this the hard way."

When the light changed, she tugged him across the street through the press of suited bodies that smelled of cologne and sweat. They followed the crowd along the sidewalk, moving with the tide of pedestrians uptown for a block or two as Harte tried not to run into any of the peddlers selling handbags and trinkets on the edge of the sidewalks.

Esta handed him something that seemed to be a hat declaring that he loved NY. "Put it on. The bill goes in the front."

He did as she instructed, pulling the broad brim low over his forehead as she slipped on a pair of dark glasses she hadn't possessed a second before.

"Where did you—"

"Thief. Remember?" she said, tossing him a sharp-toothed smile. If he didn't know her so well, he might have missed the pain and tightness bracketing her mouth. "Come on. I think I see a pharmacy up there. It'll have what we need."

The shop was like nothing he'd ever seen before—not even in 1950s San Francisco. The lights felt brighter. The products more garishly colorful. The whole store smelled of bleach or some other sort of astringent and stale air.

Grabbing a brightly colored basket from a stack by the door, Esta dragged him past row after row of metal shelving filled with a dizzying array of products. Occasionally, she would toss something into the basket. When they reached an aisle with packages emblazoned with red crosses, she grabbed even more, tossing items into the basket without seeming to consider her choices.

Harte followed wordlessly, overwhelmed by the abundance and astounded at the lack of shopkeepers. One surly-looking woman glared at them as she stocked shelves at a slow, plodding pace, but she didn't offer to help. She glanced away just as quickly as she'd noticed them. He'd never seen a pharmacy where you could simply walk through and select your own merchandise. But he barely had time to marvel at the system before they'd reached the clerk at the front of the store. Esta placed the basket filled with supplies on the counter to be tallied up, and while the old man pushed buttons on a strange contraption that must have been a cash register, she tossed a couple of chocolate bars onto the counter. Somehow, he wasn't even a little surprised to see Esta pull out a leather wallet filled with cash as she waited for him to finish ringing them up.

The man looked up at his machine and started to read the total, but he paused. His eyes narrowed and then focused on something behind them. "Hey, wait a minute. . . ."

Harte turned and found himself face-to-face with . . . himself. The shelf behind him held newspapers, and he and Esta were there, right on the front page.

"You're them," the man said. "The maggots they're looking for." He backed away, fumbling for something under the counter, and somewhere in the distance, a siren started to wail.

THE ALGONQUIN

1980—Times Square

Ever since Harte had noticed that she was bleeding, the wound in Esta's side had been aching more and more, but when the clerk behind the counter recognized them, that pain fell away. From the way he was searching blindly under the counter, he'd probably already triggered a silent alert. She had to get them out of there, but her affinity was still fuzzy, and they needed the supplies.

"We're not—" she started, but the old man pulled out a gun before she could finish. It was a small snub-nosed pistol, but the size didn't matter much in such close quarters. He was already pointing it in their direction.

"Put your hands up," he demanded. "The reward for the two of you is dead or alive, so I don't care if I have to shoot you."

Esta felt Harte go still next to her, freezing at the sight of the gun, just as she had. She reached for her magic again, and she could *almost* grasp her affinity. But it still felt slippery and just beyond her reach.

"We don't want any trouble," Harte said as he lifted his hands. He was using his most charming voice, the one he'd used onstage when he wanted to entrance an audience.

"Then you should have stayed the hell out of our city," the old man sneered. All the while the sirens were drawing closer.

"We'll leave," she told him, wondering if she could still grab the basket as she backed away slowly. "We're going now."

"Like hell you are," the old man said, drawing back the hammer on the pistol as he aimed it toward Harte. "You're not getting away again.

Not after you kidnapped that poor girl and murdered her in the subway."

Esta knew what was about to happen. There was too much anger and hatred radiating from the clerk for him to stand down. Even without her affinity, time seemed to go slow. His thumb had already cocked the hammer of the gun. His finger was on the trigger, was easing it back.

On instinct, she leaped in front of Harte, pushing him aside as she reached once more for her affinity, and . . . *there*. This time her fingertips brushed along her magic, and she managed to pull the seconds slow just as she careened into Harte and knocked him to the floor.

Heat erupted through her arm. Her connection to the old magic already felt unsteady, but now it felt like holding a live wire. But she gritted her teeth against the discomfort and held tight.

With the world frozen around them, the sound of the gunshot echoed like a far-off cannon, long and low, and there was an icy energy coursing through her arm. Her affinity still felt too unsteady—too dangerous—to focus on anything but holding tight to the seconds. She closed her eyes and focused on her connection to the old magic, but it slipped from her fingers as another shot rang out. The linoleum tile shattered next to where they'd fallen.

"We have to go. *Now*," she told Harte through gritted teeth as she reached for the seconds again.

Her affinity was there, but the cold that had rocketed through her when the bullet grazed her was getting worse. The icy throbbing in her arm felt like it was radiating from the wound, numbing her and wreaking havoc on what little of her affinity she could sense. The seconds still felt slippery and wild, and she didn't know how long she could keep hold of them.

As Harte pulled her to her feet, he saw that the bullet had grazed her arm. "You're hit."

"I'm fine," she told him, brushing off the fear in his stormy eyes. It wasn't completely a lie. She'd been grazed by a bullet before, so she knew this one hadn't done any real damage to her body, but she couldn't shake the feeling that it had done something to her magic. Her arm burned like hell, if ice could burn, and the pain seemed to be spreading. She couldn't think too much about what that might mean, though—not until they were safe. "Get the basket of supplies."

Harte grabbed the plastic shopping basket, and then he ripped the gun from the clerk's hand for good measure. Together, they ran. Her arm screamed as she pushed open the heavy glass shop door, but she managed to keep hold of the seconds this time, despite the pain.

Outside, the streets around Times Square were frozen. People were halted mid-stride across busy intersections. The yellow flash of unmoving taxicabs dotted the crowded streets. Lights gleamed steadily, no longer flashing or twinkling. The persistent drone of the city, with its blaring horns and constant noise, was silent.

It was almost a comfort. Esta had done this so many times before. When things had gotten to be too much for her, when she needed a break—when she'd needed to feel in control of *something* in her life— she'd come to Times Square to watch the tourists take photos of every-thing and get swindled on fake Rolexes. She'd been just a kid then, but it had felt miraculous every time. Then, her magic had felt like a lifeline, the only thing that made sense. Now, with the tenuous grasp she had on the seconds, her affinity felt like a liability. They had to get moving.

She started walking without any idea about where they should go. There was a whole city they could hide in, but thanks to whatever tale Nibsy told the Guard, everyone was searching for them. Esta's mind raced, trying to think about where she was. *When* she was.

The subway wasn't an option, and neither was a taxi, so getting away from Times Square would be tricky. But there had to be somewhere they could hide for a while and regroup without anyone seeing them.

When they rounded the corner, they nearly ran into a trio of police-men frozen in time, and at the sight of them, Esta's magic slipped for just a second, and the world slammed back into motion. The noise of Times Square—squealing breaks and blaring horns and the drone of traffic and people—assaulted her. She saw the instant the police recognized them, but she couldn't quite grasp her magic.

"Run," she told Harte, ignoring her arm as she pulled him away from the police.

She could hear the cops behind her, shouting for the two of them to stop, but she plunged on, darting down the crowded sidewalks, dodging around pedestrians until—*there*—she finally managed to grasp the seconds.

The world went silent again, but she didn't stop tugging Harte onward through the tableau of now-frozen pedestrians. Her connection to the old magic felt even more unsteady than it had a moment before, and the ice in her arm was definitely spreading.

Then Esta realized where they could go. It was perfect. Times Square had changed dramatically since 1902, and most of the buildings that rose around them now hadn't been there at the beginning of the century. But she knew one that had. They could even slip back into the past without ever leaving, if they needed to.

"This way," she said, pulling Harte farther east along Forty-Fifth Street. They'd gone only a few yards when her magic slipped again, but this time no one seemed to notice that the two of them had basically just appeared out of nowhere. With the injury to her arm, she decided to let time spin on for a little while. She'd need her strength for what was coming next.

When they reached Sixth Avenue, they turned south and went one more block until she saw the cream stone and hunter-green awnings of the Algonquin Hotel. Despite all the changes in this part of town, the Algonquin had been a constant.

"Don't you think we should get away from this area?" Harte asked, frowning a little when she slowed to a stop in front of the hotel. He tossed a nervous look behind them.

"Probably," she admitted. "But running ourselves to exhaustion isn't going to help anything. It'll be safe enough here if we can get into a room without being seen."

Harte looked unsure until his gaze fell to her torn sleeve and the blood staining the side of the overalls. "Okay, then," he said. "If that's what you think."

She didn't want to know how bad she must look that he'd given in so easily. "How's your affinity?" she asked.

He shook his head. "Nothing but whispers. Not enough to risk anything."

It would have been nice to know that they could depend on Harte's magic to take care of any unexpected problems they might run into. If she could just keep hold of time, she could get them to safety, but her whole upper arm felt encased by ice now. Unsure what that meant, she worried instead about focusing on her affinity. Her connection to the old magic felt tenuous as the world when silent, and she had to grit her teeth to not lose hold of it. "Let's go."

They'd barely made it through the large, heavy doors when the seconds slipped from her grip and the soft sounds of the hotel wrapped around them. She reached for time again, but it took two tries before she was able to make the world go still.

Once they were through the entryway, the lobby of the Algonquin was all gleaming dark wood and luxury. Dark pillars flanked the space, reaching up to the ornately coffered ceiling above. Giant palms softened the overall impression of the room, creating cozy nooks around deep leather sofas and plush carpets. Esta would have given pretty much anything to collapse into one of those chairs and rest, but there wasn't time. Her connection to the old magic was still too unstable. She'd rest once they were in a room.

On one side of the space, golden elevator doors waited to take them up to safety, but Esta steered them to the other side of the lobby instead. There, the main check-in desk was staffed by two men in dark suits, and a yellow tiger cat sat on the counter, an unexpected sentinel sightlessly watching the still, silent room. She couldn't stop the seconds from slipping again as they approached the front desk, and she was sure the cat saw them before she could pull time tight.

Behind the counter, she found a small office. On one side, luggage was stacked and tagged, waiting for its owners, on the other side, the wall was covered by a large board with rows of metal pockets, like a filing system. Each of the pockets was labeled with numbers that corresponded to the floors of the hotel and the rooms they contained. A little of her worry eased. It would be easier to steal a room this way—like plucking that wallet filled with cash in Times Square had been easier. New York in the eighties might be gritty and dangerous, but it was also a city before computers had taken over. Before cameras watched the subway and credit cards were the most common currency. Cash, at least, was untraceable. Just as their use of a room would be.

"What are we doing back here, Esta?" Harte asked, frowning.

"We're getting a room," she told him.

He frowned. "We could have just picked a lock."

"Maybe," she agreed. "But this way no one will bother us."

It took her a minute to figure out the system, but once she did, it was easy enough to locate a room that still had a key hanging on the corresponding holder. She slipped the white notecard from the metal pocket, and with a pen she found on the counter, she wrote a false name on the card before placing it back into the corresponding room's slot. It looked like someone had been officially checked in now, so there wouldn't be any worry about an unexpected arrival. A Do Not Disturb sign on the door would take care of the rest.

She held up the key, feeling almost hopeful. But they were barely across the lobby when her head spun unexpectedly. Her connection to the old magic pulsed, sending a shock of heat through her, and she stumbled as she lost her grip on time again. She teetered on unsteady legs, but Harte was there to catch her. She didn't want to admit that his arms were the only thing holding her upright. Even once he set her back on her feet, she couldn't stop herself from leaning on him.

"Elevator," he growled, wrapping her closer to him and leading them both to the bank of golden doors.

EVERY WEAKNESS

1902—Bella Strega

James riffled through the stack of papers that Jianyu had been so generous to liberate from Morgan's mansion, but he couldn't quite believe what he was reading. He'd known J. P. Morgan was a collector, known as well that the Morgan mansion must have contained numerous secrets—he never would have maneuvered Dolph and Leena into infiltrating it otherwise. But he hadn't really expected *this*.

Never underestimate the ambition of men to dig their own graves.

He flipped over another sheet of paper and marveled at the secrets it contained. Line after line told the story of the men of the city, both past and present. Every weakness. Every possible indiscretion. Morgan, clearly, had been angling for more power for some time now. With this information at his disposal? He should have been able to claim the highest position in the Inner Circle. Had it not been for the bumbling mistakes of his nephew, perhaps he would have.

The collected scraps and bits of parchment told a history of the Order that was unlike any James had ever encountered. Here was evidence of their every victory and failure. It was a *true* accounting, rather than the narrative of half-truths and myths they currently wrapped themselves in.

The Aether danced when he picked up one of the sheets of parchment, an overlarge document compared to the others. Its ink had long ago browned and faded with age, but he knew at once that it was the most exciting—and perhaps the most important—of them all.

Newton's Sigils. There they were, clearly sketched on the page, just as

Werner and Logan had described them. According to the document, the thin discs were made of mercury, not silver. The Sigil of Ameth had been carved into their surface, just as it appeared in the painting of Newton with the Book that currently hung over the bookcase.

Here at last were the answers he had been searching for: the sigils could be used as a key. They could be used to get through the Brink.

It wasn't their original intent. Newton had designed them to neutralize the power of the Book. He'd infused them with some of his own power, because *Newton had been Mageus.*

He hadn't been a Sundren searching for power that wasn't his to claim, as the story went. No, he'd had a connection to the old magic already, but genius that he was, he'd learned that he could harness *more.* Just as alchemists sought to transform lead into gold, Newton understood that the Ars Arcana contained a piece of old magic, a shard so pure that it could transform *him.*

Myth and legend called what he was attempting to do to the philosopher's stone, the key to eternal life. But these documents made it clear that the philosopher's stone wasn't an object. It was a ritual that gave victory over *time* itself. But Newton had never finished that ritual. Something had happened. He hadn't been strong enough to look into the fire and live. He'd nearly gone mad from what the ritual had done to his affinity, so he'd fashioned the sigils to contain and neutralize the power in the Book.

With them, he created a space where the Book's power could be constrained.

Newton had given the Book of Mysteries and the artifacts to the men who would form the Order. He'd given them the sigils as well, a safeguard against the Book's power.

A hundred years later and those men had forgotten the danger in those pages. They had only remembered the promise. They either forgot the risk or believed themselves stronger than Newton, and they'd used the Book and the artifacts. They too failed in completing the ritual and created the Brink instead. Too late, the forefathers of the Order realized their error and found themselves trapped within a boundary of their own making. But they still had the sigils. And they found a way to use them.

He'd known that Cela Johnson's location would be important—the Aether had pushed him toward her and the objects she was hiding. But James hadn't imagined how essential the sigils could be.

With them, he could control the Brink.

More importantly, with them, he could control *Esta*—and with her affinity, he could finally claim the power of the Book for his own.

A knock came at the door, but the clock on the shelf told James that it was far too early for news of the sigils' location. Tucking the papers back into the leather envelope, he called for whoever it was on the other side to wait. Then, after Morgan's papers were secured, he opened the door to find Logan on the other side.

"Razor Riley is downstairs in the Strega," Logan said, looking clearly uncomfortable about this news. "He's asking for you."

"Why?" James sensed the Aether bunching somewhere far off, but the vibrations were steadily growing. Something was coming. Something new was happening, and whatever it was, it left him feeling uneasy.

Logan shrugged. "He wouldn't say. He wants to talk to you."

"Fine." He locked up the apartment and led the way down to the saloon.

Just as Logan had said, Razor Riley was waiting near the bar along with one of the other Five Pointers, Itsky Joe. Razor always looked like he was on the edge of exploding, but Joe looked uncomfortable. The shifty way their eyes took in the barroom, the defensive hunch to their shoulders, told him that the premonition he'd felt earlier hadn't been wrong.

Catching their attention from across the room, James gave a jerk of his head for them to follow him to his usual table. He sat with his back safely against the wall while they stood before him. He didn't bother to invite them to sit.

"I hope you're bringing me good news from Atlantic City?" He cocked a brow in their general direction expectantly.

Razor Riley was older than James by at least a decade, probably more. He had an ugly face made worse by a nose that had been broken one too many times. He might have been a large guy, a bruiser as good with a knife as he was with his fists, but he wasn't all that bright, not like Johnny the Fox. Yet next to Itsky Joe, Riley seemed like an actual genius.

Neither of them spoke at first, and James watched as they exchanged nervous looks. "You were stationed there, weren't you, Joe? I thought Torrio told me he'd sent you personally to watch the Johnson girl?"

Joe glanced at Razor Riley, but it was Itsky Joe who spoke. "Look, Lorcan, I'm gonna cut to the chase. Joe here'd been watching the girl for the last week, just like he was supposed to, but today she didn't come out of the hotel after her normal shift. We looked everywhere for her. She's gone."

"What do you mean she's gone?" James demanded, trying to keep his voice cold and level as he stared at the two men across from him.

"He means she's gone. She wasn't in the hotel, and she never went back to her rooms. I know because we searched them," Razor told him. "Somebody got to her before we did."

"Did you find anything in her rooms?" James demanded.

"No," Razor said. "All her things were like she'd left them. Seemed like she was planning on coming back. We tore the place apart looking, though. Even cut open the mattress and checked the floorboards. We didn't find any silver plates."

The Aether seemed to be laughing at him now.

"Someone has to know where she went," James said.

"The maids won't talk," Joe said. "Razor here spooked them, and now they're shut up tight as clams."

James cursed, low and vicious, as the Aether bunched around him again, the uncomfortable murmuring louder now than before.

"Get back to Atlantic City and keep your eyes open," he told the two of them. "People don't just disappear."

"We don't take orders from you," Razor told him.

James stood, gripping the silver gorgon and taking comfort in her cool sharpness. "Don't you?"

"No," Joe Itsky said with a sneer. "We don't."

"It would be a shame if our alliance shattered over something so terribly . . . *stupid*." James glared at them as he grasped the cane topper, as he felt for the link to the marks through the silver Medusa's coiling hair.

All at once, the entire saloon seemed to change. Like a wind rustling through trees, a tremor of unease rippled through the people in the barroom, causing them to go strangely silent. As one, they turned toward the two men, and the air felt suddenly frantic with magic.

"Find her," James said once more.

This time the two Five Pointers weren't idiotic enough to refuse.

A WARNING

1902—Little Naples Cafe

By the time Viola made her way from Little Africa over to the Bowery, night had long since fallen. Her brother's place, the Little Naples Cafe, looked oddly quiet. When Paolo had been running things, raucous noise would have spilled out through the open windows and doors late into the night. But Paul was sitting in the Tombs waiting for a trial, and the lights of the Little Naples had remained low, its doors closed to those who weren't Five Pointers ever since.

With Paul still in prison, Johnny the Fox had stepped effortlessly into her brother's position as head of the Five Pointers. But her brother had made his bed, and now he could lie in it as far as Viola was concerned.

But Torrio had made a mistake. By aligning himself with Nibsy Lorcan, he'd chosen his side in the ever-churning battleground that was the Bowery. And by sending the Five Pointers after Cela? He'd made himself *her* enemy as well. If any harm at all came to Cela Johnson, Viola would make him regret it.

She watched a little longer as Razor Riley and another man scurried toward the Little Naples like the rats they were and disappeared inside. It didn't worry her none that they were there. Better to make it clear to all of them at once that she was done with their games.

Gathering herself, she crossed the street and gave the door a vicious kick. A knife was already in her hand as she stepped into the room, and without hesitation, she let it fly at the first of the Five Pointers dumb enough to charge her, pinning him to the wall through the meaty part of his arm. Then she let her affinity unfurl, felt the beating of every heart in the sparsely filled space, and brought them all down. Pulling at her affinity, she slowed their hearts until they fell unconscious, one by one, until it was only Torrio staring at her with undisguised hatred from across the room.

He stood to attack, but she sent a pulse of her magic through his blood until he too stumbled and fell back into his seat, clutching at his chest.

"Where is she?" Viola demanded as she stalked across the room. "Where have you taken her?"

"Who?" Torrio gasped, grimacing against the hold Viola had on him.

"Cela Johnson." She took a step forward, increasing the pressure slightly until Torrio's eyes widened. "I know you have her. You can tell me where you've taken her, or we can finish this now."

"I don't have the girl," he told her.

"Lies." She tightened her hold on his blood, not caring that his lips were turning blue. "I know you have her. And I do not care if I have to kill every one of your men before you give her up."

"I told you, I don't have her," Torrio said, his eyes desperate and his hands still grasping his chest as he spoke through gritted teeth.

"You were watching her for Nibsy Lorcan."

"I *was*," Torrio agreed. "But these two idiots let her slip away." He nodded toward Razor and another man.

Viola eased her grasp on Razor Riley's heartbeat until he groaned. She kicked his leg as she drew another knife from her skirts and commanded him to get up. Razor staggered to a sitting position and then to his feet slowly, leaning on the table for support.

"Where is Cela Johnson?" she demanded.

Razor glared at her, but he didn't speak, so she pushed more of her affinity into Torrio.

"Tell her," Torrio growled, his voice rough with the strain of what she was doing to him.

"Gone," Razor said, hatred burning in his eyes. "I told Lorcan already, someone else got to her first."

"I don't believe you," she told them. She *couldn't* believe them. Because Cela had to be with them. They *had* to know where she was. The alternative was unthinkable. "If you can't tell me the truth, you're useless to me."

Torrio groaned as she tightened her hold on him, but he sneered up at her. His face was colored with the same hatred as Razor's. The same disgust that her own brother often turned on her. "You can't kill me."

She pulled his blood slower, pressed at his heartbeat. "Certo?"

He gave her a leering smile. "You won't. Not if you ever want to see your mother again."

Viola's hold on her affinity slipped a little as the meaning of his words hit her, and she heard another moan come from the men who'd fallen. She had not thought of her mother in the weeks after the Flatiron Building. Pasqualina Vaccarelli had made it quite clear that she preferred her son and would side with him no matter what he had done. But Viola had not considered what that might mean with Paolo in jail. She'd simply assumed that with Paolo in prison, her mother would remain in her apartment close to the Italian community on Mulberry Street and that her mother's life would go on as always, the daily cycle of mass and market and martyrdom that characterized the lives of so many women in the Bowery.

She'd been shortsighted not to consider that Torrio would see their mother as a pawn in his play for power. She should have expected that he would take their mother into his keeping. Not to protect Pasqualina, though that's how he would make it appear. But as insurance. In case Paolo was freed from the Tombs and in case Viola herself had any thoughts to meddle with his affairs. Because Torrio knew that neither of them would put Pasqualina's life in danger.

"Paolo would gut you if you laid a single finger on her," Viola said.

"Your brother's currently indisposed," Torrio told her. "And if you kill me—if you touch any one of my men, nothing will protect her from what I can do."

Her heart was pounding, and panic was churning through her as Torrio pushed himself up to his feet, struggling against the power of her affinity. "I told you: I don't know where Cela Johnson is, and frankly, I'm finished taking orders from maggots."

"Are you?" Nibsy Lorcan stepped through the still-open doorway. "Viola," he said with a nod. "It's been a long time."

"Not long enough," she said, trying not to let her fear show. Already, she could feel the creeping ice of the mark's warning on the skin between her shoulder blades.

"Perhaps not," he agreed. "I'm going to need you to step away from my associate. We have things to discuss."

"Like hell," she said, taking a step toward Nibsy. She was already directing her affinity toward him, already sensing his blood and heart with her magic.

But Nibsy was faster. Pain shot through the ink that was inscribed in her skin, pain so sharp it brought her to her knees. She couldn't hold on to her affinity any longer, not when she felt it slipping away from her— being *ripped* from her.

"I don't want to hurt you, Viola." Nibsy continued to approach as she struggled to keep from writhing against the mark's magic that was tearing at her skin. "You could be an asset to the Devil's Own. To *me*. Just as you were to Dolph."

She was shaking her head, trying to find the strength to refuse him even as she felt herself flying apart.

"This is just a warning, Vee. It's just a small taste of what I'm capable of now." He crouched down before her. "In a moment I'm going to release you, and you're going to turn around and walk out of here. Because if you don't, that will be the end of you."

Tears were streaming down her cheeks, but she couldn't speak. "And if you die here, now, who will protect your friends? Who will protect your dear, *dear* mother?" He stood then, looming over her. It did not matter that his build was slight or that she could have easily beaten him in an actual fight, not when he had the marks.

All at once, the pain in her back ebbed, and she gasped with the relief of it.

"It's time for you to go, Viola," Nibsy commanded. "Get out of here and think about what I said. Soon you'll need to make your choice."

But she'd already made her choice—hadn't she? Then why couldn't she bring herself to say it? She felt frozen, caught in a way she never had before. Cela. Her mother. Jianyu. The Devil's Own. Dolph. The responsibility of far too many souls made it impossible to stand.

"Go," he commanded. "Before I change my mind."

Once again, the warning flared beneath her skin, and this time Viola did what he commanded. She ran.

LISA MAXWELL

SAFE ENOUGH

B y the time the elevator opened onto the eighth floor, Harte was practically holding Esta upright. To his relief, when the doors slid open, the hallway was empty.

The wall across from the elevators was lined with mirrors, and he paused, shocked for a second to see just how bad the two of them looked. He still looked gaunt and pale from his illness in California. There were heavy, dark circles under his eyes, and his hair was standing up at all angles. With his jacket covered in filth from the subway tunnels, he looked like he'd just tumbled out of an opium den and was in need of his next hit on the pipe.

Esta's eyes met his in the mirror. She was tired-looking and dirty as well.

And wonderful. Because she was there, safe and alive and still his Esta. It didn't matter that her hair was a dark riot around her face or that her overalls were torn and dirty. But his eyes found the gash in her sleeve and the other dark patch of dampness at her side where her clothes had been ripped during her fall from the train.

"This way," Esta said, pulling away from his examination and ignoring her reflection in the mirrored wall. "We need to get into the room before someone notices us."

Beyond the bank of elevator doors, the hall split in either direction. Softly glowing lights hung overhead, and plush Oriental carpeting muffled their footsteps. Distant music drifted through the air from some unseen source. Harte kept his arm under Esta's, just to be sure, until they were finally standing in front of room 803. She used the key she'd taken from the office in the lobby without any problem, and once they were both inside, she bolted the door securely behind them.

The room reminded Harte a little of the hotel they'd stayed in back in San Francisco, where he'd recovered from the worst of his bout with the plague. That room had felt miraculous with its modern bed piled with goose-down pillows, unlimited hot water, and flickering television. This room was smaller—definitely cramped in size—but somehow it still felt like *more*.

The space was decorated with the same gleaming dark wood, richly colored carpeting, and golden accents as the lobby, but where the lobby had been grand, the room itself felt intensely intimate. Peaceful, even. On the left wall stood a single, enormous bed covered with a heavy burgundy jacquard quilt.

Esta went to the windows on the far end of the small room, where gauzy white curtains covered the bowed panes of glass. The same rich, burgundy jacquard framed the view beyond. She pushed back the filmy curtains to look at the street below. "No sign of trouble yet," she said, letting the curtains fall back into place. "I think we're safe enough for now. If anything changes, we'll be able to see from here—the entrance is below."

Harte nodded, but the lack of immediate trouble wasn't overly reassuring. He still couldn't quite reach his affinity, but the muffled silence and soft luxury of the space caused the tension in his chest to unwind a little.

He lifted the strap of the satchel over his head and, for the first time since he'd left the body that looked so much like Esta in the underground station, he set the Book and the artifacts down. They weren't really all that heavy, but he hadn't realized the weight of them—of what they meant, of what they could do—until he was no longer carrying the burden.

Taking Esta's arms gently, he turned her to see the tear in the side of her overalls. The fabric there had long since turned dark with her blood, and from the look of it, she was still bleeding. "We should take care of this."

Esta grimaced. "I need a shower first," she said, pulling away from him. "I feel like I've rolled through half the sewers in the city."

He had to force himself to let her go, to turn toward the window and focus on the steady traffic of Forty-Fourth Street to give her some privacy. But Esta didn't even bother to close the bathroom door. A minute or two later Harte heard the water starting, and he was instantly reminded of another time—it felt like a lifetime ago—when she'd installed herself in his apartment at Dolph Saunders' bidding. She'd been damn near euphoric to discover the hot running water and the porcelain tub.

He'd barely slept at all that night just from the thought of her soaking in the steaming water of that tub.

So much had changed between them since then. Perhaps there was no need, but Harte forced himself to stay at the window. Still, he couldn't stop thinking about Esta behind that door. Removing the mangled overalls. Stepping beneath the steaming spray of the modern shower.

With an exhausted sigh, he slipped off his soaked shoes and filthy jacket before sinking into the velvet club chair in the corner. He still felt far too filthy to lie on the bed, but the chair was deep and plush. He couldn't help but rest his eyes—just for a minute or two. Just until he could help Esta with her wounds.

When he opened his eyes again, he wasn't sure how much time had passed. Outside, day had turned to night, and the city lights seemed brighter than ever. Esta was standing over him, touching his arm gently to wake him.

"Harte?" She was frowning at him like she was worried.

"I'm fine," he said, trying to shake off the sleep that had overtaken him so soundly. "Sorry. I didn't mean to drift off."

Esta had wrapped herself in a thick white robe. As she moved, the front gaped a little, exposing flashes of her smooth, tawny skin. Her dark hair tumbled about her face, only barely damp from her shower.

"I waited as long as I could to wake you," she told him, lowering the sleeve of her robe to expose the soft curve of her shoulder.

He felt his gut go tight at the sight of her bare skin, clean and flushed from the heat of the shower. Without thinking, he stepped toward her, but he stopped short when she lowered the robe farther to expose the angry gash on her arm where the bullet had torn away skin. The wound had already started to fester and rot. Its ragged edges were a worrying shade of nearly black, and the skin around it was turning an unnatural gray. He didn't miss the brush of cold energy that sifted through the air when the wound was exposed.

He took her arm and examined the puckered, darkened skin. "You shouldn't have waited to wake me up."

"You needed the sleep," she said with a shrug.

He only glared at her, because he didn't trust himself to say anything else.

"My whole upper arm is starting to feel almost numb," she admitted. "It's like my blood and skin are turning to ice. And I think it's affecting my magic."

He looked over at the desk, where he'd placed the gun he'd taken from the clerk. "It must have been the bullet." His chest tightened at the thought of how much worse it would have been if the bullet had done more than simply graze her. What if it had actually gone through her arm?

"You're going to have to cut it out," she told him.

Releasing her arm, Harte stepped back. "There has to be some other answer. Maybe the Book—"

"It's spreading, Harte. I can feel it. Every second that passes, it gets worse," she said with a small shudder. "I could try to do it myself, but I'm not sure I could get everything."

"Esta, no—"

She'd already pulled the sleeve of the robe back up and turned to the pile of things he'd left on the table. When she found Viola's knife, she pressed it into his hands. "Please, Harte. You have to. Before it gets any worse."

Harte stared down at the glinting blade, horrified at the thought. "You know what this is capable of."

"I do," she said, turning her attention to the basket of supplies they'd taken from the store earlier.

"I could cut too deep," he argued. "What if I hurt you, Esta?"

"You won't," she argued. But she wasn't paying attention to him. She was too busy laying out clean towels and supplies. Gauze and some kind of ointment. A small sewing kit with the name of the hotel emblazoned on the case.

"You don't know that." He was staring down at the silvery blade, but all he could see was Esta broken and lifeless on the station floor. And then that was replaced with the thought of Esta bleeding to death there in that room. "I can't. I can't hurt you again—" His voice broke as the memory of her dying crashed through him, and he looked away, focusing on the swirling design in the carpet at his feet.

He sensed Esta stepping toward him, and when she was standing in front of him, he finally forced himself to look up from the floor. To meet her eyes. The fear and pain that had been in her expression a moment before had softened. She brushed the hair back from his forehead, but guilt turned his entire body cold. He tried to look away again, but she gently took his face in her hands, forcing him to look at her. "You *didn't* hurt me. She wasn't me, Harte."

He tried to pull away, but she stopped him.

"*She wasn't me,*" she repeated, more forcefully this time. "You *knew* that."

"Did I?" he whispered as doubt took the place of certainty.

"Of course you did," she told him.

"I didn't even try to find another solution." Nibsy had offered him an out, and he'd taken it. Had he really known it wasn't Esta? Now that they were out of danger, now that he could really think, he wondered if he'd been lying to himself. Maybe he'd just wanted to escape, like he always did.

"Whatever stupid thing you're thinking right now, you need to stop," Esta told him. "You did what you had to do to keep going, to come find me. You're not going to hurt me now."

He wished he could believe her, wished that he were half as certain as she sounded.

"I'm *already* hurt, Harte." Gently, she pressed a small, encouraging kiss to his mouth. "I trust you."

"You shouldn't," he told her, unable to stop himself from kissing her back. Softly. A brush of lips that made him want to lean in and take whatever she offered.

But she was injured, and he was a bastard for wanting more. He forced himself to pull back, to keep his hands clenched at his sides instead of pulling her closer like he wanted.

She stepped away, but she tossed an impish smile in his direction, as though she knew the direction his thoughts had taken. As though she maybe even approved. But she didn't move back toward him. She left him holding the knife, stuck in indecision, as she searched through a case of small bottles provided by the hotel. She found what looked like whiskey and downed the whole bottle, along with a handful of aspirin. Then she grabbed another bottle of something clear and downed it as well, wincing at the taste.

The knife in his hands felt cool, an impossible weight, as he watched her prepare the chair he'd just been sitting in, covering its arm with towels. "It'll be easier if I have something to support me," she told him, rolling the sleeve of her robe completely off before she took her place on the chair.

This time, not even the bare expanse of skin was enough to distract him. She was right. Even now he could see that the rot in her arm was spreading. Something had to be done. There was no other choice. As much as he couldn't imagine ever wanting to hurt her, he was going to have to do this. He was going to have to spill her blood and hope that Viola's blade didn't do worse.

"You'll tell me if I'm hurting you," he told her, a command more than a question.

"You can't hurt me any worse than this already is," she said.

Harte wasn't so sure. He'd seen Viola's dagger slice through solid wood and skewer a man's heart. He knew how badly it could cut Esta if he wasn't careful. Even once everything was ready, it took Harte a long couple of minutes to finally gather the courage to press the deadly blade into her skin.

ONE WAY OR ANOTHER

1902—Mott Street

When Viola returned with news that neither the Five Pointers nor Nibsy had Cela—or knew where she was—Jianyu knew of only one place he could turn. But as he navigated unseen through the city toward the mansion-like building at 20 Mott Street, he could not help but wonder whether he was making a mistake.

Once, he had been a regular visitor to Tom Lee's home. Once, he had been so favored by Lee and the On Leong Tong that most people in the Bowery had believed him to be Lee's nephew. But he had not stepped across the threshold of Lee's home since he had pledged his loyalty to Dolph Saunders the year before. His leaving was the ultimate betrayal, because he had left not only Lee's organization but also the closely knit community of his own people. In doing so, he had made an enemy of the self-proclaimed mayor of Chinatown. To Lee, Dolph Saunders had been yet another gwáilóu determined to keep the Chinese people in the city from claiming the success they rightly deserved, and the Devil's Own was simply another gang intent on stopping him from expanding their community and his prosperity by preventing Lee from claiming any more territory in the Bowery.

At the time, leaving the tong had been worth the risk. Lee might have helped to smuggle Jianyu into the country, and the On Leongs might have provided safety and employment once he had arrived in the city, but Jianyu had grown increasingly discontented with his role as Lee's most powerful weapon. Fleecing small family businesses was not the sort of job that had allowed him to sleep at night. At least with Dolph, Jianyu had felt like something more than a common criminal. He had felt as though he could make some small difference for Mageus in this terrible city and, hopefully, for his own people as well.

But the Bella Strega was no longer his home, and Dolph Saunders was no longer around to provide him protection. Now, Jianyu's only concern was for Cela's safety—and to keep Nibsy Lorcan from gaining any more power before Esta and Darrigan returned with the Book. He could no longer sit by and wait, willingly allowing the players in the city's game to continue without him. It was time to draw his own alliance.

With the threads of light pulled open around him, it had been easy enough to slip unseen down the busy thoroughfare that was Mott Street, the heart of Chinese life in the city. There, Jianyu was immediately surrounded by the sights and smells of his first days in New York. A wave of nostalgia swept through him, and he felt almost as though he were coming home. But with the amount of real estate Lee himself owned on the street, it was perhaps the most dangerous place he could be.

Jianyu passed 14 Mott Street, the headquarters of the tong, where Lee ruled with an iron fist. Next door, at 16 Mott Street, was the Chung Hwa Gong Shaw, or Chinatown's unofficial City Hall. There, Lee's influence was perhaps less violent but no less subtle. Lee had established himself as the leading Chinese figure in the city years before, when he aligned himself with Tammany and the police. Since then, he had acted as their deputy sheriff. It was only recently that Mock Duck and his Hip Sings had threatened that power.

Finally Jianyu reached 20 Mott Street, where Lee lived in an enormous three-story home. Its tall windows flashed in the morning sun, while balconies of fanciful wrought iron clung to its brick facade. There was not another family in the Chinese quarter that could afford three floors of luxury, and only a few of those who depended upon Lee for protection and support had ever been inside. Far fewer of the ordinary working poor could ever hope to amass even a fraction of Lee's prosperity.

In front of the building, a trio of highbinders stood guard in plain sight. In the past weeks, the Hip Sing Tong had grown bolder with its attacks on Lee and his territory. It was no doubt the result of the packet of information Nibsy Lorcan had given Mock Duck weeks before as payment for Jianyu's capture.

The rest of the city often dismissed Chinese men with their long queues and decidedly non-Western dress, viewing them as effeminate. As not *truly* masculine or virile. Few newspapers paid attention to the squabbling between the tongs, and even fewer citizens understood that these young men were every bit as deadly and dangerous as the Italian Mafia or Black Hand.

Jianyu knew better. The trio of Guards waited, sharp eyed and alert, ready to protect their employer from any danger. Well armed with knives and guns, they would shoot to kill any who might threaten their territory.

With his affinity strong and sure, Jianyu slipped easily past the high-binders. He waited a little longer until a peddler's cart clattered by, and then, using the noise to disguise the opening of the door, he let himself into Lee's mansion.

Inside, very little had changed since the last time Jianyu had been there. J. P. Morgan himself would have felt at home in the opulent space, with its plush carpets and gleaming furniture. There was even a grand piano holding court in one corner. The style of the large porcelain vases and colorful Chinese paintings gracing the walls were the one difference between the splendor of Morgan's mansion and the luxury of Lee's. But each piece of Lee's collection was particularly astounding in their beauty and rarity. Even a Westerner would easily be able to appreciate their value. Every detail of the home sent a message: Here was prestige. Here was *power*.

Perhaps once Jianyu had been swayed by the gleaming luxury of Lee's house—the promise that such prosperity could one day be his as well. Now he understood the truth. Lee had built his power and collected his riches in the same way Morgan and the other men of the Order did—on the backs of those who had no power to stand against them. On the backs of peasants who had no other choice.

Jianyu found Lee exactly where he expected him to be at this time of day, alone in his chambers. It was a simple thing to slip in undetected, but once he closed the door behind him, Lee knew he was no longer alone.

"I wondered when you would come back to me." The older man spoke in the Cantonese they shared. Turning in the direction of the door, Lee was almost uncanny in his ability to find the exact spot where Jianyu waited. But then, he had always been able to sense when Jianyu was near, even when he was wrapped in the light. "That is, I assume you are return-ing. Otherwise, you should have killed me already."

The old man looked the same. His full goatee was white with age, though the hair he had pulled back into a queue was still dark. Even now, after so many years of success and power in this new land, Lee still wore his hair long, in deference to a dynasty that currently held little power over his life. But the queue also meant that he could return to his place in Chinese society. It meant a way out should Lee ever desire one—an escape no longer available to Jianyu.

Under the cover of his magic, Jianyu lifted his hand to his own shorn hair, remembering the night a group of men had surrounded him in the Bowery, beat him, and cut his queue. But that terrible memory brought up another—the night Cela had trimmed the ragged ends of his hair, shaping them into a Western style. Her fingers soft but sure against his scalp.

He had to find her. He would do anything—even if it meant submit-ting to Lee—to ensure her safety.

Lee lifted one dark brow, his hooded eyes calm and sharp as he waited, ever unflappable. Ever sure in his command of the situation.

Releasing his affinity and allowing the light to close, Jianyu stepped forward, visible now. "I did not come to kill you."

"That, I think, is only the first of your many mistakes." Lee's mouth flattened.

"I do not fear your threats any longer," Jianyu said, perhaps foolishly. But he had lost his adopted home and mentor. He had lost the Delphi's Tear. And now he had lost Cela as well. What more did he have to lose?

"Perhaps you should," Lee said, his eyes flashing as brightly as the diamond stickpin in his lapel.

Jianyu inclined his head as though to agree. But he did not voice the sentiment. He would not give Lee so much this early in the negotiation. "I have not come to fight."

"I have nothing else to offer," Lee told him. "You cannot imagine you would be welcomed back with open arms."

No, Jianyu had not expected a warm welcome. In truth, he had no wish to be counted as one of Tom Lee's men again. But he needed them. And so he would do what must be done.

"I know of your problems with the Hip Sings," he said softly.

"You know nothing," Lee told him.

"Then the whispers I hear in the air are incorrect? Your men have not been picked off by Mock Duck's highbinders, while Tammany's police do nothing? Your fan-tan parlors have not been raided by the very police that promised to protect them, all because they believe that Sai Wing Mock can offer them more?" He paused, letting this information resonate. "People throughout the city are talking. They fear a new tong now, a new leader in the Bowery, one who threatens the rule of Mott Street."

Lee's cheeks were turning an angry red. "People are fools. Sai Wing Mock has no standing with Tammany. He can offer no protection to the Chinese people in this city, and his men are nothing but common criminals."

Jianyu nodded. "And yet his name is whispered from mouth to willing ear."

"Idle chatter."

"Perhaps, but people will believe it nonetheless. And bloodshed is not so idle," Jianyu said. "People grow wary of the war that is brewing."

"You tell me nothing I do not already know," Lee said. His eyes narrowed. "Why are you here?"

"I have a proposition for you. One that could be beneficial to both of us."

Lee laughed. "What good is your proposition when your word means nothing? You broke a blood oath already," he said. "And for what? A dead man cannot protect you."

"Then listen not to my words, but my actions." He took a rumpled package of papers from where he had tucked them inside his tunic and tossed them onto the table that stood between them.

Tom Lee's expression never shifted, but Jianyu could see the interest in his eyes.

"What is that?" Lee asked, making no move to pick up the packet of papers.

"Information," Jianyu said simply. "Perhaps the most powerful currency in the Bowery. You wish to know how the Hip Sings seem to anticipate your every move? You wish to know which bosses have their sights on Mott Street?"

"Everyone has their sights on Mott Street," Lee said, waving a hand dismissively. "I know this already."

"But do you know which enemies might strike, or when?" Jianyu nodded toward the package. "Once I was your eyes and ears in Chinatown, but for Dolph Saunders I did much more. I helped him build his territory and his power with the secrets I collected, and I could do the same for you."

"I have men enough for that," Lee said, sneering. "Did you believe you were so irreplaceable?"

"Can your men make Tammany bend to your will?"

Lee didn't bother to hide his interest. "Explain."

"You have long had an understanding with Tammany, and yet how many fan-tan parlors have their police raided this month?" Jianyu asked. But he did not wait for Lee to answer. "Why do you think their officers no longer honor your alliance? Because they seek more power. They see Mock Duck as the future of Chinatown. Tammany does as well. You must show them they are wrong."

There was doubt etched into Lee's features, but he was interested.

"Even now, Tammany is struggling to reassert themselves as the leaders in the city in opposition to the rich men who run the Order. But how can Tammany establish their power when the Order's patrols of mercenaries continue to stir chaos in the streets? The police have been unable to stop them. They sweep up Mageus and Sundren alike, and they make Tammany look weak. But if someone could provide information to stop these patrols? If the police knew where and when they might strike, would Tammany not be grateful?"

Lee was silent at first, considering the proposal. "I am to believe you can provide this information?"

"And more," Jianyu promised. "Think of it. With me as your eyes and ears, you will no longer be at the mercy of the Hip Sings' violence. You can reassert your place with Tammany as well."

"And in return? What do you expect?"

"Very little," Jianyu said.

"I doubt that," Tom Lee said, cutting his eyes in Jianyu's direction.

Jianyu inclined his head. "I need assistance in locating someone beyond the reach of the city," Jianyu explained. "A friend who is missing and likely in danger. I cannot leave the city, but your men could."

Tom Lee considered this, but his eyes were steady, and his expression gave nothing away. Finally, he spoke. "How can I be sure of your loyalty?"

"Name your price," Jianyu said.

"I want the Devil's Own," Lee said simply. "I want them all, and the territory now held by the Bella Strega along with them."

Jianyu fought to keep his expression from showing even a flicker of the horror he felt. "You cannot truly believe it is possible for me to deliver you the loyalty of so many."

Lee's brows rose. "Do you not think I understand that Nibsy Lorcan is aligned with Mock Duck? He has chosen a side, and in doing so, he has entered the war."

"I would happily make Nibsy pay for all he has done," Jianyu said. "But the Devil's Own, they are too vast, too diverse for me to guarantee their loyalty to you."

"You are not the only one who hears whispers in the streets," Lee said with a dark smile. "Nibsy Lorcan has a cane that once belonged to Saunders. I hear it has a certain power over the marks the Devil's Own have inscribed in their skin. I will find your friend and offer my protection, and in return, you will deliver me that cane. This is the price of the alliance you propose."

Jianyu thought of the mark on his own back and knew exactly what it would mean to hand Dolph's cane over to Tom Lee. He would be handing over his life and the life of every person who had ever trusted Dolph.

But Cela was missing. Somewhere beyond the city, beyond his ability to help her, she was in trouble, and it was in large part his fault. He had sent her away unprotected, too shortsighted to consider that Nibsy could reach far beyond the Brink. He would buy her safety now, whatever the cost. And he would see to the safety of the others later. "I will take your bargain."

"I thought you might," Lee said. He went to a tall rosewood cabinet that stood on the far side of the room. From it, he took a black braided silk band and, unfastening the ends, he turned to Jianyu.

"What is that?" Jianyu said, suddenly uneasy. The thin piece of cord looked like nothing at all, and yet his skin crawled with the cold energy coming from its clasp.

"You are not the only one with access to magic," Lee said. "I cannot trust your word, but I can trust this. You will wear this to seal our agreement. I will have command over you and your affinity . . ." Lee's expression was cold, hard. "One way or the other."

HIDDEN DEPTHS

1983—Times Square

A t first Esta didn't feel the cut, but then all at once, she felt the cold magic of Viola's knife as the blade sank into her arm. She couldn't stop herself from gasping. It hurt worse than she'd expected, and she'd expected it to hurt a lot. Harte stopped with her sharp intake of breath, but she told him to keep going.

"The faster this is over with, the better," she told him. "The liquor's already helping."

It wasn't, really. Not nearly enough. But the thing about pain, really bad pain, is that there's a point at which it all starts to blend together. There's a point where the body almost stops feeling it.

Almost.

Gritting her teeth, Esta refused to so much as whimper again as Harte methodically ran the tip of the knife around the gash in her arm. He would stop again if he knew how much it *actually* hurt, and he couldn't stop. There was no way she could do this to herself.

She hadn't allowed herself to think about what the wound had meant until they'd made it safely into the hotel room. She'd known immediately that the wound had felt wrong. But when she'd taken off the ruined overalls in the bathroom, she'd still been surprised. The gash in her side was simple enough to deal with, but the festering edges of the skin where the bullet had grazed her told a truth she couldn't deny—it wasn't a natural injury. The bullet had contained some kind of ritual magic that hadn't existed in her version of the future. Even after she'd showered off the filth and scrubbed her arm clean, it looked like the infection had gotten worse. The cold still felt like it was spreading.

Harte worked slowly and carefully, his face tense with the concentration of slicing the tip of the knife through her skin without cutting too deeply. It was excruciating, but slowly, the cold magic of the wound was replaced by the warmth of her own blood. And then, finally, only the normal burning ache of a fresh cut remained.

When Harte was finished, blood welled, but there was no sign of the rotten magic that had drained the color from her skin and the affinity from her fingertips. When she reached for her affinity, it felt almost normal. The net of time hung around her, ready to be taken in hand, and only the barest whisper of Nibsy's trap remained.

"You're going to need stitches," he told her, examining the bloody wound.

"I can probably manage that," she said.

But he reached for the sewing kit and got to work.

The needle repeatedly piercing her skin hurt, but compared to the knife, the poking was almost bearable. By the time Harte had finished a row of six surprisingly neat stitches, the alcohol she'd gulped down had truly taken hold. The whole world felt softer, despite the throbbing pain in her arm.

"Not bad," she said, glancing up at him. "Who knew you were an expert tailor?"

He ran a hand through his hair and let out a ragged breath. "I couldn't afford a seamstress when I first started my act," he told her. "I had to figure things out until I could hire Cela."

Hidden depths. Sometimes she forgot how solitary he'd been for so long, living alone in the city with only his wits and charm and magic to get by. *Not alone anymore, though.* Not ever again.

After he dabbed ointment onto the stitches and wrapped her arm in gauze, Harte glanced up at her, his stormy eyes fringed with dark lashes. They'd been through so much together, but she suddenly understood what it must have been like for him back in San Francisco to be so help-less and dependent on her.

But his eyes on her—the serious way he was studying her, the care he had taken with her—made her skin feel warm. It made her *everything* feel warm. They were in a gorgeous hotel room, and now that the danger of the bullet had been taken care of, they were maybe even safe. At least for the time being. It didn't matter that her arm ached and that her side still needed to be tended to. Harte was standing there, shirtless and deter-mined, and she couldn't stop her thoughts from turning to that moment in the tunnels, when he'd touched her. She couldn't stop thinking about how she wanted him to touch her again.

"I wonder what happened to Cela," Esta said, trying to distract herself from the direction of her thoughts.

She'd met the seamstress from Wallack's during those weeks when she'd been working as Harte's assistant at the theater, back when she had been trying to con him for Dolph. Cela had been more than happy to make a costume to help Esta get back at Harte for his heavy-handedness. She'd been so brilliant with a needle and thread that Esta had barely been able to believe how stunning the finished piece had been.

Harte frowned as he secured the end of the gauze. "What do you mean?"

"Nibsy shouldn't have had the Delphi's Tear, Harte. I didn't steal that ring for him until well into the twenty-first century. I was thirteen when I took it from a party in the 1960s. But that other girl—the version of me that died—she never had Ishtar's Key. She wouldn't have been able to slip through time. Which means that Nibsy shouldn't have had the ring."

"You think he got to Cela," Harte said.

"I think it's possible," she admitted. "Something certainly changed."

"Maybe Nibsy got the ring later. We sent Jianyu to protect her. . . ."

"Maybe Jianyu wasn't enough." Esta pulled her robe back up around herself. The gash in her side still needed to be taken care of, but she could deal with that on her own.

Esta's mind was spinning furiously, trying to pull the pieces together. The answer was there; she could nearly see it. And then she did. "The diary."

"What diary?"

She ignored the question until she'd located the small notebook in the pile of papers they'd taken from the library on Orchard Street, the same one that the scrap of the Book had fallen out of earlier. The one that showed their fate. She curled her leg beneath her as she sat on the bed and opened the diary.

"What is that?" Harte asked, tilting his head to get a better view of the indecipherable writing. "And why can't we read it?"

"I think this is a record of Nibsy's life," she told him. "But for some reason, those events aren't certain anymore." Flipping through a few of the pages, she watched as the words morphed into new letters, new arrangements, bubbling up and then disappearing back into the page in a never-ending dance. "I've seen this before, or something like it. When I first came back, I brought a news clipping with me, and when I changed the events, the print did this. I used it to keep myself on track."

"You're thinking that Nibsy had access to this in the past?" His gaze shifted from the diary to her. "That he used it to find Cela?"

"I think we have to consider the possibility. The Nibsy you knew—the one I met back in 1902—wouldn't have known how to actually use the Book or the artifacts," she told him. "The Professor that I grew up with would have had to send his younger self something so he'd know what his older version knew. It makes sense that he'd send himself *every-thing*. He'd want to give himself every opportunity to avoid any possible pitfall and ensure his victory."

Harte took the diary and thumbed through it, his brows bunched together the whole time. "So at some point, something happened to change the course of his life."

"Or *he* changed something," Esta told him. "Like getting the ring from Cela."

"We can't know that for sure," he argued. "It's completely unreadable."

"But we don't know *when* it became unreadable," she said. "We don't know how long Nibsy might have had clear knowledge of his own future."

"If that's true, he would have known everything that happened," Harte realized. "Every victory. He could have avoided every past failure. He could have used this to change fate."

She took the diary from him. "I think that's exactly what he did," she said, flipping to the entry for December 21, 1902—the night of the Conclave. She handed it back to him and waited as he read. She knew when he'd reached the relevant part.

He looked up at her and then turned back to the page as though reading it again would change the words. "That can't be right," he told her, adamant. "I *refuse* to believe that *this* is what happens."

She understood his reaction. Hers had been similar, and the shock of it had nearly cost her everything. "When I first found the diary, it was only Viola and Jianyu, but the second I thought about going back to save them, it changed to that."

"No," he said, adamant. "It's wrong. Or it's another of Nibsy's tricks. Now that we know—now that *I* know—how can *that* still be the future when we know to stop it?" He closed the diary and tossed it onto the bed. "I don't believe it," he told her. "I refuse to believe that's just *it*. We have to be able to change it."

"There has to be a way to," she told him. "With the newspaper clipping, I changed things—or I changed the possibility of things. Nothing else about the past has been set in stone. Why should this be?"

"Or maybe we don't go back," Harte told her.

"That isn't an option," she reminded him. "We have to set things right. For North and Everett and Sammy. For everyone. And Ishtar's Key has to go back. Even if there were a way to keep time from unraveling, look what happens if I *don't* send the girl I was forward. You saw the girl I might have been. To Nibsy, she was nothing more than a sacrifice waiting to be made. Can you even imagine what her life must have been like to have been kept endlessly ageless, all for the sake of catching me? Despite what he did to her, she believed in him enough to risk everything for him. He broke her somehow, worse than he ever broke me."

"He never broke you, Esta," Harte told her, his voice dark with emotion. There was a rawness in his stormy eyes that made Esta feel strangely vulnerable—more exposed than she'd felt just a few minutes before when she'd been basically bared to him.

She thought at first that he might reach for her. The seconds stretched, and time felt as though it was holding its breath. She waited, wanting something she couldn't define. Needing him to touch her again.

But Harte stepped back instead.

"I'm going to wash up," he told her, his posture suddenly distant and his voice stiff.

He was avoiding her and avoiding the question of their future as well, but she let him go. She waited until she heard the bathroom door close, and when she heard the muffled sound of the water running, she finally let out a breath, wincing a little at the ache in her side, a reminder that she needed to get it bandaged.

Everything was a mess. They were stuck in a time line where Thoth hadn't been destroyed and Jack Grew had become a saint. They had an entire city hunting them—their faces were in every newspaper, on every news report. They could take a few hours to rest and regroup, but they couldn't stay in the soft, quiet luxury of that room indefinitely. Outside, the world waited. In the past, their likely deaths waited as well. Time held its breath, watching for what would come.

ENEMIES AND ALLIANCES

1902—The Bowery

The church smelled of incense. Once, the cloying sweetness of frankincense and myrrh had been a comfort to Viola. Now it reminded her of a tomb. On the altar, the priest murmured in Latin, his low voice rolling through familiar litanies as the people dotting the hard wooden pews mumbled their responses.

Viola's mother was among them. Pasqualina Vaccarelli sat in her usual position on the left side of the aisle, where she could face the Blessed Mother. Like the other women in attendance, her head was covered by a heavy mantle, and Viola knew that wooden beads turned dark by age would be spilling through her mother's fingers as Pasqualina moved silently through the prayers of the rosary. The beads had been her grandmother's, carried like a treasure across the ocean. Now they would never be Viola's.

From her own pew at the back of the church, Viola kept her veil pulled close around her face and her head bowed. She lifted her eyes only enough to take stock of the situation. There were at least three of her brother's men stationed at various points around the nave. The Five Pointers were familiar enough with the mass that they were virtually indistinguishable from the other worshippers as they stood and knelt, their hands clasped in prayer as they sang the appropriate responses to the priest's call. But the early weekday mass was populated mostly by women or those too old to work. Young and hardened by the streets as they were, Paul Kelly's men stood out.

Not Paolo's, Viola reminded herself. They were Torrio's now.

Mass ended, and the worshippers began stirring to leave. If her mother knew the men were there, she did not show it. Despite the stifling heat of the church, Pasqualina pulled her shawl around her as she left the pew, genuflected to the altar, and then turned to go. She passed Viola without seeing her.

The men began to stir, preparing to follow the older woman.

Viola allowed her magic to unfurl, but only a little. Her soul might be forever marked, but there were certain lines she would never cross. Killing here in the presence of god himself was one of those. She slowed their blood just a little, enough to have the men sinking back into their pews. Enough so she could follow her mother into the vestibule without them seeing.

"Mamma?" Viola whispered, catching her attention before Pasqualina could leave the church.

Her mother turned, dark eyes wide and a look of shock—of fear—on her wrinkled face. But the expression quickly softened to something more like confusion. "What are you doing here?" she asked in the Sicilian of her childhood. The language wrapped around her, but the harshness in her mother's tone grated against Viola's already frayed nerves.

"We have to go, Mamma," she urged. She took her mother gently by the arm and started to lead her toward the open door. Outside, the streets bustled, and freedom waited.

Her mother frowned and pulled away. "What are you talking about?"

"We need to go. Away from here," she said. "You're not safe, not without Paolo."

At her brother's name, Viola's mother's face turned hard. "You speak his name to me after what you have done?"

Unease skittered through Viola. "What *I've* done?"

"It's your fault that my Paolo, that my boy, is in that terrible place," her mother said. "Mr. Torrio, he told me everything. He told me how you betrayed your brother."

Viola took a step back. "*Torrio* is the one who betrayed Paolo, Mamma. Not me."

Pasqualina glared at her. "You think I believe this? After so little care you have for your own blood?"

"Mamma, Paolo is a dangerous man. He's made many enemies in this city," Viola explained. Enemies who had already threatened to use Pasqualina against both Viola and her brother. "And Torrio, he is one of them."

"Bah!" her mother said, throwing down the rag. "If you had any salt in that gourd of yours, you could have caught the Fox. He would have made you a fine husband, but no—"

Their time was up. Two of the Five Pointers from the church entered the vestibule. The taller of the two spoke to Viola's mother. "Signora Vaccarelli, is this girl bothering you?" He glared at Viola with a hardened expression that told her the man knew *exactly* who she was.

"Mamma," Viola pleaded. "Please. You have to believe me."

"Mr. Torrio sent us to see you safely home," the other scagnozzo said easily. "He worried that something like this might happen."

"*Please,*" Viola pleaded. "Please come with me."

Her mother glanced at the two men looming over them, but when she turned back to Viola, her expression was as cold and unfeeling as the marble icons in the church. "Paolo, he gave you a home, gave you his protection, and what did you do in return? You chose sconosciuti over your own blood. *You* are the reason Paolo is in jail, not Mr. Torrio. You—"

"Torrio is a *rat*, Mamma. He'll use you against Paolo," she said, wishing she had more time to explain. "Johnny Torrio won't keep you safe. Neither will his men here."

"And you will?" Her mother's mouth pinched in disgust. "What? Will you take me to your melanzane?"

"Don't call them that," Viola said. Her voice was sharper than she intended it to be, but she didn't apologize, and she wouldn't retract her words.

Her mother pointed at her, jabbing at her chest to punctuate her words. "*There* is the truth. You could be here, working to help your brother until he returns, but still you choose others over your own blood."

"I haven't—"

"Now who lies?" Pasqualina shook her head. "I tried, Viola. I tried to be a good mother to you. I tried to make you into a good, god-fearing woman and to teach you what is right, to teach you the importance of the family. But I've failed. *Madonna*, how I've failed. Look at you. At your age I was already a wife, a *mother*. Instead, you run around the city like a crazy woman, come una *puttana*. I am finished trying." She turned to the men. "It was kind of Signore Torrio to think of me. Please, I would like to go now."

"Mamma—" She stepped toward her mother. "You can't go with them." It was the exact thing she'd come there to prevent. "You would choose Johnny Torrio over your own daughter?"

Pasqualina blinked, unmoved by the emotion in Viola's voice. She lifted a hand, as though brushing the past—and Viola with it—aside. "I have no daughter. Not anymore." Then Pasqualina Vaccarelli lifted her chin, proud and resolute, and brushed past Viola as though she were a stranger. The Five Pointers followed, and as the third passed, he gave her a rough shove with his shoulder.

Before she could even consider what to do, they were gone, leaving Viola alone in the stream of worshippers departing the church. At first, she could not move. The finality of her mother's words had turned her feet to lead. Strangely, it wasn't grief or regret that overwhelmed her now but a hollow sort of relief.

It was over. There was no returning from this, no way back into her family's arms. Not ever again.

Viola wasn't sure how she got herself back to the apartment. Navigating the bustling streets of the city felt like walking through a terrible dream.

Jianyu was already there when Viola arrived. He was sitting on the lone bench in the room, his shoulders hunched and his finger running along the underside of a black silken bracelet secured around his wrist. He was examining it so intently that he didn't notice her come in. There was an unsteady buzzing cold in the air, unnatural magic.

"What is *that*?" she asked, closing the door behind her.

Finally, he looked up at her. "It is done," he said, his voice sounding strangely hollow. When he looked up at her finally, there was a quiet desperation in his features. There was determination as well, though. "Tom Lee has agreed to our alliance. I will once more become his spy, and in return, his men already have been sent to seek out Cela."

"And that," she asked, nodding to the bit of unnatural magic tied around his wrist. "It is his price?"

"It is *part* of his price." Jianyu grimaced. "He will have my loyalty, or he will take my magic."

Viola frowned. "Only part of his price? What else does he want?" she asked, knowing already that she wouldn't like the answer.

Jianyu looked more miserable than she'd ever seen him. "He knows of Dolph's cane. I am to retrieve it for him."

Understanding settled through her. There could be only one reason Tom Lee would want the cane Dolph Saunders had carried—the same reason Nibsy Lorcan wanted it. "He wants the Devil's Own." *He* wants *us.*

Jianyu nodded.

"You can't have agreed to such a thing," she said, horrified. It was bad enough to have discovered that Nibsy Lorcan had the cane, and with it, the marks. But for Tom Lee, a Sundren who wanted only territory and wealth to have it? *No.*

"I had no choice," Jianyu said. "Cela is missing, and the fault for that lies with us. With *me.* We need Lee and his men. They can go beyond the Brink where we cannot. They can keep Nibsy too busy to cause trouble as well."

"But the marks . . ." She shook her head, unable to imagine a world where Tom Lee controlled the most powerful Mageus in the city.

"I have no intention of giving Tom Lee any more power than he already has," Jianyu told her. "Until his men find Cela, I have some time."

Viola nodded. "If they find her?"

"*When* they find her," he corrected. "I will do what I must. But I will not hand over the Strega or anyone who was loyal to Dolph. I will die first."

This was exactly what she feared.

It was a terrible plan. With his connections to Tammany, Tom Lee was far too powerful a force to toy with for long. Then another thought struck.

"We will figure this out," Viola promised. There had to be a way to remove that cord around his wrist without handing over every Mageus who had ever been loyal to Dolph. "Once I get Libitina back—"

"He assured me that he would know if I tried to remove it. If I do, he will enact the charm and take my magic . . . and my life." Jianyu gave her a weak smile, but the resignation in his eyes told the truth of the situation. There would be no easy way out of this. But he was right. He could have made no other choice, not when she had already failed so spectacularly to put pressure on Torrio. Trapped as they were behind the Brink, they needed help. They needed allies, even dangerous ones.

A knock sounded at the door, disrupting the heavy silence that had fallen over them. Together they turned in unison, hearts in their throats. No one but Joshua and Abel should know where they were, and both should have been in Atlantic City searching for Cela. But both would have known the rhythm to signal their identity.

Viola exchanged a look with Jianyu, a silent conversation that had both of them nodding. She readied her affinity as he eased toward the door, opening it just a crack to see who waited on the other side. And then suddenly he was flinging it open.

In the doorway stood Theo Barclay, and with him was Cela Johnson.

DISTRACTION

1983—Times Square

Harte soaked until the bathwater had gone nearly cold, but still he remained in the tub, not yet ready to face Esta again. How could he when he'd read Nibsy's diary, when he'd seen with his own eyes what their fates held?

No . . . He wouldn't let that be the future that waited for them. He'd do whatever it took to make certain of it.

His vows didn't help his conscience, though. He felt like the worst kind of ass. He'd just sliced her open and stitched her up. He'd just seen her death, there on the page of Nibsy's diary, and all he could think about was how soft her skin had felt beneath his hands. How much he wanted to touch her again.

But he was delaying the inevitable. He couldn't hide in the bathroom indefinitely. On the other side of the door, Esta was waiting. They had decisions to make, work to do.

Pulling himself from the tepid bath, he dried off and wrapped himself in a robe like the one Esta had been wearing. His reflection caught his attention, and under the bright garish glow of the modern electric lights, he was struck by how much he had changed in the last few weeks. His hair was too long. He'd always kept it neatly cut, and now it curled over the collar of the robe and fell into his face. Beneath his eyes, dark hollows told the story of too many days with no real sleep, and his once-sharp features now verged on gaunt. He looked like someone who had been sick recently, which . . . he *had* been. But he didn't want to see that weakness staring back at him. He didn't want to remember how completely *helpless* he'd been back in San Francisco.

He definitely didn't want Esta to remember that, either.

Pulling his shoulders back, he lifted his chin. *Better.* Or if it didn't make him look any better, it was as good as he was going to get.

Esta was sitting cross-legged on the bed. The robe she was wearing had come loose a little, and now it gaped, exposing the skin at the base of her throat. Maybe it was the graceful curve of her neck or maybe it was the smooth, exposed stretch of her leg that did him in, but suddenly it took everything he had not to go to her. He wanted to untie the robe and let it fall aside. He wanted to run his hands across the soft expanse of her skin. He wanted to see every inch of her. He wanted to take his time.

Touching her in the tunnels hadn't been nearly enough. Then again, Harte had a feeling that nothing would ever be enough when it came to Esta. But he forced himself to stay still. She'd been through enough in the last few hours. She'd been burned and bloodied, and now she needed time to heal. He was going to keep his hands off her.

He was going to try to, at least.

At first she didn't notice him. She was too deep in concentration, gnawing absently on her thumbnail as she studied the Ars Arcana, which was open on her lap. Stacks of Nibsy's papers were lined up around her on the bed. It looked like she'd been sorting them. When he took another step into the room, she finally looked up. He couldn't quite read the emotion in her whiskey-colored eyes.

"You didn't waste any time," he said, trying to keep the note of disappointment from his words. He knew they had to deal with what lay ahead, but he'd hoped they could set it aside—at least for the night. He wasn't ready to face the truth of what had to be done. Esta was right. They had to go back—he *knew* that—but that didn't mean he was ready to accept the possible future that Nibsy's diary had shown them.

When she frowned at him, frustration and maybe even hurt flashing through her eyes, he felt like an ass.

"I'm sorry," he told her. "That isn't what I meant. It's only that—" How was he supposed to put everything he felt into words.

Her expression softened. "I know."

He took another step toward the bed. "Well, did you find any answers yet?"

"Maybe." She swallowed hard enough that he could see the column of her throat move, and then she turned back to the pages open before her. "Jack's made our job easier with all the translations and notes he's left. I think I found the ritual we need to use the Book as a container for the stones."

It should have been a victory, but Esta didn't seem happy or even relieved. Her eyes were still too serious. "That bad?"

"No, that one is simple enough," she said. "Mostly because of what the piece of magic in the Book can do." She closed the Book and stared down at the cover.

There was more. He could see it there, on her face.

"What else did you find, Esta?"

She didn't answer at first, but when she finally looked up at him again, he knew he wasn't going to like what she said.

"We need to talk, Harte. There are things I need to tell you. About Chicago."

"You already told me—"

She shook her head. "Not about that. About what happened on the stage when Jack was about to kill you. About what the piece of magic in this Book can do and about the promise I made."

Unease slid cold down the back of his neck. "*What* promise?"

"You might want to sit down."

He took a seat on the other edge of the bed, away from the papers and definitely away from the danger inside the Book. Then Esta told him everything she hadn't yet—about the conversation she'd had with Seshat, the danger of having a piece of magic held outside of time—how it threatened the world and reality itself if it were controlled by the wrong person or, worse, exposed to the killing power of time. Because if that piece of magic died, everything died with it. She told him, too, about the vow she'd made to finish what Seshat started. The promise to complete the ritual and place the piece of magic back into the whole.

"Why would you promise such a thing?" he asked, horrified at the implications of what she was saying.

"You were about to die," she told him. "I would have promised *any-thing* to stop that from happening."

"Esta, no—"

"You would have done the same, Harte. But it wasn't only that," she told him. "I believed her. What she told me about the danger that piece of magic poses to the world—she wasn't lying. She was desperate. She just wanted to fix her mistakes."

"She wanted to destroy *you*," Harte reminded her. "She wanted to use you to destroy the entire world. I know because I *felt* it. Her anger. Her absolute desperation."

"Only because she believed there wasn't any other way," Esta argued. "She truly believed that her unmaking the world would be a kindness compared to what would happen if that piece of pure magic escaped. I offered her another way, and she accepted."

He started to argue, but she cut him off before he could form words.

"Seshat didn't have to accept the bargain, Harte. She already had me. She could have done whatever she wanted. She could have pulled me apart, taken my affinity, and *finished* it. But she didn't."

She had a point, but he didn't want to admit it. "It doesn't matter anymore. Seshat isn't a danger now, Esta. She's trapped in the Book again. We're safe."

"What if we're not?" Esta asked. "What if she wasn't lying? Seshat damaged magic. By taking it out of time, she put everything at risk. If we don't finish the ritual, if we don't place that piece of magic back into time, anyone could touch it. Especially now, with the artifacts united. If the ritual remains uncompleted, magic will die, and when it does, it will take everything with it."

"But, Esta, Seshat might have still been lying. Think about it—you grew up in a time even farther beyond the one we're currently in, and magic hadn't died yet. The world hasn't collapsed. Nearly a hundred years passed from the time I first stood on that bridge until the time you came back, and magic was *fine*."

"It wasn't fine, Harte." Esta was frowning at him, and he could sense her frustration. "Magic was basically extinct. Hardly anyone had an affinity. No one remembered what their families had even been. No one remembered what *magic* had been."

"But the world spun on," he argued, unable to stop the desperation he was feeling from seeping into his words.

"Maybe. But how much longer would it have lasted?" Esta's eyes softened. "She let me save you, Harte. She gave me another chance. I have to honor that. I have to try to complete the ritual she started."

Esta wasn't going to be swayed. He could tell by the set of her mouth and the determination in her eyes.

"Did she tell you *how* to finish the ritual, by any chance?" Harte asked sardonically, because anger was easier than fear. Safer, too.

Esta didn't take the bait. "No, but I think *you* know." She looked down at the open page and read words he'd heard not that long before. "*To catch the serpent with the hand of the philosopher*—"

"No." He tried to stop the memories of what had happened on the subway platform from flooding back. "No, Esta. Not that. You can't be serious. That ritual *killed* the girl."

"I know," she told him. "I need you to tell me what happened, Harte. I need to know what happened with the other girl—the other version of me."

"Esta, I can't—"

Moving aside a stack of papers, she scooted across the bed to where he was sitting. She was close enough now that he could smell the flowery scent of the soap on her skin, close enough that her leg rested against his. Gently, she took his hand. "Please, Harte," she said softly. "I need every detail. It's important."

He couldn't deny her. Slowly, he forced out the words. One by one, he handed his memories over to her and described everything he could remember: the ritual of drawing the circle on the floor, how she'd sliced open her finger and pressed it to the Book while she spoke words he couldn't understand. How he'd felt her affinity linking the stones, uniting them and using them to pull Seshat out of him.

"After that—you were still trapped inside the circle?" she asked. "Kind of like we're trapped inside the city by the Brink."

"And the same as Seshat was trapped when Thoth betrayed her," Harte said, drawing the connections between the rituals, between the memories.

"But you got out." Esta tilted her head, her brows drawing together. "Seshat couldn't get out of the circle Thoth trapped her in, and no one can get through the Brink."

Shame flooded through him. "I told you—I used my affinity. I forced her to give the rest of her magic over to the ritual. It drained her, and when her magic was gone, so was she."

Esta touched his cheek, pulled his face gently to hers, and kissed him softly. "It's okay," she said, kissing him again. "You did what you had to do. You *survived*."

He pulled away from her then, willed her to understand. "I had a choice, Esta. I didn't have to kill her."

"You knew she wasn't me," Esta said.

"I'm not sure that it matters," he said.

She considered that. "I think it does. If you hadn't done it, you both would have died, and that would have been terrible. Because this isn't over, Harte. There's so much more to do, so much more to make right. There's still so much at risk," she told him, and he heard the honesty in her words. "But I think what the girl did is the answer to how we fix magic. I think we need to replicate the ritual she used, but instead of putting Seshat into the Book, we need to put the beating heart of magic back into time."

Suddenly, he understood. She was talking about giving herself to it, just as the girl had done. And for what? For a half-mad demon who would have used her and tossed her aside.

"No." He was shaking his head. "I watched you die once already. I can't go through that again."

"Maybe I don't have to die. Maybe there's another way," she said. "You lived with Seshat inside of you for months. Do you really think she did the original ritual intending to die?"

"No," he admitted.

"With power *willingly given*, mercury ignites. Elements unite," she read. She tapped the page thoughtfully, and then looked up at him. "Power willingly given . . . Maybe it isn't a matter of living or dying. The girl in the station didn't give her affinity, not willingly. You *forced* her. Maybe that made the difference. Maybe if I'm willing to give up my affinity, I can finish the ritual without giving up my life."

She looked up at him through dark lashes. "Maybe I can fix everything, Harte. The Brink. The old magic. *Everything.*"

But for Harte, "maybe" wasn't good enough. "The promise you made to Seshat was to protect me—to protect the *world* from her insane desire to tear it apart. But Seshat isn't a danger anymore, Esta. Not to me, and not to the world. She's trapped in the Book again, like she was before we disrupted the flow of history. There isn't any reason to take that kind of a risk."

"Harte—"

"No, Esta," he said, refusing to listen to even one more word about the topic. "I won't allow it."

"You won't allow *what?*" she asked, and from the ice in her tone, he knew he'd said the wrong thing.

But he didn't have the strength or energy to fight her. *"Please—"*

"The answers are here, Harte. I *know* they are."

He let out a long, exhausted breath. "Maybe they are. But what if you're wrong? People don't walk away from losing their magic, Esta. My mother didn't. The girl today didn't, either."

"I think there's another way," she told him. "Seshat's trapped in the Book now, isn't she? We can use her power. Think about it. You used that other Esta's affinity to give the ritual what it wanted—the magic it demanded—and you walked out of that subway station alive. What if we use Seshat the same way? She's the one who started all of this. With the artifacts united, we can control her. We can use *her* affinity to complete the ritual in the Brink, and maybe we can walk away from that the same as you did?"

"How are we supposed to use the artifacts while they're inside the Book, Esta?" His brows were creased with worry. "If we remove them in the past, we're liable to lose them because they'll cross with themselves."

"There has to be a way," she pressed. "I've only scraped the surface of this, Harte. With all the power Thoth collected—all the knowledge and rituals—there *has* to be an answer in the Book. We can't have come this far only to stop now."

"What if you're wrong?" he asked.

"I don't think I am," she told him, far too certain for his liking.

"Are you really willing to risk everything without knowing for sure?" He moved toward her. "What about *us*, Esta? What about the future we could have together? Seshat isn't a risk. She's trapped in the Book. We don't have to do *anything*. We can go back and stop Jack and just be together."

"But the Brink—"

"The Brink is still out there," he told her, pointing toward the strange, modern city beyond. "It's terrible, but it doesn't mean we couldn't be together. The Brink isn't the thing holding us back."

"It's holding *you* back," she told him softly. "I really think that we could use Seshat to complete it. I don't think I have to give my life to do that. But more than that, Harte, could you really live in a future knowing you could have changed everything for the better but you didn't?"

He cupped her face gently. "*You* are my better," he said, letting his hands drift down her neck, down to her shoulders. He pulled her close. "I could live in any world as long as you're there with me."

"Harte . . ." Her voice was softer now.

He could not listen to any more of her arguments because he couldn't bear even one second of thinking of a world without her in it. Damn the Brink, and damn magic as well. Nothing mattered but her. So he kissed her. Fiercely. Ardently. He put everything he had, everything he was into the kiss. Because he had to stop this disastrous line of thinking. He had to convince her that this could be enough, that *they* were enough. They could go back and stop Nibsy. They could even stop Thoth. But she didn't have to die.

He couldn't lose her again.

She pulled back from him. "I know what you're doing, Darrigan."

"What?" He kissed her again, this time on that delicate skin where her jaw met her neck.

"You're trying to distract me," she said, her voice going breathy.

"Is it working?" he asked as he nuzzled into her neck.

"Maybe," she said with a sigh.

He nipped down to where her neck met her collarbone. "Then what's the problem?"

"I'm not exactly sure." She tipped her head to the side. "I just wouldn't want you to think you're getting away with it."

Drawing back, he gave her his most charming grin. "Noted."

Harte leaned in again, and this time she met him halfway, her lips parting for him. This time she was the one who deepened the kiss, who pulled him under. It wasn't her magic that made time feel like it was standing still. The whole world narrowed to her mouth against his, her fingers threading through his hair, her body moving closer to him.

Her hands slid under his robe, her palms brushing against the flat planes of his chest. Pushing his robe off his shoulders, she leaned toward him, practically climbing into his lap to get closer still.

His hands were already beginning to untie the belt of her robe when he realized what he was doing. It took every ounce of his strength to pull away from her. To stop.

"We can't do this," he said, barely able to catch his breath. She was looking at him with a dreamy expression that made him only want to lean in again.

"I think the train to Chicago proved that we absolutely can, Harte." She smiled as she kissed him again, and he couldn't resist the happiness of her mouth against his. But when she started to lower her robe, he stopped her.

"You're hurt, Esta."

"I'm fine," she said, lowering the robe a bit more, until her shoulders were bare to him and he could just see the gentle slope of her chest.

He tried to give her a stern look. "I just stitched you up."

She shrugged, looking down at the bandage on her arm. "You did." She glanced up through her lashes at him. "And I haven't properly thanked you."

Her hand was on his leg beneath his robe, and he couldn't stop from trembling at her touch. But when she started to inch her fingers upward, he pushed her away.

"We can't," he said. "There's too much of a risk. Until you're married to me, and—"

She pulled back, her brows snapping together. *"Married?"*

"Of course," he said, uneasy with her sudden stillness.

"I'm way too young to think about getting married," she told him.

He frowned. "You're older than half the brides in the Bowery."

"Maybe in 1902," she told him. "In my own time? People don't just run off and get married at seventeen. I can't even vote."

"Women can vote?" he asked.

She blinked, as though thrown off by his question. "Yes, but that's beside the point. You don't have to marry me, Harte. I don't need you to make an honest woman of me."

"I know I don't *have* to marry you, Esta." He suddenly felt a sinking sense of dread. "And I don't think *anyone* could make an honest woman of you."

She smacked him playfully. "I mean it. We can be together without all of that. Marriage is so . . . permanent."

"What if I *want* to marry you?" he asked. "What if I want permanent?"

Esta stared at him without speaking. Her silence was unreadable. He'd just assumed . . . After all they'd been through, he thought she felt the same.

"Unless that isn't what you want?" he asked. "I would never want you to feel any pressure—"

The corner of her mouth had twitched in amusement at that sentiment, as though to say *Good luck trying to make me do anything I don't want to do.* Some of his fear eased at the sight of it.

She was close enough that he could smell the soap from her hair, the mint on her breath. The entire world had narrowed to Esta. "I'm just saying that maybe that was a really shitty proposal, Darrigan."

He felt almost dizzy. "You'll marry me, then?"

She did smile then, satisfied like a cat who'd managed to drink all the cream. "One day. When this is all over." She leaned in and kissed him, softly at first and then more deeply, until he thought he'd never be able to come up for air. She was pushing down his robe now.

He pulled back. "We shouldn't, Esta. You're injured, and there's still the risk of a child. We can't do this."

She let out a long-suffering sigh. "Yes, Harte, we can." She climbed off the bed to go sort through the basket they'd taken from the pharmacy. When she found what she was looking for, she tossed him a package.

It took him a second to figure out what he was looking at, and then he realized. *Prophylactics.*

"I'm not going to pressure you," she told him. "But if you don't want this, I'm going to need you to tell me right now."

He looked up at her, afraid to say yes. Unwilling to say no. Knowing he wasn't anywhere near worthy of her, he felt himself nodding.

She smiled and untied her belt, and then she dropped her robe to the floor.

BOUND

1902—Uptown

Cela Johnson had barely stepped into the room before she found herself wrapped in Jianyu's ironlike embrace. She was aware of Theo closing the door behind them, of Viola's rapid spurt of Italian, but only barely. She'd been awake for nearly two days now and had already started to feel that slightly off-kilter dizziness that comes from exhaustion mixed with fear, but the second Jianyu's arms were around her, everything fell away. The fear. The worry. The room itself. For a moment it was only the strength of him, solid and secure, towering over her and the scent of him, cedar and sage, wrapping around her. Blocking out all that had happened.

But before she could register how easily they fit together, how perfectly his body aligned with the softness of hers, and how much returning to him felt like coming home, Jianyu was releasing her. Stepping back. He looked as shocked by his actions as she felt. Adorably, color pinkened the sharp lines of his cheeks and the tips of his ears.

"Cela," he said, his voice rough. "Where—" He shook his head, looking between her and Theo as though he could not believe either of them were real.

"Where have you been?" Viola demanded, cutting off Jianyu's attempt to form questions. "We thought you'd been taken."

"I nearly was," Cela told them. "But Theo found me first."

Viola turned on him, her eyes flashing. "*You?* Abel found her room torn to pieces. He is beside himself with worry. We all were! We thought Nibsy had gotten to you, or worse."

Shame flashed through Cela. "I'm sorry. I told Theo we should send word, but he thought it was too dangerous." She glanced at Theo, silently willing him to explain.

"We couldn't contact anyone," Theo told them. "Not until I was sure it was safe."

"Until *you* were sure?" Viola asked, stepping toward Theo, her finger jabbing in his direction as violently as any blade she'd ever held. "What are you even doing here? After all we did to get you out of that building, away from the Order's suspicions? You should still be in France."

"I was, but—"

"But *what?*" Viola let out a string of angry—and probably filthy— Italian curses. "Explain yourself."

"He is trying to, Viola." Jianyu placed what he probably intended as a calming hand on her arm, but she jerked away.

"I arrived back from the Continent two weeks ago," Theo said.

"You didn't send word," Viola said, frowning. She looked shocked by the news, and maybe even disappointed.

"There hasn't been time," Theo told her. "They've been watching me since I've returned. My family and the Order as well."

"You are not safe from the Order's suspicions?" Jianyu asked.

Theo shook his head. "Not completely. Thanks to you, they couldn't prove anything, and with how everything turned out back in June, they're angrier at Jack than anyone else. But Jack said enough about my involvement that they're still unsure. They don't exactly trust me."

"Still." Viola pouted. "You could have sent word. You should have let us know."

"I haven't had a minute to myself since my father summoned me back," Theo explained. "I barely had time to gather my things before my ship left. And from the minute we docked in the harbor, they've kept me busy. My father found me a position at his bank, and I started immediately upon my return. In the evenings, when I'm not working, I've been doing translations for Morgan. The Order is pretending that everything is fine, but they made it clear that I'm being tested. They've been keeping their eye on me. I couldn't risk trying to contact you, not when they were still so suspicious. I could have led them right to you."

"Yet you are here now," Jianyu said, pointing out the contradiction.

"Something happened that made it necessary," he explained. "When I was working on Morgan's papers, I overheard a meeting the Inner Circle was having. I don't think they realized the venting between the rooms was so connected, or they likely wouldn't have spoken so freely. But it was clear that the Order had information about Cela. Someone had tipped them off about her involvement with what happened at the Flatiron. They knew she was working at the hotel in Atlantic City, and they were planning on bringing her in for questioning. I had to get to her first."

Cela looked to Viola. "Once he got me out of the hotel, we had to get Newton's Sigils from where I'd stashed them at my boardinghouse. But there were men watching it. It took two days for them to give up so that we could get close."

"Two days and you could not send word?" Viola demanded.

"The last thing we wanted was to lead them back here," Theo repeated.

Cela lifted the satchel from where it was secured across her body and handed it to Jianyu. "They tore apart my room, but I had these somewhere safer—the floor of the boardinghouse's root cellar. They didn't find them."

Viola snatched the bag from Jianyu. In a matter of seconds, she'd pulled her dagger from it. Her attention only on her blade, she handed the satchel back to Jianyu.

"I'm sorry I brought them back here," Cela said, feeling like she'd failed. "I've put you all at risk by coming back, but I didn't know what else to do."

Jianyu's expression softened. "You did well. Exactly as you should have."

"But Nibsy will be able to track you now," Cela said.

"He already can." Jianyu said darkly. "Better to have our weapons here. Better to meet him on our own ground than leave ourselves exposed and unprotected."

Cela bristled a little at this. "I can take care of myself, you know. Thanks to you and my brother's heavy-handedness, I have for months now." But when she saw the guilt that flashed in Jianyu's eyes, her frustration faded. "But you're right. I'm glad to be back. This city is my home. I won't let Nibsy Lorcan or the Order chase me from it again. This is where I want to stand and fight."

"It isn't only the Order and Nibsy we have to worry about now," Viola said, looking to Jianyu with an unreadable expression. "Not with Tom Lee's noose around your wrist."

Cela turned to him, confused. Her gaze dropped to his wrist and, just as Viola had said, there was a braided bit of silken cord tied there. "What is that?" She looked up at him and saw the frustration—the fear—in his eyes.

"We thought Nibsy had taken you," he explained. "We needed an ally who could move outside the city."

"But my brother could," Cela said, her stomach already flipping.

"He was already searching," Jianyu said. "We—I—could not leave it all upon Abel's shoulders."

"You went to Tom Lee for help?" Cela asked. He'd told her before how Tom Lee had treated him before he'd left the On Leongs for Dolph Saunders gang. "Why would you do that?"

"Because you were missing," Jianyu told her, the words infused with so much emotion that Cela took an actual step back.

"Well, call it off," Cela said. "You don't need him now."

Jianyu shook his head. "It is not so easy."

"It's *exactly* that easy," she told him, unnamed panic already creeping along her spine.

Jianyu only shook his head.

"But I'm *here*," Cela argued. "There's no one to look for any longer."

LISA MAXWELL

"He made an agreement that he cannot break," Viola said. "Not so long as that bit of dangerous magic lives on his arm."

Cela didn't have to ask to know the answer to her next question. There was no way Tom Lee would simply remove that bracelet of thread, not if he'd managed to trap a Mageus as powerful as Jianyu with a little bit of string.

THE CHOICE OF FATE

1983—Times Square

The throbbing in her side and arm woke Esta sometime in the deep hours of the very early morning. Still hazy with sleep, she heard the sounds of the modern city coming to her through the closed windows. The far-off honking of horns and the steady hum of traffic punctuated by the rumble of a heavy truck had been the lullaby of her childhood, the background noise of her entire life, and for a second she thought she was back in the room she'd grown up in on Orchard Street with the Professor. Her brain registered the weight of an arm thrown across her waist and the heat of the body pressed against her back. Then she remembered.

She smiled to herself in the darkness as Harte's breath fluttered against her neck. Other than her injuries, her body felt warm and relaxed. Her skin felt alive, buzzing with the memory of how Harte had touched her. Like she was something important. Valuable. Like she was *his*.

Her whole life, Esta had never felt like she fit—not with the crew she'd grown up with on Orchard Street. Not with the Devil's Own. Maybe Dakari had been different, but that hadn't stopped her from feeling the constant need to prove herself worthy. Of respect. Of love. With the Professor, she'd always needed to earn her place, and she had. But there, with Harte, Esta felt a kind of calm that she hadn't before. He'd seen the worst of who she was. He'd seen her at her weakest, and somehow it didn't matter. Somehow, he was still hers.

But then he shifted behind her, moving his arm so it pressed on the bandage at her side. A sharp burst of pain shot through the injury on her torso, and she had to clench her teeth to keep from making any noise. Once the worst of the pain had passed, she gently lifted his arm and slipped out from under it.

Wrapping the discarded robe around herself, she found the bottle of aspirin and took a couple more to dull the ache. Even with the noise she'd made, Harte still hadn't moved. He was sprawled beneath the mountain of bedcovers, his face slack with sleep. The sharpness of his cheekbones was a reminder that it hadn't been that long ago that he'd nearly died. As if she could ever forget.

Now that she was awake, she was too restless and unsettled to fall asleep again. Rather than climbing back into the bed, she grabbed the satchel that held the Book and Nibsy's papers, along with a package of Oreos from the minibar. She took everything into the bathroom, where she could turn on a light without waking Harte. The second she popped a cookie into her mouth, she realized how ravenous she was. And how much she'd missed junk food. The hit of sugar and hydrogenated oil tasted like a miracle. Maybe before, she would have barely thought about the ordinary, packaged snack, but after months of living in the past, the sweetness—the *normality*—of it felt like coming home.

She ate another as she opened the Book. The Ars Arcana was a marvel. It wasn't a single volume, as she'd always believed. Instead, it was a collection, which made sense considering that Thoth had used it as a record of the power he'd collected over the years. There were places where new pages had been added or sheets of parchment had been pasted in.

The pages were written in every language imaginable, including some that Esta didn't recognize. It was a record of Thoth's many lives over the ages. Symbols and diagrams littered most of the time-worn pages, but occasionally she came across an image painted in brilliant colors that seemed to defy its age. The Book was a startling repository of ritual magic from all corners of the world. Here were spells from the Far East, others from the southernmost tip of the Americas. Some of the writing looked to be done in Egyptian hieroglyphs. Jack had somehow translated some of the unfamiliar languages, but the parts written in more modern languages were—thanks to her training—easy enough for Esta to read.

Esta stopped at the pages she'd been studying earlier, especially the one that seemed to depict the ritual Newton had tried to perform ages ago. It was the same ritual used to create the Brink, and from what Harte had described, also the one the other version of herself had used to unite the stones and force Seshat back into the Book.

On one page, the image of the Philosopher's Hand shimmered in ink flecked with gold. The symbols above each of the fingers seemed to float within the page. The crown glinted and the star and moon almost appeared to glow. In the center of the palm, a fish sat within living flames that looked so real, she wondered how the Book didn't burn itself from within.

She'd seen this image before. It was a fairly common symbol traded among alchemists. Those who studied the occult sciences or who practiced the type of ritual magic of the Order understood the picture of the Philosopher's Hand as a recipe. In legend, it depicted the key to the transmutation of elements. With it, alchemists believed they could turn lead to gold or transform a simple mortal life into godlike immortality.

It was what Thoth wanted. To be infinite—and to be infinitely powerful.

You could have that power as well.

She frowned to herself, wondering where the thought had come from. She didn't want that power. She'd *never* wanted that power.

Running her finger over the gilded page, Esta could feel the grooves carved into the parchment by a desperate pen. The various objects represented the classical elements, and the flames represented mercury, which could unite them. But another name for mercury was Aether. *Time.* She thought of what Everett had said about Newton's quest for the philosopher's stone—how he was trying to form a boundary out of time—and she thought of what Seshat had been trying to do as well. Maybe myth and history had it wrong. Maybe the philosopher's stone wasn't an object but a place—a *space*—carved out of time. After all, Seshat had never intended to live forever. She'd wanted to make the old magic infinite—both outside of time and *part* of all time at once.

On the opposite page, Esta found markings that mirrored the burned wounds on her arm. The page was complete now—the other version of herself must have put the two together. The cipher was also complete, and she could see that what had appeared as symbols when torn in two were actually some kind of Greek. It was archaic, to be sure, but readable.

The answers are here. You need only be strong enough to take them.

Her hands trembled as she grabbed a pen and some of the hotel stationery and started to work.

Time dissolved around her—or it felt like it did. By the time she was done decoding the page, her hand was cramping, but Esta barely noticed. She finally understood.

Running a finger over the intricate sketch of the Philosopher's Hand, she wondered how she'd missed it before. The icons on the hand were connected by the element of mercury—*Aether*—just as the stones had been, both in Seshat's ritual *and* in the ritual that created the Brink.

And in the ritual the girl completed.

The boundaries formed by uniting the stones were made from time—or rather, Esta realized—they were made from time's *opposite*.

Her own affinity didn't *control* the seconds; it simply found the spaces between them and pulled them apart. Because magic lived in those spaces. It waited there, ready to unfurl, as time kept it constrained and ordered. In perfect balance. When Esta reached for her connection to the old magic, when she used her affinity to slow the seconds, she pulled those spaces apart, and in doing so she asserted power over the order imposed by time.

It was the same when she slipped through the years using Ishtar's Key. Esta didn't *control* the years. All she did was pull the layers of time *apart*. She found the spaces and used her affinity to open them so she could slip through. After all, what was magic but the possibility of power contained within chaos? Her slipping through time had done nothing but insert chaos into the time line.

Nibsy had been wrong. Aether wasn't time itself. Aether was so much *more* than that. It was the indefinable quality of the spaces between, the substance that kept everything in balance. Her affinity wasn't for time but for its opposite. For the chaos inherent in magic itself.

That was why Seshat had been able to remove a piece of the old magic from the whole. It was the reason she could put its beating heart into the book she'd created. Not because she could touch the threads of time but because she could move them and manipulate them by controlling *magic itself.* That was also why Thoth needed Seshat, why he had *hunted* her over the ages. Without her power, he couldn't reach the pure piece of old magic trapped within the Book, and he certainly couldn't control it.

But *with* her power . . .

It was why Nibsy had used the girl to put Seshat back into the Ars Arcana. He needed Seshat's power as well.

Esta thought again of the night of the convention, of all that Seshat had told her and shown her. That night so long ago, she'd been trying to rectify her mistake. She had tried to correct the imbalance that she'd created by inventing ritualized magic.

She'd removed a piece of pure magic from the whole and infused it into the Book. But the power in those pages wasn't *inscribed*. It wasn't the stable writing of ritual. It was chaos, still pure in its possibility. A piece of magic that transcended the ordering of time.

It was why the Book could hold the stones. The magic within it was outside of time, beyond time's reach. It was also what made the Book so dangerous. If that power was released, it could destroy time and reality itself.

Esta placed her hand over the inscription of the Philosopher's Hand so that the symbols there floated above her own fingers. She turned her hand over, inspected her palm, and considered the burning fish in the drawing. *Aether.* Within herself. Outside as well.

Seshat had a similar affinity. She'd used her power to unite the stones, just as the palm united the fingers of the hand. Whole and complete, unite through the Aether that connected all things. A perfect circuit.

Had Thoth not interrupted and stopped her, Seshat would have reinserted that piece of magic back into time. But how?

She would have given up that piece of magic and the power that came with it, Esta realized. *By giving* everything *up*.

She read Newton's inscription again: *With power willingly given, mercury ignites. Elements unite. The serpent catches its tail, severs time, consumes. Transforms power to power's like.*

Power willingly given. Seshat had given nearly everything to perform the ritual. She'd placed almost all of her own affinity into the stones. *Would she have given the rest?* The girl had. That other version of herself had given up her entire connection to the old magic—or she'd been forced to.

Would it have turned out differently if the girl had been willing rather than coerced? Would the girl have survived, as Seshat would have survived? Or had Seshat always intended to die?

Somehow, Esta doubted it. Seshat believed that she would become something more by completing the ritual. The goddess didn't seem like the type to martyr herself.

But Seshat had never been able to finish the ritual. Thoth had stopped her before she could reinsert that piece of pure magic in the Book to the whole of creation, and for centuries, he'd been trying to use her power to replicate the ritual she'd never finished.

Not to save magic, as Seshat had been attempting to do. But to capture and control it.

Because maybe that's what the ritual does. "Transforms power to power's like," Esta read, puzzling over the words.

Seshat never would have just given up, and nothing about the goddess had ever struck Esta as purely altruistic. She wouldn't have sacrificed her power unless she thought she'd receive something in return. Seshat must have believed she would get something from the ritual—something more than simply saving the old magic—the same as Thoth.

Esta flipped to another page and reexamined the way the old alchemist's writing had gone from the straight, steady script to something more erratic that bordered on madness. Newton had believed the ritual was the key to the Philosopher's Stone—the answer to endless riches and eternal life. Thoth had likely used that desire for fortune and immortality to control him, the same way he'd used Jack's hatred.

Newton had been willing to *kill* for the power in the Book. He'd created the stones by sacrificing the lives and affinities of the most powerful Mageus he could find. But something had stopped him from finishing the ritual. *What was it?* Maybe he hadn't been strong enough, or maybe he hadn't been willing to give up everything—not his power and not the beating heart of magic, either.

Maybe that was the answer. Seshat had never intended to keep the magic in the Book for herself. She'd been ready to reinsert the piece of pure magic back into the whole once it was protected. She would have given it up, and in doing so, power would be transformed.

But maybe Newton had been unwilling to do that. The Order certainly had been unwilling to. They'd used the artifacts to create the Brink to *keep* their magic, but they never completed the ritual. Either because they weren't able or they refused to do what Seshat had been willing to do—to give her own power over to the ritual to complete it. To give up the power of the Book as well. *Power willingly given.*

Maybe that was why the Brink continued to take the power of Mageus who tried to cross out of the city—because it was still waiting for the final piece of the ritual. Thoth had told Esta that *time will always take what it is owed.* So too, it seemed, would magic.

But it would never be enough, Esta realized. The Brink was waiting for a power that no single Mageus could contain. It was waiting for the beating heart of magic.

That was how Seshat's ritual could still be completed. The Brink was created by the same ritual that Seshat had performed eons ago—a ritual formed by Seshat's power to touch the strands of time, just like Esta herself could. They could use that ritual. The piece of magic in the Book could be returned to the whole, and with it the Brink could be transformed into what Seshat had always intended for the ritual to create—a space where magic could not die. *Part for the whole. Like to like.* Magic could be saved.

But only if someone was willing to pay the ultimate price.

But it doesn't have *to be you. The demon goddess could be used . . .*

There *was* a way to control Seshat's power—through the stones—as Thoth had always intended. If Thoth could use the artifacts, so could Esta. She could help the goddess finish what had been started eons ago without giving up her own life.

Esta pressed her hand to the pages of the Book, as she had done in her dream, but nothing happened. She closed her eyes and tried to sense some indication of Seshat's power or her presence, but she wasn't Harte. The pages told her nothing of the life within them.

Running her fingers over the tightly bunched symbols on the page, she almost felt bad for Seshat. Maybe the ancient being *had* tried to kill her—and tried to destroy the world along with her—but once she'd been a woman who had only been trying to do the right thing.

How was Seshat any different from Esta herself? Hadn't Esta also tried to do right by magic and failed? Hadn't she, too, tried to change the course of history and made things immeasurably worse? Being trapped within lifeless pages had to be nothing short of misery. Why did Seshat deserve that fate when Esta herself now had a chance to walk free?

Whatever pity Esta might have felt, one fact remained: now that they had the Book and the artifacts, they could do what Thoth had planned all along—they could use Seshat's power to complete the ritual. They could go back and put history on the course it should have been on all along. With Seshat's power, they could fix the Brink, and by reinserting that piece of magic back into the whole, they could fix *everything.*

The problem was Nibsy.

He wanted her to return to the past. That much had been clear, even if his reason wasn't. There must be something he still needed from her. Maybe her power? Maybe he still needed to use her to control the Book.

It would be so much easier if they could just eliminate the threat he posed.

But they couldn't kill him. Otherwise, who would be waiting in the future to find the girl and to raise her? Who would send her back, so that she could remain on *this* path? It meant dooming that girl to a life being raised by a monster.

Esta had seen what this version of Nibsy had done to the girl. With her own eyes, she'd witnessed what she could have become in another life under his control. Could she really doom that other girl to that fate, just so she could claim a future with Harte for herself?

FUTURES PAST

1983—Algonquin Hotel

Harte woke from a deep sleep with a jolt. All at once he remembered what had happened in the subway station. Remembered Esta, broken and dead, and his own magic the reason it had happened.

Panicked, he struggled to free himself from the mess of blankets and sheets, but they felt like a serpent wrapped around him. Strangling him.

"Harte?" The mattress sank with Esta's weight as she sat next to him. "Are you okay?"

Not dead. The rest came back to him then as well. The rush through the city, the night they'd shared. Finally, he managed to free himself from the covers enough that he could sit up. Esta was there—*alive*—looking at him with concern.

"Fine," he told her, trying to wake himself fully. The nightmare of what had happened in that subway station still felt too close, too real. "I'm fine. Just a dream."

They were in the hotel, safe from the forces hunting them. Daylight streamed through the gauzy curtains, and he could hear the rumble of the city beyond.

He realized then that he wasn't wearing anything beneath the sheets, and though his cheeks heated at the memory of the night before, he felt desire pull low and sweet in his gut. He wanted to tumble her back into the bed and forget about everything else.

But Esta clearly had other ideas. She was already dressed—not in the robe she'd wrapped herself in the night before but in an outfit he'd never seen. A soft, oversized sweater in seafoam green concealed her shape, and pale denim pants covered the legs that had been bare just hours before. The clothing looked warm and comfortable. And he hated it.

"Where'd you get the clothes?"

"I raided the luggage in the bellhop's office," she told him. "Don't worry. I didn't let anyone see me. I got you some things too."

"Later," he said, and reached out his hand. She took it, and he tugged her toward him until she'd fallen into bed. Once she was situated across his lap, he took his time kissing her.

She hummed happily and leaned into the kiss, opening her mouth against his as she tangled her fingers in his hair.

Better. He ran his hands beneath the sweater, careful not to disturb the bandage on her side, and found the strap of her undergarments. His thumb was poised to unhook the fasteners when she went still. "Harte, wait . . ."

He did what she asked, but he left his fingers splayed across her back. Her skin was so warm beneath the thick clothing. "Do you really want me to stop?" He rubbed his thumb along the pearls of her spine until she shuddered.

"No, but—"

He kissed her before she could finish the thought, and by the time she pulled away breathless, he'd managed to unfasten the undergarment.

"Harte—" Her voice turned to a whisper as his hand ran across her skin and his thumb brushed the underside of her breast.

"Yes?" He paused, waiting for her. Dying a little with every second he didn't touch more of her.

Her head fell to his shoulder, and he felt the warmth of her breath against his skin. "I wish I could stop time forever," she whispered. "I wish we could live here in this room and this moment. Then we would never have to face what comes next. I want you—"

She leaned back to look at him, and he let her go. Let his hand fall away.

"But," he said softly, echoing her earlier statement.

　　　　　　　　　　　　　　　　　　　　LISA MAXWELL

"But," she agreed with a sigh.

It was only the wanting he saw there in her golden eyes that kept him from shattering completely.

For a long beat, he wondered if she would reconsider, but eventually she reached back beneath her sweater and refastened her underthings. Then she retrieved a small notepad from the chair where she must have been sitting before he woke.

"While you were sleeping, I've been working," she told him. "I think I've figured out some things."

His stomach sank. She was talking about going back, about returning the piece of magic to the whole. She was talking about risking everything for an ancient goddess who would give nothing but death and destruction in return. He'd wanted to forget about those problems—he'd wanted *Esta* to forget as well.

"I think I'm going to need to put on some pants before I hear about them," he told her.

He wrapped a sheet around himself and, taking the trousers she offered, retreated into the bathroom, where there wasn't enough cold water in the world to wash away the morning's desire.

When he could finally fasten the pants comfortably, he reemerged and found her sitting curled in the velvet armchair, deep in concentration as she read through a stack of Nibsy's papers. She noticed his entrance immediately this time, and when she looked up, her eyes raked over his body, taking in his shirtless torso and the soft woolen trousers. A part of him thrilled at seeing the heat in her gaze, but he needed her to stop looking at him like that if they were going to talk.

"Shirt?" he asked, his voice coming out more strained than he'd expected.

She blinked, and her cheeks flushed a damn delicious shade of pink.

"There are a couple to choose from," she said, visibly pulling herself together. She nodded at a pile of clothes near the television. "I wasn't sure what you'd like."

Once he was dressed, he took the chair at the desk, not trusting himself near the bed. Not when Esta kept looking at him like *that*. It took everything he had to listen to all she'd managed to puzzle out. But as she talked, some of the tightness in his chest eased.

"You really think that's the answer?" he wondered. "To use Seshat as Newton would have?"

"I do," she told him. "We have the Book, and with the artifacts, we can control Seshat. We can go back and use her power to fix the Brink. We can stop Jack before he causes any damage. We can save our friends."

The diary. Harte reached for the small book and skimmed through it until he found the date of the Conclave. He read the part of the entry that was still legible. Most of it was obscured, the details hidden by the strange changing letters, but one point was clear. "If we go back to save them, you die at the Conclave." He showed her the entry. "I *kill* you, Esta."

"*No . . . ,*" she told him, as though the words weren't there, stark and accusing. And the truth. "I trust you with my life, Harte. You wouldn't hurt me."

"Maybe you shouldn't, because according to this, I already did," he said. "It's already done." He scrubbed his hand over his face, wishing he could erase the words from his memory. When he spoke again, he softened his voice. "What I don't understand is how. How the diary can be so sure—when we're here now? Years after this supposedly already happened."

Esta took the diary from him, frowning down at the page. "It didn't change to this scenario until I found it in Nibsy's library. I think the diary is certain because we are. We *will* go back. We've decided it, and one way or another, we'll change the past. We'll change it to *this*."

"But we know now," Harte pressed. "Shouldn't that fact change *everything*? Shouldn't we be able to avoid it?"

Esta's brows bunched as she considered the diary. "Maybe," she told him. "The details are still indistinct. They're still unsettled, so maybe the outcome is still undetermined."

"Except *that*," he said, pointing to their names, stark on the page.

"Except that," she repeated softly, staring down at the words as they undulated on the open page. Neither of them seemed to know what to say at first. "Maybe Nibsy knows too much. He must have had this diary in the past along with his affinity. Maybe he's seeing what we're seeing. If he has this diary, he'll always see us coming. He'll be able to outmaneuver us." She looked up at him then, a spark of determination in her golden eyes. "But he doesn't win."

"It sure as hell looks like he does."

She shook her head. "No. He *doesn't*. If he won—if he was able to get the Book and artifacts—the rest of this diary wouldn't be unreadable. History would have already settled itself into something more certain than this. And if he had won? Nibsy wouldn't have been the weak old man we just met. He would have used the Book and taken its power, and the world would already be unrecognizable." She flipped through the unreadable pages. "I think this means that there's still a way to beat him. There *has* to be."

"If we could kill Nibsy before the Conclave—"

"We can't," she told him. "We can't kill him at all."

"Why the hell not?" Harte asked.

"Once the Brink is fixed, we have to send Ishtar's Key forward with the girl. That fact hasn't changed. She still needs to be raised by the Professor, so he can send her back to find the Magician and search for the Book. Otherwise, none of *this* can happen." Her expression bunched in concentration. "I can't exist as I am now—*this* can never be—unless that happens," she told him, frowning. "Even though I die in this scenario, someone must have given the girl the stone and sent her forward. Otherwise—"

"It would have unraveled everything," Harte realized. But then another thought occurred to him. "If someone else could give the girl Ishtar's Key, maybe someone else could raise her too?"

The words in the diary wavered a little, as though suddenly the past was no longer set in stone.

"What do you mean?" she asked.

"Maybe it doesn't have to be Nibsy that raises you," Harte said, watching as the entry became more unsteady. Esta's name was still there alongside Viola and Jianyu's, but the ink almost seemed to vibrate with a new possibility. It had to mean that he was onto something.

"What if someone else could find her when she jumps forward and raise her to do what you did?" Harte pressed, thinking it through. "If there was someone else there in the future, waiting for her, we could eliminate Nibsy before *this past* becomes the truth."

Esta's expression was unreadable. "It would be such a risk to change the time line that much," she told him, chewing thoughtfully on her lower lip. "And even if we were willing to take that risk, who would we choose? Who could we trust?"

But they didn't have time to find the answer. Outside their window, a siren started to wail.

Esta leaned over and looked out through the gauzy curtains. The curse that came out of her mouth would have made a longshoreman blush.

"What is it?" Harte asked, but in truth, he already knew.

"They've found us."

PART

III

ALLIANCES

1902—The Bowery

K eeping the early-afternoon light wrapped around him, Jianyu made his way down Prince Street toward the heart of the Bowery and the stretch of the boulevard that held the Bella Strega. His pockets were weighed down with the coins he had collected from two opium dens and a fan-tan parlor, payment from the owners of each for Tom Lee's protection. The coins jangling in a pocket against his leg were a constant reminder that he was no longer his own man—that he had not been for weeks now. The circle of silk on his wrist was another reminder. One that was becoming more urgent.

Since he had accepted the piece of ritual magic in exchange for Tom Lee's help to locate Cela, the silken cord around his wrist had been easy enough to ignore. As long as Jianyu spent most of his days serving as lap-dog to Lee, the tong leader had been happy enough and had not pushed the arrangement. Week after week, Jianyu had supplied information about the Order's patrols to Lee, who passed it on to the men at Tammany Hall. As the number of abductions and disappearances decreased, the police took the credit for calming the chaos in the Bowery, and Lee's standing with Big Tim Sullivan and Charlie Murphy had grown more secure.

But the Order had pulled back in the past two weeks. Without information to deliver to Tammany, Lee was becoming impatient. And with the On Leong's established ties to the political machine, things were growing more tense in Chinatown. Mock Duck's Hip Sings were becoming more brazen and violent in their attacks. Two days before, they had ransacked a gambling parlor that Lee protected and sent one of Lee's men to the hospital with numerous knife wounds. The attack was a reminder to Lee that control over the Bowery was still anyone's game, and Jianyu had not yet fulfilled his promise to deliver the Strega.

That morning, Jianyu had noticed that the bit of silk seemed to be tightening around his wrist. It was growing colder as well, like the blade of a knife poised and ready to slice. It was a message—of that Jianyu was certain. Tom Lee would not wait indefinitely for results. It did not matter if Cela was safe. As long as the silken cord tied him to Lee, their agreement stood. There was no breaking it, not even with Viola's blade. If he did not give Lee Dolph's cane—and control over the Devil's Own—he had no doubt that the braided silk would rip his affinity from him. But handing over Dolph's cane and his people to Tom Lee was an impossibility.

He would not betray the Strega or the Devil's Own, but to appease Lee, Jianyu had to make a show of his efforts to retrieve the cane. And so he had set his course toward the Strega.

Turning east, Jianyu pulled the light more securely around himself and kept a brisk pace through the nearly deserted streets. It was late in November, and the air was already starting to turn cold. Soon, winter would arrive, and with it, the punishing cold that Jianyu hated perhaps more than any other part of this terrible land. He missed the humid heat of his homeland on those cold, dark days. But there was no going back, no escape from the city, and no retreat from the course he was on.

Now that summer had closed its final pages, now that he was staring into the promise of winter's wrath, Jianyu did not know what was to come. Darrigan and Esta still had not returned. Nibsy wore the Delphi's Tear securely on his finger. And the Order's Conclave was ever closer on the horizon.

We have Newton's Sigils, he reminded himself. For reasons he could not guess, Nibsy had not tried to retrieve them again. If they could get the papers back from Nibsy, they might be able to figure out how to use the silvery discs. Because if he had to die, he would make sure his friends were safe.

As he made his way through the Bowery, the city seemed to be holding its breath. Throughout the dirty streets and shadowed alleyways, a strange, uneasy silence had simmered all through the summer. But the recent calm of the streets was only a mask for the chaos that waited beneath. It was only a matter of time before a spark would ignite the tinder of the city, and the streets would erupt once again.

How could it be otherwise? The danger of what was to come crept like a warning against his skin.

When Jianyu finally arrived at the Bella Strega, he paused, overwhelmed by a sense of loss he had not expected to feel. From across the street, he watched the entrance of the building that had once been his home, making note of people who came and went through the familiar, heavy door. Nibsy was likely inside, sitting in Dolph's seat in the saloon as though it had been his all along. Jianyu could picture him clearly: the boy's slight build, the glint of his thick spectacles, and the coldness in his eyes. How had none of them recognized the ice in him? How had none of them seen the snake in their midst?

And how could they hope to defeat him, when Nibsy held the power of the marks in his hands?

Finally, the person Jianyu had been waiting for emerged from the saloon. Werner Knopf had once worked for Edward Corey, the owner of the Haymarket. Before Bridget Malone had died in a fire there, Werner had helped her keep control over the often-rowdy dance floor. He had a particular affinity, one able to stop the air in a person's lungs. It made him dangerous in his own right, but Werner had never been a leader. He had always been content to take orders—first from Corey, then Dolph, and now from Nibsy.

Jianyu still was not quite sure how Dolph had managed to lure the boy to the Devil's Own or whether collecting Werner had been a good idea. But Jianyu had seen Werner's fear in the Flatiron. That night the boy had been willing to ignore Nibsy's orders to save himself. Perhaps he would be willing to do so again.

Once more, Jianyu pulled the light around himself, and then he began to follow Werner north along the Bowery, matching the other boy's pace. It was a risk, following him like this, because it was possible Werner would be able to sense him there, but it was a risk he had to take.

He followed Werner down one street and then another, until he realized the other boy's final destination was the Little Naples. When he disappeared into Paul Kelly's cafe, Jianyu found a place that was out of sight, and he settled down to wait.

It was nearly dark before Werner emerged, looking more than a little harried. Jianyu released his affinity and took one step from the shadows of the doorway he had been waiting in. Werner quickly noticed him waiting there, but to Jianyu's relief, the other boy did not take his breath. Not immediately at least. Werner's eyes shifted, right to left, as though he felt he was being watched, and then he gave a small jerk of his head, which Jianyu took to mean he should follow.

When they rounded the next corner, Werner turned on him. It was almost a relief when Werner slammed him up against the wall, placing his hand against Jianyu's throat.

"What are you doing here?" Werner demanded. "How did you find me?"

Jianyu did not even bother to shake him off. If Werner had wanted him dead, he already would be. "I followed you from the Strega."

"You can't be here," Werner told him, looking more panicked now. "If Nibsy knew I was talking to you—You're gonna get us both killed."

"I need to speak with you."

"*You* need to speak with *me*?" Werner repeated, incredulous.

"I understand that Nibsy has the marks," Jianyu said.

"Then you should've known better than to come here," Werner snapped. "What if the Fox had seen you? What if one of his men tells Nibsy?"

Jianyu tilted his head. "You fear Johnny the Fox? A Sundren you have sworn no oath to?"

Werner's mouth twisted in disgust. "Yeah, well, we all swore an oath to the Devil's Own, didn't we? You included."

"I have not broken that oath," Jianyu told him.

"No?" Werner asked. "Then what are you doing here, lurking in doorways instead of joining the rest of us in the Strega?"

"My loyalty is to Dolph, not to the one who murdered him."

Werner could not quite hide the surprise in his expression. But it quickly shifted to doubt and distrust. "Says the one who ran off and sided with Darrigan after he stabbed us in the back. Everyone knows the Five Pointers took out Dolph."

"And yet you walked out of their lair unharmed," Jianyu said. "Strange, is it not, how quickly Nibsy made allies of Dolph's supposed murderers? And now you run between them, an errand boy doing the devil's bidding."

"You don't understand nothing," Werner said. But he released him.

"Nibsy Lorcan is the one who killed Dolph," Jianyu said. "And now he uses all that Dolph built—the people Dolph once protected—for his own interests."

Werner looked unsettled, but his jaw was tight. Denial was clearly more comfortable than truth. "So what if he did kill Dolph?" Werner asked finally. "It's done, ain't it? He has the marks now. He runs the Strega. Anyone who tried to stand against him would be a fool."

"I have been called far worse," Jianyu assured him.

"You'd fight him?" Werner laughed. "What? You think you could take over the Strega and lead the Devil's Own?"

"I think that what Dolph Saunders worked for is worthy," Jianyu said. "I believe the Devil's Own should be more than Nibsy Lorcan's puppets."

"What do you want from me, Jianyu?" Werner said, sounding almost exhausted now.

"Your help."

Werner shook his head. "No, thanks."

"Not even if I can offer you a way out?" Jianyu asked.

Werner's eyes shifted. "A way out of what?"

"Everything. You would no longer have to fear Nibsy's control if you could leave the city," Jianyu told him. "Help me, and you could have your freedom from Nibsy Lorcan. You could have the entire world beyond the borders of this island."

Werner huffed out a laugh. "You're as mad as everyone says."

"Nibsy knows how to get out of the city," Jianyu told him. "Or has he not shared that information with the rest of the gang?"

That seemed to get Werner's attention, but suspicion clouded his eyes. "There ain't no way out of the city for Mageus like us."

"There is," Jianyu said. "There is a key to the Brink—a way for Mageus to pass through it without being destroyed. I have the tools. You saw the sigils Viola stole from the Order? We can use them to create a doorway. A safe passage for our kind."

Werner shook his head. "That ain't possible. People would know."

"People *did* know," Jianyu said. "The Order's Inner Circle knew. Once, long ago, it was information that the highest members protected, even from their own."

"So if you know so much, why are you sitting here talking to me?" Werner's eyes narrowed, but his interest was still keen.

"Because I do not yet have the ritual needed to use them," Jianyu admitted. "Nibsy took some papers from me a few weeks ago, papers I had stolen from J. P. Morgan's office. In them were the instructions. With those papers, the sigils could become a key to the Brink."

"You want me to get the papers," Werner realized. "You really think I'm going to stand against Nibsy for *you*?" He shook his head, a look of utter disgust on his face. "Maybe I should help *him*. Maybe I should get those discs back from you."

"Nibsy will never let you go, Werner," Jianyu said. "Your affinity is far too useful. Even if he had the discs, he has you by the mark you accepted. You are his. Unless you leave. Unless you go far beyond where he can reach. Help me get what I need, and I will make sure you are free. I can make sure anyone who has the mark can be free of Nibsy's control."

Werner was shaking his head, ready to reject the offer.

"Take your time," Jianyu said. "Ask Mooch what he thinks. Both of you could be gone before Nibsy Lorcan even understood what had happened. We can keep the both of you safe."

"Mooch is dead," Werner said, his voice hollow.

That news made Jianyu pause. "The Order?"

"He ran his mouth about what happened the night of the solstice, and Nibsy had enough." Werner rubbed his hand on the back of his neck. "He made an example of him."

The marks. Nibsy had used them in a show of power.

"I am sorry. But you cannot let yourself be next," Jianyu told him. "Nibsy Lorcan must be stopped, but Viola and I, we cannot do it alone. We need your help. We need the Devil's Own to remember what they once stood for, to stand again for what Dolph believed in. Think of it, Werner. Freedom from the Brink. Freedom from this city."

Werner shook his head. "I saw what Nibsy can do with those marks. I can't cross him."

"That is probably the smartest thing you've said since I met you." Logan Sullivan stepped out from around the corner then. His hands were tucked in his pockets, but the expression on his face was anything but relaxed.

Color drained from Werner's face. "You can't tell him, Logan. Please."

"Think about my offer," Jianyu said.

"He doesn't need to," Logan told Jianyu. Then he turned to Werner. "Take care of this. It's time to go."

But Jianyu had already pulled the light around himself. Before Werner had time to reach for his affinity, before he could attack, Jianyu was already gone.

A DIFFERENT LIFE

R uby Reynolds ignored the brisk chill of the late-November breeze tearing at her hair as she studied the Manhattan skyline from the upper deck of the SS *Oceanic*. It would be a while still before they docked in Manhattan and disembarked. First the ship had to wait at the quarantine checkpoint for smaller boats to pull up alongside and transfer the new immigrants in steerage to Ellis Island.

Looking at the city in the distance, she could hardly believe it had been more than five months since she'd been sent to Europe, exiled by her own family because of what had happened at the Order's gala in the spring. Not because of the danger she'd been in, but because someone had seen her kissing Viola. Now she'd been summoned home, back to the life she'd trapped herself into. The life she'd trapped Theo into as well. But she was returning a different woman than she had been before.

When her family had decided to send her away early in the spring, Ruby had been furious. But as her sister Clara grew bored with shopping for a bridal trousseau, she'd given Ruby more and more time to herself. Time to write and to think. Time for Paris to change her.

She hadn't been looking for anything in particular when she'd wandered into the small, cluttered bookseller's shop on the left bank of the Seine, but behind its leaded glass doors, she'd found another world. Week after week, she'd met women who were permitted to have minds of their own. Women who had made entire *lives* on their own. While her sister went off to discuss the gossip from back home, Ruby was transfixed by a world where women cared more for art and politics than whose ball was the crush of the season. There Ruby saw that a different future was possible. In Paris, something was beginning, and in those rooms, she had begun to dream.

But as summer eased into fall, her mother had begun to suspect that Ruby was simply avoiding what waited when she returned to the city. Marriage. Duty. And then the endless march of days as a wife.

Theo's wife, she reminded herself. Dear, sweet Theo. Now trapped as she was in the situation *she* had created.

Their engagement had been her idea. When the first of her group found happiness in church bells and white lace, Ruby had turned to Theo, because she knew that if she *had* to marry—and really, there was little choice in her world—he, at least, would be comfortable. He, at least, would not try to press her into the mold that society had provided for a wife and mother. Theo understood her as no one else did. He would allow her to breathe, as much as anyone could breathe in her world.

She could not deny that meeting Viola had changed everything. Marriage to Theo had become less a solution than another weight to bear. But in Paris, Ruby had started to see that if she and Theo must marry, they could still make a life together that suited them.

They would return to the Continent, far from the prying eyes of New York society. Ruby could see herself in Paris, perhaps writing as Mrs. Wharton did. She could see herself establishing a salon, like Miss Stein's on the rue de Fleurus, and continuing to send her missives about life abroad to be published back in the States, as she'd been doing all summer. She could see Theo there in Paris as well, spending his mornings studying endless art in the many museums and his afternoons discussing his findings in the many salons. Theirs did not have to be a life of misery. It did not even have to be a life of regret.

And if Ruby often thought of a pair of violet eyes and the way her entire world had come into focus at the press of a single pair of soft lips? It did not matter. It *could* not matter. Viola had made that point quite clear. If Viola was not an option, Ruby would fill her life—and her heart—with other things.

Or at least, that was what she was telling herself as she pasted on a bright smile and prepared to follow Clara and Henry down the gangplank.

As she disembarked, she found Theo waiting in the crowd of the docks. It had been weeks since she'd seen him—almost as long since she'd had a letter from him—and she felt her whole self brighten at the sight of him there. She began to wave before she noticed his expression. He looked so very lost standing there in the midst of the smiling crowd that her stomach had turned itself into knots by the time she finally reached him.

"Hello," she said, feeling suddenly and unbearably awkward as she looked up at his familiar handsome face.

He leaned down and placed a chaste kiss on her cheek, as he'd done a hundred times before. "I've missed you," he said, and Ruby felt the truth of his words. But she knew implicitly that something was wrong.

"I've missed you too," she told him, meaning it. "I haven't heard from you in so long, I almost feared you'd forgotten me."

He frowned at her. "I wrote to you," he said. "Every week."

"I haven't received any letters." She turned to Clara with a silent question and saw immediately the brazen satisfaction in her sister's expression. "You *took* his *letters?*"

Clara raised her nose, imperious as ever. "We thought it best."

"Then you don't know?" Theo said before turning to Clara and Henry. "Tell me you've at least told her?"

"Told me what?" Ruby asked as her confusion grew.

"Everything's been prepared," Clara said. "What was there for her to know?"

"What was there for her to—" Theo rubbed his hand across his mouth. He looked at Ruby. "We're to be married."

"I know that," she told him, confused at the frustration in his tone.

His mouth drew itself into a flat line. "We're to be married on *Thursday.*"

"Thursday?" That couldn't be right. She was supposed to have time—to plan, to prepare. She needed time to tell Theo about the life she dreamed they might have one day.

Theo was glaring at Clara. "I can't believe you kept this from her." He ran a hand through his usually perfect hair, mussing it in a way that was distinctly un-Theo. "What else doesn't she know?"

Clara lifted her chin. "It isn't the business of a wife to question."

"What else is there?" Ruby demanded.

Her sister's mouth grew grim. "I've only done what was necessary. It's for your own good."

"Her own good," Theo mocked. He was well and truly angry now. "If you were stopping my letters, you should have prepared her."

"Prepared me for *what*?"

Theo let out a ragged breath as he turned his attention back to Ruby. "We leave for my new post with the bank the day after our wedding. There won't even be time for a wedding trip."

Ruby looked at her sister, who was still tight-lipped and unrepentant, but she barely cared about Clara's betrayal or secrecy. Even as she tried to understand what Theo was telling her, she knew. They were being sent away, exiled again. This was the Order's doing. She was sure of it.

"Where are they sending us?" Ruby asked, trying to keep her voice steady.

He grimaced. "I can't believe Clara took my letters. I'd already explained all of this. . . ."

"*Where*, Theo?"

His shoulders sank. "Kansas City."

"*Kansas City?*" It might as well have been on another planet entirely. From the look of utter misery on Theo's face, she knew he wasn't any happier about the situation than she was.

"I'm sorry, Ruby. I've tried to fight this, but there's nothing more I can do. If I don't take the post, Grandfather will cut me off. I would have no way to support us."

Because she sensed that Clara was still watching, Ruby forced herself to be calm. She tried to give Theo a brave look, but she could not manage any words of comfort. Not when they both knew the truth. They were still being punished for what had happened in May.

Half-numb, she allowed Theo to lead her farther and farther away from the ship as they followed Clara and Henry through the boisterous crowd that lined the docks. *Married.* Before the week's end, if their families had their way.

"I *am* sorry," Theo said as they walked a few paces behind her sister. "I had no idea they were keeping this from you."

"It's not your fault," she told him, looking up into his eyes. "We'll make do. We'll be together at least."

"I read your last column in the *Post*," Theo murmured a little while later.

"The one about Pompeii?"

He nodded. "It was beautifully done."

"I *was* happy with that one," she said, feeling suddenly wistful for those days in the Mediterranean sun. "It seemed somehow more important than the usual drivel I'd been writing about the width of women's skirts."

"The emotion you put into it," he told her. "The beauty of the land and the people. It's all there, clear as day on the page how you feel."

Ruby looked out over the water. She knew exactly what had made that particular article different. She'd been to Italy before, but this time she'd seen Viola everywhere she looked.

"I'm not sure if Viola saw it, but if she had . . . I think she would have understood," Theo said.

"I don't know what you're—" Her footsteps stopped along with her words. She and Theo had always had honesty between them. "It doesn't matter if she saw the piece," Ruby told him with a sigh.

"No?" he asked.

She shook her head, but she couldn't quite look him in the eye.

"I have an aunt in Edinburgh who would be happy for company," he told her. "I could get you a ticket on the very next steamer available. You could leave as early as tomorrow. She'd have you as long as you'd like."

Clara tossed a look back at them, looking more than a little disgruntled that they'd stopped. Theo pulled her along gently.

Ruby understood what he was offering, but she knew that Theo's aunt was no real answer. Edinburgh was far too cold and gray and damp. Agnes Barclay was a lovely old woman, even if she did smell of the mothballs she used to store her furs, but she wasn't a solution.

"Are you truly encouraging me to jilt you by sailing away to your spinster aunt mere days before our wedding?" Ruby lifted her hand to her chest in mock horror. "Society would never allow you to forget. The tale would follow you for years."

"Perhaps . . . Though it would have to travel across a few hundred miles to find me on the edge of the prairie," he joked.

"Perhaps you would find some strapping young pioneer woman to bear you sons," she said, trying to make light of the situation they'd found themselves in.

But her words fell flat. Instead of a joke, the statement sounded more like an accusation. It was unfair and awful of her. It was she who had roped Theo into their agreement and then turned around and kissed another. She was the one who had fallen desperately for someone else. Did he not also deserve the same?

Theo simply looked at her with his usual calm, unflappable kindness.

"Is that what *you* want?" Ruby asked, surprised to hear her voice breaking.

"What I want is for neither of us to settle," he told her, his words heartbreakingly kind. "For *neither* of us to be unhappy."

She placed her hand on his arm. "I could never be unhappy with you, Theo. A life with you wouldn't be settling."

He gave her a knowing look. "Darling . . ."

Ruby shook her head. "It's not a lie. The whole idea for the two of us to marry, it was never about *settling*. It was a way for us to somehow escape from—" *From what?* From the only lives they'd ever known? Lives that so many would give *anything* for.

She let out a long, tired breath and released his arm. "What happened to us, Theo? We had such dreams. You with your art and me with . . . *everything*."

"Everything is exactly what I want for you," Theo told her simply.

"But everything isn't possible, is it?" Ruby asked. "Maybe it never was. Perhaps we were kidding ourselves all along, and this is all that life was ever supposed to be—one long march of expectations and meaningless social responsibilities."

"We can still have adventures, darling." He gave her a small smile that barely lit his face before he grew serious again. "You know I've always loved you."

"Like a sister," she said dryly.

He wouldn't quite meet her eyes.

"Like a sister, Theo?" Ruby frowned at him, confused at the way his cheeks had gone pink. "Isn't that what you've always said?"

He took her hand in his then, but he didn't answer her question. "You're my best friend in all the world, Ruby. There isn't anything I wouldn't do for you. Be my bride. Walk away now. Whatever you want, I'll stand beside you and weather whatever storms may come our way."

She could leave. She knew in that instant that he was giving her permission to upend their lives and follow a different path. She could jilt this sweet man and return to the Continent to find her freedom. She could become a stranger in her own family, the lost spinster aunt. She might even find happiness.

Before, she likely would have taken the lifeline he'd just tossed her. Even now, if there were any chance at all that Viola could leave the city, that Viola might go with her out into the world, Ruby might have risked all. But if she could not have Viola—and she could *not*—then she would do whatever she must to make Theo's life one that he deserved.

Dear Theo. She took his face between her gloved hands.

"Ruby?" His cheeks went pink. "People are watching."

"Let them." It wouldn't be the first time one of her kisses created a stir. She pulled him to her. Softly, she pressed a kiss against his lips. They were warm, and he was so familiar, but she did not feel the fluttering kick of her heartbeat racing as she had when she'd kissed Viola.

"My jilting you is not a possibility," she told him.

"You're sure?"

She nodded, blinking away the tears that threatened to fall, and gave him a brave smile. "I'm sorry for what your family is doing to you, but together we will find a way through."

WHAT LIVES INSIDE

1983—Times Square

Esta's mind raced as she counted the dark vans on the street outside the hotel. *Seven.* They completely blocked Forty-Fourth Street. Surrounding them were men and women in the same boxy coats they'd encountered back near Orchard Street—more of the Guard. One spoke into a walkie-talkie while others stood ready near the vans.

It was clear: they'd been tracked somehow. The Order or the Brotherhoods or whoever it was that the Guard now worked for had found them. They didn't have any more time to plan or consider. They needed to move. Now.

"There are some shoes that should fit you," she told him, nodding toward the pile of clothing she'd stolen from the luggage room as she gathered Nibsy's papers, the Book, and the artifacts. "They'll start searching the rooms soon. We probably don't have much time."

As soon as they were clothed and had gathered everything they needed, Esta took Harte's hand and pulled time slow. Her affinity felt sure and strong, as it had earlier. That, at least, was a relief.

When they slipped out into the hallway, a pair of Guards were frozen with their fists raised to pound on another of the doors. It was only luck that had them starting at the other end of the hall. A bleary-eyed businessman stood in one of the doorways, clad in nothing but boxers and a scowl, watching.

They took the steps down to the lobby, darting past more of the dark-suited Guards. The hotel was crawling with them, and when they reached the lobby, others were stationed at the exits and near the elevators, clearly trying to block any escape. The leader—a man with an extra set of medals across his chest—was speaking with the person behind the desk while the same yellow tiger cat stood silently by.

"They know we're here. We need to expect anything."

"Maybe we should go a different way," Harte said. "Is there a kitchen or—"

"It doesn't matter," she told him. "They would have blocked all the exits. At least this way, we have a straight shot to the street. It's gotta be close to the morning rush hour. We'll find a crowd and disappear."

Esta kept hold of time easily enough as they darted past the Guards in the lobby. As she suspected, there were Guards at the front doors as well. Through the glass, she could see more waiting outside.

"Do you think it's safe?" Harte asked.

"I don't think we have a choice," she told him.

He lifted her hand to his lips and kissed the back of it. "Then let's go."

She gave him a sure nod, and they went for it, bursting through the front doors as though every Guard in the hotel had been chasing them. She'd forgotten it was winter, and the burst of cold once she was through the door felt like a slap. For a second she thought she felt her affinity waver, but she'd barely taken another step before it was fine again. The world stayed frozen in time.

Then, all at once, the Guard waiting near one of the black vans turned toward them, and when he spoke, a familiar voice, dry as ancient parchment, came out of his mouth.

"I have waited a long time for you, Esta Filosik," the Guard said, stepping toward them with the jerky motions of a marionette dangling from strings.

"Thoth," Esta said, her voice barely a whisper. Her hand tightened on Harte's as she checked her affinity. The entire world stood still and waiting except for this one Guard. Except for Thoth.

Harte tugged at her, but she felt frozen in place. More, she had the sense that it was pointless to run. If Thoth could be anywhere, he could find her again and again.

"How are you here?" she asked. "I killed you back in Chicago."

The man-thing laughed in Thoth's eerie voice. "You killed the shell, girl. You *freed* what was inside."

"Esta," Harte said, his voice an admonition as he tried to pull her away. "We have to go."

The Guard's impossible eyes, black as an endless night, turned on Harte. "Where will you run?" the man mocked in a voice that was no longer human. "The city is mine." He spread his arms wide. "The whole *world* belongs to me."

"Not for long."

Before Esta realized what he was doing, Harte had already drawn the snub-nosed pistol he'd taken from the clerk at the pharmacy, aimed it at the man's chest, and fired.

"Oh god . . ." She looked at Harte. Then back at the man, who was already slumping to the ground. "Harte—"

The Guard was clutching his wounded stomach, and blood was already dripping from between his fingers. The darkness that had consumed his eyes was receding, and as it did, the man's face contorted in agony. But when the man looked up at the two of them, Harte saw something ancient shift across the man's features. "You cannot run," Thoth said. The Guard's teeth were red with blood, and when he coughed, more bubbled from his mouth. "You cannot hide."

"Watch us," he said.

This time Harte wasn't gentle. With a vicious jerk of her arm, he pulled Esta away from the dying man and into the crowded city beyond.

THE PRODIGAL

1902—The Docks

Jack Grew shoved his way through the crowd at the ferry docks, his stomach turning at the stink of humanity that surrounded him. He was glad to be back, even if it was without invitation. He'd been born in New York, and now that he'd seen much of the country, he was sure there was no place better. But as much as he'd missed Manhattan's finer points—the food and fashion and especially the women—he hadn't forgotten the impoverished urchins that tainted everything. He hadn't missed that at all.

The docks were littered with ragged, worn-out men and women freshly off the boat from whatever hellhole they'd left. The air stank of garlic and unwashed bodies. It seemed as though a steamer ship had skipped Ellis Island completely. Old women in babushkas and men with beards far too long and bedraggled to be fashionable waited for the next step in their journey. With any luck, they would continue on to some other place, but he wished they would just go back to wherever it was they'd come from.

Jack shoved his way past a group that might have been a family or might have been a pack of vagrants for all he knew. He kept moving until the crowded docks were finally behind him, past the line of dark carriages that waited for hire, and on to the private carriages beyond, where he found his mother's coachman, Adam—or was it Aaron?—waiting.

"Good afternoon, sir," Adam—or Aaron—said, taking Jack's bags and opening the door for him. "Did you have a pleasant holiday?"

"Holiday?" Jack asked. "Is that what the family has been calling my absence?"

Adam—or Aaron—blinked, but he didn't have a response. He turned to deal with the bags with a mumbled apology.

Jack hadn't been given a choice when he'd been shipped off to Cleveland to do inventory at one of his uncle's offices last summer. However his family had explained his absence to the rest of the world, Jack knew the truth: The position had been his uncle's way of getting him out of the city—and out of the Order's way.

But those long weeks of exile in the wilds of the Midwest had only served to convince Jack that there was no longer any use in trying to play the Order's game. Not when he could make plans of his own.

His mood darkened further the second he opened the carriage and saw his cousin J. P. Morgan Jr. waiting inside.

"Hello, Jack," Junior said without an ounce of warmth in his voice.

"How delightful. A welcoming committee of one," Jack drolled. There wasn't much choice but to take his seat on the bench across from Junior. Their knees practically touched in the cramped interior. "I assume your father sent you." He waved a dismissive hand, unwilling to allow Junior's unexpected appearance to throw him. "You might as well say whatever it is you've come to say, so we can both get on with our lives."

Junior frowned. "Come now, Jack. Can't one welcome his cousin home without so much animosity?"

"Perhaps . . . if the one offering the welcome wasn't completely full of bullshit." Jack waited, relaxed and completely at ease. Why shouldn't he be? He had the Book tucked securely against his chest, and now he had even more.

"I come on behalf of the family, of course," Junior began.

"Of course," Jack echoed, as though he cared a fig for what the rest of the family had to say.

"It worried us all when we received news that you'd relinquished your post in Cleveland," Junior began.

Jack shrugged, keeping his expression bland. "I found that the work didn't appeal to me. I gave notice, as required."

Junior frowned at Jack's impertinence. "You *disappeared*. For most of the summer, the family had no idea whether you were even still alive."

"I sent Mother a postcard. . . ." Jack gave him an indifferent smile.

"That was back in *August*," Junior sputtered, his tone every bit as imperious as the expression he wore. "It's nearly the end of November now."

"I also sent notice that I was returning," he pointed out, as though that fact should be obvious, considering Junior's current presence.

Junior bristled. "Jack, you aren't a boy anymore—"

"I'm *well* aware of that fact, even if the rest of the family regularly overlooks it."

"Be reasonable—"

"I am. More than," he said, cutting Junior off. "Your father stuck me in an insufferable position in an insufferable city. I did my duty, taking orders from the most ridiculous little man who smelled of onions and wore suits four seasons out of style, but after more than a month, I'd heard nothing from the family. I had no idea how long I was to waste out in the middle of nowhere, so I decided to take control of my life."

"You've been gone for *months*," Junior exclaimed. "Where on earth have you been?"

"I traveled around the country a bit, took in the sights." *Found what you could not.* "A grown man needs more of the world than the four walls of an ugly, cramped office, you know."

"The last time you tried to see more of the world, it ended rather badly," Junior said dryly. "Or have you forgotten what happened in Greece?"

Jack clenched his teeth and refused to give his cousin even a glimmer of temper. He wouldn't allow him the satisfaction. "Why, exactly, are you here, Junior?"

Junior let out a heavy breath, as though everything about the situation exhausted him. "The city isn't quite as it was when you left us."

"You mean when I was sent away."

His cousin glared. "The fact of the matter remains that things are . . . unsettled."

Jack lifted a single brow, inquiring. "That sounds rather unfortunate."

"After the solstice, the Inner Circle has done everything possible to silence any talk of what happened at the consecration ceremony. But the Order's alliance with the upstarts at Tammany is in tatters. We have been searching for those involved in the thefts, but with Tammany actively working against us, it's been impossible."

"You mean they won't allow you to ransack their wards as they did last winter?" Jack said, not bothering to hide his amusement. The richest men in the city, and they couldn't even manage to take in hand the filthy immigrant upstarts that ran Tammany Hall. So much for their hallowed institutions. So much for their supposed *power*.

Junior bristled. "The situation is delicate, and the family—the Inner Circle as well—has sent me to remind you of how much is at stake in the coming weeks. The Inner Circle has decided that you will remain uninvolved."

Jack didn't bother to cover his surprise. "What do you mean?"

"You'll receive this news officially soon enough, but Father believed it was important to prepare you. To avoid any unbecoming scenes," Junior said.

"What are you talking about?"

"The High Princept and the rest have decided that you should not attend the Conclave," Junior told him. "You are no longer invited to the gathering."

"Have they revoked my membership, then?" Jack asked, feeling a cold anger wash over him. In his front pocket, the Book seemed to tremble, understanding his fury.

"Not yet," his cousin told him. "But everyone involved believes it would be best if you are not present the night of the solstice. There is far too much at stake."

"Is that so?" Jack asked, forcing his voice to remain level.

"For the moment, yes. They've made their decision."

The carriage stopped at the Morgan mansion, and Junior alighted. When Jack didn't immediately follow, Junior turned to him. "The members of the Inner Circle are inside, along with the Princept. They require your presence."

"Consider their message already delivered. I'm afraid I have other plans," Jack said, keeping his voice pleasant.

Junior gave an exasperated sigh. "Come, Jack. Meeting with them now is the first step toward regaining their confidence."

"To be perfectly honest, I don't particularly care whether the old goats of the Inner Circle have confidence in me or not," Jack told him truthfully. "I actually *do* have another engagement—one I'd arranged before my arrival, as I wasn't expecting company on my ride into the city."

"Jack—"

"I'm finished dancing to their tune, Junior." Jack pulled the door shut and knocked on the roof of the carriage, leaving Junior to deal with the Inner Circle and the rest of the Morgan clan without him.

As the carriage rattled on through the city, Jack took two cubes of morphine and crushed them between his teeth simultaneously. *Finally.* Little by little, the tension in his head eased, and as the morphine lit his blood, the Book grew warmer, like a brand against his chest.

Fifteen minutes later the carriage stopped again, and Jack descended into the grime of the seaport. The area around the docks was lined with weather-beaten warehouses and teemed with longshoremen and other laborers, who looked at Jack from the corner of their eyes as he made his way through the maze of buildings.

He'd been away for months, but the warehouse he rented stood as it ever had, far at the end of the line of other low-slung structures. Making quick work of the lock, he entered the dark, dust-filled building.

Looming in the center of the space, the remains of his once-glorious machine waited. Before he'd left for Cleveland, he'd managed to rebuild the base and had been working on one of the circular arms, but he hadn't gotten much further. Now his progress was coated in dust.

He took the valise that had not left his side for the last few days and set it on the dusty tabletop. He didn't even care that the fine leather was being marred by the grime, because the contents were far more import-ant. He opened it and took out an object he'd obtained only a few days before. *This* was what had drawn Jack away from the post where his fam-ily had deposited him and out into the wilds of the country.

With satisfaction, he held the piece up in the flickering lamplight. The ornate dagger gleamed, and the unpolished garnet in the hilt seemed almost to glow from within. He thought he might understand why leg-end called it the Pharaoh's Heart, because even now he could almost sense the throbbing power coming from the stone.

In a single, fluid motion, Jack brought the blade down, lodging it into the wood of the table. The stone in its hilt pulsed, blood red in the dim light of the warehouse, and Jack finally allowed himself to smile.

Let the Inner Circle believe what they wanted of him. They could try to push him out and keep him away, but they would inevitably fail. With the Book's knowledge and the power caught inside the stone, he would finish what he'd started so many months before.

Whatever the Inner Circle said, he would be at the Conclave. They could try to push him out and keep him away, but they would inevita-bly fail. It was time to show them all *exactly* what he was capable of. He would build his machine and harness the power of the Book, and then, when the time was right, Jack Grew would show the Brotherhoods what true power was.

All he needed was a maggot strong enough to bring all his plans to life. Fortunately, he knew how to find one.

THOSE WHO ARE LEFT

1983—Grand Central Terminal

The icy winter air nipped at Harte's cheeks, but he barely felt the cold. All around him, the world had frozen in time, caught in Esta's magic. He had no idea where he was going as he tugged Esta along. All he knew was that they needed to get away.

"How was he able to do that?" Harte asked.

"I don't know," she told him. "He always could."

The sidewalk was crowded with early-morning commuters, and Harte expected each person they passed to blink with night-dark eyes or break free from the hold Esta had on time. But no one did, and he didn't slow until they'd gone two blocks. Finally, Esta stopped him.

"We have to keep moving," he said.

"I know, but we can't just run ourselves to exhaustion. We need a plan," she told him, looking around as though to get her bearings. "I need to *think*."

"How are we going to plan when Thoth could be anywhere?" he reminded her. "He can be *anyone*. And your affinity doesn't touch him."

"So we need to go somewhere there's not a lot of people," she murmured. Suddenly her expression shifted. "I know where we can go."

She didn't explain as she took the lead, guiding him through the maze of enormous buildings that had grown up since the early century. They dodged across streets, winding through stalled traffic, until suddenly they came to a building that looked like something from the past. The cream-colored stone facade was dingy with pollution and age, but unlike the boxy, window-covered structures around it, this particular building featured towering columns and arched windows. It was crowned with a large, ornately gilded clock. Above, winged statues watched over the streets below.

"Where are we going?" he asked, trying to get his bearings in a much-changed city. All around him, skyscrapers towered. The crown of one flashed a brilliant silver in the winter sun.

"Grand Central," she told him.

On the other side of the doors, Harte found himself standing in a cavernous room topped with an arched ceiling. A train terminal. It was strangely gloomy for such a huge place, but perhaps that was because one wall of windows had been covered by a large advertisement for Kodak. Or maybe it was because the ceiling had been painted a dark cerulean blue. He thought he could almost make out the shape of constellations in the murkiness of the false sky, but he couldn't tell beneath the soot and the age of the paint. On the far end of the station, crowning what must have been the entrance to the trains, a large illuminated clock waited in vain to advance the next second forward.

Around them, crowds of travelers were caught in Esta's magic. Groups of suited men and women were clumped throughout the cavernous space mid-stride. Most had the determined expressions of people on their way to somewhere else.

"There are too many eyes here, Esta," Harte said, warily searching the crowd for any sign of movement. He wasn't going to be caught off guard again.

"I know, but it'll be faster this way," she told him. "He can't control everyone."

Harte shot her a doubtful look, because they actually *didn't* know what Thoth could do. But Esta didn't notice. She was too busy looking up at the large board on one wall.

"I'll have to let go of time," she said as she studied the tracks and the arrival times.

"No—"

"The train can't get here if it can't move, Harte. The next 6 train should be arriving in a few minutes. Until then, we can use the crowd for cover."

"Why do we need another train when we could go on foot?" he asked, not liking the idea of her letting time go.

"We could," she admitted. "But the place I have in mind is a good distance from here. Probably over an hour's walk."

That *was* a long time to risk being seen. And Thoth didn't seem to be bound by Esta's affinity, so it didn't much matter whether time was still. Better to get wherever she had in mind quickly. "Fine," he told her with a nod. "I trust you."

Warmth lit her golden eyes, and suddenly the station sprang to life. The sepulchral silence of the terminal was instantly replaced by the droning murmurs of the hundreds of people filling the large hall.

"The trains are over there," she said, pointing toward the doorway capped by the large glowing clock. Its seconds hand was steadily inching around the dial now. "We should try to time it so that we get to the platform right about the same time as the train. In case we've been spotted, we won't tip anyone off to the direction we're going until it's too late."

"I'm not jumping off any more trains," Harte told her, remembering the grime of the tunnel the day before.

"We shouldn't have to." Her eyes cut to him. "As long as your affinity's working?"

He reached for his affinity and felt the connection to the old magic that had been with him his entire life, sure and strong. He nodded.

Having his affinity back didn't make him feel any more confident. It was a sign that Esta had been right. Nibsy intended for them to return to the past. But Harte wasn't in any hurry to meet the fate waiting for him in the pages of that diary.

Looping her arm through his, Esta pressed her body close to his. "Let's go."

The tunnel that led to the trains was even more crowded than the large hall they'd just left. Dim chandeliers that might once have been ornate had too many lights missing to truly illuminate the passageway. Esta seemed unbothered by the crush of people that jostled them as they pushed their way through, but every bump and brush with a stranger put Harte more and more on edge. Along the passage, a few police officers in crisp dark-blue uniforms watched the crowd, but thankfully, there wasn't any sign of Guardsmen. And there was no sign of Thoth.

When they arrived at the platform, they still had three minutes until the train they were waiting for arrived. Esta led them over to a place by one of the steel pillars that lined the tracks and curled into him, tucking her face close to his neck. His heart raced at the scent of her so close to him before he realized what she was doing—hiding her face from the crowd. Following her lead, he dipped his head toward hers, blocking the view of their faces with the bill of his hat. It was a ridiculous-looking thing with "I ♥ NY" scrawled across the front, as though anyone could love this trap of a city.

"Just a few minutes more," she whispered, her breath warm against his neck.

"I don't mind the wait," he said honestly. Especially when she was so close to him.

She'd only just smiled up at him when he heard a commotion coming from the tunnel that led to the platform they were currently standing on. The shrillness of a whistle cut through the noise, and Harte sensed the people around them shifting. It didn't matter that the squealing of the approaching train was already echoing into the station. No one cared about its arrival, because everyone was craning their heads to look back and see what was happening. Esta stepped back from Harte, and her expression conveyed the same thing he was thinking—trouble had just arrived.

Somehow neither of them noticed that a small older woman had sidled up next to them until she was too close to avoid. She moved faster than anyone at that age had any right to, and before either of them could step back, she'd latched on to Esta's wrist.

"Let her go," Harte growled, but the old lady ignored him.

She was a tiny thing, but she must have been stronger than she looked, because Esta couldn't seem to shake her off. Or maybe she wasn't trying to? The old woman's eyes were clouded with age, but there was no inky blackness staining them.

"Gram, let that lady go," a woman with curly blond hair said. She looked at Harte with an apologetic expression. "I'm sorry about this. She doesn't mean anything."

"I know what I mean, Ella," the old lady said. "Go make yourself useful and keep them occupied."

"Gram—"

"Go!" the old woman told her. "You know what to do."

"But the Guard . . ." The frenetic energy of whatever was coming toward the platform was growing.

"Did I raise you to be a coward?" the old lady asked, which caused the younger woman to blink. "Take care of it."

The woman looked like she wanted to refuse but then thought better of it and darted off into the crowd.

The old lady turned to Esta. "We don't have much time. They're coming for you."

Esta seemed transfixed by the woman's hand around her wrist. "Who are you?"

"Someone old enough to remember," the old lady told her with a wry curve of her mouth. "I was just a girl when the Devil's Thief nearly destroyed the Order. We *all* remember."

Panic flashed through Esta's expression. "I'm not—"

"Don't play games, girl," the old lady snapped. "There isn't time. The Guard are coming, and you're injured. Worse, you're marked."

"Marked?" Harte asked, still not sure what was going on. "What are you talking about?"

The train was sliding into the station, but the wind Harte felt lifting his hair was somehow stronger than its arrival should have created. Warm energy coursed through the air, reminding Harte of the noisy music hall he'd found in the Bowery. There had been magic there as well.

"It's how they'll find you," she said. "It's how they find all of us not smart enough to keep hidden. Hold still now, and I'll do what I can."

Esta gasped, and Harte felt magic surge again. Behind them, the doors of the subway car were sliding open, and people were beginning to pour out onto the platform.

"We have to go," Harte told them, desperate to get Esta away from whatever was coming, and away from the woman as well.

Esta glanced at him, startled confusion in her expression, but she didn't seem afraid. Whatever the old lady was doing didn't seem to be harming her.

Suddenly, the old lady gasped and released her, stumbling a little. Esta reached for her, catching her before she could crumple. "Go," the woman said, trying to push Esta away. "I did what I could, but I couldn't remove the trace. Not completely. They'll be able to track you through your magic, so be careful. We can buy you some time, but if you don't go now, it'll be for nothing." She pushed Esta away as the wind on the platform increased. "Go!"

Esta was staring at the woman as though she didn't know what to do, so Harte made the decision for her. "Come on," Harte said, trying to drag Esta toward the train.

"We can't just leave her there," Esta told him.

"I'll be fine," the old lady said. She was leaning against the column now, her eyes closed. "We'll do what we can to protect you."

"Who will?" Esta asked.

The old woman's eyes opened. "All of us, dear. All of us who are left."

RESTLESS

1902—Uptown

As she waited for the water to heat, Cela heard the bells of the grandfather clock chime in the offices of the *New York Age* below. They marked another hour gone by without word from Jianyu.

Maybe she should have been used to his absences. He was up most days before dawn and rarely returned until long after dark. They didn't usually hear much from him while he was off to do the bidding of Tom Lee, working to fulfill the bargain he'd made with the tong boss to save her life. It didn't matter that she was safe. Lee had his spy, and he kept Jianyu busy from morning until night doing his bidding.

But that day, Jianyu *wasn't* working for Lee. He should have been back.

Both she and Viola had been against the idea of Jianyu going to find Werner Knopf. Viola didn't believe that the Devil's Own could be swayed to turn against Nibsy so long as he had possession of the marks, and Cela, who'd had her own experience with Werner's particular brand of magic, didn't think it was worth the risk. But neither had been able to dissuade him. Jianyu had been growing increasingly restless over the past few weeks. More and more often, he talked of the Strega and the people there, because he still believed that they could turn back to the path Dolph had set them on.

He had too much faith. Viola thought it was a fool's errand, and to a lesser extent, so did Cela. But she understood. Each day without answers meant another with Tom Lee's shackle on his wrist.

The last few months had been difficult. It had been a long, frustrating stretch, filled with days trapped in the small apartment and nights trying to save Nibsy Lorcan's castoffs. Danger was always imminent, but nothing ever seemed to happen. As summer eased into fall, hopeful patience had been replaced by consternation and desperation. No wonder Jianyu had gone. She likely would've done the same.

Finally, the sputtering from the percolator stopped, and she removed the coffee from the stovetop and took the pot to where Viola and Abel were sitting. Cela's brother had come by for an early dinner before he had to go. His train left at eight.

She'd been distracted by thoughts of Jianyu, but now she realized that Abel had been telling Viola of his plans to help them by spying on passengers.

"You can't be serious," Cela said. "If anyone suspects what you're doing, you'll be lucky if all you lose is your position. And then what?"

"I'll be fine. And there will always be another position," he told her, nodding his thanks as she poured him a cup of the freshly made coffee.

"Abel—" Cela started.

But he didn't let her finish. "The Order knows who you are, Rabbit. They wouldn't have been looking for you if they didn't think you were involved with that mess back in June. But you won't run, so I'm going to do whatever I can to protect you. I can't be here every day, but there are things I can do out there, beyond this city. There are men who would love to see the Order brought low—cattlemen and ranchers, businessmen and bankers, who are all tired of New York being the only place that matters. The other Brotherhoods are hungry, Cela. They want a piece of the power that the Order has held for too long."

Her nerves were already on edge waiting for Jianyu, but now fear and guilt churned in her as well. There was no way she could let him put himself into that kind of danger for her. "What, exactly, do you think *you* can do about it?" she asked, her voice sharper than she'd intended.

"The people who can afford Pullman berths aren't your average travelers," Abel reminded her. "They're people like the men in the Order. They don't even bother to hide their secret insignia or conversations from me. I'm just the porter." He shrugged as he took another forkful of food. "To them, I barely signify. But I hear things. A lot of people wonder just exactly how ready the Order is for the Conclave. They've heard whispers about some of the things that have happened—the fire in Khafre Hall, the move to a new set of headquarters—and they wonder if the Order is hiding something. Maybe they don't need to wonder anymore."

"They wouldn't listen to you," Cela pointed out.

Abel frowned. "Probably not, but they'd listen to one another. All it would take is a telegram or two delivered to the right people."

"How would you know the right people?" Viola wondered.

"We listen and watch," Abel said. "Me and Joshua, we know plenty of other porters who would be willing to gather some information. We know people on different lines who could send messages from the right locations. With their help, we can make it believable. If the other Brotherhoods think the Order is weak, they're more likely to cause trouble. Maybe if we cause enough problems for the Order, they'll be too busy to think about Cela here and start worrying about their own selves."

"It's too dangerous," Cela argued.

"It's no more dangerous than you staying here in the city." He shrugged, taking a careful sip from the steaming cup. "You know how white people are. They talk around the help. Listening isn't going to do anyone any harm."

"You're not talking about just listening, though," Cela said. "You're talking about forging telegrams. You're talking about involving yourself in ways that could get you killed."

"Rescuing the Order's castoffs every other week could get *you* killed, and I can't seem to stop you," he pointed out. "It's bad enough you won't leave the city. You don't have to keep risking everything in these midnight rescues."

Guilt washed over her. "I do, Abel."

"No, you don't." He put his fork down and took the napkin from his lap. "You don't owe them a thing. Certainly not your life."

"It's not because I owe them," she argued. How was she supposed to explain to him why she went with Viola and Jianyu on those midnight runs? It wasn't because she didn't understand the danger. And it was more than the rush of excitement she felt when she put on the trousers and the vest she wore to disguise herself. She'd spent her whole life living in a city where the haves could take whatever they wanted from the have-nots. But on those nights that she rode in the box of the wagon and steered them all to safety, she helped to right that imbalance—if only a little. "I owe it to myself, Abe."

When he frowned in confusion, she took his hand.

"Could you live with yourself knowing you could have saved a life, but you sat by instead?"

His mouth tightened, but he shook his head.

"Then how do you expect me to?" She gave his hand a squeeze, knowing that he would go through with his plan. Knowing that she would let him. "We're both cut from the same cloth, Abel Johnson. You and me. We aren't built to sit by."

"I'm going to go outside and wait for Jianyu," Viola said softly, excusing herself from the table. "This is a conversation for family."

Even once Viola was gone, Abel still didn't speak.

"I'm sorry I dragged you into this, Abe," Cela said finally.

He wrapped his other hand around hers. "You didn't drag me anywhere, Rabbit. I've thought this through, you know. It's going to work, and when it does, we'll have a whole network in place of people working together. Think of what we can build with that. Not just for your friends but for *our* people too. The world's changing, Cela. Pretty soon it's not going to be this place or that. This Conclave that the Order is throwing is just one example. The country's coming together, one way or another. We have to be ready too."

THE INVITATION

The bite of the late-November air was exactly what Viola needed to shake off the mood that Cela and Abel's bickering had put her in. She had already been on edge, waiting as they were for Jianyu to return from his foolish attempt to convince Werner to join them, but to see the siblings' love for each other—their mutual respect and concern, so starkly different from her own family—was too much.

It had been a long summer and a longer fall waiting for something to happen, but nothing had. Darrigan and Esta had not yet returned. Nibsy seemed content to let them suffer as they waited for him to make his move. Even the Order seemed more restrained of late—or perhaps they'd just run short of victims.

Meanwhile, Viola had been mostly confined to the small apartment they all shared above the offices of Abel's friend's newspaper. Nibsy had the marks and control over much of the Bowery, and John Torrio had the Five Pointers and control over the rest of it. Her mother no longer had a daughter. Even if she could walk the streets freely, even if she hadn't been worried that one of their enemies might follow her back and harm Cela and Abel, where would she go?

Theo seemed to be keeping his distance as well. It was necessary, she knew. His family still didn't quite trust him, and he didn't want to risk leading anyone from the Order to their location. But he was Viola's only real link to Ruby. Without his steady, sunny presence to remind her of how good he was, it was too easy for Viola to allow herself to imagine a different world, where Ruby might be hers.

Pushing away her maudlin thoughts, Viola wrapped her thin shawl around herself more tightly to ward off the chill. Luckily, the *Age* building was far enough uptown that it had a small garden in the back, if one could call a plot of dirt patched with scrubby weeds a garden. At least there, she could be under the sky. She could pretend she wasn't trapped like a rat.

She'd been out in the yard honing her blade for no more than fifteen minutes when Jianyu opened the gate. At the sight of him, some of the tension drained from her shoulders.

She lifted her hand in greeting, but the expression Jianyu wore made her pause.

"I take it that your meeting didn't go as well as you hoped?" she asked.

Without answering, Jianyu lowered himself to sit on the stoop next to Viola. "I suppose it went well enough. He did not kill me where I stood."

"Small blessings," she said dryly. "He won't join us."

"No," Jianyu said, sounding utterly deflated. "Werner's fear is too great. So long as Nibsy has Dolph's cane, he has the Devil's Own. So long as Nibsy has the Strega, the Devil's Own will suffer."

Viola frowned. "Why is their fate so important to you? Most of them never truly accepted you even when Dolph was alive. Saving them won't change that."

"It is not about their acceptance," he said, turning to her. "I had that and more with the On Leongs."

"Then what?" she asked, truly curious. They'd lived and fought side by side for so long, but she'd never really understood the strange clockworks that drove him. "Dolph is gone. You can't keep fighting for him."

"I have never fought only for him, Viola." His mouth curved grimly. "When I left the tong, it was not for Dolph. It was for myself, because I wished for something more. Dolph believed in a vision of what the world could be—for magic. For everyone. I believed in that vision."

"He was no saint, Jianyu," she said, remembering the truth of her old friend. "He hurt many people in his quest for this world he believed in."

Jianyu nodded. "He did. He helped many as well." He paused then, and the seconds stretched in silence as the city hummed around him. "I came to a point in my life when I made a choice between the man I was and the man I wanted to be. And the man I want to be would not allow innocents to suffer under Nibsy Lorcan's rule. Not the Devil's Own. Not anyone."

She looped her arm through his and leaned over to rest her head on his shoulder. "You're a good man, Jianyu," she told him. "But the world doesn't care for goodness. Only for strength."

He patted her arm. "Then I shall be strong as well."

They sat in companionable silence as the wind whipped through their hair and made their cheeks turn cold. When Jianyu spoke, his voice was serious.

"I cannot help but feel that something is starting, Viola. Beneath the peace in the streets, danger is churning. With every passing day, the Conclave grows closer, and Nibsy grows more certain of his power."

"And Darrigan hasn't returned," she acknowledged, speaking the truth that they'd both been avoiding. "You expected him by now. Esta, too."

"We are running out of time," Jianyu said. "If they do not return before the Conclave . . ." He shook his head.

Viola laid a hand upon his knee. "If they do not return, we will do what we must." But though her words were filled with confidence, the dread within her had been growing every day. They had no artifact, no allies. No idea what was coming next.

"Cela is inside?" Jianyu asked, pulling himself to his feet.

Viola nodded. "Abel as well. He has a plan to help," she said, unable to hold back her smile at the thought. Strange allies, indeed. "But he leaves on the eight o'clock train."

Jianyu was staring at the back door, not bothering to hide the concern in his eyes. Or the wanting.

"She won't go with him," Viola said. "Ask her as many times as you want, but her answer will be the same."

Jianyu let out an exhausted-sounding breath. "I know."

"At least here we can watch over her while Abel's gone."

"Perhaps." Jianyu frowned at Viola. "It is the one thing I blame Darrigan for, putting Cela at risk when he had no right."

"Only one? I have an entire list," Viola said, moving her hands far apart as though to show just how long it was.

Jianyu shook his head, amusement chasing some of the shadows from his eyes. "Perhaps I do as well."

"You should tell her how you feel," Viola said softly.

He turned to her, his expression guarded.

"I see it whenever you look at her. Anyone could," Viola told him with a shrug.

"Cela Johnson is not for me," Jianyu said stiffly. The easy companionship they'd had between them before was now replaced by formality.

"Perhaps you should give her a say in that decision," Viola suggested. "Perhaps she would feel otherwise."

But Jianyu only frowned at her a moment longer before jogging up the steps into the building.

Viola remained on the porch, thinking of bottle-green eyes and curling blond hair as she watched twilight cast shadows and the night cool to a chill. She understood Jianyu's reluctance, his fear.

She can never be mine. But how Viola wished it were otherwise.

The sky was growing deeper now, a lavender-gray that felt as somber as Viola's own mood. She wasn't ready to go in quite yet, so she stood and took her knife from its sheath. With a fluid motion, she sent it sailing toward the fence. Some of the tension in her eased a little at the sound Libitina made as her blade found a home in the weathered wood.

She went to retrieve it and then returned to the spot and threw it again. And again. And again, until she felt her muscles aching and her back beading with sweat despite the coolness of the night air. With the feel of the knife leaving her hand and the sureness of her aim, she could breathe again. She could almost forget.

Suddenly, a sound came from behind her, and she turned, her knife already raised and poised to be launched. Theo Barclay stood there in the shadows, as though her thoughts had somehow summoned him. His hands went up as if in surrender, and he stepped into the light just as Viola managed to stop herself from turning him into a pincushion. Her hands shook a little as she sheathed her knife.

"Why do you people never use a front door?" Viola asked, embarrassment and heartache turning to temper. "I could have killed you just now."

Theo smiled. "I appreciate your restraint." Then his smile faltered. "Ruby arrived today," he said, rocking back a little on his heels. "Her ship came in just this afternoon."

"You must be happy to have her back," Viola said. She itched to throw the knife again. To send it sailing through the air. To feel the burn in her muscles and the satisfaction of it landing in the wood.

Theo nodded, and silence stretched between them.

"Is there something else you wanted?" Viola asked, wishing that she had any right to ask after Ruby. Wishing for all the world that she didn't care how the pampered heiress was.

"I came to bring you an invitation." Theo stepped toward her, extending an envelope in his well-manicured hand.

"An invitation for what?" Viola looked at the parcel suspiciously before she finally, reluctantly, took it from him. Immediately she was struck by the softness of the paper, the thickness of it. Her name was written in a wild flourish of ink across the front.

"For the wedding," he told her, looking down at his feet as he spoke. "Ruby and I are finally going through with the ceremony we've been putting off for so long."

Viola's eyes snapped up in surprise. "When will it be?"

Theo gave her a small smile that looked more like a grimace. "Thursday."

"So soon," Viola murmured, her throat growing tight.

"I'm sorry I didn't come sooner, to tell you. This is the first I've been able to get away." Theo let out a long breath. "There's more. After the wedding, I'm starting a new position. In Kansas City."

"You're not leaving?" It had never occurred to her that Theo or Ruby would simply *leave*. But then, she'd forgotten that, unlike her, they could.

"It's more that we're being sent away," Theo said sourly. "The Order clearly wanted to be sure that neither of us would be in the city for the Conclave. While we were away, everything was arranged for us."

Viola was still staring at the looping scrawl on the invitation. "Who is it that's inviting me?" she asked, her traitorous heart clenching a little.

"I am," Theo said softly.

She should have known that it wouldn't be Ruby. After everything Viola had said at the gala when Ruby had taken the chance and kissed her? Viola had no right to expect anything more.

"No." Viola handed the envelope back, pushing it toward him when he wouldn't take it. "I'm sorry. I wish you happiness, but this, I cannot accept it."

But Theo only tucked his hands into his pockets. "Keep it," he told her. "Please. I hope that perhaps you'll even consider coming."

To see Ruby Reynolds married? Her head seemed to be shaking of its own volition. "I can't—"

"If not for me, come for Ruby," he told her. "She'd want to see you there."

"You can't ask this of me," Viola told him, studying the flowing script of her own name once more, because she could not quite manage to meet his eyes.

"It *is* rather selfish of me, isn't it? Especially after you went and saved my life not once but twice." Without even looking, Viola could hear the smile in his voice. "But sometimes I find myself an exceedingly selfish and completely preposterous creature."

It was a lie. Of all the many qualities that Theo Barclay possessed, not one of them was selfishness. There was a reason Ruby had chosen him, a reason Ruby *loved* him. It was the reason that he—and maybe *only* he—was deserving of her.

But Viola's traitorous heart wanted to deserve Ruby too.

Theo turned to go then, but he hadn't quite made it ten paces when he turned back. "I've been Ruby's friend since we were still in the cradle. She's often difficult, you know. When she sets her mind to something, it's nearly impossible to sway her—even if a better option is standing right in front of her. Still, I want you to know that I'll do anything necessary to keep her safe and make her happy."

Viola pressed her lips together, swallowing the emotion that had caught in her throat before she spoke. "Why do you tell me this?"

"Because I think you feel the same," he said gently. "Because you're maybe the only other person I'd trust her to—her safety and her happiness together." He tipped his finger to the brim of his hat and then stepped into the shadows.

Viola realized her hands were trembling as they held the invitation. She'd never seen or felt paper half so fine. Theo's words swirled through her mind with memories of the girl she should not want. Ruby Reynolds was a frivolous piece of fluff with her pink cheeks and silken dresses.

Except that she isn't. Beneath the silk and lace, Ruby had a spine of steel and courage like a lion. She was rich and protected and disgustingly perfect. Viola hated her and wanted her just the same, and Viola didn't need to open the envelope to know that she had no place in Ruby Reynolds' life. Or at her wedding.

OTHER PASTS, OTHER FUTURES

1983—Grand Central Terminal

Esta allowed Harte to lead her into the waiting subway car just before the doors slid shut, but her arm was still buzzing with warmth from the old lady's magic. From between the various graffiti tags that covered the windows, she watched the woman droop to the floor while the people on the station tried to hold on to their hats or held their hands up to ward off the swirling wind.

There was still magic in the city, maybe even more than when she had grown up. There were still *Mageus* there, too, despite Thoth and the Order and everything Esta herself had done to the course of history. Maybe the Brink was still standing, and maybe the Order had more of a presence, but she remembered the old lady's words and wondered if what she'd done in Chicago had helped others like her. Maybe instead of forgetting, instead of simply allowing magic to die, more had decided to *fight*.

"What was she doing to you?" Harte asked as they found two empty seats. His voice was barely audible over the clacking of the car.

Esta rotated her arm and tested her injured side. "I think she was healing me?"

He frowned, as though he didn't quite believe anything could be that simple. She wasn't sure that she believed it either, but her side no longer ached. The wounds on her arm no longer felt tight and sore.

"But what was all that about being marked?" he asked.

"I don't know," she told him. "I've never heard of any kind of trace or mark before—not in any time. But who knows what Thoth has been capable of since I freed him."

"You tried to stop him," Harte reminded her.

"It doesn't matter what I *tried* to do," she argued. "Not when the results hurt people."

"I know," he told her, and there was a pang of regret in his words. She didn't have to ask to know he was thinking about Sammy.

She leaned into Harte, resting her head against his shoulder, and he wrapped his arm around her, nestling her into his embrace. They didn't need to say anything else, not when they both understood each other so perfectly. She wished she could let herself imagine that they were any young couple on their way uptown together. Safe. Content. Normal.

But Esta had never been normal, whatever that meant, and there wasn't time for playing pretend. She had no idea what the trace was that the old woman said they'd been marked with, but she suspected that it was the reason the Guard had found them at the Algonquin. She'd used her affinity to get them the clothes and likely had set off some sort of magical alarm. It meant they couldn't use their affinities or any magic without summoning the Order. It meant they likely wouldn't be safe as long as they were in that time, in *that* version of the city.

"We have to go back, Harte. And we have to go soon."

Harte let out a tired-sounding sigh. "I know." Those two words carried every ounce of the fear and regret that she felt herself. "So what's the plan? Where are we going right now?"

"North," she told him. "We need a safe place to secure the artifacts in the Book, and I know a place in Central Park that should work."

The twenty-minute trip felt like it took ages. It was a miracle that they didn't run into any other problems, but every time the car's doors closed without an attack, Esta didn't relax. They weren't truly out of danger. If what the old woman said about them being marked was true, the second they started the ritual to keep the stones safe, the Guard would likely know.

They disembarked at the 110th Street Station. Luck was on their side, and the small, dark platform was mostly empty. When they reached the street above, they walked for a few blocks until they came to the northern edge of Central Park.

As they approached the entrance to the park, Esta noticed the changes. The bricks lining the sidewalk were buckled, and half of them were missing. Trash lined the low stone wall that circled the park, and the path leading into it was cracked and uneven. Someone covered with a heap of filthy blankets was lying on one of the benches flanking the entrance. Beneath the sleeping figure, a paper-wrapped bottle had fallen over, spilling its contents onto the slush-covered walk.

Inside, Esta didn't find the park she'd grown up exploring. The grassy areas were riddled with sparse bare spots beneath the melting snow, and the pathways looked like they hadn't been repaved in years. She pulled Harte to the side before he could step on a bent syringe, but there was no avoiding the trash littering the area.

At least there weren't many people around. The farther into the park they ventured, the quieter it became, and soon the sounds of the city were no more than a gentle buzz in the background. Above, the trees caged them in with craggy, bare branches. It took her a second to remember the way, especially with how different everything looked, but eventually she found the path that led to the Blockhouse.

"This place looks older than I am," Harte said, peering up at the stone structure.

"It is." While she might have preferred the comfort of a hotel, there were too many people there. Too many exits to be blocked. Too many passages to be trapped. "You've never been here?"

He shook his head. "What is it?"

"An old Revolutionary War fort," she said. "The war ended before it ever saw any action, but we should be safe enough inside to get the artifacts secured." Or if not safe, at least they'd be able to see danger coming.

She shivered when a cold gust blew through the trees. "I should've found us warmer coats."

Harte cocked a brow in her direction. "Are we planning on staying long?"

"No," she said. The old woman's words made it clear that they didn't have time to get comfortable. They needed to secure the artifacts and get out of there. It was time to go back.

"Good," he told her, frowning up at the structure. "I've never really been one for the outdoors."

She thought of his apartment, of the enormous white tub and the hot running water that would have been a luxury at the time, and she laughed. "I think that's probably an understatement." Then she grew serious. "We should get started. The sooner we get the stones secured, the better."

They used Viola's blade to cut the rusted padlock off the barred door, and then they climbed through the low-hanging entrance. From the trash lining the small, stone-walled space, Esta could tell that they hadn't been the only ones with the idea of using the fort recently. She nudged aside a used condom with her foot and shuddered.

"Let's set up over there." She pointed to a spot near one of the openings in the block. "You can keep a lookout while I take care of the artifacts."

Harte took the satchel from where he'd slung it across his body and handed it to her, and in the matter of a few minutes, she had everything ready—the Book of Mysteries was open to the page that described the ritual, and the artifacts were arranged nearby. Viola's knife was in her hand. But she hesitated.

"What is it?" Harte was frowning down at her from where he stood a few feet away.

"I thought we'd have more time," she admitted. "Back in the hotel, I thought we were safe. It felt like we could stay there for a while. Just the two of us. I wouldn't have stopped you if I had known—" She pressed her lips together and fought back the tears burning at her eyes. She wanted too much, and she was afraid she couldn't have any of it.

He came over to where she was and wrapped her in his arms. "It's okay," he said.

"What if it's not?" she asked. "What if that was our chance, and I wasted it?"

His hands were rubbing her back gently as if to warm her, but there was a cold fear lodged deep within her that she couldn't quite shake.

"I keep thinking about what you said back at the hotel," she told him. "About someone else raising me. And the more I think about it, the more I realize how selfish I'm being. Even if we figure out a way for me to survive the Conclave, can I really send that girl forward in time to be raised by Nibsy now that I know what he's truly capable of?"

Harte's hands went still.

"You saw what he did to her," Esta continued. "He's worse now than he was before. He's more dangerous because he knows everything. Even if I'm willing to sacrifice her like that, even if I'm willing to send her forward, it means I have to let Nibsy live. And if I let him live, he's never going to stop hunting us. He's never going to give up trying to get the power in the Book."

"What are you saying?" Harte asked. "If you don't send her forward with the stone, you'll disappear. It'll be like you never existed."

She stepped back from him, because it was too hard to think when he was touching her. It was too hard to want something that maybe never should have been hers.

"Maybe I shouldn't have," Esta told him.

"No, Esta—"

"Think about it, Harte. You heard what Everett said: *A life is singular.* But mine isn't. It hasn't been since Nibsy mistakenly sent me forward in time as a toddler. I'm myself, and I'm that other version as well." She showed him her wrist with the scars of injuries she shared with another person. "We're separate, but the same. We're connected in a way I don't understand. Maybe that's not supposed to happen. Maybe I *am* an abomination," she told him, repeating what Jack—Thoth—had told her weeks ago in Colorado.

"I don't believe that," he said. "I *refuse* to believe that."

She smiled softly at the vehemence in his tone. "Maybe abomination is too strong a word. But I'm certainly an anomaly. I've introduced chaos into the time line just by existing." Her smile faded. "Maybe the only answer is for me to set that right. Maybe I'm supposed to go back and fix the mistakes I made. I can finish the ritual and make the Brink whole. Without the Brink, the Order would be powerless, and maybe magic could go on. But what does that matter if Nibsy is still a liability, more dangerous now than ever? If I wasn't worried about surviving, we could eliminate him and the danger he poses."

"You'd really kill him?" Harte asked. "I know what killing Jack did to you, Esta. You can't tell me you're really willing to take another life so easily."

"It wouldn't be easy," she said honestly. It had been terrible, and for the rest of her days, she would have to live with the memory of Jack's life seeping out beneath her hands. But if it meant ending all of this? If it meant saving someone else from carrying that burden? "But I saw what he did to that other version of me, Harte. He tortured her and twisted her into something I never want to be. How can I send a child forward to him, knowing that? How can we let him live, knowing that if he survives, no one will ever be safe? He won't stop, Harte."

"What about the girl?" Harte asked. "What happens to her if you sacrifice yourself and kill Nibsy?"

She'd been thinking about that problem ever since she realized that she could end the madness. She'd be dead, but that other version of her could go on. The girl could have the life that Esta should have lived, one not tainted by manipulation. One where she felt like she belonged.

"You could raise her," Esta told him. "You could give her the life I never had."

"No," he told her, adamant. "Absolutely not."

"Think about it, Harte," she told him.

"I won't," said. "I *can't*." He threw up his hands. "Esta, even if I was willing—and I'm *not*—it wouldn't work. Or have you forgotten? If you don't send the girl forward, then you never come back to find the Magician—and that's the end of me as well."

Esta froze. She *had* forgotten. She'd been so wrapped up in the horror of what Nibsy had done to that other version of herself that she'd nearly forgotten that Harte's destiny and hers were interlocked.

"You're right," she said, feeling more defeated than ever before. To choose between the girl—herself—and Harte? She couldn't. She *wouldn't.* "I don't know what I was thinking."

Harte sighed and took her in his arms, holding her tightly in the familiar comfort of his embrace.

"It's going to be okay," Harte said. "We have time, and if we don't, you'll steal us more. We'll figure out a way to deal with Nibsy Lorcan, but you have to promise me that you won't give up and do something rash."

"I just don't see how we can beat him," she whispered. Not when he knew so much.

Harte leaned forward until their foreheads were touching. "Hey," he said gently. "You're a thief, aren't you? And I'm nothing but a very talented con. We'll steal a future for ourselves, one way or the other."

"You're right," she said, still feeling unsettled.

"Promise me you won't do anything rash," he said. "Whatever happens, we do this together."

"I promise," she told him, meaning the words.

Then he kissed her. His lips were cold, rough from the dry winter air, and she felt his relief in the kiss. But she did not allow herself to get lost in it.

"Okay," she told him, pulling back. "We'll figure it out."

He stepped away, and she took a deep, steadying breath as she lifted the tip of Viola's knife to her finger once more.

"Be careful," Harte said, retreating farther.

We'll figure it out. She had to believe that. She had to think that this hadn't all been for nothing.

Gently, she pressed the blade into her finger, making the smallest cut possible. Blood welled at once, and without hesitating, she did what the ritual required and began to trace the symbol on the page open in front of her. Almost immediately, she felt something shift. Cold and hot energy climbed her arm as the page began to glow and the dark line of blood sank into the page. Three times she traced the figure, and then suddenly the page burst with light. A strange, humming energy brushed her cheeks, and she knew it was time.

She took the necklace first. The Djinni's Star gleamed in the wan winter sunlight, the turquoise stone sparkling with silvery flecks that looked like a hundred universes. It seemed only fitting she take this one first, since it was the first she'd ever stolen, years before. Maybe it was superstitious of her, but she had the sense that there was some power to the repetition. She lifted it over the glowing pages and then, remembering how Jack—how *Thoth*—had used the Book, she lowered it and watched as it disappeared into the pages with another flash.

It had no sooner disappeared than she heard a far-off sound—a steady, pulsing whir that second by second grew closer. They were coming. She reached for the Delphi's Tear and hoped there would be enough time to finish what she'd started.

INEVITABLE

1983—Central Park

When Esta had explained how they could use the Book to hold the artifacts, Harte had trusted her, but he hadn't understood. The idea that the Book could serve as some kind of magical container outside of time had seemed impossible and too good to be true. But as he watched the heavy glittering necklace sink into pages that certainly weren't thick enough to hold them, he began to believe that their plan might actually work.

The ring went next. The Delphi's Tear with its heavy, clear stone and ornate golden setting disappeared into the page, the same as the necklace had. Then Esta reached for the Dragon's Eye and was careful to keep the blood welling from her fingertip off the piece. The fantastical golden crown had cost his brother Sammie his life, and as Harte watched it disappear into the Book, he was reminded that, whatever the diary might prognosticate, he had no choice but to return to the past. It was the only way to give his brother a different future—a different fate. And he would find a way to save Sammie without sacrificing Esta's life.

The Pharaoh's Heart glowed blood red as Esta took it and began to feed the dagger into the Book, and when it had disappeared, the Ars Arcana pulsed with light as though it was hungry for more. Esta closed it securely instead. Ishtar's Key would remain where it belonged, snug in the silvery setting against her upper arm.

"We need to go," she said, looking up at the heavy winter sky. "They know we're here." She was already rewrapping the Ars Arcana in one of the Algonquin's fluffy white towels.

Harte realized then that the far-off droning hum of the city had changed. It was getting louder, growing closer.

Esta looked up at the sky above at the roofless room where they were standing. Then she tucked the covered Book back into the satchel and slung it over her shoulder. "We have to get out of here and find some cover."

The sound was even louder now, a steady mechanical chuffing that pulsed ominously as it grew in volume. Harte wasn't sure what the sound was, but he sensed that he didn't want to find out. Without hesitating, he took her hand, and together they hurried out of the fort and down the uneven stone steps into the park.

"This way," Esta told him, leading him onward.

"Why don't you use your magic?" he asked as the sound grew louder.

"I can't. Not if it's the way that they're tracking us." She picked up her pace. "And slowing time has never stopped Thoth. If we get far enough away, maybe we can lose them in the park."

He had no idea where they were going. He'd been to Central Park plenty of times, but never this far north. And even if he had, everything looked different now.

Esta led them from the path into more dense overgrowth, but the bare trees provided little cover. Their empty branches exposed them to the heavy gray winter sky above. They were moving as quickly as they could through the drifting snow on the forest floor, but they didn't get far before the source of the sound was upon them.

Harte felt the wind picking up as it had in the station, but this time it had nothing to do with magic. When he looked up, he saw an enormous beetle-like creature hovering over them.

No, not a creature. A machine.

He'd known that people had discovered flight. In San Francisco, he'd seen the silvery bodies of what Esta had called airplanes swimming through the sky, like minnows in a pond. But this was different. More horrifying and immediate. The dark metal insect loomed over them, and the sound it made was deafening. Thunderous. The pulsing, thumping beat echoed the frantic rhythm of his own heart as he and Esta raced along.

As though there was any chance of escape.

It happened so quickly. They were running hand in hand. Harte took one step, trying to navigate the snow-covered forest, and the next, the ground was gone. Suddenly, the world was turning itself inside out. Harte was falling. He felt himself torn apart, shattered into a million pieces, and then pressed back together. His head spun and he stumbled, barely catching himself before he went down.

Everything had changed. The snow was gone, and the forest was carpeted with moss and vines. The sky above was a brilliant blue, and the trees were green with fresh growth. The air no longer held the bite of winter. It hadn't yet warmed to the sweltering heat of summer, but the promise was there.

But they weren't far enough back. In the distance, he heard the blasting of a horn and the rumble of engines. Through the branches of the trees, he could see that the future city still loomed, enormous and impossible.

"When are we?" he asked, as Esta's steps slowed.

"I don't know?" She looked as shocked as he was.

"You didn't take us back?"

"I was going to," she told him. "I started to, but—I don't know. I hesitated. And then I saw this moment, and I just thought—" Her eyes were wide. "I didn't mean to . . . But I couldn't. Not yet." Her voice broke.

He understood. How could he not? She didn't want to face the choices that were coming any more than he did. Neither of them wanted to face the fate that waited for them in the pages of that damnable diary.

"It's okay," he told her, wrapping his arms around her. Because he could. Because the future hadn't unfurled yet in all of its terrible inevitability. His stomach still felt as though it had been turned inside out, but at least they weren't dead. "You stole us some time."

"I screwed up," she told him, trying to pull away. But he didn't let her. "I meant to go back. We're ready—"

"We're not." He brushed a piece of hair back from her face. She looked tired. Exhausted really. More worried than before. "We might have the stones tucked away, but simply having the Book and the artifacts doesn't mean we need to rush into whatever traps Nibsy has waiting for us. You made the right choice. You gave us time so that we don't have to run back unprepared."

She looked up at him, and the emotion swimming in her golden eyes felt like a punch to his gut.

"I know it's selfish of me," she told him. "But I want more time."

"So do I," he told her. "I want forever."

The glimmer of a smile tugged at her full mouth. "Me too, but I think we should probably settle for a day or two. We can find another room, rest, and make a plan."

"If we find another room, I'm not sure a day or two is going to work for me."

She did smile then, clearly amused despite herself. "We'd just be delaying the inevitable, Harte."

"Maybe." He wrapped an arm around her. "But I don't think anyone would blame us."

"*Harte—*"

"The past will still be there waiting for us, Esta," he reminded her. "It isn't going anywhere. We'll go back, but on our terms. Because we're ready, not because we're on the run."

She nodded. "You're right. We'll need clothes and supplies. We can't go back wearing this stuff. We'll need money, too." She looked out at the waiting city as though formulating a plan. But then she glanced at him from the corner of her eye. "You know, I *have* always wanted to stay at the Plaza."

"I have no idea what that is, but it sounds promising."

Her expression faltered as she stepped away from him. "I don't know how this trace thing works, but we should get moving. Maybe they can only track us if they know to be looking for it, but I don't think we should count on that. I took us back a few years. Not very far. Our arrival might have already triggered something."

He slipped his hand into hers. "Then by all means, let's go find this Plaza you spoke of before they arrive."

A TANGLED KNOT

1980—Central Park

Esta wasn't sure if her slipping them through time had triggered any sort of alarm. The old lady at Grand Central said she had a trace, but if her magic had activated it, no Guard arrived before she and Harte had left the area.

When the helicopter had been chasing them, she'd had every intention to take them all the way back, but as she'd sifted through the layers of time, she'd lost her nerve. And something about the moment—the soft green of spring or the calm peace of the undisturbed park, maybe—had called to her.

Or maybe that was her own cowardice. Because the truth was, she wasn't ready. One night with Harte wasn't enough before they rushed back and launched themselves into the final endgame. She accepted that Nibsy's diary might show her fate, but she wasn't ready to charge headlong toward it. Not yet. Not if there was *any* other way.

Once they were fairly certain that there wouldn't be any more helicopters coming after them, they left the underbrush and kept mostly to the paths. But the farther south they went, the harder it became to avoid people. Central Park in the early 1980s wasn't the park she knew. It looked worn out and run down, and most of the people they passed had hungry eyes. There were too many lumps of blankets and bags being guarded by bedraggled-looking souls. At the sight of them, Esta straightened her shoulders and walked a little faster.

"Don't look at them," she told Harte when she sensed him gawking.

She kept her own eyes straight ahead. "I'm not in any mood to fight off a junkie who might think we're dumb tourists and easy targets."

"I know this place," Harte told her when they came to the Reservoir. And as they continued on, he mentioned features of the park that he recognized from his own time, marveling at how much they'd changed.

"I knew the eighties were rough, but this place is a mess," Esta told him as they passed through a large open field with patchy grass and the frames of what might have once been fencing. In her own childhood, these fields had been manicured baseball diamonds. Now the grass between them was spotty, with bare earth showing through most of the field. Trash was strewn everywhere. "This is nothing like the park I grew up in."

They walked a little farther, and Harte noticed a building beyond the edge of the trees that he recognized. "There used to be a reservoir here."

Esta nodded. "They covered that over in the thirties."

"The sheep are gone," he noticed.

"Not a lot of room for sheep in the city these days," she told him, amused at his surprise. "Still plenty of rats, though," she said, as one scurried across the path a few feet in front of them.

"What else did they change?" he wondered. "Is the obelisk still there?"

"Cleopatra's Needle?" she said. "It's still there, over by the Met. You can't see it from here, though." And there wouldn't be time to go later. They could take a few days to plan, but they couldn't risk much more, no matter how much she might want to.

As they drew closer to the edge of the park, the noise of the city grew, and soon enough they came to where the park butted up against Fifty-Ninth Street.

"The Plaza's just there," she told him. "We'll need more cash to get a room without magic. For the clothing, too, but that should be easy enough. Tourists line up a couple of blocks over for carriage rides. We can head that way now. It shouldn't take long to find a few marks."

He followed her down the uneven, buckled sidewalk, toward where white carriages stood waiting with sad-looking mares. But her feet came to an abrupt stop before they were even close. Suddenly, her heart was in her throat.

"Esta?"

She heard Harte speaking to her, felt him move closer to make sure she was okay, but she couldn't respond.

"What is it?" he asked, gently guiding her to the side of the pathway.

"Dakari." She smiled through the burn of tears as she watched a young Dakari whisper something to his horse and pat it gently.

"Your friend Dakari?"

She nodded. She'd told Harte about him—about the kindness he'd showed her as a child. About how Nibsy had murdered him in cold blood to force her to return to the past with the Book.

"He's here?" Harte asked, now searching the line of carriages.

"There," she told him. "The white carriage with the gray horse."

Dakari's was the second in line. He was younger than Esta had ever known him. He was still tall and broad-shouldered, but he wasn't much older than a teenager. His deep brown skin wasn't yet creased in the lines that would come later, and he hadn't yet filled out. But his expressions were the same as he worked on brushing down the gray mare, his lips moving steadily as though he were speaking to the beast.

"Is he supposed to be here?" Harte wondered. "Or is this something else we've changed?"

"He's supposed to be here," she told him. But in all of the chaos of the previous days, she'd nearly forgotten that Dakari's existence was a possibility. "He arrived in the city in the early eighties. But Professor Lachlan didn't find him right away. He worked here for a few years before the Professor brought him on board." She wiped the tears from her cheek and choked back a laugh. "He looks so young—he can't be that much older than we are."

When she was a child, Dakari had been such an imposing figure, so sure of himself. His steady presence had been so much a part of her childhood, and he'd helped to make her who she was. She'd never imagined him like this, on the cusp of adulthood with his whole future in front of him. But now that she saw him, young and unmarked by Professor Lachlan, her heart ached for the man who died in the library that night. What might he have been if Nibsy hadn't gotten ahold of him? What else might he have done?

"Do you want to speak to him?" Harte asked.

She shook her head. "I couldn't." She felt another tear slide down her cheek, and she dashed it away. "What would I even say? 'Hi! You don't know me, but eventually you'll change my diapers?'" The thought made her feel ridiculous. "I just . . . I never thought I'd see him again."

Harte stilled. "You said that he knew you as a baby?"

She sniffled a little as she nodded. "Well, as a toddler. He was already working with the Professor when I showed up. He was older then. He'd been with Professor Lachlan for a while by then."

"Esta . . ." Harte's voice was barely a whisper when he spoke, as though he were afraid of time or fate or whatever powers existed hearing him. "What if Dakari is the answer?"

Confusion shadowed her expression. "The answer to what? Don't you remember? It's my fault that he's going to die."

"*Is* he going to die now?" Harte wondered. "Think about it. We just left Nibsy. He took his own life. How can he kill Dakari?"

Esta frowned. "Maybe he won't. Or maybe it's still a possibility. If we go back and set history on the course it should have been, then the Professor who just killed himself would never have happened."

"I don't know," Harte told her, scrubbing his hand through his hair until it stood on end. "How can *any* of this work? Time doesn't exactly seem to flow in straight lines."

"Doesn't it?" she wondered. "We created the Devil's Thief, and we saw the effects of that action on history." But it wasn't really that simple. If it were, Esta would have already been an impossibility.

"If that's true, why go back?" Harte asked. "Wouldn't the past remain unchangeable?"

"Because it's the only way to make a better future," she told him, her mind whirring as she considered something new. "I'd always imagined that we'd created a break somehow, that history veered off course. But maybe I was wrong. Maybe time isn't a line."

"What is it, if not a line?" Harte asked.

"It's something more complicated," she told him. "It's a tangle. A knot."

But that didn't quite fit either, not when she could sift so easily through the layers of minutes to reach a different time.

"Professor Lachlan said that time was more like a book," she told Harte. "Maybe he was right. Maybe you can change some of the words, but the basic story stays the same. Even if you removed whole pages, the book itself remained. The story is still there."

"But he believed the ending could be changed, Esta." Harte was frowning at her. "He wouldn't have sent you back to find me, to find the Book, if he hadn't believed that it could change his future in some substantial way."

"You're right," she told him. "He believed it would take something monumental to change time. Something that would be the equivalent of destroying the metaphorical book completely." She considered the implications of that, the way the Professor's metaphor aligned with the existence of the Book itself. He never would have destroyed the Book. He wanted its power too badly.

"Maybe we can write *over* the pages," she said, still thinking the idea through. "Maybe that's what we've been doing all along. We aren't erasing anything. Maybe the other versions *are* still there, waiting, and all the possibilities still remain somehow. At least until something happens to make them impossible."

"What if Dakari is the answer to rewriting *your* story?" Harte asked.

She stared at him, not understanding.

"You told me he was a mentor to you," Harte reminded her. "You told me how he basically raised you. What if he was the one who *actually* raised you?"

"You mean we could send him to find me?" Esta told him. "Maybe that's why time hasn't taken me yet, because *someone* can still be there."

Harte nodded. "You need to send the girl forward," Harte said. "And she needs to be sent back. But why should it matter who raises her?"

Maybe he was onto something. Maybe she was still living and breathing and part of the world because *someone* was still there to raise her. It could still be Nibsy. When they went back, they might still do something to make it possible for Nibsy to survive. But what if they didn't? What if it could be someone else who found the girl? Who raised her, and protected her, and sent her back?

"I don't know, Harte." Esta worried her lower lip with her teeth. "That's changing so much. Anything could go wrong. It could change *everything*. We could destroy Dakari's future."

"Or we could *give* him a future," Harte insisted. "He could be his own man, free from the Professor. And if we do it right, nothing else has to change."

"There are too many variables," she argued.

"Are there?" He drew her hands into his, and she felt the warmth of his magic sizzle across her skin. "Give me your past, Esta, and I can make sure Dakari keeps it on track."

Realization hit. "Your affinity."

He nodded.

"But that would take away his choice, his free will." She shook her head. "I can't do that to him."

"He's going to end up dead on Nibsy's floor, Esta." Harte's grip around her hands tightened. "We can give him a future. We can make sure that even if Nibsy makes it through alive, Dakari knows what's coming. We can make sure he survives."

She could protect him. She could make sure Dakari wasn't time's victim.

"It might not work," she said, chewing her lip as she watched the line of carriages.

Harte leaned in close to her until he could smell the soft scent of her hair. "But what if it does?"

SOMETHING BORROWED

1902—St. Paul's Chapel

As her mother adjusted the gauzy tulle around her face, Ruby couldn't help but think about how strange it was to be both solidly in your own body and somehow apart from it. She felt quite numb. The past three days had been a blur, and now that she was there at the church, dressed in the confection of silk and lace that Clara had selected, it all seemed so very absurd.

How quickly her life had changed, but not only in the last three days and not only because of the impending ceremony. If she were being truly honest with herself, her life had changed in the span of a single *second*. When her lips had touched Viola's at the gala, everything had come into focus. For the first time in her life, Ruby had the strangest sense that she could finally *breathe*.

But then it had all been ripped away.

Maybe if she had never kissed Viola. No . . . perhaps if she had never *met* Viola, there would not be this sinking feeling of regret. But there was no going back, no way to rewrite the past and make other choices. Now there was only the aisle before her, leading to a future that would not be terrible. She *knew* that. She was not marching toward her death or even toward a future filled with pain or suffering. She was simply walking toward Theo.

Somehow, though, that didn't seem to matter.

There she was, standing in the narthex of St. Paul's chapel, waiting for her own wedding to begin, and she would have rather been anywhere else. With her veil casting a white haze over her vision, Ruby could suddenly see more clearly than she ever had before. She'd never really intended to marry Theo. She'd always assumed *something* would come up to get them both out of their promises.

But nothing had. Now there was no escaping the path she'd put them both upon. Soon the organ would trill its opening notes and announce that any possibility of claiming the life she had once hoped for was officially at an end.

Her mother lifted the tulle over Ruby's face long enough to place a cool kiss on her cheek before she went to take her seat in the church, and then it was only Ruby and Clara's humorless husband, Henry. Because *of course* there would be a man. She was not even permitted to give herself into this new future.

The organ began to trill the familiar tune, and Henry offered his arm.

Ruby looked down at it and truly considered running. But she had never been one to run *from* something—only toward. And with her life suddenly unrecognizable, where would she even go?

"I don't believe I have to tell you how happy it makes all of us to know you'll finally be taken in hand," Henry said softly as they stepped into the open door and waited for the crowd in the church to rise. "Although I often have my doubts that Barclay will ever be man enough for that particular job."

Ruby swallowed down her anger and turned to him with what she hoped would look like a blinding smile to anyone close enough to see. "Dearest brother," she said through her clenched teeth. "Isn't it funny? We had the same fears about you on Clara's wedding day. But I doubt Theo will be half the disappointment to my family as you have been."

She could feel his arm tighten as her barb hit its mark, but Ruby stepped forward, starting down the aisle and forcing Henry to follow.

St. Paul's was a beautiful old chapel, with its white columns and arched vaulted ceilings overhead. At the other end of the aisle, waiting on the marble steps that led up to the great altar, was Theo, looking impossibly handsome in his morning coat—and impossibly nervous as well. He loved her. She *knew* that. He loved her enough to go through with this mad plan of hers, but what they were about to do here before god and these witnesses would end all other possibilities. Headstrong as Ruby might be, she was not fickle. Nor was Theo. They would take their vows seriously, and once they were wed, neither of them would be untrue.

They would not be miserable, but Ruby also suspected they would neither be truly happy—not as they might have otherwise been.

When Ruby had taken the first step into the church, the aisle seemed endless, but in no time at all she found herself standing at the altar next to Theo. He wore a smile, but his eyes betrayed the more complicated truth of how he felt. She imagined hers did the same. She understood the sadness in his expression—a bittersweet mix of affection and pain—because she felt the same echoing emotions. Before she realized it was time, Henry was already taking her hand and placing it upon Theo's. The rector was beginning to speak.

She met Theo's eyes through the haze of ivory tulle. *We don't have to do this*, she wanted to say. You *don't have to do this.*

But he only squeezed her hand in return. *It seems we do.*

On and on, the rector droned through the well-worn prayers, but Ruby heard none of it. All she could think was that this was a mistake. All she could feel was the enormity of her own guilt for forcing them to this point.

It will be okay, Theo's expression seemed to say. And Ruby knew he wasn't wrong. It *would* be okay. They would make a fine life with each other, but it would only ever be the shadow of the life she had dreamed of before she'd even known what to dream.

". . . speak now or forever hold your peace," the rector was saying. He paused then, waiting for someone to speak as the silence of the church threatened to crush her.

Theo turned to the few friends and family who had come to witness their union. His eyes searched the small group of their guests, but then something suspiciously like hope lit in his expression. It was enough to make Ruby turn as well, to see what it was.

In the rear of the chapel, sitting far off from anyone else, a pair of violet eyes met Ruby's. Ruby turned back to Theo, unsure of what was happening even as the rector continued with the ceremony, completely unaware that anything had just changed.

"What is she doing here?" Ruby whispered.

"I think she came for you," Theo told her, which was about the most preposterous thing he could have said.

"I require and charge you both, here in the presence of God," the rector droned, "that if either of you know any reason why you may not be united in marriage lawfully, and in accordance with God's Word, you do now confess it."

Theo's eyes suddenly didn't look quite so sad. "You can throw me over right here and now," he whispered, a small smile playing about his lips. "I wouldn't blame you one bit."

Ruby's heart felt as though it would burst in her chest. "It's impossible," she told him, feeling so many eyes upon them. The weight of expectations and promises not yet kept. But Ruby was already turning back once more to where Viola was sitting.

Viola looked like a woman carved from stone.

The rector was asking whether Ruby would take Theo as her husband, forsaking all others, but she wasn't listening. She was still looking at Viola. *Could she? Could they?* She had seen the women in Paris, the women who lived lives that she'd once thought impossible. . . .

But Viola could never go to Paris, Ruby realized. Not so long as the Order controlled the Brink.

". . . as long as you both shall live?" the rector asked.

The church was draped in silence, and it seemed that everyone—everything—was hanging on her answer. Past and future together meeting here in this one instant. This one *impossible* moment.

Ruby glanced back at the people in the church once more. But Viola was no longer sitting there. She was making her way out of the church. She was leaving.

"It's okay, darling," Theo told Ruby, giving her hand a soft squeeze before releasing it.

"Miss Reynolds?" the rector said, clearly growing impatient.

Ruby opened her mouth, her throat tight with fear and hope. But in the end . . .

"I do," she said, her voice cracking.

She couldn't decipher the look Theo gave her as he slid his ring upon her finger, but it didn't matter. It was done.

The priest lifted his arms. "Those whom God has joined together, let no one put asunder."

The congregation murmured amen, and it was over. Her fate was forever sealed to his.

"You may kiss your bride," the priest told Theo, who looked just as shocked as she did that they'd actually gone through with it.

His cheeks went pink, and she gave him a small nod to let him know it was okay. Slowly, he stepped toward her, reached for her veil, and lifted it.

But his lips had barely brushed hers when she felt her bouquet start to vibrate. Surprised, she drew back. Something was happening to her flowers. They were moving and quivering as though they were alive, and then they began *melting*.

"What the—" Theo took an instinctive step back.

The people in the pews were murmuring, and Ruby was frozen with shock as her once lush bouquet began to melt, liquefying down the front of her full white skirts. As the flowers dissolved into a lurid mess, they began to release a strange green fog-like substance.

Horrified, Ruby finally managed to toss the bundle of flowers—and the strange fog—away from her, but the instant it landed, the entire bouquet exploded in a burst of cold flames. They crackled as they grew, flashing with peculiar colors.

Fear rippled like a wave through the wedding guests, as row by row they realized that something was happening—and then they all seemed to realize the danger. The flames climbed quickly, spreading as though the entire church had been doused in kerosene, and despite the lack of heat, a dark smoke began to fill the space. Within it, energy crackled like lightning about to strike. The smoke churned and gathered, moving as though directed and molded by unseen hands. By the time the terrible roaring began, the congregation had already dissolved into chaos. But Viola had long since gone.

TO CHOOSE OR COMMAND

1980—East Fifty-Ninth Street and Fifth Avenue

Esta watched Dakari from down the block, still unsure about whether she could really do what they were planning to do to him. Could she take away his free will by imposing a future upon him that wasn't of his choosing? How did that make her any better than Nibsy?

Over the past few days, they'd looked at every possibility from every angle, and they hadn't been able to come up with anything else. Maybe Harte was right. Maybe it was the only way to *give* Dakari a future. He hadn't been all that old when Professor Lachlan killed him. Once he raised the girl and sent her back to 1902 to find the Magician, once he completed the time loop, he could go on and have the life he deserved.

But it still wouldn't be the life he'd chosen for himself.

She thought of the last few days with Harte. They'd spent them gathering the clothing and supplies they needed without any real trouble and making their plans. They'd spent them *together*. It had been a reprieve, but nothing they did had yet changed the writing in the diary. No plans they made swayed the future inscribed there in Nibsy's own hand. Still, she'd been happy, even knowing that it was all about to end—even knowing that she could be returning to the past to face an unavoidable fate.

Maybe there was a chance they could outsmart Nibsy and change the entry in the diary. But was that possibility of a chance enough to do this to Dakari? Could she really choose her own life, her own happiness, over his?

No. She couldn't.

"Harte . . ." Esta turned toward him so that she didn't have to look at the line of horses and carriages. "I can't take his free will from him."

"Esta, we've been over this a thousand times," Harte told her, looking suddenly panicked.

"I know, but that doesn't change the fact that Dakari was under Professor Lachlan's control the whole time I knew him. I can't make him into my puppet. I can't do that to the one person who was *always* there for me."

"Esta—" Harte reached for her.

"No," she said, stepping back. "I can't. I'm sorry, but I just *can't*."

"Please," he said, taking her hand. "We can talk about this."

But she only shook her head, knowing there was nothing more to say.

"He's more important to you than I am?"

She saw the frustration cloud his face and the anger sparking in his stormy eyes, and she wished it were otherwise.

"Don't do that, Harte. You know this isn't about the choice between you or Dakari. It's about *me*. It's about what I can live with and what I'll live to regret. And having *this* regret? Even if everything works—if we survive the Conclave and manage to fix the Brink and neutralize the danger of the Book—even if we do all of that and succeed, knowing we'd hurt Dakari would poison everything between us."

He scrubbed his hand over his face. "What if it's not forced?"

"What do you mean?"

"What if I don't compel him?" Harte told her. "Maybe I could just suggest?"

"And what? Dakari just goes through life making choices without knowing why he's making them?" She shook her head. "No, Harte. I can't—" Then another idea occurred to her. "But if he agreed to it . . . It would be different if we could talk to him and if he understood what he was undertaking. Maybe if he had the *choice*."

Harte stared at her, dumbfounded. "What are you planning to do? Walk up to him and say, 'Hello. You don't know me yet, but you will. And, by the way, could you raise the baby that I used to be twenty years from now?'" He shook his head. "He'll think you're mad, Esta. Hell, *I* think you're mad, and this was mostly my idea."

"Maybe," she said. "But what if he doesn't? What if he agrees to help us?"

Harte shook his head, and she knew he wanted to argue.

"I want a future with you, Harte, but I can't have that—not even if everything else goes right. Not if I'm dragging the past along behind me."

"Fine," he said, drawing her close to him. "We'll try it your way."

"There's only one problem," she told him.

"There's a lot more than one," he said with a sigh. But he sounded more amused than exhausted. A few nights of uninterrupted sleep and a couple of good meals had done wonders for him. For *both* of them. The gauntness of his cheeks was nearly gone, and his eyes were no longer shadowed by the heavy hollows that had haunted him since San Francisco.

"If you're not compelling him, we won't have any way of knowing what choice he makes," she said. "We won't know if it's safe to eliminate Nibsy or not."

Harte considered the problem. "Maybe there is a way. . . ."

"Well?" She looked back at him. His mouth was so close to hers, and his gray eyes were smiling at her. "You're not going to tell me?"

"No. I don't think I will." He kissed her softly.

"Harte—"

"You'll have to trust me on this one, Esta." He kissed her again. "If it works, you'll know."

"We won't be able to touch Nibsy until—unless—it does," she told him. "If I can help—"

"You can't," he told her. "We'll have to leave it up to fate."

Too bad fate was a fickle bitch.

She took one more opportunity to lean into Harte, to allow herself to enjoy the way he touched her now like they'd always been together. The way her heart raced, even with the familiarity of him. They were going back, and for her, it would likely be the last time. If they made it through the Conclave alive, she'd have to give up Ishtar's Key, and maybe even her affinity. If they didn't . . . well, she wasn't going to think about that.

Still, the modern city—even this version of it, dirty and broken as it was—had always been her home, and even if everything went right, she'd miss the towering buildings of Midtown that felt like walking through a cavern. She'd miss the spacious hotel where they'd burrowed and planned. She'd miss all of it. But if they could get Dakari's help, if they could bend time and fate to their will, she'd have Harte.

"Are you ready?" he asked.

"Not even a little," she said, throwing one of his standard lines back at him.

It wasn't a lie, because before they could go back, she had to face her past. She had to face Dakari.

Esta swallowed against the tightness in her throat and willed herself not to start crying like a fool as they approached. Instead, she focused on what needed to be done and pasted on the kind of smile that could hide the emotion beneath. It was the smile she'd learned as a child, the one that had let her pretend everything was fine when all she'd wanted was for someone to gather her up and tell her she was enough.

They walked toward the line of carriages, arm in arm. To anyone they passed, she would appear to be nothing more than a girl with her boyfriend, madly in love. And because it was New York, hardly anyone looked twice at their clothes, styled for nearly a century before.

They were there too soon, standing in front of Dakari's rig, with the old gray mare that she knew was named Maude. He was wearing a ridiculous suit meant to mirror the clothes of old New York. But its thin fabric was stretched across his broad shoulders, and the cheap top hat appeared to be every bit the prop it was.

"You folks looking for a tour?" he asked when he noticed they'd approached.

"Possibly," Esta said, suddenly nervous. Suddenly unsure about their plan.

What had she been thinking? Now that she was standing in front of Dakari, facing him as a stranger, she couldn't seem to form words.

She stalled by distracting herself with the mare. Tentatively, she put her hand out and brushed her palm across its smooth coat. "She's a pretty horse."

"She's the best you'll find in the city," Dakari said with a smile. He looked so young. So fresh and unbothered. She wondered again who he could have been if Nibsy had never gotten his claws into him.

"The cars don't bother her?" Esta asked, knowing the question was completely inane but wanting to draw the time she had with him out a little longer.

"Nah," Dakari said. "Old Maude here is as steady as they come. She never spooks. She'd be happy to take you both for a tour of the park. Thirty even for half an hour."

Harte's brows shot up. "Dollars?"

"He still isn't used to the big-city prices," Esta said, laughing at the look on Harte's face despite herself. It was enough to remind her why she was doing this and what was at stake.

She wasn't ready to give him up.

"Actually," she said, trying to keep her voice steady. "We didn't come looking for a ride. We came looking for you, Dakari."

Dakari's brows rose, and he took a step back toward his horse with wariness clouding his expression. "Who are you? Who told you my name?"

"It's a long story," she said. When Harte squeezed her hand encouragingly, she continued. "But if you have a few minutes, it's one I think you should hear." She reached into the inner pocket of her jacket and took out a small object wrapped in a piece of flannel. She'd carried it with her everywhere—had managed to protect it through every danger of the last few months—because it was a connection to her own, true past. And to the one person she'd always loved.

Unwrapping the small knife, she offered it to him.

"Where the hell did you get that?" he asked, already reaching for his own jacket pocket.

"You gave it to me." She met his eyes. "More than thirty years from now."

Dakari took the same knife from his own pocket, a twin to the one he'd given her—the one she'd lost in the past and then found again. He looked down at the two matching blades. "My father carved this knife," he told her. "There shouldn't be another one like it."

"I know," she said, feeling a little more certain. "He gave it to you when you left for New York."

Dakari let out an uneasy breath and looked at her with a mixture of wonder and fear. "I think I'd like to hear that story of yours now."

MALOCCHIO

1902—St. Paul's Chapel

Viola had known that she was a fool three times over for venturing to St. Paul's the day of Ruby Reynolds' wedding. What business did she have at the church where Ruby would be wed? What had she hoped to accomplish by putting herself through such a thing? She'd gone out that morning with the purpose of trying to forget the event was even happening, and somehow her feet had directed her to the chapel just the same.

At first she hadn't gone in. Before the ceremony, Viola had watched from across the street as the guests began to arrive, all dressed in silk and lace. Then came the carriage decorated with swags of flowers and greenery, and within it, the bride. Viola had seen Ruby only from the back, a blur of ivory silk and tulle, but as she mounted the steps of the church, Viola felt her dark heart twist.

Suddenly, she hated Theo. She hated Ruby as well. Or she tried to.

She should have left. If Viola had even a little bit of anything at all between her ears, she would have. But her feet would not seem to go any direction but closer. When the bells had called out the hour and the organ had summoned the bride down the aisle, Viola could not stop herself from slipping into the back of the chapel. She waited until Ruby had finished her journey and had been given over to Theo's keeping before she took a seat at the back of the church, far from the rest of the guests. But she still felt too close.

At the altar, Ruby stood next to Theo, hand in hand. Fair and slender and perfectly matched. But when Ruby turned to the guests sitting in the church, there was no joy in her expression. Then Ruby's eyes found Viola's, and the sadness turned to surprise. Perhaps even hope?

Viola's heart had risen into her throat—but almost as soon as the moment had arrived, it was gone. Ruby turned back to the priest, who was asking for her intentions, and Viola realized it had all been a mistake. Her coming there. Her ever having hoped. *A terrible mistake.*

She didn't remember standing, didn't realize her feet were carrying her away from the church until she was nearly hit by a carriage when she stepped into the street. She'd pulled back just in time not to be flattened by hooves. Standing on the sidewalk, she ignored the curious looks of passersby as she tried to catch her breath. As she tried to keep her heart from crumbling to dust in her chest.

Finally, she forced herself to leave. She crossed the road without any care for her own safety. Darting between the carriages, she knew only that she had to get away—to escape—and she was nearly to the other side when the sound of an explosion drew her attention back toward the chapel.

Smoke was pouring from the church she'd just left, and the wedding guests were all fleeing, coughing and shouting as they fled from whatever was happening inside the sanctuary.

Viola didn't hesitate. She ran toward the church, only barely conscious of the cold energy that flowed from within it. Without stopping, she plunged headfirst into the fleeing crowd, shoving past women clad in silk and men in crisply pressed wool as she pushed her way back to Ruby.

Inside, she could barely see through the thick smoke. The flames climbing up the walls behind the altar had started to spread. They were a strange greenish blue, but despite their brightness, they gave off no heat. Instead, they continued to produce more of the thick, pea-soup fog that had filled the sanctuary. It crackled with an unmistakable cold energy. But however much the fleeing guests were shouting about Mageus, Viola understood the truth. This was the work of corrupt magic, debased by ritual and controlled by someone without any affinity.

Which didn't make it any less dangerous.

There was something else in the air as well—the sickening sweetness of opium. Its presence was cloying and heavy in the dense fog. Whoever had done this had come prepared.

From the front of the church, Viola heard a woman's scream, and sending her affinity out into the chaos, she found the familiar pulse of Ruby's heartbeat. It raced along, erratic, but alive just the same.

Viola took a shallow breath, trying to avoid the threat of the opium as she struggled through the fog until she'd reached the altar. She stopped short when she saw Ruby near the front of the church, not far from where she'd taken her vows with Theo at the altar.

At first Viola couldn't understand what she was seeing. There was an enormous creature lurking over the altar. It was shaped something like a man—impossibly broad, *impossibly* tall. But the arms were too long and the neck too short for any human, and when it opened its mouth to roar, the strange flames burst forth from its open jaws, and more of the dark smoke flooded out. It looked as though it had been taken from a nightmare. It seemed to be made of darkness, or perhaps it had been formed from something like the strange fog that filled so much of the sanctuary. But Viola knew it was solid and alive because it was holding Ruby over its shoulder like she was no heavier than a rag doll.

Theo was trying to free Ruby by attacking the creature with the blunt end of a tall candelabra, but the heavy base sliced through the monster without so much as touching it. Its fog-formed body simply rippled, even as its enormous arms continued to hold Ruby tight. When Ruby screamed a warning to Theo, a ribbon of fog slid across her face, obscuring her mouth as completely as any gag.

Suddenly, Jianyu was there next to Viola, gasping for breath.

"I followed you," he said simply, before she could even ask. He gave no more explanation but wore a look that said she should be thankful he had.

"It reminds me of the gala," she told him. This creature wasn't made from stone, but it seemed very much the same. Like that other creature, she could not sense a heartbeat. It contained no true life, no true magic.

Jianyu nodded his agreement. "If it is false magic, its master must be here, close. Rituals such as this cannot work without someone to direct them."

"Jack Grew," Viola said. He had wanted to frame Theo for stealing the ring, and he'd wanted Ruby dead long before this. Who else could it be?

"Possibly," Jianyu agreed.

"He must be cloaked in some kind of magic. I can't sense him," Viola said, frowning. There was no sign of any additional heartbeat. "We need to find him." But she couldn't bring herself to leave Ruby or Theo alone with this monstrous thing.

"You stay. Help them," Jianyu said, as though reading the direction of her thoughts. "I will find Jack."

"The opium—"

"Will not kill me. And I do not need my affinity to deal with Jack Grew," Jianyu reminded her with a steely expression. He plunged into the fog, leaving Viola to help Theo and Ruby on her own.

Viola stepped toward them, drawing Theo's attention. When he saw her, relief briefly flashed across his face, but then the creature swiped at him, drawing his focus back.

Theo swung the candelabra again, but the brass base barely left a mark on the rocklike hide of the beast. "I can't get her free. It's like fighting a ghost."

In the beast's grip, Ruby had gone limp and was no longer struggling to get away. Her skin was turning an ashen gray, and her eyes had fluttered shut. The creature was crushing her. Even now, her affinity already beginning to go numb from the opium, Viola could sense Ruby's heartbeat slowing.

Only a few minutes before, Viola had felt herself cracking in two because she had believed that Ruby had been lost to her. She realized now how very wrong she had been. *This* was something far worse. Viola would see Ruby married a hundred times over before she'd accept her death.

"We have to hurry, or it will kill her," Viola said. "Can you draw its attention toward you?" She was already reaching for Libitina, sending up the desperate prayer of a sinner to her god. "If you keep it busy, I will carve her out."

False magic for false magic. Please let this work.

Theo looked doubtful, but he did what she said and doubled around the creature before launching another attack from its other side. Swinging the heavy base of the candelabra once more, he sliced through the fog that formed its legs, again and again, until the creature turned on him.

It was all the entrance Viola needed. In a flash, she lunged for the billowing body of the thing, plunging her blade into the fog that formed its arm as she focused her intentions through the dagger and sliced downward. The blade tore through the smoke, ripping it apart as easily as if the creature had been made of paper. As the dismembered arm evaporated into nothing, Viola barely had time to try to catch Ruby and break her fall as she tumbled free.

The creature itself went suddenly still before exploding into a burst of flame and dark smoke. Viola braced herself over Ruby to protect the still unconscious girl from the icy blast. She murmured another desperate prayer as she touched Ruby's too-pale cheek.

"Please," she whispered, urging Ruby to wake up. She tapped Ruby's cheek gently.

Ruby gasped, drawing air back into her lungs, and opened her eyes. Immediately she jerked away from Viola as though she were still struggling against the creature that had held her. It was only when Viola backed up, her hands raised in surrender, that Ruby finally calmed herself enough to truly see who had hold of her.

"Viola?" Confusion flashed through her expression, but then her eyes fluttered shut again.

Theo had already come over to where Viola was cradling Ruby on the cold marble floor of the altar. "Is she—"

"She'll be okay," Viola said before Theo could so much as speak the words. "But we must go," Viola told him. "This smoke, it's too much. . . ."

Her affinity felt so far from her now that she could no longer feel Ruby's heartbeat. Nor could she sense anything or anyone else. The cold flames were still climbing, the strange murky smoke still billowing. She had no idea whether Jianyu had found Jack and managed to stop him.

"We need to get her into the air," Viola told Theo. And then she would return and put a stop to this madness alongside Jianyu.

Theo helped to lift Ruby, supporting her with his arm around her waist, as Viola stood.

"Theo?" Ruby was waking now, coming back to herself. She blinked, then saw Viola standing there. "Viola? You came back. . . ."

"Come," Viola commanded, looking away. It was too painful to see the warmth there in Ruby's bottle-green eyes, too painful to hope. "We must go. While we still can."

"I'm afraid it's too late for that," a voice said.

Jack Grew stepped from the smoke as another enormous creature began forming itself from the smoke that billowed behind him.

Theo ran for Jack, but he didn't notice the beast forming from smoke and fog until it was too late and he was already caught up in the monster's clutches.

Jack was murmuring something, some strange gibberish as the whites of his eyes began to go black as the night. It looked as though light and life had flooded out, leaving only emptiness.

Malocchio. As dangerous as the devil, and Viola knew that no cornicello would protect them from this perversion. This dark, adulterated magic had no place in this world.

Viola kept her blade raised and ready—it seemed enough to keep the deadly fog away—keeping one eye on the large figure as it formed behind Jack and another on the creature who held tight to Theo. She could not risk throwing her only weapon, but if she could get past Jack, she could slice through the demon and free Theo by destroying it. If she could only slow Jack's heart, it would have been easy enough. She would not even regret it, taking his life here on the altar consecrated to god. But her affinity was dead to her by now, an effect of the opium that was thick and sweetly cloying in the smoke around them.

She had no idea where Jianyu was—or if Jack had gotten to him first. She could attack maybe one of the creatures, or she could attack Jack himself, but any attack would leave Ruby unguarded.

She lifted her knife, aiming for Jack.

"Kill me if you think you can," he told her, a sneering laugh in his voice. "But it won't stop my creations from ending you."

Viola froze. When she threw her knife at Jack, she would be completely defenseless. If Jack Grew wasn't lying, if these creatures somehow could exist without his direction, she'd be weaponless and without a way to defend Ruby or to rescue Theo. She could attack him herself, but it meant leaving Ruby without protection. Torn, she kept her knife poised, when she heard a voice whisper close to her ear.

"Give me your knife."

OUT OF TIME

1980—Central Park

Harte could practically feel Esta's nervousness as they rode in Dakari's carriage into the park. He hadn't said no or called her a madwoman, but that was a long way from him agreeing to help them. It was one thing to listen to a fantastical story. It was another completely to say yes to what they would be asking him.

As Dakari steered the carriage into the park, away from the crowds on Fifth Avenue, Harte wrapped his arm around Esta's shoulders and rubbed his thumb against her arm, trying to calm her. With the clothes they were wearing and steady clippity-clop of the horse's hooves, Harte could almost imagine they were already back, that they were already living another life. He and Esta, together.

But there was so much that needed to happen for that future to become real, and Dakari was the key. Even if Esta thought she had everything figured out with the Book and the Brink, there was no future for them as long as Nibsy's diary remained stubbornly unchanging. They had to take Nibsy out of the picture, and they needed Dakari's help to make that possible.

The diary still seemed like some kind of a trick Harte couldn't quite figure out. He would never hurt Esta on purpose, much less *kill* her. That fact alone should have made the words on the page impossible. And yet the entry had remained stubbornly consistent. The only thing that had affected it at all was their current idea to involve Dakari, but even that hadn't changed the words. It only made the ink on the page seem less sure of itself.

Dakari steered the carriage into an out-of-the-way corner of the park, and they alighted while he secured the horse and gave it an apple.

"You can do this," Harte whispered, urging Esta on. Then he listened to her spin the story of her life.

She started from the beginning. Or maybe it was the end. She told Dakari everything—everything except his own death. And when she was done, when she had lain out everything they needed of him, he frowned for a long, uncomfortable minute.

"And you think *I* can help you with this?" Dakari asked, his voice filled with doubt.

"You're the only one who can," Esta said. "I know it's asking a lot . . ."

Dakari shook his head. "That's an understatement. I don't know, man."

Harte had the sudden sense, then, that Dakari would refuse.

"You don't have to decide now," she told him. "It's your choice, completely."

"You're telling me I could change everything?" He didn't seem as though he believed her.

She nodded. "The Guard. The Order. The way they hunt our kind now? It's not supposed to be like this. You could live in a different world. You were *supposed* to live in a different world."

He looked down at the two pocketknives that rested in the palm of his hand. The knife his father had carved. The knife there should have only been one of. "Dammit."

"I know," she said. "I always was a pain in your ass."

He smiled a little at that. "I can't promise you anything," he told them.

"You don't have to," Harte said. "I can give you everything you need."

"And nothing you don't," Esta reminded Harte, cutting her eyes in his direction.

"The choice will be yours," Harte told him. But he wondered if he could really walk away, knowing Dakari was likely their only chance.

Dakari thought for a long stretch of minutes while the wind whistled in the trees above them. The horse nickered softly, tired of waiting for its next destination.

Esta suddenly slipped her hand into Harte's, and the world went silent around them.

"What are you doing?" he asked, panic rising. She was risking the Guard finding them by using their magic.

"He's going to say no," she told him.

"Maybe not," he said, but he didn't sound convincing even to himself.

"He is." She sounded certain. "And when he says no, you're not going to do anything."

Harte's brows drew together. "You're sure?"

She nodded.

"You know what that might mean, Esta." He had to clench his jaw from saying more, from begging her to reconsider. But she was right. If he forced Dakari—if he coerced the one person who had always loved her—it would always be between them.

"When he refuses, we're going to let him go," she told him. "You're not going to use your affinity to take away his free will."

"Even if it means the entry in the diary might come to pass?" he asked.

"You would never hurt me, Harte." She was pressing her lips together, and he could tell she was fighting back tears. "I will take every single second I have with you. But I won't steal any more than I deserve." She kissed him softly. "I love you too much to do that to either of us."

She released time before he could react and before he could respond. The city was humming around them again, but the world had narrowed down to Esta. Her whiskey-colored eyes drinking him in, her hands warm and sure in his.

"I know," he told her.

"What?" Dakari frowned for a second, confused. But then his expression cleared. "Fine," he said. "I'll do it."

"You will?" Harte asked, hope shooting through him.

"I can't promise things are going to work out like you want, but I'm willing to try," Dakari told them, looking down at the pocketknives. "I don't have any other way to explain this. And I think my father would have wanted me to try. He always did say my traveling here was for a reason. Maybe this is it."

"Thank you," Esta said softly, her eyes shining with tears.

"Don't thank me yet. We're not anywhere near done." He looked to Harte. "So, how do we do this?"

Harte held out his hand. "It's simple."

Dakari hesitated for a second, but then he took Harte's outstretched hand, and the second their skin connected, Harte focused on his affinity and sent everything through the bond between them. Dakari's eyes widened as though he sensed the intrusion, but then a calm, dazed expression fell over him.

"Don't forget—" Esta started, but Harte shook his head to shush her. He had one chance to get this right. He needed to concentrate on what he was trying to do.

The change happened almost immediately. It was as though they could feel the echo of something shattering in the atmosphere. Just like when they'd crossed back into the city, the air seemed to shift, and then the sirens began. Harte thought of the trace they'd been marked with, but he didn't allow himself to panic. There was more he needed to give Dakari. Unspoken instructions that might mean the difference between defeating Nibsy or the fate in that diary. He wasn't finished yet. . . .

"Hurry," she told Harte.

He shook his head slightly, as if to say, *Not yet,* but the sirens were getting louder, closer.

They were out of time.

TOO LATE

1902—St. Paul's Chapel

Jianyu coughed as the smoke from the strange flames clawed at his throat. Because of the opium in the air, he had all but lost his hold on the light. He had found Jack and followed him to the front of the church, where Viola was struggling to hold back the bride. Theo Barclay was there as well, struggling against one of the creatures formed from the strange, unnatural smoke. Even as Viola tried to keep the girl from danger, she had her knife raised and aimed for Jack Grew. But behind Jack loomed another of the monsters.

Viola's eyes went a little wide at Jianyu's request, and at first she did not relinquish her blade.

"*Now*, Viola!" he insisted. "With your blade, I can free him. Allow me to try."

She never turned away from Jack or the creature, but tucking her knife behind her back, she relinquished her dagger into Jianyu's hands.

"Please, Jack," the bride pleaded, her voice ragged with fear. "Theo's done nothing—"

"Nothing?" Jack asked, his voice suddenly hollow and cold. "He helped the maggots attack the Order. He helped them take the Delphi's Tear and Newton's Sigils. He tried to *ruin* me." Jack's eyes glowed unnaturally bright with glee. "Now he'll pay for daring to cross me."

"You're insane," the bride said, going suddenly still. It was as though she had only just realized Jack Grew's madness.

Jack simply laughed. "I'm far from insane, Ruby. I am simply more than your feeble, utterly *female* mind could ever begin to imagine." Jack gave the girl a cold smile. "I have taken possession of magic far more powerful than you—or your maggot friends—could ever hope to understand."

Jianyu used the cover provided by their conversation to edge his way ever closer. Hidden by the light and the fog, he positioned himself near the creature. Desperately, he considered the way it was built, searching for some weakness. He understood he had only one attempt to bring it down before Jack realized and turned it on him as well.

"I don't need to understand your pathetic false magic to destroy it," Viola said, drawing Jack's attention back to her.

Jianyu did not hesitate. Though he felt his affinity slipping away from him, he lunged. With a flash of steel, he plunged Viola's knife into the smoke and tore the creature open. Where the slice of the blade created a gash, blue-gray flames erupted, immolating the beast with a burst of otherworldly fire.

At the same time, the last bit of his hold on the light slipped from him, and he knew he was exposed.

Jack Grew turned on Jianyu, and when he realized what had happened, his expression turned murderous. He charged at Jianyu as the other creature began to move toward Viola and the bride.

"Get Ruby out of here," Theo shouted to Viola.

"I won't go without you," Ruby told him, struggling again against the hold Viola had on her.

As the two argued, Jianyu's focus was on the creature that was moving steadily toward them. He could cut it easily with Viola's blade, but with his affinity numb and impossible to reach, he no longer had the element of surprise.

By now the girl had torn herself away from Viola, but the other creature was already coming for her. Jianyu could see what would happen— the beast would reach her, and she would not be able to fight it off.

Jianyu leapt, trying to reach the figure of smoke, but Theo was faster. He put himself directly in the creature's path, using a candelabra to try to fend it off. The creature only billowed larger, rippling with something that might have been laughter if the roaring noise it made had been anything remotely human. It towered now, fifteen or more feet in the air. Three times the size of a normal man.

Theo was not dissuaded. He batted at it again, trying to force it back, but the candelabra sliced through the fog of its body without touching it. In an instant, the creature had grabbed him by the neck and lifted him into the air.

"Theo!" the bride screamed.

"Take her," Theo shouted, his face turning a sickening purplish red. "Viola! Get her out of—"

His words went silent as the creature tightened its grip, and the man's body jerked, a terrible, lurching convulsion, before he went completely limp.

Jianyu felt as though the entire world had focused down to the image of Theo hanging lifeless from the monster of smoke that towered over them.

"*Theo!*" The bride was screaming and tugging against Viola's hold on her, her face a mask of grief and horror that Jianyu felt echoed deep in his own bones.

The bride turned on Viola suddenly, clutching her by the shoulders as though she would shake the very life out of the assassin, who looked every bit as horrified as Jianyu felt. "You have to save him," she begged Viola. "It's not too late. Not for you. You can save him."

Jack took a slow step forward, as though there was no urgency at all. As though the sanctuary around him was not swirling with chaos and terror.

"Oh, it was too late for Theo Barclay the second he aligned himself with maggots who would try to destroy the Order," Jack said. "Or rather, I suppose it was too late for him the second his antics affected me."

"No . . ." The bride's moaning wail tore through the noise and confusion.

Jack looked almost amused. "He interfered where he should not have, and because of it, he nearly destroyed *everything*."

"You're a monster," the bride said, her voice angry and hollow. "You won't get away with this. I'll make sure everyone knows what you are."

"Take her," Jianyu commanded, finally breaking through Viola's shock.

She did not move, but simply stared at him, wide-eyed, as though she was unsure of what to do.

"You must take her from this place," he told her. The girl would only get herself killed if she stayed making threats she could not keep, and Jianyu owed Theo Barclay too much to allow his intended to die like this. "Now. Go!"

"I won't go!" Ruby screamed, tearing at Viola like a hellcat bent on escape as she tried to reach the creature still holding Theo's limp body. Her face was stained with tears, and her voice was raw with grief and fury. "Not without him."

"I wasn't planning on allowing you to anyway," Jack said, and as he lifted an arm, the beast lurched forward again. "Such a shame, isn't it, that the *maggots* chose today of all days to attack your wedding? What a *tragedy* that both the bride *and* the groom were killed by their dangerous, *feral* power. Something really should be done about it."

As Jack Grew's words dissolved into laughter, Jianyu leapt for the monstrous smoke, slicing at the body with Viola's knife. This beast was larger than the others by far, and this time it did not immediately burst into flames. Instead, it reared back as if in pain, trying to dislodge Jianyu. In the process, it dropped Theo to the floor, and his body hit the hard marble below with a sickening thud.

"We have to help him. You have to *help* him!" Ruby cried to Viola.

But it was already too late. There was nothing Viola would be able to do for Theo, not anymore.

"You must go," Jianyu ordered as he tried to wrestle the beast back with the dagger. "Would you deny Theo the last thing he asked for?" Jianyu asked Ruby as the monster stalked ever closer.

With his words, the fight seemed to drain out of the bride, and the girl fell into Viola's arms.

"Your knife," Jianyu shouted, ready to toss it back to Viola. She would need something for protection.

"Keep it," Viola said. "I *will* come back for you."

"I know," Jianyu told her simply. "Go."

As Viola tugged the bride away, disappearing through the dense fog, Jianyu turned back to Jack Grew.

Jack Grew had gone completely still and was examining Jianyu with narrowed eyes. "I've been looking for one like you," he said. Suddenly the fog around Jianyu began to swirl. Anticipation lit Jack's eyes. "The things I'll do with the power that lives within you."

"You are certainly most welcome to try," Jianyu said as he prepared for the attack, hoping that Viola would be swift.

THE DIARY

1980—Central Park

The wailing sirens were growing closer, but Harte wasn't done yet.

"Hurry," Esta told him, but his eyes were still closed, and his hand was still wrapped around Dakari's. He shook his head slightly, as if to say, *Not yet.*

She considered using her affinity. Maybe she could grab the two of them and hold them in the net of time until Harte was finished, but her power over the seconds had never stopped Thoth.

They needed to go, and they needed to go *now.* They had to lead the Guard and Thoth away from Dakari before anyone saw him. He'd already died once because of her. She wouldn't put a target on his back by letting the Guard find them together. Even if it meant dooming herself to an unknown future.

Esta jerked Harte away, breaking his hold on Dakari's hand, hoping he'd done enough. Dakari gasped as though surfacing from water, and Harte shuddered, stumbling a little before he caught himself.

"What happened?" Dakari asked. "Did it work?"

"They know we're here," she told him, as another siren cut through the air. "But we're not going to let them find you."

Dakari blinked in confusion. He looked almost drunk, and she didn't want to leave him there unprotected. But in the distance she heard the rhythmic thumping of a helicopter. They were out of time. They couldn't take him with them, and there wouldn't be a chance to come back to see him again. Once she was in the past, there would be no returning, not if she sent the child forward with Ishtar's Key. But somehow saying goodbye felt impossible.

It didn't matter that this rangy-looking teen wasn't really *her* Dakari. She launched herself at him anyway and wrapped him in a hug. For a second he just stood shocked, and then his arms were around her.

"Is that all really going to happen?" he asked, whispering close to her ear.

She nodded. "But it doesn't have to. You can change things, but it will be your choice." She squeezed a little tighter, wishing she could tell him everything she'd never said. "Whatever you choose, there aren't any regrets. You made my life bearable. You made it everything."

He looked shaken. "It's a lot to take in."

"I know. I'm sorry." She thought about that night she went back, about the night he died. "Whatever you do, don't trust the Professor," she told him. "He'll use you until he doesn't need you anymore. It doesn't matter what he promises. He's never going to put you before his own interests."

Releasing him, she stepped back, wishing she could stay. She would have liked to know him now, before he'd been trained by the Professor and honed into the weapon he'd later become. But there wasn't time. There were Guards in the park. She could see the black of their boxy coats through the thick foliage and hear the confused exclamations from the people they were searching.

"You're going to need this," Harte told him, handing over the small diary.

"What are you doing?" Esta asked. This wasn't part of the plan.

Harte glanced at her. "You're going to have to trust me on this." Then he turned back to Dakari. "You'll know what to do with it when the time comes." He held out his hand, and Dakari took it, pulling him in for a rough hug.

There was some unspoken conversation between the two of them, but eventually Dakari stepped back and climbed into his rig. With a flick of the reins, he spurred the horse onward, and then he was gone.

"Good-bye," Esta murmured, watching the carriage disappear around the corner. Then she turned to Harte. "Promise me that you didn't—"

"I wouldn't betray you like that, Esta." He slipped his hand into hers. "I promise."

"You really didn't, did you?"

Harte shook his head, and suddenly Esta wondered if she'd made a mistake. They could have known what Dakari would do. They could have been sure.

And she would have hated herself every day because of it.

"It's in fate's hands now," Harte told her.

"No," she said. She swallowed down her fear. "It's in Dakari's. We have to give him a chance, though. We need to lead the Guard the other way."

They started to run back toward the entrance to the park, until they came face-to-face with a squad of Guard. When they were sure that the men had seen them, Esta squeezed Harte's hand. She reached for her affinity and slowed time as she stepped toward him, and as the world hung silent around them, she kissed him. She only meant to hold on to the seconds long enough to capture the Guard's attention, but the second their lips met, Harte pulled her into the kiss.

He kissed her fiercely, like she was something precious. He kissed her like he was saying good-bye.

She was left breathless and wanting and without any idea of what she was supposed to say.

"This is going to work, Esta."

But they didn't know that. Dakari was one of the best men she knew, but time was a tricky beast, and the past was waiting. "You gave him the diary," she said. "We won't know what we're walking into."

"It doesn't matter," Harte told her. "I am never going to do anything to hurt you. I don't care what that page says. I'd die myself before I took your life."

"If we don't get out of here, it's not going to matter," she told him, trying to brush away her fear.

"Ready?" Harte asked, releasing her.

"Let's go," he said, and the second she let go of time, they ran, leading the squad of Guard down the winding path away from the direction Dakari had gone. When they reached the pond, they followed the path around rock formations covered in graffiti that rose out of the bedrock. And when she thought they were far enough away for Dakari to be safely out of range, Esta slowed time around her again.

The city went silent as they slowed, trying to catch their breath. Their pace was slower as they rounded a corner and headed toward one of the arching tunnels that carried one path over another. They were halfway through the tunnel when something changed. The world was still silent, caught in the web of time and Aether, but a line of Guard stepped into the opening on the other end to block their way. Their eyes were an inky black.

She cursed, but when they turned back to retreat, the path they'd just taken was blocked as well. More Guard had filed into the tunnel opening behind them. Their eyes were also empty of light and color.

Around them, the wind shifted unnaturally, and she thought she heard laughter.

"It's time, Esta," Harte said, his hand firm around hers. "We're ready."

One of the men lifted something that looked like a large fire extinguisher and aimed it in their direction. Harte jerked her back as the device began spraying a thick, bluish fog. They couldn't retreat too far, though, because on the other side, the other line of Guard was approaching.

But it didn't matter. They *were* ready, and it was time for them to go.

Esta was already focusing on her affinity, already riffling through the layers of time and history, until *there*. She had just reached the layer she needed when the fog began to swirl. She pulled them both through just as a cold wave of energy blasted over her. She felt her hold on time slipping, but she gritted her teeth and forced herself back, back, back.

But her magic lurched, and her hold on time went erratic.

It didn't feel like when she'd been shot by that bespelled bullet. Her affinity didn't seem to be slipping from her or draining away like before. Instead, her connection to the old magic felt like something wild and alive. The power flowing through her and tethering her to this time, to *this* place, went simultaneously hot and cold, and her grip on time—on *Harte*—began to slip.

All at once, time itself began to change. The layers of history, those years piled one atop the other, began to blur. She could no longer see the distinct layers of time, each minute anchored to this one, singular place. Now she saw *everything*. The minutes and seconds multiplied, twisted, until each minute contained *all* minutes. Each second held the promise of every possible second. And she saw, suddenly, what she had missed before—the possibilities inherent in the Aether, the way it connected *everything*.

The spaces between things weren't empty. They were filled with all that had been and all that might ever be.

The city flashed and blurred around her, and time became a living thing. There, within the layers—within the promise of each second—she saw every possibility, all at once. Simultaneously present and past and future.

There was the city as an untouched place, infinite in what it might become. There was *her* city as it had once been before she saved the Magician or became the Devil's Thief. Before she'd changed the flow of time. That past was still there, a ghost or memory within the layers of time. She couldn't reach it, but it wasn't gone. Because it was still *possible*.

One possibility among infinite possibilities.

Her affinity felt like a separate thing. No longer only a part of her, but a part of *everything*.

You could have all of this. The thought came unbidden, stark and absolute, and she knew somehow it was true. With the power in the Book, she could remake the world. *You could remake time itself.* She could reclaim all that she thought was lost.

Because it *wasn't* lost. Every time line, every change she'd created, it was still *there*. Within the seconds. Waiting.

It could be yours. The life you never got to have. Any life you might claim.

Her affinity flared, and she saw into the spaces between. For a blinding instant, she saw all that the city could have become had it taken a different course, had the Brink never severed it from its place in creation. But then she saw a different future. She saw *every* future, the beautiful and the terrible all at once. She saw futures where they won and the old magic grew and futures where they lost everything.

And then she saw the Brink fall, felt the terror of time turning to nothing—of the world and existence ceasing to be. And she understood *that* future, *that* possibility, was there waiting as well. Reality came undone as the city became an aching maw that was not time or place. It was only emptiness and lack.

Esta didn't realize at first that she'd begun slipping there into the nothingness of that unmade city, unmoored from time. But then she felt the familiar pull of time, the same terrifying sensation she'd felt back in Colorado of flying apart and being unmade. In a panic, she reached for her connection to the old magic, but whatever the Guard had doused her with was doing its worst. Her affinity was cold now. Distant. The seconds felt slippery, and the layers were flashing by too quickly for her to see any single time or place.

With all her strength, she reached for the city she had known, struggling against everything to find a layer where the city still stood and where she could still exist. But she'd only barely glimpsed it, had just started to grasp those seconds, when everything went dark.

DANGEROUS MAGIC

1902—St. Paul's Chapel

Viola struggled to drag Ruby from the church without harming her. She understood why Ruby was fighting her; she didn't want to leave Theo or Jianyu with Jack and his creatures, either. But Ruby was a liability. She was fragile and devastated, and Viola could not both protect her and help Jianyu at the same time.

"We can't leave him there," Ruby wailed, again trying to turn back.

"He wanted you safe," Viola reminded Ruby. Fear coursed through her even as she felt the crack in her heart growing, expanding so wide and deep that it felt like soon it would spread through her entire body. With one more heartbreak, she might shatter completely.

"You can save him," Ruby said with a desperation that only made the crack in Viola's heart ache all the more. "If we go back, you can save him."

"I can't." Viola shook her head as she fought back tears, wishing it were otherwise. She had seen the way Theo had jerked and gone still in the monster's grasp. She'd heard the sickening sound of his body when it hit the floor, and she knew that he was no longer with them. She could mend a wound or rend a heart in two, but she had no power over death. Though she would have perhaps traded whatever was left of her very soul if she could have only stopped Ruby's keening grief.

"You did it before. I watched you remove a bullet from his body. You saved him before," Ruby charged, her eyes wide and half-delirious from the shock of what had happened. Then she released Viola and stepped back. "Or is it that you won't?" Her voice had become cold and hollow, and her eyes were as hard as the diamond band that now sparkled on her finger.

Viola's throat was so tight she could barely speak. "I would if I could, but not if he's—" She couldn't say the word. She could not be the one to make this real for either of them. "Please. You must come with me now. Come, and I'll return for Theo," she promised. "I'll bring him back to you."

She could not tell Ruby the truth. She could not explain to Ruby that each second she wasted could be the moment that one of those creatures did to Jianyu what they'd done to Theo. Viola *had* to go back. She had to return to the dangers within the church, but only for Jianyu, because Theo's life was beyond her reach now.

Her promise to return for Theo worked, though. It was enough to allow Ruby to relent, and Viola was able to pull her through the side door of the chapel, where they found themselves in a graveyard. Viola led Ruby past the worn stones and uneven ground, breathing as deeply as she could. She willed the effects of the opium to wane enough that she might be able to again grasp the edges of her affinity. She needed something more than a single knife when she returned to the battle.

Compared to the chaos within the church, the graveyard was starkly silent. The day itself was unbearably bright. Despite the cold in the air, the sky above was an indecent blue, clear and absurdly serene. Viola hurried Ruby to the side of a mausoleum and found a place shielded from view.

"You must stay here," she told Ruby. "Keep yourself out of sight. Please." Viola's affinity had not yet returned to her, but that didn't matter. Even without her magic, she could certainly destroy a man who had become a monster. "Promise me that you'll stay here."

Ruby nodded. "I promise. I'll wait right here, out of sight. Please, Viola. Save him for me."

Unable to lie, Viola turned without answering and started to move toward the door, but she hadn't even gone four steps when flames erupted once more, blocking the exit they'd just used. A blast of cold energy, every bit as dangerous as the Brink had ever been, careened through the churchyard, nearly bowling Viola over with its power.

Ruby was on her feet, already charging back toward the chapel, but Viola snagged her and held her back. Flames were now completely blocking the door they'd just come from. There was no way to retrace their steps, no way to reach Jianyu.

"The front," Viola commanded Ruby, hoping against hope that Jianyu had managed to escape before the fire engulfed the building.

Together, they dashed through the graveyard, stumbling over ancient headstones, until they reached the front of the church. A crowd had already gathered on the sidewalk, barely far enough from the building for safety. Viola held Ruby back as the front doors of the church flew open and Jack Grew appeared with Theo draped over his shoulder.

All at once the flames that had been crackling in the doorway died down and the smoke began to dissipate. The crowd went completely silent as Jack descended the steps of the chapel slowly, like a hero returning from battle.

When Ruby recognized who was draped over Jack's shoulder, she moaned. It was a broken sound, filled with pain and devastation. She lurched forward to run toward the front of the church—to run to Theo—but Viola kept hold of Ruby by the waist and didn't let her go. Together, they watched in horror as Jack reached the bottom of the chapel's steps. The crowd parted just enough to make room for him to lay Theo's body on the gravel walkway.

Theo's body was limp and lifeless, and his head lolled back at an unnatural angle.

Ruby whimpered, still struggling to break free of Viola's grip.

"Shhh," Viola told her gently, tugging her back farther from view. Her instincts were prickling, and she cursed the opium that was still thick in her system. She did not have her blade, and she could not grasp her affinity.

"We have to find the bride!" Jack shouted. "Ruby Reynolds. They took her. Mageus did this. They killed Theo Barclay. I tried to stop them from killing his bride as well, but I was too late." His voice rose in near hysteria. "They're *monsters*. Look at what they've done to this hallowed building. *Look* at what they've done to my friend."

"Lies!" Ruby screamed, but Viola clamped her hand over Ruby's mouth before she could draw attention their way.

"We have to go," Viola said, but Ruby was still fighting her.

"We can't let him lie," Ruby told her, desperate with her grief. "Let me go, and I'll tell them I'm fine. I'll tell them Jack is lying. That he's the one who did this." She struggled to get away from Viola, scratching and clawing to be free. "Let me go, Viola."

Viola didn't listen. "Jack won't let you live, not after what you've seen. He would never allow you to speak against him. If you go out there, if you show yourself now, you're dead. He'll kill you as he killed Theo."

"Then let him kill me," Ruby sobbed, still trying to push away from Viola. "Let him show everyone the monster he is. It's no worse than I deserve."

Viola could feel her affinity starting to return to her—*too late*—and found Ruby's heartbeat, wild and erratic. Viola let her magic flare, only a little, just until Ruby went limp in her arms.

FRAGILE

1902—Uptown

Cela heard the carriage approaching right about the same time she got a sort of chill down her spine. She put down the trousers she was stitching and stepped out onto the front stoop of the building as Viola was helping another white lady down from a hired carriage. The other lady was dressed for a wedding—her own, it looked like—and her face was nearly as pale as the lace that was framing it. She didn't seem to be completely conscious, but she leaned on Viola in a dazed sort of way.

If Viola was bringing home the bride, something had gone terribly wrong.

"Where's Jianyu?" Cela asked, coming down the steps to help Viola with the girl.

Viola didn't so much as look at her when she answered. "I don't know," she said, her voice tighter than usual. "Help me get her inside?"

"Who is she?" Cela asked.

"Theo's," Viola said simply, and the way her eyes welled up was all Cela needed to know before she took the bride's other arm and helped Viola get her up the steps of the front stoop.

Abel was off on a Pullman run. He wouldn't be back for two weeks, but his friend Joshua was there, hanging around to keep an eye on her like he usually did when her brother was away. He looked up from his papers and gave Cela a questioning look as she helped the white girl into the room. All Cela could do was shrug.

They got the girl situated on a cot in the back room, but she just sort of sat there, slumped—as much as anyone could slump in a corset—and stared into the distance.

"Looks like she can't hardly breathe in that thing," Cela said, frowning at the way the girl didn't seem to respond to anything they did. "Help me loosen it up, would you?"

Together, they unfastened the endless row of buttons that secured the dress in the back and then undid the laces of the girl's corset to loosen the boning. Beneath, her pale skin was marked with angry red lines. The girl didn't so much as stir. She just sat there like some sort of fancy porcelain doll, but when the corset was finally off, the girl took a deep, shuddering breath. And then she began to cry.

Good lord, Cela thought. Abel was going to kill her if he came back to yet another problem.

"Shhh . . ." Viola eased the girl back down onto the cot and tucked her beneath a heavy blanket. As quickly as the girl's tears had started, they stopped. Her eyes fluttered closed, and she began breathing more softly, all peaceful-like.

Viola didn't say a word about anything until she and Cela were back in the kitchen, and even then, she didn't settle. Instead, she propped her hands on the sink and stared out the window.

Cela traded looks with Joshua, who was watching Viola warily now. She understood. Viola was being so unusually quiet that it was starting to make Cela nervous too.

"Come on now," Cela said, putting a light hand on Viola's shoulders. "Whatever happened out there, it's gonna be okay."

When Viola turned to her, there was nothing but raw pain in her strange violet eyes. She looked so completely vulnerable—so *unlike* herself—that Cela let out a small sigh.

"Come sit down here," Cela told her, offering her a chair. "And when you're ready, you can tell me everything."

"I'm going to head back down to the office," Joshua told Cela, giving her a meaningful look that she knew meant he'd be close if she needed him.

Cela drew some water from the pump at the sink and filled two cups. Then she took the seat across from Viola and offered her the drink. "You look like you could use something stronger, but I think we better start with this."

Viola took a sip, reluctantly, but once she started drinking, she didn't stop until the cup was drained. Then she let out a sigh that telegraphed exhaustion and pain.

"I should have stayed away," Viola said, staring into the cup without lifting it to her lips. "I had no business there, but . . . Oh lord, if I hadn't been there." She buried her face in her hands. "If Jianyu hadn't followed to help . . ."

"What happened?"

Viola only shook her head. "There was an attack at the church." She looked up at Cela then. "Jack Grew came for them—Theo and Ruby both. He wanted to punish Theo for what happened on the solstice."

"Where's Theo now?" Cela asked, already knowing by the grief in Viola's eyes what the answer was.

"Jack killed him," Viola said, her voice as hollow as her expression. "There was nothing I could do." She said the words like an apology.

Cela's chest felt so tight at the realization that Theo was gone, she could barely draw breath. She reached across the table, to take Viola's hand. "Viola . . . Where is Jianyu?"

Viola only stared at their interlocked hands, and Cela had the same twisting, sinking feeling of dread as when she had thought Abel had been killed. *No . . .*

Viola looked up and met Cela's eyes. "I don't know."

She told Cela then what had happened in the church, what Jack Grew had done.

"And you left Jianyu to deal with Jack and those creatures on his own?" Cela asked, panic warring with anger.

"He told me to go," Viola said numbly, as though she couldn't believe the words she was saying. "Why did I *listen* to him? I saw what those creatures, what that *madman* could do, and left him there."

Cela's heart felt like it was in a vise. There was an ache in her chest and one behind her eyes as well. She wanted to rail at Viola for leaving Jianyu behind, but she understood immediately that blaming her would do no good. Panicking would do no good.

Jianyu will be fine. He'd slip out of there and be back to them in no time. *He has to be.*

"I failed them," Viola murmured, utterly bereft. "I left them both behind."

Cela wanted to agree, but instead she squeezed Viola's hand firmly. "You saved that girl's life, just like Jianyu told you to."

Later, they sent Joshua out to see if he could gather any news, and then they sat together for a long while after that, not so much talking as just holding a silent vigil until the world outside turned to night. Cela finally stood to light the lamps, so they wouldn't have to sit around in the dark. She was just finishing when the bride appeared in the doorway to the kitchen.

Cela knew good work when she saw it, and whoever had made the girl's gown was a talented seamstress. An expensive one too, from the look of it. The frock must have been truly stunning earlier that morning, with all the lace and embroidery still crisply pressed. But now the hem of the white satin was marred with the grime of the city, and the lace flounces hung limp from her shoulders.

Viola stood immediately, but she seemed frozen, like she suddenly didn't know what to do. Cela took one look at her, the way she was looking at Ruby Reynolds with her heart in her eyes, and suddenly everything became clear.

They stood there for a long stretch, stuck in the moment and unable to shake themselves free. Cela thought that maybe they each understood just exactly what the others were feeling, that mixture of longing and loss that made her throat feel tight. That made her want to scream and cry and tear at her skin all at once.

Jianyu will come back, she told herself, not quite understanding why that point seemed so essential. But Theo Barclay would not, and beyond the tremor of fear that Cela felt in the pit of her stomach, she felt the ache of loss. Still, she knew that it was nothing compared to what this poor girl must feel.

"I see you're awake, Miss Reynolds." She paused, regretting her mistake. "Or should I call you Mrs. Barclay?"

The girl stared at her for a long second, like maybe Cela hadn't spoken the English she was born with.

"Ruby," she said finally, not answering the unspoken question. "Just Ruby."

Cela nodded. "Well, Ruby, let's get you something else to wear." She went around the table, took the girl by the arm, and guided her up the stairs.

"I'm going out." Viola was practically vibrating, and Cela knew that she wasn't thinking straight. She was overwhelmed with grief and anger, and she was likely to do something stupid if she went out alone.

"That's a bad idea, Vee," Cela told her. Nothing good could come from running on fury and grief. "Just sit back down and wait with us."

She was shaking her head. "I can't."

"Of course," Ruby said, her voice tinged with something too close to spite for Cela's liking. "You pretend to be so strong and powerful, but when you're up against anything, what do you do? You *run.* You ran at the gala, and you ran back at that church. You're a coward, Viola Vaccarelli. It's your fault Theo's dead."

Viola's expression turned unbearably bleak.

"Shhhh," Cela said. "You don't mean that."

The white girl turned on her. "I *do.* I mean it." She looked at Viola. "Theo was only mixed up with the Order because of *you.* Because you and your friends needed to steal some stupid artifact from them. I know all about what you did. He told me how he helped you, how he put himself at risk for you."

"I tried to stop him," Viola said, her voice breaking. "I never wanted him to risk himself for us."

"But he did, didn't he?" The girl's voice turned hollow. "He saw what you were doing as some silly adventure. He thought he was helping his friends. But you were never his friend. You never should have let him put himself at risk. *That's* why Jack Grew came after us today, because of what happened last June. All because of you and your friends. And you don't even have the Delphi's Tear to show for it. The Order still wins. *Jack* still wins. Theo would be alive right now if he'd never gotten mixed up with the likes of *you*. Theo died for *nothing*."

The viciousness in the girl's voice nearly had Cela leaving her to fend for herself. But Ruby was leaning on her too much to let her go, and Cela understood what grief could do to a person's tongue.

But it was too late to defuse the situation. She watched the color drain from Viola's face and her violet eyes go glassy with tears. There wasn't time to step forward and comfort Viola. She rushed from the room before Cela could take one step to stop her.

Before Cela could go after Viola, the girl collapsed. Her legs went right out from under her like the porcelain doll she appeared to be. Cela slid down with her, wrapping her arms around the girl, who was quivering now like a leaf in the wind.

"I didn't mean it," Ruby whispered, and then she burst into tears.

"Hush," Cela soothed. "It's going to be okay."

The girl let out a shuddering sob. "No, it's not. She's going to hate me."

"Viola doesn't hate you," Cela said, thinking of the pain and especially of the longing in Viola's eyes every time she'd looked Ruby's way. "Viola's been nothing but nerves since she dragged you in here, all because she's *worried* about you. She'll be back soon enough, once she cools off. And then you two can make nice. You'll see."

She finally got the girl calmed down and helped her out of the wilted white dress. For a long time, they waited together in the halo thrown by the oil lamps all night for some kind of news, but when the first rooster crowed, neither Viola nor Jianyu had returned.

PART

IV

ADRIFT

1902—Central Park

One second, Harte had been stuck in the tunnel, trapped between two lines of the Guard that had pinned them in, and the next, he was falling through time. At the same instant he'd felt a blast of icy energy from the Guards' fog, the heat of Esta's magic flashed through him. The ground disappeared beneath them, and he felt himself tumbling into nothing. Time tore at him until he thought there was no way he would survive it. He knew this was it. Time would rip him apart. And then the pain grew so great that he *wished* it would.

He didn't even realize Esta's hand was no longer in his, not at first. He landed hard, unable to stop himself from slamming into the unforgiving ground. His head was still spinning, and his stomach felt as though it would turn itself inside out.

It felt worse every damn time it happened, and this time he couldn't stop himself from retching. After his stomach was completely emptied and his mouth tasted like a Bowery gutter, he finally began to catch his breath. Only then did he realize he was alone.

Harte scrambled to his feet, nearly falling over because of the dizziness still plaguing him, but Esta was nowhere to be seen. The Guards were gone, but so was she.

Beyond the trees, the city had changed. The enormous buildings that had swept the clouds had now disappeared. In their place, the city of the past had returned. It looked like his city. It sounded like his city as well—there was no squealing of sirens, and the steady rumble of automobiles had drowned away to nothing. The clip-clop of horse hooves had him scrambling to the edge of the tunnel.

Dakari.

But it wasn't Dakari's white open carriage on the road that ran over the tunnel. Instead, a wooden coal wagon plodded along, pulled by a mismatched pair of old nags. Harte realized then that the trees were nearly bare. The last of late autumn's gold clung to a few of their branches instead of the lush spring greens he'd been expecting.

This wasn't the plan.

They'd intended to slip back as close as possible to when they'd left—not long after Khafre Hall and the events on the bridge. They knew they would need time to use the Book and fix the Brink, to discover if their plan with Dakari had worked, and to try to stop both Jack and Nibsy. They knew, too, that they had to stop the rumors of the Devil's Thief. It should have still been late spring. The air should have been warm with the promise of the sweltering summer to come. But it wasn't. The wind kicked up, and a clutch of dried leaves swirled around his feet, thickening the air with the scent of their rot. The coolness in the breeze spoke of winter and snow.

He didn't know *when* this was, but he knew Esta was gone. If he happened to find himself in a time she couldn't reach—

No. It wasn't possible that he'd lost her. As soon as Ishtar's Key cooled enough to travel again and as soon as whatever was in that fog wore off, she would come. She *had* to come.

He waited late into the night. At some point, he drifted off to sleep, and he woke the next morning chilled to the bone and shivering from the overnight frost. But he still didn't leave, because leaving meant accepting, and he wasn't ready to do that. Not yet. *Not ever.* He kept watch all through the day. Waiting. Knowing the world would right itself. That Esta would appear.

Near twilight, he realized he had an audience—a small newsboy who'd stopped to stare.

"You okay, mister?" The boy's hat was askew, and he had a bruise beneath his eye that had turned a yellow-green.

"No," Harte told him. Because the truth of what had happened was beginning to become undeniable. "Not even a little."

"Buy a pape'?" The boy lifted the stack of newspapers he had slung under his arms, unconcerned with Harte's answer or mood.

"No," Harte said, waving him away. "I don't want a damn paper— Wait. *Yes.* Yes, I do." He stood, shaking off the stiffness in his joints as he took a bill from his pocket. He didn't care what the denomination was—anything but a coin would have been far too much. He just wanted a paper. He needed to know.

"Mister?" The newsie sounded confused.

"Just take it," Harte said, shoving the money toward the boy. "I don't need any change."

Wide-eyed, the newsie took the bill from him and handed over the whole stack of papers. He darted away before Harte could change his mind.

Harte barely noticed him go. His eyes were already scanning the header of the newspaper for the date, and when he found it, he nearly collapsed with relief.

December 1, 1902.

Feeling suddenly light-headed, he leaned against a nearby tree to keep himself upright as he let all but the one newspaper he was holding flutter to the ground. It was okay. He might not be in the right month, but Esta had gotten him to the right year. She *could* still reach him, and they hadn't missed the Conclave. They weren't too late. She might already be here.

And if she doesn't come?

Harte hated the voice in his head, hated the question as well. But he knew the answer. He'd fight for her. He'd carry on. He was in his city now, and he had allies waiting. He had only to find them.

He turned back to the tunnel, still empty. Still without any sign that Esta would appear. There was a part of him that wanted to stay, in case she arrived. But he couldn't live in that tunnel, waiting for endless hours and days like some kind of vagrant. The police swept through the park regularly enough that they'd notice him, and that was only if one of the gangs didn't get to him first.

They had a plan, didn't they? Whenever she arrived, they'd find each other, and then they would set things right.

Harte took one last look, and then he started walking toward the Bowery. He had been away only a matter of months, but his travels had changed him. After San Francisco and Chicago, after seeing a New York that towered and rushed around him, this city felt different, and he felt different within it. He'd seen what it would become, and he could almost see that promise now, waiting like a sleeping beast ready to rouse itself. The world felt like it was holding its breath, waiting for the future to arrive.

Or maybe it was waiting for something else. . . . There was an atmosphere in the streets he couldn't quite place. An uneasy hum of something about to begin.

He headed south. Cela Johnson would be waiting. So, too, would Jianyu and Viola. He would need allies in the weeks ahead if there was to be any chance of them stopping Jack or Nibsy, of using the Book or stabilizing the Brink. Hopefully, Esta would arrive before the Conclave. Or maybe he hoped she was late. Maybe he hoped the terrible future written in the diary would never happen if she simply missed it.

Either way, Harte had to find the others. He would have to prepare them for what was coming, because he knew he'd need their help.

But when he turned down the street where Cela lived, he found only the burned-out remains of what had once been her home. He couldn't tell how long ago the fire had occurred—trash and other detritus had accumulated in the corners of what was left of the building—but there had been no move to rebuild.

In the distance, he heard the clanging of a fire bell. The whining of hand-cranked sirens.

He'd left his mother with Cela at the house that had once stood on that lot. He assumed his mother was gone. She'd been in bad shape when he'd left her to Cela's care. But had his mother passed from the opium Nibsy had doused her with before the fire? Or had she been trapped in the flames that had consumed the home?

Had Cela made it out?

He looked around at the buildings that were still standing, silent and uninterested in his distress. He had to find Cela, or he'd never know. Which meant he had to find Jianyu.

But Jianyu could be anywhere in the city.

With one last look at the burned remains of Cela's home, he turned his feet toward the Bowery, toward the one place that might have the information he needed. He only hoped he wasn't already too late.

HELLCAT

Bella Strega

James Lorcan had almost grown used to the strange rumbling under-current in the Aether that had plagued him since not long after the summer solstice, but when the Aether shifted violently that night, he knew immediately that something was coming. Still, he felt no fear at the trembling that signaled an approaching danger. He felt only anticipation. He'd long since placed the players on the board, and finally the game would begin.

When the doors to the Bella Strega burst open with a gust of cold, he wasn't surprised to see that it was Viola. He'd been expecting her for so long, she was practically late. With a knife in her hand and her eyes flashing fury, she entered the barroom ready to fight like the hellcat she was. Everyone in the saloon went silent, because everyone in that barroom knew what she could do—with the blade *and* with her magic.

Werner stepped forward, but James gave a subtle shake of his head to stop him. Viola had none of her usual cold, calculating calm. Something had unhinged her, and because of it, she'd made a mistake by coming here unprotected. It would make what was to come that much more entertaining. So he'd let the game play out. When Viola finally came to her inevitable end, it would be his hand that ended her. Not Werner's.

"Bastardo!" she hissed, finally spotting James from across the dimly lit space. The people standing between them parted like water as she stalked toward him.

"Viola," he drawled, keeping his voice easy and unconcerned despite her rapid approach. "How nice of you to visit. I see you haven't lost a bit of your charm."

"I'll show you my charm," she said, lifting the knife and pointing the tip at his throat.

It wasn't *her* knife, which was interesting. And she didn't skewer him. Nor did she touch him with her magic. He knew she wouldn't. She was there for blood, but for some reason, she wasn't ready to draw it quite yet.

"To what do I owe this delightful visit?" he asked. He leaned forward a little, unafraid of her blade, but he kept one hand tight around the cane at his side.

Her eyes shifted to the silver Medusa, and he understood that she knew what he was capable of. He saw fear flicker in her expression—just a glimmer—before she shook it away and narrowed her eyes.

"I hope you're here to accept my offer," he said, knowing already that she wasn't. "Perhaps you've come to repent of your sins and rejoin your family?"

"You are no family of mine," she said through clenched teeth. "And I have nothing to repent, other than letting you live for so long. But I think that's a mistake I maybe can be correcting. *Adesso.*"

He didn't bother to conceal his amusement. "Don't you think you have that backward? After all, I'm the one with control of the marks. You live by my mercy alone."

"You aren't worthy of the oath I made," she sneered. She let her gaze travel around the room, and she spoke to the Strega now, to the Devil's Own. "This one, this *snake*, he's not worthy of *any* of your lives. He's done nothing but take and take."

She found Werner in the crowd and focused on him. "Tell them," she commanded. "Tell them all how he sent you to die on a fool's errand. Dolph would never have done such a thing."

"Dolph did far worse," James drawled. "I assure you."

"I *know* what Dolph did," she said, turning on him, as vicious as she ever was.

"And you forgive him?" James wondered. "He took Leena's affinity, stole it without her knowledge or her permission, and in doing so, he destroyed her."

His words had the effect he intended. The crowded barroom rustled as people murmured about this new information. Saint Dolph, the martyr. Not so saintlike anymore.

"All because he wanted power," James added. "Power over us. Over you as well." He stood then, bringing himself to his full height. He no longer needed the cane, but he kept it in his hand just the same. Sent a flash of energy through the silver Medusa until Viola visibly flinched. "He wasn't worthy of this power."

"And you think you are?" she mocked, still grimacing against the slight pressure he was sending through the mark.

Not enough to kill. But enough to distract her. Enough to remind her who was truly in charge.

She straightened. "Tell them what you do, Nibsy. Tell them how many of those who don't wear the mark you've sacrificed to the Order's patrols." She turned to the barroom. "Dolph Saunders protected those who couldn't protect themselves. But this one, he uses the weakest among us. How many are missing today because of *him*?"

Her voice broke on the last word as he sent another bolt of warning through the magic that connected her tattoo to the cane.

"Why did you come here, Viola?" James asked. "Clearly you didn't come to make amends."

She stepped toward him. Her shoulders were back, but he knew the stiffness in her step was because of the steady pain he was sending into her mark. Her ability to ignore it would have been admirable if she weren't such a nuisance.

"I came for the ring."

"You can't imagine that I'd ever give it to you." He laughed softly, amused despite himself.

"Then I'll take it," she growled. "Dead men don't put up so much of a fight." She lifted her blade, preparing to hurl it toward his heart.

Before she could, his eyes shifted to Werner. And Viola went down.

SHATTERING

Viola came back to consciousness racked with unspeakable pain. Terrible energy was flooding through her body, turning her blood to ice and making her feel as though she were about to fly apart. The pain went on and on, until suddenly it stopped and everything went dark.

She wasn't dead. Not yet. But her body felt as though it had been run through with electricity, and she could imagine very easily wanting to die. She could imagine giving herself over to death without any regrets if that pain came again.

She was tied to some table. Her eyes were closed, because it was too much effort to force them open, but her lack of sight made all her other senses more aware. Her body ached against the unforgiving table, the smell of stale beer and tobacco made her stomach turn, and her mouth tasted of coppery blood.

Maybe it would have been easier to just simply give in. To relent and be dragged under by death. The end would have been a comfort compared to the terror and pain she currently felt. But she forced herself to draw in another shallow breath that made her ribs feel like they were being cracked open. And then another.

"Ah," a familiar voice said. "I see you're still with us . . . for now."

Viola didn't respond. She didn't so much as stir. It was taking every bit of energy and strength she had just to live.

She'd been a *fool*.

It had been a volatile mixture of grief and desperation combined with the truth in Ruby's words that had pushed Viola onward through the city, determined to end Nibsy Lorcan's life once and for all. Theo was dead, and Ruby would hate her forever because of it. What did she have to lose? She had been determined to get the ring back from that traitorous snake. If Theo was dead, she'd wanted to make sure his death hadn't been for nothing.

She opened her eyes a little and tried to make them focus. There, at the level of her gaze, was Leena's likeness. The silver Medusa with her friend's face stared blankly, unseeing. Mocking her.

Had she been thinking clearly when she left the *New York Age*'s building, maybe she would have made a plan. Maybe she would have waited until her anger had eased before charging into a pit of vipers. Instead, she'd gone to the Bella Strega convinced that she didn't care what happened—not to herself, not to any of them. If the Devil's Own broke apart, if they were devoured by the snakes who ran the Bowery, then so be it. It would be their own fault since they were standing by and allowing Nibsy to pervert what Dolph had built.

When she had marched into the Strega, she'd been desperate. She had already lost her home, her family, her . . . hope. She had nothing left to lose.

Oh, but she had been wrong about that, she thought as Nibsy's hand adjusted itself on the silver topper of the cane. The ring was right there, secure on his finger, and the clear stone seemed to wink at her, taunting her.

He crouched down, until they were eye to eye. Through the thick lenses of his spectacles, he looked her over, amusement shining in his light eyes.

"It doesn't have to be like this, Viola." Nibsy's voice was gentle, coaxing, but she knew it was all an act. His cloudy blue eyes glowed with amusement behind the thick lenses of his gold-rimmed glasses. "You can still repent. Renew your oath and join me. Come back to the Devil's Own. Come *home*. Be my blade, and I'll let you live."

She reached for her affinity to show him exactly what he could do with his false promises, but her magic slipped through her fingers. Her blood felt heavy and slow, like she'd been doused with opium or Nitewein.

"*Tsk-tsk*," he said, amusement curling in his voice. "Always so vicious."

The mark on her back flared with icy energy again, and she felt herself jerking up off the table she'd been tied to. Pain shot through her, *unspeakable* pain, and she felt that essential part of herself—her connection to the old magic—starting to crumble.

Just when she thought it was the end, the pain ceased, and her body slumped back to the table. She felt the energy in the barroom shift. The people had not left. They were watching, murmuring and waiting. They were allowing it to happen. *Because it wasn't happening to them.* But there was a thread of discontent in their nervous heartbeats. There was a fear growing that had not been there before.

Viola knew that Nibsy was playing with her, just as she understood that he was nowhere close to done. Her suffering amused him, certainly, but it served a purpose. She'd allowed herself to become an example to those standing around the barroom—of his power, of what happened to anyone who crossed him.

And still, no one stepped forward to help her. Theo was dead, and Ruby hated her. Cela would not know where she was, and Jianyu would be too late, if he wasn't dead himself. She had always felt apart, but now she understood what it felt like to be truly alone.

"Have you learned your lesson, Viola?" Nibsy asked. "It's not too late. Even now I would welcome you back, if only you give me your oath."

"I'd rather die," she told him.

"That," he said without any emotion at all, "can be arranged."

Suddenly, she felt hands upon her, and then the coolness of air on her back as someone tore her blouse in two, exposing the tattoo inked between her shoulder blades. It had nearly gone numb from the icy-hot ache of Nibsy's previous attempts to break her, but now the ink was boiling in her skin. It screamed of the danger she was in.

"Good-bye, Viola," Nibsy said, lifting the cane.

Her skin already hurt too much to feel the Medusa's kiss. She barely sensed the pressure, but then all at once, cold and unnatural magic shot through her. If the pain she'd experienced before was terrible, *this* was worse. She could not stop the scream that tore from her throat.

She would not survive this.

Viola knew with the same certainty that she had felt every time she reached for her blade that she would not live to see the next day. She would never be able to tell Jianyu how much she valued his friendship or to thank Cela for forgiving her. She would not live to see the Order destroyed or Nibsy Lorcan struck down. And she would never be able to tell Ruby how she truly felt.

That was the biggest regret of all. The Order could go hang. Nibsy Lorcan could as well. But she'd lied that night at the gala when Ruby had opened her heart and Viola had rejected it. She'd lied to Ruby, and she'd lied to herself about what she was willing to risk.

How foolish she'd been to be afraid of love, when this terror—this *pain*—she now felt existed in the world. How stupid of her to reject such a gift.

Viola's eyes flew open, and she searched the crowd surrounding her for some sign of pity, of mercy. Werner was standing there, white as a sheet. Unmoving.

Please—she mouthed, her voice no longer working. He could stop Nibsy. He could stop all of this. *Please.*

But she saw the fear in his eyes, and she understood he would not stand against his new boss. Not now. Likely not ever.

Viola was flying apart, her body separating from her soul. She was being ripped to shreds right along with her magic. She felt herself shattering, felt her magic crumbling away, and her life with it.

And then, suddenly, everything exploded.

TAINTED MAGIC

Harte took out Werner first. It was the only choice, considering what Werner's affinity could do. The single shot did exactly what he'd expected and launched the people in the Bella Strega into chaos. It wasn't exactly the most elegant form of misdirection, but it served his purpose.

After finding Cela's house destroyed by fire, there was only one place he could think of to go where he was sure to find some answers—the Strega. He hadn't known what to expect, not after all they'd done to change the course of time and history. But when he'd reached the saloon, he realized that even his worst fears hadn't come close to the reality of the scene he found there. Viola was tied to the table that Dolph once favored—the one where he'd once gathered his closest friends—and Nibsy Lorcan was using Dolph's cane to unmake her.

If Viola was there, somehow trapped and under Nibsy's control, where was Jianyu? What could have possibly happened over the past months to make *this* scene a possibility?

If he didn't save Viola, he'd never find out.

Harte hadn't even paused. There wasn't time to worry about whether Werner deserved to die, because Harte had seen a similar scene play out before. He'd watched when Dolph had destroyed a man in this same way years before—it was the reason he'd never taken the mark himself. He refused to let that fate happen to Viola, not when he was there to stop it. When he'd lifted the snub-nosed pistol he'd taken from the future, he hadn't aimed to injure. He needed Werner to stay down, because he knew he'd have only one attempt to get Viola out of there alive.

As Harte stalked through the frantic crowd, he touched an exposed wrist here, a bare neck there. He hadn't used his affinity so much in months. Hell, he'd never used his affinity that much at all, but he didn't hesitate now. Wrapping his magic around him, he reached through the shells of humanity and commanded as many as he could. He had only so many bullets left in the gun, after all. By the time he reached the other side of the barroom, he already had the pistol aimed at Nibsy's chest. No one moved against him.

Instead, the barroom descended into an unsettled quiet. A couple of the Devil's Own were trying to save Werner, but most had realized that something else was happening. No one stepped forward to help Nibsy or stop Harte. But the whole room turned to watch the drama that was about to play out.

"I wondered when you might show up again, Darrigan," Nibsy said, glancing over Harte's shoulder to the door he'd just come through. "But you seem to be missing something. Or will Esta be joining us later?"

Harte ignored the taunting calmness in Nibsy's voice. The knowing glint in his eye. "Let her go, Nibs."

Viola's dark hair had fallen from its pins and now covered her face, so Harte could not tell if she was conscious. Her shirt had been torn open, from neck to waist, and her corset had been cut away to expose the skin on her back. There between her shoulder blades, something that might have once been Dolph Saunders' mark had been transformed into a bloody mess. Her skin looked blistered and torn, and the once-black tattoo had turned the color of blood. The mark itself—or what was left of it—was glowing, as though there were a fire beneath her skin, burning her from within.

"I don't see why I should." Nibsy touched the silver head of the cane to her back again, and cold energy flashed through the room.

Harte felt the hair on his arms and neck rise as Viola screamed. The skin on her back bubbled and blistered as the snakes inscribed into her skin began to move. As they rippled and pulsed, the ink turned bloody, and Harte knew that if he didn't stop Nibsy, she wouldn't last much longer.

He drew the hammer back on the pistol. "I'm not going to ask you again, Nibs. Let Viola go, or I'll pull the trigger right now."

"You can't kill me," Nibsy said, not making any move to release Viola from the Medusa's kiss.

"Try me," Harte challenged.

"If I die, Esta dies as well," Nibsy said with an amused shrug. "I'm necessary to her very existence. And she's necessary to *yours*."

He was right. Harte had no way of knowing where Esta even was—or *when* she was—but if Dakari didn't follow through, then Esta's existence depended on Nibsy Lorcan's life. He couldn't risk killing him. *Not yet.* Not until he got the sign he was waiting for. But that sign had not yet appeared.

"I don't have to kill you to make you regret hurting her," Harte warned. "The bullet in this gun doesn't need to take your life to destroy your magic. Tell me, Nibsy, what do you think your life would be like without your affinity?"

Nibsy's expression faltered a little, and Harte could see him calculating. Reading the room or the Aether—or whatever it was that he did to get three steps ahead of everyone. The cold power swirling through the room eased a bit, even if Nibsy didn't move the cane from Viola's blistered and bloodied back.

"This gun happens to be a little gift from the future," Harte explained, taking another step forward. "The bullets in it are tainted with ritual magic made to destroy Mageus. I've seen up close what it's capable of. One strike and your affinity will be virtually useless. And if you don't manage to cut out the rot in time? The damage will spread. It won't kill you right away, but you'll wish it had. Now step away from her, or I'll be more than happy to demonstrate."

Nibsy hesitated, calculating still, but then suddenly he seemed to have a change of heart. He lifted his hands, raising the cane above his head as well. "Fine," he said. "Take her, for all the good it will do you."

"Back up," Harte said. "And tell your guys there to stay back as well.

Anyone moves, anyone tries *anything*, and you're the one who'll get the bullet."

Nibsy spread his hands wide, but Harte didn't accept his cooperation as a given. He kept the gun leveled at him the whole time, waiting for the trick.

"Tell that one to untie her," Harte commanded, nodding toward an unfamiliar blond boy about his own age. He'd noticed the interest in the blond's expression the second Nibsy mentioned Esta's name, and he had the sense he knew who the guy might be.

"Logan," Nibsy said, confirming Harte's suspicions about the boy's identity. "Go ahead and cut Viola free."

Logan had been one of Professor Lachlan's. He'd grown up with Esta, but Harte didn't know whether it was loyalty or desperation that had made him Nibsy's.

As Logan was working on cutting the ropes securing Viola's legs, Harte sidled up behind him, brushing the back of his fingers along the boy's neck. He sent a quick pulse of magic through him, a command to ensure his complicity. When Logan was done cutting the ropes from Viola's wrist, he lifted her gently in his arms without being told and brought her over to where Harte was waiting. All the while, Harte kept the gun aimed at Nibsy's chest.

Viola let out a moan in response to being moved, but she didn't seem to be conscious. Her head hung back over Logan's arms, her limbs loose and limp.

"Are you taking him as well?" Nibsy asked. He'd lowered his hands by now and had them resting on the silver Medusa's head.

"For now," Harte said.

"Keep him." Nibsy shrugged. "He's too soft to be of much use anyway."

Harte wasn't sure he trusted Nibsy's appraisal of Logan, who had once been loyal enough to the Professor to bring Esta back as his prisoner. But for now, under the thrall of Harte's affinity, Logan had his uses.

He considered the cane resting beneath Nibsy's hands, but it would have to wait. He had to get Viola somewhere safe before the uneasy interest in the barroom turned to something else. At that moment, he couldn't risk anything more than surviving.

Harte nodded to Logan. "Let's go," he said, never lowering the gun as they backed out of the Strega.

A dozen or more pairs of eyes watched as they retraced his steps, leaving through the front door of the saloon. No one made any move to stop them, though it would have been easy enough to block their path and make things more difficult. He hadn't charmed *that* many people. Maybe it was shock, or maybe it was simply unwillingness to involve themselves in dangers that didn't directly affect them. Whatever the case, it never would have happened under Dolph. Had someone attacked the Strega as he just had, the Devil's Own wouldn't have stood for it.

Whatever the reason for their silence, Harte hoped that it held. There were only a couple of bullets left in the gun, and if the Devil's Own did decide to attack, he couldn't shoot them all.

He didn't want to, either.

Once they were outside, Harte kept the gun firmly in his grasp, but he reached out to grab Viola's wrist. It took only a second to discover the information he needed.

A block over, they found a covered carriage for hire, and with a quick shake of the driver's hand, he made sure that the fellow wouldn't remember them once he dropped them at the address he gave. They didn't seem to have been followed from the Strega, not that it made Harte relax any. If Nibsy let them go, there was a reason.

Viola was still unconscious when they finally arrived at the address Harte had taken from her memories. It was a brick building, three stories tall, with a large sign that pronounced the offices of the *New York Age* across the front door.

He alighted from the carriage and then took Viola from Logan before the other boy jumped out as well. She was barely breathing, and her skin was a ghastly gray.

Logan stood there, still half in a daze under the control of Harte's affinity. "Go knock on the door. See if Jianyu is in there," he commanded.

But Logan hadn't even crossed half the distance to the building when the front door of the building flew open and Cela Johnson emerged.

"Harte Darrigan?" she said, her eyes as wide as if she'd seen a ghost. Then she realized who he was holding. "Oh, god. Viola."

Another woman had emerged from the building as well. Tall and lithe, the blonde took one look at the scene in the street, focused on Viola hanging unconscious and unmoving in Harte's arms, and shoved past Cela. "No," she said, brushing the hair back from Viola's face. "She can't be—"

With the girl tugging at Viola, Harte could barely keep hold of her.

He struggled to adjust his grip so he didn't drop Viola. "Cela, if you could—"

Cela was already taking the blond girl by the shoulder and pulling her back.

"She's not dead," Cela told the girl.

Harte knew Cela understood. The worry in her eyes spoke more loudly and clearly than even her words could.

At least not yet.

FOR SPORT OR SLAUGHTER

The Docks

Jianyu opened his eyes to darkness. The floor was cold and hard beneath him. It smelled of dirt and dampness, and when he tried to lift himself from it, he found that one of his ankles had been secured. The shackle felt unnaturally smooth—unnaturally cold as well. And though he could not see what held him, he knew it was no simple piece of metal. When he stood, he could take no more than two or three steps in either direction. He had been chained in place, like some kind of animal. But whether he was being kept for sport or for slaughter, he could not tell.

He did not know where he was. In the distance, he could detect a gentle murmuring that he could not quite discern; it was too far off. In the space around him there was only silence. The air was thick and close, choked with dust and the scent of something heavy and metallic—and also with the cloying sweetness of opium. All around him, he felt the cold energy of counterfeit magic. He reached for his affinity, but with the sweetness of the opium, he was not surprised to find a numb hollowness where his connection to the old magic should have been.

Jack Grew knew what Jianyu was, and it seemed that he was taking no chances.

He had been so close to escaping. After Viola had taken Theo's bride to safety, Jianyu had nearly slipped away himself. But before he could make it to the back of the church, another of the beasts had formed itself from the thick smoke, billowing up as unexpectedly as a nightmare. It happened so quickly—far more quickly than before—and before he could react, Jianyu had been caught up by the throat. He rubbed at the soreness that ringed his neck now, remembering what it had felt like to struggle . . . and to lose.

He was not sure how long he sat there, waiting for whatever would come, but the darkness was severed suddenly and unexpectedly by a flash of light not so very far away. The block of brightness might well have been a doorway opening to another world. Jianyu's eyes ached as he squinted against the glare, but he knew immediately who the figure silhouetted against the brightness was.

"I see you're not dead," Jack Grew said, lighting a lantern and then another until the space was completely illuminated.

Jianyu did not bother to respond. While Jack busied himself with the lamps, Jianyu took stock of his situation. They were in a warehouse, and in the center of the space was a large metal structure that could only be the terrible machine Darrigan had described to him. The machine that had killed Tilly. The machine that could destroy all magic for a hundred miles. The Magician had destroyed the machine, but there it was. Whole once again.

As Jianyu had suspected, his ankle was chained to a stake cemented into the ground, but the shackle was a single, unbroken piece of dark steel without any hinge or latch. There was no keyhole—no lock to pick— and the cold energy of the corrupted magic was strong enough that it made the dangerous piece of silk wrapped around his wrist feel like no more than a whisper. A few feet away was a broad table piled with papers and tools. Among the clutter was Libitina, too far away to be of any use on the shackle.

Jack carried with him a burlap sack and a ceramic growler. As he approached Jianyu, he took a small paper-wrapped parcel from the bag and tossed it at Jianyu's feet, just within reach of the end of the chain. Then he set the growler beside it, before unpacking the rest. The bag contained another of the paper-wrapped parcels, some notebooks, and a flask of something that smelled strongly of whiskey when it was opened.

Jack took a sip from the flask and then set it aside on the makeshift table before he began to unwrap what appeared to be a sandwich.

Jianyu only watched. He did not move to inspect the package Jack had dropped on the floor at his feet. Nor did he try to reach for the growler. His thirst was of less concern than understanding Jack's plans.

"It's not poisoned, if that's what you're worried about," Jack said, glancing at Jianyu as he chewed. "If I wanted you dead, you already would be."

Considering his current predicament, that particular reassurance meant very little. It guaranteed even less.

"I know full well you can understand me. You might as well eat," Jack said, and then took another long drink from the flask. "You'll want to keep up your strength for the escape I know you're already planning."

Jianyu's stomach rumbled at the thought. Reluctantly, he opened the parcel to find a hard-crusted roll filled with odd-smelling meat. His nose wrinkled, but Jack was right—he did need to preserve his strength, because he was not planning on remaining a prisoner for long. He took a bite, but it was nearly impossible to choke down the terrible food, and the water in the growler was little help. It was overly warm and tasted bitterly of sulfur. He set both aside, disgusted with the food and with himself.

"I'm sure you're wondering why I haven't killed you," Jack said after he'd finished his own lunch.

He had, actually, but Jianyu simply stared at Jack. There was little to be gained by conversing with a madman.

"Or perhaps you'd prefer to enjoy the surprise of what's to come?" Jack asked pleasantly.

Jianyu remained silent. He *would* prefer to know, but he had no interest in playing these games. Better to watch. Better to wait. Eventually someone as volatile as Jack would misstep.

Jack removed an object from within the jacket he wore. He held it up and showed it to Jianyu. "Do you know what this is?"

Even if Jianyu had not known anything at all about the Ars Arcana, the strange energy coming from the small leather book in Jack's hands—the heady warmth of the old magic and the cold warning of counterfeit magic mixed together—would have told Jianyu that the book was more than it appeared. But Jianyu knew the Book. He had seen it before in Esta's possession. Jianyu also knew that Esta and Darrigan had taken the Book with them when they left the city. They had used its power to pass through the Brink, so they could search for artifacts and retrieve them before Nibsy did. For Jack to have the Book now . . .

Jianyu's mind was racing. If Darrigan and Esta had died on the train, as the news reports had suggested, it meant they were not searching for the artifacts—*had not been searching all this time*. If they were gone, they would not be returning at all.

There was no one coming to save them.

Jack had already opened the Book. His mouth was forming the shape of strange words, and his voice rose so that the droning sound of the unknown syllables filled the air in the warehouse. As he spoke, Jack's eyes had gone impossibly black. It looked as though the pupil had grown, consuming the iris and the white as well, until there was nothing but darkness, nothing but emptiness within.

Except, when Jack turned to him, he realized that the darkness was not empty. He thought he saw something shift there in that void. Something apart from the man seemed to lurk within.

Jianyu noticed the circle then. How had he missed it? Someone had traced it into the dirt of the floor, just beyond the reach of his chain, but now it was beginning to glow with a dangerous energy that brushed against his skin in warning. The air around him went thick with magic, and suddenly his arms and legs felt as though unseen hands were jerking him upward until he was floating above the ground, splayed out and helpless to fight against it. Around his wrist, the silken band had gone as cold as ice.

THE POWER WITHIN

Jack Grew felt more than the warmth of the morphine in his blood. The power within him had taken over and was whispering the ancient words that caused potent magic to begin swirling through the warehouse. He gave himself over to that power, reveled in it, as the very Aether lit around him.

The maggot was hanging, caught in the Aether, his arms and legs stretched as though pinned to some invisible rack. He was grimacing as he tried to free himself, but he'd give up soon enough. He should have realized that it was pointless to fight against the Book's power.

Jack took the Pharaoh's Heart from the sack and noticed the maggot's interest.

"Do you recognize this?" Jack asked. "No, don't try to pretend otherwise. I see it there in your eyes. You know what it is. Perhaps you've seen it before? Maybe you were there in Khafre Hall that night when your friends destroyed it." He held the blade up a little, noticing how the bloodred garnet in the hilt seemed to glow in response to the magic coursing through the air. "The Pharaoh's Heart. An apt enough name, I suppose, since I will be using it to cleave the magic from your heart."

The Chinaman remained silent, but he could not completely guard his emotions. There was fear in his narrow eyes.

Jack took the rest of the supplies from his satchel, including the large onyx he'd found out west. He turned the crystal back and forth in the lamplight, admiring the way it gleamed. He'd been right. It would be perfect for what he planned to do.

"What will you do with me?" the Chinaman asked through clenched teeth.

"You aren't really in any position to be asking questions," Jack mused. "But since you've so little time left, I'll have pity. You see, you're about to become a part of history."

He took the dagger in hand and walked toward the maggot, relishing the brush of power as he stepped over the boundary line of the ritual.

"That doesn't appeal to you?" he asked when the Chinaman didn't react. "Think of it, a filthy immigrant like yourself, destined to always be other, and now your feral magic will help me change the world."

"Are you so sure the world can be changed?" the maggot asked quietly.

"I *know* it can be changed," Jack said, snapping with temper at the Chinaman's impertinence. "And I am the one who will finally accomplish what the others could not. I will be the one to finally rid this city—this *country*—of the threat from maggots like you."

He stalked forward, feeling sureness of his purpose heat his blood. Or perhaps that was the morphine.

"The old men who rule over the Order are convinced that the Brink is the solution to protecting the city from feral magic. They believe that the maggots who have sullied our streets can be contained." Jack knew otherwise. If it were possible simply to *contain* undesirables, the Chinese vermin overrunning Mott Street with their violence and filth would never have even entered the city. They, at least, were easy enough to spot. But maggots in general? They hid too easily among the refuse of the city's streets.

And they were still coming, more each day. The Brink did nothing to dissuade them. It certainly didn't *stop* them.

It was the central problem that the old goats like his uncle failed to recognize—*refused* to see. The Brink could never be a solution to the dangers of feral magic because it *depended* on the power it harnessed from the maggots who dared to cross it. It *needed* them. It allowed them to live, to *exist*, because it had to.

LISA MAXWELL

"The Inner Circle refuses to understand. Vermin cannot be contained. Like the rats that plague our streets, they must be *eliminated*. And it must be now, before the danger grows any greater.

"Perhaps before, they could have bought themselves a few more years by strengthening the Brink. Perhaps with the Delphi's Tear they could have even managed to convince the Brotherhoods of their continued importance. But now?" He reached up and gave the maggot a couple of quick, sharp slaps on his cheeks. "Thanks to you and your friends, the Order has nothing. No artifacts. No Book of Mysteries. No hope to regain their footing." He smiled at the thought of their demise. Of his inevitable victory. "Soon they will have even less, and I will be the one to step forward and remake them."

Jack walked over to the machine and ran his hand over the curve of one of the heavy metal arms. He gave it a gentle push and watched as the entire contraption lurched into a slow, graceful movement. The arms orbited around the center console, dodging past one another like an enormous gyroscope.

"We live in a modern age, an age of wonders. Why should we depend on antiquated magic when science can augment our understanding of the occult?" He stopped the swinging arms. "This machine is powered like every other machine—with electricity. It only requires something to harness the energy it harvests, so that energy can be used. Think of it—I will be able to protect the country from the feral power of maggots like you while providing enough energy to power a bright new future. All I needed was something like this," he said, gesturing to the dagger.

The Chinaman remained silent, but Jack could tell he was impressed. He could see the utter fear in the maggot's expression.

"There is the problem of scale," Jack said, frowning. "A single machine can do only so much. With this one stone and the machine installed in Tesla's tower, I could reach a hundred miles, more than enough to exterminate the vermin in this city. But what good would that do for the *country*? One machine doesn't solve the problems we face, not when maggots are now pouring in through other ports as well."

"You would make five machines," the Chinaman murmured, his eyes wide with terror.

Jack only laughed. "You're thinking of the other artifacts." Which only confirmed his likely involvement with their theft. "No. I will make enough of them to cover the entire country. From sea to shining sea, as it were."

He smiled at the confusion on the maggot's face. "You seem to be making the same error in logic as the old fools of the Inner Circle have made," Jack told him. "They believe their artifacts are so precious, so utterly unique."

The Chinaman's dark brows drew together. He seemed interested despite himself. "Are they not?" he asked.

"Oh, the Order's artifacts are precious. They're ancient pieces taken from the ancient dynasties. They're powerful as well. But they are not *singular*. Once, they were the same as this." Jack took the glittering black stone and lifted it to the level of the Chinaman's eyes. "Nothing more than a gem, beautiful and pure. They were symbolic, but otherwise powerless until they were transformed by the Ars Arcana. It's all here, in these pages. The ritual is complex, but not impossible to re-create. It only requires a maggot powerful enough to complete it."

He placed the stone on the floor directly beneath the man's body. "Luckily, Barclay and his bitch of a fiancée provided the perfect opportunity to find one."

"The attack on their wedding was a trap," the maggot realized.

"Well, it wasn't *only* a trap," Jack told him. "Barclay caused me enough trouble last June that he deserved his fate. I won't mourn him in the least. But yes . . . I had hoped to ensnare more than Theo and his blushing bride. I knew that he must have had help to escape from the Flatiron Building, and I assumed that whoever saved him once would be willing to rescue him again. I was right. As I expected, you and your maggot friends came running to his defense. But you were too late, and you weren't strong enough. Feral magic never is.

"Now I have everything I need. The power in the Book. The feral magic beneath your skin. And an enchanted blade to cut that magic from you," Jack told him. "With the Pharaoh's Heart, I'll use you to transform this hunk of stone into something more."

"You'll create another artifact," the Chinaman realized.

"Nothing so precious as an *artifact*," Jack corrected. "I'll create something more common, an object that can be reproduced as long as there are gemstones to mine and feral magic to harvest. With it, I'll finally be able to balance the power of this machine. And with my machine, I'll be able to destroy those who threaten our land. I'll change *everything*. And the old men of the Order will have no choice but to step aside. What little power they've built over the last century will be mine to wield, and I will do even more than those old goats ever dreamed."

"The Order cannot want you to take their power. . . ." The Chinaman couldn't hide his confusion.

Jack scoffed. "Perhaps, but they'll be too busy to realize what's happening until it's already done," he said. "You see, the Conclave is destined to be attacked by dangerous maggots desperate to destroy the Order, just as they destroyed poor Theo Barclay. In the chaos, the Brotherhoods will be tossed into disarray. But I'll be ready. The Order will finally recognize my greatness, as will the other Brotherhoods. And I will claim my rightful place as their leader. It's a shame you won't last long enough to see my victory."

"You would attack your own?" the Chinaman dared to ask.

"I would *save* my own," Jack corrected. "The entire city is already awash with fear after what happened at St. Paul's. They will blame your kind for the terrible tragedy at the Conclave, just as they already blame you for Theo Barclay's death. Imagine their fear when the richest and most powerful men of our time fall. The entire city—no, the *country*—will understand the threat that maggots like you pose.

"And in the wake of that tragedy, I will be the one to lead the Brotherhoods into a world built free from the dangers of feral magic. When the Brink falls, my machines will take its place, and with them, I will build a country clean of the maggots who would bring us low—a new century free of the dangers of feral magic." Jack paused, cocking his head slightly as he considered the man. "And to make all this happen, all I require is a small sacrifice."

The Chinaman suddenly seemed to realize the true danger he was in and began thrashing impotently against his invisible bonds.

"Now, now . . ." Jack smiled. "There's no use fighting the inevitable, is there?"

He lifted the dagger and sliced the shirt from the man's chest. There was more than the warmth of morphine in his blood now. The power within him, that voice that urged him on and guided him, was thrumming with anticipation. It was further proof of his worthiness, further evidence that victory must soon be his.

The maggot was shaking now, fighting against a power he could not hope to defeat. Jack ignored his protests, reveled in his fear, and pressed the point of the dagger to his chest. The bloodred garnet in the hilt grew brighter, and Jack could feel the power within it calling to him.

His hands almost did not feel like his own as they began to guide the blade, slicing into the Chinaman's chest to create the intricate pattern from the front of the Ars Arcana. Blood welled from the maggot's skin, and Jack felt the beginnings of feral power stirring in the air as the Aether around him vibrated. He finished his first cut and continued on, carefully replicating the symbol from the Book on the Chinaman's bare chest. As he cut, the maggot tried to keep himself from crying out. His face twisted with the effort of holding back evidence of the pain, but in the end, he broke. A ragged, guttural moan tore from his throat as the sigil was nearly complete.

Energy pulsed wildly around him, like a small storm building in the otherwise silent warehouse, but the magic seemed erratic. It wasn't as powerful or sure as he would have expected.

He was nearly done—there were only a few more lines to connect—when someone started pounding on the warehouse door. At first Jack thought to ignore the intrusion. But the pounding grew more urgent, and in the end, he lowered the dagger. He'd waited too long to rush this and miss the moment of completion. He'd get rid of the intruder, and then he would *savor* it.

It wasn't like the maggot was going anywhere.

On the other side of the door, his mother's coachman, Adam—or was it Aaron?—waited, looking uneasy.

"You aren't supposed to be here yet." He'd paid the man handsomely to do what he asked and to keep quiet about it.

"Sorry, sir, but I didn't have a choice," the driver said, looking nervous. "It wasn't your mother that sent me. Mr. Morgan himself wants to see you."

Jack cursed. "You didn't tell them where I was?"

"No," the driver said. "They didn't ask. Just told me to go fetch you and make it quick."

"Give me a minute," he told the man, and then slammed the door in his face.

He considered the body of the maggot suspended a few yards away and cursed again. The rest of the ritual would have to wait. It was too delicate a procedure to rush and risk a mistake, especially when he couldn't be certain that he could find another maggot with so much power again before the Conclave. And he couldn't make his uncle wait. Not now, when he was so close. If the Order suspected what he was doing, they might realize what he had in his possession, and they'd certainly try to take it for their own.

He couldn't allow that to happen. His plan to unseat the Inner Circle from power depended on the element of surprise.

Jack tucked the dagger beneath his jacket and then secured the Book of Mysteries in its usual hidden pocket, close to his heart. He left the maggot where he was, suspended in the Aether. Once he dealt with his uncle and whatever demands Morgan felt like issuing, he'd return and finish the job. By the time tomorrow dawned, he would have the stone he needed, and the machine would be complete.

LONGING

Uptown

C ela still couldn't quite believe that Harte Darrigan was standing there, alive and in the flesh. She didn't *want* to believe that it was Viola in his arms, bloody and unconscious and looking like she was two steps from the grave. But denial wouldn't keep her friend alive.

"What happened to her?" she asked.

"Nibsy Lorcan," Harte told her. "She's hurt pretty badly."

At this declaration, Ruby wailed and tried to break free of Cela's hold. But holding the near-hysterical heiress back, Cela waved Harte inside.

"Take her upstairs," she told him. "Third floor. The room she's been using is the second door on the left."

Harte turned to the blond boy that Cela recognized from the night at Evelyn DeMure's apartment. Logan was his name, or at least that's what Jianyu had told her. He'd been with Nibsy Lorcan before, but now he was standing next to Darrigan with a dazed expression on his face.

"You listen to Cela," he told the boy. "Any order she gives, you do it. And you don't talk to anyone else until I come back. Understand?"

Logan blinked with a far-off look and nodded.

Seemingly satisfied, Darrigan headed toward the house with Viola still draped in his arms. Cela watched him go, far too aware of just how bad off Viola must be to not even stir when he jostled her as he mounted the steps.

Cela looked at Logan. She didn't have any idea what she was supposed to do with him. The last thing Mr. Fortune would want messing around with his newspaper business was another white boy. "Go on upstairs to the kitchen. Have a seat at the table and don't go nosing off anywhere."

"Yes, ma'am," the boy said, and then followed Harte into the building.

Ruby was still making a sort of terrible keening sound as she sobbed in Cela's arms. Any second now, she was going to break completely, but Cela didn't have time for that. Not with the two white boys making trouble in Mr. Fortune's building. She took the white girl by the shoulders and, pushing her back a little, gave her a firm but gentle shake. "You gotta stop that noise," she told her. "Hush, now. Your tears aren't helping anyone."

"My fault," the girl moaned.

Maybe it was and maybe it wasn't, but Cela didn't have the energy to deal with Ruby's hysterics. She'd worked in theaters with less drama. "Then do something about it," she snapped, realizing too late how sharp her tone had become. She let out an exhausted breath, knowing she wasn't really upset at Ruby. She was scared for Viola, same as the girl.

"I'm going to need some supplies," Cela told Ruby, trying to make her voice a little gentler. "We'll need some hot water to clean her wounds. Find whatever clean towels and blankets you can, and you'd best grab my sewing basket, just in case."

Ruby simply stared at her.

"You can do that, can't you?" Cela asked, her voice sharpening again. "I know you've probably had women like me running your baths since you were a baby, but if you want to take responsibility for what happened to Viola, then you'll get yourself together. She needs us."

The girl wiped the wetness from her eyes. "You're right," she said with an undignified snuffle. "I can do it. Towels and water. I'll fetch them for you."

Cela didn't know who Ruby was trying to convince, but if it stopped the other girl from wailing, she didn't much care.

"Good. I'm going up to check on them," Cela said, releasing her shoulders. "Make sure that other boy is in the kitchen where I sent him, and then bring everything to Viola's room when you have it."

She gave the girl a quick, sure embrace. "She's going to be okay, Ruby."

Ruby wrapped her arms around her in return, and for a second they just stood there in the open air of the street, an unlikely pair brought together by even more unlikely circumstances.

"She has to be," Ruby whispered.

By the time Cela reached the doorway of the small room where Viola slept, Harte had already laid her facedown on the narrow bed. Cela stopped short when she saw Viola's back. "Jesus," she whispered, lifting her hand to her mouth. She'd never seen anything like it.

"I don't know how Nibsy got a hold of her," Harte said. He was kneeling by the edge of the bed, peeling the blood-soaked fabric away from Viola's skin with the long, noble fingers that had once manipulated locks. "The Viola I knew would've killed him before she let him touch her."

"She'd just watched a friend of hers get murdered, so I don't think she was exactly thinking straight," Cela said softly.

Taking a breath to fortify herself, she stepped into the room and pushed Harte aside gently so she could see what needed to be done. Viola's back was a bloodied mess. A dark tattoo of two intertwined snakes lay between her shoulder blades. Had it not been split open and bleeding, it would have looked like the one Jianyu also had etched into the skin of his back.

"I've never seen damage like this," she murmured, almost afraid to start. "I can't even begin to picture the weapon that caused it."

"He used the mark against her." Harte's voice sounded hollow. "When I found her, he already had the silver cane top pressed against her."

Cela's brows bunched in concern. "This is what happened because he tried to take her affinity?"

Harte nodded. "He started to. It looked like he was ripping the magic out through her skin. If I'd been a few minutes later . . ."

Jianyu and Viola had tried to explain about the marks and the control that Nibsy had over them, but Cela hadn't realized. Not really. She knew their magic was a part of them, but now she could see exactly what that meant. It looked like her skin had burst open, like her body had turned on itself.

There was a gasp from the doorway behind her, and Cela knew Ruby had arrived with the supplies.

"If you're not going to be able to handle yourself, just leave the stuff there and go," Cela told her, tossing a stern look over her shoulder.

Ruby looked like a ghost, but the edge in Cela's voice must have shaken some sense into her. Cela watched something harden in Ruby's expression as she drew herself up. If she'd thought the girl nothing but a porcelain doll, she now started to revise her judgment. There was steel in Ruby's eyes. Determination likely born from getting whatever you wanted for an entire life.

Cela nudged Harte away, and together with Ruby, they began the terrible, painstaking process of working on Viola's back. Once the crusted-over blood was washed clean, Cela could see the true extent of the damage. It was worse, somehow, than she'd expected. Viola's back looked like a piece of shredded silk, but luckily Cela had plenty of experience with mending far more delicate things.

"How does it look?" Harte asked.

"She's going to need stitches," Cela said, stretching her neck. With all the damage, it would take a while to put her back together. "But she's still breathing, and I'm not sensing any infection yet. I think she might come through."

"Do you know where Jianyu is?" Harte asked. "I expected to find him here with you."

Cela couldn't stop her cheeks from heating, though she knew that wasn't what Darrigan meant. She shook her head. "He's not here," she told him, not sure how she managed to keep her voice steady. Darrigan's unexpected appearance and Viola's injuries had been enough to distract her, but now the worry returned like a wave crashing over her.

She couldn't keep the emotion from her voice as she told him how Jianyu had followed Viola to Ruby's wedding and how he hadn't returned. And when she glanced back, the expression on Darrigan's face—the pity in his eyes—let her know that he saw the truth of her feelings.

"So the two of you are . . . ?" he asked awkwardly. His ears had gone red.

"We're friends," she told him stiffly. "Nothing more."

Darrigan only frowned silently as he studied her. She wasn't sure what he saw in her eyes or in her expression, but when he spoke, his voice had softened. "Does he know?"

Cela thought about denying what Darrigan's words implied. She could have pretended that she didn't understand or that he was out of place in his asking, but all she could think about was the way Jianyu had taken her in his arms when Theo had brought her back to the city. The strength and sureness of his embrace had made her think that he might feel as she did. But he was always so careful, and it was only sometimes that she caught him looking at her when he thought she didn't notice.

She could have brushed off Darrigan's question, but whether prayers or curses or ritual spells, there could be power in words. With Jianyu missing, with Viola bloodied and bruised before her, Cela couldn't bring herself to lie.

"Sometimes I think he does," she whispered. "Sometimes I think he maybe even feels the same." She turned back to working on Viola's back, though her hands didn't move. "But he has ideas about who he is and what he deserves."

"We all do," Harte told her. "And we're nearly always wrong." He paused, and Cela wondered what he was thinking. She didn't need to wonder *who* he was thinking about. "Jianyu's a good man."

"One of the best," Cela agreed with a small, terrified smile.

"I'll see about looking for him while you're finishing up here," Harte told her.

She hadn't realized how tense she was until the worry coiling within her eased a little at Darrigan's words. "You think you know where he might be?"

"Not yet," Harte said. "But maybe Logan can help with that."

"Be careful, Darrigan," Cela warned. "This isn't the same city you left. A lot has happened while you've been away."

He gave her an unreadable look. "You have *no idea* how true that is."

Once he was gone, Cela turned back to Viola and reached for her needle and thread. With the first poke and pull of the thread, Viola released a ragged, whimpering moan. Cela took that as a sign that she wasn't dead yet and kept stitching.

SECOND CHANCES

Harte had complete confidence that Cela would be able to close up the ragged skin on Viola's back, but he wasn't sure if that would be enough. Dolph's cane touched more than the surface of a person. The power within that silver gorgon's head went far below the skin to destroy the person's connection to old magic, but that connection—that part of any Mageus, no matter how strong or weak their power might be—was an essential part of them. Intrinsic and interwoven. Removing it, or even attempting to, usually meant death.

The fact that Viola wasn't already dead made her damn lucky. She'd be even luckier if she walked away with her magic intact.

Logan was sitting at the kitchen table, right where Harte had told him to wait. He was staring off absently in the direction of the sink, or maybe he wasn't looking at anything at all. He looked lost, like he was unsure of where he was or what he was supposed to be doing. But when he saw Harte enter the kitchen, he got to his feet. He opened his mouth like he wanted to say something but then thought better of it.

Finally, when he did speak, Logan didn't ask any of the questions Harte had expected.

"Back at the Strega, James made it sound like he expected Esta to be with you." Logan took a step toward Harte. "Do you know where she is? I need to find her. I have to talk with her."

Harte eyed the other boy, sizing him up. He tried to see what Esta might have seen and wondered if this guy had meant something to her once. "What do you want with her?"

The guy shook his head, lifting his hands a little. "No, it's not like that. She's like a sister to me."

Harte only glared at him. "You brought her back here at gunpoint," he reminded Logan. "Not exactly very brotherly of you."

Logan at least had the grace to look embarrassed. "Look, man, I'm sorry about that, but I can't undo it now. I just want to get back to my own time, back to my old life. Esta's the only one that can do that for me, so if you know where she is, you gotta tell me. Please. I'm *begging* you."

Harte knew Logan wasn't anywhere close to begging, and for a second or two he considered reaching forward and grabbing Logan's wrist. It would be so easy to let his affinity flare, to issue another series of commands. They could use a spy in the Bella Strega, one they could depend on. It might be worth the risk, even if Nibsy would likely expect it. But Esta's voice was in his ears, brushing against his conscience about taking Logan's free will.

It didn't seem to matter that he'd already killed a boy today. He hadn't hesitated in ending Werner's life to save Viola's. But he hesitated now. He wasn't sure if that meant he was getting better or just getting soft.

It wasn't that he trusted Logan, not after what he'd done to Esta. Not after he'd been standing there, healthy and unharmed and clearly part of Nibsy's crew in the Strega. But Logan seemed sincere enough, and Harte Darrigan knew better than anyone that everyone deserved a second chance. And if he could use Logan? All the better.

"I don't know where Esta is right now," he told Logan honestly. "But she'll find us eventually. In the meantime, I need your help to find a friend of ours."

Logan crossed his arms over his chest, and the expression he wore gave his answer before his words did. "Why would I want to help you?"

"Because Esta will be here soon enough, and when she arrives, she's not going to have a lot of incentive to help you, not after what you've done." Harte shrugged. "But maybe if you helped a friend of hers, *maybe* she'd be more willing to listen to your sob story about how Nibsy made you do it."

Logan's nostrils flared with frustration.

"We can do this the easy way, or we can do this the easier way," Harte told him, ready to use his magic if he needed to.

"What's that even supposed to mean?" Logan asked, his face screwed up in confusion.

"It means I want to give you the choice, but I don't have the patience to wait forever." He'd lost too much time already.

Logan considered him. "Fine," he said. "I'll help you find your friend, but when Esta arrives, you're going to convince her to help me."

"I'll do my best," Harte said, clapping Logan on the shoulder. "But if you know Esta at all, you'd already know there's no convincing her of *anything*."

Logan exhaled. "Yeah. I know." He glanced at Harte. "I take it I'm looking for the Chinese guy?"

"Jianyu," Harte corrected. "He has a name."

Logan lifted his hands again. "Sorry."

Harte glared in warning. "You should be able to find him if you track the bronze mirrors he carries."

"I know," Logan said. "But I'm not some kind of oracle. I'm more like a metal detector. I need to get close enough for a read to find someone. And Jianyu could be anywhere in this city."

"Maybe," Harte agreed. "But I know a couple of places where we can start."

An hour later, they parked the wagon they'd borrowed from the *New York Age* at the edge of the warehouses that lined the dockyards. They'd already driven by Jack's town house near Washington Square without any luck.

"Well?" Harte asked, but he already knew the answer from the way Logan's expression had gone tight.

"The mirrors are here somewhere," Logan told him. Apparently, he was smart enough not to lie.

Across the street from where they were parked, the warehouses blocked the view of the water, but Harte could feel the Brink in the distance, waiting. He'd been down to this area near the docks before, but that was months ago, and in the gloom of the early evening, the low-slung structures all looked the same. He wasn't sure which one had been Jack's.

"You're coming with me," Harte said, hopping down and securing the horse to a nearby hitch.

The day had already been cold, but now that the sun had gone down, the temperature had dropped even further. The chill in the air made Harte wish he'd thought to bring a coat. A gust of wind came in off the river and brought with it another brush of icy energy. A warning and a promise of what the Brink would do to any who crossed it.

Esta could change that. The thought rose sudden and unwanted. Harte tried to push it aside but found that he couldn't. Esta *could* change it. She had the Book and the artifacts, and she had an affinity for Aether. Esta believed she could do the ritual and use Seshat as the sacrifice to complete it. She believed that being willing to give up everything would be enough to let her live, but Harte wasn't so sure. He'd seen that other version of her perform the same ritual. *And I watched her die.*

He refused to watch her die again.

But standing so close to the shore, he wondered if it was his choice to make, even if he could find a way to stop her. It had been easy enough to forget about how terrible it was to live there, trapped in the city, once he'd been beyond it. But now that he was there, close enough to the Brink that he felt the edges of fear creep along his skin, he wondered if he had any right to doom countless others for his own selfish happiness.

Maybe he had to trust her. Maybe he had to let her try.

"Are we doing this or what?" Logan asked, rubbing his arms and looking every bit as uneasy as Harte felt.

"Yeah," he said, mentally shaking himself free of the direction his thoughts had taken. "Let's go."

Logan grabbed him by the sleeve and nodded in the opposite direction from the way Harte had turned. "It's this way."

THE MYSTERIUM

The Flatiron Building

J ack Grew bristled with impatience as he sat in the visitors' gallery of
the Order's headquarters high above Madison Square Park. Two floors
above, the new Mysterium stood empty, as powerless as the feeble
old goats who had summoned him like a dog to heel. The city glittered
below, waiting for its future to unfold—a future he was determined to
take for his own.

Soon, he promised himself. The Book echoed the sentiment by pulsing twice softly in the breast pocket where it rested against his heart. He
heard the whispered encouragement rise within him. Soon he'd show
them the dog had teeth.

It was all a game to the Inner Circle. The summons. The waiting. But
they had entered a game board they did not truly understand, and they
were playing a match they had no hope to win.

When the doors finally opened behind him, Jack turned from the
window, putting the city to his back. He arranged his face in an expression of bland curiosity as the High Princept entered.

"Sir," he said with a small deferential nod.

The old man barely blinked. "If you'll come this way?"

It wasn't like he had much choice.

Jack followed the High Princept from the sterile quiet of the visitors'
waiting room into the lush inner sanctum of the Order. As they traversed
the winding passageways designed to disorient any would-be attackers,
Jack could not help but wonder why they had summoned him. He'd

remained quiet and out of the way these past weeks, just as they'd requested. What could have possibly drawn their attention? And why was the Princept himself acting as escort?

Finally they came to the library where everything had gone to shit on the solstice. The doorway to the Mysterium stood open in the ceiling above.

"After you," the Princept insisted, waving his hand in the direction of the steep metal staircase that led upward.

Interested despite himself, Jack accepted the invitation. When he emerged into the room above, it wasn't empty. His uncle was there, as were the other members of the Inner Circle. They were draped in ceremonial sashes, and each wore a golden medallion with the Philosopher's Hand hanging from a cord around their necks. Only his uncle betrayed any irritation that Jack had arrived.

Like the library below, the Mysterium felt hollow and somehow less impressive than it had the night of the solstice. In the center of the room, a sculpture of iron and gold meant to represent the Tree of Life waited, its branches empty of the artifacts that should have lived in the spaces designed to house them. During the solstice, the tree had glowed with an otherworldly light, protection for the one artifact that had slipped away. Now its gilded branches stood cold and powerless.

But as interesting as it was to be summoned by the Inner Circle and escorted personally by the High Princept, his patience was at an end. The Chinaman waited with all the promise of his feral magic. Jack didn't have time for these games.

"I assume that eventually you'll get around to telling me why you've called me here tonight," Jack said, enjoying the way his uncle visibly bristled at his irreverent tone.

"Watch yourself, boy," Morgan growled. "You stand in a sacred place."

"Not by my own choice," he reminded them. "I was told that your summons couldn't wait."

"What could you possibly have to be so busy with?" Morgan asked, sneering down his large nose. "More of your chorus girl trollops? Do the family a favor and keep the next one alive."

Jack felt his blood go hot, but the High Princept stepped between them.

"Enough," the Princept said, lifting a hand. "We called you here because of the events that transpired earlier today."

Jack waited, barely breathing, as the Book seemed to pulse in warning against him. *They can't know.* He'd been so careful to make sure that no one would suspect that the events at St. Paul's had been his doing.

"It seems that we've underestimated you," the Princept said, glancing at Morgan.

His uncle wore a look as though he smelled something rotten, but he didn't reply.

"What you did at Barclay's wedding was . . . admirable," the Princept continued.

"It would have been more admirable had Barclay's grandson not ended up dead," Morgan muttered.

Jack realized then that the older Barclay was missing from the meeting. "I'm sorry I couldn't do more," Jack murmured. "Theo's death was a true tragedy."

"It was murder." Morgan's nose twitched as he narrowed his eyes at Jack as though he suspected. "The Barclay boy didn't even get his wedding night, and the bride is gone. Vanished without a trace. Likely dead, and if not dead, then ruined beyond saving."

Jack remained silent. There was nothing to be gained by speaking.

"But those beasts," the Princept said. "You cannot deny that Jack was instrumental in helping to quell the danger."

Quell . . . Inspire. It was all of a piece, really.

"It's put us in a damned impossible position," Morgan bristled.

"I'm sorry my actions today inconvenienced you," Jack said, refusing to show even a glimmer of the amusement—or the temper—he felt stirring. "Perhaps next time I should stand aside when maggots attack our people."

"There was nothing wrong with what you did today, my boy," the Princept told him. "You likely saved the chapel with your quick thinking. But news has spread quickly, and the events that transpired today are unfortunate for more reasons than the tragic loss of Theo Barclay." He stepped over to the windows that faced out over the city, turning his back to Jack as he spoke. "As of late, we've heard murmurings throughout the Brotherhoods, concerns about our ability to remain in control of the maggots in this city."

"Somehow word has spread that we may no longer be in possession of those objects that gave us our power so long ago," his uncle added, glaring at Jack.

"If you are implying that I told others—"

"No," the Princept said. "That isn't what we're saying."

His uncle was staring at Jack as though he disagreed.

"But things between the Brotherhoods are . . . delicate. Until today, we have managed to deflect the rumors about the missing artifacts," the Princept told him. "But what happened at the chapel is already making its way around to the various organizations. I've already heard from the Veiled Prophet. They want to know what is happening in this city. They have questions about their own safety and about whether the Order of Ortus Aurea is fit to lead. Which is why we've called you here tonight."

Jack waited, impatience buzzing along his skin.

"The other Brotherhoods will surely learn of your actions today, if they do not already know. It is essential that we present a united front when they arrive in this city." The Princept turned back to him. "You'll be attending the Conclave after all, it seems." It wasn't a request, but Jack wouldn't have refused it anyway.

"I see." Satisfaction simmered within him.

"This is a mistake," Morgan said to the Princept. "You can't possibly imagine that his attendance at the Conclave will end any differently than the other travesties he's been involved with."

"We don't have a choice," the Princept told Morgan. "If he isn't there, standing beside us as one Order, what do you think Gunter and Cooke and the rest will think? The hero of St. Paul's, not invited? It will only make the rumors seem plausible. We cannot allow anyone to think that the Order itself is fractured. No, we must stand united. We must make them believe that nothing has changed, that there is no distress from within our ranks. It's our only chance to make it through that night and retain the power we currently hold."

He turned back to Jack. "But make no mistake, boy. Every one of the men from the other Brotherhoods will come to the Conclave hoping to find our weakness. They've been talking to one another—trading telegrams and stirring discord. They're waiting for an opening to take the seat of power from New York, and you aren't going to do anything that gives it to them."

Jack clenched his teeth, but he could not stop himself from speaking. "Did you call me here only to berate me like some unruly schoolboy? After all I've done, all you've witnessed me—"

"Shut up, Jack," Morgan snapped. "You haven't done anything but screw up since you went off on your Grand Tour. First that mess with the girl in Greece, and then you were duped by the maggots who destroyed Khafre Hall. And still that wasn't enough. In these very rooms, you let the Delphi's Tear slip away. Now Barclay is dead and his bride is gone, and the entire country is whispering about the Order of Ortus Aurea's failure. Because of *you*. All the parlor tricks in the world wouldn't give you the right to speak to us as equals."

"That's enough, Morgan," the Princept said. Then he turned to Jack. "We can't rewrite the past, but we can make sure to claim the future. You'll come to the Conclave, as I said, and you'll stay out of trouble. We cannot afford one of your spectacular disasters. Too much is riding on that night. The Conclave is more than a gathering of the Brotherhoods. It's the anniversary of our Order's founding, the anniversary of our greatest achievement." The Princept pointed toward the windows, where a dark ribbon of water divided the island from the rest of the country. "But if we are unsuccessful in reconsecrating the Brink, everything will be lost."

On the evening of the solstice, the power of the sun had illuminated that boundary through the crystal of the windows. Then, he had been able to see it, wavering and unstable already.

The Princept looked out into the darkness beyond the city. "The world is changing, Jack, and the Brotherhoods are becoming impatient to claim power of their own. Other cities are growing in wealth, and every day more and more of those with feral magic come to our shores and threaten what we have built. The other Brotherhoods see themselves as worthy of partnership rather than fealty. They want a seat at the table, and they want the power that comes with it."

"But we have no interest in sharing," Morgan added.

"None whatsoever." The Princept turned back to him. "We will welcome the Brotherhoods, but we have no intention of divesting ourselves of our place as their leaders. Before the destruction of Khafre Hall and the theft of our treasures, it would have been easier. We had already fortified the powers in the stones, and with them, we would have transformed the Brink—and the city with it.

"This city was carved out by magic," the Princept explained. "Its very design was intended to augment the power of those who had mastery of the occult sciences. We would have used what our forefathers created here—the Brink, the streets and hidden rivers, all mapped onto the power that runs through everything—to demonstrate our power to the other Brotherhoods. To show them that Manhattan was *truly* singular, and with it the Order. Every Mageus who dwelled in these streets would have had their magic ripped from them, and the Brotherhoods would have understood what was possible."

"Quite impressive," Jack murmured, trying not to show his true reaction. He hadn't realized their plans went beyond the Brink itself. He had never thought the old men of the Inner Circle capable of such imagination. He'd assumed them to be relics of the past, naive to the threats of the modern world.

"It's more than impressive," Morgan sputtered. "It was to be the future of the Order, the future, perhaps, of the world."

No, Jack thought to himself. He refused to believe or accept that. Not when the Book urged him on and promised a future that these old men could only begin to imagine. Not when the voice inside him whispered that the future belonged only to *him*.

"What will you do now?" Jack wondered. They had no artifacts, and he had possession of the Ars Arcana.

"We'll do what must be done to preserve our power," the Princept told him. "We are not without resources. The city itself will provide the answer. We may not have the artifacts, but we still have the power built into this land."

"The grid," he realized. The city hadn't been built along the traditional measures of longitude and latitude, but in alignment with ley lines infused with power. All connected to the Brink itself.

The Princept could not stop himself from gloating. "Yes. The artifacts would have made things easier, but the modern age has given us *other* tools to provide the power we need to reconsecrate the Brink and maintain our power over the other Brotherhoods and the city. *Electricity.* Lightning made by man. The modern and the ancient brought together."

It was an impressive idea, possibly even a plan that would work, except for one small issue. "And the Brink? I thought Newton's stones were necessary to stabilize it."

The Princept and his uncle exchanged an uncomfortable look, and Jack knew in an instant that whatever they said, this plan would not fix the problems with the Brink. Without the artifacts, they could not hope to reconsecrate it, and this plan would not make it stronger. It would not protect the city.

"We're confident that the increased energy will provide the Brink the power it needs until we are able to locate the stones," the Princept said.

They weren't confident of anything, but they were clearly willing to lie to him and to the other Brotherhoods. Worst of all, they were willing to lie to themselves.

"What we require is that you refrain from mucking it up," Morgan said. "The other Brotherhoods will expect you to be present, but you will stay out of the way. And if you do anything at all to put the Order or our power in jeopardy, I will make sure that you are sent so far from this city that you never return."

Jack watched his uncle, gratified at least to see that Morgan was unhappy about this entire situation. "You have nothing to worry about, gentlemen. I'm grateful for the opportunity to witness the Order's rebirth, and I would never dream of doing anything to put our city or our hallowed organization at risk."

Morgan muttered something under his breath, but Jack ignored him. His uncle had never believed in him. He'd done nothing but hold him back, probably because he was threatened by his promise. But in the end, he'd see. They all would.

Jack had no intention of coming to heel. This new information helped to bring his plans more clearly into focus. Let them believe that he was penitent and docile. They'd learn otherwise soon enough. In fact, the Inner Circle would have ringside seats to witness the birth of Jack's power. And J. P. Morgan would be the first one to fall.

ANOTHER STONE

The Docks

Harte and Logan passed three buildings before Logan finally stopped, and Harte recognized where he was. It looked like the others, but there was a marking on the door and a padlock too expensive and shiny for the filth of the docks.

The building was secured, but Harte made quick work of the lock, and in a matter of seconds they were inside. Lamps weren't necessary because the far side of the warehouse was already aglow. There, in the light of the ritual circle, Jianyu was suspended in midair, his arms and legs stretched out as though held by invisible cords. His tunic had been torn open, exposing the bloodied skin of his bare chest.

Harte rushed across the room, only barely registering the lurking metal structure in the center. He knew what it meant—Jack had rebuilt the machine—but it was pointless to waste time destroying it again. He'd just build another and another until they stopped him for good.

"Jianyu?" Harte stayed outside the ritual circle, not sure what would happen if he crossed over it.

Jianyu opened his eyes slowly, lifting his head with clear difficulty to try to find the source of his name. When he saw Harte standing there on the other side of the glowing circle, his brows drew together. "*Darrigan? You returned.*"

Harte didn't love the note of disbelief in Jianyu's voice. "I told you I would."

"You seem to have taken your time about it," Jianyu said, giving him a droll look that turned into a grimace of pain.

"Hold tight," Harte said, taking stock of the situation. "We're going to get you out of there."

"We?" Jianyu grimaced again.

Looking back over his shoulder, Harte saw that Jianyu was right. Logan was gone.

He should have gone further and used his affinity. At least then he'd have some help. And he could have been sure that Logan wouldn't become yet another weapon in Nibsy's arsenal.

Cursing softly at his soft-hearted stupidity, he thought about going after Logan, but he dismissed the idea almost immediately. It was more important to get Jianyu out of the mess he was in.

"I don't think I should cross that line," Harte said, examining the ritual circle. He'd seen circles like it trap Mageus enough times before. The last thing he wanted was for Jack to return to the warehouse and find *him* stuck inside it as well, like some kind of early Christmas present.

He searched the room for some answer to getting Jianyu out of that circle and considered a couple of different ideas before his gaze snagged on a familiar flash of silver resting on a nearby table. He pushed a pile of Jack's notes and diagrams aside and found Viola's knife sitting there.

"How did *you* get here?" he wondered, taking up the blade. The last time he'd seen it, Esta had secured it in the satchel before they'd talked to Dakari. Of course, that was a later version of this knife. Not the one in his hand.

"Viola," Jianyu groaned, gasping in pain. "Did she—"

"She's with Cela," Harte told him. No sense in making him worry until they knew anything for sure. There would be time enough for him to tell Jianyu everything. But first . . .

Harte crept closer to the circle, feeling the brush of cold energy as he approached. He didn't really know what he was doing or whether it would work, but if the blade could cut through pretty much anything, maybe it could cut through ritual magic as well. Like answered to like, after all.

Edging the tip closer, he held his breath, and with a quick, sharp push, he sliced through the dirt floor of the warehouse, severing the circle. The line went dark where the blade had cut it, and Harte released a relieved breath at the sight. Once more he edged the tip closer and pushed, and as the cold energy licked dangerously against his skin, a portion of the circle went dark. He did it twice more, widening the opening until there was a space large enough for him to step through.

He considered the situation—the ritual circle, the missing piece, and his friend suspended on invisible bindings, hanging in the air. And the strange dark crystal sitting beneath him. Suddenly he understood.

Jack's making another stone. Which would give him all the power he needed to make the machine functional. There wasn't time to wait. He had to get Jianyu out of there, and he had to get him out *now*.

He stepped through the opening in the circle and hoped he wasn't making a mistake. Then, on instinct, he drove the tip of the knife through the black crystal, and as the blade sank through the stone, it cracked in two, and a burst of icy magic passed over him like an explosion. His magic flashed hot in response, and Jianyu fell to the ground.

Harte helped him up, looping Jianyu's arm over his shoulder and pulling him out of the now-dead circle.

"Jack has the Book," Jianyu told him.

"I know," Harte said.

"What happened?" Jianyu asked. "Where is Esta?"

"She's coming," he said, because it was the only thing that could be true. "Right now we have to get out of here before Jack comes back."

They'd nearly made it across the warehouse when he heard a carriage approaching.

Harte looked around the warehouse for some other exit or somewhere to hide, but the open space offered no cover. "If that's Jack—"

There wasn't any other exit. All they could do was run for it and hope it wasn't Jack, but Harte's hopes were dashed when he eased his head out and saw Jack Grew's familiar figure alighting from the carriage. He was giving some kind of order to his driver, who looked more than a little tired of taking them, and Harte and Jianyu took the distraction as an opportunity to slip out of the warehouse and ease around the corner.

Once they were out of sight, they started to run.

STRENGTH

Uptown

Viola didn't know how long she'd been unconscious. Pain made time unsteady, and at some point she'd lost track of the hours and minutes. When she finally woke, it was to the sound of weeping. She wasn't the one crying, though she probably had every right to be, considering the pain she was currently feeling. She opened her eyes but didn't have the strength to turn her head and find the source of the sniffling sobs. Still, even with only the wall in front of her, she recognized where she was. She'd stared at this wall often enough in the last few weeks.

But how? She remembered the Strega, remembered the flash of temper and grief that had spread through her, and then remembered hearing an explosion. Werner. Nibsy. The Medusa's kiss. They were all mixed up in her memory. Who had come for her? How had they saved her when Nibsy had been so determined to destroy her?

She shuddered a little at the memory of what that had been like—to be captured and helpless. To be unmade by Leena's magic.

The pain had been terrible, but more unbearable was the knowledge that she'd done it to herself. She'd known what Nibsy was capable of and what power he had at his disposal, and she'd gone anyway.

Perhaps she had died.

But no, hell would not be so soft as the bed beneath her, and heaven certainly wouldn't hurt so much. She wasn't dead, as much as she might have preferred it right then.

Gathering her strength, she tried to turn her head, and suddenly the sniffling sobs stopped.

"Viola?"

It took everything she had to push through the pain of moving, but when she turned, there was Ruby Reynolds, sitting in the lamplight. Her eyes were red and her nose swollen and pink from tears, but she was not looking at Viola with hatred.

"No," Ruby said, rushing over to her. "You shouldn't move. You'll tear the stitches."

Viola realized then that her back was covered with some kind of cloth that had been wrapped around her torso. A bandage of some sort.

"I need to sit," Viola told her. "I've been in this position so long, my neck feels like it'll never be straight again." But Ruby didn't owe her anything. Not after all that had happened—not after Theo. "Is Cela here? She can maybe help me up."

"Let me," Ruby said softly.

Viola wanted to say yes. She wanted to accept Ruby's help, to feel Ruby's hands upon her skin. But yes seemed a dangerous word. It was too much to believe that Ruby was real and whole and here. Too much to hope that Ruby would want to help her, to *touch* her.

"Please?" Ruby asked, mistaking Viola's silence for some other emotion.

Viola nodded, trying to keep the tears from welling over.

Gently, Ruby took her by the arm and helped to ease her upright. She understood then what Ruby had meant by tearing the stitches—every movement brought fresh bursts of pain to the skin on her back. It felt tight and hot with the aching.

"Water?" Ruby asked, offering a tin cup to Viola.

She shook her head. "Why are you here? Why are you helping me?" She could not stop herself from asking. "After all I did to you, to Theo . . ."

"You didn't do anything to Theo," Ruby said with a soft sob. "You tried to save him."

"But I didn't," Viola said, closing her eyes against the memory of Theo's broken body falling from the monster's grasp. "I couldn't," she whispered. "It's my fault he's dead."

"No, Viola." Ruby took her hand. Her skin was soft and warm, but Viola could feel her trembling. "I never should have said those things to you. I never should have blamed you. I was so sad, so angry at myself."

"You did nothing," Viola said, not understanding.

"What happened to Theo was my fault, Viola. It wasn't yours."

Viola ignored the pain she felt when she moved her hand and did it anyway, to brush the tears from Ruby's face. "No—"

"Theo was only marrying me so I wouldn't have to marry someone else," Ruby told her.

Viola's brows drew together. "He loved you."

Ruby nodded. "He did, but he never should have married me." She withdrew her hand from Viola's. "We were just children when I forced him into the engagement."

"Forced?" Viola frowned.

"Well, maybe not *forced*," Ruby admitted. "But I pushed and pushed until he agreed, and I always told myself that he could back out at any time. Except I realize now that Theo never would have." She shoved back the hair that had fallen into her face and looked at Viola. "He gave me an opportunity to jilt him," she admitted. "When I arrived a few days ago, he offered to help me run off to stay with an elderly aunt of his in Scotland."

"You didn't go," Viola said, wondering what that meant.

"No," Ruby told her. "But if I had been brave enough to free him from our childish agreement, he wouldn't have been there at the church. He wouldn't be—" She stopped suddenly, and the tears started again.

Viola laid her hand on Ruby's arm. "I didn't know Theo so long, but the time I did know him? Theo wasn't the type of man you could force."

Ruby was looking at her through watery green eyes.

"I tried to talk him out of helping us. I threatened him, too, maybe a little, but no." She shook her head. "It didn't matter the danger. Theo made up his mind, and that was that. That one, he was stronger than most."

"He was, wasn't he?" Ruby said, wiping a tear away.

Viola took her hand again and squeezed it. "He wouldn't want you to do this, to blame yourself. If he was at that altar, he was there by his own choosing."

Ruby's lips pressed together as she nodded, but at first she didn't speak.

"I wanted someone to stop it," Ruby whispered finally, as though this confession was almost too terrible to make. She was staring at their two hands. "I was standing there before god and our families, with Theo's hand in mine, and the rector had just asked my intentions, and all I could think was that I wished that something would make it stop. *Anything.*"

Viola's heart felt like it was being squeezed in a vise. She wanted to tell Ruby that what happened wasn't her fault, that her wanting and wishing didn't make evil grow there in that holy place. Not when the evil was inside Jack Grew. But she couldn't find the words to say anything. She was too afraid to break the moment hanging between them.

Ruby looked at Viola through her lashes. "I wanted it to be you."

MORE THAN ENOUGH

R uby watched Viola's reaction to the words that had just escaped
from her mouth—the slight widening of her eyes, the panic that
shifted in those violet depths—and she wondered if she had
made a mistake.

She hadn't planned on saying any of the things she'd just said to Viola.
She wasn't even sure that she'd known the truth of those words until they
were already tumbling out of her mouth, changing her life and her world
just by their existence.

She hadn't wanted to marry Theo. Truth.

She'd trapped him because of her own selfishness. Another truth.

She'd stood on that holy altar, pledging her life to him before god and
the world, but she'd been thinking about another. She could not deny it.

Maybe if Ruby had never been sent off to Europe, things would have
been different. Maybe if she hadn't spent months watching women who
had built lives with one another, who were happy together. Not content.
Not settling. Fulfilled. *Together.* Maybe then she could have forgotten
about Viola. Perhaps she might have finally accepted Viola's rejection back
at the gala and moved on toward a happy future with Theo Barclay. But
Paris had changed everything. It had shown her what was possible. It had
whispered to her that Viola's rejection had been nothing but fear.

As a journalist, her lodestar was the truth, and so she had to admit that
truth now, most of all, to herself. The truth was simply this: She would
have given anything right then to stop the world from spinning, to stop
her life from being forced down a path she could never return from.
Anything. She would have even given Theo.

Of course, desperate bargains were easy enough to stomach when they seemed impossible. It was a far different thing to face the reality. Theo was gone. She was, at least, in part to blame.

"You didn't cause this," Viola told her. "Nothing you did, nothing you wished for. You aren't the reason Theo died."

Ruby closed her eyes to hold back the tears. "I wish I could believe that."

"Do you know how many times I've sat in a church, pleading?" Viola asked. "Bargaining with and begging whoever might be listening?"

Ruby shook her head. She had no idea what a girl as strong and brave as Viola would ever need to beg or bargain for.

"Too many times," Viola said, glancing away. "My whole life I've spent sitting in churches just like that one, promising anything—offering *anything*—to be free from this connection to the old magic that lives in my skin, that beats with my blood. My whole life, no one has answered those prayers. Because god, he don't work like that. He's not gli folletti, flitting through the air to grant our wishes."

Surprised, Ruby looked up. Why would Viola want to give up that essential part of her, that piece of light that made her so uniquely herself? "But your affinity, it's part of you. Why would you ever wish it away?"

"Bah," Viola exclaimed with disgust. "It's nothing but a curse."

"No," Ruby said, squeezing her hand. When Viola wouldn't look at her, she scooted closer on the bed, took Viola's face in her hands, and turned her head. So that she would have to see, have to understand. "It's part of you, Viola. It's nothing to be ashamed of."

But Viola backed away from her. "I don't understand you. You know what I am, what I've done. The lives I've taken. The people I've killed." She shook her head. "Why do you not see?"

"See what?" Ruby asked.

"The truth," Viola said.

Ruby realized then what she hadn't understood before. It was so easy to look at Viola, all brash temper and headstrong fire, and think that nothing could touch her. Maybe she should have seen it sooner—maybe it was what had drawn her to Viola in the first place—how similar they were. Neither one of them fitting in the world they were given. Both of them wanting more. But someone had hurt her.

"Who was it?" Ruby asked.

Confused, Viola looked back at her. "What do you mean?"

"Who convinced you that you're not enough just as you are?"

This time it wasn't panic Ruby saw but pain. Shadows darkened Viola's violet irises, and she tried to turn away again.

But Ruby wouldn't allow it. She shifted so Viola had to look at her. "You can't see yourself clearly at all, can you?"

"I know what I am," Viola whispered.

"Do you?" Ruby wondered. "I've seen you with your friends. I've seen your heart, Viola Vacarrelli. You can't hide it from me."

Viola tried to shrug off her words, but Ruby would not allow her to.

"*You* can't hide from me," she said. "I don't know who convinced you that your affinity was evil, but they were wrong. Maybe you're brash, with a temper to go along with it. But you're strong because of it. You're *good*, Viola. Clear to the center of who you are." A lock of hair had fallen from Viola's usual low chignon, and Ruby tucked it behind her ear as a tear escaped from Viola's eyes. "Beautiful, too."

She leaned forward, slowly, so that there was every opportunity for Viola to escape, and when she didn't, Ruby kissed her. Gently at first, a question. And then, all at once, Viola leaned into her, and the whole world focused down to the truth of Viola's mouth, the feel of her lips against hers, the *taste* of her. When Viola lifted her hands, threaded them through Ruby's hair, and brought her closer, she was lost.

It was too easy to forget that earlier that morning she had been someone else's bride. Too easy to forget where she was, *who* she was, and what had just happened.

But suddenly Ruby felt something between them shift, and Viola stopped.

"We shouldn't be doing this," Viola said, nearly breathless.

"Why?" Ruby challenged. "Because some crusty old men told us it isn't possible to live a life without them?"

Viola blinked. "That's not—"

"They're wrong," Ruby told her. "I've seen how wrong they are." She saw the confusion, the interest in Viola's expression. "In Paris, I saw the lives women can lead. *Together.* In the open. Happy."

Viola shook her head. "That's not what I meant. But don't you see? It doesn't matter, because I'll never go to Paris. I'll never leave this city."

Because of the Brink. How stupid she'd been to forget. "Then we'll make our Paris here."

Viola only stared at her, and Ruby began to think that maybe she'd been wrong about what was between them. She'd just assumed that Viola felt the same, and with that kiss—

"And what of Theo?"

Theo. She waited for the guilt and shame to wash over her . . . but it never came. When she thought of Theo, when she thought of what had happened to him today, grief creased her heart. But not shame. He'd wanted this for her. He alone had understood. And because of what he gave—for her, for them—he would always be a part of the bond she felt with Viola. He would never truly be gone.

"I think he'd approve," she told Viola. "You know, he talked about you and your friends when he came to visit me this past summer. He told me everything about what you'd done, what he was helping you with. He admired all of you so much, but I think he loved you most of all."

"He's the one who invited me to your wedding," Viola said, her eyes glittering with unshed tears.

"Maybe he knew what both of us needed," Ruby told her.

Viola leaned forward, rested her forehead against Ruby's. "Sei pazza. You know that?"

"Maybe a little," Ruby told her with a shrug. "But I've been called far worse."

Viola choked out a surprised laugh.

"I want this, Viola. Whatever it is between us," Ruby confessed.

"Ruby—"

"No," she said, unwilling to allow Viola to brush aside what she knew was there. She'd tried this once before, but she'd made a complete mess of it. She would get it right this time. "I'll mourn Theo for the rest of my life. His death will always be a regret that I carry with me, but not telling you how I felt? Not making you understand? What I feel—all of *this*—it's not some silly whim of some silly rich girl. I understand what might lie ahead if we choose this—if we choose each other. I understand how hard all of it might be, but it doesn't matter."

"It matters," Viola argued. "Do you think I could ask that of you, to drag you down to my level?"

"Why can't you see?" Ruby shook her head. "Viola, I lost *everything* today—my family, my best friend, and the life I once had—and none of it mattered compared to how I felt when they brought you in earlier, broken and bleeding. You're better than all of them put together, and you would never drag me down. Whoever it was that made you believe you weren't enough, they were fools, and I won't let them get between us now. Let me stand next to you. Choose me, choose *us*, and the rest will figure itself out."

Viola stared at her for a long beat, and the world began to tilt. Ruby was certain her life was destined to be colored by loss and disappointment. But then Viola leaned in and kissed her.

"Pazza," Viola whispered. But she kissed Ruby again.

Someone cleared their throat in the doorway.

"Glad to see you're still with us," Cela said to Viola.

Viola started to move away from Ruby, but Ruby caught her hand, held tight, and looked Cela right in the eye.

Cela's mouth quirked a bit. "I'll give the two of you a minute, but Darrigan's back with Jianyu. And you're probably going to want to hear their news."

THE BLACK CORD

Jianyu hissed in pain as Cela tended to the wound that had been caused by the silk cord around his wrist. He had not told anyone how the cord had grown smaller in recent weeks, but when he had removed his shirt so that Viola could take care of the wounds on his chest, there had been no way to hide it. Not when the black silk was so tight, it had practically embedded itself into his skin. Viola had healed the cuts Jack had made with a small burst of her magic, but her affinity had not touched the corrupt power in the shackle around his wrist.

"Sorry," Cela whispered, grimacing a little at the pain she was causing him. But she did not stop her examination.

There was no denying it any longer. The black cord had been growing progressively smaller, but when Jack Grew had tried to harvest his magic, the bracelet had become like a garrote. The more power Jack had pressed into Jianyu's body with the tip of the dagger, the tighter the braided silk had become.

"I don't think there's anything I can do," Cela told him with a frustrated sigh. "Why didn't you tell us it was getting so bad?"

"There was nothing you could have done," Jianyu said, pulling away and immediately regretting the loss of the comforting warmth of Cela's hands. "The bargain was mine to make. So too are the consequences."

"Che cassata!" Viola snapped. "You should have told us. We aren't any of us alone in this. Not anymore."

She was right. But he had not wanted them to worry about things that could not be changed.

"It was not so tight as this until Jack Grew touched me with the dagger." He did not know how to explain that the cold ritual magic it contained seemed stronger now, too. It radiated up his arm and down through all his fingers. He opened his hand and closed it, wincing at the stiffness there.

When he noticed Cela watching him with a worried frown, he stopped and clasped his hands together.

"Maybe Lee already had a claim to your affinity," Darrigan said, eyeing the black silk on Jianyu's wrist. He was leaning against the counter, slightly apart from those sitting around the table, as he had been the entire time Viola and Cela had tended to Jianyu's wounds.

Jianyu frowned, remembering the way he had felt nearly torn in two as the dagger and the silk had warred for control over his affinity. "You think this cord might have offered protection?"

Harte shrugged. "It's possible. When I found you, it looked like Jack was nearly done with the ritual. But you walked away with your magic intact. Maybe that bit of thread saved you."

"He doesn't look saved to me," Cela told Harte. "He looks like he's about to lose a hand if we don't figure out how to get this off him."

"Only Tom Lee has the power to remove it," Jianyu said. "And he will not until I deliver what I have promised him."

"You've done nothing *but* deliver," Cela said sourly. "He keeps you running day and night. Nothing is ever enough."

"Perhaps, but I have not yet given him what he wants most," Jianyu reminded her.

"I know. And after seeing what that cane did to Viola's back, I understand," Cela said with a sigh. "Even if you could get it from Nibsy Lorcan, you wouldn't hand it over to Lee—or anyone else."

Jianyu was not sure why a part of him uncoiled at the realization that Cela knew him so well. When had he ever been seen so clearly? Perhaps not since Dolph. Perhaps not even then.

"Maybe another solution will present itself," Jianyu told them, not at all believing that such a fantasy would come to be.

The truth was that Tom Lee would never let him go. The truth was also that Jianyu would never offer up the Devil's Own.

"But you don't believe it will," Cela said, her voice hollow with understanding. "You've already made up your mind, haven't you?"

"Nothing is certain," he told her, wishing that he felt the truth of his own words. "But this piece of thread is the least of our problems."

"That piece of thread will *kill* you," Cela argued.

"If Jack Grew destroys the Brink, it will kill us all," Jianyu reminded her. He had already explained what Jack had revealed to him.

"I still don't understand," Ruby said. "Wouldn't that solve your problem? Without the Brink, anyone with the old magic could leave the city. None of you would be trapped here." She turned to Viola. "You could leave. We could go anywhere."

"It's not that easy," Harte said. He stepped toward the table. "Jianyu's right. If Jack brings down the Brink, it doesn't mean freedom for Mageus. It means the end."

"Of magic?" Ruby asked.

"Of *everything*," Jianyu told her.

Ruby frowned. "How can that be?"

"Because everything is connected," Harte said. "All of the magic the Brink has taken over the years is still linked to all of the old magic in the world *and* to all Mageus who still carry an affinity for it. If the Brink is destroyed, it would destroy everyone who has a connection to the old magic."

"That would kill hundreds—maybe thousands—just in this city alone," Cela said, her eyes meeting Jianyu's.

"It would destroy magic itself," Viola corrected.

"You would all die?" Ruby asked, her eyes wide with new fear.

"Not only us," Jianyu said softly. "The old magic is not some spell to cast or control. It lives in the spaces of all things."

"End magic, end the world," Viola said.

"Doesn't Jack know that?" Cela asked, clearly horrified. "How could he not?"

"I'm sure you could fill whole libraries with all that Jack Grew doesn't know," Ruby said wryly. "If what you're saying is true, we have to stop him."

"We?" Viola looked at her.

"I'm with you now," Ruby said, taking her hand.

Jianyu watched as color rose in Viola's cheeks and the two women shared a secret look, a silent conversation between them. He glanced at Cela, who was watching as well, and then suddenly she looked up at him, and he felt his world shift.

He looked away first, unwilling to consider the warmth building inside his chest. Unwilling to let himself hope. Cela Johnson was not for him. Who was he but an outsider to this land? Trapped in the city, trapped now too in a country that did not want his kind. She deserved far more than he could ever offer.

But he did not have to look to know that Cela was watching him still.

"He's not going to bring down the Brink," Harte said. "Or, at least, he didn't before."

Darrigan told them then about the future he and Esta had seen in St. Louis and the years beyond.

"In the future we saw, the Conclave is the turning point. Because of the attack on the Conclave, the entire country will turn against the old magic," Darrigan said. "People who live far from Manhattan, people who maybe haven't ever thought about Mageus, will learn to fear those with the old magic. The whole country will come to see the old magic as a threat, and they'll outlaw it. The Defense Against Magic Act will make magic and anyone with a connection to it illegal. After the DAM Act, every Mageus on these shores will be in constant danger of being discovered and rounded up.

"But now we know—it isn't Mageus who attack the Conclave." He turned to Jianyu. "If what Jack told you is true, it's going to be Jack himself who attacks."

"Just as it was he who attacked the church yesterday," Jianyu confirmed.

"That's not surprising. He's done this sort of thing before—or he will," Harte told him. "He'll use the power he's gained from the Book to make it appear that Mageus are at fault, and then he'll swoop in as the hero of the day."

"We have to reveal what he's doing," Ruby told them. "People need to know that Jack's the one who attacked the church and killed Theo. They need to know he's planning another attack."

"Who will tell them?" Viola asked.

"I can," Ruby said. "I can go back, write article after article. Do you know how many papers my firsthand account will sell? Someone will publish it. They won't be able to resist."

"No one will believe it," Viola said. "When do they ever believe a woman's words? They won't want to believe what you write, no matter the truth. I saw the crowd outside of St. Paul's when Jack brought Theo's broken body like a trophy to lay at their feet. They never questioned him because they *wanted* to believe the tale he told. It only confirms the hate and fear that live in their hearts about our kind."

"Viola's right," Darrigan said. "It's not enough to reveal Jack's plan and hope the authorities step in. Hell, the authorities are probably on his side."

"So we kill him," Viola said, her eyes flashing.

"That will only confirm the public's beliefs," Jianyu told her.

"We can't kill Jack," Darrigan told them. "Remember? Esta tried that, and it only released the demon inside him. It made things worse."

Jianyu believed the tale Darrigan had spun about ancient beings and cursed souls. He'd seen the living blackness take over Jack Grew, had he not? And the danger of the goddess that inhabited the Book matched too closely to what he'd overheard in Morgan's mansion.

"Perhaps there is a way to control the danger that lives within Jack Grew's skin so we can eliminate the threat of them both," Jianyu told Darrigan. "We have Newton's Sigils."

Darrigan frowned in confusion.

"If what Morgan said is to be believed, the sigils were created to control the power in the Book—a power you say might have been this goddess, Seshat," Jianyu explained. "Could they not also control the power in Jack?"

"But we have no idea how to use them," Viola reminded him.

"Nibsy has Morgan's papers, which means he has the answers we need," Jianyu said. "If we retrieve those documents, perhaps we could use the sigils and eliminate the threat within Jack before the Conclave."

"It's worth a try," Darrigan told them. "Since I never took the mark, I should be the one to go. Dolph's cane can't touch me."

"You cannot go alone. You have not seen the papers we require," Jianyu said.

"No, Jianyu," Cela said. "I saw what that boy did to Viola. You can't go running into danger as well. Not as long as you're wearing the mark."

The worry in her voice warmed him and terrified him just the same.

"I do not fear Nibsy Lorcan," Jianyu told her. "This twist of magic around my wrist is no less dangerous than anything he can do. One way or another, my life is marked."

"You're talking like you've given up," Cela said, her brows drawing together.

"No," Jianyu corrected. "But fate has thrown its dagger. Perhaps if I reach for the handle, I will not be caught by the blade."

"Or maybe you'll be sliced to bits," Cela said darkly.

He inclined his head, acknowledging her point. "But the danger in the Strega might prove useful in other ways," he told her as he considered the dangerously tight cord around his wrist. "Tom Lee may have more patience if he believes I am still seeking the cane. Perhaps I might buy myself some time."

"We need to act, and we need to do it before the Conclave." Darrigan looked suddenly lost and unsure as he scrubbed his hand through his hair. "So much has happened, and the Conclave is only a couple of weeks away. I thought we'd have more time. We were supposed to have more time. If Esta doesn't arrive before then—"

Darrigan stopped as though he'd said too much.

"I think," Jianyu said carefully, "it is far past time for you tell us where Esta is."

BAIT

They waited a week for Esta to arrive before they made their move on the Bella Strega, and during that week, Harte grew less and less sure in his belief that she would find him. How could she not have appeared by now? His affinity had long since returned from the substance the Guard had doused them with. It only stood to reason that Esta's should have as well.

Each day that passed made him worry that something more was keeping her. Perhaps something had happened to Ishtar's Key, or perhaps she had landed in some danger that they hadn't expected and was trapped by one of their enemies.

He worried too that he was the cause of her absence. They couldn't eliminate Nibsy unless they were certain that Dakari would do what he'd promised. Harte had believed he found a way. He had hoped to return to 1902 and find evidence of that possibility, but the sign he was looking for had not materialized. Now he began to worry that what he had done—the minute change he'd inserted into Esta's history—had some larger effect that he hadn't intended.

Without the diary, he was flying blind, and without Esta, he was growing desperate.

He kept those worries to himself, just as he kept his knowledge of what would happen to his friends should they not take care of Jack before the Conclave. He told himself that the future could still be changed. He told himself that what had been written in Nibsy's diary need never come to be. But he wondered if they didn't deserve some right to their own fate.

They had waited long enough. Each day that passed was one day less they had until the Conclave was upon them—one day less to plan, to prepare, and to neutralize the threat that Jack posed to the march of history and the future of all magic. They needed the instructions for using Newton's Sigils. Until they had those documents, they could not be sure that the strange silvery discs could do what Jianyu believed.

Harte still had trouble believing that Newton's Sigils could be the answer to dealing with Jack. But the day had arrived for them to find out.

"She will come," Jianyu said as though sensing the direction of Harte's thoughts.

They were heading toward the Bowery and were both wrapped in Jianyu's affinity, protection against any who might be searching for them.

Harte could have denied his worry, but he found that he no longer had the energy to pretend. "What if she went too far?" Harte asked, voicing the one fear that had haunted him through the days and nights without Esta. "If she was thrown off course by the Guard's attack, anything could have happened. If she went too far—or not far enough—if she landed at a time when Ishtar's Key already existed—if it crossed with itself—she'd be stuck. Trapped. Maybe for good."

And if that happened, if it became impossible to give the cuff to her younger self . . . she'd be gone.

"I might not ever know," he whispered, his greatest fear of all.

Jianyu stopped and clapped him on the shoulder. His grip felt sure and strong. "She *will* come, Darrigan."

"How can you be so sure?" he asked.

Jianyu released him with a small shrug. "I have no other choice."

In the days since the attack on the wedding, the mood in the Bowery had shifted. The increased police presence was enough to have the various gangs drawing inward. But the factions in the Bowery were chafing under this new control. Each day Jianyu brought word from the On Leongs that Lee was growing impatient to act. It was the perfect situation to stir into a distraction so they could get to the papers Nibsy had stolen.

They left the park and headed south once more, the sky heavy and gray above them. As they walked, snow began to fall, coating the world and erasing the grime and filth of the city. In moments like this, Harte could almost believe that a different life was possible. He could almost fall in love with the city that had born him and raised him and made him who he was. *Almost.*

Without Esta, the city was nothing but a prison once again. But with her . . .

They went to the Little Naples Cafe first and then to find Sai Wing Mock and the Hip Sings. With Jianyu's help to keep them unseen, it was simple enough for Harte to use his affinity and put their plan into action before they headed back toward the Bowery. Back to the Strega.

Under the cover of Jianyu's affinity, they watched the door of the saloon from under the cover of a shop awning farther down the block. The sign over the entrance bore the likeness of a golden-eyed witch— Leena, the woman Dolph had loved. But now, the more Harte looked, he saw Esta in those features too.

His heart clenched.

"This will work," Jianyu promised as they waited for some sign that their morning's work had borne fruit. "Nibsy will be forced to deal with the problems we have created for him. It will give us time."

It was the best distraction they could think of. Both the Five Pointers and the Hip Sings had formed tenuous alliances with the Devil's Own because of what they believed Nibsy could do for them. But as of that morning, the leaders of those two organizations would begin having second thoughts about the trust they placed in Nibsy Lorcan. The commotion caused when they both showed up at the Bella Strega at the same time would, with luck, be enough of a distraction to allow Harte and Jianyu to steal back the documents Nibsy had.

But Harte knew how slippery Nibsy could be. He wished he felt half as sure as Jianyu.

"Maybe we should have told the others," he said, watching the street for some sign that their plan was working.

It didn't take long before John Torrio arrived with a large group of Five Pointers, including Razor Riley. Torrio and Riley went into the Strega, leaving their men to stand guard outside. When the group of Hip Sings arrived not long after, they found their way blocked by Torrio's men. The mood on the streets changed quickly as the two factions began to circle each other, with Sai Wing Mock demanding entrance into the saloon.

Harte and Jianyu didn't wait to see who won that particular argument. They hurried around to Elizabeth Street, where the back entrance of the Strega waited, unguarded. But just before they were inside, Harte paused.

"I'm sorry about this," he said, and sent a pulse of magic into his friend. "But it's better this way."

Jianyu's gaze went a little fuzzy, but he did not release his hold on the light. "What?"

"Wait outside and don't let anyone see you," Harte told him. "If I'm not back in ten minutes, it means something's gone wrong, and you can let the others know what I've done. But don't you dare come back for me alone."

Then he released Jianyu and started up the steps to the apartment that had once belonged to Dolph Saunders.

The lock was a surprise, though perhaps it shouldn't have been considering what he knew of Nibsy. It was easy enough to pick, and in a matter of seconds, he was inside.

He didn't waste any time, did he? Harte thought, looking at the changes Nibsy had made in the once-familiar space. His gaze snagged on the painting above it. The one he'd seen just days before in the Professor's office. It was another reminder of the future that might unfold if they didn't manage to change the course of history.

It wouldn't take Nibsy long to realize that the simultaneous arrival of both Johnny Torrio and Mock Duck was nothing more than a distraction, so Harte didn't hesitate. He went to the bookcase, searching for the leather folder Jianyu had described. He'd sorted through one of the shelves when he heard the door open behind him.

He turned at the same time he heard a metallic *snick*. Nibsy already had a pistol primed and aimed directly at his chest.

Nibsy stepped into the apartment, not bothering to close the door behind him. "I wondered when I'd see you again, Darrigan. I have to say, I expected you sooner than this."

Harte lifted his hands slowly, keeping his attention on the gun. But he didn't miss what Nibsy was holding in his other hand.

"I assume you're looking for these?" Nibsy lifted the leather portfolio and then tossed it onto a nearby table. "Well, there it is. Not that it'll do you any good."

"Don't you think you should be downstairs with your guests?" Harte asked. "Careful, or you might lose your saloon."

Nibsy only smiled, his eyes flashing with amusement behind his thick spectacles. "Your care is touching, Darrigan, but my people are far too loyal and too powerful to let anyone get the best of them. They'll handle the problem. It's not like they have a choice. Torrio and Sai Wing Mock should know better than to come into my territory making threats. And their alliance means nothing, not in the grand scheme of things."

Harte realized that they'd made a tactical mistake. Both he and Jianyu had assumed Nibsy would protect his troops since they were all that stood between him and losing everything. They'd been wrong. It was clear now that Nibsy would sacrifice everyone in the barroom if it meant he might get his hands on the Book.

"I should have killed you," Harte said, realizing that without Jianyu's help, he had no way out.

"Such a shame you didn't. Now you'll never have the chance," Nibsy told him with a small, amused smile.

He kept the gun on Harte as he poured a glass of Nitewein.

"Here." Nibsy set the glass on the floor between them. "Drink it. I don't want any unfortunate incidents with that affinity of yours."

Harte stared at the glass and then looked back at the gun. He could try to lunge for him. He still had his affinity. But Nibsy's skin was covered almost completely, and the gun would likely go off before he could use his magic.

"It's the wine or a bullet, Darrigan," Nibsy said. "I don't need you alive, but it would make things so much more entertaining."

Stay alive. It was the only thing that mattered.

He reached for the glass slowly, but at first he wouldn't do more than look at the dark liquid inside. He had to delay a bit longer, until his command wore off and Jianyu realized he was gone.

What had he said? Had he commanded him to leave? He suddenly couldn't remember.

Delay, he thought as he stared at the Nitewein. *Someone will come.*

Someone *had* to come. It wasn't possible that he'd been so stupid to step right into Nibsy's trap again.

"Oh, don't worry so much, Darrigan," Nibsy said as Harte considered the Nitewein. "You aren't the one I want. You're only the bait."

THE MESSAGE

Central Park

E sta opened her eyes, and the darkness that she'd fallen through transformed itself back into the tunnel. She felt unsteady from all that had just happened—all she'd just seen—but the second she realized that the weather was bitterly cold and snow covered the ground beyond the tunnel's entrance, she sprang to her feet. Her head swirled at the sudden movement, but she tried not to panic. Though it was damn hard to stay calm when her affinity was dead, the city was covered in snow, and Harte was nowhere to be seen—*and* when the memory of the unmade world was still clinging to her like old cobwebs.

Against her arm, the stone in her cuff thrummed with an unsteady warmth. At least she still had Ishtar's Key. It meant that she hadn't gone too far off course. She hadn't crossed herself and the stone. Even though it wasn't spring, as they'd planned, it meant that she still had a chance to sift back through the layers of years to Harte and to get things on track. Once the stone cooled, she could get back to where she'd intended to go. She could find Harte. Once her affinity returned.

If it returns.

Esta let out an uneasy breath at the thought. She couldn't let herself go there. Not yet. *Not ever.*

Rubbing her arms for warmth, she considered her situation. It was snowing. Large, white flakes tumbled from the heavy gray sky. From the shelter of the tunnel, she could see the city clearly through the bare branches of the trees. Gone were the soaring skyscrapers of mirrored glass and steel. Brick and stone structures lined the park. It looked similar to the city as it had been in 1902. Maybe she was close to the right time.

Her gaze caught on a set of markings low on the wall of the tunnel. Her name. Someone had written her name in chalk. Along with the words "New York" and "age."

She crouched down, ran her fingers along the letters, wondering what they meant, wishing she could understand what they signified by simply touching them. She tried to tell herself that there was any number of reasons that her name would be there, but she knew the only reason was if Harte had been there as well.

But how long ago did he write this?

There wasn't anything she could do as long as her affinity was dead, so she figured she might as well figure out what the words meant. And whether Harte was here as well.

The words turned out to be a newspaper, and through a little investigation, she finally found the large brick building that held the paper's offices. It was far uptown, away from the Bowery and the areas their friends would have frequented.

She studied the front entrance for a long while before realizing that she had no other real options. As long as her affinity still felt cold and empty, there was nothing to do but try to find someone she knew, someone who could tell her what might have become of Harte.

Inside the main vestibule, Esta shook the snow from her hair and shoulders before knocking on the heavy office door. A middle-aged man with light brown skin and a pair of pince-nez spectacles on his nose opened it and gave her a look somewhere between irritation and resignation.

"You'll be looking for Abel and his folks," the man said before Esta could even open her mouth to speak. "Upstairs."

He shut the door in her face.

Esta didn't know any Abel, but the man had been confident enough that she figured it would be worth trying the apartment upstairs. When she knocked on that door, she heard shuffling from within, and then suddenly the door was thrown open and Cela Johnson was standing there, a look of absolute shock on her face.

"Who is it?" Viola's voice called from somewhere in the apartment.

But Cela didn't answer. "Is it really you?" she asked Esta in a voice close to a whisper.

Esta nodded. "Is Harte here?"

Before Cela could answer, Viola was pushing her aside.

"Chi é—" Viola froze, her violet eyes wide, and then suddenly the prickly assassin launched herself at Esta and wrapped her in a fierce embrace.

Esta felt the burn of tears as she returned Viola's embrace. She wasn't too late. They weren't gone. *Not yet*. She could save them. "Where's Harte?" she asked. "Is he here?"

Viola nodded as she looked her over. "I can't believe it. Darrigan, he said you'd come, but after a week, we weren't so sure."

"So Harte *is* here?" Esta asked, her stomach flipping. She hadn't lost him. "What's today's date?"

"The eighth of December," Cela said.

"But what *year*?" Esta asked.

Cela frowned. "It's 1902. What other year would it be?"

Relief washed over her. They weren't where they intended to be, but at least they were together. And they could always go back if they needed more time.

Once they were inside, Cela introduced Esta to Joshua, who seemed to be a friend of her brother's, and a blond girl, who seemed to be Viola's. But there was no one else there.

Confused, she turned to them. "Where's Harte?"

Then she saw the uncomfortable look Cela and Viola were exchanging.

"What?" Esta asked. Her mind spun with a thousand scenarios for a thousand things that could have happened to him. The Order. Nibsy. Jack. "He's okay, isn't he?"

"Yes, of course," Cela told her. "He's out with Jianyu."

Again, the uncomfortable silent exchange between the other women.

"What's going on?" Esta said.

"We thought they were checking for you," Viola told her. "Every day he goes to see if you've come. To make sure that his message is clear."

"It was clear," she told them with a wobbly smile. "He must have missed me."

Viola cursed under her breath as she cut her gaze to Cela. "You know where they went, no?"

"They wouldn't . . ." Cela's brows drew together. "Not without telling us."

"They're men, aren't they?" Viola asked. "Of course they would!" Then she turned back to Esta. "They've gone to the Strega to get back what Nibsy took from Jianyu."

"They've been gone all day. Even if they went to do something as stupid as that, they should have been back by now," Cela said. Again the silent look exchanged with Viola.

Viola was already reaching for her shawl and her knives. "After we rescue them, I'm going to murder them myself."

PREDICTABLE

The Bowery

Though Cela urged the tired nag onward through the city, the small delivery wagon they'd borrowed from the *Age* could not move fast enough for Esta. Winged horses wouldn't have been fast enough, not when she knew that Harte had been brash and reckless enough to go after Nibsy on his own.

She told herself that it must mean his affinity had returned, because he couldn't have possibly been so stupid to go to the Strega with nothing but his wits for protection. It should have given her some hope, because it meant that whatever the Guard had used on them was only temporary. But it was hard to hope when her own affinity remained cold and empty. No matter how hard she concentrated, she couldn't reach it.

As the wagon navigated the cluttered confusion of the early-century streets, Viola and Cela tried to fill Esta in on what happened since she and Harte had left in May. Ruby sat in the back of the wagon, listening as well. She'd been unwilling to be left behind. Speaking in stops and starts, they weaved the tale that made clear how much she'd missed—and how much had happened because Jack had possession of the Book.

But the Conclave was still two weeks away, she reminded herself. They could still stop Jack and Nibsy, both. And if Cela and Viola were to be believed, there might be a way to control Thoth long enough to unmake him completely. She was determined to save her friends from the fate she'd seen in the Professor's diary—to change the fate written on those pages and to save them all.

When they came down Elizabeth Street, Viola ordered Cela to stop the wagon after she noticed Jianyu waiting outside the Strega's back door. He looked lost, like he was in some kind of a daze, staring at the door without seeming to see it. Esta barely waited for the wagon to stop before she leaped down and was already trying to shake Jianyu from whatever stupor he was in before Cela could tie off the reins.

"Jianyu, where's Harte?" She shook him again when he didn't respond. "Was he with you? Is he inside?"

Jianyu finally blinked away the daze he was in and focused on her. Shock and surprise flashed through his expression. "Esta?" He lifted a hand like he was about to touch her and make sure she was really there, but then thought better of it. "You have finally returned to us?"

"I have," she told him. "But I need to find Harte. Do you know where he is?"

Jianyu didn't immediately answer. He had the telltale glassy look to his eyes and the docile confusion that often came with having your consciousness invaded. "Where is he, Jianyu? I need you to *think*. What was the last thing you remember?"

"The Five Pointers and Hip Sings had just arrived, as we planned," he told her, his focus already growing sharper. "We sent them—Darrigan sent them—as a distraction. We were going to find Morgan's papers." He took a sharp breath, like something had just startled him. "Darrigan was not supposed to go in alone. This was not the plan."

"But it sounds like something he'd do," she said, looking up at the silent windows of the building. *Dammit, Harte.*

"I'll need your help," she told him. "My affinity's not quite steady right now. Can you get me inside?"

"Certainly," he told her, looking more settled and alert now.

"You can't go in there again," Cela said, catching Jianyu's arm before he could reach for Esta. "You know what could happen." Cela turned to Esta. "Please. You can't ask him to do this. That boy has the marks. He nearly took Viola apart."

"It does not matter," Jianyu said, pulling away from Cela.

"You saw what he did to Viola," Cela told him, her voice breaking with emotion. "Don't ask me to piece you back together too."

He lifted his hand, touching her cheek with a tenderness that surprised Esta. It seemed that so much had happened while they were gone.

"Jack attempted to destroy me with the Pharaoh's Heart and the power of the Book, and he could not," Jianyu told Cela. "Let Nibsy try."

"Why would you give him the chance?" Cela asked. "There has to be another way."

"There is no time," Jianyu told her.

"I'm coming too," Viola said, her knife already in hand.

"No." Jianyu held up his hand as though to stay her, and to Esta's surprise, Viola actually paused. "Please. I need you here. Watch over Cela and make sure no harm comes to her."

Viola looked like she wanted to argue, but one look at Cela had her changing her mind. She nodded instead. "Hurry. And come back safe."

"I don't need watching over," Cela argued, bristling in frustration.

"Then let me stand by you instead," Viola told her.

Jianyu offered his hand. "If you are ready?"

"Let's go save Harte from his own stupid bravery," Esta told him, taking it.

Almost immediately, she felt the buzz of warm magic wrapping around her as the world went wobbly.

"Come back to us safe," Cela told them, but she was looking at Jianyu when she spoke.

Esta saw his expression soften, but he didn't respond. Instead, they turned and pushed into the back entrance of the Strega, leaving the noise of the streets behind.

It had been only a few months since Esta had been there, but it might as well have been an eternity. Once, the scent of Tilly's bread would have warmed the air, but now only the smell of stale ale and tobacco smoke welcomed them. A racket was coming from the direction of the barroom, but she ignored it and followed Jianyu up the back stairs, invisible in the cloak of his affinity.

"So, you and Cela?" she asked as they climbed.

"Cela has been a true friend in these weeks," he answered, and it was only the bit of pink that warmed the tips of his ears that gave anything away.

"She's pretty great," Esta told him.

"Cela Johnson is not for me," Jianyu said.

She glanced at him from the corner of her eye. "She sure looks at you like she wants to be for you."

He turned to her like he would argue. But instead, his mouth went tight, and he continued onward without speaking.

Soon enough they were at the doorway of Dolph's apartment, and Esta stopped. She couldn't seem to make herself take that next step and walk through the door.

Jianyu gave her a questioning look, but she only shook her head to tell him she was okay.

She had to be okay. She had to focus, because Harte was likely on the other side. She would not think about the time she'd spent in that apartment with Dolph, never suspecting her true connection to him. It was too late to go back, too late to grasp those minutes like the treasures they had been. Now there was only forward, to Harte. To whatever the future held.

The door to the apartment was ajar, and a familiar voice carried through the gap.

Nibsy.

Silently, they slipped into the apartment.

Harte was standing on the other side of the room with his hands raised. He was wearing a sleepy, almost drunk look, and he was smiling despite the gun Nibsy had aimed at his chest. On the table next to Nibsy was a leather folder. In the hand not holding the gun, Nibsy leaned upon Dolph's cane.

They'd barely gotten through the door when Nibsy visibly stiffened, like a predator catching the scent of prey. Suddenly, Esta heard Jianyu gasp. She felt the warmth of his magic dissipate as a shock of ice burst around them.

Jianyu let go of her hand as he went rigid. His back arched, and he fell to his knees, writhing against some invisible torture. She wanted to help him, but she didn't dare move as long as Nibsy had Harte held at gunpoint. She couldn't save them both, and now that Jianyu's affinity was no longer cloaking them, she might not be able to save anyone.

Even drugged as he seemed to be, Harte's expression sharpened the second he realized she had come for him. His stormy eyes were dark with emotion—hope and fear and love all at once. He started to get up, but Nibsy lifted the gun as a reminder and gestured for him to remain where he was.

I'm okay, she wanted to say to soothe the fury and the terror in his eyes. *We'll be okay.*

Nibsy stepped to one side, keeping the gun on Harte as he turned to face her. "I thought you might join us," he said pleasantly. "Jianyu as well, I see." Esta saw Nibsy's fingers tighten on the cane, and Jianyu jerked in pain.

"Let them go, Nibsy," Esta said.

He pretended to consider her request. "No," he said after a thoughtful beat. "I don't think I will."

Jianyu cried out again, his face contorting in agony. He'd gone nearly white with the pain of what was happening to him.

Harte's expression turned murderous, but he didn't move. He didn't dare to with Nibsy's gun still aimed at his chest.

"You don't really want them." Esta lifted the strap of the satchel over her head. "You want this."

Nibsy stilled, and even without her affinity, time felt like it were standing still. "You brought it? Just as I always knew you would."

She nodded. "The Book and the artifacts, too. But you need me to work the ritual. I'm willing to make a bargain. You let those two go, and it's yours. Take me instead of them."

Harte's expression turned to horror. "No, Esta. Don't—"

"Hush," Nibsy said, easing back the hammer of the pistol. "I've heard about enough from you."

She didn't look at Harte. She couldn't risk it, not so long as Nibsy held the gun that could end his life. "If you hurt him—"

"You'll what?" Nibsy said. "You aren't in the position to be making any demands."

She took Viola's knife and placed it at her own throat. "Aren't I?"

Nibsy considered her offering, his eyes narrowing in suspicion. She knew he didn't trust her or believe her, but he didn't have to. He just had to take his attention off Harte long enough so they could get away.

"You can have one," Nibsy said finally. "And I'll see the contents first."

Esta pretended to consider this offer and then, slowly, she lowered the knife.

"Fine." She allowed herself a quick glance at Harte, who was still shaking his head, trying to deny the bargain she seemed to have struck. Even through his half-drunken stupor, she hoped that he already understood what she intended to do. "I'll take Jianyu."

"Interesting choice." Nibsy's mouth twitched with amusement.

Jianyu screamed, his body twisting in pain.

"I'll take Jianyu alive and *whole*," she said. "If you hurt him or kill him, the deal is off."

"Show me what's in the satchel," Nibsy demanded. "Open it."

Esta saw the doubt in his expression, but there was hope as well. Yearning. She moved slowly, carefully unlatching one buckle and then the other. She looked at Harte once more. Willed him to understand.

"No, Esta—"

But she was already moving. With a violent twist, she swung the bag toward Nibsy's face. He reacted on instinct, reaching for it and taking his attention off Harte just long enough to give them a chance.

In that fraction of a second, Harte lunged. One shot went off, but it flew wide, shattering a window without hitting anyone. Before Nibsy could fire again, Harte was on top of him, pinning him to the floor and trying to wrestle the pistol from Nibsy's grasp.

Esta went to Jianyu. His wrist was bleeding, and his hand was already coated in his own blood. It was coming from a black bracelet of some sort cutting into his wrist, and the cold energy coming from it told her that ritual magic was involved. But there wasn't any way to stop it. She couldn't figure out how to get it off him.

Out of the corner of her eye, she saw Harte punch Nibsy—once, twice—until blood was pouring from his nose, and he only barely tried to get away. The fight seemed to have been beaten out of him, but he was laughing like some kind of lunatic.

"So predictable," Nibsy said, blood dripping from his nose into his mouth. "Always so predictable."

Harte tore the gun from Nibsy's hand and pointed it at his chest. "Am I predictable now?"

"Eminently," Nibsy said with a leering smile.

Cocking back the hammer, Harte aimed at Nibsy's chest. "You don't deserve to live. You don't deserve to take even one more breath."

"You won't kill me," Nibsy said, suddenly deadly calm. "You can't. You *need* me."

"No—"

"He's right," Esta said. "You can't kill him now." *Not without dooming me.* "Unless you know?"

Harte kept the gun still aimed squarely at Nibsy's chest, but his mouth went tight. He shook his head.

"Then you can't," she said. "As much as he might deserve it."

Harte's features hardened, and Esta watched as he waged a battle within himself that she understood too well. Deciding, Harte tossed the gun to the side and punched Nibsy once more, viciously, squarely in the nose.

Nibsy wasn't laughing anymore. He wasn't even moving. But considering she was still there, Esta figured he'd survive. Harte's stormy eyes were burning with fury as he drew back his fist again.

"Leave him," Esta said.

But Harte didn't move off Nibsy's still body. He seemed frozen, his hand clenched into a fist, ready to strike.

"He's not worth it." She was trying to help Jianyu up from the floor, but with the agony of the bracelet cutting into his wrist, he wasn't exactly steady on his feet. "I need your help."

That seemed to be enough to have Harte hesitate and lower his fist. He climbed off Nibsy slowly, reluctantly, and got to his feet. He started to move toward her, but Jianyu held up his hand.

"The cane," Jianyu said through clenched teeth. "The papers as well."

Harte pried the cane from Nibsy's hands and then scooped the leather folder from the table, tucking it securely inside his coat. Then he helped Esta get Jianyu up from the floor.

Harte hesitated at the door, turning back to look at Nibsy's unconscious body. "It's a mistake to leave him."

"Probably," she said.

"He's not going to stop, Esta."

"I know." But there was nothing they could do. *Not yet.* First, they needed to get out of the Strega without any more problems. They needed to save their friend. "Jianyu is more important right now. He's bleeding pretty badly, Harte. And I can't get him down the steps alone."

Harte cursed when he finally noticed the blood dripping down Jianyu's hand. "It's worse," he said softly, and the worry was clear in his expression.

"What is it?" she asked.

He shot her a dark look. "Later."

As they descended the steps, they heard voices growing louder, closer.

By the time they reached the bottom of the staircase, Jianyu was no longer writhing. He was almost able to walk on his own. But at the bottom of the stairs, a familiar face stepped into their path, blocking their escape.

Bella Strega

When Logan Sullivan had realized that James wasn't going to do anything about John Torrio and Mock Duck brawling in the Bella Strega, he'd done what any sane person would do. He'd hidden behind the bar and waited for the goons who followed James to deal with the threat.

It took longer than he expected. As the barroom had erupted into chaos, people seemed to realize that James had already left. It hadn't taken long before they started leaving as well. Marked and unmarked alike, few seemed willing to be drawn into a Bowery brawl that didn't benefit them, and in a matter of minutes the only people left were the Five Pointers and the Hip Sings, tearing the whole place apart.

Which worried Logan. He hated the damn saloon, but it was the one safe place he'd found in that godforsaken version of the city, and James was the one shield Logan had against the dangers of this stupid time. But if James wasn't going to stick around, neither was he. The first chance he had to get the hell out of there, he did.

But if the arrival of Torrio and Mock Duck had been a surprise, finding Esta descending the back stairs was a complete shock.

"Logan?" Her mouth parted. She didn't exactly look happy to see him.

"Esta." Her dark brown hair was shorter than he'd ever seen it, and there was a sharpness to her features that he didn't remember her having before. She'd always been confident and brash, reckless and impertinent, but now there was also a calmness beneath it all. A sureness that went beyond simple confidence. He wasn't sure he liked it one bit.

For a second, though, he was too surprised to do anything but stand there like a complete moron, staring at the group of intruders who had clearly just come down the back steps. Along with her was Darrigan, the damned magician who had twisted Esta's loyalty and made her betray the Professor and their team. They were helping the Chinese guy, who didn't look so good, down the steps.

"What are you doing here?" Then he saw James' cane in Darrigan's hands, and everything started to come together. "It was you, wasn't it? The fight in the saloon. *You* made it happen, didn't you?"

Esta's eyes went wide. "Please, Logan. You don't understand—"

He stepped more squarely into their path. "What the hell have you done, Esta? Do you have any idea what's happening in there? They're destroying the place." Then another thought occurred to him. "Where's James? What did you do to him?"

Her features hardened. "Get out of our way, Logan."

"*That's* all you have to say to me?" he demanded. "After the mess you made? After you *left* me here?"

"Please, just step aside and let us go," she told him. "I don't want to fight you."

"I don't particularly care what you want." He crossed his arms. "I'm not moving an inch until you agree to take me back."

"Back?" Her brows drew together.

"Yes, back," he said, then considered. "Or forward. Whatever you want to call it. The bottom line is that I want out of here. I want to go back to my normal life in the normal world. You have no idea— You can't understand how terrible it's been for me here." She was frowning at him, but he didn't care. "I miss reality. I miss television and iPhones and reliable running water. I miss penicillin. Hell, I even miss the streets only smelling like piss and garbage instead of like horse shit on top of that. You want to get out of here? Fine. But I'm going with you, and the only place we're going is back to where we belong."

Esta glanced at Darrigan, who still looked murderous. They seemed to exchange a silent conversation between them.

"I *am* where I belong, Logan," she told him. "Here, with my friends. Fighting with them for what's right."

Panic inched along his skin. He'd practiced this conversation a million times in his head. He'd thought of every possible variation, but he hadn't considered that she'd want to stay here in this hellhole of a time. "These aren't your friends, Esta. And you don't want to stay here. There's nothing for us here."

The pity in her eyes made his skin crawl. "I can't take you back," she said.

"Can't?" he asked. "Or *won't?*"

"Does it really matter?" she asked. "Either way, it's not happening. I don't have time for this right now, Logan."

"Really?" he said, feeling suddenly furious. "*You* don't have time for it? You have all the time in the world, Esta."

"Not now I don't," she said. Her jaw went tight, and he knew she would dig her heels in harder.

"Esta, you have to listen to me—"

"No, Logan," she snapped. "*You* need to listen. The world you knew doesn't exist anymore. When you brought me back here? That changed *everything.*"

He ignored the tremor of unease he felt at her words. They had to be lies. She'd been turned by the Magician, and now she'd say anything to keep Professor Lachlan from winning.

"I don't believe you, and I also don't care," he told her. "So what if it's a different world? As long as there's indoor toilets and the internet, it's where I want to be."

"You don't get it," she snapped. "I've been back—or close to it—and no amount of indoor plumbing can make up for what it's like. It's not the world you left. You're safer here."

He thought of the battle raging in the saloon and knew she was insane.

His heart was pounding in his ears. "You just don't want to help me. He's twisted you, *changed* you."

"She's not lying," Darrigan said, as though anyone could believe a con man like him.

"Get out of our way, Logan." Esta adjusted her grip on Jianyu. Her gaze shifted to the door behind him and then back. "I'm warning you. Step aside. You don't need to get hurt."

"No," he said. "You're not going anywhere." He squared his shoulders and prepared to do whatever he had to so she couldn't slip away again.

COLLATERAL

V iola did not kill the boy, though Jianyu could tell from the fury in her violet eyes that she wanted to. But she did use her magic to remove him from their path. One minute, Logan Sullivan was standing against them and issuing demands, and the next, the warmth of old magic coursed around them, and Logan was on the floor.

"Come," she commanded, beckoning them forward, toward the open door. "Cela is waiting with the wagon."

At the mention of Cela's name, Jianyu felt a flash of panic. "She should not be here."

"Neither should you," Viola scolded. "We're a team, no? You and Darrigan should have included us. Maybe *this*"—she gestured toward his clear injuries—"wouldn't have happened."

Or perhaps it would have been worse, Jianyu thought. But he knew better than to start a pointless argument when Viola was snapping with temper.

In the distance, Jianyu could hear shouting coming from the saloon. It sounded like an argument or brawl. The voices were louder, and the uproar far more violent than he had expected. Something crashed, like glass shattering.

What had they done?

Jianyu had never intended to put the Devil's Own in danger, only to keep Nibsy occupied. Which clearly had not worked. Nibsy had not been distracted, and now the Strega sounded as though it were at war.

He thought to go, started to turn in the direction of the noise. They needed to stop the madness that Darrigan's affinity had inspired, but he was only upright because Darrigan and Esta were supporting him.

"Whoa," Esta said gently. "Wrong direction."

"But the Strega—"

"We don't have time," Darrigan told him.

They were already dragging him out the back door of the building before he could argue any further.

Outside, snow swirled in the air. The clouds had grown heavier above, making the daylight seem slanted. Everything looked softer somehow, cleaner and quieter than it had before. Or maybe that was the loss of blood and the pain making him delirious.

They were barely out the door when he saw the familiar wagon from the *New York Age* waiting across the street. There was Cela sitting on the driver's perch, watching the building, her long legs clad in trousers and a man's cap pulled low over her brow. There was nothing about her that looked remotely like the boy she was playing at being, especially not once she noticed they'd emerged. The instant her eyes locked on him and saw that he was injured, she was moving.

But the change in her expression—the fear in her eyes—had warmth blooming inside him, pushing away the pain despite the icy wind and the cold energy radiating through his arm. That warmth felt too close to joy. Too close to wanting.

He could not allow himself to believe that the concern he had seen flash across Cela's features was for him alone. She would have felt the same no matter who was injured. He would not start thinking that he had any right to her care. He *could not* begin hoping for that.

Cela opened the gate of the wagon, her expression still painted with fear, and she watched as they helped Jianyu into the back. He felt like a fool—weak as a child—as Cela helped Darrigan and Esta get him into the wagon, but he did not have the strength to bat them away. He kept his jaw clenched tight, though, so he wouldn't cry out and betray the amount of pain he was currently in.

Once everyone had climbed into the back, Cela hesitated. Her gaze had caught on the bloody mess of his hand, and when she lifted her eyes to meet his, he could not read the emotion there. It was not pity. It was not even fear any longer. She closed the door, securing them, before Jianyu could begin to understand why the look she had given him made him feel so very . . . unsettled.

The jerk of the wagon starting off shot a fresh burst of pain through him. He could not quite stop the grunt of pain that escaped. At least the others were too busy with each other to notice how badly he was hurt. Harte was looking at Esta as though he had just unearthed a rare treasure, taking her face in his hands and examining her for any sign of injury. Viola was checking that Ruby was unharmed as well.

"I don't know why you're worried about me when Jianyu's the one who's *actually* hurt," Ruby said, brushing her aside.

Viola turned then, as though she had forgotten, and from the way her expression shifted and the color drained from her cheeks, Jianyu understood exactly how bad he must look.

"Madonna," she whispered, looking down at his arm. "What happened in there?"

"Nibsy," Darrigan said darkly, which seemed to be all the explanation that any of them needed.

"What did he do to your arm?" Esta asked, gesturing at the place where the black cord had embedded itself into Jianyu's skin.

It was worse than it had been. There was no denying that fact. Before, the piece of braided silk thread had been cutting into his skin, which had been bad enough. Now, the bit of thread had changed, transformed by the corrupt magic it contained. It no longer appeared to be a solid, braided cord. It seemed to be transforming, as though the silk had been liquefied by the magic within it and was melting into him, fusing with his skin. The braided threads appeared to be separating as well, and now some had begun to vine up his arm, like deadly tendrils seeking out the affinity that lay within him. More crept down beneath the blood coating his hand, and they were still moving, slowly but steadily creeping and spreading their terrible cold energy with every passing second.

"That isn't Nibsy's work," Viola told Esta. "It's part of the bargain this one made with Tom Lee." As the carriage bumped and rattled and Jianyu tried to keep himself from crying out in pain, Viola explained the situation that had driven him to make his foolish alliance. "He wanted protection for Cela, but that bit of evil was the price of the agreement."

"It was necessary," Jianyu argued. He would not regret the choice he had made. It did not matter that Cela had been safe all along. She had been in danger, and if Theo Barclay had not reached her first, his bargain might have been the only thing to protect her. It was worth it, mistake though it might have been. Cela's life would always be worth it, whatever the price might be.

"You could have waited," Viola argued.

"Would you have?" he asked, glancing from Viola to Ruby and back.

She understood his silent message, and at least she was honest enough not to say anything more.

"He put his affinity up as collateral for Lee's help?" Esta said.

"And Lee seems to be ready to call in the deal," Darrigan said. He lifted Jianyu's wrist to examine it, eliciting a fresh grunt of pain from Jianyu.

"Enough." Jianyu drew his arm back to cradle it against his chest and protect it from the rattling of the carriage.

"But I don't understand," Esta said. "If that thread is linked to Tom Lee, how was Nibsy able to tap into it?"

"I do not think he was," Jianyu told her.

"I saw what happened," Esta argued. "Your arm didn't start bleeding until we were there with Nibsy. He did something to you, and whatever that thread is doing now, he was the cause of it."

Jianyu grimaced. "Only because he was trying to use the mark against me."

"It happened again?" Viola asked, frowning.

"I believe so," Jianyu told her. "It felt much like when Jack tried to perform his ritual. This bit of corrupted magic asserted its previous claim over my magic once more. This is the result."

"It protected you again," Harte told him.

"Protection? *This* you call protection?" Viola asked, horrified. "*Guarda!* Even now it's growing. This is no protection. This is a curse, and if you don't remove it, you're going to lose your hand."

Jianyu wished it were so easy. The pain radiating through his arm was from more than a simple wound. The silk cord's icy magic felt as though it was seeping into his bones. "From the way this feels? I worry I will lose more than my hand."

"There has to be something we can do," Esta said. "There has to be some way to get out of your bargain."

"There is no way to remove the charm without Lee knowing and taking his payment in full," Jianyu said with a grimace.

Viola eyed the cane. "You have what you need," she told him, nodding toward the silver Medusa's head. "Take it to Lee. Get that piece of evil off you while you still can."

"No, Viola." Jianyu hissed in pain when the carriage hit another rut in the road. "No. I will not do that. I *cannot*. Whatever happens to me, Tom Lee cannot have possession of the cane. He cannot be given that kind of power or control over the Devil's Own. No one should have that sort of control over another."

"Be reasonable, Jianyu," Viola begged, eyeing the black vines crawling up his arm. "Lee won't wait forever, and you won't last if this continues."

He could not stop himself from groaning as the wagon hit another bump and a fresh bolt of pain lanced through him. She was right, but he did not see what there was to do about it.

"See?" she told him. "If you allow this to continue, it will kill you."

"You would let Lee control you?" he asked. "Because if I give him this cane, that is what will happen. He will control everyone who was once loyal to what Dolph tried to build. He would have you, Viola. He would use you and your magic for whatever purposes he desired."

Viola lifted her chin. "He could try."

Jianyu bit back a smile at his friend's fire, but this was bigger than either him or Viola. "Even if you were willing to risk it, could you truly hand over the lives of all of those who were once our friends? All those we once vowed to help Dolph protect?"

She had no answer to that.

"Giving Lee the cane is not the answer," he told her, sure of this if nothing else. "I pledged my loyalty to the Devil's Own, and I will not betray them. I will not betray *you*, either, my friend."

"They wouldn't do the same for you," she told him.

"But you would. You already have," he said, thinking of all they had been through.

Viola did not seem to agree. She was not going to let the issue go. "Jianyu—"

"I have no plans to be a martyr, Viola."

"What is your plan?" Esta asked.

"These past weeks, I have been considering the issue, and I believe there may be a way, at least to buy more time." He looked at Darrigan. "You retrieved the papers?"

Harte nodded, patting the front of his shirt.

"Perhaps they hold the key," Jianyu said, hoping that his reasoning was correct. "Morgan believed that Newton's Sigils could create a protective barrier. Perhaps we can use them as protection from the magic Lee is using against me."

Viola's eyes widened. "Why would you not tell us this?" Viola asked. "We could have retrieved those papers *weeks* ago."

"What was there to tell?" Jianyu shrugged. "It was a theory only, not enough to put anyone at risk."

"Your *life* was worth that risk," Viola told him.

Her fierce belief warmed him, even if she was wrong. "We have the documents now. Perhaps the answers we need are there."

Viola shook her head. "Even if Newton's Sigils work, even if we can figure out how to use them, that doesn't stop this," she told him. "Only Lee can do that. You must go to him. You must take the cane and be done with this."

"That's not quite true," Esta told them, her expression thoughtful. "I could do it."

"How?" Jianyu asked.

"My affinity," she told him. "It's more than just slowing down time. I can touch the Aether that holds everything together, which means I can also pull it apart. I could unmake the ritual magic for you."

Jianyu did not understand how that helped. "But if Lee realizes you are trying to tamper with the cord, the magic in it grows more powerful. Every time we have tried to remove it, it has only made things worse."

"If Newton's Sigils do what you believe, they'll cut Lee off from his connection to that thread, right?" she asked. "Without that connection, he can't hurt you. If the sigils work, if you're right, I can unmake that cord while you're within the sigil's protection. At least, I think I can."

She was looking at Harte now, and there was some silent conversation happening between them. He nodded, and Jianyu understood that something more was happening. Something more had been decided.

"It might work," Harte said before Jianyu could ask what else they planned to do. "You just need to hold on until we can get back."

The cart lurched suddenly to the left, and they all scrambled to find something to hold on to. Pain lanced through Jianyu's arm, and Viola cursed as she tumbled over. They'd barely had time to right themselves when the wagon lurched again.

"Che diavolo?" Viola said, trying to steady herself and Ruby.

The sliding window at the front of the wagon opened, and Cela's face appeared in the small opening.

"We're being followed," Cela told them.

"Who is it?" Jianyu asked.

Viola was already moving toward the back gate, where she could take care of their pursuers.

"I'm not sure," Cela said. "Hold on, though. I'm going to try to lose them."

CASTOFFS

E sta barely had time to comprehend what Jianyu had just revealed—that Newton's Sigils could be the answer to stopping Thoth—before the delivery wagon rounded another corner, throwing her into Harte. He caught her solidly in his arms, but she didn't have time to appreciate the strength of his arms around her or the relief of knowing that she hadn't lost him, not when they were being followed.

"Can you tell who's chasing us?" she asked Viola, who had opened the back gate just enough to look out at the traffic behind them.

"I don't know," Viola said, cursing when the carriage lurched as it took a turn to the right. "I can't tell for sure."

Jianyu was holding his arm, trying to keep himself steady, but she could tell the effort was costing him.

The wagon swerved again, and Harte looked at Esta. "Newton's Sigils aren't going to help anyone if we don't get out of this mess."

"My affinity—" She stopped, felt it stirring there. *Maybe.* She kissed him soundly and felt her world click into place at the feel of his mouth on hers. "I'll be right back."

Esta crawled through the small doorway that opened into the driver's cab. There, Cela was urging the exhausted-looking horse onward, dodging through the traffic as they climbed northward through the city. She had no idea if her affinity was strong enough yet or if what she planned to do would even work.

"We're going to try something," she said, offering her hand to Cela, who didn't hesitate to grasp it. Focusing everything she had on her connection to the old magic, Esta forced the seconds to a stop. Everything went still—the world, the horse, and the wagon as well.

It wasn't the same as a car, she realized with a sinking sense of dread. The horse was a living thing, caught in the spell of her affinity along with everything else.

As Esta released time, Cela stared at her, completely unaware that anything had happened. "Well?" she demanded.

"I'm going to need you to drive as straight as you can. And whatever you do, don't let me go," Esta told her.

Cela blinked at her in confusion. "What are you—"

But Esta was already leaning far over the front lip of the driver's perch. She tightened her grip on Cela's hand and leaned forward to touch the back flank of the horse. As soon as her fingers brushed the coarse hair of the animal, she reached for time. Using all her concentration and strength, she slowed the seconds.

Cela gasped, and the wagon started to slow.

"No!" Esta shouted. "Keep driving. Steady as you can."

Her hand was damp with sweat, and her skin felt warm with the effort of holding on to Cela and the seconds, all while keeping a precarious balance over the front of the wagon. When they hit a pothole and slid a little through the snow-covered street, Esta nearly lost her grip, but she fought hard to keep them all—herself and Cela and the horse—in the net of her power. By the time they'd put entire blocks between them and whoever was following them, Esta was damp with sweat. The icy winter air lashed at her face, but she ignored the sting of it.

As they rounded another corner, she realized they were close to Washington Square. The arch wouldn't be built there for years to come, but it was easy enough to recognize with its stately homes and manicured pathways. Exhausted, she pushed away from the horse and fell backward onto the driver's perch as the world slammed into motion around her.

Cela tossed a disconcerted look in her direction. "What *was* that?"

"Hopefully enough to get us away," Esta said, looking back around the side of the wagon. The streets held the occasional carriage or wagon, but they seemed to have lost whoever had been chasing them.

"Well? Any sign of them?" Cela asked.

Esta looked again, and this time she noticed the logo of the newspaper emblazoned on the side of the wagon. "We can't go back to the *Age*," she told Cela. "If they saw the name on the wagon, they'll know where to find us."

Cela's eyes widened. "We have to go back. We can't just leave Joshua and the rest to fend for themselves," Cela said. "They need to know that trouble is coming. We have to warn them."

"We will," Esta promised. "But first we have to get Jianyu somewhere safe."

Fear tightened Cela's features, and she looked torn between two terrible options. "It's bad, isn't it?" she whispered.

"Really bad," Esta told her gently. "I want to make sure your friends at the newspaper are safe, but that bracelet Tom Lee put on him is still changing. I think it's going to kill him if we don't get it off."

Cela's mouth pressed into a thin line. She looked like a woman at war with herself. "*Can* we get it off?"

"I think there's a way, but we can't do it in the back of this wagon," Esta told her. "Is there somewhere else we could go? Somewhere safe?"

Cela nodded. "There's a safe house we've been using for the people we've rescued from the Order." She still looked torn in two, but she turned the wagon west and headed toward the water.

The building they stopped next to looked like any other tenement in the city—drab brick with uneven steps, fire escapes cluttered with clothing despite the freezing weather, and windows covered by white curtains. But there was something about the place that set Esta's teeth on edge, something that made her want to turn around and go the other direction.

"Where are we?" Esta asked, following Cela down from the driver's perch.

Cela busied herself with securing the horse and wagon. "You'll see soon enough."

When they opened the back of the wagon, Jianyu looked worse than he had a few minutes before. The blood was nothing now compared to the veining darkness that was creeping steadily up his arm. Climbing ever closer to his heart.

Esta sensed Cela coming up behind her, and she felt fear in the other girl's sharp intake of breath at the sight of Jianyu and his arm.

They helped him down, but when Jianyu saw where they were, he began to panic. "No, Cela. We have to leave. This is far too dangerous," he argued. "We can't risk leading our enemies here. If the Order or Nibsy or anyone knew of this place—"

"It's the only place I could think of," Cela told him. "It's been safe for months now."

"I cannot risk them—"

"You're going to have to," Cela snapped. "You don't have a choice."

Esta wasn't sure what the subtext of their conversation was, but they didn't have time to argue, not with how much worse Jianyu's arm currently looked. "She's right. We need to get that thing off you, and it needs to happen now."

Jianyu was still trying to argue and fight against Harte's support, but the pain he was in was making it difficult.

"It will be safe here," Viola said. "There's no reason to think otherwise. But that wagon, it will give us away."

"You'll need to move it," Esta told her. She was aware of Harte watching her as though she might disappear, but there would be time for that later.

"I need to take it back," Cela told her. "It belongs to my brother's friend. I can't risk anything happening to it, and I need to warn the others," Cela said. She looked like she didn't want to leave them. "Whoever was after us will have seen the newspaper's name. If they can't find us, they'll go after the *Age*. I can't leave Joshua unprepared."

"And Abel," Jianyu said. "Is he not expected tonight as well?"

Cela nodded. "I need to warn him, too."

"You cannot go alone," Jianyu argued. "We should all—" The words were barely out before his whole body contorted in pain and nearly collapsed to the snow-covered ground.

They all rushed toward him to keep him upright, but Cela moved fastest of all.

"We need to get him inside," Esta said, looking up at the building and feeling that same creeping unease. "If you're sure it's safe."

"No," Jianyu said.

"It's fine," Cela told her at the same time. She turned to Jianyu. "You need to stay here and let your friends take care of you."

"I need to protect those inside," he whispered.

"You already have." She kissed his cheek softly. "It's your turn now."

When she stepped back, Cela had tears in her eyes.

"Maybe Harte could take the wagon," Esta suggested, knowing that Cela wanted to stay.

She could tell that Harte hated the idea—and she didn't blame him—but Cela shook her head before Harte could even start to refuse. "It wouldn't be right for anyone but me to go."

As the others helped Jianyu into the building, she watched Cela climb back into the wagon.

"Be safe," she told Cela.

"You take care of him, okay?"

Before Esta could do more than nod, Viola shouted for her to wait. She was already handing Jianyu over to Esta and Harte.

"I'm going with her," Viola told them.

"I'll come too," Ruby said.

But Viola shook her head. "You'll be safer here with them," she told Ruby. "And I'll be back soon." She looked at both Esta and Harte. "Jianyu will show you the way."

"You should stay," Cela said as Viola climbed into the wagon. "They'll need your protection."

"They have plenty inside to keep them safe," Viola told her. *"Andiamo."*

Cela hesitated a second longer more before she snapped the reins and launched the wagon into motion. In a matter of seconds, the wagon disappeared into the falling snow.

Almost as soon as they were gone, Jianyu's legs nearly went out from under him. Esta caught him up, supporting him with Harte's help. "We need to get him inside."

She looked back up at the building, and despite all her misgivings, she helped Harte keep Jianyu upright as they made their way through the darkened entryway.

Inside, the building was strangely quiet. The tenement houses Esta had been in before were always noisy. They were crowded with homes and places where people lived out loud, because it was pointless to try to go unheard. The walls were too thin, and the rooms were too crowded for any hope of privacy. But the hallways of this building didn't echo with voices. There was an uneasy silence that filled them, like all sound had been sucked away. It was cold as well, and the hallway was filled with the chill of corrupted magic.

Jianyu directed them through the main hall, and Ruby led the way as they took the back staircase up three floors.

"What *is* this place?" Esta whispered as she helped him up the steep stairs. It felt almost dangerous to speak out loud.

"A safe house that Dolph used." Jianyu groaned. "He showed it to me before he died."

"It feels . . . *wrong*," Esta said with a shudder.

"You get used to that," he told her. "It's the magic."

"Not natural magic," Ruby said with a shiver. It seemed that she could feel the wrongness of the place too.

"No," Jianyu agreed. "Not natural magic. Dolph had it charmed somehow to keep the uninvited from entering." He paused, though whether gathering his strength or remembering the past, Esta couldn't tell. "I never understood why he showed me this place. It was as though he knew somehow that we would need it."

"He trusted you," Harte said softly. "He knew he could rely on you if anything happened to him."

Finally, they arrived at their destination, an apartment on the third floor. With some difficulty, Jianyu managed to rap his knuckles in a rhythmic pattern on the door. There was rustling from within, a pause, and then the clicking of locks being unlatched.

An older woman poked her head out of the opening, and when she saw Jianyu, she opened the door, but her eyes went wide when they stepped from the dark hallway into the light of the apartment. "What happened to him?"

"Nibsy," Harte said, which was apparently all the answer the woman needed.

Immediately, her expression changed from horror to determination. "Well, what are you waiting there for? Bring him in and let's take a look—" Then her eyes lifted to Ruby, standing behind them in the doorway, and she frowned, looking suddenly anxious. "Wait . . . I know her." She took a step toward Ruby, fear suddenly shadowing her features. "She's the one they're looking for. The heiress bride. What is she doing here? If the Order discovers her here—"

"She's with us," Jianyu said simply.

"But not one of us," the woman said, still looking horrified.

Esta realized then that she recognized the woman. Months before, Dolph had taken her on his rounds and introduced her to the families in his keeping. Golde and her children were one of many stops on the tour.

"Golde?" Esta said, trying to remember if that was her name.

The woman frowned at Esta, but then her eyes widened. "I remember you," she told Esta. "You came that day, with Saunders."

Esta nodded. "How are you? What are you doing here?"

"Later," Jianyu told them with a groan. "Please. I cannot—" But he grimaced again before he could finish.

Golde gave one more nervous look at Ruby but then ushered them all inside. As they followed her through the apartment, Esta realized it had not been divided up into small, cramped rooms like most tenements, and it felt larger than it should have been inside. The entry parlor was larger than most New York apartments. Beyond it was a wide corridor lined with doors, and as they passed by, people began to emerge from the closed rooms, curious to see who had arrived. The warm buzz of magic in the air told her they were Mageus.

"Go on, the lot of you," Golde said, turning to shoo back the growing crowd. "There's nothing for you to see here."

They stayed back, but they didn't retreat.

"Who are they?" Esta asked. She was aware of them still watching from a distance.

"They're Dolph's," Jianyu told her. "They were in trouble and needed a safe place."

Golde grumbled. "Maybe they were Saunders' before, but they're my trouble now."

"No one forced you to live here," Jianyu said with a groan. But humor laced his words.

"Who else was going to?" Golde sniffed disdainfully. "It's not like you know how to cook or clean, and I wasn't going to let my Josef go without good food in his stomach or a strong hand to keep him in check." The woman's mouth wobbled a little.

"He still has not spoken to you?" Jianyu asked softly.

She shook her head. "Not yet," she whispered.

"He will come around," Jianyu told her. "It is not you that he is angry with."

"You don't deserve his anger," she said with a sigh. Golde turned to Esta. "It's thanks to this one that my boy is even alive."

"I don't understand," Esta said.

Golde's expression was serious. "My boy, Josef, and the others, they're all hiding from the Order's patrols. If not for Jianyu and Viola—"

"We can tell this tale later," Jianyu said as they finally settled him into a chair. He looked at Harte. "The papers. I do not think I have much more time."

A DECLARATION OF WAR

Cela's heart was in her throat as she guided the wagon through the slick streets of the city. Snow was still falling, heavy and constant, but she didn't have time to notice its beauty. If the people pursuing them had seen the name emblazoned on the side of the wagon, they might already be on their way to the offices of the *Age*. Joshua might already be in danger. And if any of the people looking for them saw the wagon she was currently in? She'd be in trouble too.

Viola was next to her in the driver's seat, silent and stoic as a statue. She seemed to understand that Cela wasn't in any mood for talking. Not when it was taking all her concentration to keep the wagon steady in the quickly accumulating snow.

They smelled the smoke a half mile away, but Cela knew before they were close enough to see the dark smoke pouring from windows that the *New York Age* building was on fire.

Her first instinct was to push the exhausted nag even faster, but Viola grabbed the reins before Cela could snap them again.

"Stop," Viola told her. "Park the wagon over there before someone sees."

She was right. The people who had been pursuing them would be watching for the wagon. They needed to stay out of sight for their own safety. But Cela needed to find Joshua and the others.

They parked the wagon in an alley so the name of the paper would be hidden from anyone who might be looking, and then, on foot, they started toward the crowd that had gathered near the burning building.

It was worse than she'd thought. Now, less than a half block away, Cela could see clearly that the entire building was already engulfed. The snow continued to tumble down, indifferent to the tragedy unfolding, but even from so far, she could feel the warmth of the flames brushing against her skin.

She felt someone tall creeping up behind her, too close. Before she could turn, she heard a male grunt of pain as Viola spun to confront their attacker.

"Abel?"

Her brother was clutching at his chest, his features bunched in clear pain.

"Let him go, Viola," Cela said, slapping at her friend, but Viola had already released him.

Abel gasped for breath and looked more than a little unsettled as he pulled himself together.

"What are you doing here?" Cela asked. "I didn't expect your train to get in until later this afternoon."

"It's nearly five," he told her.

She realized then that the darkening sky was from more than the snow flurries or the black smoke pouring from the *Age*'s building. It was later than she'd realized.

"When I got here, there were already white men surrounding the place," he told her. "Order patrols from the looks of it. They've rounded up the people inside."

"Joshua?" Cela asked.

Abel's jaw went tight. "Mr. Fortune, too."

"Then let's go and get them," Viola said, already moving toward the building.

Abel caught Cela's arm before she could follow Viola. "You can't go back there, Rabbit. It's too dangerous."

"We have to stop her from doing something stupid," Cela told her brother. "She's going to make everything worse."

As soon as they reached the spot where Viola had stopped, Cela realized that it *couldn't* get any worse. Just beyond the edge of the crowd, a group of men with guns had Joshua and some of the other employees of the *Age* on their knees. Along with them was Mr. Fortune.

Joshua saw them in the crowd. He met Cela's eyes and then Abel's, shaking his head a little as though to warn them away. But he looked terrified.

Rightly so. The men who had them hostage were too bold, too confident, considering the crowd that had gathered.

Cela recognized their type easily enough. The rough-cut clothing, grease-stained hands, and the excitement that sparked in their light eyes at the power they'd been handed marked them as men the Order had hired. Cela and her friends had been trying to stop those patrols all summer, but there was always an endless supply of white men angry enough to be used as weapons.

One had Ruby's wedding gown in his hand. He was holding it high enough for the crowd to see and explaining that the men were all guilty of aiding the abduction.

Another placed a gun to Joshua's back.

He never had a chance to fire. The man went down unexpectedly, crumpling like a puppet whose strings had been cut. The others turned, startled by the man's collapse, but they didn't have time to act. One by one they fell.

Cela didn't have to see the look of determination and fury in Viola's eyes to know the cause. She grabbed her arm. "You have to stop this."

Viola only shook her off. Two more men went down.

"Tell me you're not killing them, at least," Cela said. It would only cause more problems.

Viola turned to her. "Tell me you don't want me to."

Cela couldn't. "It won't help."

The final man went down, freeing the *New York Age*'s employees. Joshua was up first. He tossed a grateful, nervous look in their direction before turning to help Mr. Fortune up from the snow-covered ground. All around them, the crowd had already surged forward to help.

"What have you done?" Cela asked, her mind spinning with the implications of what had just happened. "They'll know for sure now that the *Age* was helping Mageus."

"They already knew," Viola said, regret clear in her violet eyes. "They had Ruby's dress."

"She's right," Abel said softly. "That was evidence enough to prove our involvement. It's all the excuse they needed."

"But she didn't need to confirm it," Cela told him. She turned on Viola because she didn't know where else to put her fear. "You put a target on the back of everyone at the paper, maybe everyone in this neighborhood with what you just did here!"

"You think those men cared about your friends helping us?" Viola asked darkly. "You know as well as I do that the payment they get from the Order is only an excuse. It's permission to do what they want to do anyway. Do you think that they would have stopped at this building?" She shook her head. "This was the opening shot. Those men, small, pathetic creatures that they are, wouldn't have stopped here. They would have continued on, terrorizing this entire neighborhood because of the license the Order's payment gave them."

"But what you just did will confirm to the entire city that Mageus did take Ruby."

"Maybe so," Viola told her. "But now those men who were forced to kneel, their families, and all these people, they will know we did not just stand by and allow others to be harmed. They will know we stand with them. That we are not their enemy, and from us they have nothing to fear."

CIRCLE OF LIGHT

The Safe House

Esta wanted nothing more than to take five minutes alone with Harte—to make sure he was okay—but she knew they were running out of time to help Jianyu. Their reunion would have to wait. The package of papers Harte and Jianyu had reclaimed from Nibsy had so much information—about the Order and their history and the Brink—but it had taken too long to sort through it all. They started to worry that maybe the instructions for using the sigils weren't even there. Nibsy could have ferreted them away somewhere separate.

"There," Jianyu said. He was doubled over now, and his skin too pale and slick with sweat. He pointed to a piece of parchment that had been folded in thirds, and Esta realized that his hand was nearly completely black now. But the cord around his wrist was clearly affecting more than his arm.

Esta looked at the page Jianyu pointed to and recognized the cramped, uneven scrawl almost immediately. It looked the same as the pages that Newton had written in the Book. "This is it," she whispered to herself and to Harte, but it took another few minutes for them to figure out what they were seeing.

The diagram on the parchment seemed to depict four discs—the sigils—connected through the Aether. "It should create a kind of force field," she explained.

"A what?" Harte asked.

"A kind of barrier," she said, trying to explain.

"Like the Brink?" He was frowning. "Or like the ritual circle the girl used?"

"I don't think so," she said, reading a note scrawled sideways in Latin. "It's not opening the spaces the way the Brink does. It's not doing anything with the Aether at all other than directing it around an area. Like a magical fence. It's easy enough, except that I think it would work best with four people. The ritual would be more stable."

"I'll help if I can," Ruby said.

Esta frowned down at the page. "I'm not sure if that'll work. It looks like it takes some kind of energy to activate the sigils. I think we need people who have a connection to the old magic."

Golde stepped forward. "He saved my boy," she told them. "I'll help with whatever you need."

"It might work with two," Esta said, considering. "You and Harte could each hold two of the sigils."

A man stepped into the room from where he'd clearly been listening in the hallway.

"What do you want, Yonatan?" Golde asked. "Here to make trouble again? Because we don't have time for your complaints."

The man was middle-aged, with thinning hair and a round stomach that strained the buttons of his shirt. "I'll help," he said.

"You?" Golde frowned at him.

"He saved my life too, didn't he?" The man seemed almost uncomfortable admitting this. "I'll help."

"Good," Esta said, before Golde could change the man's mind. "That's three." She looked past Yonatan, to the others waiting in the hallway. "It shouldn't be dangerous. You just have to be willing to try."

At first none of them moved.

"Cowards, all of you," Golde said, stalking over to them. "You stand and gawk, but none of you are man—or woman—enough to help the one who keeps you safe."

The people watching from the hallway remained silent. A few looked uneasily down at their feet, while a few looked defiant.

"We didn't ask to be brought here, Golde," a woman with curling blond hair said. "We didn't ask him to keep us here away from our work and our families."

"Neither did you ask the Order to hunt you for sport," Golde said, her anger simmering through her words.

"Maybe he saved us from the Order, but he sure didn't save Dolph." The speaker was a boy Esta recognized from her days at the Strega. He was a tall, rangy kid with acne shadowing his jaw who might have been named Henry or Harry.

Another stepped forward. "From what I hear, he's the one who got Dolph killed."

"That's not true," Esta said, frustrated and at the end of her patience. "Jianyu had nothing to do with Dolph's death. Neither did Viola."

"That ain't the way Nibsy tells it," the first kid said.

"Nibsy Lorcan is a liar and a traitor," Harte said. His voice had a dangerous edge to it. "He's the one who killed Dolph, and he's the one who sold every one of you over to the Order."

"And we should believe you?" the kid asked, narrowing his eyes. "You were never one of us."

"You don't have to believe him. Not when Nibsy told me himself," Esta said. "He killed Dolph, just like he killed Leena. He arranged everything so he could take the Strega and the Devil's Own."

Golde stepped forward. "Do you think I don't understand how you feel? Do you think it was any easier for me to accept that a boy like Lorcan could bring down the great Dolph Saunders?" She shook her head. "But I know what happened with my Josef. I went to Nibsy and asked him to save my boy, but he wouldn't. He refused because my son hadn't taken his mark. He laughed at my fear. Jianyu," she said, turning back to where Jianyu was struggling to stay upright. "He helped with no question of payment or price. He helped with no promises."

A door opened in the hallway, and a ripple went through the crowd as a younger teenager stepped forward. He was short, small even for his fourteen or fifteen years, with Golde's same ashy brown hair and hazel eyes.

"Josef?" Golde's heart was in her eyes.

"I'll be the fourth," the boy said, glancing at his mother before turning his attention back to Esta. "Tell me what I need to do."

They didn't waste any more time. Esta arranged them in a circle with Jianyu in the center. He looked worse than ever, but she couldn't let herself worry about that—only about the ritual ahead.

The silvery discs felt strangely cool to the touch, a mark of the corrupted magic within them. On the surface was a design similar to the one on the Book—it wasn't exactly the same, more like a blurred version of the original. Like a copy of a copy. She took the first of the sigils and had Harte hold out his hands. Gripping the sigil on the edges like a vinyl record, she used her thumb to send it spinning, with her two middle fingers as the pivot.

It spun slowly at first, but just when she feared it might stop, the silvery surface began to glow, as though it had caught fire, and the sigil began rotating faster and faster. When it was spinning fast enough that the disc looked like a ball of light, she placed it over Harte's outstretched hand. It hung there, suspended in the Aether, above his palm.

"Focus your affinity through this," she told him. "You need to try to connect with the part of yourself that can speak to the old magic."

He nodded, and she could see the concentration on his face. When she was sure he had it, she took her hands away, and the disc remained floating in the air, a shimmering sphere of light.

She'd never done ritual magic herself, so she wasn't prepared for the way it tingled across her skin and lifted the hairs on her neck. She wasn't prepared for the brush of power that felt exhilarating—like flying and falling all at once. It was nothing like the comfort of her own affinity. That was warm and soft, like an old friend. But this? She wasn't prepared for how much she wanted *more*.

Esta repeated the same process with Golde next, and then with Yonatan. Finally, she placed the last of the glowing spheres over Josef's outstretched hands. The boy flinched when the sigil flashed even brighter. All at once, cold magic swept through the room as the four sigils connected in a blinding flash of light.

Almost immediately, Jianyu's entire body went limp. He was no longer contorted in pain, but Esta wasn't sure if it was because he was protected from Lee's connection to the black thread, or if it was because—

"He's still breathing," Harte said, as though reading the direction of her thoughts.

She looked at him, his face aglow with the strange power of the sphere of light he held in his hands, and he nodded encouragingly. *You can do this*.

"Let's get that thing off his arm," Esta said, and she stepped across the boundary and into the circle.

QUESTIONS OF AETHER

Bella Strega

James Lorcan didn't know how much time had passed between when Darrigan had managed to escape and when Logan found him unconscious and bloody on his own living room floor. He immediately noticed what was missing: the portfolio from Morgan's mansion and the cane.

"Did the boys take care of the problem in the Strega?" James asked as he sat himself upright. He gingerly dabbed his battered nose, wincing at the slight pressure. Then he tilted his head back, so the blood could run down his throat instead of all over his rug. He'd have to find another healer to fix it, and soon. Preferably before he showed himself in the saloon.

"I don't know," Logan told him, looking distinctly more uneasy than usual. "I didn't stick around to find out."

"You didn't stay?" James glared at him.

"The others were leaving," Logan said, feeling suddenly uneasy. "If your own people aren't going to fight, I'm not getting my head busted in for some stupid saloon."

"Who left?" James asked.

"I didn't take down their names," Logan told him. The boy was jangling with nervous energy, coward that he was. "But Marcus and Arnie for sure."

James frowned. Marcus and Arnie were old blood. They wore the mark, but they hadn't stood and fought for the Strega?

The Aether shuddered around him. That stupid, constant droning seemed louder now, more perverse in its insistence that something was coming and more determined to hide it from his view.

He shoved over the small table, shattering the glass that had been sitting atop it and splattering Nitewein on the Persian carpet. The way it marred the ornate pattern in the weave, like drops of blood on fabric, settled something in him. Any time he chipped away at the perfection of Dolph's life gave him a thrill of satisfaction.

"Come," he ordered, and without waiting to see if Logan would follow—of *course* he would—James took the steps down to the bottom floor and entered the barroom.

It was a disaster. Chairs lay broken in heaps and glass littered the floor. There were a handful of his people there, looking morose and dejected as they stared at the mess. But Logan had been right. The majority of the Devil's Own were nowhere to be found. They'd fled like rats from a sinking ship. Not even the fear of the marks had been enough to have them stand and fight for the place that served as their home.

The few who remained stood when he entered, but they didn't make any move to explain.

He called over Murphy, one of the new boys he'd recruited in the weeks after the Flatiron, when the heat of a city summer stirred tempers and made men volatile. Murphy, like other new faces that had come to call the Strega their own, had gladly accepted the mark. He, like so many others, had yearned to be part of something. James' possession of the ring, along with his new alliance with the Five Pointers, had been enough to convince them that *this* was what they were willing to die for.

Unlike those who had followed Dolph, the new boys never asked inconvenient questions, never pressed. The newer ones, like Murphy, were easier to control without their inconvenient memories and misplaced loyalty to Saunders and with the freshly inked snakes entwined on their skin.

"Find the others," he told them. Then he turned to the bar to see if any of the whiskey had survived.

When John Torrio and Razor Riley had entered the Strega a few hours earlier, no one had paid them any attention. Maybe it was because the two had become regulars since Torrio had made the alliance with the Devil's Own as payment for the help James had given him to wrestle control of the Five Pointers from Paul Kelly. Or maybe there was another reason why none of the Devil's Own noticed the pistols carried by the two as they stalked through the crowded bar toward the table where James usually held court. Not until Torrio had it pointed directly at James' head.

It seemed that the stupid dago was tired of waiting. He wanted the territory he'd been promised, and he wanted it immediately.

James had managed to talk him down, but who knows what might have happened if Mock Duck hadn't arrived a few minutes later, shoving into the Strega like he and his highbinders belonged there.

But it wasn't a coincidence that his two newest allies had both shown up that day at the same time, both primed for a fight and ready to brawl.

"The attack was a distraction," he said.

Logan blinked at him.

"Esta's back," he told Logan, cataloging the guilt he saw flash through the other boy's eyes. "But you already knew that, didn't you?"

At least Logan had the good sense to look away. "I tried to stop her, but . . . I don't know what happened, James. One second I was blocking their way, and the next . . ." He looked more than a little unsettled by it. "I woke up on the floor, and they were already gone."

"Viola, if I had to guess," James said. Though it could have just as easily been Logan's own incompetence or cowardice. "But it doesn't matter. If Esta's back, it means the Book is back as well. She wouldn't come without it."

Logan frowned, his brows drawing together in confusion. "I didn't sense it."

The Aether lurched uneasily.

"That's impossible. Esta wouldn't leave it unguarded. She'd have it with her." He focused and felt the Aether, trembling and uncertain. Something wasn't right. Something hadn't gone according to plan.

"If it's still in the city, I can find it for you," Logan said, ever earnest.

"I know," James told him. "It's why I've kept you around despite your complete ineptitude. Esta and Darrigan aren't going anywhere. For now I want you to find me someone to take care of this broken nose. You can track the Book for me after."

There was one bottle of whiskey left unbroken. After taking two long swigs to help with the pain in his broken face, James went to the sink and pumped some cold water into the basin. Carefully, he washed away the blood that had already started clotting around his nose and lips. The shirt was ruined, but he took it off and soaked it anyway.

There was a part of him, an impatient boy deep inside, who cursed himself for not going after Newton's Sigils weeks ago. He'd wanted to. He'd thought of nothing else ever since he'd taken Morgan's papers and realized what they could do, what he could use them for. But every time he tried to form a plan, the Aether counseled patience. Any scheme, any attack that he began to map out sent uneasy vibrations through the ethereal substance around him and dread down his spine.

He needed to wait. He trusted his magic, and the Aether had never led him wrong, but he could not understand why. *Especially* now that Darrigan and Esta had bested him.

There had to be a reason.

He left the mess of the Strega in the hands of the people who hadn't run at the first sign of struggle and headed back up to his apartment, dabbing at his still-bleeding nose as he went.

Once inside he took stock. They'd taken Morgan's papers, but he already knew the contents of those. They'd taken the cane as well, which would make things more delicate. But he still had the Aether, and he still had the Devil's Own.

Settling himself on the couch while he waited for Logan's return, he took the small diary from his pocket and flipped through the entries. Most of it remained unreadable except for one page. But something there had changed. The future was becoming more certain.

Esta was back, and now the entry about the Conclave was settling itself.

Perhaps there was a reason he wasn't supposed to have the sigils yet. Words rose up on the page, hints of a future that could become. Perhaps he didn't need them *quite* yet.

They had taken the papers and had Newton's Sigils as well. Neither were weapons that could be used against him. The sigils were strange, powerful occult magic with the ability to protect Mageus from the Brink and to control a power as dangerous as the Book. He'd let them take the risks, and then, when the time was right, he'd step in and claim the rewards.

Let Esta and Darrigan believe they'd won this round. James knew the truth. Closer and closer, the final gambit was coming, and if the Aether was true and the words in the diary were correct, they were positioning themselves exactly where he wanted them.

Until then, he had work to do. He could not allow the alliances he'd made to crumble, not so long as they were useful. And he could not lose his hold on the Devil's Own.

GHOSTS OF THE PAST

Uptown

Viola refused to apologize for killing the bastardi that had destroyed the building that belonged to Cela's friends. She had not acted in a fit of rage. *No.* She had acted to save the lives of those who had stood by her, and she had sent a message in the process. This is who she would stand beside. This is who she would fight for. And if the Order and their scagnozzi came for Cela's friends, they would have to come through her.

And if she dreaded having to tell Jianyu what she had done? She would deal with it when she saw him. When he was well.

If he was well.

"Can't this thing go no faster?" she growled as the streetcar plodded steadily south.

Cela shushed her, while the other riders pretended they hadn't heard.

"We'll be there soon enough," Cela told her, but Viola could hear the fear in her friend's voice.

It took too long, that trek back down to Dolph's safe house near the river. She still couldn't quite believe that her old friend had been able to hide such a thing from her. She did not have any trouble understanding why Dolph had confided in Jianyu, but she still wondered why he hadn't told her as well.

Finally they arrived, Abel along with them, and it was Cela who was first through the cold warning of the front doors and led the way up to the third floor, where the apartment waited. Viola and Abel followed closely behind, but Viola paused before she entered. She hated visiting this place. She knew how they saw her—they thought her a murderer at best, and they feared her when she was around. It didn't matter that she'd helped to save every life within those walls. Somehow it still wasn't enough to erase the distrust in those they'd rescued.

She closed her eyes, girding herself for the judgment that was sure to come, and took a deep breath. The hallway was silent, peaceful, and she wished she could just wait there until it was over. Her attention snagged on a movement at the other end of the corridor, where a doorway to the back stairs stood open, but when she looked, nothing and no one was there.

Still . . . With all the dangers that surrounded them, it wouldn't hurt to be careful. And she was in no hurry to go inside. She wasn't yet ready to know whether their mad plan to save Jianyu had worked . . . or had failed.

At the end of the hallway, Viola found the staircase empty. She listened, just to be sure, and considered checking the other floors. But she knew she was being stupid. No one else could enter the safe house—Dolph had made sure of it. She was only delaying the inevitable. She took another deep, steadying breath, and along with the dust, she breathed in the scent of old books—aged leather and parchment and the acrid scent of drying ink—that reminded her somehow of her old friend.

She wished Dolph were still there. She wished he had lived to see the leader Jianyu was becoming and the peace that she herself had found. She wished most of all that they hadn't failed him so utterly and completely.

A shout came from the open apartment door that shook Viola out of her melancholy. *Ruby.* Forgetting the ghosts of the past, she ran.

Her knife was already in her hand when she reached the large back gathering room. She found Ruby immediately, huddled in the corner of the room with her face turned away from the scene.

"Are you okay?" Viola asked, touching her face, her neck, her arms. "Where are you hurt?"

"I'm fine," Ruby said, her eyes squinting against the brightness in the room. "I was only startled. It's just so much—"

Cold magic crackled through the air as Viola turned to take in the scene playing out in the center of the room. Darrigan and Golde along with Golde's son and one of the others were holding blinding orbs. A visible wall of energy connected them to form a curtain of light, and behind that boundary, Esta was bent over Jianyu's body. His eyes were open and the muscles of his neck were corded with his screaming, but she couldn't hear anything other than the low roar of counterfeit magic swirling around them.

On the other side of the circle, Abel was holding Cela back.

Viola stepped closer, trying to see beyond the boundary of energy and light. Esta looked like a girl made of fire. Her eyes were closed as she gripped Jianyu's arm, and as Viola watched, she felt a wave of warm magic swirl around them, warring with the cold energy in the air.

Then the blackness that had sunk into Jianyu's skin began to ripple.

GONE

The Safe House

Esta had felt the difference the second she'd stepped into the circle of light. It was like the atmosphere within the boundary created by the sigils was different somehow. Her ears had crackled, threatening to pop from the pressure, and her skin had gone hot and cold all at once as the corrupt magic brushed against her. Sound had drained away, leaving only silence, and when she'd reached for her affinity, she had found it strong and sure.

She knelt next to Jianyu, who was no longer conscious. He was still breathing, just as Harte said, but time was running out. Examining his wrist, she suddenly wasn't sure what she was supposed to do. It had seemed so simple before, but now that she was standing at the threshold, she hesitated.

What did you think you were, child? Seshat had purred. Esta was like Seshat. The same as Seshat.

Esta hadn't wanted that knowledge then, but she'd felt the truth of it in Chicago. She'd been so close to just *destroying* every bit of hatred in that arena. *You can touch the strands of time. . . . You can tear them apart.*

Esta had tried with Thoth, but she had failed. She'd only made things worse.

But you didn't have the sigils, she reminded herself.

Shoving her misgivings aside, Esta closed her eyes as she reached for time, that indelible net of creation within which all things were suspended. It hung clear and distinct around them, but she noticed that the time inside the circle was somehow different from the rest. It was as though it had been severed, set aside as a space beyond.

She filed that information away, and this time when she pulled, she focused on Jianyu—on the silken cord that had woven its way into him. Little by little, she called on the spaces between things, pulled and tugged, until . . . *there*. She could feel the very molecules that made the thread—the protein and carbon and every atom within it. The silken thread was breaking apart as chaos rushed in. She reached in, grabbed hold of the very essence of the thread.

And then she tore it from the world.

She unmade it completely by allowing the spaces between—the chaotic power of the old magic—to swallow the thread whole, like a snake devouring its prey.

Suddenly, Jianyu gasped, and his arm jerked awkwardly.

Esta jolted as her connection to the piece of silk evaporated as though it had never been, and when she looked down, the silk was gone. Jianyu's wrist was bleeding, but there was no sign of the dark veining magic that had threatened his life.

She turned to Harte, who had been watching, and the smile on his face matched her own. But when she stepped toward him, she realized she couldn't get close. Whatever boundary the sigils created kept her in just the same as it kept Tom Lee's connection out.

"You have to break the ritual," she shouted, but the flash of confusion on Harte's face told her that he couldn't hear anything. She pointed to the spinning ball of light and mimed breaking a stick in two.

Harte immediately understood. He lowered his hands and stopped the sigil from spinning, and with a burst of icy energy, the chain of magic that had formed the boundary around them broke. Then he caught her up in his arms and held her tight.

"You did it," he whispered. Then he kissed her, long and full. When he drew back, there was no mistaking the pride in his eyes, or the heat. "I knew you could, but . . . You know what this means?"

She did. The world tilted a little as the effort—and the importance—of what she'd just done nearly knocked her over.

Cela was there—Esta hadn't even noticed her return, but she was kneeling beside Jianyu, who was already coming to. Abel was standing close by and helped them both up from the floor.

Esta let herself lean into Harte's body. It wasn't just that she was exhausted—or it wasn't only that. *This* was the answer they'd been looking for.

She'd tried to kill Thoth once before by killing Jack, but it hadn't worked. She thought she'd unmade Thoth then, but now she felt the difference. Now she understood. Maybe if they could trap Jack using Newton's Sigils, they could contain Thoth until she could rip him from the world in truth this time. They could make sure he never walked the earth again in *any* body, in any form. Maybe they could destroy Jack *without* killing him.

"We can finish this," she told him, feeling more certain with every passing second. "We have everything we need. We have the Book and the artifacts. We'll use the sigils to take care of Thoth, and once we do, we can stop Jack as well. There are still two weeks before the Conclave. And then we can use Seshat's power to take care of the Brink."

She saw the doubt in Harte's eyes, the worry. "The stones, Esta. How are we supposed to touch them here? Nibsy has the ring, and Jack has the dagger. That's at least two that we know for sure will disappear the second they're out of the Book."

"Don't you see?" She kissed him again, unable to stop the joy from bubbling up within her. "The sigils are the answer—to finishing Thoth *and* to using Seshat's power. I felt it, Harte. The boundary they make cuts off everything, even *time*. We can use them to take the artifacts out of the Book, and then we can complete the ritual. We can unite magic and time, and we can finish this once and for all."

Harte still looked unmoved. "We don't have to rush anything."

"You know that isn't true," she whispered. "This has to be done. *Before* the Conclave."

He didn't have an argument for that. He knew what the diary she'd taken from Nibsy foretold: the deaths of Jianyu and Viola. Esta's as well. He refused to let *that* particular future come to be.

"If we find Jack before the Conclave, we can use the sigils to trap Thoth within them, and I can eliminate the threat he poses."

"And once we trap the demon?" Viola asked. "Then can I kill the bastardo who murdered Theo?"

Ruby took Viola's hand and gave her a watery-eyed look of approval.

"I'm not sure it's going to be that easy," Esta told her as she remembered the sickening suck of the dagger sliding into Jack's chest and the way he'd looked at her—him, not Thoth—right before he died in Chicago. They couldn't risk making him a martyr as she had before. "If we're the ones who kill Jack, it's only going to reinforce how dangerous people with the old magic are."

"What do I care what people think?" Viola asked. "I care only that Jack would be dead."

Ruby murmured her agreement, but Esta knew she was right about this. "Jack's the least of our problems. We can take care of Thoth, but the Brink is more important. If I'm right, these sigils could be the answer. We could do what Dolph always wanted to do. If we use the Book, we can stabilize the Brink *before* the Conclave. We cut the Order off at the knees and take away the danger Jack presents at the same time."

"It's true, then?" Jianyu said. "You have the Book and the artifacts within it?"

Esta nodded. "We have everything. We can end this." She walked over to where she'd left the satchel on a chair in the corner and brought it to the large kitchen table as the others gathered around. She unfastened the satchel and took out the first-aid kit and other supplies so she could remove the thick white towel they'd wrapped the Book in early that morning before they left the Plaza.

Even before she touched it, she had the sense that something was wrong. Her hands began shaking as she removed the towel from the bag.

The second she grabbed it, she knew there was nothing inside, but her brain refused to accept it. Even once she unwrapped the folded towel, she didn't want to believe it. But there was no denying the truth. Inside the towel, there was nothing but dark ash.

Everything was gone. The Book, the artifacts within it, and any hope they had of ending this.

Esta shook out the towel, certain that it would reveal the Ars Arcana if she just willed it hard enough, like a magician revealing a trick. Nothing but ash tumbled out.

"Well?" Viola demanded. "Where is it? Where's the Book of Mysteries?"

A feeling of unbelievable dread was coursing through Esta as she looked at the empty towel. "We should have realized," Esta whispered, still too struck by the horror of what had happened to fully process it.

They had been so careful. They had planned and schemed and found the answers they needed. They had known not to cross the stones, but why hadn't they considered that the Book itself might follow the same rules?

Why would they have considered *that*? They couldn't have known, because unlike the stones in the artifacts, the Book had never crossed with itself through time. *Not until now.*

"It's gone," she said, her voice hollow with defeat. "It was here. We had it. We had *everything*, but now it's gone. And the artifacts are gone with it."

They had no Book and no artifacts, save the cuff around Esta's arm. And there was no guarantee that Dakari would take on what they'd asked of him—no guarantee he'd even made it out of the park before the Guards found him. They might never know if they could take Nibsy out of the equation.

No, it wasn't *exactly* where they'd started. Somehow, it felt worse.

"The Book isn't gone," Jianyu told her. "It's here, in the city. With Jack. I saw it not even a week ago."

"Jianyu's right," Harte said. "If Jack is here, then the Book is as well.

We can still get it back from him. We can still stop him, Esta. And now that we have the sigils, we can destroy Thoth."

That thought buoyed her spirits, but only a little. Because it wasn't enough. The version of the Book with Jack wasn't *their* Book. It wouldn't contain the artifacts or the angry goddess who had been trapped within the pages of that other Book.

"But what about the artifacts?" she asked. "They're still out there. Without them, there's no chance of stabilizing the Brink. Even if we had them, Seshat's gone."

Her eyes met Harte's, and she knew that he understood exactly what she meant.

Without Seshat, there was no way to fix the Brink—not without sacrificing herself.

PART

V

HARTE

The Docks

As Harte Darrigan waited, tucked back into the shadows of one of the long warehouses that lined the docks, he thought of another night not so long ago. For him, it hadn't been that long since those terrible, lonely nights after the job at Khafre Hall, when he was an enemy to everyone—the Devil's Own, the Order, and Esta as well. He'd been utterly alone as he had executed his careful plans, but being alone had been necessary—it had been the best chance of slipping past Nibsy's defenses and to protect Esta and the others as well.

Then, the city had felt like his inevitable tomb. He'd had no hope of escaping. He had not expected to live beyond the following day, much less escape the Brink and travel across a continent and through time itself.

After all he'd been through, he suddenly found there was a strange comfort in the familiarity of the city—of *his* city. He'd seen Manhattan soaring to impossible heights, had seen the speed of the world by train and automobile, had seen another sea as well. None of it had brought him the peace he'd been searching for. None of it had been enough.

Esta's profile was clear against the softness of twilight, and as he looked at her, something in him settled, as it always did.

"What?" she asked, noticing his attention.

He shook his head as though to say, *Nothing*, but when she continued to frown, he attempted to explain. "I was considering how strange it feels to be back."

Her expression softened then. Sadness eased the tension around her eyes. "I'm sorry, Harte," she whispered, misunderstanding his meaning.

"Don't be," he told her. "I'm exactly where I want to be." He leaned down and kissed her.

"Me too," she told him. "But I wish it could have been different. We were so close. . . ." She let out a long sigh. "We wasted so much time when we should have just come back and taken the Book from Jack here and now. So many people got hurt because of it."

"There's still time to change that," he told her. "We'll figure it out soon enough, but right now it's time to pay Jack a visit."

Jianyu appeared suddenly. "He is inside, just as we expected. Viola is waiting nearby, close to the building, to make sure he cannot leave."

"It's time," Esta said, sounding suddenly nervous. Her breath hung in a cloud around her.

"This is going to work," Harte told her, slipping his hand into hers. "We have everything we need. Jianyu will get us in, Viola will slow Jack down, and before he even knows what's happening, we'll have him trapped with the sigils. Once we take care of Thoth, we'll worry about the Book and the artifacts with one less enemy at our throats."

"But what if I can't destroy Thoth?" she asked. "It was challenging enough to take care of a piece of silk, but that bit of counterfeit magic was nothing compared to what Thoth has been able to accumulate over the centuries."

"You can do this," Harte told her. "And this time, Thoth won't be able to get away."

Esta nodded, but she wasn't wearing her usual brash confidence, so he drew her close again and gave her the kind of kiss that told her everything he felt. *You can do this. We can do this. It will be okay, because I believe in you.*

"You *can* do this," he told her, in case she hadn't received the message, and then kissed her once more.

"If the two of you are finished?" Jianyu looked vaguely uncomfortable to be witnessing their show of affection.

LISA MAXWELL

Harte gave his old friend a grin. "I don't think I'll ever be finished with that particular activity, but we're ready enough."

Esta smacked him softly, but he could see the tension had eased from her a little. A small, secret smile had replaced the worry that had been bracketing her mouth.

They took Jianyu's hands, and Harte felt the world wobble, as it had on the bridge that day so many months ago, when Jianyu had saved him from the death he'd originally planned for himself. Around them, the city shivered and breathed, and for once, the familiarity of it felt like a comfort. He knew this city. He'd mastered it once, and he would reclaim it.

They were nearly there when Viola came flying out of the darkness. "He's leaving," she said, pointing toward the narrow alleyway between the warehouses.

Harte could just make out the silhouette of a man running in the opposite direction.

"I couldn't stop him," Viola told them. "There's something blocking my magic. I can't even hear his blood."

"Thoth," Esta told her, as they saw Jack turn toward the water.

The four of them took off after him, but as they rounded the corner, Jack was already getting into a boat. Harte knew they'd never be able to reach him if he was able to pull away from the shore.

Esta must have had the same thought, because they'd barely taken another step when the world went silent around them. After grabbing Harte's hand, she reached for Jianyu's as well and brought him into the circle of her affinity. Together, they ran toward the water's edge and the waiting boat, but with their hands joined they couldn't go half as quickly as any one of them might have alone.

They were nearly to the boat when Jack emerged from the small pilot's house and tossed off the lines attaching the craft to the dock.

Not only Jack, Harte thought. *Thoth.*

The Brink's icy power was a cold warning the closer they came to the dock, but they pushed through, desperate to reach the boat and Jack.

But it was too late. Jack was already moving away from the dock, steering the craft out into the water, away from the shoreline.

They couldn't let him escape, not when he was so determined to destroy the Brink. Esta knew what it would mean if he succeeded. She'd seen that future as she fell through the years, and she could not allow that to happen.

Esta started to leap for the boat, but Harte held tight to her.

"You can't," he told her. "Not with the Brink."

Jack stood on the back of the craft, his eyes as black as the night itself, watching them. As the boat drifted silently out into the East River, toward the Brink and away from any chance of catching him, Harte heard a laugh carrying across the water to him. Not Jack's, but someone far more ancient and powerful.

THE GAME OF FATE

The Safe House

E sta paced in front of the windows, occasionally glancing out to the snow-covered street outside Dolph's safe house. She could tell it was beginning to annoy her friends, who must have felt every bit as frustrated and disappointed as she did, but she needed to move. She should've been out there, doing *something*.

But what could she do? Jack was gone, beyond the Brink. And he'd taken the Book and any sign of his machine with him. All they could do was wait for word from Abel and his friends, who had left the city in an attempt to track Jack. But none of them were good at waiting.

She still couldn't quite believe that she was there, back in the past. She couldn't believe that everything had gone so very wrong. And it had happened so quickly.

Back in the future, before they had talked with Dakari and before the Guards' attack had thrown everything off, Esta had felt certain they could succeed. They'd had the Book and the stones, and because of that, they had Seshat's power to control. But in a matter of seconds, she'd managed to screw everything up. If she could have just held on a little tighter as they slipped through time, maybe they would have had longer to plan. If she had only been a little stronger, maybe things would be different. Maybe even without the Book, they could have changed more.

By arriving so late in the year, they'd missed their opportunity to stop any of the events that happened after they'd handed Jack the Book months before. The Order's gala, the heist at the Flatiron Building, even the attack on Ruby's wedding—those events couldn't be changed now, unless she was willing to change the lives of the people she cared about.

Esta couldn't do that—*wouldn't* do that—especially not now that she'd met Ruby and Cela. Not once she'd understood the bonds that her friends had formed with those women because of what they'd been through together while she and Harte were gone. She couldn't take that from them, especially when there wasn't any guarantee that going back farther would make anything better. Because even if they went back, they still wouldn't have the Book or the artifacts.

The only real choice was to stay, to go forward from this point and fight with all they had. But while they all understood that their failure to catch Jack before he slipped away meant that they may not have another chance to stop him until the Conclave, Esta and Harte more than the others knew the additional dangers that event held.

"Would you sit down already?" Viola barked with a frustrated huff. "Back and forth all day—you've been wearing a hole in the floor, and I can't watch you no more. It's driving me mad."

Esta's feet came to a stop as she realized everyone was looking at her. "I'm sorry," she told them, feeling suddenly awkward. "I just—I don't know what to do next, and I've never been good at waiting."

"Come and sit," Jianyu said gently. "We all feel the same."

Harte slid the chair next to him back from the table, and she took it, grateful for his presence. At least she still had him. At least they had this time together.

Cela came in a few minutes later, brushing the snow from where it had settled in the curls of her dark hair as she took off her heavy coat and hat and set them aside.

"Any news?" Esta asked, even though she knew Cela would have led with the information if there had been any.

She shook her head. "Abel's got people on almost every line running out from New Jersey. If Jack shows up, we'll know. But so far there hasn't been any sign of him."

"He's staying close," Harte said, his voice heavy with the same regret they were all feeling. "He's not going to run. He's just finalizing his plans."

"I can't believe we let him go," Viola said, temper lashing her words. "I should have killed him when we first found him, before he had the chance to run. That should have been the plan." She paused then, her expression heavy with regret. "But I couldn't even stop him from running."

"Because he's more than Jack," Esta told her. "He's been able to slip past my magic as well."

"Jack will return," Jianyu assured them. "He was too determined to take power from the Order, too certain of his victory to turn away from it. Now we must put aside our regrets and begin to plan. Jack will attack the Conclave and attempt to destroy the Brink. We must find a way to stop him there."

But at the mention of the Conclave, the memory of Nibsy's diary sent a bolt of fear through Esta. *If they stand with you, they're sure to die. You've seen their future. You know their fate.*

She couldn't allow that to happen. She couldn't allow them to die there. But she'd seen that vision of what a future without the Brink could be. She'd felt the emptiness, the hollow nothingness of a world unmade, and she could not allow that to happen. Still . . .

"The Conclave is too dangerous," Esta said. "There has to be some other way, some option we haven't considered."

"What other option is there?" Jianyu asked. "Jack told me of his plans. We cannot allow the Brink to fall. What is it that you haven't told us?"

Esta looked at Harte, who knew the truth, but he only shook his head.

"We have to tell them," she said.

"Tell us what?" Viola asked.

"Esta, nothing good can come from this," Harte warned.

"We tried to avoid it, but we're here now. They have a right to know." She turned to her friends, who were watching her with barely leashed frustration, and she told them about Nibsy's diary, about what it had shown. "If we try to stop Jack at the Conclave, there's a good chance you'll die."

"You kept this from us?" Jianyu asked Harte.

"Because I didn't believe it." Harte closed his eyes as though gathering strength. "I *don't* believe it."

"Did you not read it with your own eyes?" Jianyu pressed.

"The diary also said that I'll end up killing Esta," Harte said, his voice like a lash. Everyone went silent at the outburst.

"This is true?" Viola asked.

"Yes," Esta told her.

At the same time Harte said, "No." He gave her a sharp look. "I refuse to let some dumb book that belonged to Nibsy Lorcan determine my fate."

Esta tried to slip her hand into his. "It's okay, Harte."

"Nothing about this is okay," he said. He was practically vibrating.

"Where is the diary now?" Ruby asked.

"We left it," Esta said, glancing at Harte. "We gave it to a friend."

"You *left* it?" Cela asked. "It told the future, and you didn't think to bring it?"

Viola threw up her arms. "Why would you do something so stupid?"

"*I* left it," Harte told them. "Esta didn't have anything to do with it, and I didn't give her a choice."

Esta looked at Harte and wondered for the hundredth time what he'd done. He still wouldn't tell her why he'd left the diary with Dakari. She knew it had something to do with Nibsy, but whatever Harte's reason, it apparently hadn't worked.

"The diary does not matter," Jianyu said finally. "Whatever it might have shown us does not signify in our decisions."

"How can you say that?" Cela demanded. "If it says you're going to die, of *course* it signifies."

"Jack *must* be stopped," Jianyu said, as though the point were as simple as that. "Should he bring down the Brink, it will mean the end of everything." He gave a small shrug. "We are the only ones who know of his plans, and so we must be the ones who stand in his way."

"I can't ask you to do that," Esta said. "I can't ask you to walk into that danger knowing that it likely won't work, knowing that you probably won't walk away."

"You are not asking it of us," Jianyu told her. "I nearly died under Jack Grew's hand. I know what he is capable of, and I will choose my own path. No matter what the consequences for my life may be."

"Jianyu is right," Viola said. "Whatever the diary might have said, Jack cannot be allowed to create this future you described where the old magic is hunted. He cannot be allowed to keep the Book."

"What we read weeks ago doesn't mean anything," Harte told them. "The Conclave is still two weeks away. We still have time to learn more. We still have time to improve our chances."

"I might be able to help with that," Ruby said. The entire table of people turned to her, waiting.

"What do you mean?" Esta asked.

"My family has been tangled up in the Order's business for years," she explained. "Do you know how many secrets my uncle and my sisters' husbands have let slip in front of me? They don't even bother to hold back, probably because they assume women are too vapid to pay attention, much less understand. If I go back after escaping from the terrible Mageus who attacked my wedding, they're likely to trust me. I could get the information you need."

"Assolutamente *no*," Viola told her. "It's too dangerous. I won't allow it."

Ruby gave her a pitying smile. "It's better for our future if you understand now that there's very little you can do to stop me when I put my mind to something."

"Please," Viola begged. "Don't ask me to stand by while you walk into that sort of danger."

Ruby stepped toward Viola and took her hand. "I can do this—I'm certain of it. It won't even be an act to play the distraught widow. They won't suspect."

"Jack might," Viola argued. "He's not so stupid as everyone thinks."

"He'd have to come back to the city to find out," Esta pointed out. "And if he returns before the Conclave, even better. We can take care of him then."

"Jack Grew killed Theo. He destroyed one of the kindest souls I've ever known. He took my best friend from me." Ruby's eyes were glassy with tears, but her voice was filled with steel. "I will do anything—risk *anything*—to make him pay for that."

"We could use her help, Viola," Esta said, earning herself a dangerous look from the assassin. But she ignored it because she understood her friend's fear. In Viola's position, she'd likely do the same. "If we have more information, we're less likely to run into trouble. Maybe we can avoid the fate that was written in those pages."

"She has a point," Cela said. "Ruby could go places and get information that none of the rest of us could even dream of getting close to."

"I'll be okay, Vee," Ruby said. "I can handle myself. You *know* that."

"Fine," Viola said eventually. "But I don't like this one bit."

"None of us do," Jianyu said, laying his hand on Viola's arm. "But the die has been cast, and the game has already begun. We have no choice but to play the positions we hold on the board." He turned to Esta. "Whatever that diary might have said, whatever our fate, we will remain beside you and do what we must. Not because you ask it of us. But because we choose it for ourselves."

Esta looked at the faces of the people sitting around the table—people who had once been strangers and now had become her dearest friends. Viola and Jianyu, Cela, and now Ruby as well. And Harte. *Always Harte.*

They were all still there, standing next to her and ready to face any danger. Unquestioning. Loyal.

For her entire life, Esta had wanted this. Friends. *Family*. People who would stand by her without question. Now they were here. Hers for the claiming. Without question or payment. She didn't deserve any of them.

But maybe one day she would.

INTO THE LION'S DEN

Madison Square Park

"How do I look?" Ruby asked, trying to ignore the way her stomach was flipping with nerves. It was one thing to propose going back to spy on the Order in theory, but now that she was once again wearing her stained wedding gown, things had grown much, much more real. She hadn't considered what it would be like to wear it, but once she slipped the dress on, she could only think of Theo. She hoped he was with her as she climbed into the carriage that would take her back to her own world and her old life—because she'd never really lived in that world without Theo there by her side.

"You know how you look," Viola told her. She was trying not to show her fear, and her worry came out as temper instead.

"That bad?" Ruby joked, earning her another sharp look from Viola that made her want to smile and cry all at once.

"What do you want me to say?" Viola asked, sounding suddenly tired. But she turned to Ruby, let her eyes drift over her face, her body, and her gown. "You look like you always look. Beautiful. You're a vision, even with the torn satin and the dirt on your hem. Like an angel come down in the night."

She felt her skin go warm at Viola's appraisal. "I guess that's a decent enough compliment for a start," Ruby told her, trying to keep their banter from turning too serious.

Viola must have noticed the nervous tremor in Ruby's voice, because her expression softened. "You come back alive and unharmed, and I'll praise your beauty and fashion until you can't stand it no more." She squeezed Ruby's hand.

"I'll come back just fine," Ruby promised. "I'm not afraid of Jack or the Order—any of them."

"You should be," Viola said. Then she shook her head. "Don't underestimate them, cara."

"I know what they're capable of," Ruby told her. "I won't let my guard down. I can do this."

"I know you can," Viola agreed. "But that don't mean I have to like it. If anything happens, I won't know. I won't be able to help you."

"Nothing is going to happen," Ruby reassured her. "Everything is going to be fine."

"But Jack, he knows—"

"For Jack to say anything against me, he's going to have to return to the city first. *Then* he's going to have to admit that he lied the day Theo died," she reminded Viola. "He's not going to do that. He has too much riding on his attempt to be some kind of hero."

The wagon stopped at the dark edge of Madison Park. "This is it," Ruby said. "I'll come to the park as soon as I can get away, just like we planned. Wait for me by the fountain. If I'm not there by two, I'm not coming. But please, don't come for me, and don't worry. I'll be fine. I'll see you as soon as I can get away."

"Two days," Viola demanded. "No more."

She couldn't stop her mouth from curving at Viola's determined insistence. "I thought you wanted me to be safe?"

"I want you here, with me," Viola told her. "Where I can kill anyone who thinks to hurt you."

"As soon as I can get away without drawing suspicion, I'll come. I *promise*." She leaned forward and kissed Viola, sighing a little as Viola responded without hesitation, lifting her hands to frame Ruby's face and gently deepening the kiss.

Ruby could have stayed there in that dark, dirty little wagon forever as long as Viola's mouth was pressed against hers. With their lips touching and their breath intermingled, she could almost forget what lay ahead. The danger she was placing herself in and the importance of the information she needed to get fell away. There was only Viola. Only *now*. In that impossible moment, the Order didn't matter, and neither did the city beyond.

She didn't notice at first when the carriage rattled to a stop, but Viola drew back. Her violet eyes glowed with a need that Ruby felt too keenly. One day, they would have hours to explore each other, hours to ignore the world. But to have those hours—to imagine that future together—they had to stop Jack. And to stop Jack, they needed information that only Ruby could attain.

Then the wagon's back gate opened, and Jianyu was there, waiting. It was time.

He helped Ruby down from the back of the wagon's bed, and then she felt the world go a little wobbly as he wrapped her in magic. It felt a bit like looking through old-fashioned glass.

"Take care of her," Viola demanded, but her eyes searched the darkness, and Ruby understood that she could not see them any longer.

She stepped forward for one last kiss, but Jianyu held her back.

"Come," he whispered.

Reluctantly, Ruby complied. With her arm tucked through Jianyu's, they set out through the darkened park hidden by his affinity. She did not allow herself to look back even once—she couldn't. If she turned back, she might lose her nerve or change her mind. So she walked onward, her head high, promising herself that she would do everything she could to create a future for them. A future where the Order and the Brink and Jack Grew had no power.

And if she could make Jack suffer for what he did to Theo? *All the better.*

It wasn't long before they were standing beneath the soaring blade of the Fuller Building—the Flatiron, as the city had taken to calling it for its strange shape.

"You do not have to do this," Jianyu said when Ruby paused, looking up at the building. "If you are unsure—"

"No," Ruby said. "I *need* to do this. I'll be fine."

"Do not underestimate the danger," he warned.

She gave him a weak smile. "I won't, but I've been pretending for these fools my whole life, and they've never suspected. What's another few days?"

She released Jianyu's arm and stepped out of the safety of his magic. When she turned back, she couldn't see him any longer, but she knew he was there. She could sense him waiting. Watching.

Her dress was a puddle of silk and taffeta chiffon, but suddenly it felt like armor. She'd worn this gown for Theo, and she felt him now by her side. Terrified though she might be, Ruby would do this in his memory. She would get the information they needed to destroy the man who had killed her dearest friend. And then she would help bring the entire Order to their knees.

Looking up, she gathered her courage beneath the star-swept night, and then, with a blood-curdling scream, she shoved her way into the building.

"Help!" she cried, bursting through the doors. "Someone, please help me!" And then she collapsed into a sobbing heap on the floor.

NEWS FROM THE CITY

New Jersey

The warehouse space he'd rented in New Jersey was not much warmer than the chill winter air outside, but though Jack Grew was in nothing more than shirtsleeves, he didn't feel the cold. Not even now, in the dead of night. How could the cold touch him when there was a fire burning within him and a voice urging him onward and onward?

His machine was nearly done, and it was *magnificent*. The gleaming steel of the curved arms glinted in the light of the lamps. He'd redesigned it for his new purposes, and sometimes the sheer magnificence of what he'd created left him breathless.

Jack hadn't succeeded in finding a maggot to power a new stone. It was his singular regret. But he had the Pharaoh's Heart, and if he failed to locate a maggot before the Conclave arrived, it would serve his purposes well enough. It was worth the risk of losing the stone to claim his new future.

A knock sounded at the door on the far side of the warehouse. That would be Aaron, he thought, wiping the grime from his hands and putting on his jacket, where the Book was tucked safely into the hidden pocket against his chest. *Right on time.*

The coachman looked half-frozen by the time Jack opened the door and let him in. While the sniveling little man shivered, Jack barely felt the burst of winter that followed in with him.

It hadn't taken much—a few extra dollars thrown his way and the help of a fairly simple spell—to ensure Aaron's loyalty. With the coach-man's position in his mother's house, he traveled between the Grews and the various Morgans often enough to be useful. Servants knew more about their employers than anyone ever wanted to think about, and more, they talked to one another behind closed doors. Aaron had been more than helpful with making Jack privy to those conversations.

"What news do you have for me?" he asked, securing the door behind them.

"David Francis has been giving the Inner Circle fits," Aaron said, rubbing his hands together to warm himself.

"From the Society?" Jack asked.

Aaron nodded. "Word is that the other Brotherhoods are coming for blood. The Inner Circle is nervous. They're not sure that the Conclave will be enough to maintain their power."

"Did you get the plans yet?" Jack asked.

Aaron took a paper-wrapped package from within his coat. "One of the maids at the Vanderbilts knows a girl who works for the High Princept at the Flatiron. One of those harem girls they keep for their ceremony. She managed to get me these." He started to offer the parcel, then withdrew it before Jack could take it. "She's risking a whole lot by taking these, though. She's going to expect something in return."

Glowering, Jack turned to his things and took a handful of bills from his wallet. "Will this suffice?" He tossed them on the table for Aaron, whose eyes lit at the sight.

"That should do," the coachman said, greed coloring his features. "At least to start." He tossed the parcel on the table and took up the pile of money, counting it before he tucked it into his jacket. "It should all be there, the plans for the Garden and the Conclave. They're doing something with the electric grid, too. Wiring it up for some kind of big exhibition."

Jack left the parcel where it was. There would be time enough to go through its contents later. "Anything else?"

"Your mother is still beside herself because you ran off again," he said. "And your uncle keeps showing up to the house demanding that she tell him where you went. Oh . . . and one other thing. The Reynolds girl, they found her."

Jack's instincts prickled. "They found Ruby?"

Aaron blew into his hands. "Yeah. She came running right to the Order. Said she managed to escape from her kidnappers."

"Has she said anything about what happened to her?" Jack asked.

"Not much," Aaron told him with a shrug. "Says she doesn't remember anything. Whoever took her must have drugged her up pretty bad. But she'll tell anyone who listens that it wasn't maggots that did it. Which makes sense, I guess. If it were maggots that took her, how would she have gotten away?"

"How indeed," Jack said, considering this new piece of information.

He ushered Aaron out and bolted the door behind him again before turning to the information the coachman had delivered. But he had trouble concentrating on the plans, detailed and revealing though they were. He hadn't expected Ruby to return. If she had any brains in that pretty head, she would have run far, far away from him.

But if she was back and telling tales about her experience, she was up to something. It meant his plans would have to change. He'd intended to arrive back in the city the day of the Conclave, early enough to make his preparations but not so early as to get caught up in the Order's drama or his family's expectations. Or to put himself at risk of being found by Darrigan and his band of maggot filth. Now he'd have to return sooner. Because he could not allow Ruby Reynolds to interfere. He was so close to victory. He would not let some stupid girl get in the way of his plans.

MORNING'S LIGHT

The Safe House

Harte woke early in the morning and reached for Esta only to find her side of the bed cold. It was still dark, long before dawn. Pushing himself upright, he rubbed his eyes and tried to wake himself. Moonlight lit the window, but the room was empty.

He wrapped a blanket around his shoulders to ward off the chill in the air and padded barefoot down the hall, knowing already where he'd find her. She hadn't been sleeping well the last few nights, and this wasn't the first night he'd awoken to find her gone.

She was where he expected, sleeping on a well-worn couch in the front parlor. It reminded him of the time he'd returned home to find her in his apartment, courtesy of Dolph. How many weeks ago had that been? He wasn't sure any longer. He'd been through years and years, back and forth through time, and the experience of it had left him turned inside out and unmoored. But the sight of Esta, sleeping there in the moonlight, settled him. Terrified him.

The Conclave was coming, and with it, the threat of the future he'd read in Nibsy's diary. It was a future he'd do damn near anything to prevent.

Esta shivered in her sleep and curled into herself more tightly.

With a sigh, Harte took the blanket from his shoulders and wrapped her in it before lifting her gently. She didn't wake as he carried her back to the room they shared or when he settled her into bed. She only sighed and moved her body closer to his warmth when he climbed in with her.

But he didn't sleep any more that night. He couldn't stop thinking about what might happen if they couldn't stop Jack before the Conclave. He couldn't stop regretting his decision to give Dakari the diary. With it, at least they might have known what was coming. For the rest of the night, he lay awake, watching Esta's fitful sleep and listening to the building settle and sigh.

It was a strange place, perhaps because of how it was bespelled or perhaps in spite of it. Dolph's building. Another secret he'd kept. Harte had to admit he was grateful, even if the building felt alive sometimes. As though the walls themselves were listening to their conversations.

He must have finally drifted off to sleep sometime around dawn. When he finally woke, the slant of the winter sun told him it was later in the morning than he usually slept. Esta was still in the bed next to him, but she was sitting up and reading the stack of Nibsy's papers that had survived their trip back into the past. She set them aside when she saw he was stirring.

"Good morning," she said, snuggling into him.

"What time is it?" he asked, maneuvering her closer, so she was tucked into his side, their bodies fitting perfectly together.

"Around ten." She kissed his neck, nuzzling into the tender skin just beneath his ear. He felt her smile against his skin. "I don't remember coming back to bed. Again. Thank you." She gave him another soft kiss that shot a bolt of heat straight through him.

He pulled her over him and kissed her until they were both lost.

They had so little time left. The Conclave was coming, and with it the possibility of fate.

"Stop thinking," she murmured against his mouth. Then she deepened the kiss and slid her hand down his body until he could not think at all.

Later, they curled together skin against skin, warm beneath the covers, and watched the light change in the room. The minutes ticked by, one by one, but even the peace of being there with her was not enough to make him forget what lay ahead.

LISA MAXWELL

"I can't lose you," he told her.

Esta let out a deep sigh and turned to him. "You're not going to lose me, Harte."

But he didn't believe that could be true. He'd ruined everything he'd ever loved—his mother, his brother. He couldn't let that happen to Esta, too.

When he didn't immediately respond, she took his face in her hands. "You aren't going to lose me. I don't care what that diary said. You aren't going to hurt me."

"I know." He looked into her whiskey-colored eyes and saw the determination there, the fierceness that he'd fallen for almost at once. "I'd die before I'd do anything to hurt you."

"You aren't going to die, either."

He couldn't stop himself from smiling softly at her determination. She spoke as though she could take fate and destiny in her hands and bend it to her will. But then, she was Esta. Maybe she could.

"I've been thinking," she told him.

"A dangerous proposition to be sure."

She smacked him playfully, but then the amusement drained. "We have to consider Nibsy."

"He's the last thing I want to think about right now," he told her, brushing his lips over the tender skin of her neck. He's the last thing Harte wanted to deal with *period*.

"Harte, be serious," she said, trying to pull away. When he didn't let her go, she let out a not-unsatisfied sigh and allowed him to work his way along her neck, trailing his lips against her jaw and then finally kissing her.

She was breathless and flushed again by the time she managed to unentangle herself. "Seriously, Harte."

"I don't want to think about Nibsy," he repeated.

"But we have to," she said. This time he let her go, because he knew she was right. They were only delaying the inevitable, and it wasn't going to help anyone to ignore the fact that Nibsy Lorcan was likely already three steps ahead of them. "He might have the diary here, in this time. If he does, he's going to be able to predict what we do. We need to do everything we can to stop him."

What if there's no way to stop him?

Harte pushed the thought aside. Just because his idea hadn't worked didn't mean that another couldn't. "What do you have in mind?" he asked.

"We should get the others," she told him. She was already sitting up, already getting out of the bed.

He rolled on his side and watched her reach for her clothes. He let his eyes take in every inch of her, memorizing the curve of her back. The golden expanse of her skin. He wanted to touch her again. "Do we have to?"

She smiled back at him. "We do."

"But maybe it could wait." He was trying for playful, but the words had come out strained.

Esta's smile faltered. "I don't think it can."

He rolled onto his back and stared up at the ceiling. There was a crack in the plaster that traversed the entire room, dark against the dingy white of the paint. "The Conclave is coming too soon," he told her. "I feel like we have so little time left."

The bed dipped next to him, and Esta was there. She'd put on a large sweater, but her legs were bare. "We're going to have time, Harte. I have to believe that."

He tried to give her a sure smile, but he couldn't quite make his mouth curve. "If anyone can steal it for us—"

"I will," she promised. "Now get dressed. We have work to do."

AN ARRIVAL

E sta threw on her clothes quickly and left Harte still lying in bed because she knew if she didn't keep moving, she'd be back there with him. As much as she wanted to laze the day away, the truth of the matter was that they *were* running out of time. It had been days since Ruby had gone back to be their spy, and they hadn't heard anything. Every day Viola went to the park to wait for her, and every day she'd been disappointed.

There was still no sign of Jack, despite Abel's best efforts, and there had been no further word from Nibsy.

It didn't feel right, the silence from the Bowery. Esta couldn't believe that Nibsy had simply let them walk away with Morgan's papers. If he wasn't coming after them, he must have a reason, and whatever that reason was, it was likely linked to the future they'd seen in his diary.

That was, in large part, what had been keeping her awake at night. Nibsy's silence—his inaction—was like a splinter festering beneath her skin. But last night she'd had an idea.

She and Harte had taken one of the empty rooms on the fourth floor, away from the people who'd already made the safe house into their home, and she took her time descending to the floor below, thinking through the ideas she'd come up with in the dead of night.

At the landing of the third floor, she hesitated. In the distance, she could hear the soft murmur of voices, but there in the stairwell, it was quiet. It seemed impossible that Dolph had somehow managed this, an entire building that no one knew existed. It was another secret about her father discovered too late. Another piece of the puzzle that might have been her life if things had gone differently.

She wondered if Leena had known about this place. Maybe she and Dolph had come here before Esta was born. Had her parents spent time in these rooms together, planning their future or helping those in the city that needed to be hidden? Or had this been a place Dolph had kept from Leena, just as he'd hidden his intentions and plan to use her magic to fuel the cane?

What a lonely existence that must have been. So many secrets and so many lies. He'd been so afraid to trust that he'd left himself isolated. Maybe if he hadn't, Nibsy wouldn't have been able to strike.

Esta forced herself to push those thoughts aside. That part of the past was a page that could not be unwritten. Leena was gone, dead long before Esta had arrived in the past—far beyond where she could go and impossible to save. Dolph was gone too. Not even Viola could bring people back from the dead. It was time to focus on the future and on what could be done to try to change it.

The building was bustling when she finally made her way to the large communal area in the back of the third floor, where everyone usually gathered. Viola and Jianyu were already there. Cela was too, along with some of the other occupants who had warmed to them.

Not everyone had. Some still held suspicions about Jianyu and Viola, because of their skin or their gender, or because of the lies Nibsy had spread. But that morning the gathering room seemed like a friendly place. The mood was light, and the sun was shining in through the opened drapes.

"You slept awful late this morning," Cela said with a knowing grin. She glanced at Esta as she sipped from her mug. "Long night?"

Esta ignored the heat in her cheeks and poured herself some coffee. "I refuse to dignify that question with an answer."

Viola laughed knowingly. "I think you just did."

Cela lifted her mug in a salute, and Viola returned the gesture. Jianyu pretended he wasn't listening.

"Where's Darrigan this fine morning?" Cela asked, still smiling. "Too worn out to join us for breakfast . . . or is it lunch?"

"Darrigan is right here," Harte said from the doorway. "And he's fine this morning, thank you very much."

"You always did have such a high opinion of yourself, Harte," Cela murmured into her cup. But her eyes were smiling when she glanced at Esta. "But is it well founded, I wonder?"

Esta's cheeks were burning, and as much as she was enjoying the gentle ribbing—the camaraderie and friendship of these women—she had little experience with either and had no idea what to do with it.

"You'd think that the lot of you would have more to do than sit around and gossip like a bunch of chickens," he muttered. But he came up behind Esta and, wrapping her in his arms, nuzzled into her neck. "I told you we should have stayed in bed." He kissed her softly before letting her go.

Esta couldn't exactly argue. The heat of his mouth on her sensitive skin brought with it memories of his mouth on other places, and she had to focus much harder than anyone should just to slice herself a piece of the brown bread Viola had baked earlier. She took her time and only turned back to the room after she'd composed herself.

But from the knowing looks on the other women's faces, she'd failed miserably.

"Esta had something she wanted to discuss," Harte told them, thankfully drawing the attention away from her. "Something to do with Nibsy."

Grateful for the opening, Esta brought her breakfast over to the table. "I've been thinking—"

"Is that what they're calling it these days?" Viola asked, her mouth twitching.

It was only Jianyu's steady, encouraging expression that let Esta shake off the teasing and get to her point.

"I think it's a bad sign that Nibsy hasn't come after us yet," she told them. "He's not the type that just lets someone beat him."

"We have been here," Jianyu reminded her. "Hidden by the magic of this place."

"Sure," she agreed. "But we've been out there, too. There's no sign that he's even looking for us."

"Maybe he already knows where we are," Viola told her. "He has Logan. He's been able to find us before, even when we thought we were well hidden."

"That's one possibility," Esta admitted. "But I worry he's not looking because he already knows where we'll end up. If he has the diary—his version of it—it's likely he knows we'll go to the Conclave. He might simply be waiting to make his move there. Especially if he's being guided by the messages from his future self."

Silence descended as they all considered this.

"It feels likely," Jianyu agreed. "But it changes little. Regardless of the threat Nibsy poses, the Conclave is where Jack will try to take power, and we must be there to stand in his way."

"I know," Esta said. "But we should do everything in our power to make it harder for Nibsy to do that."

"What are you thinking?" Harte asked.

"I'm thinking that we have to start with the cane," she told them. "If we could use the sigils to destroy Tom Lee's bracelet, we can do the same with Dolph's cane. We can't chance it falling back into Nibsy's possession."

"You would unmake it," Jianyu said, considering the proposal.

Esta nodded. "And once it's been destroyed, we make sure that people know. We make sure that the Devil's Own understands that they're free."

"You'd take his army," Viola said approvingly.

"No," she told them. "We'd *free* them."

"They may not want to be freed," Jianyu said finally.

Esta acknowledged that he had a point. "But at least they'd have the choice."

Golde had stepped into the room. "I'm sorry to interrupt, but there's someone outside. I think it's the boy who was hanging around with Lorcan. He's looking up at the building like he knows that we're here."

Everyone around the table went still, and she knew what they were likely thinking. Maybe she'd spoken too soon about Nibsy coming for them.

"Is he with anyone?" Esta asked.

The woman shook her head. "He's just standing there alone. But he shouldn't be. He's making the others nervous."

Esta went to the window that looked over the front of the building and peered down. "It's Logan," she said, then turned back to the others. "I'll go out and talk to him."

"Not alone you won't," Harte said.

Viola was already standing as well. "I'm coming, too."

PLAYING THE ANGLES

I t took real effort for Logan Sullivan to stay where he was, standing in the drifting snow in front of the building. Something about the place made him want to turn and walk away, and the longer he stood there, the more painfully desperate that urge became. There was no chance of him going up to the front door, even though he wanted to. Even though he knew Esta was inside. Even staying there on the sidewalk was a struggle.

He'd been searching the city for days to find the Book, just like he'd been commanded, but every day that he couldn't find it was another day closer to James finally losing his patience. Logan couldn't risk that. Since he'd let Esta and Darrigan slip away that day the Strega got trashed, James had been nothing but fury. He had a group of new boys who were still standing by him—big, rough, bruising types who took the mark happily and displayed it where it could be seen. Guys like Murphy, whose cold eyes gave Logan the creeps.

James had made it well known that anyone who'd abandoned the Strega the day of the attack was no longer welcome. If they couldn't stand and fight for the Devil's Own, they were on their own, mark or no mark, without protection from the Hip Sings or the Five Pointers. But Logan had been around enough meetings that he knew the truth. It wasn't only that James would no longer protect the people who'd left that day. He was using the deserters to shore up his alliances by handing over their names and locations. Between the new boys and his allies, he'd declared open season. And Logan knew it was only a matter of time before he was next.

He wasn't going to let that happen.

Maybe he hadn't found any trace of the Book within the city's borders, but could sense Ishtar's Key, and that was enough to keep his feet bolted to the sidewalk, no matter how unpleasant the sensation of staying was. He was going to talk to Esta. He was going to demand that she take him back. If he just waited long enough, he knew she'd be forced to appear.

He wasn't wrong. It took longer than he'd expected, but finally the front door of the building opened, and Esta came out, alive and in the flesh. Following close behind her was Darrigan. Viola was with them as well, looking more alive than Logan had expected her to be considering that he'd watched James nearly tear her to pieces with that cane of his. When Darrigan had carried her out of the Strega, Logan had assumed she was a goner. Especially considering the lack of medical care available in this godforsaken time.

But he didn't want to think about that. He'd probably never get over the sight of her naked back or the way her affinity had bubbled up in blood and fire straight from within her skin. He didn't want to remember, and he'd resisted taking the mark himself because he didn't want to be next.

"Esta," he said. "Thank god I found you."

She was frowning at him. "What are you doing here, Logan?" Her eyes were sharp, narrowed in suspicion.

"Look, I'm sorry about the other day," he told her. It was almost the truth.

"Are you?" she asked, her voice flat and angry. "You nearly got us killed."

He ran a nervous hand through his hair and started having second thoughts about this plan. Or maybe they were third thoughts, since he'd already second-guessed himself a few times.

"Look, I didn't mean to be so difficult back at the Strega," he told her. "I wasn't thinking straight, you know? You surprised me."

"Enough with the bullshit, Logan," she said. "I know you meant everything you said back there. You would have stopped us from leaving if it hadn't been for Viola, so cut to the chase. Why are you really here, Logan? I've already told you I can't take you back."

He had the sudden insight that this wasn't *his* Esta. She might have looked like the girl he'd practically grown up with, but there was something fundamentally different about her now. It felt like he didn't know her, like maybe he had never really known her.

"Well?" She crossed her arms over her chest.

"I'm here because I'm done with James," Logan told her. "He's not the guy we knew."

"He is," Esta disagreed. "He's *exactly* the man we knew. We just never saw it because we didn't want to."

She wasn't exactly wrong. This younger version of Professor Lachlan at first had seemed like a completely different person, but the longer Logan had been with him at the Strega, the more he'd seen the seeds of the man their Professor would become.

"Look, the bottom line is that I can't stay there anymore, Esta," Logan told her. "He's going after anyone he thinks isn't completely loyal. Or he's sending his allies after them. And the thing is, he gave me one job—to find the Book—and I already know it's impossible. You don't have it."

Viola had a knife in her hand, and she lifted it in his direction. "I should have killed you then before you could cause us any more problems," she told him.

"Wait, Viola," Esta said, staying the Italian girl with a silent look. Then she turned back to Logan, her expression as implacable and unreadable as ever. "You're sure I don't have it?"

"I don't sense it, and I've known you long enough to know you wouldn't leave it somewhere. You'd keep it on you so you could protect it."

Esta glanced at Darrigan, and some indecipherable conversation happened silently between them.

"You still haven't told us what you want," Esta said, turning back to him.

"I can't go back to the Strega without the Book," he told her. "If I walk in there and tell James you don't have it, that it's nowhere? I'm dead. I need to get out of here. You have to help me."

"I can't," she said, frowning.

"I know you, Esta," he said, leaning into his plea now. "You can snap me back in an instant. It wouldn't be anything for you."

"You don't understand, Logan." Her expression was intractable. "There's nothing to 'snap' back to. The life you led, the world you knew? You changed all of that when you dragged me back here at gunpoint and handed Nibsy the diary."

"You know about that?" he asked.

"I didn't for sure," she admitted. "But I do now."

"Please," he begged. "I'll do anything you want."

Esta considered his plea for long enough that he started to get nervous. She wouldn't really say no to him, would she? No one ever really said no to him.

"There's only one thing you can help us with," she told him.

"Anything," he promised.

"Get us the diary," she said. "You do that, and I'll take you back after the Conclave."

"That's impossible," he told them. "He never puts it down."

"That's the deal," Darrigan told him.

"Even if I could get it without getting myself killed, it's not enough. I can't just wait around for you to finish playing with fate. If I get the diary, you take me back. *Immediately.*"

"I can't," Esta said. "There's too much at stake. It's after the Conclave or not at all."

Logan felt like tearing out his own hair. "That's more than a week away. Do you know what he could do to me in that time?"

"You'd have a place here," Esta said. "We'd keep you safe."

"No," Logan said. "It has to be now."

"You're not listening, Logan." Esta looked like she was about to lose her temper. "There is no *back* if we don't stop Jack from attacking the Conclave. If he does, he could bring down the Brink. But if we stop him, we can get the Book, and then maybe—just *maybe*—there will be a future for you to go back to."

"Jack has the Ars Arcana?" Logan asked. It didn't explain why he couldn't sense it, though.

Esta nodded. "He does, and if we don't take it from him, then everything changes. Everything about *your* future depends on what happens at the Conclave, Logan. You think things were hard in the world we grew up in? They'll be worse in a country where magic itself—and those with a connection to it—is made illegal. But Nibsy's going to try to stop us, and as long as he has that diary, he might be able to. Get the diary, and maybe we can stop Jack. If that happens, you get to go home."

But what if James wins?

Logan knew better than to voice the question aloud. "You're sure I'd be safe here?"

"I swear it," Esta told him.

He considered his options, but finally he decided. All he wanted was to go back to his normal life. He wanted to go home. If Esta was offering him a chance, he'd take it.

Esta exchanged a long, silent look with Darrigan, and when they'd finished whatever conversation they'd just had, they turned to him.

"There's no going back once you're with us, Logan," Esta told him. "If James kills me, it's game over for your dreams of getting back to your own life. And if he kills any one of my friends? I won't be feeling generous enough to take you back."

"I know that." He wouldn't let them see his nerves. *I just want to go home.*

"You're sure we can trust him?" Darrigan asked.

"No," Esta told Darrigan, never once looking away from Logan. "But if he turns on us, Viola will take care of him."

"Happily," Viola said, her violet eyes as sharp as her knife.

Esta did look at Darrigan then. "It's our best shot."

He didn't look happy about it, but eventually, the Magician held out his hand. "I don't like this, but I trust Esta. So welcome to the team."

UNSETTLED

Once Logan had disappeared around the corner, Jianyu released his hold on the light. It was a dangerous gamble to send Logan back to Nibsy as a spy and even more dangerous to let him carry the knowledge that they wanted the diary.

"Do you believe you can trust him?" he asked Esta.

"No," she said sadly. "That isn't the Logan I knew. When I went back to the future the first time, my world had already changed. Logan and even Dakari were different from the people I'd grown up with. So I don't know anything about this Logan, but it doesn't matter. Harte took care of that."

Harte nodded. "Even if he's not for us, he won't be able to betray us."

"Do you think there is any truth to what he said?" Jianyu wondered. "What he told us about what Nibsy is doing with the Devil's Own."

"Probably," she said. "It sounds like something he would do."

They turned together to go back into the warmth of the building, and as they climbed the stairs to the rooms on the third floor, the problem of the Devil's Own pressed at him.

It had been his idea to play the Hip Sings and the Five Pointers against one another to distract Nibsy. But the idea had not worked. Nibsy had sensed that the distraction was a ploy, and he had left the Devil's Own to protect the Strega. When they had run—as any sane person would—he had viewed their actions as a betrayal.

Because Nibsy Lorcan did not view those who wore the mark as friends or partners, not in the way Dolph had. James viewed them as expendable.

When they reached the door to the apartment, Jianyu stopped them just inside the parlor. What he had to say was for his friends alone.

"You need to destroy the cane," he told Esta. "You were right. Nibsy Lorcan can never be allowed to hold that power again. But as long as it exists, someone can use those connected to it as weapons. As cannon fodder for their own selfish desires."

"He's right," Viola agreed. "We need to make sure it's not a liability."

"It needs to be done today," Jianyu told them.

"We can do it right now," Esta said.

They started toward the back room, but when they reached the larger gathering space where the cane rested under the watchful eye of Golde Salzer, he stopped before entering the room. Cela was there too. Her eyes met his, and he understood the silent question she was asking.

Is everything okay?

He nodded. *All is well.*

Good, her eyes seemed to say. *Come get warmed up.*

The ease of their silent conversation was a comfort, but he took a step back. What right did he have for comfort when people were being hunted for Nibsy's sport because of him, because of the events he had set into motion?

There, sitting around the corner, were a handful of the people he had helped to free from the Order's patrols. Some seemed content enough to while away their days with menial tasks to keep them entertained. But he had already started to hear the whispering. Many were growing tired of being away from their lives. It did not matter that without the protection of the building, they might not have lives to return to.

They were safe, but what good was safety when they were trapped? How was this building, with all its protections, any better than the Brink?

All that he had tried to do, and none of it was enough.

"What is it?" Viola asked when she sensed Jianyu's hesitation.

"Why do we wait?" he asked, stepping into the room. "We have the sigils, and we have Newton's diagrams. We have the Order's records as well. We know what the silver discs are capable of. We could free people and release them from this city."

"We've been over this," Esta told him. "We can't risk losing the sigils. Not until we use them on Thoth."

"There's a way out?" A boy stepped forward—Golde's son, Josef. "You could help us escape from the Order and Nibsy Lorcan both, but instead, you're keeping us here?"

The others had gone quiet, and he knew they were listening.

"We're not keeping you here," Darrigan said, but his voice was too tight. "You can leave anytime you want."

"No, we can't," Josef argued. "Out there, the Order knows who I am. So does Nibsy. What do you think he would do if we left? He'd find us, and he'd use whatever he could to force us into telling him about this place. But if we could get out of the city—"

"Can we?" another of the tenants asked. "Is it really possible?"

"It is," Jianyu told them.

"We *think* it is," Esta corrected. She turned to the gathering crowd. "It's true that the Order used the sigils to get through the Brink more than a hundred years ago, but we don't have any idea what they would do now. We can't risk them, and we can't risk *any* of you to test some theory written a century ago."

"We saw what happened with Jianyu's wrist," Josef pressed. "I *felt* it. You know they'll work."

"*Josef*," Golde said, stepping toward her son.

"No, Mutter," he snapped, stepping back. "They're *lying* to us. Can't you see that? They're no better than Lorcan or Dolph Saunders or anyone who would control us."

"They saved you," Golde said. "They risked their lives, and then they gave you a roof over your head and a safe place to sleep, and what have they asked for? *Nothing*."

"There's always something," Josef said. "Besides, I wouldn't have needed saving if I had taken the mark like I wanted to."

His mother reached for him again, but he jerked away and stormed off. A few seconds later, they heard a door slam.

"I am sorry, Golde," Jianyu said.

"You have nothing to be sorry for," she said with an apologetic shrug. "He's young. He doesn't understand."

Jianyu turned to Esta. "We cannot keep people here forever."

"We won't," she told him. Then she turned to the others. "I know it's hard," she said. "I know it's difficult to believe, but I've seen the world that this will become if we don't stop Jack Grew. I wish we didn't need to wait. I wish we could take every one of you outside the Brink right now, but if we lose the sigils, we lose everything."

"If we keep people trapped here, against their will, perhaps we already have," Jianyu argued.

"You can't think that," Cela said.

"No?" he asked, feeling suddenly uncomfortable with the intensity in her expression and the fire in her dark eyes.

"*No.*" It was Yonatan who spoke now. He'd helped with the ritual to remove the cord from Jianyu's wrist, but he mostly kept to himself. "The boy is wrong. He's too young to know how wrong he is, but I see what you've done here. The lives you've saved." The man shrugged. "Maybe it's hard not to be free, but when has our kind ever been truly free in this city? You've given us safety, and now we'll give you our patience. And we'll trust that you'll keep your word."

"We will," Esta told them. "I promise. After the Conclave."

It seemed to settle the mood of the building, but Jianyu was still bothered by what Logan had said. There were still people in danger because of what he and Darrigan set into motion.

"Darrigan, could I have a word?"

Harte glanced to Esta, who nodded, before following Jianyu out to the front parlor, where they would be less likely to be overheard.

"What is it?" Darrigan asked once they were alone.

"I cannot help but think about what Logan told us—about the

destruction we caused and the people we have put in unnecessary danger."

The Magician frowned, but his expression held interest. "What are you thinking?"

"It will not be enough to destroy Nibsy's cane if he has others to command," Jianyu said. "I think it is time we pay another call on John Torrio and Sai Wing Mock."

He considered the proposal. "I think you're right. Let me just go tell Esta and the others what we're doing. They should be able to handle the cane while we're gone."

"I'll wait for you outside."

The air was warmer than it had been all week, but it still chapped Jianyu's nose and lips as he waited for Darrigan.

"So you're leaving, just like that?" When Jianyu turned back around, Cela was standing in the doorway at the top of the stoop. "Running off to save the world without so much as a good-bye?" she asked, descending the steps slowly toward him.

He felt caught in her gaze as she approached him and tipped her head up to look at him. Her brown eyes seemed even deeper, and now he could see the flecks of green near their irises. He was not sure at first what to say. "There is something I must do."

Her expression softened. "There always is."

Confused by her words, he started to move back, to put the distance between them that he always maintained. But she caught his hand.

"Not this time," she said. "Where are you going, anyway?"

"To make amends for a problem I caused," he told her.

"You know you didn't make Torrio and Mock Duck mean as snakes, don't you?" She was closer now, and he could smell the scent of her, floral and tropical, with a note of something woodsy and clean. "You've done more than anyone could have asked."

He did not respond to that statement. He had no idea how.

Cela looked up at him. "Tell me something."

"Yes?"

"You keep yourself so busy being good, proving that you're worthy of a dead man's approval, but are you ever going to deal with this?" she asked, waving her hands between them. "Are you ever going to address what there is between you and me?"

Panic froze his tongue.

Cela let out a tired-sounding sigh. "I can practically see that brain of yours churning through all the reasons there shouldn't be a you and me. But while you're thinking, consider this, too."

She rose onto her toes and pressed her mouth against his. Soft and sweet. He closed his eyes, unable to resist her, and suddenly he could no longer feel the cold.

But the kiss was over before it began. She looked up at him, smug satisfaction shining in her expression.

"That's what I thought." And with a small smile, she turned on her heel and left him standing there in the bright cold of a winter's day.

Jianyu didn't even hear Darrigan approach until the Magician let out a long, amused whistle. "You're going to need to breathe there, sport. And just a suggestion, but maybe next time? Kiss her back."

VAGUE PROMISES

From his usual table at the back of the Bella Strega, James Lorcan watched over the crowd. They were quieter than usual and had been since Torrio and Sai Wing Mock's boys made matchsticks of the furniture and tore the barroom apart. But in the days since then, he'd put things back together—his alliances, his saloon, and his control over the Devil's Own.

And if there were those who had disappeared into the Bowery despite wearing the mark? He would not let that concern him. There were others who would replace them, others who already had.

It was nearly midnight when Logan entered the saloon and looked around warily. The boy was always nervous, jittery, and unsure of himself, but for the last few days, he'd been different. Every time he entered James' presence, the Aether shifted and bunched. Unlike the others in the Devil's Own, Logan had no loyalty to the Strega or to James other than what was inspired by desperation and fear. But desperation pushed people to do things they otherwise wouldn't, and fear had the nasty habit of making them stupid.

In the days since Esta had slipped away from them, James had been allowing Logan some freedom—enough rope to either help him catch a thief or to hang himself. But tonight the vibrations had grown more insistent about Logan's possible duplicity.

It was time to ensure he wasn't a risk.

He called out and waved the boy over. When he saw the summons, Logan hesitated. He looked suddenly ill, and when he finally started to move, he came slowly, with his eyes shifting around the barroom the entire time.

"Well?" James asked, rubbing his thumb across the Medusa's coiling hair. "What have you discovered for me?"

"I found her," Logan told him. "I tracked Ishtar's Key to a building north of Washington Square. But she doesn't have the Book. Or if she does, she's not keeping it there," Logan told him, unable to meet his eyes.

It was no more and no less than what he'd suspected. The Aether had been whispering of missed opportunities for days, but now it seemed to whisper of deception as well. Logan, it seemed, had made a choice. A rather unfortunate one.

"That certainly is terrible news," he said. "For you especially."

Logan looked up then, fear in his expression. "For me?"

"Yes," James agreed. "You have no connections to this city, no talents other than to find magical objects, and you've failed to do that. You've refused my offer of the mark again and again. Because you believe that you're destined for other places . . . or because you aren't truly loyal?"

"No, James," Logan said, his eyes growing wider. "That isn't it at all."

"Isn't it?" James pretended to consider the situation.

"No," Logan said. "I wouldn't do anything against you, James. You have to know that."

"Do I?" He nodded to Murphy, indicating that he should come over as well. "Maybe you're right. You haven't given me any real reason to doubt your intentions—not yet, at least. But I can't help but wonder . . . What use are you to me if you can't accomplish the task I've kept you around for?"

By now Logan had noticed Murphy's approach and understood he wasn't safe. Fear shivered through him, coward that he was.

"Unless you *do* know something more?" James asked, glancing over his spectacles. "Something you wish to share?"

Logan looked distinctly uncomfortable, and James watched as the war played out within him.

"She's never going to take you back, Logan. Whatever Esta might promise you, whatever she might have told you, she's lying." James shrugged. "It's what she does. She was trained to deceive. But she will not win. When everything is settled and when the dust clears, Esta Filosik will meet the fate intended for her. If you trust her, if you take her side against me, then you'll share her fate as well."

"She doesn't have the Book," Logan said again. He glanced up at Murphy. "I wasn't lying about that. I wouldn't lie to you, James."

"If she doesn't have the Book, then where is it?"

Logan shook his head, his eyes wide. "I don't know. Maybe it's not in the city."

But it would be. The diary had assured him of as much.

"What aren't you telling me?" he asked, testing the Aether as he spoke. "What are you trying to hide?"

"I wouldn't—" He stopped when Murphy's hands landed on his shoulders. His eyes went wide. "Esta knows where the Book is going to be. She's making plans."

"Sit down, Logan." James nodded to Murphy, who pressed Logan forcibly into the empty chair on the other side of the table. "I want to know what you found out. And this time you'll tell me everything."

He listened to the Aether as Logan evaded his questions, and the more he struggled, the more convinced James became that someone had gotten to him. He'd been compromised, likely by Darrigan. But the question was how—had he submitted to Darrigan's magic of his own free will, or had he been trapped?

And could he still be used?

James considered him as he tested the Aether around him. The humming was insistent today, more unsettled than the usually buzzing unease he'd almost grown accustomed to.

The Conclave was coming, but he was no closer to understanding the directions fate would push him. And all the while, that incessant vibration in the Aether taunted him. He'd figure out soon what it meant and silence it once and for all.

"Do you trust me, Logan?" he asked.

"Sure, I trust you, James. You made me what I am—or you will."

"I sincerely hope that isn't true," he said. "But I'm willing to give you another chance. Maybe you can make up for your failings."

Logan licked his lips nervously. "Whatever you want, James."

"Since you claim that you can't bring me the Book and that you don't know any of the traitors' plans, maybe it's time for you to make a statement of who you stand with and who you're against."

"You want me to take the mark." The color drained from Logan's face. "I don't know . . ."

"That is the heart of the problem." He leaned forward. "You *don't* know. You're unsure of where your loyalties lie."

"No. That's not it—"

"But it is," he said sympathetically. "And I'm afraid I can only offer protection to those who are loyal to the Devil's Own—those who are loyal to me alone. What are you afraid of, Logan? Darrigan stole the cane. The mark is nothing more than your promise to me and to those whom I protect."

Logan swallowed hard, clearly understanding the threat. "Give me some time to think about it, would you? A day or two."

If he gave Logan a day or two, he'd run straight to Esta. The truth was there, clear on his face.

James got to his feet. "You can have the night." He gave Murphy another small nod, the indication that perhaps Logan would be more amenable to making that choice with a little encouragement.

He didn't stay to watch what happened next. He didn't particularly care. Logan would take the mark, or Murphy would take care of him. Either way, it didn't seem to have solved anything. Despite pinning Logan into a corner, the Aether still hummed uncertainly.

Back in his own apartment, James took out the diary that Logan had brought him from his future self and again looked over the impossible pages, cursing their refusal to reveal everything as they once had. The future was his to make, to bend and form to his will, but for weeks now the diary had refused to show him the path.

Now something seemed to be changing. The future was coming into focus.

The Ars Arcana would soon come back into the city—this diary made that fact clear, and Logan had confirmed the truth of it. When it did, Esta and Darrigan would go after it. They and the other traitors would risk everything to try to take it back from Jack Grew, and James would let them.

The Aether vibrated with encouragement at this decision, and he knew it was the right path. He would let them fight, and then, when the risk was over, he would make them fall.

In the end, the Book would be his.

THE BIND

The Safe House

Esta was sitting next to Harte around the table in the back room of the safe house with Cela and Abel, waiting for the others to arrive. Jianyu and Viola would be along in a while as well, and then they could go over everything together. Until then, they had the news Abel brought them. The pressure he'd been helping apply to the Order seemed to be working, and he could get firsthand news outside the Brink that they could trust.

"The delegation from California won't be in until the day of," Abel told them, running through the list of names in front of him. "Their trains are set to arrive the afternoon of the twenty-first. But the men from out west—the Ranchers' Syndicate—and the ones from St. Louis are planning to be here the night before."

"You mean the Veiled Prophet Society," Harte said darkly, glancing at Esta.

She had a sense of what he was thinking about. The regret in his eyes was for Julian, who hadn't deserved any of what happened to him.

"They don't really wear veils, do they?" Cela wrinkled her nose.

"Just the head guy," Esta told her, remembering the ridiculous costume and the fateful fear that the men hid beneath it.

"Veils or hoods, it doesn't make much difference when the marrow's all the same," Abel said.

"So they're Klan?" Cela asked.

"Not exactly, but they're all part of the same family tree," Abel explained. "The Society got their start busting up railroad strikers about twenty years or so ago. The city fathers in St. Louis didn't like the way all the workers were coming together, Negro and white alike, so they made sure to stop that before it got anywhere at all."

"Of all the Brotherhoods, they're probably the most organized," Darrigan told them. "They're likely the closest to making a play for power. If we can stir up something there, it might put more pressure on the Order."

"I'll let Mr. Fortune know," Abel told him. "He's familiar with the Veiled Prophet nonsense, and after what Viola did to save him and his men, he's more interested than ever to go after the Order and their like any way he can."

"I can't imagine there's a Negro in this city that won't have something to say about the Order welcoming Klansmen right out in the open, no matter what they might call themselves," Cela told her brother.

"Probably not," he said. "And I'm sure that the men involved with the Order wouldn't want the publicity if the other papers pick up the story. There's a reason the Klan wears hoods, and here in the north? People like to pretend they're not as low as all that."

Esta wasn't sure that involving more innocent people in their current mess was the answer. "I don't want anyone else getting hurt. Especially not Mr. Fortune. If the Order retaliates—"

"He's not worried right now," Abel told her. "With the fire, there was no proof at all that he was housing Mageus, much less the missing Reynolds girl. And then when she showed up *wearing* the wedding gown that the patrol supposedly found?" He shrugged. "Everyone's backing away from the story. The Order's pretending they didn't have anything to do with it."

"What about Jack?" Harte asked. "Any sign of him yet?"

Abel shook his head. "Sorry. No one's caught word of anything that might point to where he could be. It's like he's some kind of ghost."

Jianyu was there suddenly, appearing in the doorway. His eyes found Cela first, as usual, and Esta watched whatever was going on between them play out silently. She wondered if Abel noticed as well. She wondered if he was as tired of the simmering emotion between the two as the rest of them were.

"You're back early," Esta said, pretending she hadn't noticed the way that they were looking at each other.

"Did you have any luck?" Cela asked.

Jianyu took a folded bundle of papers from his sleeve and placed them on the table. "The Inner Circle are keeping to themselves. Outside of their new headquarters, they do not say much about the arrangements of the Conclave. But the Garden does not seem to have the same concerns about secrecy. I found these in their offices."

"Seating charts?" Darrigan asked, frowning. "Not sure what kind of help those will be."

"It's always good to know the players on the board," Esta told him, giving Jianyu an encouraging smile.

"I have the floor plan as well," Jianyu said, pointing to the sketches he had made from the originals. "The Order will hold events throughout the building. From what I gather, they will start here, with speeches in the main arena, but the ritual will take place in the open air. Here . . . on the roof. There's more. . . . Timetables for the catering and staff."

"So Jack could strike anywhere," Esta realized.

"But he is most likely to strike during the ritual," Jianyu told them.

"Which means we should focus our attention on the roof," Harte said.

"Any word from the Bowery?" Esta asked.

Jianyu's expression grew more serious. "There is still no sign of Logan. Nibsy seems to be keeping him close."

Esta's stomach sank. It had been a risk to draw Logan into this. She should have just turned him away. Despite what he'd done to her, she hadn't wanted to see him hurt. He was a pawn as much as anyone.

"And what about Nibsy?" Harte asked.

"He remains within, safely surrounded by those who still stand by him," Jianyu told them. "He seems in no hurry to make any move."

"That doesn't mean anything," Esta said, thinking of the diary. "He knows what's coming. He just has to wait."

She hated that Nibsy had that luxury while they were scurrying around like rats. The truth of the matter was, they were running out of time. The Conclave was mere days away now, and they weren't anywhere close to ready.

A COMPLETE FOOL

Jack Grew didn't tell anyone when he returned to the city. He kept his movements to himself, electing to stay at a hotel instead of his own, more comfortable town house. He hadn't contacted his family or the old fools in the Order. He'd been watching and listening, waiting for the perfect time to make his presence known.

When he arrived at a banquet the Order held the night before the Conclave, he wasn't surprised to find Ruby Reynolds there, dressed completely in black and whispering into the High Princept's ear as though they were old confidants.

"Jack . . . What a surprise. We weren't sure we'd see you here tonight." His cousin, Junior, sidled up next to him. A crystal glass of something light and sparkling dangled between his fingers.

"I was invited," he said stiffly, his eyes still on the Reynolds bitch. "The High Princept issued the invitation himself."

"I see," Junior said. But his tone made it clear it was a decision the family hadn't been consulted about.

He turned to his cousin. "Is there something you wanted, Junior?"

Junior's eyes narrowed, and his almost affable expression turned more severe. "My father wanted me to remind you that you aren't to do anything that would put the family at risk."

"I would never," Jack said dryly.

"And yet . . ." Junior shrugged. But the expression he wore didn't match the bored indifference in his voice. "You're on your last bit of goodwill, Jack."

"Goodwill?" He tilted his head. "Is that what this is? How delightful," he said flatly. Then, before his cousin could even sputter a response, Jack cut him off. "You and your father—the family—have nothing to worry about. I'm here only because I was summoned. I'd rather be anywhere else than this gathering of overstuffed old men. I will be on my very best behavior."

Junior blinked at the severity in Jack's tone. "Well . . . see that you are."

Before Junior could drift back to the crowd, Jack caught him by the sleeve. "The Reynolds girl's back, is she?"

"I believe she's officially Mrs. Barclay now, despite the tragedy," Junior said. He was frowning in her direction. "She turned up a week ago, ranting and raving at the Order's headquarters."

"It's good to see she survived her ordeal," Jack said, infusing his tone with sincerity. "The High Princept seems quite taken by her, but then, beautiful young women often do have that effect on old men."

His cousin sneered at him. "In this case, I think his interest goes far beyond her beauty."

Jack lifted his brows and gave his cousin a questioning look.

"He still believes it was maggots who captured her," Junior explained. "He believes he can get information about them and their plans if he keeps her close."

Jack was sure that the Princept believed a lot of things, old fool that he was. But Jack would discover the truth. And if the situation worked to his own benefit? All the better.

He waited until Ruby had wandered away from the Princept's side not long after the meal, and he followed her. She went to the coatroom first, and Jack waited behind one of the large columns that anchored the entryway to see what she would do. Instead of leaving once her cloak was wrapped around her shoulders, she turned back into the mansion. With no more than a glance in the direction of the party, she continued toward one of the unused hallways that led deeper into the heart of the mansion.

Jack followed far enough behind that she couldn't detect him and watched as she let herself into a locked room using a hairpin.

Apparently her new friends had taught her all manner of skills.

He gave her time to get into the room before he followed, and she turned in surprise, knowing already that she was cornered. He looked around the room and realized that it was Vanderbilt's private temple. There was an altar in the center and a Tree of Life painted on the wall. Ruby, it seemed, had been helping herself to the cloaks that had been folded there in preparation for the Conclave.

"Miss Reynolds," he said, placing himself between Ruby and her only chance for escape. "You seem to have lost your way."

She straightened. "It's Mrs. Barclay now," she corrected, her mouth going tight. She lifted her chin, regal as a queen, but her eyes betrayed her nerves.

So she isn't a complete fool.

"You were a wife for so short a time," he said mockingly. "I'd forgotten."

"I haven't," she told him. "I remember my wedding day like it was yesterday. I remember *everything.*"

"Such a tragedy," he said, not bothering to hide his amusement. The evening was becoming far more entertaining than he'd expected. "My condolences on your loss." He waited a beat, allowing her nerves to tighten.

"What do you want, Jack?"

"As I said, you seem to have lost your way," he told her. "Or perhaps you haven't. You don't have them fooled, you know."

Ruby's mouth was still pressed tight. "I've no idea what you're talking about," she said, moving forward. The items she was taking were still tucked beneath her cloak. But he stopped her, catching her by the arm.

Fear flashed through her bottle-green eyes, and Jack smiled, tightening his grip until he saw pain join it. "Your family really shouldn't allow you to wander about unescorted," he told her, keeping his tone easy.

"You're a bastard, you know that?"

"Such language from a lady," he mocked. "But I'd rather be a bastard than a corpse."

She backed away from him then, and this time he allowed her. But as she passed him, he whispered a string of ancient syllables into the air. He felt the words, strange though the language was, bubble up from within him, wrap around them, and settle over the room.

Ruby stopped, and he saw her eyes go glassy.

"You seem a bit confused, Mrs. Barclay," he said pleasantly, looping her arm through his again. "Please, do allow me to escort you."

He allowed her to take the cloaks, because it suited his plan even better than he could have imagined, and then he led her quietly back the way they came. He left her standing in the entryway. "I assume you can see yourself out," he told her, snapping his fingers and then walking away.

ANOTHER SUNSET

Viola waited under the cover of trees in the Grand Army Plaza, the portion of Central Park directly across from the Vanderbilt mansion. It was a ridiculous structure, all peaked rooflines and decorative gables, dark brick and smooth stone that glowed in the lamplight. At this time of night, the traffic on Fifty-Seventh Street was practically nonexistent, but it didn't calm her any. She wouldn't feel like she could breathe until the girl she loved was no longer in that nest of vipers.

Finally, she saw Ruby emerge from the front doors of the mansion, her blond curls glinting in the moonlight. She stopped just outside the door and waited beneath the enormous portico, her icy breath wreathing her head, until her carriage was brought around. Viola forced herself to be patient, and then, when the carriage departed, pulling up alongside the park, she made her move, using her affinity to make the driver drowse just enough that he wouldn't notice her opening the door and slipping inside.

"What's wrong?" Viola asked, her stomach turning at the expression Ruby wore. "What happened in there?"

"I'm not sure . . ." Ruby blinked at her, but there was a fuzziness in her eyes, like she was walking through a dream. "I got the robes." She took the pile of fabric out from the folds of her thick velvet cloak and looked down at them as though she had never seen them before. "The members and their wives will all be wearing them. It should get everyone in safely."

Viola took them and set them aside before squeezing onto the cushioned bench next to Ruby. She hated the way the black widow's weeds made Ruby look drawn and pale, but tonight it was worse.

"Something happened," Viola said, taking Ruby's hands in hers.

"Your fingers are freezing," Ruby told her, blinking away the last of whatever daze she'd been in.

"It's winter," Viola said with a shrug.

"You aren't wearing nearly enough." Ruby unfastened the neck of her cloak and opened it, adjusting herself so Viola could wrap it around herself as well.

Ruby's hair smelled of flowers and her clothes of cigar smoke. On her breath, Viola could detect the sweetness of champagne. All of it, scents from a life she could not imagine.

But it didn't seem to matter. With a contented sigh, Ruby settled into Viola. "I've missed you," she said.

Glad for the darkness of the carriage, Viola felt her cheeks go warm. "I'm sure that big, soft bed of yours and all the servants have been a trial," she told her.

Ruby chuckled. "Truly. They're just awful." Then her voice grew more serious. "It really is awful, Vee. I don't belong there anymore. Maybe I never did."

"This will be over tomorrow, and you can leave," Viola told her. "You can go wherever you want."

"I don't think I'll be leaving the city," Ruby said, leaning her head into Viola's.

Viola closed her eyes and savored the feel of the other girl against her. How easy it was to sit like this, together. How *right*. "Theo would want you to live your life," she said finally, speaking through the tightness in her throat. "He told me about how happy you were in Paris. You should go."

"I'm not leaving unless you come with me," Ruby told her. She took Viola's face softly between her hands.

"You know I can't." And nothing had ever hurt so much as that simple, undeniable truth. "Not so long as the Brink keeps me here."

Ruby kissed her softly. "Then I suppose we'll have to find a place uptown."

"Ruby—"

LISA MAXWELL

"You're right about one thing, Viola. Theo would want me to live my life," Ruby said. "*My* life. The one I choose. I will miss him every single day I have left to live. I will mourn him just as long. But I'll bless his memory as well, because by marrying me, he gave me freedom I never expected. Our families tried to tie him to me with my dowry, but since we officially married before he died, that money is mine alone now. No one can tell me how to use it. And when this is over, we'll be together."

Viola knew she should argue. It was impossible, what Ruby was proposing. To stay here beneath the watch of Ruby's family, in the city where her magic would only ever be a liability? But she couldn't bring herself to. For this one, small moment, she wanted to dream.

But the truth of Nibsy's diary waited to reveal itself, and dreams were dangerous distractions.

"The cloaks should get you in without any trouble," Ruby repeated. Then she explained what she'd gleaned of the Order's plan. The streets would turn deadly, and the Brink would be recharged. "They're going to be using electricity," Ruby said. "They're so proud of themselves harnessing the power of science to fuel their magic that they couldn't keep it a secret. If Jack's going after the Brink, he'll likely do it there. It's his best chance to have the biggest impact on their ritual."

The carriage was rolling to a stop, and Viola knew their time was nearly up. Another sunrise, another sunset, and the die would be cast. Their fates would be known.

Unable to help herself, she leaned forward and kissed Ruby until the other girl melted and opened for her. Until she could taste the expensive champagne on Ruby's lips.

"You shouldn't be there tomorrow," Viola said, feeling more than a little breathless. "It's too dangerous."

"I'll be there," Ruby said. "For you, and for Theo. For the end of the Order and Jack Grew. We'll finish this, and then we'll start the life we both deserve."

PLENTY OF TIME

It had been six days since Cela had acted a fool and kissed Jianyu. Six days of wondering what was going on in that head of his. He'd been avoiding her. But she was done with waiting. The Conclave was tomorrow, and she wasn't about to let him go running off headlong into his possible doom without forcing him to confront the truth about the feelings between them. If he didn't reciprocate them, fine. But she wasn't going to spend the rest of her life wondering.

She found him up on the roof of the building, right where she'd expected him to be. Ever since the dustup a few days before with Golde's boy, he'd been avoiding the other occupants in the safe house every bit as much as he'd been avoiding her.

The second she opened the door onto the roof, he turned. If he was surprised to see her, it didn't register. He watched her walk toward him with the same measured calm he always wore.

Armor. It had taken a while for her to understand, but now she thought she might. He kept himself closed up, calm and steady no matter what, as a kind of disguise. It meant that people were less likely to notice him, despite the color of his skin or the magic that ran in his veins. It kept him safe.

"Tomorrow's the day," she said, trying for lightness. But her voice betrayed the fear she'd been trying to hide.

He nodded, still looking at her with those fathomless eyes of his. She suspected he saw everything as well.

Then he surprised her. She'd expected him to do any number of things, including to pretend he didn't know why she was there or to deny the connection that felt undeniable between them. She hadn't expected him to touch her. But that's exactly what he did.

Slowly, he lifted his hand to her cheek, and despite the promises she'd made to herself to stay stoic and strong, her traitorous body responded by leaning into the warmth of his hand.

"Your skin is freezing," he said, frowning, as though he'd just noticed she wasn't wearing more than a shawl.

"I'm fine." And she was. She didn't even feel the bite of the wind with him touching her.

With an exasperated huff, he stepped back to remove his heavy over-coat and draped it around her shoulders. All at once, she was engulfed in the scent of him—the warm amber and sage and the not unpleasant musk of his sweat.

"Now you're going to be the one freezing," she told him, unable to hold back the smile that threatened.

"You did not come here to talk about the weather," he said. His expression was unreadable.

"No," she admitted. "I didn't."

"You came to talk about our earlier discussion," he said. He looked out over the city, as though he could no longer hold her gaze. "You gave me quite a lot to think about."

"Have you?" she wondered. "Thought about it?"

A long beat passed, and she heard his soft exhale of breath. "Every second of every day."

Cela hadn't realized how nervous she'd been until those words unlocked a wave of relief. "And?" She turned toward him. He was still looking out over the city, toward the river beyond. The lines of his face were sharp against the hazy blush of twilight, and while he studied the city, she studied him. "What did you come up with?" she asked finally when she couldn't stand to wait anymore.

"I will never leave this city," he told her, "but I still cannot claim it as my home." He turned to her then, looked deeply into her eyes as though willing her to understand. "Even if tomorrow goes well, even if the fate inscribed in Nibsy's diary can be changed, I have no future to offer you."

Unease inched up her spine, made her heart feel unsteady in her chest. "Jianyu—"

"No," he said gently. "You must understand this. In this land, I will never belong. But even if I could go back, even if I could pass through the Brink unharmed, even if I wanted to travel back across the seas to the land of my birth, I could not."

"Is that what you want?" she asked. She'd never considered it before, never even imagined that he might want to return. "To go back to your homeland?"

"No," he told her. "I also do not belong there any longer. I find myself a man between worlds, with no home in either."

She slipped her hand into his. "So make your home with me."

The city settled around them. The low, steady hum that had rocked her as a baby and guided her days seemed to wrap around Cela now as she waited for his decision.

He kissed her then, and though his mouth was firm and resolute against hers, it felt more like a question than an answer. "You make me want things I cannot have."

"Why can't you have them?" she asked, her mouth so close to his that she could taste the jasmine tea on his breath.

"Sometimes I forget the reasons," he told her, and he kissed her again. But this time was no question. He wrapped her in his arms and claimed her mouth as his own.

She allowed him to, offering herself up and giving everything over to him, to what lay between them. Because tomorrow was another day, another danger. Because today was all they ever had. Here, this beautiful, terrible, impossible now.

They were both breathless when they broke away from each other.

"There is nothing I can offer you," he told her. "I cannot even promise you tomorrow."

"So give me today," she said, slipping her hand into his. "Give me tomorrow as it comes."

He pulled her into a tight embrace, resting his face against her neck. "It would be a difficult life. I would make you regret my choices."

She laughed then. "Have you ever been able to make me do anything?"

"Your brother will want to murder me," he murmured.

"Let me handle Abel," she told him, but then she thought about his point.

"Cela—"

"No," she said before he could go and ruin what they'd just shared. "Don't you dare say another word." She kissed him again, softly this time, so he couldn't change his mind.

"Tomorrow is going to be fine," she told him. "We're going to stop Jack, and we're going to get the Book, and then the two of us are going to have plenty of time to figure everything out. But until then, I have an idea that might help with your problem in the Bowery."

A CHANCE

Esta Filosik was a thief, and a damn good one at that. She'd slipped out of a thousand impossible situations, had evaded her enemies countless times. But nothing in her life—no failure or mistake—had prepared her for the situation she currently found herself in. There was no slipping out of this, no evading her destiny, and there was no time left to steal.

Thanks to Ruby, they had an idea of what the Order's plans were. They were going to use the street grid to charge the Brink with electricity in an attempt to display their power for the Brotherhoods. Thanks to Abel and his friends, the Order was running into the Conclave on the defensive. But they still didn't know what Jack had planned, and they didn't know how to evade Nibsy—or if they even could. And the time for planning was up. In just a few hours, the Conclave would begin, and one way or another their fates would be sealed.

"Once we're inside, we need to find Jack," Esta said, trying to focus on what they could still control. "If we can corner him before he does anything, maybe we'll get to him before he can start the attack."

"I still say we should just kill him and be done with it," Viola told them.

Esta felt the same. But she knew it wouldn't work.

"It's not enough to kill Jack," Esta reminded her. "If Thoth gets free, then he can find someone else to do his bidding, and we haven't solved anything. And if he gets free *tonight*? There's a few hundred likely options for him, each one of them every bit as willing as Jack was. We need to trap Jack first, so I can destroy Thoth before he can get free."

"*Then* I can kill him,"Viola told them.

"No,Viola.You can't," Esta said, wishing it were otherwise. But she remembered the sickening suck of the dagger sliding into Jack's chest, the way he'd looked at her—him, not Thoth—right before he'd died in Chicago, and she knew it wasn't the answer. Not for her, and not for Viola, either.

"If we kill him, we prove the Order right.We make those with the old magic into the villains, the same as what happened before. That's what caused the DAM Act and everything else that followed.You're going to have to trust us. The last thing we want to happen is to turn him into some kind of martyr."

She thought of the first time she'd seen Jack, when he was a middle-aged man at Schwab's mansion, back in the twenties. *That's* the future they needed for him. One where he wasn't important or even respected.

"We don't need to kill him, but we need to make sure he loses all credibility after tonight. He has to look like such a fool that no one will ever listen to him or take him seriously again."

"I like him better dead," Viola said with a pout.

"I'm not disagreeing," Esta said. "But if Jack dies, it can't be by our hand."

"We must take his victory from him," Jianyu said. "We must protect the Brink."

"Not just the Brink," Esta told them. "The Order as well."

Viola cursed her displeasure, but Esta had already explained this to them. "If Jack succeeds, people will die tonight. Rich people—*important* people. Not the kind of people that let things go."

"The Inner Circle," Jianyu said. "We should begin there. He would destroy them all if he could."

"The High Princept?" Harte wondered.

"Maybe," she said, wishing they'd taken the time to learn more while they were in the future. "Ruby will try to stay close to him and signal us if there's anything happening, and Viola will stay close to Ruby," Esta said before Viola could interrupt.

Viola huffed her agreement. "Finally you talk some sense."

"The most important thing is to keep the attack from happening, and if it does happen, we have to protect the Order. The fate of every Mageus in this country for another century depends on that."

"So it has come to this," Jianyu said. "Our only chance is to help the very people who would destroy us or risk being destroyed ourselves."

Viola cursed. "First you want us to save the Brink, the terrible magic that can rip our very lives apart, and now we must save the men who would kill us where we stand? So much risk, and for what? If we succeed, everything will go back to how it was. The Brink will stand. The Order will survive. And those of us who have the old magic will be no better off."

Esta hated that she was right. "We can still stop Jack," she reminded Viola. "Harte and I saw what happened when he had power. I know this isn't the situation we hoped for, but we can still change things. We can stop that other future from happening."

"The Conclave isn't the end," Harte said. "We still have the sigils."

"You mean if we don't all end up dead," Viola said darkly.

"That's not going to happen," Harte told them.

"It might. We don't know what Nibsy has planned," Viola argued.

"Thanks to Yonatan and some of the others, Nibsy will likely be too busy dealing with a minor uprising tonight to bother with us," Jianyu said.

"They agreed?" Cela asked.

"You were right," he told her. "They were more than willing to help."

"What are you talking about?" Esta asked.

"It was Cela's idea," Jianyu said.

"I only suggested that maybe you all should include the others in this," Cela told them.

Esta's stomach sank. "It's too dangerous."

"They live with danger every day, Esta." Cela shook her head. "I've spent enough time here listening to conversations and learning who these people are that I understand why they want to help. Nibsy Lorcan took everything from them, and they're ready to take some of that back. They've never been cowards. Isn't that why you saved them?" she asked Viola.

Viola was forced to admit that it was.

"The people living in this building, the ones you've been so good to protect, are the ones who *didn't* break," Cela reminded them. "They didn't break then, and they won't now."

"They might not wear the mark," Jianyu told her. "But they are still loyal to what the Devil's Own was supposed to stand for. Not to a man or a building, but to an ideal."

"They're going to wage war on the Strega?" Esta asked.

"No. They're going to demand an end to Nibsy Lorcan's rule," Jianyu told them. "Even if Nibsy himself is not distracted, they will occupy the people he has left. They will do what they can to give us a chance."

A chance. It almost seemed like too much to hope for, but Esta would take it.

Eliminating Thoth and taking the Book back from Jack wouldn't solve the problem of the Order's control over the city or the danger of the Brink, but it would give those who had the old magic a chance. At least Jack wouldn't be a threat. At least the path of history could come closer to what should have been: There would be no DAM Act without Jack's attack on the Conclave, no Reticulum without his possession of the Book. No President Grew. And maybe one day they could do more.

"If we can get the Book from Jack, a different future is still possible," Esta said. "As long as we stop Jack tonight, we can start again. We know where the artifacts are waiting. We know how to use the Book. And we have Morgan's papers, along with all the secrets the men in the Order might want to hide. The Conclave is just the beginning."

She could feel Harte looking at her, and she knew what he was thinking—about the Book and the artifacts. About what it would cost her to use them to destroy the Brink.

Golde knocked on the doorframe to announce her arrival. "I'm sorry to interrupt," she told them. "I know you're busy, but there's something that's happened. Something you should know. My Josef—he's gone."

AN UNEXPECTED VISITOR

Bella Strega

Josef Salzer was a coward. The boy was so terrified of the choice he'd made that he was shaking like he had a palsy. He's been a coward to let his mother keep him from taking the mark months ago, and he was a coward now. But at least he had turned out to be a useful one.

"And Esta believes they can use the sigils to trap this demon?" he asked the boy.

Josef nodded. "That's their plan. They're going to go to the Conclave and try to find Jack Grew before he can attack anyone. Once they unmake the monster that's inside him, they'll take the Book."

"You've seen this ritual?" James asked. "With your own eyes?"

"She took care of the curse on that Chinaman's arm," Josef told him. "I was one who helped. I held one of those magic discs they have while it was spinning like a ball of light. And then Esta stepped inside to work on that curse. She broke it too. Healed him up fine. Then we all stopped our discs so they could both get free."

James' interest peaked. "She was trapped?"

"I don't know," Josef said, looking suddenly even more frightened—if that were even possible. "I suppose she was."

James considered this news and felt the Aether lurch around him in ways that made his blood race. That wretched hum still pulsed in the background, but it was barely noticeable now. Barely a nuisance.

With a small nod, he let Murphy know to dispose of the kid, and he made his way back to the privacy of his apartments, where he could study the diary.

It remained mostly unreadable, but more had been revealed—enough that he could tell the Salzer kid hadn't been lying. The sigils were part of it.

He leaned back in his chair and considered the problem in front of him. He'd known since the beginning that he would need someone with an affinity like Esta's to touch the power in the Book. If the sigils could trap a demon, perhaps they could trap her power as well.

No wonder the Aether had urged patience for so long.

He'd let Esta and the others take all the risks. Once Jack Grew had been taken care of and the demon had been destroyed, James would make his move.

One by one he'd let her watch as he destroyed her friends, plucking away her layers of protection. He'd enjoy seeing the end of those who should have been following him all along. He'd make them regret their choices. Jianyu, Viola, and the Sundren trash that trailed behind them.

His only regret was that there wouldn't be time to savor Darrigan's end. After all that damned magician had done to him, after all he'd put James through . . . But obtaining the Book was more important than enjoying Darrigan's pain. His own *future* was more important.

And then, when Esta was at her weakest, when she had no one to step in and save her, he'd take *everything*.

He took the silver gorgon's head from where he kept it beneath his shirt. It wasn't exactly comfortable to walk around with the hard metal tucked under his arm, but it was necessary. He'd had the replica made not long after he'd taken it from Saunders. From the very beginning he'd known that possessing the cane would unlock control over the Devil's Own, but he'd expected it to put a target on his back as well. Just as it had for his old boss. Unlike Dolph, however, James was smart enough to protect what was his.

If Dolph could take Leena's affinity and place it into that bit of silver, why couldn't he do the same with Esta's? Once he had her magic, he could use it at will. And once he had the Book, he was one step closer to unlocking its power.

Parts of the future might still be undetermined, but the diary showed him what was certain: Esta would attempt to regain the Book. He'd allow her to, just as he'd allow her to take care of the unfortunate issue of whatever it was living within Jack Grew.

And then Esta Filosik would die.

THE INFINITE NOW

As the carriage carrying them toward the Conclave rattled on through the city, Esta could not help but think of a night not so long ago when she'd sat in another carriage next to Harte. That night, she'd planned to betray him. It hadn't mattered that she'd felt a connection to him like she'd never felt with anyone else. That night she'd forced herself to see him only as the Magician, as her opponent and enemy. Because she'd believed that the future of magic had been riding on her choices.

She hadn't exactly been wrong. Everything *had* been riding on that night. But Esta hadn't understood *anything*. Because she believed the Professor, because she'd trusted him to guide her—because she wanted to be worthy of his approval—she'd made the wrong decision.

Tonight would be different. The world, again, was hanging in the balance, but this time she knew who she was fighting for. She knew who she was fighting *with*. Tonight she and Harte would stand together against the Order, against Nibsy as well. And with any luck, together, they would change the course of time.

"Do you remember the night we took the artifacts from Khafre Hall?" Harte asked as though reading the direction of her thoughts.

"*We?*" She turned toward him all mock offense. "If memory serves, *you* were the one who took them. And you left *me* sitting onstage in a room full of people who would have cheerfully murdered me if they had the chance." There was no anger in her tone, though. Only distant amusement. She nestled into him more. "Or am I thinking of someone else?"

"Definitely someone else," Harte agreed, all false innocence. "I would never—"

"You would," she corrected, slipping her arm through his. She tilted her face up to his. Their lips were inches apart, and she could smell the mint on his breath, the soft scent of his skin, clean and warm, and that indefinable scent that was only Harte. "You *definitely* would. Apparently I go for that sort of thing."

"Thank god for that," he said, his stormy eyes dancing.

Her smile slipped from her face. "It was raining that night."

"Better than this insidious cold," Harte told her, rubbing his hands to warm them. "In the middle of the summer's heat, I always think I want winter to come, until it actually arrives."

"I didn't want to leave," she said, still remembering that night. "I didn't want to betray you or to leave you behind."

She'd gone back through time to stop the Magician, but instead she'd found a home. She'd hated every second of the drive to Khafre Hall, because she had known what was coming. Once she had her cuff—along with the Book—she had known she had to betray him. And she'd believed that there was no coming back. By then she'd come to love the city as it had been and the people she'd met there. If she were honest, by then she'd come to love Harte.

But then, maybe she'd loved him from the beginning, just as she'd always loved the city.

In all its seasons. Through all its years and ages, she'd never wanted to live anywhere else. While Harte had always wanted to escape, this island of Manhattan had been Esta's only home, and even when she'd been able to leave, nowhere else had ever quite fit her the way these streets did. Nothing except for Harte had felt as right to her as choosing to come back.

"I never should have chosen anyone but you," she told him.

He lifted their interlocked hands to his mouth and placed a soft kiss on the back of hers. His stormy eyes never left hers. "You never have to choose again. Tonight it's both of us together. Or it's nothing at all."

But she wasn't sure he was right.

She hadn't told Harte about all the things she'd seen as she fell through time to find him. At first, it had been hard enough to remember or to know whether any of it was real. But in the past weeks, those memories had grown more certain, more insistent. The more she'd thought about what she'd seen when she was caught in time, the more she'd started to wonder if those visions held the answer to the final, unthinkable fate that Nibsy's diary had revealed.

They were nearly there. Outside the carriage window, Esta could see the blade of the Flatiron Building. At its base, Madison Square Park was lit by hundreds of glowing luminaries, and beyond that the enormous structure of the Garden was lit like a temple.

In her own time, Madison Square Garden was in a completely different location. It had been moved in the 1920s and then rebuilt again in the 1960s. The Garden she'd grown up with was the longest-standing and perhaps the most iconic. But the enormous, round arena that stood atop Penn Station wasn't nearly as beautiful or striking as the ornate building that stood on the corner of Thirty-Sixth Street and Madison Avenue in 1902. This version of the Garden was barely a decade old, and it would be a few years still before its famed architect would be murdered on the rooftop he'd designed by the jealous husband of a showgirl he'd been sleeping with. It had the look of a Moorish palace, with its roof lined with towers that looked like minarets.

The tallest of the towers soared over the park, rising like a finger pointing toward the heavens. It was only *barely* smaller than the Flatiron Building itself. At the top of the tower, Augustus Saint-Gaudens' *Diana* glistened in gold, her naked body caught in an elegant arabesque as she held her bow aloft, ready for the hunt.

Esta could see why the Order had chosen this location for their Conclave. The beauty and size of the building, and the grandeur of it as well, lent an immediate air of power and importance. The Flatiron Building nearby was a statement of the city's innovation, a preview of the modern era to come. The entire area around Madison Square was awash with light. Electric bulbs had been strung along the walkways of the parks, and enormous columns of light shot up from the rooftops of nearby buildings. The roof of the Garden was perhaps the brightest spot of all.

That was where it would happen. Thanks to Ruby, they knew for sure that the final ritual would be held on the rooftop of the Garden. There, with the grid of the city visible below, the Order would use an electrical current to replicate the power of the stones and the Book. If Jack was to attack, he would do it *there* high above the city streets, at the apex of the Conclave, during that final, essential ritual. If they wanted to stop him, if they wanted to take back the Book and eliminate Thoth, they had to do it before that final ritual.

The cold energy coming from the silvery disks Esta carried beneath her cloak gave her a chill that had nothing to do with the wintery night air. Their plan could work. If they found Jack in time, they could corner him and use the sigils to trap him—to contain Thoth so that she could destroy the creature he'd become. Once that was done, they could stop whatever attack he intended.

It was a simple enough plan, but so much could go wrong. If the words in Nibsy's diary had any truth to them, a lot likely would.

As traffic inched along, bringing them ever closer to the building and their awaiting fate, Esta turned to Harte. "There's something I need you to promise me."

"Anything," he told her without any hesitation. But there was a question in his storm-colored eyes.

"There's a distinct possibility this won't end well," she told him.

"Esta—"

"No, Harte, listen. I saw what was written in that diary, the same as you. And as much as I want to ignore it, we can't."

"I'm not going to kill you," he told her. "I *couldn't*."

"You could," she said softly. "The words on that diary page prove it's a possibility, however unlikely it might feel."

His brows snapped together in frustration. "I'm not having this discussion. We are going to make it out of this tonight, and we're to make it out together."

"I hope so," she told him. The sureness in his voice had brushed away some of the icy dread clinging to her. "But I trust you, Harte. I know that you wouldn't hurt me. If you killed me in some version of tonight, you must have had a reason, and that reason must have been an outcome worse than my death."

"There is no worse outcome for me than your death," he told her.

He was wrong. She'd seen it herself, hadn't she? She'd seen futures more terrible than death, and she'd felt a terrifying nothingness that waited as a possibility lodged in time.

Esta fought back the tears that threatened. "I feel the exact same way, Harte. But whatever happens in there, I need you to promise me that you'll do whatever you have to in order to keep Nibsy from winning. Especially if he tries to take my affinity."

Harte went very still. "How could he?"

"If he got hold of the sigils—" She stopped. It felt too dangerous even to utter it out loud. But she'd seen the world as it would be if the Brink fell.

"We have Viola," Harte reminded her. "Nibsy won't get anywhere near you or those discs."

Esta leaned her head on his shoulder. "All I'm saying is that if everything goes wrong and if there is no other option, you should do whatever you need to do to keep him from winning."

"He can't win if he's dead," Harte said.

"But you can't kill him," Esta reminded him. "Even if I'm about to die. Even if everything else is falling apart. If there's any chance at all that you or the others can get away, there has to be someone to send the girl forward to. Or it will doom everyone." She glanced at him. "Unless you know?"

Harte was frowning at her. He shook his head slightly.

It meant that there was a good chance that the fate they'd read in Nibsy's diary would be realized tonight. It felt impossible. How could she believe Harte would ever hurt her, much less kill her outright? Unless . . .

A thought occurred to her then, one that she'd been trying to ignore ever since she'd read those words written in Nibsy's own hand. There *were* fates worse than dying. She'd seen the possibility of a world torn apart. She also remembered the pain and terror of nearly being torn apart herself when she'd originally brought the Book to Professor Lachlan and he'd tried to take her affinity to control it.

There had been a reason Professor Lachlan had wanted them to return to the past. Maybe it was because the diary had shown him how to win.

"There might not be a choice," she whispered, horrified at the thought of it. "If we're not successful tonight, if Nibsy somehow gets the upper hand . . ." She couldn't bring herself to finish that statement. "It might be the only way to stop him."

Confusion shadowed Harte's expression. "What, exactly, are you saying, Esta?"

"The diary," she told him. "Maybe it doesn't show the worst-case scenario. If he managed to get control of the Book, or worse . . . control over my power? Maybe it isn't Nibsy who has to die tonight. Maybe it's me."

"*No,*" Harte said. "I refuse to believe that's possible. It's not going to happen. I won't *allow* that to happen."

"Harte . . ." She closed her eyes, because she couldn't look at him, not when she asked *this* of him. "If Nibsy is about to win—if the worst has happened and he somehow manages to get control of my affinity—you have to take me out of the equation."

"No, Esta—"

"We *cannot* allow Nibsy to control the Book," she said, her mind spinning furiously. "Ever since that day in the library, I've been trying to figure out why the Professor would have wanted us to come back here. I knew there had to be a trap of some sort. I knew he had to have some bigger plan. Maybe it's been right in front of us the whole time. He needs my power to control the Book. It's possible he'll find a way to get it."

"I would kill him first," Harte vowed.

"But you *can't*. The girl has to go forward, or everything we've been through—all that we've done and all that we've lost—will have been for nothing. If she goes forward, we still have a chance to start again. If she goes forward, maybe in another time line there's some other possibility where we *do* win. But if that girl doesn't go forward, or if there's no one waiting to send her back, then it's over."

A heavy silence filled the carriage before Harte responded.

"You're not actually asking me to kill you, Esta?" he asked, his voice straining with emotion. He pulled away from her. "Absolutely not."

"If everything is falling apart, you might have to, Harte," she told him. "Nibsy *cannot* be allowed to control the Book with my affinity. He cannot be allowed to have that kind of power. If he has me, if I'm going to die anyway, then take the possibility of victory away from him. It would be a mercy."

"I can't," Harte said, his voice breaking a little. "It's not possible."

"But it is. You've already done it," she told him. "Don't you see? We found that book eighty years from now. It's already happened. There is a time line where you do kill me, and because you do, Nibsy doesn't win. He ends up a bitter old man, waiting for a future that never comes."

"Please, don't ask this of me," he told her, his voice breaking. "Even if the world is cracking in two. Even if the Brink is about to erupt and everything will end because of it. I can't be the one."

"You're the *only* one who can, Harte. You're the only one I would trust with this." She cupped his face gently and forced him to look at her. "My life isn't worth the entire world."

"*Yes*, it is," he told her, taking her hand from his face and clasping it in both of his. "It *absolutely* is." His eyes were shadowed with pain, their stormy depths like the wave-tossed sea. "Don't you understand? Everything I've done since I decided to stay in the city, since I met you on the bridge that day, has been for you. To me, you're the only thing that matters. The world can go to hell if you're not here in it."

His words made her feel like she would break into a million pieces, but she couldn't let them sway her. "You don't really mean that," she told him.

"I do," he said softly.

"Promise me, Harte," she whispered, begging him. "Please. I need to walk in there knowing that there is no possibility of Nibsy winning. *Please*."

"Fine," he told her. "I'll promise. But only because I'm not going to ever need to make good on it. We're going to do this, Esta. We have our way in, and we know how to stop Jack. Nibsy is not going to touch you. It's going to be okay." He kissed her then with an ardent fierceness that let her know just how terrified he was. And just how determined as well.

The carriage came to a stop in front of the entrance to the Garden, and before she could say anything more, it was time to face their fates. They lifted the hoods of the cloaks Ruby had stolen for them up over their heads until they shadowed their faces and hid their identities. Then Harte alighted first, reaching back to help Esta down as well.

The walls of the Garden were aglow with electric lamps that cut through the depth of the night. Flanking the door were enormous cauldrons burning with multicolored flames. She looked back only once to see Cela on top of the driver's perch, dressed in a top hat and cloak. They nodded up at her silently, and she tipped her hat at them before steering the carriage away.

Harte offered Esta his arm, and knowing that the time for argument was over, Esta accepted it. Together, they followed the line of robed figures up a path that glowed with electrical lights toward the Garden.

As they stepped up to the entrance and handed over their stolen tickets without any trouble at all, Esta thought that maybe she'd been wrong to demand his promise. She'd asked too much, but not because she was afraid. Tonight, fear could not drive them. Only certainty. Tonight, the future could be anything they made it. Arm in arm, they pressed into the crowd of the Conclave, walking steadily onward toward their destiny.

WHAT LAY AHEAD

On the night of the Conclave, Jack Grew didn't particularly mind being one of the faceless masses seated in the Garden. As far as he was concerned, it was better if his uncle and the rest of the Inner Circle believed he had accepted their edict to keep out of trouble. Let them assume that he was no better than one of the sheep sitting around him. At least there in the crowd, no one was paying him any attention. It would make it that much easier to step forward when the time came and accept his place as their savior.

He could not deny there was a sense of anticipation in the air that night that went beyond his own. The grand arena was filled with men from around the country, along with their wives or consorts. Many, clearly, had never been outside their own backwater towns before. Jack had enjoyed watching them as they descended from their carriages, craning their necks to look up at the buildings around the park. They marveled at the size of the Garden and at its beauty.

Perhaps some had come with the idea to wrestle control from the Order. They all had come ready to judge whether the Order still had any right to claim supremacy over the Brotherhoods. But none had any idea at all of what lay ahead. By the end of the night, the tides would have changed, and Jack himself would be the one to bring their boats to shore.

The first half of the evening's event was filled with endless speeches and posturing. He'd expected that. Planned for it. It gave him time to settle himself, to take another of the morphine cubes and let its bitter warmth fortify him. He barely paid attention as, one by one, the leaders of each of the Brotherhoods stepped forward to present themselves and their platforms to the Conclave as a whole. They spoke of their growing numbers, of the burgeoning cities, and of their plans for the future. They exposed their craven desperation for power and importance and their distinct lack of good breeding.

Jack saw the threat they posed, but unlike the Inner Circle, he understood that you couldn't simply bat them away like the annoying insects they were. They'd only come back for another try. No, the only way to deal with men like this was by giving them what they wanted—a sense that they were equals to the titans of New York. Only then could the Brotherhoods be brought together under one banner—but it wouldn't be the Inner Circle who led them.

By the time the night was over, *his* era would begin.

Eventually, the time for talking finally, *blessedly*, came to an end. The High Princept called for a brief recess to allow the group to move from the general assembly hall to the rooftop, and Jack followed along amiably, a wolf among sheep. The Book pulsed against his chest in anticipation, urging him on toward a future that could only be glorious. And within, the voice that had become his second conscience purred its approval.

The rooftop of the Garden was usually closed in the winter, but the ritual ahead required open air and a sense of drama that the vaulted hall below could not provide. Jack couldn't deny that the setting was an excellent choice. In addition to the space it afforded and the grandeur of the star-swept sky above, it provided an extraordinary view of the city beyond. The buildings already climbing toward the clouds. The electric lights turning night into day. The promise of it all. The *power* held within its streets.

The Flatiron Building, like the prow of a ship, was impressive, but it was only the newest feature of a larger, far older design. New York itself was a city made for magic, elegantly planned and meticulously designed. Now it was on the cusp of unimaginable greatness. Only here could the men from the other Brotherhoods—those from the middle and far west, who had neither polish nor cultural refinement—see that *this* city was the center of everything. Only here would they understand that a new century was just beginning, one that would carve itself out from the chaos of feral magic. A new world.

The sharpness of the icy December night was a welcome relief after the hot air that had been spouted in the preceding hours. The night sky was clear enough to view the steady progress of the constellations that watched over their proceedings. All around the roof, the towers of the Garden loomed like sentinels, dark fingers against the light of the city beyond. At the top of the highest tower, a naked Diana was illuminated from below, her arrow pointing southward toward the Bowery, as though she, too, were interested in hunting the vermin in their midst.

Along the outer perimeter of the roof, large iron cauldrons churned with flames that sent plumes of incense-laden smoke into the air. Other than alchemical lamps that had been positioned along the aisles of seats and the stars above, the cauldrons provided the only light. It gave the whole area an ancient, mystical atmosphere that it never had during the summer months, when the small stage was used for reviews featuring long-legged chorines and singers in spangled gowns. It was impressive, even to Jack's jaded eyes, but it was also perfect for his own uses. The shadows cast by the flames were exactly what he needed.

As the robed men of the various Brotherhoods began to settle them-selves into seats that had been arranged in a half circle, facing the direction of the park, Jack found the person he'd been watching for all evening. He made his way through the crowd to where Ruby Reynolds stood not far from the High Princept. He saw her stiffen when she realized he was approaching and felt pure satisfaction when he saw she understood that there was no way to avoid him without drawing attention.

"Miss Reynolds," he said, inclining his head slightly.

"Mrs. Barclay," she corrected primly, lifting her chin. She was still studying the crowd, her eyes searching for something or someone.

"I wasn't aware you'd had a wedding night," he said, amused at the way her head snapped around and by the fire in her eyes. It would be gratifying to see that fire go out. "I wonder," he drawled. "*Is* a marriage that remains unconsummated *truly* a marriage?"

"You're a pig, Jack," she told him. "And tonight you're going to get *exactly* what you deserve."

"One can hope," he told her pleasantly, and when she turned to leave, he caught her by the arm. "Best if you watch yourself tonight, Ruby. It would be a tragedy if you joined your dearly departed husband sooner rather than later."

She tried to free herself from his grasp, but before she could storm off, Jack whispered a single, ancient word.

"What did you say?" she asked, looking suddenly unsteady.

"I simply said to enjoy your evening." Then, before she could escape, he jerked her close and whispered the word again while slipping a small pistol into her hand. It was a delicate little thing with a pearl handle. Exactly the type of weapon a woman would select for herself. When he released her, Ruby had a dazed look in her eyes, and she stumbled off without a word, taking the gun along with her.

He watched her go until her hooded figure had disappeared into the crowd.

"I thought we made it clear that you weren't to make any sort of scene."

Jack turned to find his uncle and cousin standing behind him, looking sour as old women. "What were you doing with the Reynolds girl?"

"I believe she's a Barclay now," Jack said, amused despite himself. "And it wasn't I who was making the scene. She doesn't seem quite stable."

"You had your hands on her," Morgan accused.

"Yes, Uncle," Jack said. "I admit that I did take her by the arm. Gentle as a child. You might thank me for stopping her."

"Stopping her from what?" Morgan asked, his large nose twitching.

"I don't know *exactly*," Jack said, feigning confusion. "But she seemed a bit hysterical. All the talk of feral magic must have brought up terrible memories. Someone might want to check on her. I don't trust that she wouldn't do something desperate. I could go, if you'd like?"

"You're not going anywhere," Morgan said, which was the exact answer Jack had planned for. "Junior can go after the chit. You sit down and try not to get in the way. Things have gone too well so far for you to make any sort of trouble."

Jack opened his hands as if in surrender. "As you wish."

Smiling secretly to himself, he went to find a seat in the center of the audience. In his pocket, the Book felt nearly alive. It pulsed in time with the steady beating of his own heart.

An intricate piece of metalwork grew up from the rear of the stage, providing a backdrop for the Order's next act. It was a larger and more intricate version of the Tree of Life that stood in the Mysterium, high across the park. In its branches, hundreds of tiny alchemical candles threw their otherworldly glow across each of the filigreed leaves. Above those topmost branches, the upper floors of the Flatiron Building were just visible. Below, beneath the platform of the stage, his machine lay hidden. Ready and waiting to rise into a new future.

Across the park, the upper floors that comprised the Order's new headquarters were alight, a crown on the bladelike building. The windows of the ceremonial library and the new Mysterium glowed with a brilliant amber that no simple gas lamp or electric bulb could have produced. It looked much like the golden light that had been visible on the solstice so many months before—molten and powerful, created by the sort of practiced and controlled magic that could bring the country into a new future. But Jack knew the truth. It wasn't magic alone that created the effect. The Order was channeling modern electricity through the ritual there, increasing its potential exponentially.

The Mysterium would be where the evening's display began. There, a group of men from the Inner Circle would be waiting to initiate the ritual that would demonstrate their continued relevance.

Too bad Jack had gotten to those men first. Too bad the Order's great gambit was destined to fail.

The wind gusted across the rooftop, causing the people around him to shuffle slightly, shuddering from the cold, but Jack Grew barely felt the ice in the air. He placed another of the morphine cubes between his teeth and let the bitterness fortify him, allowed its heat to invigorate him.

Soon it would begin. Jack had only to watch and wait. With the Book in his pocket, with fate on his side, he would be the one to direct his destiny and bring about the Order's end.

UPRISING

Bella Strega

On the winter solstice, night came early, covering the city with a blanket of darkness that would remain undisturbed for hours to come. The longest night in the coldest part of the year marked the turning from winter toward spring. For James Lorcan, it would mark the turning of his destiny.

Far uptown, the Order would be beginning their Conclave. Men from all across the land had arrived to do what countless civilizations had done for centuries, to keep watch for the dawning of a new day. To mark a moment of rebirth. They were dressed in their finery and jewels, wrapped in the confidence of their wealth, but they could not predict what was coming.

In the Bowery, it wasn't spirits who roamed the streets that night, but men. The anger and frustration that had been slowly simmering for months beneath the uneasy peace of the surface was beginning to boil over.

James heard the shots fired in the distance, the clanging of bells, and the shouts in the streets below, but he ignored them and turned the page of the small diary. The words on the page shimmered, coming ever clearer into focus.

Tonight, all would be revealed. Tonight, his destiny would be known.

Around him, the Aether felt frantic. The buzzing drone that had plagued him for months was barely noticeable now. It bunched and lurched, stirring his anticipation. Pushing him, guiding him, as it had always done before.

A pounding sounded at his apartment door, and when he opened it, Logan was waiting on the other side. "There's a problem in the saloon."

"What kind of problem?" James asked.

Logan grimaced, as fearful and uncomfortable as ever, despite the new ink he wore on the underside of his wrist. "It's hard to explain."

The Aether lurched, murmuring its uncertainty.

"Torrio?" James asked. The damned Five Pointer had been unsettled ever since he and his men had torn the Strega to pieces fighting the Hip Sing highbinders.

"It's not Torrio or the Chinese guys," Logan told him. "I don't know who they are, but there's a lot of them. There's hardly a place to stand. They're screaming and chanting. They're shouting for *you*."

The Aether trembled then, urging him on. "It's nothing but a distraction."

"It's an *uprising*," Logan argued. "They're demanding to speak to you tonight, or they're threatening to tear the place apart. You need to go down there before everything blows up."

"What do I care?" James told him. The Strega had always been a means to an end. After tonight, he'd have far more to rule over than a sordid saloon on the Bowery. "Let them have it."

Logan stared at him, incredulous. But then, how could he possibly understand?

The Aether leaped and danced in anticipation. The vibrations were so frantic now he could no longer hear the buzzing that had bothered him for months.

"It's starting," he told Logan. And when the night was over, he would hold the key to controlling far more than a simple Bowery barroom. Soon he would have the Book of Mysteries and everything he needed to unlock its power.

He'd have the world itself in the palm of his hand.

"Get your coat," he told Logan. "I need you to come with me."

DEVIATIONS

Madison Square Garden

J ianyu was growing impatient. He and Viola were waiting on the main level of the Garden for some sign of Ruby Reynolds, who should have been along before now. He looked up at the grand clock at the end of the cavernous hall and wondered what was keeping her—and how much longer they could afford to wait.

It was not that he had any fear of being discovered. Both of them were still wrapped in his affinity, hidden from sight within the strands of light, just as they had been since the beginning of the evening. They had slipped into the hall with the rest of the attendees, rich men and women who had come from across the continent to celebrate the solstice and decide the fate of their Brotherhoods. While men who were boiling with fear and raging with hate had given speech after speech, he and Viola had stolen away from the crowd and taken the opportunity to search the building for some sign of what Jack was planning.

In the end, their search had turned up nothing. The corridors and back rooms were clear of any obvious danger, and nothing seemed amiss on the roof either. It would have been easier had they found some small hint as to what Jack had in store. Without any clues, all they could do was watch and wait.

But first they had to find Ruby.

"She'll be here," Viola said, but Jianyu wondered who she was trying to convince—him or herself. She was vibrating with her usual impatience, but tonight there was an edge to it.

Ruby should have already arrived. She was supposed to have slipped away from her escorts while the crowd found their seats on the roof above, long before the ritual was to begin. Jianyu alone could have ferried her out to the carriage where Cela and Abel would be waiting to take her back to the safe house, but Viola had insisted on being involved.

"We cannot wait much longer," Jianyu told her. Cela and her brother would not be able to circle the block very many times before someone noticed their carriage.

There were many reasons that Jianyu had fought to keep the Johnsons outside the Garden that night. After the attack on the *New York Age's* offices and Viola's subsequent decision to end the men who had perpetrated it, the Order clearly suspected a connection between the Mageus and the Negro Community. They would not have requested a staff of only white workers for the evening's festivities otherwise. Because there would have been no way for the Johnsons to blend in without discovery, Jianyu had refused to put either Cela or her brother at any more risk than they already were.

She had been livid, but it was better this way. With Cela safely outside, he could focus on the dangers ahead without worrying about which of them might touch her. He would get through the night—he would *live* through the night—and when it was over, only then would he allow himself to consider what they had spoken about earlier. Only then would he let himself remember the feel of her lips against his.

"There," Viola said, pointing toward a single robed figure descending the back staircase. The woman's hood had flopped back as though Ruby did not care who saw that she was not where she was supposed to be. "See? I told you she would come."

But Ruby did not immediately head for the place where they had agreed to meet. Instead, she paused at the base of the stairs and considered her options. When she reached the midpoint of the room, she stopped and looked around as though she did not know where she was supposed to be.

Jianyu hesitated.

"Andiamo," Viola said, impatient as ever. "You wanted her to come, and now you hesitate. What are you waiting for?"

Jianyu frowned, unsure of the reason. But he waited longer still, until Ruby began moving in their direction. She stopped short of their meeting place.

"Hello?" Ruby whispered, searching the empty room for some sign.

Only then did Jianyu release the light, making them both visible once more.

Ruby let out a relieved breath at their appearance. "Thank heavens," she said in a hurried breath. "You have to come with me."

"No," he told her. "Cela has already been waiting too long. Harte and Esta will have expected us by now."

But Ruby was taking Viola's hand. "Please, you must come. You have to see this."

"Viola," Jianyu warned, because he could see that she was already softening. "This is not the plan. We are supposed to get her outside, remember? The whole point was to get her to safety."

"You must come," Ruby urged again. "Please. Come this way, and I can show you . . ." She was already leading Viola in the opposite direction of the exit.

"Stop," he said. "We need to get you outside. Cela cannot wait forever, not without drawing attention."

"But this is important," Ruby said, pleading to Viola. "It's the machine. Jack's machine. It's here."

Jianyu went very still. "Are you certain?" There were very few things that could have turned his feet from the path they had decided upon, but the mention of the machine, the terrible contraption that Jack had designed to eliminate those with the old magic, was one.

How could they have missed something so large? "We checked the entire building," he told her. "We found no sign of the machine."

"You didn't check everywhere," she said. "Hurry. We don't have time to waste. He's going to use it tonight. And if that happens, everyone within a hundred miles with the old magic will die."

Jianyu looked back toward the entrance of the Garden and then again at the large clock hanging over the main floor. Cela would be waiting for Ruby. There was no time to tell her of any change in their plans, not before the final events of the evening began. But if the machine was there, somewhere in that building, they needed to find it.

They needed to destroy it.

"Fine," he told Ruby and Viola both. "Take us to the machine, but be quick. There is no time to waste."

They hurried through the empty arena to a door hidden by the fabric that had been draped to cover the bare brick of the walls. It was a door that he had not discovered in all his trips to map the floor plan of the arena.

"This way." Ruby moved back the fabric so they could enter. "It's just down here."

The hallway beyond was narrow and dark, lit only by the flickering of the occasional dim bulb. They followed the hall along the length of the arena, and when they turned a corner and found another doorway, he felt the cold warning and stopped.

"Quickly," Ruby urged again.

Hair rose along the nape of his neck. "The machine is down there?"

Ruby nodded. "It's just a little farther."

"Well?" Viola asked, looking as uncomfortable about the cold energy emanating from the door as he felt.

"Can you sense anything?" he asked.

"No one," Viola told him. "But then, I couldn't sense Jack before. So why should I now?" Her mouth tightened. "We could get the others?"

They'd already wasted too much time. Esta and Darrigan were waiting on the rooftop above, and Cela was expecting him, but if the machine was there, it could not wait. Not if Jack planned to use it that night.

He shook his head. "There is no time for the others."

"Wait here," Viola told Ruby. She handed her the copy of Libitina that Esta had brought back from another time. "If anyone comes, you use this." Then she turned to Jianyu. "Let's go."

Opening the light, he wrapped Viola in his magic, and they stepped inside. But the second he crossed the threshold, he felt a shift. Cold pulsed around him, and he heard a grinding of metal as a barred gate began to descend across the entrance of the chamber.

Instantly, he released his affinity and lunged for the opening they had just passed through, but when his hands hit the bars, he pulled back. They were cold as ice, charmed or infused with some dangerous, corrupted magic.

"Ruby," Viola said. "Quickly. My knife."

Ruby's eyes were wide and unseeing. She stood, staring into nothing, the knife dangling from her fingertips.

"*Ruby*," Viola called again.

But Ruby showed no signs of hearing her. She continued to stare, and her pupils were so dilated that they nearly overwhelmed the green. The knife dropped, clanging to the floor.

Without another word, Ruby turned and left them there, even as Viola called to her.

They were alone. Trapped in the dark, where no one would think to look for them.

Somewhere in the distance, a thunderous crack echoed, and the building began to quake.

CONSECRATION

Harte stood next to Esta at the edge of the crowded rooftop, waiting for Jianyu and Viola amid the crush of robed men. He knew their types. He'd met men like them in St. Louis and San Francisco, and he'd heard about Esta's brushes with their brothers in Colorado. He knew what each of them was capable of, but he paid them little attention. Jack was the true danger that night.

Jack, however, didn't seem to be in any hurry. He'd been careful to keep himself in the middle of the crowd, where it was impossible to get him alone and corner him with the sigils. He also didn't seem to be planning or plotting anything.

"Why is he just sitting there?" Esta whispered, pulling her cloak low over her forehead to keep from being seen. "Shouldn't he be *doing* something by now? Preparing or . . . *something*?"

"I don't know," Harte said. He didn't particularly *want* Jack to do anything, but the lack of action didn't make him feel any safer.

She frowned. "So far he looks as bored as we are."

"Maybe that's the point?" Harte studied Jack. He looked far too relaxed, too confident. Like he was already sure that he would succeed.

Harte looked around the rooftop again, but other than the strange alchemical torches and flickering cauldrons, nothing seemed capable of causing the kind of destruction Jack had to have been planning.

"I'd feel better if Viola and Jianyu were here," Esta whispered. "What do you think is keeping them?"

"They had to wait for Ruby," he reminded her. "It's likely she couldn't slip away as quickly as she'd planned. She knew how important it was not to call attention to her departure."

"Well, they'd better hurry."

Suddenly, a drumroll interrupted the softly murmured conversations. The robed men who were still standing and milling about began to shuffle quickly toward their seats, while those already sitting straightened a little taller to see what was happening as the lights around the rooftop flickered and dimmed.

"It's starting," Esta whispered.

And Jack still hadn't made any move. He was still just sitting there in the middle of the row, just to the left of the stage, shoulder to shoulder with the men next to him. It would have been impossible for him to do *anything* without drawing attention to himself.

The drumroll continued, swelling in volume and intensity, until the crack of a rim shot ended in a flash of light that revealed a line of barely clad women at the back of the seating.

"Figures," Esta muttered, sounding annoyed with the whole scene.

Harte knew it had been nothing more than simple stage magic. There was no burst of hot or cold energy, but the illusion was effective enough to have the crowd gasping and murmuring with excitement. Or perhaps that was caused by the lack of clothing on the women. They were dressed in nothing more than glimmering silk sarongs, and their bodies had been painted the same gold as the Diana that balanced above them. Around their necks hung cut crystals, each to symbolize a digit of the Philosopher's Hand: the key, the crown, the lantern, the star, and the moon.

Another drumroll began, and the women parted to reveal five robed men.

"That must be the Inner Circle," Esta whispered.

The group followed the women who were silently processing down the middle aisle, toward the stage that had been erected on the side of the roof facing the park and the Flatiron Building. Slowly they walked, with every eye on the roof watching the sway of their hips as they continued up to the stage and then began to climb.

On the stage, an iron tree glimmered with a hundred lights. It was large enough for the women to sit within its branches, Harte realized. Like gilded birds, they took their places, lounging in positions to best display their impressive. . . assets. And the crystals that hung around their necks.

The Inner Circle mounted the stage not far behind them. Unlike the dark robes worn by the other Brotherhoods, the old men of the Inner Circle were dressed in ceremonial robes made of golden silk. The High Princept was easily recognizable in silk so white it seemed almost to reflect the light of the moon. Harte supposed that the outfit was meant to give him a regal appearance, but the winter wind made the fabric of his robe billow and made the old man look small and almost shriveled in comparison.

The Princept raised his arms, and the crowd grew silent.

"We welcome to our city our fellow brothers of the occult sciences. To the steadfast men of the Veiled Prophet Society, we bid welcome. As above . . ."

An entire section that could only have been the delegates from St. Louis responded, droning, "So below."

"To the courageous settlers of the west, the Syndicate, we bid welcome. As above . . ."

Again a portion of the rooftop erupted in answer: "So below."

"And finally, our newest brothers, those who guard our westernmost shores, the Vigilance Committee. We bid you welcome. As above . . ."

"So below" came the echoing reply.

"As above, so below, and so we bid all welcome to our city, to this bastion of hope and prosperity," the Princept said. "From its earliest days, this island has been a shining light. Centuries ago, it served as a foothold in the wilderness, and the men who carved civilization out of chaos became exemplars of what was possible for the worthy in this great and noble land. And so, on this darkest night in the deepest part of the year, we commemorate their work and bind ourselves to the mission of the Brotherhoods. We gather to reconsecrate ourselves to the power of the occult sciences as we look onward into the new century."

The crowd erupted into applause, and the Princept basked in their adulation. Harte watched the muscle in Jack's jaw twitch as he clapped slowly along with the rest. The Princept raised his hands to quiet the crowd before he continued.

"For decades now, the Order of Ortus Aurea has protected this great city from the darkness threatened by feral magic. During that time, we have led all those worthy of the occult sciences into a new, golden dawn. For more than a century, our work here has protected this city, and the country beyond."

Again came a smattering of applause, but this time it seemed contained to the portion of the roof where the Order sat.

Harte sighed. "They do love droning on about nothing, don't they?"

Esta nodded, biting back a smile. "Endlessly."

"Our Founders saw the threat to these shores, the creeping danger of feral magic, and were not satisfied to allow the danger to go unchecked. They were determined to protect this land of opportunity and plenty, and they used their great skills—their sacred artifacts—to protect the innocent. Their fortifications have stood steadfast, and tonight we reconfirm our commitment to this noble calling and our commitment to this nation and its people. Tonight we reconsecrate the power that has been at the heart of our country's safety for so long. Tonight we reaffirm our commitment to these streets and to the land beyond."

"Where are they?" Esta wondered again, looking back over her shoulder to the entrance of the roof. "They should *definitely* have been here by now."

"They will be," Harte told her, hoping he was right.

Esta frowned, searching the crowd on the rooftop. "They'd better be. We can't do this alone."

Out of nowhere, a thunderous crack echoed through the air, and the top of the Flatiron Building flashed, bursting with light. Harte watched as the light grew into a churning ball of otherworldly flame, and then, suddenly, a bolt of something that looked like amber-colored lightning shot out through the crystalline windows of the Mysterium to the fountain at the center of Madison Square Park.

The crowd on the roof gasped in appreciation and applauded again.

Worth Square was barely big enough to be considered a park, and its obelisk—a tombstone for some long-dead general—was a modern piece, not anything as large or authentic as the Egyptian obelisk that stood in Central Park. Now, though, everyone's eyes were being drawn to that small plot of land. The monument had started to glow from within, the gray stone turning brighter and brighter, until another thunderous crack echoed through the air and another bolt of light erupted from its tip and shot across the park, meeting the bolt from the Mysterium.

As the two lines of energy intersected in the center of the park, it formed a ball of light that started to swell. As it expanded, the alchemical flames that had illuminated the park leaped and danced, and the cement pathways of the night-dark park began to glow.

Harte realized then what he maybe should have realized before: The walkways of the park formed another symbol. Another *sigil*. Perhaps it wasn't as ornate or intricate as the one on the Book or the ones carved into the silver discs, but as those pathways turned to shimmering, he couldn't deny the cold power that was rising into the air.

Hadn't Ruby told them that the Order built the city—designed the very grid of streets—to channel occult power? Hadn't Jianyu and Viola explained how the Manhattan Solstice had transformed those streets during the Golden Hour? Harte hadn't quite understood, but now he did.

The Order no longer had its artifacts or the Book of Mysteries. They'd lost Newton's Sigils as well. But they had this, the city itself. The power that had somehow been built into it as part of the design. This was how the Order would convince the other Brotherhoods of their supremacy.

This was how they would attempt to recharge the Brink . . . and this would be where Jack would attack. He'd use this display somehow in his attempt to bring everything down around them.

But as the sidewalks of Madison Square Park burned bright, the pathways like carpets of undulating flame, Jack did not make a move.

"Why isn't he *doing* anything?" Esta asked. "And where are Viola and Jianyu?"

Harte didn't have answers to either of those questions. He was too busy trying to predict what might happen next.

"Something's wrong," Esta told him. "We need to find them."

"No," he said, touching her arm softly to steady her. "We need to stay here with Jack. We have to trust them."

There was something stirring in the air, a strange energy that had his hair rising and his instincts sparking.

"My brothers," the Princept called out. "Behold the mastery we have attained. Behold our city alive with power, ready to accept the future fate has held in store."

Another crack sounded, this time closer yet, and Harte jerked Esta back to protect her, ducking like everyone else on that roof as sparks flew from the tallest of the Garden's towers. High above, the goddess Diana began to glow as energy coursed through her body. She was a woman aflame, and then, just when she had turned nearly incandescent, the energy being channeled through her bolted out from the tip of her arrow and careened through the air to join the other currents in the park below.

The crowd murmured in appreciation as the cauldrons flashed, their colored flames rising into the night, and the pathways of the park pulsed with light. And then, little by little, the light from the park began to move. To *spread*. The bright energy might have been magic or electric or something between, but it moved like molten molasses creeping toward the pathways of the streets, and little by little, it began to light the city from within.

OVERCHARGED

Jack watched as the three bolts of light came together as one in the center of the park and reveled in the feel of electricity and power thick in the air. Everything was going exactly to plan. The Order had no idea that it had already initiated its own inevitable end.

Already, the electrical charges were coursing into the center of the park, hitting the precise location where multiple ley lines came together. The Order had believed themselves to be so clever, using the ley lines to carry the charge to the Brink. They'd believed it would be enough to simply give the magic surrounding the city a bit more energy, creating a visual demonstration that would keep their would-be usurpers quiet. What they *didn't* realize was that the amplification of the ley lines, focused as they were through the grid of the city, could do more than illuminate the Brink. It could destroy it.

The Order hadn't considered what would happen if the Brink were to be *overcharged*. They never suspected that the trustworthy minions they'd put in charge of starting the ritual might fail to stop it at the appropriate time. They had no idea how easily the Brink could shatter and fall, and with it, their control over the city.

But Jack would never allow the danger of feral magic once contained by the Brink to escape and pollute the country beyond. Once the Brink had fallen, Jack himself would step forward with the answer. With the push of a lever, he would show the Brotherhoods what the future could be. Not an antiquated boundary, limited by the magic of a bygone world, but a glorious machine. He would make them believe in what was possible—a world filled with machines capable of cleansing the entire continent.

Jack reached into his pocket and let his fingertips stroke the cracked and aged leather of the Ars Arcana. A voice inside him whispered of a promised future, of a glorious rise, and he thought he could *almost* feel the power within those pages crackle and pulse. Ever since he'd set himself on this path, as his plans had begun to come together over the past few weeks, the Book had seemed different somehow. Stronger. The power in those pages felt as though it was ready to awaken, and the voice inside him whispered that if he were brave enough, he could grasp it. *Use* it. Bend it to his will.

Murmuring a string of ancient syllables under his breath, Jack traced the symbol on the cover, and he felt the Book shudder. The cauldrons around the edges of the roof had been burning steadily with undulating flames of every color, but now, called forth by his words, they began to smoke. Unnoticed by those on the rooftop too interested in the pyrotechnics lighting the park below, a dark greenish-gray fog began to creep and grow.

By now the pathways of the park were molten with energy. Like lava, it flowed outward, following the grid that had been designed so many years ago to channel the power deep within the city's core. Steadily, the light flowed and spread toward the land's end, where the dark strip of water—and the Brink—was waiting.

OUT OF SIGHT

Cela was still near livid at Jianyu for keeping her out of their plans. She wasn't much happier with her brother, who'd agreed without hesitation that it was better for her to stay *outside* and wait.

Outside. As though anything was going to happen *outside*. She huffed to herself, annoyed at the heavy-handedness of the men in her life.

"I know you're not happy, but those noises you're making aren't going to convince me it's a good idea to go in there," Abel said from his seat on the driver's perch.

"Ruby should've been out by now," Cela told him. They'd been circling the blocks around Madison Square for the better part of an hour, waiting for some sign that things were progressing as planned inside, but none had come. The blond heiress was long overdue.

"There's still time," Abel said, steady as ever. "The final ritual doesn't even start until after midnight."

"Still," she said. "There should have been some sign by now."

"If something has gone wrong, we'd know."

"How?" she asked.

"We just would," Abel told her. But she realized he was sounding less sure by the minute.

"I still don't see why we couldn't help."

"We are helping," he told her. "Someone has to be the getaway driver."

"Some help," she muttered.

Abel had a point, as much as she refused to admit it. Whatever was going to happen tonight wasn't likely to be something her friends could just stroll away from. Someone had to be ready with a fresh horse and a good, solid carriage.

"Look, Rabbit, just because Mr. Fortune isn't nervous about the Order these days doesn't mean I'm going to take any chances with you," Abel said. "Maybe they've backed off publicly, but those men aren't stupid. They know that the patrols they sent to burn down the paper's building didn't die natural deaths. They know that Fortune and his people had protection, and they'll be looking for any excuse to come after not only us but the whole community."

She let out a resigned sigh. He was right. It wasn't just their lives on the line. Cela might have been willing to risk that. But she knew what could happen when a whole community got blamed for a single man's actions. It had cost her father his life, and others right along with him. She wouldn't be the cause of that, no matter how much she might be worried about her friends.

When the first thunderous crack reverberated across the sky, Abel cursed and had to fight to keep the horses from bolting.

"I told you she should have been here by now," she said, climbing into the driver's perch with him. "It's starting."

When the second bolt crashed, they both knew something had gone wrong.

"We can't just sit here," she told her brother.

He didn't respond, but she could see the worry lining his face.

When the third thunderous crack reverberated across the sky, she looked up to see the goddess of the tower's bow lit and a bolt of light like an arrow's path coursing down to the park, and she decided.

Abel was too busy looking up to notice her climbing down until she was already standing on the street.

"What the hell do you think you're doing, Cela?"

"I'm going in there, Abe," she told him.

"Like hell—"

"You can either come with me or you can wait here," she said, but she was already turning and running toward the entrance.

Abel caught up with her before she'd reached the main entrance and directed her off to the side. "Are you crazy?"

"I have to get in there," she told him, trying to pull away.

"Not that way." He jerked his head, nodding toward an unmarked employee entrance down the block a little farther.

For a second, she didn't think she was hearing him right.

"Let's go," he told her. "Before I change my mind."

They made it into the building without any trouble. Nobody was around to see them slipping through the service hallways. Thanks to the work Jianyu had done to map out the building, they found their way to the arena without any trouble.

They arrived just in time to see Ruby emerging from a split in the heavy, draping fabric that covered the walls.

Relief bolted through her, but Cela barely took a step in Ruby's direction before Abel caught her arm.

"Wait a second," he whispered.

"Where's she going?" Cela asked as she watched Ruby turn away from the exit.

"Looks like she's headed up to the roof."

Ruby looked back, as though checking to make sure she hadn't been followed, before turning toward the stairs.

"Did you see her eyes?" Cela asked. Ruby'd had a blank, dazed look to her. "Something's not right."

They watched as Ruby took the steps up toward the ritual on the roof.

"We need to get out of here, Rabbit," Abe told her.

"Where did she come from?" Cela asked, studying the place where Ruby had emerged from the curtains. "There shouldn't be any kind of passage back there."

"Maybe Jianyu missed something," Abe said. "We're not staying to find out. If the rich white girl wants to go play with her rich white friends, I say we let her."

But Cela's instincts prickled. She'd gotten to know Ruby over the past weeks, and nothing about what she'd just seen felt right. Something had gone terribly wrong.

They could go after Ruby and make sure she was okay, but that meant going up to the roof. It meant being seen by any number of people who might connect her or Abel to the *New York Age* just by the color of their skin.

Or she could find out where Ruby had just come from.

One or the other.

"I'm not leaving yet."

"I will carry you out of here," Abel threatened.

"You can try," she said. "But it'd be a lot easier if you just came with me. Something's back there. I got a feeling we need to go check it out."

Abel looked like he about wanted to murder her. "You're sure about this feeling?"

"I wish I wasn't."

The hallway was a long, narrow passage with barely any light, but she didn't let the darkness bother her. The second she saw it, she knew that there was no legitimate reason Ruby should have been back there. Her instincts buzzed again, and they pushed onward.

When they rounded the corner and saw the bars blocking her path, Cela thought for a second she'd been wrong. Abel was already taking her by the hand, starting to turn back, when Jianyu shifted out of nothingness and appeared. Viola was there beside him suddenly as well.

"Cela," he said, stepping toward the bars. But he came short of touching them. "Why are you here?"

"It seems like I'm rescuing the two of you," she said, pointing out what should have been obvious.

"You should not be here," he told her. She would have been angry at his greeting if his voice hadn't been ragged with fear. He turned on Abel. "How could you let her come?"

"She had a feeling," Abel told Jianyu with a resigned shrug.

"How did you find us?" Viola asked.

"I saw Ruby leaving this hall," Cela told them.

"Was she alone?" Viola's expression was a study of worry. "Where did she go?"

Cela nodded. "There wasn't anyone with her, far as I could tell. But she was heading up to the roof."

"Jack," Jianyu said softly. "He is the only one who could be behind this."

"You have to go after her," Viola pleaded. "If Jack has her . . ."

Cela noticed Viola's blade on the ground not far from the bars. "We're not going alone."

ANTICIPATION

The sky hung dark and heavy above as James walked through the city with Logan following like a dog a few steps behind. He hadn't bothered to check on the saloon. Why should he? His destiny lay north, where the Order stirred corrupted magic and where the possibilities he'd seen flash across the diary's pages waited.

His cheeks burned with the cold of the winter air, but he craved the bite of pain and the way the frosty air focused him. Block by block they marched, past brawling in the streets. Past homes closed off from the dangers of the night. He could have taken a cart or a streetcar, but this felt right somehow, his feet meeting the solid earth beneath him. Steady as he traversed the city that would soon be his.

A few miles north, the Order would be beginning their evening's festivities. He could imagine them, the men who would one day bow to him. He could practically see them there, not knowing the future he was about to create.

Finally, they made it to the part of town where the Flatiron Building sliced through the night. The park was lit with hundreds of luminaries lining the walks with an ethereal glow that could only be the result of corrupted magic. Beyond the park, the Garden was awash with light. The sky above them glowed so brightly, it nearly blocked out the stars.

"Where are we going?" Logan asked, breaking what had been a more preferable silence.

"To the Conclave," he said, as though that should have been clear enough.

They cut through the park, and as they walked, James felt the brush of cold energy on his cheeks. He thought he felt vibration beneath his feet, a steady pulsing like the city itself had a heartbeat. With each step, he fell in time with that ancient rhythm. With each step, the Aether stirred, joined the song, and pushed him onward. Something trilled suddenly within the Aether, and he paused, waiting.

"What is it?"

"Shhh—" He held up his hand to silence Logan.

The buzzing was back. Clearer now. Like a hive of bees growing closer.

He thought something moved in the shadows, but when he turned, nothing was there.

"Do you sense anything?" he asked. "I need to know if any of Esta's friends are close by."

Logan frowned but shook his head. "I don't think so. Not here."

"You're sure?" The buzzing throbbed now, a warning that inched across his skin. "There's nothing?" He took Logan by the lapels. "Be *sure*."

"No—" Logan's eyes had gone wide. "There's nothing here but those lamps."

All at once, the buzzing ceased. Faded.

The Aether pulsed softly again, returning to its previous order, but James didn't feel any relief. He wouldn't until the Book was in his hands and Esta's power was under his control.

"Come on," he told Logan, and set off toward the Garden once more.

Outside the entrance, he looked up toward the rooftops. If Josef Salzer's information was right, the ritual would be held there. His own destiny would unfold there as well.

The Aether seemed to approve.

"Is Esta inside?" he asked. He needed to be sure.

Logan hesitated before confirming she was. "She's in there. I can feel Ishtar's Key." He frowned. "They're close, and . . . something else. Another of the artifacts?"

The Pharaoh's Heart. Right where he'd wanted it to be.

"And the Book of Mysteries?"

Logan looked up to the roofline, where otherworldly flames sent their fragrant smoke into the air. "It's there."

The Aether danced in anticipation, pushing him on. He tested the possibilities and found the one that assured his victory. And if the faint unsettled hum was still present? It no longer signified. It was time.

Suddenly a crack of thunder split the night, and an impossible light flashed through the darkness. James lifted his hand to shade his eyes as he squinted against the glare of the brightness. Magic crackled and cold power brushed along his skin, beckoned and threatened all at once.

He felt the Aether lurch, and he turned to see that Logan was walking away from him. He was heading toward the entrance of the building.

Because Logan believed Esta could still save him. James had sensed this possibility for days now. But he'd come prepared for this eventuality, even if he had hoped Logan would have been smart enough to choose otherwise.

It was a shame, really. The boy could have been so useful.

Taking the silver gorgon from within his shirt, he focused his affinity through the ring on his finger and pushed them both through to the magic that lay within. He could feel its connection to the newly inked mark on Logan's wrist, and he sent a small pulse of power through.

Logan froze, but James could sense the boy struggling against his hold.

"What were you planning to do, Logan?" James stepped toward him slowly. He pressed his affinity through the ring, through the silvery topper, and Logan turned. He tried not to. He struggled against the hold that James had on him, despite the pain he must have been feeling, but he turned just the same.

"Did you think you would run to her?" James asked, tightening his hold on Logan's mark—on his *will*. "Did you think she would save you from me?" He laughed softly.

"You think I don't know what you want? Do you think I'm not aware of what you've been planning for, even as you pledged yourself to me and took the mark? Esta was never going to take you back," James told him truthfully. "That possibility has never existed. It was never an option."

He pushed more of his affinity through the silvery snakes, shoved his power through the mark, and Logan screamed. He was still frozen, unmoving, but blood was beginning to drip from his wrist.

"Please—"

James was unmoved by the desperation in Logan's eyes. Desperation made people weak, and there was no place for weakness in the world he would build.

"I gave you a chance to choose differently," he told Logan. "Even after I knew you went to Esta and Darrigan, even after I knew you'd promised to betray me, I gave you the opportunity to turn from that path. I tried to make you see the truth."

The boy was clearly straining from the effort of fighting against the hold of the mark. But there was no possibility of fighting against that magic, not when the Delphi's Tear was snug on James' hand. He focused his affinity through that ancient stone and sent another command through the Aether that had been his guide for so long.

Logan struggled against the compulsion, but he never had a chance. Bloody tears streaming down his cheeks, he knelt there before James.

"You could have been so much more," James said, feeling only the hint of regret. *Such a useful tool.*

Then, with another sure push, he used the mark to tear the magic from Logan's very soul.

Logan collapsed, a bloodied heap on the ground as another crack sounded and another arc of light shot through the sky overhead.

James looked up to see the flames in the cauldrons rising and great beasts beginning to form themselves from the smoke.

With the Aether jangling in anticipation, James stepped into the Garden to claim the glorious future that was his and his alone.

THE LADY ON THE TOWER

E sta watched as the bolts of electricity and magic that had illuminated the park crept through the city. The streets lit one after
another, until finally the strange light met the water that encircled
the island. She knew when that energy hit the Brink, because suddenly a
flash of blinding light turned the midnight sky into day.

The robed figures on the rooftop gasped in awe and then applauded
the spectacle, but Esta had a sinking sense that something was wrong.

"Here, in the depths of darkest night, we bring to the world a
brilliant new dawn," the Princept called from his place on the stage.
"From our ritual this night will come a new era. Golden in promise.
Powered through the mastery of the occult sciences and the modern
world."

In the distance, a wall of light shimmered against the star-draped sky.
Colors of every type wove through the glistening curtain of power as the
Brink became visible, magic made real. It wrapped around the island, as
far as the eye could see, throwing up enough light that it wiped the stars
from the sky.

But Jack still hadn't made a move. He was sitting in the same place,
placidly watching the proceedings with only the barest hint of interest in
his expression. If they hadn't known he was going to attack, if they hadn't
been sure of it, Esta would never have suspected him.

"Why isn't he doing anything?" Esta asked.

"I don't know," Harte said. "But he will."

"What if he doesn't?" she wondered. "What if we're wrong?"

"It's Jack, Esta." Harte took her hand. "He's completely predictable, and this isn't the first time he's tried to frame Mageus by attacking. He's done this before. There's no reason to think we're wrong."

In the distance, the Brink pulsed and shivered. The colors within it flashed, twisting and twirling.

"Our forefathers brought the Brink into being through the force of their will," the Princept continued. "Through the powers bestowed by angels and demons, they carved from the Aether protection for these shores, for this world. But there are those among us tonight who would question our glorious Order. There are those who came here tonight not in the bounds of brotherhood."

The crowd felt suddenly unsettled at the change in the Princept's tone, but he continued, undeterred.

"There are those who have come here this hallowed night because they believed the Order of Ortus Aurea to be weak and feeble. There are those who came not as brothers, not to join with us in the good and noble quest to eradicate feral magic from our shores, but as enemies from within."

A rustling erupted through the gathering as men from the various Brotherhoods began murmuring among themselves. The sounds of their voices grew as they voiced denials and accusations.

But the Princept didn't pay them any mind. He simply held his hands aloft, and the hundreds of alchemical flames contained within the branches of the tree behind flared from soft green to a blinding gold. The women perched there glistened, and the cut crystals around their necks flickered with the reflection of the flames.

Drawn by the spectacle like moths to flame, the crowd went quiet again.

"Do not come here with lies on your tongues," the Princept said, his expression furious. "Come instead ready to kneel in penitence for your hubris and greed. *Kneel!*" he commanded, his voice rising above the din of the night.

Beyond, the city was awash with energy, and the Brink flashed again, as if in warning. But on the rooftop, the robed men went still, as though caught in the spell of his words. Slowly, one by one, they did what he commanded and began to kneel.

Jianyu and Viola were there suddenly, appearing out of nothing next to them.

"Where have the two of you been?" Esta asked, searching them for some sign of injury. But they seemed whole and well.

"Jack," Jianyu replied darkly.

"But he's been here the whole time," Harte told them. "He's never once left his seat there."

Jianyu frowned as though he wanted to argue, but he looked beyond Esta to where Jack was sitting in the crowd. "You're sure?"

"Positive," Esta told him.

"Have you seen Ruby?" Viola asked.

Esta shook her head. "She didn't come find you?"

"She did," Jianyu said, but before he could explain, an earsplitting scream tore through the crowd.

Esta turned to find the crowd rippling with fear, but at first she couldn't figure out what was happening. Jack was still there in his seat, serene and unbothered as he'd been all night.

"There!" someone shouted.

The crowd rippled again as hundreds of faces turned, looked upward to the highest tower of the Garden.

"That explains where Ruby went," Harte murmured darkly.

"What is she doing?" Viola asked. She gripped Esta's arm, and there was no mistaking the fear that cut through her voice.

"I don't know," Esta told her.

Ruby was standing on the topmost ledge of the tower, far above them. Her hood had been pushed back, and with her brilliant blond hair shining in the night, everyone below could see who it was. But she wasn't alone. In her hand was a small silver gun, and she had it pointed directly at her companion's head.

"She has your boy, Morgan," someone shouted. "Isn't that Junior?"

It was clear from the way his face had drained of color that he was terrified. His hands were raised, and he was pleading for his life as Ruby nudged him toward the edge.

"No," Viola said. "This can't be. She wouldn't—"

"She's not," Esta said, glancing back at Jack, who was watching the events unfold with amusement glinting in his watery blue eyes. As she watched, she saw his pupils expand and his eyes darken. "He has her under some kind of spell or charm. She's not in control right now."

"I'm going," Viola said.

"No!" Esta grabbed Viola's arm and grimaced as she felt the lash of her affinity. "Viola, no. We have to get to Jack. That's how we'll stop this. *That's* what will save Ruby."

"I can't leave her there," Viola said.

"If you go running up there now, who knows what will happen," Harte told her. "You're likely to startle her into doing something that can't be undone. We need to take care of Jack. Now, while the crowd is distracted."

"What if she falls?" Viola asked. Her violet eyes were glassy with tears.

"We cannot leave her there," Jianyu said. "I will go. I can approach without her knowing. I can stop her from this course." His mouth went tight. "I can try."

Esta considered the situation. "Okay." Even if she knew it was a distraction. "We can't let her fall, and if Ruby kills Morgan's son, it'll create a new problem."

"I will not allow that to happen," Jianyu said, but his gaze drifted to a spot just over Esta's shoulder. "There is more trouble coming. You need to get to Jack before it arrives."

Jianyu was gone before he could explain, but when Esta looked back over her shoulder in the direction Jianyu had been looking, she understood.

"Madonna," Viola said, crossing herself. "These ones are bad news."

The cauldrons that had been burning with fantastical fires all night were now smoking, and as Esta watched, the green-gray fog-like smoke began to swell and grow until they were not columns of smoke at all but enormous beasts made of fog.

AS ABOVE

Jianyu opened the light around himself and, beneath the cover of his affinity, he dashed for the tallest tower at the far end of the rooftop, hoping he would not be too late. Taking the steps two at a time, he ran up toward the tower where Ruby Reynolds was holding J. P. Morgan's eldest son at the end of a gun.

She must have been bespelled earlier. It was the only explanation for why she had led them into that trap of a chamber. It was the only explanation as well for why she would threaten the life of one of the most powerful men in the city—possibly even the country.

Jianyu was nearly to the top of the tower when he heard someone let out a bloodcurdling scream. And then came another.

Picking up his speed, he pushed himself until his lungs ached and his legs burned with the effort. Finally, he reached the top and saw that both Ruby and the Morgan heir were still there. No one had fallen. No one had died.

But the rooftop below was awash with chaos.

They should have expected this. They should have predicted that Jack would use the same tricks as before. Jianyu watched with a sense of too-familiar horror as three enormous beasts hewn from fog and smoke began to attack the crowd. But he could not help those people now. Not when the Morgan heir was pleading for his life.

Jianyu considered the problem. Any move he made to reveal himself might cause Ruby to jump or fall or fire the gun. He could not do anything to startle her, especially since he had no idea what kind of charm she was under. He had no idea what might trigger a reaction.

The only solution was to stop her before she understood what was happening. He could only hope that whatever corrupted magic had her in its grasp would not sense him before he could get to her.

Without hesitating any longer, he reached for her, and in one swift and sure movement he swiped at her, hitting the point on the side of her neck that would stun her into unconsciousness. When Ruby began to collapse, he released his hold on the light and reached for her, catching her before she could fall. The pistol she'd been holding tumbled from her hand and landed in the middle of the chaos below.

The man she had been holding at gunpoint startled but caught himself on the edge of the building before he fell. As Jianyu pulled Ruby to safety, Morgan's son managed to climb back inside the tower. He froze when he saw Jianyu crouched over Ruby, trying to wake her, and there was such hatred in his eyes that it felt like an actual slap.

"Filthy maggot," the Morgan heir said, glaring at the two of them. He inched around the top of the tower, avoiding Jianyu.

It did not matter that he had just saved this man's life. Morgan's son, like his father before him, would never believe that there was any good in those with the old magic.

"I give you your life, and still you hate us?" he wondered.

Morgan's son did not answer. He stayed silent, cowering in the corner.

Beyond, the city looked like it was aflame. From that height, Jianyu could see the entire expanse of streets. The neatly laid-out lines looked like a grid of molten gold, and beyond, the Brink had become a wall of power and light. It was shuddering with the power being channeled into it, and Jianyu realized that the streets themselves were answering in reply.

He felt something more then. The building beneath him was quaking, and the tower was beginning to sway.

This is how he will do it. The realization was both immediate and terrible.

"Why have they not stopped the ritual?" Jianyu demanded.

"I bet that's exactly why you're here, isn't it? To stop the ritual. To watch the Brink fall," Junior sneered.

"I do not want the Brink to fall this night," Jianyu said. "You must tell me how it works. Where is the power coming from? Why has it not stopped?"

"Lies," Junior said. "I won't fall for your tricks. I'm not telling you anything."

"You do not understand," Jianyu said, pointing out over the city toward the wavering wall of power beyond. "Look at the streets. They are near to breaking apart. This cannot be what you intended."

Junior did look, and his expression clouded.

"The Brink *cannot* fall," Jianyu told him. "If it does, so too does the city. So too does all of creation."

"You're lying," Junior told him, but there was fear in his eyes now—more fear than there had been a second before. "I know your type. This is some kind of trickery. You and the Reynolds chit are in this together. You're trying to confuse me. Well, I won't be confused. I won't be distracted."

Distraction. How had they not seen it? The attack was nothing more than misdirection.

They had been trying to discover what Jack would do to destroy the Brink. They had imagined he might use some ritual, perhaps even his great machine, but the truth was there—clear as the night sky above. He would destroy the Order with its own weapon. Ruby's attack on Junior had afforded the necessary distraction, and now, as energy continued to pour into the streets, Jack would simply allow it to become overloaded.

It happened all the time in the city. The fragile electrical grid would overload with energy, and the lights would flicker and dim from the excess. The same would happen to the Brink if they did not stop it.

"Do you not see what is happening?" Jianyu asked. "We must stop the ritual."

The ground was rumbling unsteadily beneath them, but Junior's eyes hardened. "*There's* the truth. You want me to stop the ritual because you want to destroy us. I won't. I won't have any part of this."

"You are a fool," Jianyu said, knowing their time was running out.

Below, another of the smoke beasts emerged, climbing up over the edge of the building from the street below. Thrown over its shoulder was Cela. She dangled unconscious, not fighting her captor.

She was not supposed to be there. Abel was supposed to take her back to the wagon to wait. . . . Unless the beasts had found them before they made it. He had to get to them, to get to *her.*

He took Ruby into his arms and wrapped his affinity around himself. He realized quickly that her weight would only slow him down, and Cela could not wait. Instead of carrying Ruby down to the rooftop, he found an alcove to tuck her into far enough back from the ledge that she would be safe. Then he ran. Junior could fend for himself. Below, the beasts of smoke were still raging, and his friends needed help.

WHERE MAGIC LIVES

E sta could do no more than watch as the smoke from the caul-drons transformed itself into beasts. Viola and Jianyu both had tried to describe these monsters, but watching the fog gather itself into solid, tangible creatures was something altogether different. All around her, the rooftop was awash in confusion as the Order and their guests attempted to escape. The robed men and women of the various Brotherhoods pushed and shoved, trampling over one another in a desperate attempt to reach the steps first.

But not everyone was lucky enough to get out. The beasts weren't attacking haphazardly, Esta realized. They were specifically going after the men on the stage. Jack was attacking the leaders of the Order—the men known as the Inner Circle—just as they'd predicted. One of the larger of the monsters had cornered J. P. Morgan and was herding him toward the edge of the roof. Morgan was attempting to use a folding chair to fend off the attack, but it was useless against the creatures. With each swing, the chair cut through the smoke, and the monster re-formed. With each swing, he stepped back, closer to the edge.

Another of the beasts had the High Princept. It had lifted the old man over its shoulder and was carrying him across the roof like a rag doll.

Viola handed Esta a blade. It was the knife she'd brought back from the Professor's library, the twin to Libitina. "Those beasts are nothing but corrupt magic made by corrupt men," Viola told her. "And like men, they can die."

But Esta knew that a knife, even one as deadly as Viola's, would never be enough. There were too many of them.

"We'll never get to them all in time," she said, watching Morgan being pushed ever closer to the edge of the roof.

"We need to go after Jack," Harte told them. "Attacking those things individually will take too much time, and it will force us to split up. Which is likely exactly what Jack wants."

"Harte's right," Esta told Viola. "If we get to Jack, maybe we can stop this. We just need to find him."

Suddenly, the building shook violently, like an earthquake had just rippled through the bedrock below. Esta grabbed hold of Harte in time to stay upright, and they clung to each other until the worst of the shaking stopped.

Viola cursed, crossing herself as she looked beyond the place where they were standing.

Esta turned to find a mass of greenish-gray smoke billowing up over the ledge of the building. The smoke continued to creep up over the edge of the roofline, rising around them as it coalesced again into another one of the beasts. Tendrils of smoke transformed into an enormous arm, and as it reached for them, Viola let out a vicious scream and sent her knife flying through the air.

It struck true, and as it disappeared into the smoke, the beast roared. Its chest split, bursting open as the creature was obliterated, but as the fog dissipated, a figure fell to the ground. It had been carrying someone within itself.

Cela, Esta realized in horror as the monster fell, releasing its victim. The knife had gone clear through its fog-formed body and had found purchase in Cela's side.

Abel screamed his sister's name and ran for where she'd fallen.

Viola started to follow, but Esta grabbed her. "We need to get to Jack."

"No," Viola said, trying to tear away from Esta. "I can save her. I can—"

Esta looked over to where Cela had fallen. Abel was there with her, holding her head in his lap. Her eyes were open, and though her face was bunched in pain, she was speaking to him.

"We *will* save her," Esta promised. "But we have to stop Jack. If we don't, more of those will attack. Until we destroy Thoth, none of this stops."

Viola's brows drew together, and Esta knew she wanted to argue. She tried to pull away, but Esta held her fast.

"You have to trust me on this, Viola," she pleaded. She'd seen a future where Jack won, where the destruction of the Brink ended everything. She could *not* let that happen. "If Jack gets away, the Brink could fall, and then everything will have been for nothing. No one will make it out. Please help me. For Cela. For Theo."

Certainty settled over Viola's features. "Fine. Show me where the bastardo is. It's time to end this."

"There," Esta told Viola, pointing to the stage, where Jack watched with amusement as his uncle and the others were being pressed back toward the edge of the roof. Soon, they'd run out of room and have nowhere else to go.

As the monsters herded the Inner Circle toward their inevitable end, Jack pressed a lever in the base of the Tree of Life, which had long since been emptied of its bare-chested birds. With a grinding of metal and gears, the branches slowly began to fold down and away, and in their place an enormous machine rose from within the stage.

Jack turned to them as his machine ascended into place. His eyes were already flooded with the inky blackness that signified Thoth's presence. "Esta Filosik," he purred in a voice older than the city. "I've been waiting for you."

Esta glanced at Harte and then at Viola, giving each of them a subtle nod to make sure they were ready. She could only hope that Jianyu had been successful in the tower and was in place as well.

She knew from the blackness that filled Jack's eyes it would be pointless to use her affinity. To capture Thoth, they had to surround him, and they had to do it without depending on their magic. But they'd planned for this very eventuality, and she trusted her friends.

"I see you've decided to join us as well," Jack said to Viola. "Convenient, though you and the Chinaman were supposed to wait for me downstairs." His mouth curled. "No matter. I can harvest your power here as well as anywhere."

Jack took the Pharaoh's Heart from within his robes and slid the ornate blade into the machine. As it locked into place, Esta felt a burst of warning cold, and when the enormous orbital arms of the machine started to rotate, the building shivered. As they rotated, dodging in and out around one another like an enormous gyroscope, the arms picked up speed, and the dangerous energy snapping through the air started to build. She felt the Aether lurch as that icy energy coursed around them, like a whirlwind of power circling through the air.

There was no sign of Jianyu, but Esta knew they were out of time.

This was the same type of machine that had killed Tilly. And if they didn't stop Jack, one like it would kill Sammie's mother and countless others in San Francisco. If they didn't stop him there and then, he'd *never* stop. Not until the old magic and everyone who had an affinity for it was wiped from this land.

Esta looked at Harte and saw the determination in his stormy eyes. Saw, too, everything he felt for her. Everything that lay between them. And she vowed that their story would not end there on that desolate rooftop at the hands of a madman. She would steal them a tomorrow. She would bring a different possibility into being.

Viola came up beside Esta, shoulder to shoulder. She straightened her spine and lifted her chin as she gave Esta a sure nod. *Now or never.*

Time seemed to hold its breath as Esta looked around the rooftop—at the chaos Jack had caused, at the steadfastness of her friends. There was no sign of Jianyu, but they couldn't wait. She had to trust that he was in place.

"Now!" she screamed, and just as they'd planned, Esta ran directly for Jack.

As she'd hoped, her attack drew his attention, distracting him long enough for Harte and Viola to get in position. They already had their sigils, were already setting them spinning, when suddenly Jianyu was there as well—appearing from the night behind Jack. He was holding two of the sigils and with his position, completed the circle with her and Jack inside.

Not only Jack.

When Esta had lunged for Jack, Thoth had surged. But she'd expected him to. She'd been ready, and he'd been so focused on attacking her that it was already too late for Thoth or Jack to stop the others from trapping them within the boundary of the sigils. Already, Esta could feel the strange, cold energy as the discs transformed into golden orbs of light and power. Harte shouted the command, and she felt the Aether shift as a boundary erupted, connecting the sigils, trapping her and Thoth within.

She barely had time to appreciate the silence within that circle, the way that she felt suddenly severed from everything around her, because in an instant, Jack was on her and it was clear that he wasn't going to go easy on her because was a woman.

But she'd expected that as well.

With a vicious twist of her arm, Esta tore herself out of Jack's grip and, letting her body move on instinct that had been drilled into her for her entire childhood, she maneuvered around him, swept his legs out from under him, and then pinned him to the ground. Her knee was across his throat, holding him in place, as she pushed her hands against Jack's chest.

"Where is your weapon, girl?" Jack—or the thing inside him—said in an ancient voice.

She gave him a cold smile. "I'm the weapon." Who needed a knife when the power within her could slice through creation? She focused on her connection to the old magic, and as her affinity swelled, she pressed her magic into Jack.

Jack suddenly looked nervous. When he spoke again, it was Jack's true voice that came from his mouth. "Please, Esta," he said, his voice breaking. "Please. I don't want to die."

She felt a pang of pity for the fear in his eyes—for the humanity he'd thrown aside. But there wasn't time for pity. Not when the world was at stake.

She pressed her affinity into him further and found Thoth's power waiting there.

"You cannot win, girl." The thing inside Jack began to laugh. And when he spoke again, the voice that came out of Jack's mouth was her own. "You cannot free the world of me, Esta Filosik. Not without destroying yourself."

She would not be distracted.

Reaching for her magic again, Esta forced the spaces apart. Tearing at time and existence and the substance that held Thoth to this world.

Jack's eyes went inky black again, and Esta could sense Thoth's fear. She felt his anger as well, but she didn't pause or hesitate. She concentrated harder, focused all her magic—that connection to the spaces between all things—into Jack, into Thoth, and then she began to slowly tear them apart.

She felt Thoth—all that he had ever been—struggle against her hold on him. She heard his laughter somehow echoing deep within herself, a wild and hysterical cackling that would have been terrifying if she didn't have his very existence in the palm of her hand.

With everything she had, she took hold once more, but Thoth reared up suddenly, blasting her with the strength of power he'd collected over centuries. The force of it jangled along the connection between them, and she felt her affinity begin to waver.

POWER CONTAINED

H arte felt the strange, unnatural energy of the barrier created by Newton's Sigils course through him like icy dread as Esta battled alone against both Jack and Thoth together. As she fought, the power within the sigils surged and pulsed more wildly than they ever had before.

The building quaked beneath his feet, and the city shuddered while darkness swirled within the confines of the sigils like some malevolent storm about to break. Esta was clearly straining now, and her expression was twisted with the determination to keep Thoth from breaking free. He felt the warmth of her magic waver and prayed to any angel or demon who might hear that her affinity would be enough.

Around the circle, he saw his friends struggle to keep hold. Viola cursed and gritted her teeth. Her expression was tense with the strain of fighting against the magic that whipped through the air around them. Jianyu's neck was corded with the effort of holding on.

"We can't let him out," Harte yelled, reminding them all of what was at stake.

He sensed the boundary they'd created was growing fragile and unsteady, and he had the sinking sense that it was too much. *Thoth* was too much. But Harte had walked through a world where Thoth's power wasn't contained by any one man, and he refused to let that happen again.

The darkness billowed within the confines of the sigils, pushing and pawing like some demon sent to destroy. But Thoth was neither god nor demon. He'd once been nothing more than a simple man who, like Jack, had tried to claim far more than he'd had any right to. The centuries might have twisted him into something more, but at heart, he was human, the same as Seshat had been. Not even Mageus. And a man could be moved.

"Take this," Harte said, gesturing to Viola that she should take the sigil he held. "Esta needs help. *Take it!*"

Viola hesitated, momentarily confused at his command, before she realized what he intended. Carefully, she inched closer, until he could set the spinning ball of power in her hand. With it, she could take his place and keep the boundary unbroken.

"Whatever you do, don't let go," he told the two of them. "*Everything depends on it.*"

"We won't," Jianyu shouted. "Go!"

Without hesitation, Harte stepped into the storm.

Inside the boundary formed by the silver discs, the air felt heavier. Magic crackled and cold power lashed at his skin. Esta was in the center, wrestling with Jack. She'd managed to pin him down, but her face was contorted in agony with the effort of holding him and Thoth. Darkness was beginning to pour from Jack's mouth, but it remained within the narrow boundary they'd created. With every passing second, it swirled faster and faster as Thoth tried to escape.

Harte knelt across from Esta, with Jack between them. Her eyes widened when she saw him there. He couldn't hear anything over the roaring that filled the circle, but he knew what she was trying to tell him. She wanted him to go, to save himself and the others, but he only shook his head.

"Together!" he shouted, and then he pressed one hand over hers and one to Jack's chest and focused everything he was into both of them. He sent the command out, felt it hit against the wall of Thoth's consciousness, and pressed onward.

Just a man.

Beneath his knees, the building quaked again, and Harte felt the blistering heat of Esta's magic sizzling along his skin.

He'd known from the beginning that she was powerful. He'd known all along that her affinity was unique. But Harte hadn't truly realized what Esta could do. Until that moment, when he felt the full force of her affinity coursing around him, he'd never *truly* understood what she was capable of. Beneath his hands, he felt Thoth's pain and fear. He sensed the ancient being's absolute terror at what was happening to him, and Harte finally understood then what Esta could do—what she was.

Like Seshat. The same.

It was why the goddess had wanted her from the beginning. Because with her affinity, she could unmake the world if she wanted to. She could tear at the threads of creation and spread wide the spaces between what was and wasn't. She could destroy *everything*, and in the midst of that swirling storm of magic and darkness, he wondered if maybe she would.

Esta gave another wrenching groan, and Harte felt her magic snapping and sizzling around him as she called to the Aether and commanded the quintessence of existence. He could feel the heat of her power, the strength of it.

The malevolent cloud around them began to churn until suddenly it broke. Not into hundreds of pieces, as it had in Chicago, but into *nothing*. He felt the instant Thoth was torn from creation, because suddenly Harte's connection to the man within was gone. At the same instant, Esta pulled her hands away from Jack and nearly collapsed.

Jack wasn't moving, but he was still breathing—not that Harte was overly concerned.

Esta started to fall over, and Harte lurched to catch her. He moved around Jack, so he could better position her in his arms. She was breathing heavily, and her skin was clammy and damp with sweat.

"Is he gone?" She trembled a little, her body exhausted from all she'd just done. "Did we do it?"

Harte nodded. "You did."

Relief flickered across her face, but then all at once her features contorted in agony, and she let out a shout of pain. Her mouth opened in a silent scream.

LISA MAXWELL

"Esta?" Harte brushed her hair back, tried to get her to look at him, but her eyes were opened, focused on the midnight sky above. "What's happening? What's wrong?"

She looked at him then, terror in her golden eyes.

Suddenly, Viola screamed, and Harte felt the boundary around them, the wall of energy created by the sigils, become dangerously fragile. Viola's body had gone rigid. Her head was thrown back, and her spine was arched. Jianyu was the same. They looked like they were being tortured.

Something moved on the edge of the roof. Harte turned in time to see Nibsy Lorcan approaching.

Harte adjusted his hold on Esta and helped her to her feet. He'd be damned if they'd face Nibsy on their knees. The boundary around them felt suddenly dangerous, and Esta whimpered. Her knees seemed to go out from beneath her, but Harte caught her up against him again.

They had to get out of the boundary.

"Drop the sigils," Harte told Viola. "Just let them go. You have to break their connection so we can get out of here." He pulled Esta toward the edge of the circle, but the cold energy surged again, pushing him back into the center.

Viola let out a keening moan, but she didn't drop the balls of light in her hand.

"Now, now," Nibsy said, mocking. "It's far too soon for you to be leaving. After all, I've just barely arrived. And we have so much to do."

Harte looked at Jianyu and Viola, but they were clearly struggling against some unseen force.

"They can't help you," Nibsy told him, taking a silvery object out of his pocket. "Not so long as I have this."

The Medusa's head from Dolph's cane. Harte stared in disbelief. "We took that," he said, his mind spinning. How had Nibsy gotten it back? "We unmade it."

"You don't really think I'd walk around carrying the real one? Unlike Dolph, I'm not some dumb mark, Darrigan," he told Harte. "But it seems you are. And with the ring to amplify my affinity, I can do so much more with this beauty than Dolph ever dreamed."

He kissed the gorgon's mouth. Viola cried out, and Jianyu groaned in pain. Esta had gone stiff in his arms. Somehow Nibsy was using his control over Viola and Jianyu to control the area within the sigils, and Esta with it.

Nibsy only smiled.

"You see, Dolph might be able to take magic through the marks they wear, but I can take their will. Thanks to the Delphi's Tear, I can make them dance like puppets on a string," Nibsy told him. And to Harte's horror, both Jianyu and Viola began to shake. "I can make them *kneel.*" The second the words were out, they collapsed to their knees.

Viola gasped, and it was clear from the way her features were twisted in agony that she was fighting something, but the cold power around them surged, and a terrible scream tore from Esta's throat.

"Your friends might try to fight me, but they'll only be hurting themselves." He stepped forward. "Convenient, isn't it, that you figured out the sigils could control a demon? Just think of what they can do to a *girl.* Thanks to your friends here and their willingness to wear Dolph's mark, I'll be able to take Esta's power just as you took that demon's. But I have no plans to unmake that power. Not when I can use it."

Esta was struggling against whatever magic Nibsy had her wrapped in, but she wasn't succeeding. Tears streamed down her face, and when she looked up at him, there was terror in her eyes.

"Such a valiant effort. But in the end, she'll succumb. They all will." He took a step forward. "You never really had a chance, you know, Darrigan. It was always going to end here, like this. I was always going to win. But then, you knew that already, didn't you?"

"Harte—"

Esta jerked from his arms, her head thrown back at an awkward angle. "You can't— You can't let him . . . Please—" She gasped in pain as her golden eyes found his. "You promised."

"No—" He knew what she was asking for, but he couldn't. The gun he'd taken from the man in the future was tucked into his jacket. There was one last bullet, and she wanted him to take her out of the equation. But he couldn't. *Wouldn't.*

Drawing the gun, he turned to Nibsy.

But the bespectacled boy only smiled. "You can't kill me, Darrigan. Not without dooming her as well." He shrugged. "I suppose she's doomed either way, but at least I will make her end mean something. With her affinity, I'll change the world."

"She's not dying, Nibsy," Harte said, lifting the gun. Taking aim. "Not today."

ONE IMPOSSIBILITY

Esta was caught up in a power she didn't understand. The sigils had been turned against her, just as she had used them against Thoth, and there was nothing she could do. As long as Viola and Jianyu wore Dolph's mark, they couldn't break free of Nibsy's hold.

The boundary around them pulsed and shivered, and she felt her own affinity drawing away from her. Nibsy was standing outside the boundary, with the Delphi's Tear on his finger and the top of Dolph's cane in his hand.

She'd read pieces of this future on the page of the diary. She'd seen glimpses of it when she tumbled back through the past. She'd known there was a chance that Nibsy could best them, but she'd convinced herself they could get around him somehow. She'd convinced herself they could avoid the fate that stupid diary had foretold.

She should have guessed he'd be as slippery as a snake. She should have known he'd find a way around them.

Now it was too late. They'd played into his hand—or he'd directed them there, pushing and maneuvering until they were right where he wanted them, just as the Professor had promised. Harte was lifting the gun, taking aim at Nibsy, and there was nothing she would have liked better than to see the traitorous bastard fall. But he couldn't. Not if there was any chance for the rest of them. Not if there was any chance for the girl to do things better the next time around.

"No!" she shouted, her voice clawing out of her throat as she struggled against the draw of Nibsy's power. She had to fight. If Thoth could, then so could she. Because she refused to succumb. She refused to let him win.

"You can't," she shouted, but her voice was barely a whisper over the roaring power around her.

He turned to her, panic and pain shadowing his eyes. "He has to die. This has to end."

"If you end him, you end me as well. You promised, Harte," she reminded him. "If you end him, there's no one for the girl to go to. It will erase everything—all that we've had together. All that we've been together. It can't happen without him."

"I can't, Esta." His voice shook, but the gun in his hand was steady. "You can't ask me to do this."

"You have to." She felt tears streaming down her face, but she struggled on. "Do it, Harte. Now. Before it's too late. Give that girl the future that can lead to us. Give her a chance to do what we couldn't. To change what we couldn't."

His jaw clenched as he refused her pleas. In his hand, the gun shook, but it was still aimed at Nibsy. "I can't. I won't lose you."

"You won't," she told him, willing him to understand. "It's the only way." Time was a twisting knot, unknowable and unforgiving. "This is only one possibility. One of infinite possibilities, but if you kill him instead of me, you end them all."

He was shaking his head. "What good are infinite possibilities if they always come to this? If this is our fate, I refuse to accept it."

Then he turned resolute toward Nibsy and lifted the gun.

Esta tried to reach for her affinity, tried to stop the seconds, but she was still caught in the buzzing power of the sigil's energy. Her power wasn't her own. "No—" she pleaded.

Viola cried suddenly, and a shot rang out. But the bullet went wide and ricocheted off a wall. It wasn't Nibsy who went down.

Suddenly Harte gasped and clutched his chest as he collapsed to the floor.

"Viola, no!" Esta screamed when she realized what was happening. "Please. No. You can't do this. You have to fight him."

"Oh, she is. For what little good it will do her." Nibsy smiled then, a slow, satisfied curve of his thin lips. "You didn't really think I'd take the chance of letting him shoot me?"

"Please, Viola." Tears clouded Esta's vision as she watched Harte struggle against Viola's power. His face was draining of color, but the gun was still in his hand. He struggled to lift it, his arm shaking as he took aim.

Nibsy only laughed, but when the shot went off, his laughter died as his body lurched. He staggered forward.

"No," Esta said as Nibsy clutched his chest like his fingers alone could keep the blood in his body.

"No," she said again, waiting for what she knew would come next. She'd felt time tear her apart before, that horrifying feeling of being unmade.

Nibsy looked up at her, but Esta couldn't see his eyes past the glare of the light glinting off his glasses to tell whether it was surprise or fear that colored his expression. And then he fell to the ground like a puppet whose strings had been cut.

The cold energy around her drained away, and she felt herself flying back together. She lunged for Harte just in time for him to lurch upward, gasping for air.

"You shouldn't have done that," she told him through her tears, because what he'd done couldn't be taken back. She didn't know how long she had before time would take what it was owed. "I told you not to kill him."

"He didn't."

Esta froze at the voice, her heart thundering in her ears as she turned to see an impossibility step out of the shadows of the roof. He wore a murderous expression, and in one hand, he held a gun.

Dolph Saunders glared down at Nibsy's body. "That shot has always belonged to me."

ONE HUNDRED TIMES OVER

Jianyu thought he knew what it meant to be trapped. How many times before had he felt imprisoned—by his own poor choices, by this jail of a city, by fate itself? But none of those struggles had prepared him for what it would mean to be truly controlled. When he felt the mark on his back flare and his will recede, when he felt Nibsy Lorcan hold his every possibility through the power in the ring, he understood what desperation truly meant.

Esta and Darrigan had been trapped in the boundary of the sigils, and he could do nothing to free them. Struggle though he might, he could not fight against the hold Nibsy had on him. There was a terrible roaring in his ears, and his back had begun to burn and blister with the effort of fighting the compulsion of the mark, but it was no good.

This hell was what the future would be if Nibsy took Esta's magic, if he used it to control the Book. And there was nothing Jianyu could do to stop it.

When the shot rang out, he barely heard it. At first he did not know what it meant. But as Nibsy stumbled and fell, the power coursing through the mark went warm and then dead. The leash that had been holding him snapped, and he fell back with the sudden absence of its pressure. In the space between him and Viola, Esta rushed to Darrigan, and from the shadows of the roof stepped a ghost.

Not a ghost, Jianyu realized.

Dolph Saunders was dead. For months now, he had believed that Dolph was dead. But . . . there had been no body. No proof except Nibsy Lorcan's word.

They had all believed that word. *Jianyu* had believed, because he could not have imagined a world in which Dolph Saunders allowed Nibsy to take all that he had built and bend it to breaking. But this was no ghost, for there was no spirit that killed with a gun. His skin was perhaps more colorless than it had been before, and his cheeks were sunken from the weight he had lost, but with the shock of white in his hair and the icy blue of his eyes, there was no mistaking that his friend was alive.

Dolph threw the gun aside as he limped to where Nibsy lay. The boy's body was motionless. No breath stirred in his chest, and even from that distance, it was clear that his magic was dead. The look in Dolph's eyes was as cold and as dangerous as the Brink itself as he glared down at the boy. Then he crouched and took the silver gorgon from his hand.

As he turned the piece over in his hand, Dolph's expression was unfathomable, a mixture of fury and regret, of loss and love. After the length of a heartbeat, he tucked it into his coat and stood.

Before Jianyu could gather his wits, Viola had already launched herself across the distance. She stopped short, just before she reached Dolph.

"Is it really you?" she whispered, slowly lifting her hand as though to touch him.

Dolph lifted a single brow. "Disappointed?" he asked wryly. But Jianyu could hear the exhaustion and the *worry* in his tone.

She smacked him. "Where have you been?" Viola demanded. "We thought you were dead. Nibsy *told* us you were dead." She smacked him again, and Dolph allowed it, taking the punishment as his due.

"I'm sorry, Vee," he told her once her fury was spent. "If there had been any other way—"

She threw her arms around him then, silencing his excuses. "You *idiot*."

Dolph seemed to melt into her embrace. Slowly, his arms came around her. "It's good to see you, too."

She drew back from him again. "You didn't need to wait so long, you know," she said tartly. "You didn't have to let him get so far."

"I did," Dolph told her. "I couldn't risk doing it any other way."

"Jianyu!" Abel was shouting from the other side of the roof, where Abel was leaning over Cela.

The sound of his name jolted him from the shock of seeing Dolph. "Viola," he called. "I need your help. Cela—"

Viola turned away from Dolph and was moving before Jianyu even finished.

Abel had Cela's face cupped in his broad hands. "Come on, Cela. Stay with me," her brother begged. "Look at me. Right here. Just keep your eyes on mine."

But Cela's eyes were wide with pain and fear. Her hands were clutching her side, where Viola's knife protruded, covered in her blood.

"Get out of my way," Viola said, but Abel wouldn't be moved. He tried to shake Viola off.

Jianyu knew it would take more than a simple touch to heal the wound made by that knife. Gently, he took Abel by the shoulders as Viola removed the small, carved seal from her pocket. "Let her work."

He held Abel firmly as Viola wrenched her blade from Cela's side. Cela cried out in pain, and Abel flinched under Jianyu's hands as blood began pouring from the wound.

Cela looked up at them, her eyes first finding her brother but then looking beyond Abel to lock on Jianyu as Viola began to work.

He had been a fool.

Jianyu had told himself that he could not burden her with the sort of life the two of them might share. He had told himself that she was not strong enough to bear such a weight, that eventually she would break and come to hate him. But as her eyes remained on his, steady and clear, he knew himself for a liar. His fear had never been for her but for himself. Because losing her would break him in a way that nothing else had been able to.

She had not asked for tomorrow but only today, and he had been reluctant to give her even that. He would not be so stupid again. He remembered being healed by that seal, the small artifact they had stolen from Morgan's collection at the Metropolitan months ago and knew that the next few minutes would not be easy for her. As the cold energy of the seal filtered through the air, he promised her silently that he would give her every tomorrow, a hundred times over. As he watched her skin knit itself together, he vowed that he would start today.

THE FUTURE'S PAST

Dolph Saunders knew he was a bastard and a fool as well. All the good that had come to him in his life—his Leena, his friends, his people at the Bella Strega—he hadn't appreciated any of it. Not truly. Not until he'd been forced to live alone, hidden away in the unused upper floors of the safe house he'd charmed, guarding against any contact with his previous life. He hadn't known what regret was until he had to stand by and watch Nibsy Lorcan destroy everything he'd built.

Because it was the only way to change everything.

But when Viola and Jianyu turned from him to help their fallen friend, he felt the bone-deep knowledge that his actions had changed more than he'd expected. He'd heard their voices these past weeks as they came up through the ceiling of the floor below. He'd watched from a distance as Jianyu had stepped forward to become the leader Dolph had always believed he could be, as Viola stood by his side without shame or regret, and he'd been glad for it. He'd been gratified that, for all his mistakes, he had somehow managed to set the foundation for something larger— something better—than he could have ever built himself. And they had done it without him. *Despite* him.

And if he felt the loss of something he could not quite name as he watched his friends, their heads bent close together across the roof, he did not regret it.

The rooftop was a disaster. It would have been so much easier if he could have stepped in an hour ago. Hell, months ago would have been preferable. But Dolph had done the hardest thing he'd *ever* had to do— he'd bided his time and *waited*. Even when he saw Nibsy in the park not an hour earlier, when he could have struck the traitorous snake down and ended the danger, he had held himself back.

While everything went to hell, he'd done nothing but watch, impotent and pointless, because he had believed it was the only way they might claim the chance to make a different world.

In one corner, a clutch of men in shining robes were huddled, fearful as children. Chairs and tables had been overturned as people scattered from the danger. One of the large cauldrons had been tipped over, and now its fiery contents were smoldering on the tiles. The rest of the Order had fled like the cowards they were.

Darrigan and the girl were getting up, and the way Darrigan was looking at Esta—the way he held her face in his hands like she was something infinitely precious—told Dolph everything he needed to know about the state of things between the two. The Magician and the Thief had become something larger and more complete together than either of them had ever been apart.

"It's good to see you, old man," Darrigan said, slinging his arm protectively around Esta. "I wondered if I would. But I should have known you'd want to make an entrance."

Dolph shrugged. "Turns out I'm a hard man to kill."

"*You* did this?" Esta asked Harte, glancing between the two of them. "You should have told me."

"You know I couldn't," Harte said. "The fewer people who knew, the more likely it was to have a chance of working. Keeping secrets is the only way I'd ever gotten around Nibsy before."

"I don't understand," she told Dolph. "If Nibsy didn't kill you, why did you wait until now to show yourself?"

"I had to," Dolph explained. He took from his jacket the small notebook that had been the bane of his existence these past months. Every time he had wanted to act, it had counseled caution, so he had waited until the words on those pages pushed him to this time and place, to this singular chance to bring the Brink's power to an end.

LISA MAXWELL

"That's why you gave Dakari the diary," Esta said, looking up at Harte. Her expression shifted suddenly, and tears made her eyes glassy. "He did it," she whispered to Harte. "He chose to help us. He *saved* us. But why the diary? How could you have predicted that would work?"

"I didn't, exactly. But I knew Dolph well enough to know he would've needed some kind of proof," Harte told her.

"He wasn't wrong about that," Dolph admitted. He likely would have ignored the warnings and premonitions if it hadn't been for the diary— the way the pages changed and adjusted themselves to the path time took.

"But how did it get here?" she asked.

"You gave it to me," Dolph told her, confused.

"I didn't," Esta said. "I never had that until a few weeks ago. I couldn't have brought it to you."

Dolph's brows rose at her insistence. "And yet you did."

She'd brought it to him with a warning and with an ingenious garment that kept Nibsy's bullet from piercing his skin. It had been a leap of faith to believe the girl when she'd first arrived, but after she'd saved his life, he'd had little choice.

Darrigan took her hand to calm her. "I didn't know if it would work, but I figured that if you could exist simply because the possibility remained that you'd go back—if the diary could tell us about our deaths, even though we still lived—then maybe other possibilities could exist as well. I took a chance with Dakari, because I hoped that if he helped us, maybe we could use the loop in time that you have to create by sending the girl back to our advantage."

Esta had gone silent, her eyes wide and unblinking. And then wonder broke over her features. "You played the possibilities," she whispered to Darrigan. "You changed a past that had already happened from a future that might never be. Nibsy wouldn't have been able to see the threat coming. Even if he'd been using the diary, he would have believed the entry there."

Darrigan nodded. "Exactly. I'd hoped to keep everything close enough that the diary wouldn't change so Nibsy wouldn't realize what I'd done."

"You're a genius!" She kissed him.

And she didn't stop.

Unaccountably uncomfortable by the display, Dolph cleared his throat.

"I hate to interrupt your moment," Dolph said, stepping closer to the edge of the roof. "But this isn't over yet." He nodded toward the city beyond. "Something is happening to the streets."

Jianyu and Viola had come over to where they stood by then, along with their friends.

"The Order was using the grid to channel power to the Brink," Jianyu explained.

"It's more than that," Dolph told his old friend as he watched the streets below vibrate uneasily with the glow of an otherworldly power. Cold energy corrupted by ritual magic was thick in the air. The whole city seemed on the verge of breaking apart. "Something has gone wrong."

"The attack on the ritual and on the men of the Order was nothing more than a distraction," Jianyu told them. "This was Jack's plan, for the ritual to run out of control. If it is not stopped, the electric power it is channeling will overwhelm magic built deep within the city, and when it reaches the Brink . . ."

"It will short it out like an overblown fuse," Dolph said. "Like half the electricity in the city does."

He'd wanted the Brink to fall. That one hope—even more than his desire for revenge—had been the reason he'd remained in hiding these past months. But he didn't want it to fall like this.

It wasn't just the building beneath his feet. The entire city was awash with terrible power. Manhattan had become a city of fire. Its streets were lit with magic that crackled and swelled, and beyond it, the Brink wavered, pulsing with the energy that was coursing into it.

"We have to cut off the power," Esta said.

She was right. If they didn't stop this madness, the grid of the streets wouldn't be able to hold the flow of electricity much longer. Even now the streets threatened to shatter.

"There isn't time," Harte told her. "We don't even know where to begin."

"With the statue," Jianyu told them, pointing up toward the gilded Diana glowing with light. "We can start there."

But when Dolph looked up to the towers, it was not only Diana who stood against the night. A girl clad in one of the Order's robes stood with her arms wide. Her golden hair glinted in the light.

"No—"Viola screamed as the girl began to fall.

FURY AND VENGEANCE

Harte watched in horror as Ruby tumbled from the tower, her dark robes like a leaf carried in the breeze, and then suddenly he felt the brush of Esta's magic, and Ruby Reynolds was there, steady and alive, standing on her own two feet.

As the others rushed forward in relief and confusion, something drew his attention across the rooftop. *Jack.*

In the shock of Dolph's appearance and the concern over Cela's injury, everyone had forgotten about Jack. They'd left him lying unconscious where he'd fallen, but in the meantime, he'd come to. Ruby's little leap must have been his doing—a distraction to ensure he could sneak off back to the machine.

Before Harte could do anything, Jack pressed the lever, and the large orbital arms started to move. Jack looked up, watching with a maniacal glee as the machine picked up speed. He was so engrossed with his victory that Jack didn't notice Harte run for him until he was nearly across the stage.

Harte crashed into Jack, pummeling him as he pushed him down, and Jack fought back, laughing like a madman as he lashed out.

"It's too late," Jack said, taking a wild swing and nearly connecting with the side of Harte's head. "Every maggot in this city is about to die."

Harte drew back his fist, and when he connected with the side of Jack's face, he gathered his affinity and pushed all of his magic toward Jack. Then he drew back his fist again. And again.

He wasn't aware that the others had arrived or that already Viola was using her dagger to slice the Pharaoh's Heart out of where it had been locked into the machine. He didn't notice the arms stuttering and slowing. All he could see was the blood spurting from Jack Grew's nose. All he could feel was the crunch of bone beneath his fist.

"Harte—" He heard Esta's voice as though from far away.

He realized he was still punching an unconscious man. Jack's face was a bloody mess, and his own knuckles were raw from hitting him. But he drew his arm back again.

"We can't kill him, Harte," Esta said softly, holding his arm so he couldn't strike Jack again. "Not like this."

She was right. Jack Grew might deserve to die, but Harte wouldn't be the one to make him into a martyr.

He let Esta tug him back, but then he saw the shape of the Book outlined beneath Jack's robes. Breathing heavily, his blood singing with adrenaline, he pushed the fabric away and opened Jack's coat. There, secured in a specially made inner pocket, was the Ars Arcana.

Harte reached for the Book without thinking. Why should he have worried? The version of the Book that had contained Seshat was gone, burned to ash when Esta had brought it back and crossed it with itself. There shouldn't have been any goddess in those pages. There shouldn't have been any danger in touching *this* Book, here in *this* past. But the second his fingers touched the worn leather cover, Harte realized his mistake.

All at once, he felt a familiar ancient power flooding through him. It wasn't like before. What had happened the first time he'd touched the Book, back in Khafre Hall, was a pale imitation of pain compared to this. Then Seshat had been too broken, too fractured to do anything more than wail. Now she attacked.

Harte screamed as Seshat breached the boundary between himself and the nothingness she threatened. He was barely able to throw up enough defenses in time to keep her from ripping him apart. The Book tumbled from his hands, falling open on the rooftop, where its pages lay open, pulsing with light.

He saw the confusion in Esta's expression, saw that she would step toward him, and he threw up his hands to warn her off. "No," he shouted, backing away.

"Harte?" Esta's brows were drawn together in concern. Her golden eyes were wide with fear, but when she looked down at the Book, he knew she understood.

Within his skin, the goddess raged.

"Seshat," he said, grimacing against another of her onslaughts.

"That isn't possible." Esta scooped up the Ars Arcana from where he'd dropped it. The pages seemed to riffle of their own free will, and the power within it lit the lines of her face. "She isn't in *this* version of the Book, Harte."

"Somehow she was," he groaned, struggling to push down the goddess's power.

Seshat was screaming, her ancient voice wailing sentences that didn't make any sense.

Esta took another step toward him, but he threw up his hands again. "Keep her back," he told the others. "Keep her away from me."

Whatever Seshat may have been trying to tell him, all Harte could sense was her anger. Her hunger. She wanted. *Desperately.* Fury. Vengeance. Her emotions made clear what her incoherent raging could not.

"Harte, Seshat was in the Book that we *lost*," Esta reminded him, as though he could have forgotten. As though that wasn't the very reason he'd been so careless. "She can't be in this one."

"There's only one Book of Mysteries," Dolph told her. His icy eyes met Harte's. "The Ars Arcana is unique, made exceptional by the piece of pure magic it contains."

Esta's expression lit, and she looked at Harte with hope in her eyes. "If that's true, it means we might still have a chance."

EVER ONE

Esta's mind raced with the implications of what Dolph Saunders was telling her. She had believed that they'd lost their chance to complete the ritual and stabilize the Brink when the Book had disappeared as they'd slipped back into the past. But maybe they hadn't. The Ars Arcana that Harte had just touched was not the Ars Arcana they had possession of . . . and yet Seshat had been waiting in those pages.

"The Ars Arcana isn't some normal artifact," Dolph explained. "Its power isn't something that can be replicated. Its singularity is the reason it has been so revered and hunted over the centuries. There are a thousand legends, a hundred myths, but one thing is always clear: There is always and ever *one* Book."

"Within time and beyond it all at once," Esta murmured, thinking of what Seshat had told her, what she'd seen with her own eyes. "Because it not only contains a piece of magic outside of time. It *is* a piece of magic outside of time." She pressed her hand to the open page, wishing it were like the Book in her dream. Wishing it would tell her what to do next.

"What does that mean?" Jianyu asked.

She thought about all she knew of time and its opposite, all she'd seen falling through the years when time had revealed its truth. If the spaces between time could contain every possibility at once, then maybe the Book could as well.

"It means we might still have a chance to fix the Brink," she told them as she flipped through the Book, searching.

When she reached a slip of paper, she stopped, and hope flared bright in her chest. It was a piece of stationery with the Algonquin Hotel's name emblazoned across the top. She held it up and showed them. "I put this in the *other* Book. But time doesn't matter in these pages."

She turned to Harte, willing him to understand. "When the Professor trapped Seshat in that other version of the Book, he trapped her in *all* versions of the Book. If we use the sigils, we can remove the other artifacts from *this* Book. We can use them and complete the ritual that will stabilize the Brink. Everything we need is right here. The Book, the artifacts . . . and me. We can get her out of you. We can still use her power to complete the ritual—to fix the Brink and place the piece of magic within this Book back into the whole—just like we planned. With the Book and the artifacts, with *Seshat*, we can end this once and for all."

The building beneath them shook again, and in the distance the Brink quivered, its bright boundary illuminating the night.

He shook his head. "You'd still have to give up your affinity," he reminded her, remembering the girl who died on the subway platform. "It's the only way to use the stones and control Seshat. I watched you do that once before. You won't walk away. There's no surviving that, Esta."

But she didn't believe that. "With power willingly given," she said, reminding him of what Newton had written. "That other girl wasn't willing, Harte. You forced her to give up her affinity. Maybe if she'd done it on her own, maybe if she'd been strong enough—"

"You can't risk your life for *maybe*," he told her.

"Maybe's all we've ever really had." She stepped toward him, wishing she could touch him now. Determined that she would soon enough.

The building quaked again, but it wasn't only the building. The entire city could barely contain the power coursing through its streets. In the distance, the Brink was a wall of wavering light. But even now she could see the dark lines beginning to creep through the brilliance of it.

"We can still cut the power," he pleaded. "There's still time. You can *steal* us more time."

But she understood the truth. All the time in the world wouldn't change the choice before her. Everything had led here, and now she had to choose. The fate of the world or herself.

She'd seen the fate of the world if she chose wrong.

"I don't know if it's possible to change the future, but I do know that I can't sit by and let the Brink fall or the Order continue to rule over the old magic in this city. I can't watch Seshat destroy you, and I can't walk away from this, not when I know I can fix it. All of it. The Brink, the Order, the future I saw—I can stop all of it."

"What are we waiting for?" Viola asked. "If Esta says it will work, it will work."

She met Viola's steady violet gaze and was surprised at the trust there.

For her entire life she'd made a point of never needing anyone. It had always been easier that way. Safer. *Lonelier, too.* She'd never depended on anyone—not until Harte. Not until she'd learned to trust the people who were standing around her now. She looked at them now, one by one. Viola and Jianyu. Cela and Ruby. And, impossibly, Dolph, the father she had never known. All of them with her.

And Harte.

"I need you to trust me, Harte. We can do this," she told him, correcting her earlier words. "But only together . . . Please. Because I can't do it by myself."

OUT OF TIME

Seshat was raging inside Harte, but everything fell away except for Esta. Proud and determined and beautiful in her conviction. She believed she could complete the ritual. She believed she could use Seshat's power and give her own without dying, but if she was wrong . . .

"I do trust you." *Of course* he did. "But what if you're misunderstanding what Newton wrote? When you give up your magic, what if that's the end?"

"I'm not wrong, Harte," she told him with that same brash confidence that had attracted him to her from the very first. "But it doesn't matter. We have to try. And if this *is* the end?" Her eyes were glassy with unshed tears. "You've given me more in the past few months than anyone could deserve in a lifetime."

"*You* deserve a lifetime, Esta." He wanted to touch her. *Needed* to touch her. But he couldn't. Not with the demon goddess in his skin.

"All I've ever wanted was for someone to see me the way you do," Esta told him, a sad smile tugging at her mouth. "For myself. Without qualification. Without having to earn it. You gave me that. Now let me give what *I* can give. Let me do what I was born to do, Harte. Stand with me. *Please.* Don't make me walk into this with any regrets."

The building quaked beneath them again. In the distance the electric power had turned the Brink into a wall of light, but that wall was cracking. Even now Harte could see the black veining through it, threatening to break it apart.

Esta was right. They were out of time.

He glanced at Abel and Cela. "We're going to need to borrow Mr. Fortune's carriage one more time."

"No way in hell," Abel said. "We're coming with you."

"We're coming, too," Jianyu said, stepping forward with Viola. "You'll need us to hold the boundary steady and keep watch."

"I can't ask that of you," Esta told them, looking suddenly panicked at the idea.

"You didn't," Viola said. She glanced up at Ruby, who laced her arm more securely through Viola's as though to indicate that she was coming as well.

Dolph walked over to Nibsy's still body and pried the ring off his finger. He tossed it to Darrigan. "We're going to need this."

"We?" Harte asked.

"Do you really think I tortured myself these last few months for something so simple as vengeance?" Dolph asked. "This is it—the one chance to finish what the Order began. I was the one who went after the Book and released this mess into the world, so I'll help to finish what I started. I owe it to those who have fallen." He looked at Viola. Jianyu. "And to those I've disappointed and betrayed. If we can stop the Brink from taking one more life, then I can go to my grave knowing I've done all I could to make up for my failings."

He'd no sooner spoke than they heard a thunderous crack. In the distance, the Brink lurched, and a wave of energy snapped through the streets, rippling through the city and threatening to shatter it.

"We need to go," Jianyu told them. "We need to get to the Brink."

Esta turned to him then, and in her golden eyes was everything they hadn't yet said. But he understood. He'd always understood.

"Let's go end this, Harte."

He wouldn't be able to touch her once more before they leapt into the unknown. He wished he could. He wanted to wrap his arms around her and keep her safe. *Forever.* But maybe all they'd ever had was the moment before them, stark and beautiful in its wonder and terror.

He could no more stop Esta from this path than he could stop magic itself. And whatever happened, he'd be with her.

"Together," he said finally. Because he knew in that instant that it didn't matter. If they died today or a thousand years from now, whatever time he had with her would never be enough.

IN BROOKLYN

Viola's fingers were laced through Ruby's as the wagon careened toward the bridge, urged on by Abel's steady hand and caught in the web of Esta's power. Beneath its wheels, the streets had been turned into buckled bits of cobblestone and concrete from the energy coursing through the city's grid.

She'd been there the night of the Manhattan Solstice. Viola had watched the sun's light transform the streets into rivers of gold, shimmering with power. She'd felt the danger and the wonder as well, but this? *This* was far worse. The three bolts of electric power, amplified by whatever corrupt ritual the Order had performed, had not stopped pouring their energy into the center of the park. The sigil in Madison Square was a beacon of light, and from it, that dangerous power flowed, feeding into the grid of streets and lighting the city from within, threatening everything.

Beneath the wagon, the streets quaked under the strain of the power charging into them. They wouldn't hold. But the bridge was ahead, just there in the distance, growing ever larger as they approached. So too was the Brink.

Viola believed Esta, trusted her as well. But that didn't mean she wasn't afraid of what was to come. Though the thought of approaching that terrible barrier willingly—of breaching it? The very idea made her recoil. Since she'd come to those shores, since her family had crossed into the city, not caring what it meant for her power, Viola had known, bone-deep, that the Brink was the deadly limit of her existence. Now she would test that limit with nothing but flimsy silver discs, ritual objects created by a simple man.

It would be worth it, she thought as she looped her arm through

Ruby's and drew her closer. If it worked, perhaps they would have a chance.

If the city didn't end them first.

"Once we get there," she told Ruby softly, "you should go. You and Cela and Abel. Get yourselves across the bridge and away from the danger."

"No," Ruby said, her fair brows knitting themselves together. "I'm staying."

"There's nothing you can do," Viola said.

"I'm not running off," Ruby argued. "I'm not leaving you to whatever fate you're about to walk into. The Brink can't touch me."

"Do you see these streets?" she asked. "Do you see what's happening all around us? It's not the Brink you have to fear right now. It's the island itself. If we can't stop this—"

"You'll stop it," Cela said from her place across the wagon. She was sitting shoulder to shoulder with Jianyu, their bodies pressed close together despite the room they had around them.

"Viola is right," Jianyu said. "You and your brother, and Ruby as well, you must get to the other side. It will be safer in Brooklyn, where the city's grid does not reach."

"It won't be safer anywhere if the Brink comes down," Cela reminded him. "Isn't that what you told us?"

"End magic, end the world," Ruby said, giving Viola's words back to her.

"We're not going anywhere," Cela told them. "None of us."

It happened too quickly and not quickly enough. The streets were shuddering with the power coursing through them. The long span of the bridge was already beginning to sway when Abel urged the wagon up over the dark waters to the wall of flame that waited.

When the wagon came to a stop, Viola turned to Ruby again, pleading. "Please," she said. "It will be better if I know you're safe. If anything happened to you—"

Ruby's eyes were glistening with tears as she leaned forward and kissed her, silencing her words. "I feel the same," she whispered. "I'm not going anywhere. I'll be here waiting, and when this is over, we're going to cross that bridge together."

Viola looked up at the Brink, visible now. Icy energy mixed with sizzling heat, and the corrupt magic and natural power it had harvested for over a century pulsed and shivered, undulating slowly. Beyond the span, in the east, the edge of the world was beginning to glow with the promise of another day.

She kissed Ruby once more and vowed that day would arrive.

BETTER MEN

Jianyu helped Cela down from the bed of the wagon despite his misgivings. He would have rather she remained aboard and left with Abel, as Viola had suggested. They would have been safe in Brooklyn, whatever happened. But he saw the set of her jaw, the sharp determination in her eyes, and knew better than to waste his words with arguing. The truth of the matter was they would succeed or the world itself would die. Safety was an illusion that none of them could afford.

He released his hold on her waist and immediately regretted the loss. As her brother looked on from his perch on the wagon, he was unsure of what to say.

"Cela . . . I—"

But she shook her head. "Don't you dare start telling me your good-byes," she said. She had pulled her bravery around her, but he did not miss the way her lips trembled or the shine of tears in her eyes. "We have things to discuss, you and I. We've got plenty of time."

"Cela," he started again. She needed to understand. "If anything happens—"

"I'll be right here," she said. "Where I belong."

He did not answer, but simply looked at her, trying to memorize every curve and angle of her face. He could not quite make himself move forward, but neither could he turn away.

She turned her face up to him and kissed him softly, there with her brother in plain view.

With his heart in his throat, Jianyu glanced up at where Abel sat, watching, but if Cela's brother had any feelings about what he had just witnessed, they did not show.

Without another word, Jianyu joined his friends. Dolph was standing not six feet from the fiery wall of the Brink, gazing up with a sort of terrible wonder.

"You could have sent word," Jianyu said as he came up next to his friend.

"No," Dolph told him, glancing in his direction. "I couldn't have. And you did well enough on your own."

Jianyu huffed. He had let Nibsy Lorcan destroy everything Dolph had built—everything they had built together.

"You held it together," Dolph told him as though reading his thoughts.

"Not enough," he said with true regret. "The Devil's Own will be glad to have you back at the head."

"I'm not coming back," Dolph told him. He turned to Jianyu. "If this works, I'm leaving. And if it doesn't . . ." He shrugged. "There's nothing in the city for me now."

"But the Strega," Jianyu said. "Everything you built?"

"It will be in good hands," Dolph told him. He took the cane topper from within his coat and examined it. His jaw tightened, and without any warning, he lobbed the silvery head out over the edge of the bridge to the waiting water below. Then he turned back to Jianyu. "Well? What do you say? They'll need someone to lead them. A better man than I've ever been."

Realization dawned as Jianyu understood what he meant. "I could never," he argued, taking a step back from the Brink and Dolph and everything that his offer entailed.

"You could," Dolph told him. "It's yours if you want it. It's yours already, if you'll only take it."

"We have to get moving," Esta said. "Something's happening."

Jianyu noticed then that the vibrations beneath their feet were growing in intensity. The streets of the city had grown even brighter and more frenzied.

"It's the sunrise," Viola said.

He understood immediately what she meant. At the solstice, the setting sun had charged the streets with power. Now the rising sun was doing the same. If it reached the correct angle . . .

"Quickly," Jianyu shouted, already taking one of the sigils he had been carrying and offering it to Dolph. "We do not have much time."

ELEMENTS UNITE

The fear in Jianyu's voice had Esta turning back to look over her shoulder at the city. With every passing second, things were growing worse. Viola was right. The sunrise seemed to be adding to the energy that was already too much for the streets to contain. A thunderous rumble split the air, and she watched in horror as the bridge swayed. At the base of the long span, the part closest to the land, an enormous crack crawled across the pavement, severing them from the city and trapping them up against the Brink. But Esta didn't trust that they'd be safe in that no-man's-land between the city they'd come from and the line that could destroy them. She remembered what had happened when she and Harte had crossed back into the city. If the Brink lurched as it had then, everything would be over.

She turned to Harte, panicked suddenly at how quickly everything was moving. They were out of time. "Whatever happens, I need you to know—"

"Don't," he said, his jaw tight. The gray of his irises was a storm-tossed sea. "Not now."

"Then when?" she asked.

His jaw tensed. "After. You can tell me whatever you have to say after."

"Harte—" Her throat was tight, and she wanted to step into his arms, wanted nothing more than to touch him.

"I can't walk into this without any hope at all," he said.

She wanted to kiss him. She needed the feel of his mouth on her lips as she walked into the flames, but Seshat still waited within his skin.

Dolph took the ring from his finger and held it out to her. "I believe you'll need this."

Esta looked up at him, the man who had fathered the child she had once been. Despite the stripe of white in his dark hair, he wasn't an old man—no more than five or six years older than she was herself. She knew then that if they made it through this, she would never be able to tell him who she was.

She couldn't tell him any of it, she realized. Because if he knew about the child, she knew he would never let her go.

There was no more time for words or hesitation. They moved together as one, as though they had always known somewhere deep within the cells of their very being that this was their purpose and their fate. Viola, Jianyu, Dolph, and Harte positioned themselves in a circle with Esta and the Book of Mysteries in its center. They each held one of Newton's Sigils, the paper-thin discs covered in mercury and inscribed with a ritual that could protect them from the Brink's claim.

One by one they set the discs to spinning. One by one the flat bits of metal flashed, transforming themselves into orbs of light. Cold energy rose around them, and the atmosphere shifted as they suddenly connected, one to another. The bridge was unsteady beneath them, and the Brink shook, pulsing threateningly in the sky above them, but inside the circle of light there was only silence.

Harte's eyes were on her, determined and steadfast, and suddenly everything seemed to drain away but the two of them. She did not say, *I love you*. She did not say that she was afraid or that she wished there had been more time. She did not say any of the things she should have. She offered none of the words she'd kept inside for so long because it had felt too dangerous to release them.

But he gave her a small nod and mouthed the words *I know*.

The bridge shook again, and one of the enormous stones tumbled from the tower above them.

"No!" Harte shouted when the boundary wavered. "Hold it steady. We move together, on my count . . ." Then he began to lead them slowly, carefully into the swirling power of the Brink.

LISA MAXWELL

As they walked, energy snapped around them. She could feel it threatening the boundary they had created with the sigils. Her hair lifted, stirred against her cheeks at the cold magnetic energy, and she felt her affinity lurch. Beyond the protection of the sigils, the Brink was still there—calling, *demanding*.

She didn't waste any more time. She flipped open the Book, and once she had found the page she needed, she placed the Ars Arcana on the ground open-faced.

With Viola's knife, Esta made a small, careful cut along the same scar from before, and then—hoping she was right, hoping she hadn't just led them all to certain death—she pressed her bleeding fingertip to the open page. As her blood disappeared into the parchment, a cold power blasted up from the pages and washed over her. The Book seemed to quiver beneath her hands.

If there was only ever one Book, if it was made of a piece of pure magic—within time and beyond it all at once—it meant that the Book they'd had in 1980—the one they'd used to secure the artifacts—was also *this* Book. Which meant . . .

Carefully, she touched the page. It felt like ice and fire all at once, but the second her fingertips brushed against the parchment, she felt a burst of energy—the crackle of something like an electric shock—and her finger dipped *into* the page. She pressed farther, until her hand disappeared up to the wrist, and then she went farther still. She couldn't see her hand any longer, but she could feel the substance it pushed through, cold and alive and strangely like it had felt when time tried to unmake her back in Colorado.

When she took her hand from the page, she had an ornate dagger in her hand.

With a shaking breath, she reached for the next.

The necklace and the crown, the dagger and the ring.

One by one, she put them on, tucking the dagger into her waistband so it could press against her skin. The stones immediately grew warm, as though they understood what was to come, and the Brink shuddered in response. Outside the circle of the sigils, wind began to swirl, tearing at her friends' clothing and hair. All around them, the icy energy of the Brink pressed in on the fragile protection of the sigils' boundary.

"Hurry," Jianyu told her, his voice strained.

Quickly, Esta turned back to the Book and turned to the page she needed.

"To catch the serpent with the hand of the philosopher . . . ," she read, whispering the words to herself like a prayer. But was the serpent time? Or was magic itself?

She hesitated with a sudden unease. What if she *had* misunderstood?

No . . . The recipe was clear enough, at least to her. She'd been raised on Latin and the occult sciences—trained and honed for this. Because the Professor had believed he could use her to do this very ritual.

Professor Lachlan had thought he could use her affinity to take this power. He had stolen her life so that he could take control of the beating heart of magic for himself. But now she would be the one to claim the ritual.

What else will you claim? The thought was as unexpected as it was unwelcome.

The stones were hot against her skin, and the wind beyond the boundary had picked up speed. But within the space that her friends were holding, there was only silence.

What else could she claim? What had Thoth told her?

You could transform time. Make the world anew.

But she didn't want a world remade. She wanted *this* world, with all its uncertainty. True, there was hate and fear, but as she looked at her friends risking everything, she knew there was beauty, too. And there was Harte.

Outside the silence of the circle, the storm was increasing. She felt the boundary grow more tenuous, and she turned back to the page open before her. The Philosopher's Hand—the recipe for the mythic substance known to change lead into gold and men into gods. Five fingers of the hand, linked to one of the five elements, aligned with the five artifacts she now wore.

"With power willingly given, mercury ignites," she read. "Elements unite."

Newton's writing seemed to writhe on the page, like the Book itself knew the moment was near. The individual letters shivered, glowing with a sudden luminescence as the Brink began to crumble.

She focused her affinity and poured it into the stones that lay against her skin. At first she wasn't sure what she was supposed to do, but then she felt it. The spaces between the stones and the magic within them, the possibility of the chaos it held. She continued, giving herself over to it— giving her affinity to the old magic willingly—and she felt the instant the stones joined, twining with her magic as they were connected by Aether. In a single, staggering burst of cold power, they united as one, and at the center, burning like the fish in the Philosopher's Hand, she felt her magic catch fire.

Caught in the thrall of that power, she could do nothing more than marvel at first. She understood why men had craved it—*killed* for it— over the eons. This wasn't only the old magic, with its warm assurance and steady strength. This was something more. *Ritual magic.* Power beyond the spaces between. Power that could be multiplied and molded.

Power that you could claim.

Sound drained away, and Esta could no longer hear the wind whipping around her or her friends' screams for her to hurry. She understood suddenly what Newton must have felt centuries ago when he'd attempted this very ritual, when he'd held the power of those stones in the net of his own affinity and saw what he could become. The awe of it. The fear as well.

But there was more. She wasn't finished, not when the Book still held the beating heart of magic, not when Seshat still raged within Harte's skin. It was time to finish what Seshat had started so long ago.

It was time to place the beating heart of magic back into the whole.

Esta felt power dance along her skin, as cool as silk and as sharp as a blade as she turned back to the page before her. The letters were glowing now in earnest, urging her on.

"The serpent catches its tail," she whispered. "Severs time, consumes. Transforms power to power's like."

The most obscure of all the lines—the most difficult and the most important. Some myths believed the serpent was time. Others, like the Antistasi, saw the ouroboros as magic itself.

Time and magic, two halves to the balanced whole that *everything* depended upon. Within the Book was a piece of pure magic, held outside the threat of time. Outside the circle of the sigils was the Brink, a boundary made from the Aether—made from *time*. One would be consumed. The other transformed.

It wasn't enough to just let the Book's power go within the Brink. That wouldn't do anything but overload the already-overwhelmed boundary. *That* much power? The Brink would shatter and fall—and it would take *everything* along with it. But there was a way to complete the ritual. There *had* to be.

If she got this wrong . . .

Her skin was singing, and her blood felt alive as she laid her hand on the open page of the Book. Focusing her affinity through the stones, she reached for the spaces between all the Book was and all it had ever been. Just as she'd found the curse sunk into Jianyu's skin, she felt it there—the piece of old magic—pure and alive and wild in its infinite possibilities. She sent her affinity into the spaces between that magic and the world, and she tore them apart.

THE SERPENT
CATCHES ITS TAIL

T he stones burned against Esta's skin as she tore the piece of pure, untouched magic from within the pages Seshat had used to hide it eons before. She ignored the sizzle of energy that felt like lightning about to strike and swallowed down the taste of blood on her tongue. It took everything she had to hold on to that power.

She understood then what Seshat had tried to do—how powerful Seshat truly must have been to accomplish such a thing as removing a piece of magic from the whole. It was like holding infinity and nothingness all at once.

The Book fell away, crumbling to ash, and the space within the sigil was transformed. She'd felt something like this sense of terrifying possibility before, when she'd slipped back to this time, but that had been nothing compared to what the Book had concealed. She could feel everything— sense *everything*—the world and time and the spaces between.

The area within the boundary of the sigils became filled with the power that had been in the Book and was transformed by it. Chaos bloomed with all its beauty and its terror. It felt like stepping into the heart of an atom, like standing in the middle of an emptiness that held within it an infinite number of possibilities.

Magic lives in the spaces. That's what Esta had been taught. It was what she had always believed, but now she understood that *living* was too tame a word for what magic contained.

No wonder Newton had panicked. No wonder he had stopped the ritual before it was complete.

But it was too late for Esta to turn back. The Book was ash at her feet, and released from its bonds, the beating heart of magic swelled, growing to fill the boundary delineated by the sigils.

Viola was screaming, and Jianyu was telling them to hold tight. Harte looked back over his shoulder at her. Esta saw the desperation in his eyes as she felt the boundary waver and began to realize how far over her head she was.

The serpent catches its tail . . . severs time . . . consumes.

If the beating heart of magic broke free of the boundary, it would destroy time—and in doing so, destroy *reality* itself. After all, what was time but that substance that kept the spaces ordered and magic's power in check? But because of what Seshat had done, the power she'd taken from the Book was beyond time's reach. If it escaped from the boundary of the sigils, it would do more than simply destroy the Brink. It would consume *everything*.

Swirling around her was chaos itself. Pure and filled with possibility. But possibility meant *everything*, not only the good. Possibility included the end.

Esta knew she had to hurry. She had to finish the ritual before the ritual could finish her.

The Brink had been made the same way Seshat had created a boundary for the Book those eons ago—the same way the other version of herself had created a ritual circle in the subway—through Aether. *Through time.* By pulling at the spaces within time, between time, Seshat and the Order had created a space that craved magic.

Esta would give the Brink what it craved. She would take the beating heart of magic, that piece of power protected from time, and push it back into the spaces left by the ritual, completing the ritual that the Order had left undone. And she would use Seshat to do it.

As the power welled, stronger and more urgent, she heard Viola curse and Dolph laugh in what could only have been amazement. But Harte was watching her as though if he looked away, she might disappear.

She had to get to Harte—*to Seshat.*

Slowly, Esta pushed through the nearly solid wall of chaotic power surrounding her. It felt like swimming through concrete, but eventually she was within an arm's length of him.

"It's time," she shouted, and then reached out her hand.

But Harte only shook his head. He was saying something, but she couldn't hear him.

"It's *time*, Harte." She held her hand out again as the boundary line continued to waver, trembling as her friends struggled to hold it steady.

"I hate this," he told her. The gray of his eyes mirrored the storm around them. She could see herself reflected there. She could see everything they might be, if only they could make it to the other side.

"I know," she said, and before he could stop her, she grabbed his wrist.

Immediately she felt Seshat lurch, and Esta threw herself—her affinity and her life—into the space between them. But the goddess would not go easily. Esta hadn't expected her to. She focused her affinity through the stones of the artifacts and pressed her magic into Harte. There, she found the places where Harte ended and Seshat began. She let her magic flare within those spaces.

She felt the goddess's power sizzling up her arm, felt the darkness beginning to swell as a desert night rose up around her. A woman whose eyes were lined with kohl stepped from the spaces into time, and as fire flashed in Seshat's ancient gaze, Esta realized her mistake.

It wouldn't work. Esta couldn't force Seshat. She couldn't use the goddess's power like so many had tried to. Doing so would make her no better than Jack or Newton or Thoth. She could try all she wanted to control Seshat—to *use* her—but Esta understood in a sudden, terrible epiphany that it wouldn't work.

With power willingly given.

That's why Newton had failed. That's why the Order had failed as well. The power sacrificed to balance magic and time, to make the two into one, had to be freely given. It couldn't be stolen, as ritual magic had stolen power for so long.

But with the horror of that discovery came new understanding. Esta could see how to fix it—the Brink, the Book, all of it. Not by forcing Seshat, but by giving *herself*—her magic—in *place* of Seshat's.

There was only one answer. She had to *free* Seshat. Even if it meant dooming herself.

Darkness was bleeding into the world, filtering through the spaces and starting to claw at her, but Esta wrenched her magic back. Focusing her affinity through the stones, she pushed Seshat away. Seshat lunged for Esta, tearing at her eyes and face with razor-tipped nails, but with the artifacts hot against her skin, Esta held her back. Held her caught in the Aether.

"I won't use you as the others would have," she told the goddess—the woman—struggling against her.

"*Lies!*" Seshat screamed. Her kohl-rimmed eyes were bright with a hatred that took Esta's breath away. "But it will not work. You seek power for yourself, but you will unmake all."

"I never wanted power," Esta told her. "I just wanted Harte, but if I can't have him, then I'll leave the world safe."

You could make the world anew.

Esta shook her head and shoved the thought aside.

"Tricks upon tricks," Seshat said, still struggling against Esta's hold. "I see the desire in you. I see the duplicity as well."

Against her skin, the artifacts burned hot, but Esta held tight to their power. Through the haze of Seshat's illusion, she could see her friends on the bridge struggling. Their faces were twisted as if in agony as they fought with everything they had to keep the sigils steady. Just behind the illusion of Seshat's face, she could see Harte's features.

Outside the safety of their circle, the Brink was wavering and threatening to fall. They didn't have much time.

Under Esta's feet the desert sand rippled, just as it had once before in dreams. A desert serpent set to devour.

Maybe this was always how it was supposed to be. Maybe everything had led her to this. What was it Thoth had told her? That she was an abomination? That time would take what it was owed.

She'd been trying so hard to find a way to keep what she had—the life she knew—but she'd ignored the possibility that maybe it was never supposed to have been hers. Time wouldn't have to take her. She'd give herself. Willingly. She'd end this, once and for all.

"Why do you hesitate?" Seshat mocked. "Now that you have me, now that you have all that you have dreamed about for centuries, can it be that you are afraid?"

"I'm not afraid," Esta said. It wasn't a lie. Afraid didn't begin to describe what she felt. She was terrified and devastated and emboldened all at once. She looked at the people surrounding her, and she would not let them down.

Esta stepped toward Seshat, and she saw the fear in the ancient woman's eyes. But caught in the power of the artifacts, Seshat could not move, much less escape. Esta held tight to the goddess and tore her from Harte. Freeing her.

The desert night evaporated, and the roaring warning of the Brink rose again. Harte was breathing heavily, and the others were screaming for her to hurry. To finish it.

Harte's gaze shifted behind her to where Esta knew Seshat was still held, caught in her affinity, and then back. He blinked in confusion, like he couldn't quite understand what he was seeing. Stepping toward him, Esta sent her affinity out into the stones, giving herself to them fully. Emptying herself of her magic and her power as she pressed a kiss against his mouth.

"Be happy, Harte," she told him. "Be *free*."

His mouth was moving, and she knew what he was saying. But she could not hear the words.

"I love you," she told him as the world shuddered. Her legs fell out from under her as the last of her magic began to draw away. Beneath her body, the bridge was quaking, and all around her the beating heart of magic threatened her affinity. Threatened to consume. But this time she didn't fight it. This time she let it go and gave herself over to it.

Above her the Brink surged. Color and light, like the beginning and end of creation. Chaos and the possibility within it. Time twisted in on itself, a devouring serpent, but as she felt herself flying apart, familiar ancient laughter rose from within her.

"Did you think you could destroy me, girl?" Thoth whispered from the deepest recesses of her soul. "How could you hope to destroy that which you carried inside you all along?"

TIME, CONSUMES

As Esta collapsed like a broken doll, Harte did not hear the low, dark laughter rolling through the silence. At first he heard nothing but the terrible beating of his own heart.

With the sigil held aloft in his outstretched hand, he could not have stopped her from kissing him, even when he knew she was saying good-bye. She was there—*right there*—her mouth against his, her breath in his lungs, and he couldn't do anything to stop her from doing what she intended to do.

He felt her magic, the same power he'd only recently come to under-stand on the rooftop when she'd torn Thoth from this world. And he knew that something had happened—something had changed. It wasn't Seshat that Esta was using to complete the ritual. She was doing it *herself*, and the terror of that realization had him almost dropping the glowing sigil he held in his hand. He felt the burn of magic, hot and bright and real, and he knew that Esta was giving herself to the Brink. Sacrificing herself for all of them.

At first he didn't hear the laughter. At first he could only hear the roaring in his ears as he looked at the vision of Seshat standing over Esta's unmoving body. She was there—a woman dressed in linen and silk, with hair dark as a desert night—and yet she was not. But it wasn't victory on Seshat's face but fear.

Seshat lifted her ancient eyes to look at Harte. "Why would she do that?" the goddess asked. "She had my power there in her hand, and she let me go."

Harte didn't know what had led her to change her mind about the plan. He only knew that Esta must have had a reason, but he didn't have time to discover the answer before everything began to fall apart.

Suddenly, Esta's spine arched and her head jerked back so she was looking up at the starless sky. Her body began to rise from the ground until it hung, suspended by nothing but the Aether she had once commanded. Her mouth was open in a silent scream. But as long as he held the sigils to keep the boundary intact, Harte could do nothing but watch as darkness flooded from Esta's eyes and mouth.

Viola cursed, threatening and railing against what she was witnessing, but she was no more able to help than Harte was. Around the circle, they all shouted for her to fight whatever power had overtaken her, but they could not drop the sigils—could not break the boundary.

Harte heard the laughter then, the dark, rolling mirth that he'd heard before in the Festival Hall when Thoth had found him—and Seshat within him—and had tried to tear her from his skin. The others were struggling against the dangerous energy of the Brink and the magic from the Book, but Harte shouted for them to hold steady. He knew that everything depended on it. They couldn't let the power of the Book loose into the world, especially not there in the center of the Brink, and they couldn't release the demon that had come to claim it.

Harte watched, powerless and horrified, as the darkness that flooded from Esta coalesced before him, a shadowy figure like a man shaped from nightmares. The shadow-man turned to him, transforming slowly into a familiar figure. As his features sharpened, Harte recognized him—the man with the head shaved bare who had doomed Seshat to centuries of misery within the pages of the Book.

Thoth.

It couldn't be. It wasn't *possible.* They'd destroyed Thoth—*unmade* him on the roof of the Garden. Harte had been there. He'd felt the full force of Esta's power as she'd ripped Thoth from this world.

"Not completely," the shadow-man whispered in a voice cast from the darkest hours of night. "Not when she had a shard of me within her own skin." He smiled his serpent's smile. "Not when she carried me with her. Once she damaged her soul by murdering that fool, it was easy enough to find a place deep in the recesses of all that she was. It was easy enough to wait for her to carry me with her until it was time to claim my final victory."

"The convention," Harte realized. When Esta had tried to destroy Thoth the first time, back in Chicago, he'd infected everyone there—including, apparently, Esta herself.

Suddenly the desert night fell around him. Gone were the Brink and the city. Gone was everything but the circle of power that contained the two ancient beings and Esta's body. The stones in the artifacts she wore were bright points of light, burning with the power she'd infused them with.

"How delightful that she's prepared herself for me," Thoth purred. "With the stones and her magic, I'll finally be able to grasp the Book's power for myself." Thoth circled closer to where Esta floated, caught in the Aether and the magic around her. "The beating heart of magic, here in the palm of my hand. With it I will remake the world anew. An infinite world that bends to my will."

"That power will *never* be yours," Seshat told him, circling closer. "I will tear you from the world, from history and memory together. And there will be no one to remember your name."

"It's too late, Seshat." Thoth laughed softly. "The game is up. The final move has been played, and I've waited too long for my victory to wait any longer."

The shadowy figure looked more corporeal now, as though he'd been gathering strength as he spoke. He began to murmur then, unintelligible syllables to form ancient words, but as his voice rose, Esta's body arched back again. Harte watched as the scars on her arm opened as though being traced by a blade of light, and power vibrated through the air as her blood began to drip.

Seshat screamed.

"Did you think I hadn't prepared for every possibility?" Thoth asked. "Thanks to the ritual magic carved into the girl's arm, her power—and the stones—are mine. And with them, I'll take yours. And then I'll take the world."

"We have to do something," Viola shouted. "We have to help her!"

"We must hold the boundary," Jianyu said.

"It won't matter if the Brink falls," Viola argued.

She was right. Already, Harte could see the darkness starting to overtake the wall of light, and within that darkness was nothing. With that darkness would come the end of everything.

"If he's using the stones, it means there's still connection there," Dolph shouted. "Use it, Dare."

Harte understood what Dolph was telling him. "Take this," Harte shouted, gesturing that Dolph should grab hold of Harte's glowing orb in his other hand. "Whatever you do, don't break the barrier. You can't let any of this get out. Especially not those two."

As soon as Harte stepped into the circle, Thoth noticed and turned to him immediately. The ancient man's eyes were voids, deep as coldest midnight.

"You've come," he said, his smile filled with anticipation. "How entertaining."

"Not for you," Harte told him. Then he lunged for Esta and pushed all of his affinity into her, just as he had done with the other version of her.

He could feel Thoth's power tearing at him, but he held on until—*there*—the last bit of Esta's affinity, still connected to the power in the stones. Without hesitation, he pushed his magic toward the united stones, just as he had in the subway tunnel weeks before.

It wasn't enough to stop Thoth. It wasn't enough to control him. But it was enough to make him stumble, and in that instant, Seshat made her move.

She lunged for Thoth and clawed at his face. Her eyes flashed brilliantly white, and Harte felt the heat of her power swirling around him. Seshat held tight to Thoth's face, and as her nails dug into his skin, there was a roaring like nothing Harte had yet heard. His ears felt like they would bleed from the sound of it as the shadowy figure began to come undone. All at once, Thoth broke apart, until there was nothing left.

The others were struggling now, Harte could tell. With only the three of them, the boundary was less even, less sure.

"Finish this," he told Seshat.

But the goddess—now no more than the shadow of a woman—only shook her head. "I cannot."

"*Finish* it," Harte demanded again. "You started this. It's time to end it."

"I cannot!" Seshat shouted, her kohl-rimmed eyes wild with fear and regret. "Once, perhaps. Ages ago, I would have given everything. My life for the world's. I would have finished the ritual. I would have created a space in this world apart from the rest. Of the world and separate from it, where magic could be cut off from the ravages of time. But that was long ago, years before I'd been reduced to a shadow of myself. Centuries before I was trapped as a spirit within the pages of the Book. Now my connection to the old magic is not strong enough. I cannot finish what I began, not alone. It must be the girl."

"No!" Harte raged. "She's already given enough."

"She must give more," Seshat told him, her eyes wild and bright. "You must help her."

Harte was shaking his head. He wouldn't. He *couldn't*. "You did this," he accused. "You tricked her into giving up her magic—"

"It was her choice," Seshat said. "Her choice alone. But she must finish what she started. Help her. Help her finish the ritual."

"No," Harte said. He refused to do that again, to listen to lies. "If I compel her, she won't be willing. I can't do that again. I won't kill her. I *won't*."

"She must finish what we started," Seshat told him. "I am no longer strong enough to finish this ritual, but she is. It's the only way. Save the world, save the girl. Save the girl, save us all. If she gives her power, there is enough of me left to help keep her alive."

"How am I supposed to believe you when I've seen your heart?" he accused.

The woman shrugged. Beneath their feet the bridge began to crack and crumble. The towers were starting to fall, block by block. Dolph shouted for the others to hold steady, even as he ducked from the flying debris.

"You don't have a choice," Seshat told him. "She knows what she had to give, and she chose it willingly. Sacrifice cannot be taken, you see. Not like those terrible stones. Sacrifice freely given is far more powerful."

"But *what* does she have to give?" Harte demanded.

Seshat smiled softly. Sadly. "Only all that she is."

"No," Harte said, refusing. He tried to shove Seshat away, but she stilled his hand.

"Look," she told him. "*Look.*" She took his hand, held it in hers, and he knew what she intended.

He sent his affinity out, into the part of Seshat that remained in this world. And he understood. There was a way to end this, to complete the ritual of the Brink. To put the beating heart of magic back into the whole.

And there was a way for Esta to live. To go on.

"She'd be a prisoner," he said. "She'd never be able to leave the city."

"I know of prisons," Seshat told him. "Hers would be a palace."

But even palaces could chafe, could constrict. Harte Darrigan knew of prisons as well. He couldn't damn Esta to this one. "I won't do that to her," Harte said, refusing.

"She has already made the choice," Seshat said. "There is no going back, and it is not for you to take this from her."

The Brink was breaking apart. Dolph and Jianyu and Viola were using every bit of their strength to hold the boundary tight, but it didn't matter. One side of the enormous stone tower began to crumble, and as it fell, the ground beneath his feet buckled and tilted. The entire span of the bridge moved, undulating like the waves in the river below. The span of road beneath her feet moved slowly at first, but soon became a terrifying rise and fall that signified the collapse that was coming.

Esta's eyes fluttered open, but she didn't see him there. Not at first. Though her mouth was moving, no sound came from her lips. But he saw what she was saying. He understood that she was still there—still alive—and she was not giving up.

The bridge was moving faster now, more violently.

"Help me," she whispered. Her golden eyes met his, and they burned with the fire he'd seen that first night they'd met. She did not blink or look away, and he knew he could not deny her. Not this. Not anything.

Tears burning in his eyes, he took her hand. "Together," he whispered.

Her eyes closed as though in relief, and he did not wait for them to open again before sending his affinity through her. The Brink flashed in a terrible brilliance, and he felt the Book's power shudder through him as the world was torn in two.

POWER TO POWER'S LIKE

First, there was pain. There was the endless ache of emptying herself until she was nothing but the shell of a memory.

The world shuddered, quaked, and Esta felt the future she had seen—that nightmare of nothingness—begin to open around her. Magic flared, hot and hungry, as it pushed the spaces wide. Consumed time. Transformed the very pieces of reality into their opposite. Magic bloomed. Time came undone. And the world began to be unmade.

She saw the bridge begin to fall, the enormous stone towers collapsing in on themselves, one at a time. The great span of steel and concrete rippling like a wave. She saw her friends fighting to keep the fragile boundary intact—fighting to keep the beating heart of magic from destroying the world.

The bridge shifted and buckled, and she felt the pull of something terrifyingly familiar. Though her affinity was all but gone now—pushed into the stones and into the ritual that hungered for it—Esta felt almost like she was falling through time. There was the bridge, about to crash into the river below. There it was, whole. There was the empty river, in the time before men had ever dared to build across such a length. Just as had happened in Colorado, she felt time flicker around her. Just as when she'd lost Harte in the trip back to this time, she felt all of the possibilities of each second. The city as it was, as it could be, as it would never be again.

And then there was nothing at all. There was only the city unmade. The world forgotten.

Esta felt herself flying apart. It was a pain she'd felt before, this terror of being ripped from the very fabric of time. Time flexed and rose around her, pulsing with a strange energy. Unsteady. Unwieldy. And it felt *hungry*. Just as it had before, when it threatened to unmake her.

A hand snagged her wrist, and Esta's first thought was for Harte. But it wasn't Harte. It wasn't any of those who stood with her that day.

"You must give the rest," Seshat told her in a voice that sounded like chaos and light. The woman was gone, and the goddess had returned. Her kohl-rimmed eyes were bright beacons. "You must give *everything*. You can keep none of what you are. Power willingly given. It is the only way to sever time, the only way to save what was."

Esta realized then that she could feel the stones—barely, but they were there. She was still tethered to them, still clinging to a thread of her own affinity. To Seshat.

"You would have given your life," Esta realized.

"My magic, my life. Time and chaos. Two sides to singular coins. I would have given everything, and in doing so, I could have created a place, a pocket within time where time could not touch the beating heart of magic," Seshat told her. "By severing time, power would have been transformed, and both time and magic could have thrived together."

A place.

Suddenly, it made sense in a way it hadn't before. Time had *always* been linked to place, Esta realized. It was how she'd slipped through the layers. Seshat would have anchored the pure, protected piece of magic to a space—a literal place in the world—to keep the whole from dying.

Wasn't that what the Order had been trying to do as well? It was why they'd originally built the Brink—not as a weapon, but as an attempt to keep what they knew they were losing. Because their magic had never taken root in this land.

"The Brink," Esta told her. "If I give my affinity to finish the ritual, the Brink will become that place, won't it? The entire city will be a space where the old magic cannot die."

Seshat nodded. "A space severed from time's power over magic. Give time what it is owed—give it your power and your life—and watch power be transformed. Within the boundaries of that space, time will have no power over the old magic or those who have an affinity for it."

"The girl," Esta realized. "If I do this, if I give everything—"

"Time's terrible power will no longer be able to touch her," Seshat said. "The space within the boundary you create will stand apart, cut from the chaos you have introduced into the world with your very existence. History can be remade. Time can be reclaimed."

"I don't understand—"

"What is history but a kind of magic?" Seshat asked. "A story written to create a truth, like ritual magic carves power with time. Make your choice, girl—your affinity or the world?—for I am no longer strong enough to complete the ritual. But perhaps *we* can. Give up all that you are, and I will help you complete the ritual I began. Together we can seal the beating heart of magic back into its place, protected in time. But it must be now, and it must be all."

Esta knew what her choice would be. There was no hesitation, no regret. She would give up her power willingly. And she would die. But there was no other choice. Not for the world. Not for her friends—or for Harte.

Esta let go of the final piece of her affinity and felt herself flying apart, but despite the fear and pain of feeling herself being unmade, she gave everything over to time. Seshat was there as well, their powers locked together in the endless void that threatened everything. Together they pushed the swirling, beating heart of magic into the spaces of the Brink and made it one with time.

And then there was nothing at all.

Not darkness. Not light. Not pain or relief. There was only silence for the span of a minute or a lifetime.

Time shuddered, and suddenly it was a desert night that surrounded her. There was Seshat, goddess and woman. Her ancient eyes were aglow with power. Within their irises, Esta saw the Brink reflected. Every color that existed and some that she could not name swirled and churned, ribbons of power. Seshat smiled then, soft and sad, and Esta knew what she was giving.

"Why?" Esta asked, screaming into the void.

"You could have taken my power, but you were not like the others. You gave me my freedom, so I will give you your life." Seshat flickered suddenly, like the room back in Colorado. There was a woman with hair like night, a goddess with eyes of fire, the image of her flashing through all the possibilities of what she could have once been—what she would never be again. "It was always my ritual to finish," Seshat told her. "This is the price. Your magic for all of magic. Your life for the world. You must remain within the space we have created here, and you will not have your affinity for the old magic. But you will have a new world. A new beginning, without time's claws to tear you from your fate. Power transforms . . ." Then she released Esta's hand, and in a swirling of light and heat, she was gone.

Esta felt the loss keen and terrible and final, but as Seshat gave herself over, Esta felt a spark. A thread of connection between them broke, and the vision of the desert fell. The world around her struggled against its unmaking, as the beating heart of magic began to fill the spaces, remaking them anew. Transforming the Brink. She felt time and magic fuse, and she felt, too, her connection to it. Her affinity as part of that completeness.

She understood Seshat's words then. She would never be able to leave. Not without severing that connection to the Brink. Not without undoing what had been done.

With a terrible crash, like the shattering of glass, she saw the Brink burst with light, and the city within its arms was suddenly separate from time. She closed her eyes, turning away and shielding her face, because she could not look into the searing brightness, not without coming undone herself.

When she opened her eyes again, the bridge had gone still. The soft light of morning was beginning to warm the sky to a lavender blush. Above her, the great towers of the bridge had been remade.

Then Harte was there.

She looked up into the stormy gray of his eyes and saw how her future could begin.

EPILOGUE

I
t was New Year's Eve, and the barroom of the Bella Strega was filled with the pleasant murmuring of people celebrating and the warmth of the old magic. Esta remembered the first time she'd ever visited, a night when the power had flickered and the strength of magic had felt electric in the air. She hadn't known then that the saloon would become a home to her and the people in it the family she'd always wanted.

She sat with Harte, curled into a booth tucked into the corner, and watched her friends. Viola stood in her familiar place behind the bar, serving drinks with a surly pout. Jianyu sat next to Dolph at the table in the back, with Cela talking animatedly at his side. Dolph laughed at something she said and adjusted the toddler on his knee.

"You're really not going to tell him?" Harte wondered.

She nestled into the crook of his arm. "What's there to tell? He has a daughter, doesn't he?" Tomorrow they were leaving, Dolph and the girl who would never have to be sent forward—the girl who would never have to become a thief and a con. "He has a fresh start, and she has a future."

"And what about you?" he asked.

She kissed him. "I have a future too."

"Stuck here in this trap of a city forever," he said, frowning at her.

It was the price she'd been willing to pay. Her affinity for a world. It felt like a bargain. No . . . it felt like she'd gotten away with the perfect crime.

Ruby burst in through the front door a few minutes later, bringing a gust of winter and snow with her. She had a stack of newspapers in her hand, and she waved them brightly to get Viola's attention. "It's here!"

Viola stopped in the middle of pouring a customer's ale and abandoned the bar altogether as every eye in the saloon turned toward the blonde.

"Well, come on, you two," Ruby said, her eyes as bright as her smile as she waved Harte and Esta over. "Don't you want to see?"

"She's not going to let us be, is she?" Harte whispered.

"Not usually," Esta said, smiling at the way Ruby's sunshine complemented Viola's dark moods so well. "We'd better go before she has Viola drag us over."

They made their way through the crowded barroom to where Ruby was already distributing copies of the *New York Sun*, which contained her latest article. She proudly handed Esta a copy.

"Look there." Ruby beamed. "We made the front page!"

The headline told of the Brink's demise and the Order's disintegration. The Brotherhoods had scattered after the attack on the Conclave. The effects of that attack had been too broad and sweeping for the Order to try to hide. The city had been thrown into disarray, its citizens terrorized by the magic that had threatened to bring everything down. And thanks to Ruby's articles, everyone knew that it had been ritual magic, like that practiced by the Brotherhoods, that had been the danger. With popular opinion turned against them, it seemed unlikely that the Brotherhoods would be making noise anytime soon.

Beneath the headline was a byline by R. A. Reynolds. Esta scanned the story, appreciating Ruby's ability to convey drama without turning it into a farce. "I still can't believe Morgan gave you that quote about Jack," Esta told her.

"It's not like he had much choice," Ruby said. "Not after what Jack did to me and to Morgan's own son. There were too many witnesses to deny it." She shrugged. "They had to do something to save face. It was easy enough to pin everything on his nephew."

"It helps that a dead man isn't likely to argue," Harte murmured.

The authorities had found Jack's body on the sidewalk beneath the Garden once everything was over. He'd fallen—or jumped—to his death after they'd left him, and the whole Morgan clan had denounced him immediately. They, along with the Order, had been happy to blame the chaos of the night on Jack's actions, conveniently forgetting their own roles.

"They paid three times my previous rate," she told Viola, wrapping her arm around Viola's waist. "With this and the rest of my dowry, we have more than enough for a place in Paris come spring." Her smile faltered. "If you still want to go?"

"Certo," Viola said, her violet eyes filled with an uncharacteristic tenderness. "With you, I'd go anywhere."

"And now you truly can," Ruby said, smiling down at her again. Then she looked at Esta. "It's because of you. Because of what you did and what you sacrificed that we can have a life together away from here. Everyone can choose."

Esta returned her smile. *Not everyone.*

Before emotion could overtake her, Esta turned to Dolph. "What time is your train?"

"We leave for Chicago at noon," he said. After all he'd built, he was leaving the city behind. Not because he was running from his past, but because he was heading toward a new future.

"Abel's on that route," Cela told him. "He'll be sure to watch out for you."

"I still can't quite believe I'm leaving," he said, his eyes taking in the saloon.

"You do not have to go," Jianyu told him.

But Dolph only wrapped his hands more securely around the small girl on his lap. "Ah, but I do, my friend," he said. "I've made too many enemies in this city to ever be truly safe here. And there are too many ghosts haunting this place. We need a fresh start. She deserves one." He kissed the top of the girl's head, and the girl giggled and looked up at him adoringly.

Esta felt her heart ache at the sight—at the tenderness of a father and daughter reunited—but she had no regrets. The girl on Dolph's lap wasn't her, and thanks to Seshat and all they did to transform the Brink, the girl would never have to *become* her. She wouldn't have to carry the burden of time. She'd have a life of her own. A real future. And a father who would protect her without question or price.

"You'll look up the fellow I told you about?" she asked Dolph, reminding him of an earlier conversation they'd had once she knew he was leaving.

"Jericho Northwood?" Dolph said.

"He goes by North sometimes," she said. "Redhead who thinks he's a cowboy. With his mismatched eyes, you won't be able to miss him. I know it's a lot to ask, but it's important. I made a promise, and you finding him would go a long way in helping me to keep it."

"I have the letter you gave me," Dolph told her. "I'll be sure to deliver it."

With any luck, the letter would set North on the path to Maggie and put him on course to the life he deserved to live. A life without the problems of the Devil's Thief or the dangers of the Antistasi. A life with Maggie and their kids. There were others they still needed to help, like Harte's brother, but this was a first step.

"It's the least I can do after what you've done for me—for all of us," Dolph told her. He paused, considering her as he sometimes did. As though he wanted to ask, as though maybe he knew. But the moment passed, as it always did when the girl on his lap squirmed and demanded another cookie. He smiled as he indulged her, but then he grew serious. "I've done nothing to deserve this second chance, but I'll gladly take it."

"What will you do about the Strega?" Harte wondered.

"I've made Jianyu my partner," Dolph told them. "He'll be running things from now on."

"Only until you return," Jianyu reminded him.

"*If* I return." Dolph laughed. "Maybe I'll discover that Chicago suits me. Or maybe, if it doesn't, we'll head farther west."

"Bah," Viola told him. "You'll be back. You couldn't stay away from this place, from this city." *From us*, her eyes seemed to say.

"Maybe," Dolph admitted. "But until then, the Bella Strega will be in good hands, and the Devil's Own along with it."

"You couldn't have made a better choice," Esta told him truthfully. It wouldn't be easy, but if anyone was up for the work of bringing together the various factions in the Bowery, it was certainly Jianyu. Especially now that he had Cela by his side.

"Enough," Dolph said. "There will be time for good-byes tomorrow. Tonight we drink to friends who have become family." He lifted his glass, and the others all responded in kind.

Family. It was what Esta had wanted since she was a girl, and now she had it. At least for this one brief, shining instant. They settled in for the evening, talking and drinking and simply being together one last time before everything changed. Together they welcomed the new year, and with it, a chance for new beginnings.

It was nearly morning when Esta felt herself nodding off and Harte nudged her. "We should go," he whispered.

They said their good-byes and promised to see Dolph and his daughter off at the station later that morning.

Outside the Strega, snow was falling on the Bowery. The soft, frozen blossoms of snow continued to tumble down, covering the trash-lined gutters and broken cobbles and turning the world around them white. A lonely milk wagon rattled by, its wheels cutting a fresh path through the snow.

"I think they'll like Chicago," Esta said, nestling into Harte for warmth as they made the long trek uptown to the apartment that had once been his alone. "I'm not sure they'll ever come back. And Viola—she and Ruby will be happy in Paris. They can start a new life."

Harte didn't respond more than to nod in agreement.

But as they walked, the thought of new beginnings made Esta's mind turn to her own future—to theirs. And when they reached Washington Square, Esta stopped. Harte pulled up beside her, but he didn't speak. He seemed to sense that she needed to say something, and he gave her patience as he waited for her words.

"I've been thinking a lot," she told him. "About everything that's happened. About the future that lies ahead." She took a step away from him, felt the quiet hush of winter in the city wrap around her. "You aren't trapped anymore, Harte. The Brink is no longer a threat to our kind. Dolph is leaving. Viola is as well. You could go too. Anytime you wanted."

"What about you?" he asked, his expression unreadable.

"You know I can't leave." It had been the price she had to pay—a price she would have happily paid a million times over.

"Does that bother you?" he asked, brushing the snow from her hair.

"No," she told him honestly. "Everything I've ever wanted is here. This city, it's home. It always has been. I never wanted to escape this place, not like you did." Her throat felt tight.

"And you would have me leave you here?" he asked, frowning.

She didn't want him to, but . . . "I don't want you to feel trapped, Harte. I know how hard you fought to be free of this place, and I don't want you to ever feel trapped again. There's a whole world out there waiting for you. You don't have to stay because of me."

"What if I want to?" He stepped closer, wrapped her in the warmth of his arms.

"You'll change your mind," she told him. "I need you to know that it's okay if you do. I don't want to be the chain keeping you here. You can go. Whenever you need to go. It won't change anything between us."

He considered her in silence as the moon hung heavy in the darkened sky and the snow swirled around them in its light. "I've already seen the world, Esta. I saw the entire country, from one side to the other. I saw a future that was bigger and more unbelievable than even I could have dreamed." He let out a soft sigh. "Everything I ever did to get out of this city—every lie I ever told, every person I ever betrayed—I was only looking for a way to be free."

"You *should* be free," she told him, meaning it. "You deserve to be."

He shook his head. His stormy eyes were serious now. "Don't you see? No matter how far I traveled, no matter when we were, the only place I ever felt anything close to free was with you."

He kissed her then, tipping her chin up so their lips could press together, and Esta felt something ease inside her that she hadn't realized was wound so tight. Ever since she'd survived what happened on the bridge, ever since she'd found herself without magic and trapped in the city that Harte had always hated, Esta hadn't been able to stop from wondering what would happen between them. She knew it was only a matter of time before Harte would decide he wanted to leave the city.

"I'm not going anywhere, Esta." His breath was warm on her face. "Not now, not *ever*."

"I don't want you to regret it," she whispered.

"I could never regret choosing you," he told her. Then he kissed her again, slow and deep, and as she lost herself in the feel of his lips, the strength of his arms, and the warmth of him, her worries began to ease.

He pulled away and broke the kiss only when a passing carriage clattered by. "Let's go home, Esta."

Home. The word meant more than their small apartment just north of Washington Square. It meant Harte and the future they could build together. It meant everything.

She looped her arm through his, and with their bodies pressed close together, they continued through the snow. They'd gone only a little more than a block when he spoke again.

"Do you miss it?" he asked. "Your affinity, I mean? I know what it was like to take the Quellant, but at least I knew that it would wear off eventually. What you did, what you sacrificed . . ."

"I wouldn't change anything." She'd be lying to say that it had been easy to adjust, but she didn't regret the choice she'd made. "I'm still not used to not having a connection to the old magic. It feels a little like losing a limb must. Like my affinity should be there. Like it *is* there, and I've just forgotten how to reach it."

"You'll never go back to your own time again," Harte said softly.

"I know." She'd made peace with that. Mostly.

They turned north to cut through the park. Gas lamps flickered, throwing their soft light on the shimmering snow. Esta looked up at the sweep of stars overhead and knew she'd be okay. With Harte next to her, with her friends safe, she would be grateful for every day that lay ahead of her. They would make their own magic. And if she would never again see a speeding car or enjoy the luxuries of her own time? It did not matter. What she'd received in return was so much more.

But in the depth of the night, it was easy to see what the city would become. It was so easy to remember the towering height, the speed and the noise. She looked up, where one day there would be a great arch anchoring Washington Square, and beyond, uptown, where one day buildings would scrape the clouds. She thought she saw the shape of something glimmering there in the night sky, the familiar peak of the Empire State Building. And she wondered . . .

The night eased around them, and her steps slowed to stopping.

"Esta?"

She slipped her hand into Harte's and watched with wonder as the glimmering tower became more clear, more *real*. Her heart began to race.

"I think . . ." But it seemed too dangerous to say the words aloud.

"What is it?" he asked.

She could not stop smiling. It couldn't be. *And yet . . .*

The city settled around her, welcoming her home. Embracing her as its own. Urging her on. There in the darkness she could see the infinite.

LISA MAXWELL

She'd sacrificed everything willingly. She'd given up her magic in its entirety. But it wasn't *gone*. Instead of being within her, it was all *around* her, anchoring her to the city. Connecting her to time itself. Her magic was still there in the spaces of the night, ready and waiting for her to reach for it. To *grasp* it.

"Come with me," Esta said, and together she stepped with Harte into the darkness, through time, to that other city waiting beyond.

ACKNOWLEDGMENTS

~

When I came up with the idea for a badass girl thief who could see in bullet time about ten years ago, I knew it felt like a big idea. But I had no way of knowing what it would become. There are so many people to thank and acknowledge for all they've done in making this book and the entire series a success. Even a book as big as this one couldn't possibly contain my gratitude. But here goes . . .

To Jason, who I usually save for last in the acknowledgments. There is no way I could write books and keep my sanity without having a true partner in my life. Thanks for letting me talk about made-up people with you any time of day or night, and thanks for always being my person. None of this is possible without you.

To my boys, Max and Harry, who absolutely *are* amazing. Thanks for supporting me through every deadline and for letting me be your mom. You're a million times cooler than I will ever be, and I can't wait to see the incredible things you'll do.

To my brilliant editor, Sarah McCabe, who has been the lifeline for these books. Her intelligence, patience, and ability to spot any time-travel paradox is unparalleled, and I'm damn lucky to have her.

To my agent, Kathleen Rushall, who has always had my back, even when I didn't. I can't imagine wanting anyone else in my corner. Thank you. For all the things.

To everyone at Simon & Schuster who has touched this book and this series. There isn't a word in this book that hasn't been made better by the intrepid copyeditors, readers, designers, and publicists who have worked on this series. I couldn't ask for a better publishing team.

To the fierce and fiery women writers I'm lucky to call friends: Abbie Fine, Christina June, Danielle Stinson, Helene Dunbar, Jaye Robin Brown, Kristen Lippert-Martin, Olivia Hinebaugh, Sara Raasch, and Scarlett Rose. Thank you for every lunch date and group text and email. A special shout-out to Danielle, who read this monster as a draft and gave me the best advice. Go buy all of their books. Seriously. Their words will make your life better.

And last but not least, thank you to the readers who have lived in this story for the last few years. Thank you for your patience and your support. I'm so glad that you love these characters as much as I do, and I'm so grateful for all you've done to promote and support the series. I hope this final chapter was everything you wanted it to be and more.

ACKNOWLEDGMENTS

LISA MAXWELL is the *New York Times* bestselling author of young adult fantasy, including the Last Magician series and *Unhooked*. She's worked around words all her life and is currently a professor at a local college. She has strong opinions about pasta and a soft spot for loud music and fast cars. When she's not writing books, you can usually find her going on adventures with her husband and two amazing boys. Though she grew up in Akron, Ohio, she now calls Northern Virginia home. Follow her on Instagram @LisaMaxwellYA, or sign up for her newsletter to learn more about her upcoming books at Lisa-Maxwell.com.

LISA MAXWELL is the *New York Times* bestselling author of young adult fantasy, including the Last Magician series and *Unhooked*. She's worked around words all her life and is currently a professor at a local college. She has strong opinions about pasta and a soft spot for loud music and fast cars. When she's not writing books, you can usually find her going on adventures with her husband and two amazing boys. Though she grew up in Akron, Ohio, she now calls Northern Virginia home. Follow her on Instagram @LisaMaxwellYA, or sign up for her newsletter to learn more about her upcoming books at Lisa-Maxwell.com.